the Confusion

the Confusion

VOL. II of
THE BAROQUE CYCLE

Neal Stephenson

WILLIAM MORROW

An Imprint of HarperCollinsPublishers

The epigraph on page 292 is from *The Leibniz-Arnauld Correspondence*, edited and translated by H. T. Mason. Published by Manchester University Press, Manchester, England, 1967.

The epigraph on page 646 is from Robert Merrihew Adams, *Leibniz: Determinist, Theist, Idealist.* Published by Oxford University Press, Oxford and New York, 1994.

The epigraph on page 707 is from G. W. Leibniz, *Philosophical Essays*, edited and translated by Roger Ariew and Daniel Hackett. Published by Hackett, Indianapolis, 1989.

HarperCollins books may be purchased for educational, business, or sales promotional use. For information please write: Special Markets Department, HarperCollins Publishers Inc., 10 East 53rd Street, New York, NY 10022.

FIRST EDITION

Book design by Shubhani Sarkar
Endpaper maps by Nick Springer
Illustration of crucible by Laura Hartman Maestro

Printed on acid-free paper

Library of Congress Cataloging-in-Publication Data

Stephenson, Neal.
The confusion/Neal Stephenson.—1st ed.
p.   cm.—(Volume two of the Baroque cycle)
ISBN 0-06-052386-7
1. France—History—Louis XIV, 1643–1715—Fiction. 2. Single mothers—Fiction. 3. Treasure-trove—Fiction. 4. Women spies—Fiction. 5. Pirates—Fiction. 6. Mutiny—Fiction. I. Title.

PS3569.T3868C55 2004
813'.54—dc22
2003059343

04 05 06 07 08 WBC/QW 10 9 8 7 6 5 4 3 2 1

To Maurine

THERE ARE MANY PEOPLE TO BE THANKED
for their help in the creation of the Baroque Cycle
of which this book, *The Confusion,* is the second volume.
Accordingly, please see the acknowledgments in
Quicksilver, Volume One of the Baroque Cycle.

Author's Note

THIS VOLUME CONTAINS two novels, *Bonanza* and *Juncto,* that take place concurrently during the span 1689–1702. Rather than present one, then the other (which would force the reader to jump back to 1689 in mid-volume), I have interleaved sections of one with sections of the other so that the two stories move forward in synchrony. It is hoped that being thus *con-fused* shall render them the less *confusing* to the Reader.

When at the first I took my pen in hand,
Thus for to write, I did not understand
That I at all should make a little book
In such a mode; nay, I had undertook
To make another, which when almost done,
Before I was aware, I this begun.

—JOHN BUNYAN, *The Pilgrim's Progress,*
THE AUTHOR'S APOLOGY FOR HIS BOOK

BOOK 4

Bonanza

So great is the dignity and excellency of humane nature,
and so active those sparks of heavenly fire it partakes of,
that they ought to be look'd upon as very mean, and
unworthy the name of men, who thro' pusillanimity, by
them call'd prudence, or thro' sloth, which they stile
moderation, or else through avarice, to which they give
the name of frugality, at any rate withdraw themselves
from performing great and noble actions.

—GIOVANNI FRANCESCO GEMELLI CARERI,
A Voyage Round the World

Barbary Coast
OCTOBER 1689

HE WAS NOT MERELY *AWAKENED,* but *detonated* out of an uncommonly long and repetitive dream. He could not remember any of the details of the dream now that it was over. But he had the idea that it had entailed much rowing and scraping, and little else; so he did not object to being roused. Even if he *had* been of a mind to object, he'd have had the good sense to hold his tongue, and keep his annoyance well-hid beneath a simpering merry-Vagabond façade. Because what was doing the waking, today, was the most tremendous damned noise he'd ever heard—it was some godlike Force not to be yelled at or complained to, at least not right away.

Cannons were being fired. Never so many, and rarely so large, cannons. Whole batteries of siege-guns and coastal artillery discharging en masse, ranks of 'em ripple-firing along wall-tops. He rolled out from beneath the barnacle-covered hull of a beached ship, where he had apparently been taking an afternoon nap, and found himself pinned to the sand by a downblast of bleak sunlight. At this point a wise man, with experience in matters military, would have belly-crawled to some suitable enfilade. But the beach all round him was planted with hairy ankles and sandaled feet; he was the only one prone or supine.

Lying on his back, he squinted up through the damp, sand-caked hem of a man's garment: a loose robe of open-weave material that laved the wearer's body in a gold glow, so that he could look directly up into the blind eye of the man's penis—which had been curiously modified. Inevitably, he lost this particular stare-down. He rolled back the other way, performing one and a half uphill revolutions, and clambered indignantly to his feet, forgetting about the curve of the hull and therefore barking his scalp on a phalanx of barnacles. Then he screamed as loud as he could, but no one heard him. He didn't even hear *himself.* He experimented with plugging his ears and screaming, but even then he heard naught but the sound of the cannons.

Time to take stock of matters—to bring the situation in hand. The hull was blocking his view. Other than it, all he could see was a sparkling bay, and a stony break-water. He strode into the sea, watched curiously by the man with the mushroom-headed yard, and, once he was out knee-deep, turned around. What he saw *then* made it more or less obligatory to fall right on his arse.

This bay was spattered with bony islets, close to shore. Rising from one of them was a squat round fortress that (if he was any judge of matters architectural) had been built at grand expense by Spaniards in desperate fear of their lives. And apparently those fears had been well founded because the top of that fort was all fluttery with green banners bearing silver crescent moons. The fort had three tiers of guns on it (more correctly, the fort *was* three tiers of guns) and every one of 'em looked, and sounded, like a sixty-pounder, meaning that it flung a cannonball the size of a melon for several miles. This fort was mostly shrouded in powder-smoke, with long bolts of flame jabbing out here and there, giving it the appearance of a thunderstorm that had been rammed and tamped into a barrel.

A white stone breakwater connected this fort to the mainland, which, at first glance, impressed him as a sheer stone wall rising forty or feet from this narrow strip of muddy beach, and crowded with a great many more huge cannons, all being fired just as fast as they could be swabbed out and stuffed with powder.

Beyond the wall rose a white city. Being as he was at the base of a rather high wall, he wouldn't normally expect to be able to see anything on the opposite side thereof, save the odd cathedral-spire poking out above the battlements. But this city appeared to've been laboriously spackled onto the side of a precipitous mountain whose slopes rose directly from the high-tide mark. It looked a bit like a wedge of Paris tilted upwards by some tidy God who wanted to make all the shit finally run out of it. At the apex, where one would look for whatever crowbar or grapple the hypothetical God would've used to accomplish this prodigy, was, instead, another fortress—this one of a queer Moorish design, surrounded with its own eight-sided wall that was, inevitably, a-bristle with even more colossal cannons, as well as mortars for heaving bombs out to sea. All of *those* were being fired, too—as were all of the guns spraying from the several additional fortresses, bastions, and gun-platforms distributed around the city's walls.

During rare intervals between the crushing thuds of the sixty-pounders, he could hear peppery waves of pistol- and musket-fire rolling around the place, and now (beginning to advert on smaller things) he saw a sort of smoky, crowded lawn growing out of the wall-tops—save instead of grass-blades this lawn was made up of men. Some were dressed in black, and some in white, but most wore more colorful costumes: baggy white trousers belted with brilliantly hued swathes of silk, and brightly embroidered vests—frequently, several such vests nested—and turbans or red cylindrical hats. Most of those who were dressed after this fashion had a pistol in each hand and were firing them into the air or reloading.

The man with the outlandish johnson—swarthy, with wavy black hair in a curious 'do, and a knit skullcap—hitched up his robe, and sloshed out to see if he was all right. For he still had both hands clamped over the sides of his head, partly to stanch the bleeding of the barnacle-gashes, and partly to keep the sound from blowing the top of his skull out to sea. The man peered down and looked into his eyes and moved his lips. The look on his face was serious, but ever so slightly amused.

He reached up and grabbed this fellow's hand and used it to haul himself up to his feet. Both men's hands were so heavily callused that they could practically catch musket-balls out of the air, and their knuckles were either bleeding, or else recently scabbed over.

He had stood up because he wanted to see what was the target of all of this shooting, and how it could possibly continue to exist. A fleet of three or four dozen ships was arrayed in the harbor, and (no surprise here) *they* were all firing their guns. But the ones that looked like Dutch frigates were not firing at the ones that looked like heathen galleys, nor vice versa, and none of them seemed to be firing at the vertiginous white city. *All* of the ships, even the ones that were of European design, flew crescent-moon banners.

Finally his eye settled on *one* ship, which was unique in that she was the only vessel or building in sight that was not vomiting smoke and spitting flame in all directions. This one was a galley, very much in the Mohametan style, but extraordinarily fine, at least to anyone who found whorish decoration appealing—her non-functioning bits were a mess of gold-leafed gewgaws that glowed in the sun, even through drifting banks of powder-smoke. Her lateen sail had been struck and she was proceeding under oar-power, but in a stately manner. He found himself examining the movements of her oars just a bit too closely, and admiring the uniformity of the strokes more than was healthy for a Vagabond in his right mind: leading to the questions, *was* he still a Vagabond, and *was* he in his right mind? He recalled—dimly—that he had lived in Christendom during one part of his sorry life, and had been well advanced in the losing of his mind to the French Pox—but he seemed all right now, save that he couldn't recall where he was, how he'd gotten there, or anything at all of recent events. And the very meaning of that word "recent" was called into question by the length of his beard, which reached down to his stomach.

The intensity of the cannonade waxed, if such a thing were possible, and reached a climax as the gold-plated galley drew up alongside a stone pier that projected into the harbor not awfully far away. Then, all of a sudden, the noise stopped.

"What in Christ's name—" he began, but the rest of his utterance was drowned out by a sound that—compared to hundreds of cannons firing at once—made up in *shrillness* what it lacked in *volume*. Listening to it in amazement, he began to detect certain resemblances between it and *musick*. Rhythm was there, albeit of an overly complicated and rambunctious nature, and *melody,* too, though it was not cast in any civilized mode, but had the wild keening intonations of Irish tunes—and then some. Harmony, sweetness of tone, and other qualities normally associated with musick, were absent. For these Turks or Moors or whatever they were had no interest in flutes, viols, theorbos, nor anything else that made a pleasing sound. Their orchestra consisted of drums, cymbals, and a hideous swarm of giant war-oboes hammered out of brass and fitted with screeching, buzzing reeds, the result sounding like nothing so much as an armed assault on a belfry infested with starlings.

"I owe an 'umble apology to every Scotsman I've ever met," he shouted, "for it isn't true, after all, that their music is the most despicable in the world." His companion cocked an ear in his direction but heard little, and understood less.

Now, essentially all of the city was protected within that wall, which shamed any in Christendom. But on this side of it there were various breakwaters, piers, gun-emplacements, and traces of mucky beach, and everything that was capable of bearing a man's weight, or a horse's, was doing so—covered by ranks of men in divers magnificent and outlandish uniforms. In other words, all the makings of a parade were laid out here. And indeed, after a lot of bellowing back and forth and playing of hellish musicks and firing of yet more guns, various important Turks (he was growingly certain that these were Turks) began to ride or march through a large gate let into the mighty Wall, disappearing into the city. First went an impossibly magnificent and fearsome warrior on a black charger, flanked by a couple of kettledrum-pounding "musicians." The beat of their drums filled him with an unaccountable craving to reach out and grope for an oar.

"That, Jack, is the Agha of the Janissaries," said the circumcised one.

This handle of "Jack" struck him as familiar and, in any case, serviceable. So Jack he was.

Behind the kettledrums rode a graybeard, almost as magnificent to look at as the Agha of the Janissaries, but not so heavily beweaponed. "The First Secretary," said Jack's companion. Next, following on foot, a couple of dozen more or less resplendent officers ("the aghabashis") and then a whole crowd of fellows with magnificent turbans adorned with first-rate ostrich plumes—"the bolukbashis," it was explained.

Now it had become plain enough that this fellow standing next to Jack was the sort who never tired of showing off his great knowledge, and of trying to edify lowlives such as Jack. Jack was about to say that he neither wanted nor needed edification, but something stopped him. It might've been the vague, inescapable sense that he *knew* this fellow, and had for quite a while—which, if true, might mean that the other was only trying to make conversation. And it might've been that Jack didn't know quite where to begin, language-wise. He *knew* somehow that the bolukbashis were equivalent to captains, and that the aghabashis were one rank above the bolukbashis, and that the Agha of the Janissaries was a General. But he was not sure *why* he should know the meanings of such heathen words. So Jack shut up, long enough for various echelons of odabashis (lieutenants) and vekilhardjis (sergeants-major) to form up and concatenate themselves onto the end of the parade. Then diverse hocas such as the salt-hoca, customs-hoca, and weights-and-measures-hoca, all following the hoca-in-chief, then the sixteen cavuses in their long emerald robes with crimson cummerbunds, their white leather caps, their fantastickal upturned moustaches, and their red hobnailed boots tromping fearsomely over the stones of the quay. Then the kadis, muftis, and imams had to do their bit. Finally a troop of gorgeous Janissaries marched off the deck of the golden galley, followed by a solitary man swathed in many yards of chalk-white fabric that had been gathered by means of diverse massive golden jeweled brooches into a coherent garment, though it probably would've fallen off of him if he hadn't been riding on a white war-horse with pink eyes, bridled and saddled with as much in the way of silver and gems as it could carry without tripping over the finery.

"The new Pasha—straight from Constantinople!"

"I'll be damned—is that why they were firing all those guns?"

"It is traditional to greet a new Pasha with a salute of fifteen hundred guns."

"Traditional *where?*"

"Here."

"And *here* is—?"

"Forgive me, I forget you have not been right in the head. The city that rises up on yonder mountain is the Invincible Bastion of Islam—the Place of Everlasting Vigil and Combat against the Infidel—the Whip of Christendom, Terror of the Seas, Bridle of Italy and Spain, Scourge of the Islands: who holds the sea under her laws and makes all nations her righteous and lawful prey."

"Bit of a mouthful, isn't it?"

"The English name is Algiers."

"Well, in Christendom I have seen entire wars prosecuted with less expenditure of gunpowder than Algiers uses to say hello to a Pasha—so perhaps your words are not mere bravado. What language are we speaking, by the way?"

"It is called variously Franco, or Sabir, which in Spanish means 'to know.' Some of it comes from Provençe, Spain, and Italy, some from Arabic and Turkish. *Your* Sabir has much French in it, Jack, mine has more Spanish."

"Surely you're no Spaniard—!"

The man bowed, albeit without doffing his skullcap, and his forelocks tumbled from his shoulders and dangled in space. "Moseh de la Cruz, at your service."

" 'Moses of the Cross?' What the hell kind of name is *that*?"

Moseh did not appear to find it especially funny. "It is a long story—even by *your* standards, Jack. Suffice it to say that the Iberian Peninsula is a complicated place to be Jewish."

"How'd you end up here?" Jack began to ask; but he was interrupted by a large Turk, armed with a bull's penis, who was waving at Jack and Moseh, commanding them to get out of the surf and return to work—the *siesta* was *finis* and it was time for *trabajo* now that the *Pasha* had ridden through the *Beb* and entered into the *cité*.

The *trabajo* consisted of scraping the barnacles from the hull of the adjacent galley, which had been beached and rolled over to expose its keel. Jack, Moseh, and a few dozen other slaves (for there was no getting round the fact that they were slaves) got to work with various rude iron tools while the Turk prowled up and down the length of the hull brandishing that ox-pizzle. High above them, behind the wall, they could hear a sort of rolling fusillade wandering around the city as the parade continued; the thump of the kettle-drums, and the outcry of the siege-oboes and assault-bassoons was, mercifully, deflected heavenwards by the city walls.

"It is true, I think—you are cured."

"Never mind what your Alchemists and Chirurgeons will tell you—there is no cure for the French Pox. I'm having a brief interval of sanity, nothing more."

"On the contrary—it is claimed, by certain Arab and Jewish doctors of great distinction, that the aforesaid Pox may be purged from the body, completely and permanently, if the patient is suffered to run an extremely high fever for several consecutive days."

"I don't feel *good*, mind you, but I don't feel *feverish*."

"But a few weeks ago, you and several others came down with violent cases of *la suette anglaise*."

"Never heard of any such disease—and I'm English, mind you."

Moseh de la Cruz shrugged, as best a man could when hacking at a cluster of barnacles with a pitted and rusted iron hoe. "It is a well-known disease, hereabouts—whole neighborhoods were laid low with it in the spring."

"Perhaps they'd made the mistake of listening to too much musick—?"

Moseh shrugged again. "It is a real enough disease—perhaps not as fearsome as some of the others, such as Rising of the Lights, or Ring-Booger, or the Laughing Kidney, or Letters-from-Venice . . ."

"Avast!"

"In any event, you came down with it, Jack, and had such a fever that all the other *tutsaklars* in the *banyolar* were roasting kebabs over your brow for a fortnight. Finally one morning you were pronounced dead, and carried out of the *banyolar* and thrown into a wain. Our owner sent me round to the Treasury to notify the *hoca el-pencik* so that your title deed could be marked as 'deceased,' which is a necessary step in filing an insurance claim. But the *hoca el-pencik* knew that a new Pasha was on his way, and wanted to make sure that all the records were in order, lest some irregularity be discovered during an audit, which would cause him to fall under the *bastinado* at the very least."

"May I infer, from this, that insurance fraud is a common failing of slave-owners?"

"Some of them are *completely unethical*," Moseh confided. "So I was ordered to lead the *hoca el-pencik* back to the *banyolar* and show him your body—but not before I was made to wait for hours and hours in his courtyard, as midday came and went, and the *hoca el-pencik* took a siesta under the lime-tree there. Finally we went to the *banyolar*—but in the meantime your wagon had been moved to the burial-ground of the Janissaries."

"Why!? I'm no more a Janissary than you are."

"Sssh! So I had gathered, Jack, from several years of being chained up next to you, and hearing your autobiographical ravings: stories that, at first, were simply too grotesque to believe—then, entertaining after a fashion—then, after the hundredth or thousandth repetition—"

"Stay. No doubt *you* have tedious and insufferable qualities of your own, Moseh de la Cruz, but you have me at a disadvantage, as I cannot remember them. What I want to know is, why did they think I was a Janissary?"

"The first clew was that you carried a Janissary-sword when you were captured."

"Proceeds of routine military corpse-looting, nothing more."

"The second: you fought with such *valor* that your want of *skill* was quite overlooked."

"I was trying to get myself killed, or else would've shown less of the former, and more of the latter."

"Third: the unnatural state of your penis was interpreted as a mark of strict chastity—"

"Correct, perforce!"

"—and assumed to've been self-administered."

"Haw! That's not how it happened at all—"

"Stay," Moseh said, shielding his face behind both hands.

"I forgot, you've heard."

"Fourth: the Arabic numeral seven branded on the back of your hand."

"I'll have you know that's a letter V, for Vagabond."

"But sideways it could be taken for a seven."

"How does that make me a Janissary?"

"When a new recruit takes the oath and becomes *yeni yoldash,* which is the lowliest rank, his barrack number is tattooed onto the back of his hand, so it can be known which *seffara* he belongs to, and which *bash yoldash* is responsible for him."

"All right—so 'twas assumed I'd come up from barracks number seven in some Ottoman garrison-town somewhere."

"Just so. And yet you were clearly out of your mind, and not good for much besides pulling on an oar, so it was decided you'd remain *tutsaklar* until you died, or regained your senses. If the former, you'd receive a Janissary funeral."

"What about the latter?"

"*That* remains to be seen. As it was, we thought it was the former. So we went to the high ground outside the city-walls, to the burial-ground of the *ocak*—"

"Come again?"

"*Ocak:* a Turkish order of Janissaries, modeled after the Knights of Rhodes. They rule over Algiers, and are a law and society unto themselves here."

"Is that man coming over to hit us with the bull's penis a part of this *ocak*?"

"No. He works for the corsair-captain who owns the galley. The corsairs are yet another completely different society unto themselves."

After the Turk had finished giving Jack and Moseh several bracing strokes of the bull's penis, and had wandered away to go beat up on some *other* barnacle-scrapers, Jack invited Moseh to continue the story.

"The *hoca el-pencik* and several of his aides and I went to that place. And a bleak place it was, Jack, with its countless tombs, mostly shaped like half-eggshells, meant to evoke a village of *yurts* on the Transoxianan Steppe—the ancestral homeland for which Turks are forever homesick—though, if it bears the slightest resemblance to that burying-ground, I cannot imagine why. At any rate, we roamed up and down among these stone yurts for an hour, searching for your corpse, and were about to give up, for the sun was going down, when we heard a muffled, echoing voice repeating some strange incantation, or prophecy, in an outlandish tongue. Now the *hoca el-pencik* was on edge to begin with, as this interminable stroll through the graveyard had put him in mind of daimons and *ifrits* and other horrors. When he heard this voice, coming (as we soon realized) from a great mausoleum where a murdered *agha* had been entombed, he was about to bolt for the city gates. So were his aides. But as they had with them one who was not only a slave, but a Jew to boot, they sent me into that tomb to see what would happen."

"And what did happen?"

"I found you, Jack, standing upright in that ghastly, but delightfully cool space, pounding on the lid of the *agha*'s sarcophagus and repeating certain English words. I knew not what they meant, but they went something like this: 'Be a good fellow there, sirrah, and bring me a pint of your best bitter!' "

"I *must* have been out of my head," Jack muttered, "for the light lagers of Pilsen are much better suited to *this* climate."

"You were still daft, but there was a certain spark about you that I had not seen in a year or two—certainly not since we were traded to Algiers. I suspected that the heat of your fever, compounded with the broiling radiance of the midday sun, under which you'd lain for many hours, had driven the French Pox out of your body. And indeed you have been a little more lucid every day since."

"What did the *hoca el-pencik* think of this?"

"When you walked out, you were naked, and sunburnt as red as a boiled crab, and there was speculation that you might be some species of *ifrit*. I have to tell you that the Turks have superstitions about everything, and most especially about Jews—they believe we have occult powers, and of late the Cabbalists have done much to foster such phant'sies. In any event, matters were soon enough sorted out. Our owner received one hundred strokes, with a cane the size of my thumb, on the soles of his feet, and vinegar was poured over the resulting wounds."

"Eeyeh, give me the bull's penis any day!"

"It's expected he may be able to stand up again in a month or two. In the meanwhile, as we wait out the equinoctial storms, we are careening and refitting our galley, as is obvious enough."

DURING THIS NARRATION Jack had been looking sidelong at the other galley-slaves, and had found them to be an uncommonly diverse and multi-cultural lot: there were black Africans, Europeans, Jews, Indians, Asiatics, and many others he could not clearly sort out. But he did not see anyone he recognized from the complement of *God's Wounds*.

"What of Yevgeny, and Mr. Foot? To speak poetically: have insurance claims been paid on them?"

"They are on the larboard oar. Yevgeny pulls with the strength of two men, and Mr. Foot pulls not at all—which makes them more or less inseparable, in the context of a well-managed galley."

"So they live!"

"Live, and thrive—we'll see them later."

"Why aren't they here, scraping barnacles like the rest of us?" Jack demanded peevishly.

"In Algiers, during the winter months, when galleys dare not venture out on the sea, oar-slaves are permitted—nay, encouraged—to pursue trades. Our owner receives a share of the earnings. Those who have no skills scrape barnacles."

Jack found this news not altogether pleasing, and assaulted a barnacle-cluster with such violence that he nearly stove in the boat's hull. This quickly drew a reprimand—and not from the Turkish whip-hand, but from a short, stocky, red-headed galley-slave on Jack's other side. "I don't care if you're crazy—or *pretend* to be—you keep that hull seaworthy, lest we *all* go down!" he barked, in an English that was half Dutch. Jack was a head taller than this Hollander, and considered making something of it—but he didn't imagine that their overseer would look kindly on a fracas, when mere talking was a flogging offense. Besides, there was a rather larger chap standing behind the carrot-top, who was eyeing Jack with the same expression: skeptical bordering on disgusted. This latter appeared to be a Chinaman, but he was not of the frail, cringing sort. Both he and the Hollander looked troublingly familiar.

"Put some slack into your haul-yards, there, shorty—*you* ain't the owner, nor the captain—as long as she stays afloat, what's a little dent or scratch to us?"

The Dutchman shook his head incredulously and went back to work on a single barnacle, which he was dissecting off a hull-clinker as carefully as a chirurgeon removing a stone from a Grand Duke's bladder.

"Thank you for not making a scene," Moseh said, "it is important that we maintain harmony on the starboard oar."

"*Those* are our oar-mates?"

"Yes, and the fifth is in town pursuing *his* trade."

"Well, why is it so important to remain on good terms with them?"

"Other than that we must share a crowded bench with them eight months out of the year, you mean?"

"Yes."

"We must all pull together if we are to maintain parity with the *larboard* oar."

"What if we don't?"

"The galley will—"

"Yes, yes, it'll go in circles. But why should we *care*?"

"Aside from that the skin will be whipped off our ribcages by that bull's pizzle?"

"I take that as a *given*."

"Oars come in matched sets. As matters stand, we have parity with the larboard oar, and therefore constitute a matched set of ten slaves. We were traded to our current owner as such. But if Yevgeny and his bench-mates begin to out-pull us, we'll be split up—your friends will end up in different galleys, or even different cities."

"It'd serve 'em right."

"Pardon me?"

"Pardon *me*," Jack said, "but here we are on this fucking beach. And I may be a crazy Vagabond, but you appear to be an educated Jew, and that Dutchman is a ship's officer if ever there was one, and God only knows about that Chinaman—"

"Nipponese actually, but trained by the Jesuits."

"All right, then—this only supports my point."

"And your point is—?"

"What can Yevgeny and Mr. Foot possibly have that we don't?"

"They've formed a sort of enterprise wherein Yevgeny is Labor, and Mr. Foot is Management. Its exact nature is difficult to explain. Later, it will become clear to you. In the meantime, it's imperative that the ten of us remain together!"

"What *possible* reason could you have for giving a damn whether we stay together?"

"During the last several years of touring the Mediterranean behind an oar, I have been developing, secretly, in my mind, a Plan," said Moseh de la Cruz. "It is a plan that will bring all ten of us wealth, and then freedom, though possibly not in that order."

"Does armed mutiny enter into this plan? Because—"

Moseh rolled his eyes.

"I was simply trying to imagine what rôle a man such as myself could possibly have in any Plan—leastways, any Plan that was not invented by a raving Lunatick."

"It is a question I frequently asked myself, until today. *Some* earlier versions of the Plan, I must admit, involved throwing you overboard as soon as it was practicable. But today when fifteen hundred guns spoke from the three-tiered batteries of the Peñon and the frowning towers of the Kasba, some lingering obstructions were, it seems, finally knocked loose inside your head, and you were put back into your right mind again—or as close to it as is really possible. And now, Jack, you *do* have a rôle in the Plan."

"And am I allowed to know the nature of this rôle?"

"Why, you'll be our Janissary."

"But I am not a—"

"Hold, hold! You see that fellow scraping barnacles?"

"Which one? There must be a hundred."

"The tall fellow, Arab-looking with a touch of Negro; which is to say Egyptian."

"I see him."

"That is Nyazi—one of the larboard crew."

"He's a Janissary?"

"No, but he's spent enough time around them that he can teach you to fake your way through it. Dappa—the black man, there—can teach you a few words of Turkish. And Gabriel—that Nipponese Jesuit—is a brave swordsman. He'll bring you up to par in no time."

"Why, exactly, does this plan demand a fake Janissary?"

"Really it demands a *real* one," Moseh sighed, "but in life one must make do with the materials at hand."

"My question is not answered."

"Later—when we are all together—I'll explain."

Jack laughed. "You speak like a courtier, in honeyed euphemisms. When you say 'together,' it means what? Chained together by our neck-irons in some rat-filled dungeon 'neath that Kasba?"

"Run your hand over the skin of your neck, Jack, and tell me: Does it feel like you've been wearing an iron collar recently?"

"Now that you mention it—no."

"Quitting time is nigh—then we'll go into the city and find the others."

"Haw! Just like that? Like free men?" Jack said, as well as much more in a similar vein. But an hour later, a strange wailing arose from several tall square towers planted all round the city, and a single gun was fired from the heights of the Kasba, and then all of the slaves put their scrapers down and began to wander off down the beach in groups of two or three. Seven whom Moseh had identified as belonging to the two Oars of his Plan tarried for a minute until all were ready to depart; the Dutchman, van Hoek, did not wish to leave until he was good and finished.

Moseh noticed a dropped hatchet, frowned, picked it up, and brushed away the damp sand. Then his eyes began to wander about, looking for a place to put it. Meanwhile he began to toss the hatchet absent-mindedly in his hand. Because its weight was all in its head, the handle flailed around wildly as it revolved in the air. But Moseh always caught it neatly on its way down. Presently his gaze fastened on one of the old dried-up tree-trunks that had been jammed into the sand, and used to prop up the galley so that its hull was exposed. He stared fixedly at this target whilst tossing the hatchet one, two, three more times, then suddenly drew the tool far back behind his head, stuck his tongue out, paused for a moment, then let the hatchet fly. It executed a single lazy revolution while hurtling across several fathoms of air, then stopped in an instant, one corner of its blade buried in the wood of the tree-trunk, high and dry.

The seven oar-slaves clambered up onto the footing of the colossal wall and made for the city gate. Jack followed along with the crowd, though he could not help hunching his shoulders, expecting to feel the whip across his back. But no stroke came. As he approached the gates he stood straighter and walked more freely, and sensed a group coalescing around him and Moseh: the irritable Dutchman, the Nipponese Jesuit, a black African with ropy locks of hair, the Egyptian named Nyazi, and a middle-aged Spaniard who seemed to be afflicted with some sort of spasmodic disorder. As they passed through the city gates, this fellow turned and shouted something at the Janissaries who were standing guard there. Jack didn't get every word of the Spanish, but it was something like, "Listen to me, you boy-fucking heathen scum, we have all formed a secret cabal!" Which was not exactly what Jack would've said under the circumstances—but Moseh and the others only exchanged broad, knowing grins with the Janissaries, and into the city they went: Den of Thieves, Nest of Wasps, Scourge of Christendom, Citadel of the Faith.

THE MAIN STREET of Algiers was uncommonly broad, and yet crowded with Turks sitting out smoking tobacco from fountain-sized hubbly-bubblies, but Jack, Moseh, and the other slaves did not spend very much time there. Moseh darted through a pointy keyhole-arch so narrow that he had to turn sideways, and led the others into a roofless corridor of stone that was not much wider, forcing them to go in single file, and to plaster themselves up against walls whenever someone came towards them. It felt much like being in a back-hallway of some ancient building, save that when Jack looked up he could see a splinter of sky glaring between blank walls that rose ten to twenty yards above his head. Ladders and bridges had been set up between rooftops, joining the city's terraces and roof-gardens into a private net-work strung high up above the ground. Sometimes Jack would see a black-swathed form flit from one side to the other. It was difficult to get a clear look at them, for they were dark and furtive as bats, but they seemed to be wearing the same sort of garment as Eliza had when Jack had met her beneath Vienna, and, in any event, from the way they moved he could tell they were women.

Down in the street—if that word could even be used for a passage as strait as this one—there were no women. Of men there was a marvelous variety. The Janissaries who made up the *ocak* were easy to recognize—some had a Greek or Slavic appearance, but most had an Asiatic look about the eyes, and all went in splendid clothing: baggy pleated trousers, belted with a sash that supported all manner of pistols, scimitars, daggers, purses, tobacco-pouches, pipes, and even pocket-watches. Over a loose shirt, one or more fancy vests, used as a sort of display-case for ribbons of lace, gold pins, swatches of fine embroidery. A turban on the top, pointy-toed slippers below, sometimes a long cape thrown over the whole. Thus the *ocak*, who were afforded never so much respect by all who passed them in the street. Algiers was crowded with many other sorts: mostly the Moors and Berbers whose ancestors had lived here before the Turks had come to organize the place. These tended to wear long one-piece cloaks, or else raiments that were just many fathoms of fabric swirled round the body and held in place by clever tricks with pins and sashes. There was a smattering of Jews, always dressed in black, and quite a few Europeans wearing whatever had been fashionable in their homelands when they'd decided to turn Turk.

Some of these white men looked just as *à la mode* as the young gallants who'd made it their business to pester Eliza at the Maiden in Amsterdam, but too there was the occasional geezer tottering down a staircase in a neck-ruff, Pilgrim-hat, and van Dyck. "Jesus!" Jack exclaimed, observing one of the latter, "why are *we* slaves, and *that* old moth a respected citizen?"

The question only befuddled everyone except for the rope-headed African, who laughed and shook his head. "It is very dangerous to ask certain questions," he said. "I should know."

"Who're you then, and how came you to speak better English than I?"

"I am named Dappa. I was—am—a linguist."

"That means not a thing to me," Jack said, "but as we are nothing more than a brace of slaves wandering around lost in a heathen citadel, I don't suppose there's any harm in hearing some sort of reasonably concise explanation."

"In fact we are not lost at all, but taking the most direct route to our destination," Dappa said. "But my story is a simple one—not like yours, Jack—and there will be more than enough time to relate it. All right then: every slave-port along the African coast must have a linguist—which signifies a man skilled in many tongues—or else how could the black slavers, who bring the stock out from the interior, make deals with the ships' captains who drop anchor off-shore? For those slavers come from many different nations, all speaking different languages, and likewise the captains may be English, Dutch, French, Portuguese, Spanish, Arab, or what-have-you. It all depends on the outcomes of various European wars, of which we Africans never know anything until the castle at the river-head suddenly begins to fly a different flag."

"Enough on that subject—I've fought in some of those wars."

"Jack, I am from a town on the river that is called, by white men, the Niger. This is an easy place to live—food grows on trees. I could rhapsodize about it but I will refrain. Suffice it to say 'twas a Garden of Eden. Save for the Institution of Slavery, which had always been with us. For as many generations as our priests and elders can remember, Arabs would occasionally come up the great river in boats and trade us cloth, gold, and other goods for slaves—"

"But where'd the slaves come from, Dappa?"

"The question is apt. Prior to my time they mostly came from farther up the river, marching in columns, joined together by wooden yokes. And some persons of my town were made slaves because they could not pay their debts, or as punishment for crimes."

"So you have bailiffs? Judges?"

"In my town the priests were very powerful, and did many of the things that bailiffs and judges do in your country."

"When you say priests I don't imagine you mean men in funny hats, prating in Latin—"

Dappa laughed. "When Arabs or Catholics came to convert us, we would hear them out and then invite them to get back into their boats and go home. No, we followed a traditional religion in my town, whose details I'll spare you, save one: we had a famous oracle, which means—"

"I know, I've heard about 'em in plays."

"Very well—then the only thing I need to tell you is that pilgrims would come to our town from many miles away to ask questions of the Aro priests who were the oracles in my town. Now: at about the same time that *some* Portuguese began coming up the river to *convert* us, *others* began coming to *trade* with us for slaves—which was unremarkable, being no different from what the Arabs had been doing forever. But gradually—*too* gradually for anyone to really see a difference in his lifetime—the prices that were offered for slaves rose higher, and the visits of the buyers came more frequently. Dutch and English and other sorts of white men came wanting ever more slaves. My town grew wealthy from this trade—the temples of the Aro priests shone with gold and silver, the slave-trains from upriver grew longer, and came more frequently. Even then, the supply was not equal to the demand. The priests who served as our judges began to pass the sentence of enslavement on more and more persons, for smaller and smaller offenses. They grew rich and haughty, the priests did, and were carried through the streets on gilded sedan-chairs. Yet this magnificence was viewed, by a certain type of African, as proof that these priests must be very powerful wizards and oracles. So, just as the *slave*-trains waxed, so did the crowds of pilgrims coming from all over the Niger Delta to have their illnesses healed, or to ask questions of the oracle."

"Nothing we haven't seen in Christendom," Jack observed.

"Yes—the difference being that, after a time, the priests ran out of crimes, and slaves."

"What do you mean, they ran out of crimes?"

"They reached a point, Jack, where they would punish *every* crime, no matter how trivial, with enslavement. And still there were not enough slaves to sell down the river. So they decreed that henceforth, any person who appeared before the Aro oracle and asked a stupid question would be immediately seized by the warriors who stood guard in the temple, and flung into slavery."

"Hmmm . . . if stupid questions are as common in Africa as they are where I come from, that policy must've produced a *flood* of wretches!"

"It did—yet still the pilgrims flocked to our town."

"Were you one of those pilgrims?"

"No, I was a fortunate boy—the son of an Aro priest. When I was very young, I talked all the time, so it was decided I would be a linguist. Thereafter, whenever a white or Arab trader came to our town, I would stay in his lodgings and try to learn what I could of his language. And when the missionaries came, too, I would pretend to be interested in their religions, so that I could learn their languages."

"But how did you become a slave?"

"One time I traveled downriver to Bonny, which is the slave-fort at the mouth of the Niger. En route I passed many towns, and understood for the first time that mine was only one of many feeding slaves down the river. The Spanish missionary I was traveling with told me that Bonny was only one of scores of slave-depots up and down the coast of Africa. For the first time, then, I understood how enormous the slave trade was—and how evil. But since you are a slave yourself, Jack, and have expressed some dissatisfaction with your estate, I'll not belabor this. I asked the Spanish missionary how such a thing could be justified, given that the religion of Europe is founded on brotherly love. The Spaniard replied that this had been a great controversy in the Church, and much debated—but that in the end, they justified it only by one thing: When white slavers bought them from black slavers, Africans were baptized, and so the good that was done to their immortal souls, in that instant, more than compensated for the evils done to their temporal bodies during the remainder of their lives. 'Do you mean to tell me,' I exclaimed, 'that it would be against the law of God for an African who was *already* a Christian to be enslaved?' 'That is so,' said the missionary. And so now I was filled with what you call zeal. I love this word. In my *zeal* I got on the next boat bound upriver—it was a Royal Africa Company longboat carrying pieces of India cloth to trade for slaves. When I reached my town I went straight to the temple and—how do you say it—'jumped the queue' of pilgrims, and went before the highest of the high Aro priests. He was a man I had known all my life—he had been a sort of uncle to me, and many times we had eaten from the same bowl. He was sitting there resplendent on his gold throne, with his lion-skin, all draped about with fat garlands of cowrie-shells, and in great excitement, I said 'Do you realize that this evil could be brought to an end today? The law of the Christian Church states that once a man has been baptized it is unlawful to make him a slave!' 'What is your point—or, to put it another way, what is your *question?*' asked the oracle. 'It is very simple,' I said, 'why don't we simply baptize everyone in the whole town—for these Catholics make a specialty of mass baptisms—and furthermore why don't we baptize every pilgrim and slave who walks into the city-gates?'"

"What was the oracle's answer?"

"After no more than a heartbeat's hesitation, he turned towards the four spear-men who stood by him, and made a little twitching motion with his fly-whisk. They rushed forward and began to bind my arms behind my back. 'What is the meaning of this? What are you doing to me, uncle?' I cried. He answered: 'That makes two—no, *three* stupid questions in a row, and so I would enslave you *thrice* if such a thing were possible.' 'My god,' I said, as I began to understand the full horror of what was being done to me, 'can you not see the evil of what you are doing? Bonny—and all the other slave-depots—are filled with our brothers, dying of disease and despair before they even get on those hellish slave-ships! Hundreds of years from now, their descendants will live on in faraway lands as outcasts, embittered by the knowledge of what was perpetrated against their forefathers! How can we—how can *you*—seemingly a decent man—capable of showing love and affection towards your wives and children—perpetrate such unspeakable crimes?' To which the oracle replied, 'Now, *that* is a good question!' and with another flick of his fly-whisk sent me off to the holding-pit. I returned to Bonny on the same English boat that had brought me up the river, and my uncle had a new piece of India cloth to brighten his household." Dappa now laughed out loud, his teeth gleaming handsomely in the rapidly deepening dusk of a crevasse-like Algiers back-street.

Jack managed a polite chuckle. Though the other slaves had probably never heard Dappa's story told in English before, they recognized its rhythms, and grinned on cue. The Spaniard laughed heartily and said, "You have got to be one stupid nigger to think that's funny!" Dappa ignored him.

"It is a good enough yarn," Jack allowed, "but it does not explain how you ended up here."

Dappa responded by pulling his ragged shirt down to expose his right breast. In the gloom Jack could barely make out a pattern of scars. "I don't know letters," he said.

"Then I'll teach you two of them," said Dappa, reaching out quickly and grasping Jack's index finger before Jack could flinch away. "This is a D," he continued, running the tip of Jack's finger along the ridge of a scar, "for Duke. And this is a Y, for York. They trade-marked me thus with a silver branding-iron when I reached Bonny."

"Not to rub salt in your wound, there, Dappa, but that same bloke is King of England now—"

"Not any more," Moseh put in, "he was run off by William of Orange."

"Well, *there's* a bit of good news at least," Jack muttered.

"From that point my story's unremarkable," Dappa said. "I was traded from fort to fort up the coast. Bonny slaves fetch a low price because, since we grew up in paradise, we are unaccustomed to agricultural labor. Otherwise I would've been shipped straight to Brazil or the Caribbean. I ended up in the hold of a Portuguese ship bound for Madeira, which was captured by the same Rabat corsairs who'd earlier taken *your* ship."

"We must hurry," Moseh said, bending his neck to stare straight up. Down here it had been night for hours, but fifty feet above them, the corner of a wall was washed in the red light of the sunset. The little slave-column doubled its pace, trotted around several more corners, and came out into a street that was relatively wide (i.e., Jack could no longer touch both sides of it at the same time). Onion-skins and vegetable-trimmings were strewn about, and Jack reckoned it to be some sort of a market, though all of the tables had been cleared and the stalls shuttered. A young, dark-haired man, oddly familiar-looking, was standing there waiting for them, and fell in stride as they passed. His Sabir was infused with an accent that Jack recognized, from his last Paris sojourn, as Armenian.

But before he'd had time to think on this, they'd spilled out into an open space: some sort of public square, difficult to make out in the dusky light, with a public fountain in the center and a few large, but very plain, buildings around the sides. One of these was all lit up, with hundreds of men trying to get in the doors. Quite a few of them were slaves, but there were many members of the *ocak,* too, as well as the usual Algerine assortment of Berbers, Jews, and Christians. As they came up against the fringes of this crowd, Moseh de la Cruz stepped aside and allowed the Spaniard to lunge past him, suddenly bellowing every vile insult Jack had ever heard, as well as diverse new-made ones, and jabbing various large, heavily armed Turks in the ribs, treading on the curly toes of their slippers, and kicking them in the shins to clear a path towards the building's entrance. Jack expected to have his head scimitared off merely for being in the general vicinity of this uncivil Spaniard, but all the victims of his jabs and insults grinned and laughed the moment they recognized him, and then derived all manner of entertainment from watching him assail whomever stood in his path next. Moseh and the others, meanwhile, followed along in his wake, so that they arrived at the front door quickly—yet apparently none too soon. For the Turks standing guard there spoke angrily to Moseh and the others, pointing at the western sky, which had faded to a deep and nearly invisible blue now, like candle-light trying to penetrate a porcelain saucer. One of the guards slugged Dappa and the Nipponese Jesuit as they went by, and aimed a blow at Jack, which he dodged.

Moseh had mentioned to him earlier that they lived in something called a *banyolar* and Jack reckoned this must be it: a courtyard surrounded by galleries divided into many small cells, one ring of galleries piled upon the next to a height of several storeys. To Jack, the overall design was much like certain old-fashioned theatres that stood along Maid Lane between the marshes of Southwark and the right bank of the Thames, viz. the Rose, the Hope, and the Swan. The big difference, of course, was that those Bankside theatres had armed men trying to keep Jack *out* whereas here they were abusing him for not having entered *soon* enough.

This, of course, was no theatre, but a slave-quarters. And yet the galleries, up to and including the flat roof of the *banyolar,* were crowded (at the moment anyway) with free Algerines, and so was most of the courtyard. But one part of that yard, off to one side of its central cistern, had been roped off to form a stage, or ring; and any number of torchères had been planted around it, so close to one another that their flames practically merged into a square window-frame of fire that shed fair illumination on the empty plot in the center.

All of the Turks packed turban-to-turban around the galleries were *very* excited, and rowdier than any group Jack had ever seen outside of a Vagabond camp. When not jostling for position or transacting elaborate wagers, they were paying close attention to certain preparations underway at the corners of the ring. As far as Jack was concerned, only two attractions could account for this degree of excitement among so many young men; and since *sex,* for Janissaries, was banned, Jack reckoned that they must be about to witness some form of *violence.*

Following Moseh towards one of the corners of the fiery square, Jack was struck—but not particularly surprised—to discover Yevgeny, stark naked save for leather underpants and a thick coating of oil, and Mr. Foot, dressed up in scarlet finery and shaking a leather purse bloated with what Jack could only assume was specie. But before Jack could push his way in closer and begin asking questions, Yevgeny went down on his right knee: in and of itself, nothing remarkable. But here it was like setting off a granadoe. Everyone near him flung himself back, making an empty space with Yevgeny in the center. The crowd in the gallery went silent for a moment—then exploded with cheers of *"Rus! Rus! Rus!"*

Yevgeny spread his arms out to their full seven-foot span, then clapped his hands together, close enough to the ground to raise a puff of dust, then spread his arms again and did the same thing twice more. After the third clap he let his right hand fall to the earth, palm up, then raised it to his face and kissed his fingertips, then touched them to his forehead. During this little ceremony the cheering of *"Rus! Rus!"* continued at subdued volume—but now Yevgeny got up and vaulted into the square and the cheering rose to a level that made Jack's ears ring, reminding him of the fifteen-hundred-gun salute. Yevgeny planted his feet in the middle of the square and adopted a strangely insouciant pose: supporting his left elbow in his cupped right hand, he rested his head on his left hand, and froze in that position.

Nothing changed for several minutes, except that the torchères blazed and the cheers rang down from the deepening night sky. Finally another well-lubricated man in leather underpants performed the same series of movements and ended up standing next to Yevgeny in the same pose: this was a very dark-skinned Negro, not as tall as Yevgeny, but heavier. The cheering redoubled. Mr. Foot, who had added an expensive-looking cape to his ensemble, now came into the ring and hollered some sort of announcement up into the galleries, turning slowly round as he did, so that every member of the audience could inspect his tonsils even if hearing him was out of the question. Having concluded this, he scurried out of the ring. Yevgeny and the Negro turned to face each other in the middle of the fiery ring. Soon they had clasped their hands together, palm to palm like children playing at pat-a-cake. Rearing their heads back they smashed their faces together as hard as they could. Jack was startled; then they reared back like vipers preparing to strike, and did it a *second* time, and he was fascinated. Then they did it a *third* time, with no less violence, and Jack started to be appalled, wondering whether they would continue it until one of them was left senseless. But then they let go of each other and staggered apart with blood running down their faces from lacerations on their brows.

Now, finally, they got down to the actual business at hand: wrestling. And this was not greatly different from most other wrestling matches Jack had seen, except messier. Immediately both men got oil on their hands, then had to back away from each other and rub their palms on the ground to pick up dirt, which was shortly transferred to their bodies the next time they closed. So within a few minutes Yevgeny and the Negro were covered head-to-toe in a paste of blood, sweat, oil, and Algerian dust. Yevgeny had a wide stance, but the Negro knew how to keep his weight low, and so neither could throw the other. The crisis occurred several minutes into the bout when the African got a grip on Yevgeny's testicles and squeezed, which was a good idea, while looking up expectantly into Yevgeny's face, which wasn't. For Yevgeny accepted the ball-squeezing with a forbearance that made Jack's blood run a little cool, and paid the Negro back with another vicious downward head-butt that produced a clearly visible explosion of blood and audible splintering noises. The African let go of Yevgeny's private parts the better to clap both hands over his devastated face, and Yevgeny easily threw him into the dust—which ended the match.

"*Rus! Rus! Ruuuuus!*" howled the worthies of the *ocak*. Yevgeny paraded around the ring, looking philosophical, and Mr. Foot pursued him holding up a yawning purse into which Turks flung money—mostly, whole pieces of eight. Jack liked the looks of this—until the whole purse was delivered direct into the hands of a large Turkish gentleman who was sitting on a sort of litter at ringside, his feet mummified in white linen and propped up on an ottoman.

"IN RUSSIA, I BELONGED to a secret society, wherein we trained one another to feel no pain under torture," Yevgeny said, offhandedly, later.

This remark dampened all conversation for a few minutes, and Jack took stock of his situation.

After a long series of wrestling-bouts, the torchères had been extinguished and the Turks and free Algerines had departed, leaving the *banyolar* to the slaves. Both the starboard and the larboard oars, in their entirety, had now convened on the roof of the *banyolar* to smoke pipes. The night was nearly moonless, with only the merest crescent creeping across the sky—out over the Sahara, as Jack supposed. Consequently there were more stars out than Jack had ever seen. A few lights glimmered from the embrasures of the Kasba, but other than that, it seemed that these ten galley-slaves had the night to themselves:

Larboard Oar

YEVGENY THE RASKOLNIK, a.k.a. "Rus"

MR. FOOT, ex-proprietor of the Bomb & Grapnel, Dunkirk, and now entrepreneur-without-portfolio

DAPPA, a Neeger linguist

JERONIMO, a vile but high-born Spaniard

NYAZI, a camel-trader of the Upper Nile

Starboard Oar

"Half-Cocked" Jack Shaftoe, *L'Emmerdeur,*
    King of the Vagabonds

Moseh de la Cruz, the Kohan with the Plan

Gabriel Goto, a Jesuit Priest of Nippon

Otto van Hoek, a Dutch mariner

Vrej Esphahnian, youngest of the Paris Esphahnians—

    for the Armenian they'd picked up in the market was none other*

"We are held captive in this city by the ineffable will of the market," Moseh de la Cruz began.

These words sounded to Jack like the beginning of a well-rehearsed, and very long presentation, and so he was not slow to interrupt.

"Pah! What market can you possibly be talking about?" But looking around at the others it seemed that he was the only one showing the least bit of skepticism.

"Why, the market in *tutsaklar* ransom futures, which is three doors down yonder alley-way, on the left," Moseh said, pointing. "It is a place where anyone with money can buy into the deed of a *tutsaklar,* which means, captive of war—thereby speculating that one day that person will be ransomed, in which event all of the shareholders divide up the ransom, minus certain duties, taxes, fees, *et cetera,* levied by the Pasha. It is the city's primary source of revenue and foreign exchange—"

"All right, pardon me, I did not know that, and supposed you were framing some occult similitude," Jack said.

"As I watched Yevgeny's bout this evening," Moseh continued, "it came to me that said market is a sort of Invisible Hand that grips us all by the testicles—"

"Hold, hold! Are you babbling some manner of Cabbalistic superstition now?"

"No, Jack, *now* I am using a similitude. For there is no Invisible Hand—but there might as well be."

"Very good—pray continue."

---

* "What are the odds of *that?*" had been Jack's response, when he'd been made aware, for he'd had dealings with the Esphahnians before; but the others had rolled their eyes and, it seemed, bit their tongues—giving Jack a clew that there were no accidents, at least where Armenians were concerned, and that the presence of a Esphahnian on his oar was anything but fortuitous.

"The workings of the market dictate that *tutsaklar* who are likely to be ransomed, and for large fees, are well-treated—"

"And ones like us end up as galley-slaves," Jack said. "And 'tis clear enough to me why *I* am assessed a low value by this market, and my nuts gripped most oppressively by the Invisible Hand of which you spoke. Likewise, Mr. Foot is broke, Yevgeny's of a daft sect whose members torture one another, Dappa is persona non grata in all lands south of the Sahara, Vrej Esphahnian's family is chronically ill-funded. Señor Jeronimo, whatever fine qualities he may possess that I haven't seen evidence of yet, is not the sort that anyone who has spent much time with him would be disposed to pay a lot of ransom for. I know not the tale of Nyazi but can guess it. Gabriel is on the wrong side of the fucking world. All plain enough. But van Hoek is some kind of a naval officer, and you are an intelligent-seeming Jew—why have you two not been ransomed?"

"My parents died of the Plague that ravaged Amsterdam when Cromwell cut off our foreign trade, and so many honest Dutchman were cast out of their homes and took to sleeping in pestilential places—" van Hoek began, rather peevishly.

"Avast, Cap'n! Do I look like a Roundhead? 'Twasn't *my* doing!"

"I was suckled by government-issue wet-nurses at the Civic Orphanage. The worthies of the Reformed Church taught me reading and figures, bless them, but in time I grew up into a difficult boy."

"Fancy that—who would've expected it from a short, Dutch, ill-tempered, red-headed step-child?" Jack exclaimed. "Still, I'd think some corsair-captain could find a use for you more exalted than barnacle-scraper."

"When I was eighteen, the canals froze, and King Louis's troops swarmed over them on ice-skates, raping everything that moved and burning all else. The Dutch Republic prepared to take ship and move to Asia en masse. Seamen were wanted. I was sprung from jail and compelled to join the V.O.C.* Following the refugees north, I went to Texel, where I was issued a sea-chest containing clothes, pipes, tobacco, a Bible, and a book called *The God-Fearing Sailor.* Twenty-four hours later I was on a man-o'-war in the Narrow Seas dodging English grape-shot and lugging sacks of gunpowder. That, and a year of manning pumps, made me a sailor. Thrice I sailed to India and back, and that made me an officer."

"Fine! Why're you not an officer *here*?"

---

* *Vereenigde Oostindische Compagnie,* or Dutch East India Company

"A dozen years I lived in continual fear of pirates. Finally all of my nightmares came true and my ship was stolen from me—you can see her riding at anchor in the harbor some days, flying the Turk's flag, and if you cock an ear, and the wind's right, you can hear the lamentations of the captives she has taken, being brought in to wait for ransom."

"I am beginning to collect that you have a certain dislike of pirates and their works," Jack said, "as any upright Dutchman *should,* I suppose."

"Van Hoek refuses to turn Turk—so he rows alongside us," Moseh said.

"What of you, Moseh? Reputedly, Jews stick together."

"I am a crypto-Jew," Moseh said. "In fact, more Crypto than Jew. I grew up on the Equator. There is an island off the coast of Africa called Sáo Tomé, which is the sovereign soil of whichever European country has most recently sent a fleet down there to bombard it. But for many years only the Portuguese knew where the hell it was and so it was Portuguese. Now, my ancestors were Spanish Jews. But two hundred years ago, in the very same year that the Moors were finally driven from Spain, and America discovered, Queen Isabella threw all of the Jews out. Those who, in retrospect, were *intelligent,* put on the stockings of Villa Diego—which is an expression meaning that they ran like hell—and settled in Amsterdam. *My* ancestors simply edged across the border to Portugal. But the Inquisition was there, too. When Alvaro de Caminha went down to Sáo Tomé to be its governor, he took with him two thousand Jewish children whom the Inquisition had torn from the bosoms of their families. Sáo Tomé had a monopoly on the slave trade in that part of the world—Alvaro de Caminha baptized those two thousand and put 'em to work in its management. But in secret they kept their faith alive, performing half-remembered rituals behind locked doors, and muttering in broken Hebrew even as they knelt before the gilded table where the body and blood of Christ were dished up. Those were my ancestors. Almost fifty years ago, the Dutch came and seized Sáo Tomé. But this probably saved my father's parents' lives, for, in all the lands controlled by Spain and Portugal, the Inquisition went on a rampage after that. Instead of being roasted alive in some Portuguese *auto da fé,* my father's parents moved to New Amsterdam and worked for the Dutch West India Company in the slave trade, which was all they knew how to do. Later the Duke of York's fleet came and took that city for the English, but not before my father had grown up and taken a Manhatto lass for his wife—"

"What the hell is a Manhatto?"

"A type of local Indian," Moseh explained.

"I thought there was a certain *je ne sais quoi* about your nose and eyes," Jack said.

Moseh's face—illuminated primarily by the red glow of his pipe-bowl—now took on a sentimental, faraway look that made Jack instinctively queasy. Undoing the top-most button of his ragged shirt, Moseh drew out a scrap of stuff that dangled round his neck on a leather thong: some sort of heathen handicraft-work. "It is probably not easy for you to see this tchotchke, in this wretched light," he said, "but the third bead from the edge in the fourth row, here—it is a sort of off-white—is one of the very beads that the Dutchman, Peter Minuit, traded to the Manhattoes for their island, some sixty years ago, when Mama was a little papoose."

"Jesus Christ, you should hang on to that!" Jack exclaimed.

"I *have been* hanging onto it," Moseh returned, showing mild irritation for the first time, "as any imbecile can see."

"Do you have any conception of what it could be worth!?"

"Next to nothing—but to me, it is priceless, because I had it from Mama. At any rate—getting on with the story—my parents put on the stockings of Villa Diego and ended up in Curaçao and there I was born. Mama died of smallpox, Papa of yellow fever. I fell in with a community of crypto-Jews who had collected there, for lack of any other place to go. We decided to strike out for Amsterdam, which was where our ancestors should have simply gone in the first place, and seek our fortunes there. As a group, we bought passage on a slave-ship bringing sugar back to Europe. But this ship was captured by the corsairs of Rabat, and we all ended up galley-slaves together, rowing to the strains of the Hava Negila; which, owing to its tiresome knack for getting stuck in the head, was the only Jewish song we knew."

"All right," Jack said, "I am satisfied, now, that it is true what you said: namely that the Invisible Hand of yonder market is gripping our *cojones* just like that Nubian wrestler did Yevgeny's. And now I suppose you're going to say we should all do like the Rus and ignore the pain and swelling and score some sort of magnificent triumph of the human spirit, or some shit like that. Anyway, I am willing to listen, as it seems preferable to bedding down in the *bany-olar* to listen to the antiphonal coughing of a thousand consumptive oar-slaves."

"The Plan will no doubt strike you as implausible, until Jeronimo, here, has acquainted us with certain amazing facts," said Moseh, turning toward the twitchy Spaniard, who now stood up and bowed most courteously in Moseh's direction.

> The *vain-glory* which consisteth in the feigning or supposing of abilities in ourselves, which we know are not, is most incident to young men, and nourished by the histories, or fictions of gallant persons; and is corrected oftentimes by age, and employment.
> —HOBBES,
> *Leviathan*

"My name is Excellentissimo Domino Jeronimo Alejandro Peñasco de Halcones Quinto, Marchioni de Azuaga et de Hornachos, Comiti de Llerena, Barcarrota, et de Jerez de los Caballeros, Vicecomiti de Llera, Entrín Alto y Bajo, et de Cabeza del Buey, Baroni de Barrax, Baza, Nerva, Jadraque, Brazatortas, Gargantiel, et de Val de las Muertas, Domino Domus de Atalaya, Ordinis Equestris Calatravae Beneficiario de la Fresneda. As you have guessed from my name, I am of a great family of Caballeros who, of old, were mighty warriors for Christendom, and famous Moor-killers even back unto the time of the Song of Roland—but that is another story, and a more glorious one than mine. I have only dim tear-streaked memories of the place of my birth: a castle on a precipitous crag in the Sierra de Machado, built on land of no value, save that my forefathers had paid for it with blood, wresting it from the Moors, inch by inch and yard by yard, at sword- and dagger-point. When I was only a few years of age, and just beginning to talk, I was taken out of that place in a sealed black carriage and brought down the high arroyos of the Guadalquivir and delivered into the hands of certain nuns who took me on board a galleon at Seville. There followed a long and terrifying passage to New Spain, of which I remember little, and will relate less. Suffice it to say that the next time I set foot on dry land I was treading on silver. The ship had taken me and the nuns, as well as many other Spaniards, to Porto Belo. As you may know, this lies on the Caribbean shore of Panama, at the very narrowest part of that isthmus, and directly across from the City of Panama, which shelters on the Pacific side. All of the silver that comes from the fabulous mines of Peru (save what is smuggled over the Andes and down the Río de la Plata to Argentina, that is) is shipped up to Panama and thence borne over the isthmus by mule-train to Porto Belo, where it is loaded on treasure-galleons for the passage back to Spain. So you will understand that when Porto Belo is expecting those galleons—

such as the one on which I had arrived—bars of silver are simply piled in heaps on the ground, like cord-wood. Which is how it came to pass that, when I disembarked from the lighter that had brought me and the nuns in from the galleon, the first thing my foot touched was silver—an omen of what was to happen to me later, which in turn, God willing, is only a foreshadowing of the adventure that awaits us ten."

"I believe I can speak for all the other nine in saying you have our full attention, there, Excellentissimo—" Jack began, amiably enough; but the Spaniard cut him off, saying, "Shut up! Or I'll cut off what remains of your poxy yard and ram it down your Protestant throat with my hard nine inches!"

Before Jack could take exception to this, Jeronimo continued as if it hadn't happened: "Not for long did I linger in this El Dorado, for we were met at dockside by a wagon, driven by nuns of the same order, save that these were *Indias*. We traveled up winding tracks out of the jungle and into the mountains of Darién, and at last came to a convent that, as I then understood, was to be my new home; and my misery at having been torn from the bosom of my family was only made more *doloroso* by the resemblance of this nunnery to my ances-tral home. For this, too, was a vertiginous fortress rising out of a crag, making queer moans and whistles as the trans-isthmian gales blew across its narrow cross-shaped embrasures.

"Those sounds were almost the only ones that reached my ears until I had grown up, for these nuns had taken a vow of silence—and in any case, I soon enough learned that the *Indias* came from a cer-tain vale in the mountains where in-breeding had been practiced on a scale exceeding even that of the Hapsburg Dynasty, and none of them could hear. The only speech I ever heard was that of the carters and drovers who came up the mountain to bring victuals, and of the several other guests who, like me, were the beneficiaries of the nuns' Christian hospitality. For at no time were there fewer than half a dozen residents in the guest-house: men and women both—who, judging from their clothes and personal effects, were of gentle or even noble families. My fellow-guests appeared healthy, but behaved strangely: some spoke in garbled words, or remained as mute as the nuns, others were continually tormented by fiendish visions, or were imbeciles, unable to remember events that had occurred a mere quarter of an hour previously. Men who had been kicked in the head by horses, women whose pupils were of different sizes. Some spent all of their time locked in their rooms, or tied into their beds, by the nuns. But I had the run of the place.

"In due time I was taught to read and write, and began to

exchange letters with my beloved Mama in Spain. I told her in one such letter that I could not understand why I was being raised in this place. The letter went down the mountain in a donkey-cart and traversed the ocean in the hold of one of a fleet of treasure-galleons, and about eight months later I had my answer: Mama told me that, at the time of my birth, God had blessed me with a gift given only to a few, which was that I fearlessly spoke the truth that was in my heart, and said what everyone else was secretly thinking, but too cowardly to voice. She told me that it was a gift normally given only to the angels, but that I had been granted it in a sort of miracle; but that in this fallen and corrupt world, many were the benighted, who hated and feared aught that was of the angels, and who would surely abuse and oppress me. Hence my dear Mama had broken her own heart by sending me away to be raised by women who were nearer to God than any in Spain, and who, in any case, could not hear me.

"Satisfied, though never happy, with this explanation, I applied myself to the improvement of my mind and spirit: my *mind* by reading the ancient books that Mama shipped over from the library of our castle in Estremaduras, which told the tales of my ancestors' wars against the Saracens during the Crusades and the Reconquista, and my *spirit* by studying catechism and—at the behest of the nuns—praying, an hour a day, for the intercession of a particular Saint who was depicted in a stained-glass window in a side-chapel of the church. This was Saint Étienne de la Tourette, and his emblems were as follows: in his right hand, the sailmaker's needle and thong with which his lips had been sewn shut by a certain Baron, and in his left, the iron tongs with which his tongue, on a later occasion, had been ripped out by the Bishop of Metz, who was later canonized as St. Absalom the Serene. Though at the time the significance of these tokens did not really penetrate my thoughts.

"But my *body* was never developed until one day, around the time my voice changed, when a new visitor came to lodge with us: a tall and handsome Caballero with a hole in the center of his forehead, something like a third eye. This was Carlos Olancho Macho y Macho: a great sea-captain renowned throughout New Spain for his magnificent exploits against the boca-neers who infest the Caribbean (which—never mind what the *English* think of it—is, to us, a pit of vipers lying astride the route from our treasure-ports to Spain; a gantlet of fire, flying lead, and bloody cutlasses that must be run by every one of our galleons). Many were the pirates who had been slain by Carlos Olancho Macho y Macho, or El Torbellino as he was called in less formal settings, and a score of galleons would not carry all the silver he had kept out of the clutches of the Protestants. But in a struggle against the pirate-armada of Captain Morgan, off the Archipiélago de los Colorados, he had taken this pistol-ball between his eyes. Ever since he had been moody to an extent that put all around him—especially his superior officers—in fear of their lives, and he had been unable to put ideas into words, unless he wrote those words backwards, with his left hand, while looking into a mirror— which had proved to be fatally impractical in the heat of battle. And so with great reluctance El Torbellino had agreed to be pensioned off to this nunnery. Every day he knelt beside me in the side-chapel and prayed for the intercession of St. Nicolaas of Frisia, whose emblem was a Viking broad-axe embedded in the exact centerline of his tonsure: a wound that had given him the miraculous gift of understanding the speech of terns.

"Now I will encompass the entirety of several years in one sentence: El Torbellino taught me, of the arts of war, everything he knew; as well as some things I suspect he made up on the spur of the moment. In this way he brought the phant'sies and romance of those musty old books within my reach. But not within my grasp; for never mind my skill with the cutlass, the rapier, the dagger, pistol, and musket. I still lived in a nunnery in Darién. As I grew into the fullness of manhood, I began to make a plan of escaping to the coast, and perhaps raising a crew of sea-dogs, and going out on the Caribbean to hunt for boca- neers, and, after making a name for myself, offering my services as privateer to King Carlos II. That King was in my thoughts every day: El Torbellino and I would kneel before the image of St. Lemuel, whose emblem was the basket he had been carried around in, and pray on His Majesty's behalf.

"But as it happened, before I could go out and find the pirates, they came to me.

"Even men such as you, so ignorant and stupid, probably know that some years ago Captain Morgan sailed from Jamaica with an armada; sacked and pillaged Porto Belo; and then crossed the isth- mus at the head of an army and laid waste to the city of Panama itself. At the time of this atrocity, El Torbellino and I were off on a long hunting trip in the mountains. We were trying to find and kill one of the were-jaguars that are spoken of, with such apparent sin- cerity, by the *Indios* . . ."

"Did you catch one?" Jack asked, unable to contain himself.

"That is another tale," said Jeronimo with obvious regret, and uncharacteristic self-restraint. "We ranged far down the isthmus, and were a long time returning, because of *los parásitos* of which the less said the better. During our absence, Morgan's fleet had fallen upon Porto Belo, and his advance parties had begun to penetrate the interior, searching for the best way over the divide. One of these, comprising perhaps two dozen sea-scum, had come upon the nunnery, and were well advanced in sacking it. As El Torbellino and I approached, we could hear the shattering of the stained-glass windows, and the cries and moans of the nuns who were being dishonored—the only sounds I had ever heard from their lips.

"El Torbellino and I were armed with all of the necessaries that two gentlemen would normally take on a long were-jaguar-hunting campaign in the ravenous and all-destroying jungles of Darién, and we had the advantage of surprise; furthermore, we were on the side of God, and we were very, very angry. Yet these advantages might have gone for naught, at least in my case, for I was untested in battle. And it is universally known that many are the young men who have filled their heads with romantic legends, and who dream of fighting gloriously in battle—but who, when plunged into a real flesh-and-blood conflict, with all of its shock, confusion, and gore, become paralyzed, or else throw down their weapons and flee.

"As it turned out, I was not one of those. El Torbellino and I burst out of the jungle and fell upon those drunken boca-neers like a pair of rabid were-jaguars descending upon a sheep-fold. The violence was exquisite. El Torbellino killed more than I, of course, but many an *Inglés* tasted my steel on that day, and, to summarize a very disagreeable story, the surviving nuns carred barrow-loads of viscera into the jungle to be torn by the condors.

"We knew that this was no more than an advance-party, and so we then turned our energies to fortifying the place, and teaching the nuns how to load and fire matchlocks. When the main force arrived—several hundred of Captain Morgan's rum-drenched irregulars—we gave them a warm Spanish welcome, and decorated the court with a few score bodies before they forced their way in. After that it was hand-to-hand combat. El Torbellino died, impaled on thirteen blades as he stood in the infirmary door, and I fought on for some while despite having been butt-stroked in the jaw with a musket. The commander outside ordered his men to withdraw and regroup. Before they could make another attack—which certainly would have killed me—he received word from Captain Morgan that another way over the mountains had been found, and that he should disengage and go via that route. Seeing that there was more profit, and less peril, in sacking a rich city, defended by poltroons, than a modest convent, defended by a single man who was not afraid to die in glory, the pirates left us alone.

"So both Porto Belo and Panama were sacked and destroyed anyway. Despite this—or perhaps because of it—the story of how El Torbellino and I had defended the nunnery created a sensation in Lima and Mexico City, and I was made out to be a great hero—perhaps the only hero of the entire episode, for the performance of those who had been charged with defending Panama was too miserable to be related in polite company.

"I knew nothing of this, for I had fallen gravely ill of my wounds, as well as various tropical maladies picked up on the were-jaguar-hunt which only now were coming into their full flower. I had taken leave of my senses, despite the prodigious bleedings, and volcanic purges, administered every day by doctors who came to the convent during the aftermath of the battles I have described. When next I was aware of my surroundings, I was on a galleon coasting along the Bahía de Campeche, approaching Vera Cruz, which, as even bumpkins such as you may understand, is the sea-port most convenient to Mexico City. I could not open my mouth. A Jesuit doctor explained to me that my jaw-bone had been fractured by the blow of the musket-butt, and that bandages had been wound tightly round my head to clench my jaw shut and hold all in place until the bone knit. In the meantime my left front tooth had been punched out to create a small orifice through which a paste of milk and ground maize was injected, using a sort of bellows, three times a day.

"In due time we threaded the Western Channel of Vera Cruz and dropped anchor under the walls of the castle, there, then waited out a sandstorm, then another, and finally went ashore, forcing our way through fog-banks of gnats, and keeping our pistols at the ready in the event of alligators. We parleyed with the crowd of Negro and Mulatto mule-thieves who make up the citizenry, and arranged for transportation to the City. The town was crowded with shabby wooden houses, all boarded up—it was explained to me that these were the property of white men, who flocked to town when the treasure-fleet was forming up around the Castle, but otherwise retired to haciendas up-country, which were more salubrious in every way. The only part of Vera Cruz that can be called civilized is the square of the churches and the Governor's house, where a company of troops is garrisoned. When the officer in charge there was informed of my arrival, he had his artillery-men fire a salute from their field-pieces, and gladly wrote out a pass for me to travel to the Capital. So we rode out of the landward gate, which had been wedged open by a passing dune, and began our passage west.

"The less said about this journey, the better.

"Mexico City turned out to be everything that Vera Cruz was not in the way of beauty, magnificence, and order. It rises from a lake, joined to the shore by five causeways, each with its own gate. All of the land is owned by the Church and so it is, perforce, a most pious city, in that there is no place to live unless one joins a holy order. There are a score of nunneries and even more monasteries, all of them rich, and besides that a numerous rabble of *criollos* who sleep in the streets and are forever committing outrages. The Cathedral can only be called stupendous, having a staff of between three and four hundred, headed by an Archbishop who is paid sixty thousand pieces of eight a year. I mention these facts only to convey how impressed I was; had my jaw not been lashed shut by many yards of linen, it would have hung open for a week.

"For several days I was squired around town and fêted by various important men including the Viceroy and his wife: a Duchess of very high birth, who looked like a horse when the lips are pulled back to inspect the teeth. Of course I could not eat any of the fine meals that were set before me, but I learned to drink wine through a hollow reed. Likewise I could not address my hosts, but I could write after-dinner speeches, which I did in the heroic old-fashioned style I'd learned from those family histories. These were very well received.

"Now I am come to the part of my Narration where I must summarize many years' events quickly. I think you know what occurs next: in time the bandage came off my jaw and I was conveyed to the Cathedral where, in a splendid Mass, I was knighted by the Viceroy.

"When the ceremony was finished, the Archbishop came up to give his compliments to me, and to the Viceroy, and to the Viceroy's wife, whom he praised for her chastity and her beauty.

"To which I said as follows: that this was certainly the most wretched piece of brown-nosing I had ever heard, for whenever I laid eyes on the Viceroy's wife I could not decide whether to give her the vigorous butt-fucking she so obviously craved, or to climb on her back and ride her around the *zócalo* firing pistols in the air.

"The Viceroy clapped me in irons and put me in a bad place for a long time, where I probably should have died.

"Letters made their way down the King's Highway to Vera Cruz and into the holds of galleons, to Havana and finally to Madrid, and other letters returned, and evidently some sort of explanation was proffered, and an arrangement made. After a while I was moved to an apartment where I recovered my health, and then I was conveyed back down to Vera Cruz and given command of a three-masted ship of thirty-two guns, and a fair crew, and told to go out and kill pirates and come ashore as infrequently as possible until I was given other instructions.

"And here I could cite any amount of statistics concerning tonnage of pirate-ships sunk and pieces of eight recovered for the King and the Church, but for me the highest honor was that, among the boca-neers, I became known as the second coming of El Torbellino. I was given the name El Desamparado, which I will now explain to you ignorant filth who know not its meaning. 'Desamparado' is a holy word to those of us who profess the True Faith, for it is the very last word uttered by Our Lord during His agony on the Holy Rood—"

"What's it mean," asked Jack, "and why'd they paste it on you, who already had such a surfeit of other names?"

"It means, Forsaken by God. For tales of my struggles, and my confinement in the dungeons of Mexico, had preceded me; from which even one such as you, Jack, who has parts missing both fore and aft, may understand why I was called this. Know that whenever I sailed into Havana I was saluted by many guns, though I was never invited to come ashore.

"Then, two years ago, the treasure-fleet was scattered by a hurricane after it had departed Havana. I was sent out into the Straits of Florida to round up stragglers—"

"Wait a moment there, El Desamparado. Is this going to be one of those yarns about how you, but only you, know the whereabouts of some sunken treasure-ship? Because—"

"No, no, it's better than that!" the Spaniard exclaimed. "After combing the sea for many days, we found a smaller vessel—a brig of perhaps seventy-five tons' displacement—trapped among sand-banks in the Muertos Cays, which lie between Cuba and Florida. The storm surge had carried her into a sort of basin whence she could not now escape, for fear of running aground on the shifting sands that encompassed her. We anchored in deeper water nearby and sent out longboats to take soundings. In this manner we discovered an aperture in the sand-bank through which this brig could pass, provided that we waited for high tide, and also offloaded some of her cargo, giving her a shallower draught. The master of this ship was strangely reluctant to follow my advice, but at length I convinced him that this was the only way out. We brought our longboat along-side and set all hands to work lightening the brig's load. And as any seaman will tell you, the quickest way to get weight off a ship is to remove those objects that are heaviest, but least numerous: typically, the armaments. And so, by means of blocks and tackle rigged to the yards, we raised her cannons up out of the gundeck one by one, lowered them into the longboat, and took them out to my ship. In the meantime other sailors busied themselves carrying cannonballs up from belowdecks. And that was how we discovered that this brig was armed, not with lead and iron, but with silver. For the strong places down below, the shot-lockers built to carry cannonballs, were stacked full of pigs."

"Pigs?!" exclaimed several; but here Jack for once was able to make himself useful. "El Desamparado means, not the squealing animals with curly tails, but the irregular bars of silver made by the refinery at the head of a mine by pouring the molten ore out into a trough of clay." And here Jack was prepared to go on at some length about the silver refineries of the Harz Mountains, which he had once visited, and had explained to him, by the Alchemist Enoch Root. But it seemed that his comrades had already heard many of these details from his own lips, and so he moved on to what he assumed was the point of Jeronimo's story. "Pigs are strictly an intermediate form, meant for one purpose only: to be taken direct to a refining furnace, re-melted, purified, and made into bars, which are assayed and stamped—at which point the King would normally take his rake-off . . ."

"In New Spain, ten percent for the King and one percent for the overhead, viz. assayers and other such petty officials," Jeronimo put in.

"And so the presence of pigs aboard this ship proved beyond argument that it was in the act of smuggling silver back to Spain."

"For once, the Vagabond has spoken truthfully and to the point," said Jeronimo. "And you will never guess what person we discovered in the best cabin on the ship: the Viceroy's wife, who still remembered me. She was on her way back to Madrid to go shopping."

"What did you say to her?"

"It is better not to remember this. Knowing that she would make a full report of these events to her husband in Mexico City, I did not delay in writing the Viceroy a letter, in which I related these events— but obliquely, in case the letter was intercepted. I assured him that his secret was safe with me, for I was a Caballero, a man of honor, and he could rely upon my discretion; my lips, I told him, were sealed forever."

There was now a long and somewhat agonizing silence there on the roof of the *banyolar.*

"Some months later, I received a communication from this same Viceroy, inviting me to go to the Governor's House in Vera Cruz on my next visit to that port, to receive a gift that awaited me there."

"A lovely new set of neck-irons?"

"A pistol-ball to adorn the nape of your neck?"

"A ceremonial sword, delivered point-first?"

"I have no idea," said Jeronimo, a bit ruffled, "for I never reached the house of the Gobernador. It is important to mention that our purpose in visiting Vera Cruz was to pick up a shipment of small arms from a merchant I had come to know there—a fellow who had a knack for taking delivery of the King's armaments before they reached the King's soldiers. Several of my men and I accomplished this errand first, in a couple of hired wagons, and then we told the teamsters to take us to the Governor's House via the most direct route, for we were running late even by the standards of New Spain. I was in my finest clothes.

"We entered the central plaza of Vera Cruz from a direction that they did not expect, for instead of proceeding up the main street with its boarded-up houses, we had come in from the depot of the arms merchant, which lay on the other side of the town. Our first hint that something was amiss came from the countless fine tendrils of smoke spiraling up from various places of concealment around the town square—"

"Matchlocks!" Jack said.

"Of course our pistols were already loaded and at the ready, for this was Vera Cruz. But this gave us warning to break out the muskets and to knock the lids from several cases of granadoes. The matchlock-men opened fire on us, but raggedly. We charged them with cutlasses drawn, intending to kill them before they could reload. Which we did—but we were astonished to discover that these were Spanish soldiers of the local garrison! At this point fire came down on us from all around: the windows of the Governor's House and of the churches and monasteries ringing the square all served as loop-holes for this *emboscada*."

"The soldiers had occupied *all* of those buildings?" exclaimed Mr. Foot, whose capacity for indignation knew no limits.

"So we assumed at first; but when we returned fire, and flung our granadoes, the burnt and dismembered bodies that sprayed out of those windows were those of monks and mid-level government officials. And yet still we were stupid, for our next mistake was to drive the wagons forward, out of the square, and into the main street of the town. Whereupon planks began to fall away from the windows and doors of the sorry wooden houses that the Viceroy's officials had put up there, and the true battle began. For it was here on this street where they had planned to make the ambush. We overturned both of the wagons, and made a fortification out of them; we shot all of the horses and piled their corpses up as ramparts; we fought from doorway to doorway; we got a runner out to my ship, and she opened fire upon the town with her guns. In return she came under fire from the cannons of the castle. We never would have survived against such a force, except that the guns set some of those buildings afire, and a wind blew the flames down the street as if those rows of wooden buildings had been trails of gunpowder. Many bodies fell in the dust of Vera Cruz on that day. Most of the town burned. My ship sank before my eyes. I escaped from the town with two of my men, and we made our way down the coast as best we could. One of my men was killed by an alligator, and one died of a fever. At length I came to a little port where I bought passage to Jamaica, that den of English thieves, now the only place in the Caribbean where I could hope to find sanctuary. There, I learned that in the weeks following the catastrophe, what remained of Vera Cruz had been taken and sacked by the pirate Lorenuillo de Petiguavas, and utterly leveled with the ground, so that it would have to be built again from nothing.

"As for myself, I tried to make my way back to Spain so that I could return to the place of my birth in Estremaduras. But when Gibraltar was almost in sight, my ship was captured by the Barbary Corsairs, *et cetera, et cetera, et cetera.*"

"It is a ripping yarn," Jack conceded, after a few moments' silence, "but the best story in the world does not amount to a Plan."

"That is my concern," said Moseh de la Cruz, "and I have a Plan that is nearly complete. Though it has one or two leaks in it, which you might be able to plug."

BOOK 5

the Juncto

The Commerce of the World, especially as it is now carried on, is an unbounded Ocean of Business; Trackless
and unknown, like the Seas it is managed upon; the Merchant is no more to be follow'd in his Adventures, than a
Maze or Labyrinth is to be trac'd out without a Clue.

—Daniel Defoe,
A Plan of the English Commerce

Dundalk, Ireland
6 SEPTEMBER 1689

To Eliza, Countess de la Zeur
From Sgt. Bob Shaftoe
Dundalk, Ireland
6 September 1689

My lady,

I am speaking these words to a Presbyterian scrivener who followed our regiments down from our points of disembarkation around Belfast, and has hung out his shingle on a hut near Dundalk camp. From this, you may draw what conclusions you will concerning which matters I will address straightforwardly, and which I will speak not of.

A queue of soldiers begins at my left shoulder and extends out the door and down the lane. I rank most of them, and so could keep the scribbler busy all day if I chose, but I will address important matters first and try to conclude our business directly so that the others may send greetings to their mums and mistresses in England.

Your letter of June 15th reached me just before we embarked for Belfast, and was read to me aboard ship by a chaplain. It is well that I made your acquaintance and took your measure in the Hague, or I would have dismissed its contents as idle and womanish chatter. Your stylings are finer than the discourse that one is accustomed to hearing aboard a troop-ship. All the blokes who overheard it were gobsmacked that such pretty phrases had been directed to one such as me. I am now reputed to be a man of parts, and a fellow with many high and mighty connexions.

Upon listening to certain phrases for the third and fourth time, I collected that you had run afoul of a French count by the name of d'Avaux, who had obtained some knowledge of you that put you in his power. The Revolution in London had caused this d'Avaux to be recalled suddenly to France. Later the unfortunate Count was despatched to Brest, the remotest port of France, and loaded aboard ship in company of none other than Mr. James Stuart, who was formerly known as James II by the Grace of God of England, etc., King.

Off they sailed to the sophisticated metropolis of Bantry, Ireland. Later you had news that they had assembled an army of Frenchmen, Irish Catholics, and Jacobites (as we now refer to James's supporters in Merry England) and established themselves in Dublin.

You are too courtly, my lady, ever to come out and say what you mean directly, and so the exact meaning of your letter was unclear to me and is unclear still. As I was situated in London, and your letter was addressed thither, you cannot have known that I'd have it read to me *during a passage to Ireland*. Or perhaps you are so clever and well-informed that you anticipated this. Surely it could never have been a request for my help? For how could I give you any aid in such a matter?

Brother Jack begat two sons by a strapping Irish lass named Mary Dolores Partry—he must have told you. She died. The boys have been raised by the kin of their late mum. I have made efforts to know them and to tender such support as I might—for example, by recruiting a few of their uncles and cousins into our Regiment. My life as a soldier has made me a poor uncle indeed. But the boys, who have inherited their dad's weakness to impulses of a perverse kind, and who have been raised by Irishmen to boot, seem to respect me all the more, the more I neglect them.

Last year, Jim Stuart, then King, conceived a malignant distrust of his very own English regiments, and brought in several Irish ones to put down our Revolution (which he styled an uprising). These were phant'sied, by ordinary Englishmen, to be Crusaders, ten feet tall, bearing French bayonets red with English blood, led by Jesuits, controlled directly from Rome, yet just as wild in their ways as Irishmen ever were.

My Presbyterian scrivener is giving me the evil eye now, for making light of them. His folk have oft felt besieged in various corners of Ulster by such—by your leave, sir, put it down just as I have spoke it.

'Twas an even worse time than usual to be Irish in England, so all the kinfolk of Mary Dolores, including Jack's boys, took passage on the first ship they could find that was Ireland-bound. This happened to set them down in Dublin—the wrong part of the island by far, as the Partrys are Connaught folk and seafarers. But Dublin they found more to their liking than they had foreseen. They'd raised two generations in London and grown used to city ways. During the same interval Dublin had grown to thrice its former size. Now these people, and Dublin, suited each other.

No sooner had they established themselves than James arrived with his motley Court, and his French generals began offering gold coins to any man who would join the Jacobite army. They had recruited a horde of naked bog-trotters whilst sloshing across the island and were calling them an army. Imagine, then, how pleased they were to encounter these fellows who had served in a Guards regiment, learnt to fire muskets, and fought in battles! Those fellows—not my in-laws, since Jack and Mary Dolores never married, but, if you will, my out-laws—were not merely accepted but embraced into James's regiments, and made sergeants on the spot. They were quartered in the houses of the Protestant gentry of Dublin, who by this time had already fled to England or America.

So now the Partrys and I are ranged on opposing sides of the battle-front, which is a sleepy one at present. If I survive, and if they do, I am invited to join them over pints of black beer and to have strange, rousing yarns related to me of Dublin under the Jacobites, and of how one Connaught family made themselves at home there.

Now during the past summer, the Ulster towns of Derry and Enniskillen were put under siege by elements of this queer French-Irish army. James's eagerness to score victories for the Pope exceeds his intelligence by an amount too great to measure. So on two occasions he dashed out of Dublin on short notice with all his entourage in the hopes of making his way north to Ulster and planting the Crusader-flag on the ruins of a Presbyterian church or two. The poor roads and scarcity of bridges hindered the royal progress, and the disinclination of the besieged Scotsmen to surrender might have balked him in any event.

My scrivener, who is at this moment glowing with pride and sniffling with emotion, will perhaps append a few lines extolling the manliness of the defenders of those two towns.

When d'Avaux—who had no choice but to accompany

James on these excursions—returned, he was given the unwelcome news that some enterprising Dubliners (described by witnesses as a pair of towheaded lads) had climbed up some vines and a drain-pipe, entered his house through a window, and stolen everything that was of value, as well as a few items that were of no use to anyone but himself.

I will leave it to you, my lady, to guess whether there may be any connexion between these events, and a letter I had sent to my Dublin out-laws a few weeks previously, in which I had described this d'Avaux, and mentioned that he was now residing across the square from the house where their company had been quartered.

Not long after, I received a nocturnal delivery of papers, written out in what I am assured, by learned men, is the French language. Though I cannot read, I can recognize some of the words, and I half phant'sy I see your name in some of them. I have enclosed them in this packet.

During our memorable meeting in the Hague, you voiced sympathy for my problem, namely, that my true love, Miss Abigail Frome, was made a slave, and given to the Earl of Upnor. You seemed to doubt that I could ever be of use to you. Perhaps it is time for a new reckoning.

I attempted to settle the issue personally on the day of the Revolution but was baffled—you may hear the story from my lord Upnor if you care to know it.

This concludes my letter. You may direct any response to me at Dundalk. I am here with a stew of English, Dutch, Huguenot, Ulster, Danish, and Brandenburg regiments, enlivened by a sprinkling of unreconstructed Phanatiques whose fathers came over with Cromwell, conquered this island, and were paid for their work in Irish land. Now the Irish have got it back, and these hectical Nonconformists are disgruntled, and undecided whether they should join our army and conquer it anew, or sail to America and conquer that instead. They shall have a good eight or nine months to make up their minds, as Marshal Schomberg—the general whom King William has put in charge of this army—is desultory, and intends to tarry here in Dundalk for the entire winter.

So here is where I may be reached, if I am not killed by pestilence, starvation, or boredom.

Your humble and obedient servant,

Bob Shaftoe

The Dunkerque Residence of
the Marquis and the Marquise d'Ozoir

21 OCTOBER 1689

BONAVENTURE ROSSIGNOL HAD MANY eccentric traits, even by the standards of cryptologists; but none more striking than his tendency to gallop into town alone when most needed and least looked-for. He had done it thirteen months ago, knowing (for he knew everything) that Eliza was in peril on the banks of the Meuse. The four-month-old infant she now carried was evidence of how it had wrought on her passions. Now, here he was again, wind-blown, mud-spattered, and horse-scented to a degree that was incorrect and absurd for a gentleman of the King's court; yet suddenly Eliza felt as if she had just sat down in a puddle of warm honey. She closed her eyes, drew a breath, let it out slowly, and dumped her burden into his arms.

"Mademoiselle, I had held, until this moment, that your recent letter to me was the most exquisite flirtation that could be devised by the human mind," said Rossignol, "but I perceive now that it was merely a prelude to the delicious torment of the Three Bundles."

This snapped her head around—as he'd known it would—because it was a sort of riddle.

Rossignol had coal-black eyes. He was gaunt, and held to be unattractive by most of the ladies at Court. He was as lean as a riding-crop, which made him look awkward in court-dress; but bulked up in a cassock and flushed from the breeze off the sea, he looked well enough to Eliza. Those black eyes glanced briefly at the blanket-wrapped object she had dropped into his arms, then flicked up to a side-table where rested a packet of moldy tent-cloth, tied up in twine. Two tight little bundles. Then, finally, his eyes locked on Eliza's for a moment—she was looking back over her shoulder at him—and traveled slowly down her back until they came to rest on her arse.

"The *last* time you galloped to my rescue thus," she said, "there was only *one* bundle to contend with; a simple matter, therefore, which you were man enough to handle." Her eyes now jumped down to the bundle in Rossignol's arms, which urped up some curdled milk onto his sleeve, coughed, and began to cry. "As we grow older the number of bundles waxes," she added, "and we must all become jugglers."

Rossignol stared, with a kind of Natural-Philosophick detachment, at the viscous streak of baby-vomit probing a fold of his sleeve. His son let out a howl; the father winced and turned his head away. A door at the other end of the room was ripped open, and a woman pounded in, already cooing for the baby; then, seeing a strange man, she drew herself up and looked to Eliza. "Please, mademoiselle, be my guest," said Rossignol, and extended his arms. He had never seen the woman before, and had no idea who she was, but it did not require a Royal cryptanalyst to read the situation: Eliza, despite being trapped and detained in Dunkerque with no money, had not only figured out a way to move into this vacant château, but had also managed to retain at least one competent, loyal, and trusted servant.

Nicole—for that was this woman's name—did not move until she had seen Eliza nod. Then she stepped forward and snatched the infant away, glaring at Rossignol—who responded with a grave bow. By the time she had reached the room's exit, the baby had stopped crying, and as she hustled him off down the corridor he began to make a contented "aaah."

Rossignol had forgotten the baby already. The bundle count was down to two. But he had the good manners not to pay undue attention to the packet on the side-table, even though he knew it to be filled with stolen diplomatic correspondence. All his attention, for now, was fixed on Eliza.

Eliza was accustomed to being looked at, and did not mind it. But she was preoccupied now for a little while. Rossignol had no feelings whatsoever for the baby. He had not the slightest intention of being its father. This did not surprise her especially. If anything, it was simpler and easier that way. He wanted her for what lay at either end of her spinal column—it was not clear which end he favored—and not for her spiritual qualities. Certainly not for her offspring.

King Louis XIV of France had found it convenient to make Eliza a Countess. Among other privileges, this had granted her admittance to the Salon of Diana in the royal château at Versailles. There she had noticed this bored and lonesome man studying her. She had been every bit as bored. As it had turned out, they had been bored for the same reason: They both knew the odds of these games, and saw little point in staking money on them. But to *talk about* the odds, and to speculate as to ways of systematically *beating* such games, was absorbing. It had seemed unwise, or at least impolite, to hold such conversations around the gaming-tables, and so Eliza and Rossignol had strolled in the gardens, and had moved quickly from the odds of card-games to more elevated talk of Leibniz, Newton, Huygens, and other Natural Philosophers. Of course they had been noticed by gossips looking out the windows; but those foolish Court girls, who mistook fashion for taste, had not considered Rossignol desirable, had not understood that he was a genius, unrecognized as such by the savants of Europe.

At the same time—though she had not realized this until later—*he* had been observing *her* even more shrewdly. Many of her letters to Leibniz, and Leibniz's letters back to her, had crossed his desk, for he was a member of the *Cabinet Noir*, whose purpose was to open and read foreign correspondence. He had found her letters to be curiously long, and filled with vapid chatter about hairstyles and the cut of the latest fashions. His true purpose in strolling with her in the gardens of Versailles had been to determine whether she was as empty-headed as she seemed in her letters. The answer, clearly, was no; and moreover she had turned out to know a lot about mathematics, metaphysics, and Natural Philosophy. This had sufficed to send him back to his family château at Juvisy, where he had broken the steganographic code that Eliza had been using to correspond with Leibniz. He could have destroyed, or at least damaged, her then, but he had lacked the desire to. For a kind of seduction had taken place between the two of them, which had not been acted upon until thirteen months ago.

It would have made matters a good deal simpler if he had fallen in love with the baby and proposed to elope with her, and him, to some other country. But this, as she now saw clearly, was unthinkable in so many different ways that to dream of it any more was a waste of time. Oh, well (she thought), if the world were populated solely by persons who loved and desired each other symmetrically, it might be happier, but not so interesting. And there would be no place in such a world for a person such as Eliza. During her weeks in Dunkerque, she had gotten better than ever at making do with what Fortune sent her way. If there was to be no doting father, so be it. Nicole was an ex-whore, recruited from one of Dunkerque's waterfront brothels. But she had already given the baby more love than he would get in a lifetime with Bonaventure Rossignol.

"*Now* you show up!" she said finally.

"The cryptanalyst to His Majesty the King of France," said Rossignol, "has responsibilities." He was not being arch—merely stating facts. "Things are expected of him. Now. The *last* time you got into trouble, a year ago—"

"Correction, monsieur: the last time *you know about.*"

"*C'est juste.* On *that* occasion, war was brewing on the Rhine, and I had a plausible reason to go that way. Finding you, mademoiselle, in a most complex predicament, I endeavoured to assist you."

"By impregnating me?"

"I did that out of passion—as did you, mademoiselle, for our flirtation had been lengthy. And yet it *did* militate in your favor—perhaps even saved your life. You seduced Étienne d'Arcachon the very next day."

"I let him believe he was seducing me," Eliza demurred.

"Just as I said. *Tout le monde* knew about it. When you turned up pregnant in the Hague, everyone, including *le Roi,* and Étienne, assumed that the baby was the spawn of Arcachon; and, when it was born healthy, this made it seem that you were that rarest of specimens: one who could mate with a scion of the de Lavardac line without passing on its well-known hereditary imperfections to the child. I did as much as I could to propagate this myth through other channels."

"Are you referring to how you stole, and decyphered, my journal, and gave it to the King?"

"Wrong on all counts. Monsieur le comte d'Avaux stole it—or would have, if I had not galloped post-haste to the Hague and co-opted him. I did not *decypher* it so much as produce a fictionalized version of it. And since the King owns me, and all my work, I did not so much *give* it to his majesty as direct his majesty's attention to it."

"Couldn't you have directed his majesty's attention elsewhere?"

"Mademoiselle. You had been witnessed by many Persons of Quality carrying out what was obviously a spy-mission. D'Avaux and his minions were doing all in their power—and they have much power—to drag your name through the muck. To direct the attention of *le Roi* elsewhere would have booted you nothing. Rather, I produced for his majesty an account of your actions that was tame compared to the fabrications of d'Avaux; it deflated that man's pretensions while cementing the belief that the baby had been fathered by Étienne de Lavardac d'Arcachon. I was *not* trying to rehabilitate you—*that* would have required a miracle—only to mitigate the damage. For I feared that they might send someone to assassinate you, or abduct you, and bring you back to France."

And now he stopped because he had talked himself into a *faux pas,* and was mortified. "Er . . ."

"Yes, monsieur?"

"I did not anticipate *this*."

"Is that why it took you so long to get here?"

"I have already told you that the King's cryptanalyst has responsibilities—*none* of which, as it turns out, place him in Dunkerque. I came as soon as I could."

"You came as soon as I incited your jealousy by praising Lieutenant Bart in a letter."

"Ah, so you admit it!"

"I admit nothing, monsieur, for he is every bit as remarkable as I made him out to be, and any man in his right mind would be jealous of him."

"It is just so difficult for me to follow," said Rossignol.

"Poor Bon-bon!"

"Please do not be sarcastic. And please do not address me by that ridiculous name."

"What is it, pray tell, that the greatest cryptanalyst in the world cannot *follow*?"

"At first you described him as a corsair, a boca-neer, who took you by force . . ."

"Took *the ship I was on* by force—pray watch your language!"

"Later, when it was to your advantage to make me jealous, he was the most perfect gentle knight of the seas."

"Then I shall explain it, for there is no contradiction. But first take off that cassock and let us make ourselves more comfortable."

"The double entendre is noted," said Rossignol crisply, "but before I become *dangerously* comfortable, pray tell, what are you doing in the residence of the Marquis and the Marquise d'Ozoir? For that is where we are, to judge from the scutcheon on the gates."

"You have decyphered the coat of arms correctly," said Eliza. "Fear not, the d'Ozoirs are not here now. It is just me, and my servants."

"But I thought you were under arrest on a ship, and had no servants . . . or did you write those things solely to make me come here the faster?"

Eliza clamped a hand on Rossignol's wrist and dragged him through a door. They had been conversing in a foyer that communicated with the stables. She took him now down a corridor into a little salon, and thence into a larger drawing-room that was illuminated by several great windows facing toward the harbor.

At some point in its history, Dunkerque must have been an apt name for this place. For it literally meant Dune-church, and one could easily see it, some centuries back, as a dune with a church on, below, or near it, and nothing else, save an indifferent creek that reached the sea there, not so much impelled by gravity as blundering into it by accident. This stark dune-church-creek-scape had over ages been complicated, though never obscured, by the huts, houses, docks, and wharves of a modest fishing- and smuggling-port. More recently it had come to be thought of as a strategic asset, and been juggled back and forth between England and France for a while; inevitably Louis XIV had made it his, and begun to aggrandize it into a *base navale,* which was a little bit like mounting cannons and armor-plates on a fishing-boat. To anyone approaching the place from England, it looked fearsome enough, with a massive stout rubble-wall along the shore for cannonballs to bounce off of, and divers fortifications and batteries set up wherever the sand would bear their weight. But seen from within—which was how Eliza and Monsieur Bonaventure Rossignol were seeing it—the place looked like a perfectly innocent little port-town that had been hurled into a prison, or had had a prison erected around it.

All of which was to say that it was not and never would be a place for a great lord to pile up a brilliant château, or a great lady to spread a fragrant garden; and while those dunes might be speckled with watch-towers and mortar-batteries, no grand *maréchal* would ever make them terrible with a high citadel. The Marquis and the Marquise d'Ozoir had had the discretion to know as much, and so had contented themselves with acquiring a compound in the middle of things, near the harbor, and improving it, building up rather than out. The exterior of the main house was still old Norman half-timbered style, but one would never know it if all one saw was the interior, which had been remade in Barock style—or as close to it as one could come without using stone. Much wood, paint, and time had been devoted to fashioning pilasters and columns, wall-panels and balusters that would pass for Roman marble unless you went up and rapped on them with a knuckle. Rossignol had the good grace not to, and attended, instead, to what Eliza wished to show him: the view out the window.

From here they could see most of the ship-basin: a pool, deepened by dredging, and a-mazed by moles, causeways, wharves, sea-walls, &c. Beyond it the view was chopped off by the rectilinear bluff of the fortress-wall. Eliza did not have to explain to her guest that part of the basin was still used by the ordinary sea-faring folk who had always dwelled here, while another part was for the Navy; as much was obvious from looking at the ships.

She gave him a moment to take this in, then said: "How did I end up here? Well, once I had recovered from childbirth—" then she caught herself short, and smiled. "What a ridiculous expression; I see now that I shall be recovering until the day I die."

Rossignol ignored the remark, and so, blushing slightly, she went back to the main thread: "I began to liquidate all of my short-term positions in the Amsterdam markets. It would be impossible to manage them from across the sea during a war. This was done easily enough—the result was a pretty hoard of gold coins, loose gemstones, and vulgar jewelry, as well as Bills of Exchange payable in London, and a few payable in Leipzig."

"Ah," said Rossignol, drawing some connexion in his mind, "those would be the ones that you gave to Princess Eleanor."*

"As usual, you know everything."

"When she turned up in Berlin with money, people there gossiped. It sounds as though you were most generous."

"I booked passage on a Dutch ship that was to take me, along with several other passengers, from the Hook of Holland to London. This was early in September. We were baffled by strong winds out of the northeast, which prevented us from making any headway towards England, while driving us inexorably south towards the Straits of Dover. To make a long, tediously nautical story short, we were captured off Dunkerque by—*voilà!*"

Eliza gestured toward much the finest ship in the basin, a Ship of Force with a sterncastle magnificently sculpted, and spread thick with gold leaf.

"Lieutenant Jean Bart," Rossignol muttered.

"Our captain surrendered immediately, and so we were boarded without violence by Bart's men, who went through and confiscated everything of value. I lost all. The ship itself became Bart's, of course—you can see it there if you care to look, but it is not much to look at."

"That is putting it kindly," said Rossignol after he had picked it out among the warships. "Why on earth does Lieutenant Bart suffer it to be moored so close to his flagship? It is like an ass sharing a stall with a *cheval de bataille.*"

"The answer is: the innate chivalry of Lieutenant Bart," said Eliza.

"How does that follow?"

"After we had surrendered, and during the time that we were en route hither, one of Bart's petty officers remained on board to keep

* Princess Eleanor of Saxe-Eisenach, impoverished widow and mother, who along with her six-year-old daughter, Princess Wilhelmina Caroline of Brandenburg-Ansbach, had befriended Eliza in the Hague

an eye on things. I noticed him talking to one of the other passengers at length. I became concerned. This passenger was a Belgian gentleman who had boarded this ship at the last minute as we made our way towards the breakwater at the Hook. He had been paying me a lot of attention ever since. Not the sort of attention *most* men pay to me—"

"He was a spy," said Rossignol, "in the pay of d'Avaux." It was not clear whether he had guessed this, or already knew it from reading the man's mail.

"I had guessed as much. It had not troubled me at all when I had thought I was going to end up in London, where this man would be impotent. But now we were on our way to Dunkerque, where the passengers would be left to shift for themselves. I could not guess what sort of mischief might befall me here at this fellow's hands. And indeed, when we reached Dunkerque, all of the passengers except for me were let off. I was detained for some hours, during which time several messages passed between the ship I was on, and the flagship of Jean Bart.

"Now as you may know, Bon-bon, every pirate and privateer has lurking within him the soul of an accountant. Though some would say 'tis the other way round. This arises from the fact that their livelihood derives from sacking ships, which is a hurried, disorderly, murky sort of undertaking; one pirate may come up with some gentleman's lucky rabbit's foot while the fellow on his left pulls an emerald the size of a quail's egg from a lady's cleavage. The whole enterprise would dissolve into a melee unless all the takings were pooled, and meticulously sorted, appraised, tallied, and then divided according to a rigid scheme. That is why the English euphemism for going a-pirating is *going on the account.*

"The practical result in my case was that every one of Bart's men had at least a general notion of how much had been pilfered and from whom, and they knew that the gold taken from my strong-box and the jewels plucked from my body were worth more than all the other passengers' effects summed and multiplied by ten. Bon-bon, I do not wish to boast, but the rest of my story will not make any sense to you unless I mention that the fortune I had lost was really quite enormous."

Rossignol winced. From this, Eliza knew that he must have seen the figure mentioned somewhere.

"I have not dwelled on it," she went on, "because a noble-woman—which I purport to be—is not supposed to care about any-thing as vulgar as money. And when Bart's men took the jewels away from me I did not feel any different from the minute before. But as days went by I thought more and more about the fortune I had lost—enough to purchase an earldom. The only thing that saved me from going mad was the blue-eyed treasure I cradled in my arms."

She purposely refrained from saying *our baby*, as this sort of remark only seemed to make him restive.

"In time I was put aboard a longboat and taken to the flagship. Lieutenant Bart emerged from his cabin to welcome me aboard. I think he was expecting some dowager. When he saw me, he was shocked."

"It is not shock," Rossignol demurred. "It is an altogether different thing. You have witnessed it a thousand times, but you'll go to your grave without understanding it."

"Well, once Captain Bart had recovered a little from this mysterious condition that you speak of, he ushered me into his private cabin—it is the one high in the sterncastle, there—and caused coffee to be served. He was—"

"Here I beg you to skip over any further adoring description of Lieutenant Bart," said Rossignol, "as I got quite enough of it in the letter that caused me to wear out five horses getting here."

"As you wish," Eliza said. "It was more than simple lust, though."

"I'm sure that's what he wanted you to think."

"Well. Let me jump ahead, then, to review my situation briefly. I am rated a Countess in France only because *le Roi* decided to make me one; he simply announced one day at his levée that I was the Countess de la Zeur—which is a funny French way of denoting my home island."

"I wonder if you know," said Rossignol, "that, by doing so, his majesty was implicitly reasserting an ancient Bourbon claim to Qwghlm that his lawyers had dredged out of some pond. Just as his majesty has made a *base navale* here, to one side of England, he would make another like it in Qwghlm, to the opposite side. So your ennoblement—startling as it might have been to you—was done as part of a larger plan."

"I'd expect nothing less of his majesty," said Eliza. "Whatever his motives might have been, the fact is that I had repaid the favor by spying on his army and reporting what I saw to William of Orange. So *le Roi* had reason to be a bit cross with me."

Rossignol snorted.

"But I had done so," Eliza went on, "under the ægis of Louis's sister-in-law, whose homeland Louis was invading, and continues to ravage at this very moment."

"He does not ravage, mademoiselle, but pacifies it."

"I stand corrected. Now, William of Orange has secretly made me a Duchess. But this is like a bill of exchange drawn on a Dutch house and payable only in London."

This commercial metaphor made Rossignol confused, and perhaps a little queasy.

"In France it is not honored," Eliza explained, "for France deems James Stuart the rightful King of England and does not grant William any right to create Duchesses. Even if they did, they would dispute his sovereignty over Qwghlm. At any rate, these facts were all new to Lieutenant Bart. It required some time for me to convey them to him, for, of course, I had to do so *diplomatically*. When he had absorbed all, and pondered, and finally made to speak, the care with which he considered each utterance was extraordinary; he was like a pilot maneuvering his vessel through a harbor crowded with drifting fire-ships, pausing every few words to, as it were, take soundings or gauge the latest shift in the wind."

"Or maybe he is just not, in the end, very intelligent," Rossignol suggested.

"I shall let you be the judge of that, for you shall meet him presently," Eliza said. "Either way, *my* situation is the same. Let me put it to you baldly. The money that Bart's men had stripped off my person was *gold* or, as some name it, *hard money*, spendable anywhere in the world for any good or service, and extremely desirable on both sides of the English Channel. Such is terribly scarce now because of the war. Living so near Amsterdam and dealing so rarely in hard money, I had quite lost sight of this. As you know, Bon-bon, Louis XIV recently had all of the solid silver furniture in his *Grands Appartements* melted down, literally liquidating 1.5 million *livres tournoises* in assets to pay for the new army he is building. At the time I heard this story, I had dismissed it as a whim of interior decoration, but now I am thinking harder about its meaning. The nobles of France have hoarded a stupendous amount of metal in the past few decades, probably banking it against the day Louis XIV dies, when they phant'sy they may rise up and re-assert their ancient powers."

Rossignol nodded. "By melting his own furniture, his majesty was trying to set an example. So far, few have emulated it."

"Now, my assets—all in the most liquid possible form—had been seized by Jean Bart, a privateer, holding a license to plunder Dutch and English shipping and turn the proceeds over to the French crown. If I had been a Dutch or an English woman, my money would already have been swallowed up by the French treasury, and available for the *contrôleur-général*, Monsieur le comte de Pontchartrain, to dispense as he saw fit. But since I was *arguably* a French countess, the money had been put in escrow."

"They were afraid that you would lodge an objection to the confiscation of your money—for how can a French privateer steal from a French countess?" said Rossignol. "Your ambiguous status would make it into a complicated affair legally. The letters that passed back and forth were most amusing."

"I am glad you were amused, Bon-bon. But I was faced with the question: Why not claim my rights and demand the money back?"

"It is good that you have posed this question, mademoiselle, for I, and half of Versailles, have been wondering."

"The answer is, *because they wanted it.* They wanted it badly enough that if I were to put up a fight, they might turn against me, denounce me as a foreign spy and a traitor, void my rights, throw me into the Bastille, and take the money. Put to work in the war, it might save thousands of French lives—and balanced against that, what is one counterfeit Countess worth?"

"Hmmm. I understand now that Lieutenant Bart was presenting you with an opportunity to do something clever."

"He dared not come out and say it directly. But he wanted me to know that I had a choice. And this little Hercules, who would not hesitate to send a ship full of living men to David Jones's Locker, if they were enemies of France, did not wish to see me taken off in chains to the Bastille."

"So you did it."

" 'The money is for France, of course!' " I told him. " 'That is why I went to such trouble to smuggle it out of Amsterdam. How could I do otherwise when *le Roi* is melting down his own furniture to save French lives, and to defend French rights?' "

"That must have cheered him up."

"More than words can express. Indeed he was so flummoxed that I gave him leave to kiss my cheeks, which he did with great *élan,* and a lingering scent of eau de cologne."

Rossignol twisted his head away from Eliza so that she would not see the look on his face.

"Some part of me still phant'sied that I'd be aboard a Dover-bound boat within hours, penniless but free," Eliza said. "But of course it was more complicated than that. I still was not free to go; for as Jean Bart now informed me with obvious regret, I was being held on suspicion of being a spy for William of Orange."

"D'Avaux had made his move," said Rossignol.

"That is what I came to understand, from hints given me by Lieutenant Bart. My accuser, he said, was a very important man, who was in Dublin, and who had given orders that I was to be detained, on suspicion of spying, until he could reach Dunkerque."

"How long ago was this?"

"Two weeks."

"Then d'Avaux might get here at any moment!" Rossignol said.

"Behold his ship," said Eliza, and directed Rossignol's attention to a French Navy vessel moored elsewhere in the basin. "I was watching it come round the end of the jetty when I saw you riding up the street."

"So d'Avaux has only just arrived," said Rossignol. "We have little time to lose, then. Please explain to me, briefly, how you have ended up in this house; for only a moment ago you told me that you were detained on the ship there."

"I was already ensconced in one of her cabins. It was practical to remain there. Bart caused the ship to be anchored where you see it, so that he could keep an eye on it—both to protect me from lusty French sailors and to be sure that I would not escape. He rounded up a few female servants from gin-houses and bordellos and put them aboard to stoke the galley fires and boil water and so on. As weeks went by, I learned which were good and which weren't, and fired the latter. Nicole, whom you saw a minute ago, has turned out to be the best of these. And I sent to the Hague for a woman who had become a loyal lady-in-waiting to me there, named Brigitte. Letters began to reach me from Versailles."

"I know."

"As you have already read them, to list their contents would be redundant. Perhaps you remember one from Madame la marquise d'Ozoir, inviting me to—nay, demanding that I make myself at home in this, her Dunkerque residence."

"Remind me please of your connexion to the d'Ozoirs?"

"Before I was ennobled, I required some excuse to be hanging around Versailles. D'Avaux, who had put me there in the first place, concocted a situation for me whereby I worked as a governess for the daughter of the d'Ozoirs, and followed them on their migrations back and forth between Versailles and Dunkerque. This made it easy for me to travel up the coast to Holland when business called me thither."

"It sounds, by your leave, somewhat farcical."

"Indeed, and the d'Ozoirs knew as much; but I had treated their daughter well, and a kind of loyalty had arisen between us nonetheless. So I have moved into this house."

"Other servants?"

"Brigitte has arrived, and brought another good one with her."

"I saw men?"

"To 'guard' me, Lieutenant Bart chose two of his favorite

marines: ones who have grown a bit too old to be swinging from grappling-hooks."

"Yes, they had that look about them. And if I may ask an indelicate question, mademoiselle, how do you pay all of these servants when by your own tale you have not a sou in hard money?"

"A reasonable question. The answer lies in my status as a Countess and benefactress of the French treasury. Because of this Lieutenant Bart has been willing to open his purse and lend me money."

"All right. It is improper, but clearly you had no choice. We shall try to improve on these arrangements. Now, there is one other thing I must understand if I am to assist you, and that is the bundle of letters from Ireland."

"After I had been living on that boat for two weeks, my mail began to catch up with me, and one day I received that packet, sewn up in tent-cloth, which had been posted to me from Belfast. It turned out to be correspondence stolen from the desk of Monsieur le comte d'Avaux in Dublin. It contained many letters and documents that were state secrets of France."

"And so knowing that d'Avaux was en route to accuse you of spying, you have held on to them as bargaining counters."

"Indeed."

"Excellent. Is there a place where I could spread them out and go through them?"

Here, though she would never show it, Eliza felt a sudden upwelling of affection for Rossignol. In a world full of men who only wanted to take her to bed, it was somehow comforting to know that there was one who, given the opportunity, would prefer to read through a big pile of stolen correspondence.

"You may ask Brigitte—she is the big Dutch woman—to show you to the Library," Eliza said. "I will keep an eye on the harbor. I believe that the longboat over yonder, just rounding the end of that pier, might be carrying d'Avaux."

"Carrying him hither?" Rossignol asked sharply.

"No, to the flagship of Lieutenant Bart."

"Good. I need at least a little bit of time."

ELIZA REPAIRED TO AN UPPER storey of the house, where a prospective-glass was mounted on a tripod before a window, and watched Lieutenant Bart receive d'Avaux in the cabin of his flagship. This cabin extended across the full width of the ship's sterncastle, and was illuminated by a row of windows looking abaft; at either end these curled around like a great golden scroll wrapped around the transom of the ship, creating small turrets from which Jean Bart might gaze forward to port or starboard. The sky was clear, and the afternoon sun was shining in through these windows.

The interview proceeded as follows: first, courteous greetings and chit-chat. Second, a momentary pause and adjustment of postures (because of a recent exploit, Jean Bart still could not sit down without suffering the torments of the damned, and d'Avaux, ever the gentleman, spurned all offers of chairs). Third, a long and, Eliza did not doubt, most entertaining Narration from Lieutenant Bart, enlivened by diverse zooming and veering movements of his hands. Slowly mounting impatience shown in d'Avaux's posture. Fourth, interrogation of Bart by d'Avaux, during which Bart held up a ledger and ticked off several items (presumably rendering an *accompt* of all the jewels, purses, etc., that had been taken from Eliza). Fifth, d'Avaux jumped to his feet, face red, and worked his jaw violently for some minutes; Bart was startled at first, and went a bit slack, but gradually stiffened into a dignified and aggrieved posture. Sixth, both men came over to the window and looked at Eliza (or so it seemed through her spyglass; they could not see her, of course). Seventh, aides were summoned and coats and hats were donned. Which was Eliza's cue to summon Brigitte and Nicole and the other female servants of her little household, and to begin putting on clothes. She borrowed a dress from the closet of Madame la marquise d'Ozoir. It was from last year; but d'Avaux had been in Dublin since then, and so to him it would look fashionable. And it was too big for Eliza, but with some artful pinning and basting in the back, it would serve, as long as she did not stand up. And she had no intention of standing up for d'Avaux. She arranged herself, a bit stiffly, in an armchair in the Grand Salon, and discoursed *sotto voce* with Bonaventure Rossignol. For Bart and d'Avaux had only required a few minutes of time to reach this house from Bart's flagship, and were being made to wait in another room, so nearby that Bart's pacing boots and d'Avaux's sniffling nose (he had caught a catarrh en route) were clearly audible.

Rossignol had had time by now to sort through the stolen letters. Certain of these he gave into Eliza's hands, and she arranged them on her lap, as if she had been reading them. The rest he took away, at least for the time being. He withdrew into another part of the house, not wishing to be seen by d'Avaux. A few minutes later Eliza sent word that the caller was to be admitted. The furniture had been arranged so that the sun was shining hard into the side of d'Avaux's face. Eliza sat with her back to a window.

"His majesty has summoned me to his château at Versailles, so that I may report on the progress of the campaign that his majesty the King of England wages to wrest that island from the grip of the Usurper," d'Avaux began, once they had got the opening formalities out of the way. "The Prince of Orange has sent out a Marshal Schomberg to campaign against us near Belfast, but he is timid or lethargic or both and it appears he'll do nothing this year."

"Your voice is hoarse," Eliza observed. "Is it a catarrh, or have you been screaming a lot?"

"I am not afraid to raise my voice to *inferiors*. In *your* presence, mademoiselle, I shall comport myself properly."

"Does that mean you no longer intend to have me dangled over hot coals in a sack full of cats?" Eliza turned over a letter, written by d'Avaux, in which he had proposed to someone that such was the most fitting treatment for spies.

"Mademoiselle, I am shocked beyond words that you would connive with Irishmen to enter my house and ransack it. There is much that I would forgive you. But to violate the sanctity of an ambassadorial residence—of a nobleman's home—and to commit theft, makes me fear I over-estimated you. For I believed you could pass for noble. But what you have done is common."

"These distinctions that you draw 'tween noble and common, what is proper and what is not, seem as arbitrary and senseless to me, as the castes and customs of Hindoos would to you," Eliza returned.

"It is in their very irrationality, their arbitrariness, that they are refined," d'Avaux corrected her. "If the customs of the nobility made sense, anyone could figure them out, and become noble. But because they are incoherent and meaningless, not to mention everchanging, the only way to know them is to be inculcated with them, to absorb them through the skin. This makes them a coin that is almost impossible to counterfeit."

" 'Tis like gold, then?"

"Very much so, mademoiselle. Gold is gold everywhere, fungible and indifferent. But when a disk of gold is stamped by a coiner with certain pompous words and the picture of a King, it takes on added value—seigneurage. It has that value only in that people believe that it does—it is a shared phant'sy. You, mademoiselle, came to me as a blank disk of gold—"

"And you, sir, tried to stamp nobility 'pon me, to enhance my value—"

"But then—" he said, gesturing to the letter, "to steal from my house, shows you up as a counterfeit."

"Which do you suppose is a worse thing to be? A spy for the Prince of Orange, or a counterfeit Countess?"

"Unquestionably the latter, mademoiselle, for spying is rampant everywhere. Loyalty to one's class—which means, to one's family—is far more important than loyalty to a particular country."

"I believe that on the other side of yonder straits are many who would take the opposite view."

"But you are on *this* side of those straits, mademoiselle, and will be for a long time."

"In what estate?"

"That is for you to decide. If you wish to continue in your *common* ways, then you will have a common fate. I cannot send you to the galleys, as much as that would please me, but I can arrange for you to have a life as miserable in some work-house. I believe that ten or twenty years spent gutting fish would re-awaken in you a respect for *noble* things. Or, if your recent behavior is a mere *aberration* perhaps brought about by the stresses of childbirth, I can put you back at Versailles, in much the same capacity as before. When you vanished from St. Cloud everyone assumed you had gotten pregnant and had gone off somewhere to bear your child in secrecy and give it away to someone; now a year has gone by, and it has all come to pass, and you are expected back."

"I must correct you, monsieur. It has *not* all come to pass. I have not given the child away to anyone."

"You have *adopted* a heretick orphan from the Palatinate," d'Avaux explained with grim patience, "that you may see him raised in the True Faith."

"*See* him raised? Is it envisioned, then, that I am to be a mere *spectator*?"

"As you are *not his mother,*" d'Avaux reminded her, "it is difficult to envision any other possibility. The world is full of orphans, mademoiselle, and the Church in her mercy has erected many orphanages for them—some in remote parts of the Alps, others only a few minutes' stroll from Versailles."

Thus d'Avaux let her know the stakes of the game. She might end up in a work-house, or as a countess at Versailles. And her baby might be raised a thousand miles away from her, or a thousand yards.

Or so d'Avaux wished her to believe. But though she did not gamble, Eliza understood games. She knew what it was to bluff, and that sometimes it was nothing more than a sign of a weak hand.

WELL-READ AND -TRAVELED GENTLEMAN that he was, Bonaventure Rossignol had learned that in the world there were countries—and even in this country, there were religious communities and social classes—where men did not always go about carrying long sharp stabbing- and slashing-weapons ready to be whipped out and driven into other men's flesh at a moment's notice. This was a thing that he knew and understood in theory but could not entirely comprehend. Take for example the present circumstance: two men, strange to each other, in the same house as Eliza, neither of them knowing where the other was, or what his intentions might be. It was a wildly unstable state of affairs. Some would argue that to add edged weapons to this mix was to render it more volatile yet, and hence a bad idea; but to Rossignol it seemed altogether fitting, and an apt way to bring into the light a conflict that, in other countries or classes, would be suffered to fester in the dark. Rossignol had been—this could not be denied—sneaking around the house, trying not to be detected by d'Avaux. A winding and backtracking course had led him to a gloomy hallway, bypassed by the redecoration project, paneled in slabs of wood that had not yet been painted to make them look like marble, and cluttered with the d'Ozoirs' portraits and keepsakes—some mounted on the walls, most leaning against whatever would hold them up. For if it was a sign of high class and elevated tastes to adorn the walls of one's dwelling with paintings, then how infinitely more sophisticated to lean great stacks of homeless art against walls, and stash them behind chairs! Reaching this gallery, anyway, he smelled eau de cologne, and placed his left hand on the scabbard of his rapier (a style of weapon that had gone out of fashion, but it was the one his father, Antoine Rossignol, the King's cryptanalyst before him, had taught him how to use, and he would be damned if he would make a fool of himself trying to learn how to fence with a small-sword) and thumbed it out an inch or two, just to be sure it would not turn out to be stuck when the time came. At the same time he lengthened his pace to a confident stride. For to skulk about would be to admit some kind of bad intentions and invite pre-emptive retribution. As he pounded along the gallery he took note of chairs, busts on pedestals, stacks of paintings, carpet-humps, and other impedimenta, so that he would not trip over them when and if some sort of melee were to break out. Ahead of him, on the left, another, similar gallery intersected this one; the man with the cologne was back in there. Rossignol slowed, turning to the left, and edged around the corner just until the other became visible. Because of this slow crab-wise movement, Rossignol's right arm and shoulder led the remainder of his body around the corner, which wrought to his advantage in that he could whip out the rapier and lunge around the corner at any foe, while his body would be shielded from any right-handed counter-attack. But alas, the other fellow had foreseen all of this, and re-deployed himself by crossing to the opposite side of the side-corridor and *turning his back* upon Rossignol so that he could pretend to study a landscape mounted to the wall there; thus, the corner was entirely out of his way, and his right shoulder was situated closest to Rossignol. A slight turn of the head sufficed to bring Rossignol into his peripheral vision. He had crossed his right arm diagonally over the front of his body and then clasped his left hand over the elbow to hold it in that position; this would place his right hand very near, if not on, the grip of the cutlass that was dangling from his hip. The pose was forced and artificial, but well-thought-out; in a moment he could draw, turn, and deliver a backhanded slash through the middle of the gallery-intersection. It was, therefore, a standoff.

It was also, admittedly, ridiculous. Rossignol, for his part, had not killed anyone in years. Jean Bart (for this had to be Jean Bart) probably did it more frequently, but never in rich people's houses. If it had somehow come to swordplay, they'd have been civil enough to take it outside. And yet they did not know each other. There was no harm in taking precautions, particularly if they were as inoffensive as standing in a certain position, and maintaining a certain distance. These measures did not even require conscious thought; Rossignol had been thinking about something he had read in one of d'Avaux's letters, and Bart (he could safely assume) was thinking about fucking Eliza, and both men had relied upon habit to plan and execute all of these maneuvers.

Bart was dressed in the habit of a naval officer, which was not terribly different from what any other civilian gentleman would wear, viz. breeches, waistcoat, Persian coat over that, periwig, and three-cornered hat. The costume's color (tending to blue), its decoration (facings, piping, epaulets, cuffs), and the selection of plumes that erupted from the folds of the hat marked him as a Lieutenant in the Navy. He was not a tall man, and Rossignol belatedly saw that he was not a slender one either (the tailoring of his jacket had concealed this at first). Bart was, by the standards of this part of France, swarthy. According to rumor he was of very common extraction—his people had been fishermen, and probably pirates, around Dunkerque for æons. If so, there was no guessing what mongrel ichor pulsed in his veins. Like many who were short; many who were stout; and many who were of questionable ancestry; he paid close attention to his appearance. He affected the great Sun King mane-wig (a bit out-moded, but no more so than Rossignol's rapier) and the ridiculous tiny moustache, like a pair of commas cemented to the upper lip, that must cost him an hour at his toilette every morning. In his costume there was rather too much of lace and of hardware (buckles and buttons) for Rossignol's taste; but by the standards of Versailles, this Jean Bart would not even be rated as a fop. Rossignol made a conscious effort to ignore the clothes and the cologne, and instead concentrated his mind on the fact that the man standing before him had recently escaped from a prison in England, stolen a small boat, and, alone, rowed it all the way back to France.

Bart made a half-turn on the balls of his feet so that he could look Rossignol in the eye. Still his right arm was wrapped across the front of his body. His eyes popped down to Rossignol's left hip and, spying a rapier, checked Rossignol's left hand for a dagger, or the intention to draw one.

If Rossignol had been dressed *en grand habit* it might have gone otherwise, but as it was, he looked no better than a highwayman. So he spoke: "Lieutenant. Pray forgive my interruption." He had prudently drawn up short of cutlass-backhand range, but now, as a sort of peace-offering, he drew back an additional pace, so that Bart was no longer in range of a long rapier-lunge. Bart noted this and responded by turning more fully towards him, causing his right hand to become visible, and then raising that hand a bit, so that his arms were crossed over the barrel of his torso.

"I have not had the pleasure of meeting you, and you will rightly wonder who I am, and what is my business in this house. As *I* am a visitor in *your* town, Lieutenant, I beg leave to introduce myself to you. I am Bonaventure Rossignol. I have come here from my home in Juvisy in the hope that I might be of service to Mademoiselle la comtesse de la Zeur, and she has done me the honor of suffering me to cross the threshold of this house and bide here for some hours. It is, in other words, my privilege to be an invited guest here, as she would tell you, if you were to go and ask her. But I beg you not to do so while Monsieur le comte d'Avaux is present, for the matter is—"

"Complicated," said Jean Bart, "complicated, delicate, and dangerous, like Mademoiselle la comtesse herself." Both of his arms sprang free, which made Rossignol jerk; but those hands were moving towards Rossignol, away from the weapon. Rossignol let his own hands drift farther from hilts, pommels, &c., and even allowed Bart a glimpse of his palms.

"I am Lieutenant Jean Bart." Bart advanced a step towards Rossignol, venturing within rapier-thrust range. Rossignol rewarded Bart's gesture of trust by extending his hands farther and showing more palm, then glided to within cutlass-backhand range. Like two men groping through smoke they found each other's hands and shook— a double-handed shake, just to be extra safe. "Though I am admittedly *disappointed*," said Bart, "I am in no way *surprised,* that a gallant gentleman has ridden out from Paris to place himself at the lady's service. Indeed, I had been wondering when someone of your description would show up."

This was triple-edged, in that Bart was admitting to an interest in Eliza, conceding Rossignol's priority in the matter, and needling him for having been too long getting here, all at once. Rossignol tried to think of a way to defuse this little granadoe while they were still safely gripping each other's hands. "I have heard some in the same vein from the lady in question," he admitted drily.

"Ha ha, I'll bet you have!"

"I do all in my power to satisfy her," said Rossignol, "and when that fails I can do no more than throw myself upon her mercy."

"It is good to meet you!" Bart exclaimed, seeming genuine enough, then let go Rossignol's hands. The two men burst asunder. But there was no more of furtive glancing at hands. "Now we wait, eh?" Bart said. "You wait for her, and I wait for d'Avaux. You have the better of me there."

"I am certain that Monsieur le comte will not tarry in Dunkerque, if that will cheer you up."

"It must be wonderful to know so many things," said Bart—a way of stating that he knew what Bonaventure Rossignol did for a living.

"Many of those things are very tedious, I'm afraid."

"Yes, but the power, the understanding it gives you! Take this painting." Bart extended a blunt, thick hand toward the landscape he had been pretending to inspect a moment earlier. It depicted rolling countryside, a village, and a church, all seen from the garden of a manor house. In the foreground, children sported with a little dog. "What does it mean? Who are these people? How did they end up *there*?" He indicated another landscape, this one in a dark mountainous country. "And what significance do all of these sieges and battles have to the d'Ozoirs?" For, despite the occasional pastoral landscape, the art in the gallery *was* heavily skewed towards massacres, martyrdoms sacred and sæcular, and set-piece battles.

"Forgive me for saying so, Lieutenant, but given the importance of the Marquis d'Ozoir to the Navy, it strikes me as remarkable that you do not know everything about his family."

"Ah, monsieur, but that is because you are a gentleman of Court. I am a dog of the sea, oblivious. But Mademoiselle la comtesse de la Zeur has instructed me that I must attend to such matters if I am ever to rise beyond the rank of Lieutenant."

"Then as we are both doomed to cool our heels as we await our betters," said Rossignol, "let me do what would most please her, and spin you a little yarn that will tie together all of these paintings and plaques and busts."

"I should be in your debt, monsieur!"

"Not at all. Now, even if you are as deaf to politics as you claim, you must know that Monsieur le marquis d'Ozoir is a bastard of Monsieur le duc d'Arcachon."

"That has never been a secret," Bart agreed.

"Since the Marquis cannot inherit the name or the property of his father, it follows, by process of elimination, that all of these paintings and whatnot are from the family of—"

"Madame la marquise d'Ozoir!" said Bart. "And that is where I want instruction, for I know nothing of *her* people."

"Two families, very different, forged into one."

"Ah. One dwelling in the countryside of the north, I'm guessing," said Bart, nodding at the first landscape.

"De Crépy. Petty nobles. Not especially distinguished, but middling affluent, and fecund."

"The other family must have been Alp-dwellers, then," said Bart, turning to regard the gloomier and more horrid of the two landscapes.

"De Gex. A poor dwindling clan. Die-hard Catholics living in a place, not far from Geneva, that had become dominated by Huguenots."

"So the two families *were* quite different! How did they come to be joined?"

"The family de Crépy were tied, first by proximity, then by fealty, and at last by marriage, to the Counts of Guise," said Rossignol.

"Err . . . I am vaguely aware that those Guises were important, and got into some sort of trouble with the Bourbons, but if you could refresh my memory, monsieur . . ."

"It would be my pleasure, Lieutenant. A century and a half ago, a comte de Guise distinguished himself so well in battle that the King created him duc de Guise. Of his aides, squires, lackeys, mistresses, captains, and hangers-on, several were of the de Crépy line. Some of these developed a taste for adventure, and began to conceive ambitions beyond the parochial. They lashed themselves to the mast, as it were, of the House of Guise, which seemed like a good idea, and served them well. Until, that is, a hundred and one years ago, when the two leading men of that House—Henry, duc de Guise, and Louis, cardinal de Guise—were assassinated by the King or his supporters. For they had waxed more powerful than the King himself."

There was a pause now to look at some rather sanguinary art-work.

"How could such a thing happen, monsieur? How could this rival House become so powerful?"

"Nowadays, when *le Roi* is so strong, it is difficult for us to conceive of, is it not? It may help you to know that much of the power that so appalled the King was rooted in a thing called the Holy Catholic League. It had its beginnings in towns and cities all over France, where local priests and gentlemen had, in the wake of the Reformation, found themselves engulfed in Huguenots, and so banded together to defend their faith from that heresy and to oppose its spread."

"Ah, here is where the de Gex family enters the picture, no?"

"I am almost to that part of the story. You are correct that the de Gexes were typical of the sorts of men who in those days founded local chapters of the Holy Catholic League. The House of Guise had forged these scattered groups into a national movement. After the assassinations of Henry and Louis de Guise, the decapitated League rose up in revolt against the King—who was himself assassinated not long after—and there was chaos throughout the country for a number of years. The new Huguenot King, Henry IV, converted to Catholicism and re-established control, generally at the expense of the ultra-Catholics and to the benefit of the Huguenots. Or so it seemed to many fervent Catholics, including the one who assassinated him in 1610. Now, during this time the fortunes of the de Crépy family went into eclipse. Some were killed, some went back to their ancestral lands in northern France and melted back into bourgeois obscurity, some scattered abroad. But a few of them ended up far from home, in that part of France that borders on Lake Geneva. It was the best, or the worst, place for Catholic warriors to be at the time. They were directly across the lake from Geneva, which to them was like an ant's nest from which Huguenots continually streamed out to preach and convert in every parish in France. Accordingly, the Catholics in that area were more ardent than anywhere else—the first to create local branches of the Holy Catholic League, the first to swear fealty to the House of Guise, and, after the assassinations, the most warlike. They had not assassinated Henry IV, but only because they could not find him. The leading nobleman of that district—one Louis, sieur de Gex—had gathered around him a small, ragged, but ferocious coterie of like-minded sorts who had been driven out of other *pays,* and gravitated to this remote outpost from all over France as the fortunes of their party had declined."

"Among them, I'm quite sure, must have been several of the de Crépy clan."

"Indeed. So your question of how they got from here, to there," said Rossignol, indicating the two landscapes, "is answered. The new-comers were fertile and affluent where the family de Gex were dwindling and poor."

"I suppose most of the people in their district who knew how to make money had become Huguenots," mused Bart.

This drew from Rossignol a sharp look, and a reprimand. "Lieutenant Bart. I believe I understand, now, why Mademoiselle la comtesse de la Zeur sees a need to instruct you in how to be *politic*."

Bart shrugged. "It is true, monsieur. All the best merchants of Dunkerque were Huguenots, and after 1685—"

"It is precisely because it is true, that you must not come out and *state* it," said Rossignol.

"Very well then, monsieur, I vow not to say anything true for the remainder of this conversation. Pray continue!"

After a moment to collect himself, Rossignol stepped over to a stack of portraits leaning against a wall, and began to paw through them: men, women, children, and families, dressed in the fashions of three generations ago. "When the Wars of Religion finally came to an end, both families, having nothing else to do, began to produce children. A generation later, these began to marry each other. Here I may get some of the details wrong, but if memory serves, this is how it went: the scion of the de Gex line, Francis, married one Marguerite Diane de Crépy around 1640 and they had several children one after the other, then none for twelve years, then a surprise pregnancy. This ended in the death of Marguerite only a few hours following the birth of a boy, Édouard. The father construed the former as a sacrifice to, the latter as a gift from, the Almighty; and considering himself too old to raise a boy by himself, gave him to a Jesuit school in Lyon where he was found to be a sort of child prodigy. He joined the Society of Jesus at an exceptionally young age. He is now Confessor to de Maintenon herself."

Rossignol had found a portrait of a lean young man, dressed in a Jesuit's robes, glaring out of the canvas in a way that suggested he could actually see Rossignol and Bart standing in this back-hallway, and did not approve much of either one of them.

"I have heard of him," said Bart, and edged out of the portrait's sight-line.

Rossignol found an older portrait of a plump woman in a blue dress. "The sister of Francis de Gex was named Louise Anne. She married one Alexandre Louis de Crépy. They had two boys, who died at the same time from smallpox, and two girls, who survived it." He pulled out of the stack a gouache of two post-pubescent girls: one older, bigger, more beautiful than the other, who peered over her shoulder, as if hiding behind her. "The older of the girls, Anne-Marie, who was unscarred by the disease, married the comte d'Oyonnax, who was much older. Anne-Marie was his second or third wife. This fellow Oyonnax had originally been a petty noble, but even that modest rank had stretched his wits and his wealth thin. His ancestral lands lay just at the doorstep of the Franche-Comté."

"Even I have heard of that!"

"Really, Lieutenant? I am surprised, for it is landlocked."

Rossignol's jest almost went by Bart, for Rossignol was not, by and large, a fount of clever *bon mots*. But Bart caught it after a few awkward moments, and acknowledged it with a smile and a nod. "It is a part of the world over which the Kings of France have been fighting with the Hapsburgs for a long time, is it not—like two enemies trapped in a longboat together and struggling for the possession of the one dagger."

"The analogy, though nautical, is apt," said Rossignol. "During the reign of Louis XIII—whom it was my father's great honor to serve as Royal cryptanalyst—Oyonnax had allowed the King's armies to use his land as a base for invading the Franche-Comté, which they did frequently. In exchange for which he had been elevated to a Count. Such was his rank when he married the young Anne-Marie de Crépy. A few years after, he performed a like service for the legions of Louis XIV, which, since it led to the annexation of the whole of the Franche-Comté to France, caused the King to elevate him to a Duke. He and the new Duchess moved to Versailles, where he got to enjoy his new status for only a few months before she poisoned him."

"Monsieur! And you accuse *me* of not being politic!"

Rossignol shrugged. "It is a harsh thing to say, I know, but it is true; everyone was doing it in those days—or at least all of the Satan-worshippers."

"Now I think you are only pulling my leg."

"You may believe me, or not," said Rossignol. "Sometimes I cannot believe it myself. Such behavior has all been suppressed by de Maintenon, with the help of Father Édouard de Gex—who probably has no idea that his *cousine* was one of the ringleaders."

"That is quite enough of such topics! What about the younger daughter?"

"Charlotte Adélaide de Crépy was scarred by the smallpox, though she goes to great lengths to hide it with wigs, patches, and so forth. Marrying her off was more of a challenge; but that of course makes it a more interesting story."

"Good! Let's have it, then! For it seems that Monsieur le comte and Mademoiselle la comtesse will never finish."

"You have obviously heard of the de Lavardacs. You may know that they are a sort of cadet branch of the Bourbons. If you have had the misfortune of seeing any of their portraits you will have guessed that they have undergone quite a bit of Hapsburg adulter-ation over the centuries. You see, many of their lands are in the south, and they make tactical marriages across the Pyrenees. Through all of the troubles with the Guises, they were stolidly loyal to the Bourbons."

"They switched religion whenever the King did, then!" exclaimed Lieutenant Bart, trying to muster a small witticism of his own. But it only drew a glare from Rossignol.

"To the de Lavardacs it is not such an amusing topic, for they suf-fered diverse assassinations and other reversals. As you know far bet-ter than I, they have developed a family association with the French Navy, which is passed on from father to son by *survivance*. The cur-rent Duke, Louis-François de Lavardac, duc d'Arcachon, like his father before him, is Grand Admiral of France. He held that position during the time that Colbert expanded the French Navy from a tiny flotilla of worm-eaten relics to the immense force it is today."

"Seven score Ships of the Line," Bart proclaimed, "and God knows how many frigates and galleys."

"The Duke profited commensurately, both in material wealth and in influence. His son and heir is, of course, Étienne de Lavardac d'Arcachon."

It was not necessary for Rossignol to add what Bart, along with everyone else, already believed: *He is the one who got Eliza pregnant.*

"I have only seen Étienne from a distance," said Bart, "but I gather he is a good bit younger than his half-brother." He gestured to a recent painting that depicted the owners of this house, the mar-quis and the marquise d'Ozoir.

"The Duke was but a stripling when he begat this fellow off a woman in the household. Her surname was Eauze. The bastard was raised under the name of Claude Eauze. He went off to India for a while to seek his fortune, and later made enough money in the slave trade that he was able—with a loan from his father—to buy a noble title in 1674 when they went on sale to finance the Dutch war. Thus he became the Marquis d'Ozoir, which I take to be a play on words, as his name, to that point, had been Eauze. Only a year before buy-ing this title, he married none other than Charlotte Adélaïde de Crépy: the younger sister of the duchesse d'Oyonnax."

"You'd think he could have found someone of higher rank," said Bart.

"By all means!" said Rossignol. "But there is something at work you have forgotten to take into account."

"And what is that, monsieur?"

"He actually loves her."

"*Mon Dieu,* I had no idea!"

"Or, barring that, he knows that they form an effective and stable partnership, and is too cunning to do anything that might queer it. They have a daughter. Our friend tutored her for a while, last year."

"That must have been before the King woke up one morning and remembered that she was a countess."

"Let us hope," Rossignol, "that she will *still* be one, when d'Avaux is finished."

"IT IS A PITY," Eliza began, "that Irishmen broke into your house, and stole your papers and sold them on the open market. What an embarrassment it must be for you that everyone knows that your personal correspondence, and drafts of treaties written in your hand, are being bartered for drinks by scullery-maids in Dunkerque gin-houses."

"What! I was not informed of this!" D'Avaux turned red so fast it was if a cup of blood had been hurled in his face.

"You have been on a boat for a fortnight, how could you be informed? I am informing you now, monsieur."

"I was led to believe that those papers had come into *your* possession, mademoiselle, and it is *you* I shall hold responsible for them!"

"What you have been *led to believe* does not matter," said Eliza, "only what *is.* And so let me tell you what *is.* The thieves who stole your papers sent them to Dunkerque, it is true. Perhaps they even entertained a phant'sy that I would buy them. I refused to lower myself to such a dishonorable transaction."

"Then perhaps you will explain to me, mademoiselle, why you have some of those very papers on your lap at this moment!"

"As the saying goes, there is no honor among thieves. When these ruffians saw that I was adamant in my refusal to do business with them, they began to seek other buyers. The packet was broken up into small lots, which were offered for sale, on various channels. To add to the complexity of the matter, it seems that the thieves had a falling-out amongst themselves. I cannot follow the business, to tell you the truth. When it became evident that these papers were being scattered to the four winds, I began making efforts to purchase them, as available. The ones on my lap are all that I have been able to round up, so far."

D'Avaux was at a loss for civil words, and could only shake his head and mutter to himself.

"*You* may be chagrined, monsieur, and ungrateful; but *I* am pleased that I have been able to repay some small part of my personal debt to you by recovering some of your papers—"

"And returning them to me?"

"As I am able," Eliza answered with a shrug. "To recover them all does not happen in a single day, week, or month."

". . ."

"Now," Eliza went on, "a minute ago, you were indulging in some speculations as to where I shall end up. Some of your ideas on this topic are quite fanciful—Barock, even. Some of them are distasteful to persons of breeding, and I shall pretend I did not hear them. I can see well enough that you have lost confidence in me, monsieur. I know that you must do as honor dictates. Go then to Versailles— for I cannot travel as fast as you, encumbered as I am with an infant and a household, and busy as I am with this project of recovering your papers. State your case to the King. Let him know that I am no noble, but a common wench who deserves no better treatment. He will be startled to learn these things, for he considers me to be a hereditary Countess. I am a dear friend of his sister-in-law and moreover have recently loaned him above a million *livres tournois* of my own money. But your persuasive powers are renowned—as you demonstrated during your posting in the Hague, where you so effectively reined in the ambitions of that poseur, William of Orange."

This was truly a knee to the groin, and rendered d'Avaux speechless, not so much from pain as from a curious admixture of shock and awe.

Eliza continued, "You may induce the King to believe anything— particularly given that you have such strong evidence. What was it again? A journal?"

"Yes, mademoiselle—*your* journal."

"Who is in possession of this book?"

"It is not a book, as you know perfectly well, but an embroidered pillowcase." Here d'Avaux began to pinken again.

"A . . . pillowcase?"

"Yes."

"In English they call it a sham, by the way. Tell me, are there any other bedlinens implicated in the scandal?"

"Not that I am aware of."

"Curtains? Rugs? Tea-towels?"

"No, mademoiselle."

"Who has possession of this . . . pillowcase?"

"*You* do, mademoiselle."

"Such items are bulky and soon go out of fashion. Before I left the Hague, I sold most of my household goods and burned the rest—including all pillowcases."

"But a copy was made, mademoiselle, by a clerk in the French Embassy in the Hague, and given to Monsieur Rossignol."

"That clerk died of the smallpox," Eliza told him—which was a lie that she had made up on the spot, but it would take him a month to find this out.

"Ah, but Monsieur Rossignol is alive and well, and trusted implicitly by the King."

"Does the King trust you, monsieur?"

"I beg your pardon?"

"Monsieur Rossignol sent a copy of his report to the King but not to you. It made me curious. And what of the monk?"

"Which monk?"

"The Qwghlmian monk in Dublin to whom Monsieur Rossignol sent the plaintext to be translated."

"You are most well-informed, mademoiselle."

"I do not think that I am particularly well- or ill-informed, monsieur. I am simply trying to be of service to you."

"In what way?"

"You have a difficult interview awaiting you at Versailles. You shall come before the King. In his treasury—which he watches with utmost care—he has a fortune in hard money, lately deposited by me. You will make him believe that I am a commoner and a traitor by describing a report you have never seen about a pillowcase that no longer exists, supposedly carrying an encrypted message in Qwghlmian, which no one reads except for some three-fingered monk in Ireland."

"We shall see," said d'Avaux. "My interview with Father Édouard de Gex will be a simple matter by comparison."

"And how does Édouard de Gex enter into it?"

"Oh, of all the Jesuits at Versailles, mademoiselle, he is the most influential, for he is the confessor of de Maintenon. Indeed, when *anyone*" (raising an eyebrow at Eliza) "misbehaves at Versailles, Madame de Maintenon complains of it to Father de Gex, who then goes to the confessor of the guilty party so that the next time she goes to confession she is made aware of the Queen's displeasure. Yes, you may smirk at the idea, mademoiselle—many do—but it gives him great power. For when a courtier steps into the confessional and has his ears blistered by the priest, he has no way to know whether the criticism is really coming from the Queen, the King, or de Gex."

"What will *you* confess to de Gex, then?" Eliza asked. "That you have had impure thoughts about the Countess de la Zeur?"

"It is not in a confessional where I shall meet him," d'Avaux said, "but in a *salon* somewhere, and the topic of conversation will be: Where is this orphan boy to be raised? What is his Christian name, by the way?"

"I have been calling him Jean."

"But his *Christian name*? He *has* been baptized, of course?"

"I have been very busy," Eliza said. "He is to be baptized in a few days, here at the Church of St.-Eloi."

"How many days *exactly*? Surely it is not such a demanding calculation for one of your talents."

"Three days."

"Father de Gex will be, I'm sure, suitably impressed by this display of piety. The christening is to be performed by a Jesuit, I presume?"

"Monsieur, I would not think of having it done by a Jansenist!"

"Excellent. I look forward to making the acquaintance of this little Christian when you bring him to Versailles."

"Are you certain I'll be welcome there, monsieur?"

"*Pourquoi non?* I only pray that *I* shall be."

"*Pourquoi non,* monsieur?"

"Certain important papers of mine have gone missing from my office in Dublin."

"Do you need them immediately?"

"No. But sooner or later—"

"It will certainly be later. Dublin is far away. The inquiry proceeds at a snail's pace." Which was Eliza's way of saying he'd not get his precious papers back unless he gave a good report of her at Versailles.

"I am sorry to trouble you about such matters. To common people, such things are important! To us they are nothing."

"Then let us let nothing come between us," Eliza said.

As Bonaventure Rossignol had foreseen, d'Avaux did not tarry by the sea-side, but was en route for Paris before cock-crow the next day.

Rossignol stayed for two more nights after that, then rose one morning and rode out of town with as little fuss as when he'd ridden into it. He must have met the carriage of the Marquis d'Ozoir around mid-morning, for it was just before the stroke of noon when Eliza—who was upstairs getting dressed for church—heard the stable-gates being thrown open, and went to the window to see four horses drawing a carriage into the yard.

The coat of arms painted on the door of that carriage matched the one on the gates. Or so she guessed. To verify as much would have required a magnifying-glass, a herald, and more time and patience than Eliza had just now. The arms of Charlotte-Adélaide were a quartering of those of de Gex and de Crépy, and to make the arms of d'Ozoir, these had been recursively quartered with those of the House of de Lavardac d'Arcachon—themselves a quartering of something that included a lot of fleurs-de-lis, with an arrangement of black heads in iron collars, slashed with a bend sinister to indicate bastardy. At any rate, what it all meant was that the lord of the manor was back. Just as he stepped down from his carriage, the bells in the old, alienated belfry down the street began to toll noon. Eliza was late for church, and that was an even worse thing than usual, because on this day the proceedings could not go forward until she and her baby arrived. She sent an aide down to explain matters, and to tender apologies, to the Marquis, and hustled out one door with her baby and her entourage just as Claude Eauze entered through another. Presently he did the chivalrous thing, viz. got his carriage turned round and sent it rattling down the street after her. But so close was one thing to another in Dunkerque that, by the time the carriage caught up with her, Eliza was already standing at the church's door. She might have given it the slip altogether if she had gone in directly. But she had paused to look at the Église St.-Eloi, and to think.

She favored the looks of this church. It was late-Gothic, and could have passed for old, but was in fact a new fabrique. The Spaniards had levelled the old one some decades past in a dispute as to the ownership of Flanders. All that remained of it was the belfry, and if *its* looks were any indication, the Spaniards had wrought a great improvement on the appearance of this town. The new one had a great rose window filled with a delicate tracery of stone, like the rosette on the belly of a lute, and Eliza always liked to stop and admire it when she passed by. Now, holding her baby to her bosom, she stopped to admire it one more time. At that moment a counter-factual vision entered her phant'sy, wherein Rossignol was by her side, and the two of them went in to be joined in marriage, and then walked down to the water and boarded ship and sailed off to Amsterdam or London to raise their baby in exile.

The dream was interrupted by the raucous vehement on-rush of the carriage of the Marquis d'Ozoir, which was about as fitting and about as welcome in this scene as musketry at a seduction. Lest she get trapped outside exchanging pleasantries with the Marquis, she hurried through the door.

The church's vault was supported by several columns that were arranged around the altar in a semicircle, reminding Eliza of the bars of a giant birdcage: a birdcage into which she had been chased, not only by the banging and rattling carriage, but by divers other sudden and frightening onslaughts as well. She could fly no farther. She was caught. Best to flutter up onto her new perch, preen, and peer about. The Marquis slipped in alone, and took a seat in his family pew. She peered at him; he peered, discreetly, at her. Jean Bart watched them watching each other. They, and several servants and acquaintances who'd showed up, joined in the standings, sittings, kneelings, mumblings, and gestures of the Mass. Jean-Jacques turned out to be one of those infants who accepts the dunking, not with hysterical protests but with aghast curiosity; this made his godfather immensely proud, while giving his mother a vision of long rambunctious years ahead. The Jesuit crossed his forehead with oil and said that he was a priest and a prophet and that his name was Jean-Jacques: Jean after Jean Bart, who became his godfather, and Jacques after another man of Eliza's acquaintance who was unable to attend the rite, being either dead, or crazy and chained to an oar. No mention was made of the child's natural father. Indeed very little notice was given to the *mother;* for the story being given out was that Jean-Jacques was an orphan rescued from some massacre in the Palatinate and only being looked after by Eliza.

Over joyous bonging from the belfry, the Marquis—who, she now remembered, was a tall man, physically impressive, and handsome in a disreputable way—insisted on a celebration at his place. The produce of local vines, orchards, and distilleries was made available to a small and select list of guests. Some hours later, Jean Bart could be seen making his way home, tacking down the street in the manner of a ship working to windward.

The comtesse de la Zeur and the Marquis d'Ozoir kept an eye on Bart from the same room where Eliza had had her audience with d'Avaux three days earlier. She and the Marquis got along very well, which, given his past association with the slave trade, rather made her flesh crawl. He took a sort of avuncular interest in Jean-Jacques, which perhaps stood to reason given that the two had been born in such similar circumstances.*

The conversation that took place after Jean Bart had gone home, and the servants had been sent away, would have been altogether different if these two had inherited their titles. As matters stood, however, there were no illusions between them, and they could converse freely and without pretense. Though to do so for a few minutes (Eliza decided) was to be reminded that inhibited and pretentious chatter was not always such a bad thing.

"You and I are alike," the Marquis said. Which he meant as a compliment!

He continued, "We have our titles because we are useful to the King. If I were a legitimate son of the Lavardacs, I'd not be permitted to do anything with my life other than sit around Versailles waiting to die. Because I am a bastard, I have traveled to India, Africa, and the Baltic as far as Russia, and in all of these places I have engaged in trade. Trade! Yet no one thinks less of me for it."

He went on to explain why, in his view, Eliza was useful to the King. It all had to do with finance, and her links to Amsterdam and London, which he described aptly. This was unusual in a French noble. The very few of them who actually comprehended what went on in a Bourse, and why it mattered, affected ignorance for fear of seeming common. To them Eliza made as much sense as the Oracle of Delphi. By contrast, the Marquis affected to understand more than he really did. To him Eliza was a petty *commerçant.* Or so 'twould seem from his next remark: "Fetch me some timber, if you please."

"I beg your pardon, monsieur?"

"Timber."

"Why do you require timber?"

"You do know that we are at war with practically *everyone* now?" he asked, amused.

"Ask the *contrôleur-général* whether the Countess de la Zeur knows it!"

"*Touché.* Tell me, my lady, what do you see when you gaze out the window?"

"Brand-new fortifications, very expensive-looking."

"Closer."

"Water."

"Closer yet."

---

* For the Marquis believed that his half-brother Étienne was the father, which, if it had been true, would have meant that Jean-Jacques was a de Lavardac bastard just like him.

"Ships."

"Closer yet."

"Timber on the shore, piled up like ramparts."

"You know, of course, of my family's connections to the Navy."

"*Tout le monde* knows that your father is Grand Admiral of France and that the Navy has grown prodigiously during his tenure."

"During his tenure as a man in a glorious uniform, attending ship-christenings and twenty-one-gun salutes, and throwing magnificent fêtes. Yes. But *tout le monde* also knows that it was Colbert who was responsible for it. In addition to Grand Admiral, my father was Secretary of State for the Navy until 1669, did you know that? Then he sold the post to Colbert, for a lot of money. Did he *want* to sell it? Did he need the money? No. But he knew that the funds had been advanced to Colbert—a commoner—by the King himself, and so he could not refuse."

"He was fired," Eliza said.

"In the most polite and remunerative way imaginable, he was fired. Colbert became his superior—for of course the Grand Admiral of France is accountable to the Secretary of State for the Navy!"

"When you put it that way, it must have been an interesting time for the Duke."

"It is just as well I was living as a Vagabond in India at the time. I could almost hear his screaming from Shahjahanabad," said the Marquis. "In any case, he was well paid for the demotion, and he went on to make a great fortune out of the ship-building program that Colbert then instituted. For whenever so much money flows from the Treasury to the military, there are countless ways for those within the system to profit. I should know, mademoiselle." And he glanced around the interior of the salon. Like much in Dunkerque, it was small. But everything in it was magnificent.

"You had your title in '74," Eliza said, "and made yourself useful as a part of this Navy-building project."

"I am always eager to be useful to my King," he said.

"God save the King," Eliza said. "I of course share the same eagerness to be of service to his majesty. Did you say you required some timber?"

"Oh, but of course. There's a war on. To this point, naval engagements have been few—a small battle in Bantry Bay when our ships were taking the soldiers to Ireland, and of course the heroics of your friend Jean Bart. But great battles will come. We need more ships. We require timber."

"France is blessed with enormous size, and deep forests," Eliza pointed out.

"Indeed, my lady." His eyes strayed inland, to the crests of the dunes, which were held together with scrub, which here and there gave way to the firm straight lines of new earth-works concealing mortar-batteries. "I do not see any forests hereabouts."

"No, this is like Holland, or Ireland. But farther inland, as you must know, are forests that cannot be traversed in less than a fortnight."

"Fetch me some timber, then, if you wish to be of service to the King."

"Would it be as useful to *le Roi,* if the timber came instead to Le Havre, or Nantes? For Dunkerque is not at the mouth of any great river, but those places are, and this would make the shipping infinitely easier."

"We have shipyards in those places, too; why not?"

Here, Eliza ought to have paused to wonder why there was a shipyard in Dunkerque *at all,* given its location; but after weeks of boredom here, she was so pleased to have been given something to do that she did not give any thought to this paradox.

"Timber costs money," she reminded him, "and I have given all of mine away."

He laughed. "To the French Treasury, mademoiselle! And you shall be buying the timber on behalf of the King! I shall send letters to the *Place au Change* in Lyon. Everyone there shall know your credit is backed by the *contrôleur-général.* Speak to Monsieur Castan there— it is he who makes payments to those who have had the honor of lending money, or selling goods, to the King of France."

"You are suggesting I am to journey to Lyon?"

"It is a terribly important matter, my lady. My coach is at your disposal. You seem in need of an airing-out. Whether the timber is delivered to Nantes or Le Havre, or even here, is all the same to me; but *you,* mademoiselle, I will meet back here in six weeks."

BOOK 4

Bonanza

Throne Room of the Pasha, the Kasba, Algiers

OCTOBER 1689

Dwelling on the Sea-coast, and being a rapacious, cruel, violent, and tyrannical People, void of all Industry or Application, neglecting all Culture and Improvement, it made them Thieves and Robbers, as naturally as Idleness makes Beggars: They disdain'd all Industry and Labour; but being bred up to Rapine and Spoil, when they were no longer able to ravage and plunder the fruitful Plains of *Valentia, Granada* and *Andalusia,* they fell to roving upon the Sea; they built Ships, or rather, took Ships from others, and ravag'd the Coasts, landing in the Night, surprising and carrying away the poor Country People out of their Beds into Slavery.

—DANIEL DEFOE,
A Plan of the English Commerce

"O MOST NOBLE FLOOR, exalted above all other pavements, nay even above the ceilings and rooves of common buildings, you honor me by suffering my lips to touch you," said Moseh de la Cruz—in a queerly muffled voice, as he was not kidding about the lips.

The Pasha of Algiers, and his diverse aghas and hojas, had to lean forward and cock their turbans to make out his Sabir. Or so Jack inferred from the rustling of silk and wafting of perfume all around. Jack, of course, could see nothing but a few square inches of inlaid marble flooring.

Moseh continued: "Though you have already been generous far beyond my deserts in allowing me to grovel on you, I have yet another favor to request: The next time you have the high honor to come into contact with the sole of the Pasha's slipper, will you please most humbly beseech said item of footwear to inform the Pasha that the following conditions exist . . ." at which point Moseh went on to relate some particulars of Jeronimo's story. El Desamparado, needless to say, had been excluded from the meeting. Dappa and Vrej Esphahnian were somewhere near Jack with their faces likewise pressed to the floor.

When Moseh was finished, a voice above them spoke in Turkish, which was translated into Sabir: "Sole of our slipper, inform the floor that we are well aware of the existence of Spanish treasure-fleets, and would make them all ours, if we had the wherewithal to assault scores of heavily armed men-o'-war in the broad Atlantic."

This led to a palpable cringing from the Turk who owned Moseh, Jack, and the others, and who was kneeling behind them; a position not only *correct* for a man of his station, but *comfortable* for one who still had very little skin on the soles of his feet. He began to bleat something in Turkish before the translation was even finished; but Vrej Esphahnian boldly cut him off.

"O glorious and sublime Floor, please make it known to the sole of the Pasha's slipper that, according to Armenians in Havana, with whom I have recently corresponded, the Viceroy who figures in this story has finished his time in Mexico and next spring, weather permitting, should be on his way across the Atlantic in his brig."

"Whose shot-lockers, it is safe to assume, will be filled, not with cannonballs, but with pigs of silver and other swag," added Moseh.

"Slipper," said the Pasha, "remind the Floor that this ship of the Viceroy's, when surrounded by the Spanish fleet, is akin to a tempting morsel lodged between the open jaws of a crocodile."

Moseh took a deep breath and said, "O patient and noble Floor, concerned as you are with preventing the Pasha's carpets from falling through into the cellar, no doubt you have scarce concerned yourself with anything so tedious and ignoble as long-term bathymetric trends in the Guadalquivir Estuary. But, half-breed crypto-Jewish oar-slaves have much leisure to contemplate such matters—so, pray allow me to try your patience even further by informing you that there is a submerged sand-bar at the place where the Guadalquivir empties into the Gulf of Cadiz. For many years it has been the case that the treasure-galleons could pass this bar at high tide and enter the Guadalquivir and drop anchor before Sanlúcar de Barrameda, or Bonanza; or even sail fifty miles up the river to Seville. Those cities, then, were long the destinations of the treasure-fleet, and accordingly it is at Bonanza that the Viceroy, at the beginning of his reign, laid the cornerstone of a palace to receive the proceeds of his relentless, corrupt, and gluttonous pillagings. It has been a-building ever since, and is now complete. But the galleons have grown ever larger, and meanwhile Allah in His wisdom has decreed that the sand-bar I spoke of should wax, and build itself nearer to the surface. For these reasons, as of three years ago, the treasure-fleet no longer ends its journey in the mouth of the Guadalquivir, but at the magnificent deep-water bay of Cadiz, a few miles down the coast."

"Slipper, inform our Floor that we understand, now, that when the treasure-fleet reaches Cadiz next summer, the swag-barge of the orgulous and thrice-damned ex-Viceroy will have no choice but to break away from it, and make the passage up-coast to Bonanza by itself. But fail not to remind the Floor that it is no more a wise idea for us to send our war-galleys across the Gulf of Cadiz to assault the sand-choked estuary of the Guadalquivir, than it would be to stage a frontal assault on the high seas."

"Floor most polished and enduring, so nigh unto what is holy, and so far from the profanities of the infidels, it would be difficult, and wholly unnecessary, for you to muddle your thoughts with the shabby fragments of knowledge that so clutter my mind: for example, that while *war*-galleys of the Dar al-Islam are distinctly unwelcome in the said Gulf, it is common for *trading*-galleys to be seen there. For whereas the former type of ship is crowded stem to stern with scimitar-, dagger-, blunderbuss-, and pistol-brandishing Janissaries, the latter is occupied primarily by wretches chained to oars, and, hence, is less likely to incite all manner of alarm in the superstitious minds of the bacon-eaters."

"Slipper, for that same reason they are useless as offensive weapons."

"Seamless Floor, for that reason they can substitute stealth for might, moving among other ships without creating alarm; and if the oar-slaves are unchained at the right moment, and if they happen to be a redoubtable crew of disgraced Janissaries seeking to recover their honor, Jesuit Samurais, harpoon-hurling wrestling champions, Caballero Desperadoes, and such-like, and if one of them happens to be personally familiar with the brig under attack; then, Floor, I put it to you that the Viceroy's hoard could be taken in the name of the Faith rather easily."

"And what then, Slipper? For if we understand the nature of the Viceroy's smuggling operation, the proceeds will be in the form of silver pigs, which, like the four-legged sort, are unclean, and unwelcome in polite company. The coin of this realm, and of the wide world, is Pieces of Eight."

"Floor, the slippers of many travelers have walked upon you and the lips of many learned scholars kissed you, and from some of these you may have learned that, while the *supply* for all the world's silver is New Spain, the *demand* is in the East. According to legend, the Court of the Great Mogul in Shahjahanabad, and the Forbidden City in Peking, are where it all ends up. And just as all the ships on a sea derive their motive power from a common wind, so do all the diverse enterprises and trading-companies of Europe and the Ottoman Empire draw their force from this perpetual eastward flux of silver. Accordingly, the best place to exchange crude silver for goods is as far *east* as possible, lest middle-men take all the profits. The vessel we will be using is a half-galley, or galleot, obviously unfit to sail round Africa and attempt the passage to the Mogul's port at Surat, and so the farthest east it can possibly travel is Cairo."

Now, a lengthy conversation in Turkish between the Pasha and their owner. Finally the translation into Sabir resumed: "Slipper, rumors have reached us that a rabble of galley-slaves propose to do battle against the Spaniards in the estuary before Bonanza, seemingly a desperate undertaking, and this would seem to raise the possibility of what the Jesuits would call a *quid pro quo.*"

"Floor, it would demean you to be subjected to the numerical calculations, which have been worked out in paralyzing detail by me and my Armenian comrade, here; but when the smoke clears, and the galleot returns from Cairo laden with coffee-beans and other treasures of the East, the proceeds—after various taxes, fees, commissions, *baksheesh,* rake-offs, and profit-takings—should suffice to pay the embarrassingly modest ransoms of all ten of the oar-slaves concerned."

"Slipper, it is written in the Holy Koran that the holding of hostages is a sin, and so it grieves us indescribably that, owing to circumstances not of our making, we have, at any given time, several tens of thousands of them languishing in our *banyolars.* Therefore the plan, as described, is not lacking in virtue. And yet all men are subjected to temptation, and Christians are evidently more susceptible than *most;* and so what is to prevent these slaves, once unchained, from assaulting their overseers, and rowing this galleot—and the silver—to freedom?"

"Floor so hard and cool, it would indeed be foolish to trust a brace of slaves in this manner. Of course, if they went south, and ran the Straits of Gibraltar, they would be caught by the war-galleys of this Citadel of Islam and suffer the Penalty of the Hook. If they went directly to shore, the Spaniards would seize them. But what, an intelligent floor might ask, if they set their course to the north, circumventing the whole Iberian Peninsula, and made for France or

England? This is a most trying question, and potentially a grievous fault in the Plan; but, thanks to Allah, there is another slave whose lips are pressed against you at this very moment and whose misfortunes have taught him much concerning such things."

Jack was wondering to himself what the Penalty of the Hook was, and so almost missed his cue; but Dappa nudged him and he began to rattle off the speech he had rehearsed, albeit with certain improvements that had only just entered his mind. "My words are addressed, not even to the floor, but rather to the dirt wedged between the tiles, as, until such time as I have regained my dignity and rank as a Janissary, I do not feel worthy to address even the Floor directly; and yet here's hoping that some of my reflections will make their way up to the ears of some piece of furniture or whatnot that is in a position of responsibility." Several more nudges from Dappa and throat-clearings from Moseh had punctuated this first part of his oration, and made it difficult for him to establish a rhythm. "Unforgivably, I allowed myself to be taken prisoner at the Siege of Vienna, and knocked around Christendom for a while—it is a long story with no clear beginning, middle, or end. Suffice it to say, O magnificent Dirt of the Floor-Cracks, that before I completely lost my mind and became the wretch that I am today, I learned that there is, in France, a Duke who has polluted the seas with hundreds of infidel war-ships, brand-new and heavily armed; and that said Duke, who dines on the most unclean foods imaginable, is not wholly unknown to the Corsairs of this city, perhaps even to the extent of investing in some of their galleys; and that he owns several of the white, pink-eyed horses considered so desirable by the exalted. This Duke, if he were made aware of our Plan in advance, could easily give orders to his fleet that infests the Bay of Biscay, and tell them to monitor the coast (for our galleot, lacking navigational aids, can on no account stray out of sight of land) and stop any vessels matching the description of ours."

Much discussion in Turkish. Then: "Slipper, if you should encounter any dirt on my floor, which strikes me as unlikely given the immaculate condition of my dwelling, tell it that I know of this French Duke. He is not the sort of man to take part in such a plan out of charitable motives."

"Floor-dirt—or perhaps that is a dust-mote that I carried in on an eyelash—said Duke would almost have to be in on the plan anyway. For the galleot will require some sort of escort to Cairo, lest she fall into the hands of the pirates of Sardinia, Sicily, Malta, Calabria, or Rhodes. The terrifying armada of this City has other errands; but the French fleet plies those waters anyway, shepherding the merchant-galleys of Marseille to and from Smyrna and Alexandria—"

But here the Pasha had apparently heard enough, for he clapped his hands and uttered something in Turkish that caused all of the slaves, and their owner, to be ejected from his audience-chamber and into the octagonal yard of the Kasba. Which Jack looked upon as bad, until he saw the smile on the face of their owner, who was being lifted onto his sedan-chair by Nubian slaves.

Jack, Dappa, Vrej, and Moseh ambled out of the gate into the City of Algiers, and happened to end up standing beneath a row of large iron hooks that projected from the outer wall of the Kasba, a couple of yards below the parapet, some with enormous, gnarled chunks of what appeared to be jerky dangling from them. But others were unoccupied. Above one of those, a group of Janissaries had gathered around a man who was sitting on the brink of the wall.

"What did the Pasha say, there at the end?" Jack asked Dappa.

"In more words, Jack, he said: 'Make it so.' " Dappa had spent a lot of time rowing with Turks, and knew their language thoroughly, which is why he had been invited along.

A solemn look then came over the face of Moseh de la Cruz, as if he were uttering a prayer. "Then we are on our way to Bonanza, as soon as the season wheels round."

Above them, the Janissaries suddenly shoved the seated man off the edge of the wall. He fell for a short distance, gathering speed, and then the iron hook caught him between the buttocks and brought him up short. The man screamed and wriggled, but the point of the hook had gone too far up into his vitals to allow him to squirm off of it, and so there he stayed; the Janissaries turned and departed.

But that was not the only reason Jack felt somewhat uneasy as he and the others made their way down into the lower city. The Pasha had, several times, gone on at great length in Turkish. And furthermore Dappa was regarding Jack with a certain type of Look that Jack had seen many times before, from persons such as Sir Winston Churchill and Eliza, and that usually boded ill. "All right," Jack finally said, "let's have it."

Dappa shrugged. "Most of what passed between the Pasha and his advisors was of a practical nature—he was far more concerned with *how* to do it than *whether*."

"That much is good for us," Jack said. "Now, tell me why you are favoring me with the evil eye."

"When you mentioned that execrable French Duke, the Pasha knew who you meant immediately, and mentioned, in passing, that the same Duke had lately been pestering him for information as to the whereabouts of one Ali Zaybak—an English fugitive."

" 'Tis not an English name."

"It is a sort of cryptical reference to a character in the *Thousand and One Nights*: a notorious thief of Cairo. Time and again the police tried to entrap him but he always squirted free, like a drop of quicksilver when you try to put your finger on it. *Zaybak* is the Arabic word for quicksilver—accordingly, this character was given the *sobriquet* of Ali Zaybak."

"A pleasant enough sounding færy-tale. Yet Cairo is a long way from England . . ."

"Now you are playing stupid, Jack—which in some jurisdictions is as good as a signed confession." Dappa glanced up at the wall of the Kasba where the man squirmed on the hook.

"Perhaps you are right about *Jack*, Dappa, but *my* confusion is wholly genuine," said Moseh.

"In Paris, Jack has a reputation," put in Vrej Esphahnian. "There is a Duke there who does not love our Jack ever since he crashed a party, strangled one of the guests, chopped off the hand of the Duke's first-born son and heir, and made a spectacle of himself in front of the Sun King."

"Then perhaps this Duke got wind of Jack's misadventures on the high seas," Dappa said, "and began to make inquiries."

"Well, as a lost Janissary, recovering from a grievous head injury, I know nothing of such matters," Jack said. "But if it will help our chances, by all means let it be known that information as to the whereabouts of Ali Zaybak is to be had—if the duc d'Arcachon will only invest in the Plan."

BOOK 5

the Juncto

Château Juvisy
10 DECEMBER 1689

AFTER CARDINAL RICHELIEU HAD RECOGNIZED, and Louis XIII had rewarded, the genius of Monsieur Antoine Rossignol, he had built himself a little château. In later years he had hired no less a gardener than Le Nôtre to fix up the grounds. The château was at Juvisy. This had made sense at the time, as the King's court had been in Paris, and Juvisy lay just outside of it.

When the son of Louis XIII had moved his court to Versailles, the son of Antoine Rossignol—who had inherited Antoine's château, his knowledge of cryptanalysis, and his responsibilities—had found himself exiled. *He* had not moved, but the center of power had, and Juvisy had all of a sudden begun to seem like a remote outpost. Another man might have sold the place at a loss, and built a new château somewhere around Versailles. But Bonaventure Rossignol had been content to remain in the old place. His work did not require continual attendance at Court. If anything, the distance, and the peace and quiet that came with it, made him more productive. *Le Roi* had ratified the younger Rossignol's decision by coming to visit him at Juvisy from time to time. In its smallness, its seclusion, and the prim perfection of its walled garden, the château at Juvisy seemed to Eliza like a perfect little kingdom of secrets, with Bon-bon its king, and Eliza its queen, or at least concubine.

The garden was of an altogether different style from what Le Nôtre had done at Versailles, being, of course, much smaller, with fewer sculptures. But it had in common with the King's garden that it was made to look splendid when seen from the high windows of the château, which was how Eliza was seeing it. Bon-bon's bedchamber was on the upper storey, in the center of the building, so that when Eliza climbed out of his bed she could walk three paces over a cold floor and stand in a dormer and gaze straight down the path that formed the garden's axis. Of course the plantings were dead and brown now, but the curlicues of its sculpted hedges still drew her eye, and gave her something to stare at while she began to answer a question that Bon-bon had just asked her.

He wanted to know, in effect, what the hell she was doing here. For some reason the question irked her a little bit.

She had showed up exhausted and dirty last night, with no thought of doing anything save putting Jean-Jacques to bed somewhere, and then collapsing into some bed of her own and sleeping for a few decades. Instead she'd been up half the night making love to Bon-bon. Yet she felt more awake, more refreshed now than if she'd spent the same amount of time slumbering. And so perhaps what she had taken for tiredness, yester evening, had been some other condition.

He'd had the good grace not to inquire what was going on. Instead he had accepted, with grace and even humor, the sudden arrival of Eliza and her entourage at his gates. She'd liked it that way, and she'd liked what had happened after. But now that the sun was up and they had gotten the sex out of their systems, there was this tedious need to explain matters. Certain parts of her mind had to be woken up, and were not happy about it. She stared at the dead garden, tracing the patterns of the hedges with her eyes, and mastered her annoyance.

"You had mentioned in a note to me that you contemplated a journey to Lyon," Rossignol said, trying to prime the pump. "That was six weeks ago."

"Yes," Eliza said. "The journey to Lyon took ten days."

"Ten days! Did you walk?"

"I could have done it faster by myself, but I was traveling with a five-month-old. The train consisted of two carriages, a baggage-cart, and some outriders and footmen borrowed from Lieutenant Bart and from the Ozoirs," Eliza said.

Rossignol grimaced. "Unwieldy."

"The first twenty miles were the most difficult, as you know."

"Dunkerque is scarcely connected to France at all," Rossignol agreed.

"Have you been to Lyon?"

"Only a little, passing through en route to Marseille."

"And did you find it strangely bleak and austere compared to Paris?"

"Mademoiselle, I found it bleak and austere even compared to the Hague!"

Eliza did not laugh at the witticism, but only turned her back on the window, for a moment, to regard Rossignol. He was propped up in bed on a mountain of pillows, exposed to the chilly air from the waist up. The man burned food like a forge burned coal, and never grew fat, and never seemed to feel cold.

"That is because you have no regard for commerce. I found it most interesting."

"Oh. Yes, I know about that," Rossignol conceded. "The great crossroads where the Mediterranean trades with the North. It sounds as if it ought to be interesting. But if you go there, you see only warehouses and silk-factories, and tracts of plain open ground."

"Of course it seems boring if all you do is look at it," Eliza said. "What renders it interesting is to take part in what goes on in those boring warehouses."

Rossignol's black eyes strayed to some papers resting on a bedside table. He was already regretting having asked her to explain this, and was hoping she'd make it quick.

Eliza stepped over to the side of the bed and swept the papers off onto the floor. Then she got a knee up on the bed and crab-walked across it until she was straddling Rossignol, sitting down firmly on his pelvis. "You asked," she reminded him. "and I have got an answer for you, which you are going to listen to, and what is more, by the time I am finished, you will confess that it is interesting."

"You have my attention, mademoiselle," said Rossignol.

"Lyon. I suppose they used to hold sprawling country-style fairs there, two hundred years ago. It was colonized, you know, by Florentines hoping to make fortunes selling goods to this wild northern place called France. There are still fairs, four times a year, but it is not so rustic. It is more like Leipzig now."

"That means nothing to me."

"It means people standing in courtyards of trading-houses, screaming at each other, and trading goods not physically present."

"But the warehouses—?"

"Silly, the goods are not present *in the trading-houses.* But neither can they be terribly remote, for they must be inspected before and delivered after the sale. Much of the traffic on the streets is *commerçants* going to this or that warehouse to look at a shipment of silks, herring, figs, hides, or what-have-you."

"That helps me to understand some of what was, to a gentleman, so incomprehensible about the place."

"You'd never guess that the place does more business than all of Paris. From the street it is desolate. You can die of loneliness or starvation there. It is not until you get inside the houses that you discover the inner life of the place. Bon-bon, all of the people who have been lured here by trade have created, behind their iron-bound doors and shuttered windows, little microcosms of the worlds they left behind in Genoa, Antwerp, Bruges, Geneva, Isfahan, Augsburg, Stockholm, Naples, or wherever they came from. When you are in one of those houses, you might as well be in one of those faraway cities. So think of Lyon as a capital of trade, and the streets around the *Place au Change* as its diplomatic quarter, where the Jews, Armenians, Dutch, English, Genoans, and all the other great trading-nations of the world have established their embassies: shards of foreign territory embedded in a faraway land."

"What were you doing there, mademoiselle?"

"Buying timber for Monsieur le marquis d'Ozoir. I required some expert help. After I had been a week in Lyon, I was joined by my Dutch associates: Samuel and Abraham de la Vega and their cousin. I had sent a letter to them before I left Dunkerque, for I knew they were in London. It had caught up to them at Gravesend. They had changed their plans and made direct for Dunkerque, which they passed through five days after I had departed. As they passed through Paris they enlisted their cousin, one Jacob Gold, and the three of them followed me down and encamped at the house of a man they knew there—a wholesaler of beeswax that he imports from Poland-Lithuania."

"Now I see why this thing took six weeks! Ten days to creep down to Lyon, a week to wait for all of these Jews to show up—"

"The delay was not a problem for me. It took me and my staff that long anyway to recover from the journey, and to set up housekeeping in Lyon. Monsieur le marquis d'Ozoir, bless him, had sent word ahead, and arranged for us to stay at the *pied-à-terre* of someone who owed him a favor. Once we had established ourselves, I had begun to make contacts among the crowd who frequent the *Place au Change*. For I knew that the brothers de la Vega would spare no effort in ransacking the wholesale timber market and finding the best wood on the best terms. But their efforts would be of no use unless I had made arrangements for a bill of exchange to be drawn up, transferring the agreed-on sum from the King's treasury to whomever sold us the timber. Likewise we would need to strike a deal with the shipper, and to purchase insurance, *et cetera*. So even if the de la Vegas had arrived at the same time as I, they should have little to do for a few days. And the need to feed little Jean-Jacques posed the most absurd complications."

It was a mistake to mention this, for now Rossignol's eyes drifted from Eliza's face down to her left breast. Earlier she had wrapped herself in a sheet, but this had slipped down as she wrestled with him.

"The de la Vegas invited me to visit them at the beeswax-warehouse where they were lodging."

Rossignol scoffed, and rolled his eyes.

"It would have seemed a very odd invitation to my ears before I had gotten to know Lyon," Eliza admitted, "but when I reached the place, I found it to be perfectly congenial. It is on a meadow that rises up above the Rhône to the east of the trading district. They have more land than they need, and let it out to an adjacent vineyard. The growing season was over and so the vines were not much to look at, but the weather was fine, and we sat under a bower on the terrace of this stone building full of wax and drank Russian tea sweetened with Lithuanian honey. The daughters of the wax-magnate played with Jean-Jacques and sang him nursery-rhymes in Yiddish.

"To Samuel and Abraham de la Vega and Jacob Gold, I said that Lyon struck me as a very strange town."

"I could have told you that, mademoiselle," said Rossignol.

"But you and I think it is strange for different reasons, Bon-bon," said Eliza. "Listen, and let me explain."

"What of these Jews? What did they think?"

"They felt likewise, but had been reluctant to say anything. And so what I was trying to do, Bon-bon, was to get them talking."

"And so were these Jews responsive to your gambit, mademoiselle?" Rossignol asked.

"You are impossible," Eliza said.

SAMUEL DE LA VEGA, at twenty-four, was the senior man present—for the elders of the clan had more important things to do. He shrugged and said: "We are here to learn. Please say more."

"I phant'sied you were here *to make money*," Eliza said.

"That is always the object in the long run. Whether we make a profit on this matter of the timber remains to be seen; but we have heard of this place and want to know more of its peculiarities."

Eliza laughed. "Why should I say more, when you have said so much? You come here not knowing whether it is possible to make money. It is a place you *have heard of*, which is no great testimony to its importance, and you approach it as a sort of curiosity. Would you speak thus of Antwerp?"

"Let me explain," Samuel said. "In our family we do not recognize a profit—we do not put it on the books—until we have a bill of exchange payable in Amsterdam or (now) London, drawn on a house that maintains a well-reputed agency in one or both of those cities."

"To put it succinctly: hard money," Eliza said.

"If you will. Now, as we rode down here with Jacob Gold, he told us of the system in Lyon, and how it works."

Jacob Gold looked so nervous, now, that Eliza felt she must make some little joke to put him at ease. "If only I could have eavesdropped on you!" she exclaimed. "For yesterday at dinner at the home of Monsieur Castan, I was treated to a description of that same system—a description so flattering that I asked him why it was not used everywhere else."

They found this amusing. "What was Monsieur Castan's reaction to that?" asked Jacob Gold.

"Oh, that other places were cold, distrustful, that the people there did not know one another so well as they did in Lyon, had not built up the same web of trust and old relationships. That they were afflicted by a petty, literal-minded obsession with specie, and could not believe that real business was being transacted unless they saw coins being physically moved from place to place."

The others looked relieved; for they knew, now, that they would not have to break this news to Eliza. "So you are aware that when accounts are settled in Lyon, it is all done on the books. A man seated at a *banca* will write in his book, 'Signore Capponi owes me 10,000 *ecus au soleil*'—a currency that is used only in Lyon, by the way—and this, to him, is as good as having bullion in his lock-box. Then when the next fair comes around, perhaps he finds himself needing to transfer 15,000 *ecus* to Signore Capponi, and so he will strike that entry from his ledger, and Signore Capponi will write that he is owed 5,000 *ecus* by this chap, and so on."

"Some money must change hands though!" insisted Abraham, who had heard all of this before but still could not quite bring himself to believe it. He was fourteen years old.

"Yes—a tiny amount," said Jacob Gold. "But only after they have exhausted every conceivable way of settling it on paper, by arranging multilateral transfers among the different houses."

"Wouldn't it be simpler just to use money?" Abraham asked doggedly.

"Perhaps—if they had any!" Eliza said. Which was meant as a jest, but it stilled them for a few moments.

"Why don't they?" Abraham demanded.

"It depends on whom you ask," Eliza said. "The most common answer is that they do not need it because the system works so smoothly. Others will tell you that when any bullion does become available here, it is immediately smuggled out to Geneva."

"Why?"

"In Geneva are banks that, in exchange for bullion, will write you a bill of exchange payable in Amsterdam."

Abraham's eyes blossomed. "So we are not the only ones who are worried about how to extract hard money profits from Lyon!"

"Of course not! For that, we are competing against every other foreign merchant in Lyon who does not share the belief, common here, that entries in a ledger are the same as money," said Samuel.

"What kind of person *would* believe such a thing, though?" Abraham asked.

Jacob Gold answered, "The kinds of people who have been here for so long and who make a comfortable living off of those ledgers."

Eliza said, "But the only reason this system works is that these people know and trust each other so well. Which is fine for them. But if you are on the outside, as we are, you can't take part in the *Dépôt*, as this system is called, and it is difficult to realize profits."

Jacob Gold added, "It is fine for those who have the houses here, the land, the servants. They transact an enormous amount of business and they find ways to live well. The lack of hard money is only felt when one wants to cash out and move somewhere else. But if that is the kind of person you are—"

"Then you don't live in Lyon and you are not a member of the *Dépôt*," Eliza said.

"We can talk about this all day, going in circles like the Uroburos," said Samuel, clapping his hands, "but the fact is that we're here and we want to buy some timber for the King. And we don't have any money. But we have credit from Monsieur Castan who in turn has credit because he lives here and is very much a member of the *Dépôt*."

"Thank you, Samuel," Eliza said. "You are correct: people trust Monsieur Castan; when one of the other members of this *Dépôt* writes in his ledger 'M. Castan owes me such-and-such number of *ecus*,' to them that's as good as gold. And what we need to do is turn that 'gold' into some timber arriving at Nantes."

"Thanks to Monsieur Wachsmann," said Jacob Gold, referring to our host, "we have some ideas as to where we might go and make inquiries about who has timber, and might be willing to sell it to us; but how do we actually transfer the money to them from the King's Treasury?"

"We need to find someone who is a member of this *Dépôt* and who is willing to write in his ledger that the King owes him the money," Eliza said.

"But that still doesn't get the money into the hands of him who sells us the timber, unless he is a member of the *Dépôt*, and I do not phant'sy that lumberjacks are invited," said Samuel.

"And it provides no way for us to realize a profit," Abraham, the ever-vigilant, reminded them.

Eliza reached out and pinched him on the nose to shut him up while she pointed out, "True, and yet wax, silk and other commodities are sold here in immense quantities, so there must be some way of doing it! And some *do* realize hard money profits, as is proved by the covert transfers of bullion to Geneva!"

Monsieur Wachsmann was therefore brought in. He was a stolid gray-headed Pomeranian of about threescore years. They explained their puzzlement to him and asked how *he* sold his goods, given that he was not a member of the *Dépôt*. He replied that he had a sort of relationship with an important businessman in town, with whom he kept a running account; and whenever the account stood in Monsieur Wachsmann's favor, he could leverage that to get what he needed. The same would be true, he assured his visitors, of any timber wholesaler big enough for them to consider doing business with.

"So a plan begins to take shape," said Samuel. "We will negotiate terms with a timber-wholesaler, denominated in *ecus au soleil,* never mind that they are a wholly fictitious currency, and then take the matter to the *Dépôt* and allow them to clear it on their ledgers. We end up with the timber; but is is possible for us to extract any profit?"

Monsieur Wachsmann shrugged as if this was not something he paid much attention to; and yet his estate showed that he had profited abundantly. "If you would like, you can route the profits to my account, and I will owe them to you, and we may plow these into later trades within the *Dépôt,* which may eventually turn into some material form, such as casks of honey, that you could sell for gold in Amsterdam."

"This is how people move to Lyon, and never leave," muttered Jacob Gold, combining in this one remark the Amsterdammer's amazement at Lyon's business practices with the Parisian's disdain for its culture.

Monsieur Wachsmannn shrugged, and looked at his château. "Worse fates can be imagined. Do you have any idea what Stettin is like at this time of year?"

"What about getting some bullion and running it to Geneva for a bill of exchange?" Abraham demanded. "Much quicker, and easier to carry to Amsterdam than casks of honey."

"There is a lot of competition for the small amount of bullion that exists here, and so you will have to accept a large discount," Monsieur Wachsmann warned him, "but if that is really what you want, the house that specializes in such transactions is that of Hacklheber. They are at the Sign of the Golden Mercury, cater-corner from the *Place au Change*."

"Now, there is a familiar name," Eliza said. "I have been to their factory in Leipzig, and been ogled by Lothar himself."

"I have never heard of them," said Samuel, "but if this Lothar was ogling you it means he is not altogether stupid."

"They are metals specialists," said Jacob Gold, "I know that much."

"When the Genoese here went bankrupt," said Monsieur Wachsmann, "it happened because the Spanish mines had hiccuped in their delivery of silver to Seville. Bankers of Geneva and other places came to Lyon to fill the void left by the Genoese. They had connections to silver mines in the Harz and the Ore Range, which flourished for a brief time, until Spanish silver once again flooded the market. Anyway, one of those banking-families had an agency in Leipzig, and the people they sent thither to look after it became linked by marriage to this family of von Hacklheber. Because of the Hacklhebers' connections to the mines, they had older ties to the Fuggers. Indeed, it is said that this family goes all the way back to the time of the Romans . . ."

Abraham snorted. "*Ours* goes back all the way to Adam."

"Yes; but to them this is all very impressive," said Monsieur Wachsmann patiently, "and by the way, now that you have had your bar mitzvah you might spend less time poring over Torah and more learning social graces. At any rate, fortune favored the Leipzig branch, and before long the Hacklheber tail was wagging the Geneva dog. It is a small house, but reputed extraordinarily clever. They are in Lyon, Cadiz, Piacenza: anywhere there is a large flux of money."

"What do they *do*?" Abraham wanted to know.

"Lend money, clear transactions, like other banks. But their real specialty is maneuvers such as the one we are talking about now: shipment of bullion to Geneva. Do you remember when I warned you that there would be a discount if you converted your earnings to bullion here? It should have occurred to you to wonder just where the missing money disappears to in such a case. The answer is that it goes into the coffers of Lothar von Hacklheber."

Monsieur Wachsmann rolled to his feet, and paced across the terrace once or twice before going on.

"I trade in wax. I know where wax comes from and where it goes, and how much wax of different types is worth to different people in different times and places. I say to you that what I am to wax, Lothar von Hacklheber is to money."

"You mean gold? Silver?"

"All kinds. Metals in pig, bullion, or minted form, paper, moneys of account such as our *ecus au soleil*. To me, money is frankly somewhat mysterious; but to him it is all as simple as wax. Or so it would seem; like honeycombs in a boiler, it melts together and is con-fused into one thing."

"Then we shall go and talk to his agent here," Eliza said.

"Agreed," said Samuel de la Vega, "but I say to you that if they simply had a few coins lying about the place, we could get this whole thing done in an hour. That this system works, I cannot deny; but this *Dépôt* reminds me of certain towns up in the Alps where people have been marrying each other for too long."

"THE NEXT DAY," Eliza continued, "I met Gerhard Mann, who is the Hacklheber agent in Lyon."

She now relaxed her grip on Bonaventure Rossignol's testicles. For in the end, this was the only way she had found to maintain Bonbon's attentiveness as she had discoursed of *ecus au soleil* and the *Dépôt* and so forth. But the mention of the name Hacklheber brought Rossignol to attention.

"Lothar von Hacklheber," she continued, "is not the sort who gladly suffers an employee to while away the afternoons sipping coffee in the café."

"I should think not!"

"He has so arranged it that Mann has more work than he can handle. This forces him to make choices. He is always dashing about town on horseback like a Cavalier. Carriages are too slow for him. Arranging the meeting was absurdly difficult. It required half a dozen exchanges of notes. Finally I did what was simplest, namely remained still at the *pied-à-terre* and waited for him to come to me. He galloped up, naturally, just as I was beginning to suckle Jean-Jacques. And so rather than send him away, I invited him in, and bade him sit down across the table from me even as Jean-Jacques was hanging off my tit."

"Appalling!"

"But I did this as a sort of test, Bon-bon, to see if he'd be appalled by it."

"Was he?"

"He pretended not to notice, which was not an easy thing for him."

Rossignol shuddered. "What did you talk about?"

"We talked about Lothar von Hacklheber."

"YOU MET *HIM* IN LEIPZIG?" Mann asked.

"It had to do with a silver-mining project in the Harz," Eliza said, "in which *he* elected not to invest: a typically shrewd decision."

Eliza explained to Mann what she had in mind. He pondered it for a few moments. At first she saw concern, or even fear, on his face, which made her suspect that he did not really wish to do it, yet was loath to refuse, for fear of what *he* might say, were Eliza to go to *him* and pout. Mann was a young man—indeed, would have to be, to last for very long, working as he did—and Eliza saw clearly enough that he had been posted to this place to prove himself, or to fail, so that *he* could decide where to send Mann next. Mann had blue eyes a little too close together, and a broad brow, so expressive that in its creases and corrugations she could read his feelings like sonnets on parchment. He was intelligent, but lacking in resolution. She guessed that someone of strong personality would one day get the better of him, and that he would end up sitting at a *banca* on an upper floor of the House of the Golden Mercury in Leipzig, peering down into the courtyard with a mirror on a stick.

After a few moments' thought, Mann relaxed, and began to sift through the vocabularies of diverse languages to express his thoughts. "It would be—" he began, and then switched to German in which Eliza could make out the word-part *"sonder,"* which to them meant "special" or "exceptional" or "peculiar." This was his polite way of telling her that the sum involved was too small to be worth his time. "But we are encouraged to make such transactions. Sometimes they are like the first trickle of water coming through a tiny crevice in a dike; the amount that comes through is not as important as the channel that it cuts along its way, which presently carries a much greater volume." Which was his way of saying that he had heard she was backed by the French government, and wanted to participate in what she was doing, now that expenditures were rising because of the war.

"It is not a similitude that shall be of any comfort to Dutchmen," Eliza said, having in mind her colleagues, the de la Vegas.

"Ah, but if you cared about the comfort of Dutchmen you would not be on such an errand," Gerhard Mann reminded her.

"So through his own cleverness Gerhard Mann had devised a way to escape from the interview without giving me or *him* any cause to be angry," Eliza said. Tired of sitting on Bon-bon, she now rolled back and sat cross-legged on the bed between his spread knees.

"I let the de la Vegas know that we had now a way to get hard money out of Lyon," she continued. "Within a few hours, they were making the rounds of the timber wholesalers, and within a day, had struck two separate deals: one for a shipment of *Massif Central* oak logs, which were stacked near the bank of the Saône a mile upstream, another for some Alpine softwood at the confluence of the Rhône and the Saône. If you'd like, Bon-bon, I can devote an hour or two, now, to explaining in detail the negotiations amongst ourselves, the two merchants who sold us the timber, Monsieur Castan, various other members of the *Dépôt*, Gerhard Mann, and certain insurers and shippers."

Rossignol said something under his breath about *la belle dame sans merci.*

"Very well then," said Eliza, "suffice it to say that some entries were made in some ledgers. A fast coach went to Geneva, which is some seventy-five miles away as the crow flies, though considerably farther as the horse gallops. Abraham got his Bill of Exchange, though the margin of profit was scarcely enough to cover their time and expense. The timber was ours.

"At this point—mid-November—we supposed the matter concluded. For we had the timber, and had arranged shipping. An Amsterdammer would consider the deal closed. For to such people it is a perfectly routine matter to ship any amount of goods to Nagasaki, New York, or Batavia with the stroke of a quill.

"We, as well as the logs, had to go north: Jacob Gold to Paris and the rest of us to Dunkerque, whence the de la Vegas could find sea-passage north to Amsterdam.

"The fastest way would have been for me to climb back into the carriage I had borrowed from Monsieur le marquis d'Ozoir and go north by road. But there was no room in it for the de la Vegas. The weather had turned cold. We were in no particular hurry. And so we decided to send the horses and carriages north by road to Orléans, where the drivers could rent mounts, or hire another carriage, for the de la Vegas.

"In the meantime, we would take the river route to the same place, arriving a few days later.* Our plan was to go to Roanne, and buy passage on riverboats as far as Orléans, which would be infinitely more spacious and comfortable than making the same passage by road. At Orléans we would make rendezvous with our horses and vehicles, which would convey us north to Paris and then Dunkerque.

---

* In the part of France she was talking about, the Saône and the Loire ran in parallel courses about fifty miles apart, but in opposite directions. The Saône flowed south to its confluence with the Rhône and thence to Marseille. The Loire ran north to Orléans, where it bent westward and continued down to the Atlantic. Several miles north of Lyon was the portage that linked these two rivers: a road, or rather a bundle of roads and tracks, that cut westward over a line of hills to the town of Roanne, about fifty miles away, which lay on the upper Loire.

"The Loire, as you know, flows on past Orléans to Nantes. So the route I have just described to you was the same as that of the timber. And so there was another advantage to the plan I have described, which was that as we went along, we would be able to keep an eye on the King's logs. In the unlikely event that some problem arose en route, we would be on hand to fix it."

"But, mademoiselle," said Rossignol, "by your account, this was almost a month ago. What on earth has been happening in the meantime?"

"A full recitation would take another month yet. You know that each of the component *pays* of *la France* controls its own stretch of road or river and has the right to extract tolls and tariffs, *et cetera*. Likewise you know that the population is a quilt of guilds and corporations and parishes, each with its own peculiar privileges."

"Which are granted by the King," said Rossignol. For he seemed a little bit nervous that Eliza was about to say something impolitic.

Which she was; but she felt safe in doing so here, in the kingdom of secrets. "The King grants those privileges in order to make people want to join those guilds and corporations! And thus the King gets power by offering to broaden, or threatening to restrict, the same privileges."

"What of it?" Rossignol sniffed.

"After a few days, Abraham joked that this voyage was impossible unless one went accompanied by a whole squadron of lawyers. But this makes it sound too easy. Since every *pays* has its own peculiar laws and traditions, there is no one lawyer who comprehends them all; and so what one really has to do is stop every few miles and hire a *different* lawyer. But I have only mentioned, so far, the entities with *formal legal rights* to impede the movement of logs on a river. This leaves out half of the difficulties we faced. There are on these rivers people who used to be pirates but have degenerated into extortionists. We paid them in hard money until we ran out, at which point we had to begin paying them in logs. Every night, others who were less formally organized would come around and help themselves. We suspected this was happening, but the night-watchmen we hired were barely distinguishable from the thieves. The only reliable sentry we had was Jean-Jacques. He would wake me every couple of hours through the night, and I would sit in my boat-cabin feeding him and watching through a window as the locals made off with our logs."

"It cannot all be as disorderly as you make it out to be!" Rossignol protested.

"There does exist an apparatus of maintaining order on the roads and waterways: diverse ancient courts of law, and *prévôts* and *baillis* who report to the local *seigneurs* and who are reputed to have bands of armed men at their disposal. But they were never there when we needed them. If I shipped logs down the river every week, I should have no choice but to come to understandings with all of those *seigneurs*. Whether this would prove more or less expensive than being robbed outright, I cannot guess. Our run down the Loire surprised many who would have stolen more from us if we had operated on a predictable schedule.

"The Loire, particularly on its upper reaches, is obstructed by sand-bars in many places, and different arrangements must be made to get past each: here one must find and hire a local pilot, there one must pay the owner of the mill to release a gush of water from his mill-pond that will heave the logs over the shallows.

"I could go on in this vein all day. Suffice it to say that when we at last reached Orléans, ten days behind schedule, Jacob Gold and I dashed north to Paris and cashed in our Bill of Exchange at a swingeing discount. Jacob returned to Orléans with the money, which he used to cover all of the unexpected expenses that had cropped up en route. I came here. Soon I'll go on to Dunkerque and meet that bastard who sent me on this fool's errand, Monsieur le marquis d'Ozoir, and explain to him that half of the logs have evaporated, along with all of our profits, and six weeks of our lives."

Dunkerque Residence of the d'Ozoirs
13 DECEMBER 1689

WHERE BONAVENTURE ROSSIGNOL HAD FIBRILLATED between boredom and disbelief, the Marquis d'Ozoir was richly amused when Eliza told him the same story. At the beginning of the interview, she had been merely furious. When he began to smirk and chuckle, she tended toward homicidal, and had to leave the room and tend to Jean-Jacques for a little while. The baby was in a gleeful mood for some reason, grabbing his feet and fountaining spit, and this cheered her up. For he had no thought of anything outside of the room, nor in the past, nor the future. When Eliza returned to the salon with its view over the harbor, she had quite regained her composure and had even begun to see a bit of humor in this folly of the logs.

"And why did you send me on such a fool's errand, monsieur?" she demanded. "You must have known how it would all come out."

"Everyone in this business knows—or *claims* to—that to get French timber to French shipyards is an impossibility. And because they know this, they never even try. And if no one ever tries, how can we be certain it is still impossible? And so every few years, just to find out whether it's still impossible, I ask some enterprising person who does not know it's impossible to attempt it. I do not blame you for being annoyed with me. But if you had somehow succeeded, it would have been a great deed. And in failing, you learned much that will be useful in the next phase of our project—which I assure you is *not* impossible."

He had risen to his feet and approached the window, and by a look and a twitch of the shoulder he invited her to join him there. Gone were the days when one could look out over the Channel and see blue sky above England; today they could barely make out the harbor wall. Raindrops were whacking the windowpanes like birdshot.

"I confess the place looks different to me now, and not just because of the weather," Eliza said. "My eye is drawn to certain things that I ignored before. The timber down at the shipyard: how did it get here? Those new fortifications: how did the King pay for them? They were put there by laborers; and laborers must be paid with hard money, they'll not accept Bills of Exchange."

The Marquis was distracted, and perhaps a bit impatient, that she had strayed into the topic of fortifications. He flicked his fingers at the nearest rampart. "That is nothing," he said. "If you must know, the nobility have a lot of metal, because they hoard it. *Le Roi* gets to them at Versailles and gives them a little talk: 'Why is your coastline not better defended? It is your obligation to take care of this.' " Of course they cannot resist. They spend some of their metal to put up the fort. In return they get the personal gratitude of the King, and get to go to dinner with him or hand him his shirt or something."

"That's *all*?"

He smiled. "That, and a note from the *contrôleur-général* saying that the French Treasury owes him whatever amount of money he spent."

"Aha! So that's how it works: These nobles are exchanging hard money for soft: metal for French government debt."

"Technically I suppose that is true. Such an exchange is a loss of power and independence. For gold can be spent anywhere, for anything. Paper may have the same nominal value but its usefulness is contingent on a hundred factors, most of which are impossible to comprehend, unless you live at Versailles. But it is all nonsense."

"What do you mean, it is all nonsense?"

"Those debts are worthless. They will never be repaid."

"Worthless!? Never!?"

"Perhaps I exaggerate. Let me put it thus: The nobleman who built these new fortifications around the harbor knows he may never see his money again. But he does not care, for it was just some gold plate in his cellar. Now the plates are gone, but he has currency of a different sort at Versailles; and that is what he *desires*."

"I am tempted to share in your cynicism, for I don't wish to seem a fool," Eliza said slowly, "but if the debt is secured by a sealed document from the *contrôleur-général*, it seems to me that it must possess some value."

"I don't wish to speak of fortifications," he said. "These were built by Monsieur le comte d'——" and he mentioned someone Eliza had never heard of. "You may make inquiries with him if you are curious. But you and I must not let our attention stray from the matter at hand: timber for his majesty's shipyards."

"Very well," Eliza said, "I see some down there. Where did it come from?"

"The Baltic," he returned, "and it was brought in a Dutch ship, in the spring of this year, before war was declared."

"No shipyard could exist in Dunkerque, unless it got its supplies from the sea," Eliza pointed out, "and so may I assume that this was a habitual arrangement, before the war?"

"It has not been *habitual* for rather a long while. When I came back from my travels in the East, around 1670, my father put me to work in the Company of the North down at La Rochelle. This was a brainchild of Colbert. He had tried to build his navy out of French timber and ran afoul of the same troubles as you. And so the purpose of this *Compagnie du Nord* was to trade in the Baltic for timber. Of necessity, this would be shipped mostly in Dutch bottoms."

"Why did he put it all the way down in La Rochelle? Why not closer to the North—Dunkerque or Le Havre?"

"Because La Rochelle was where the Huguenots were," the Marquis answered, "and it was they who made the whole enterprise run."

"What did *you* do, then, if I may inquire?"

"Traveled to the north. Watched. Learned. Gave information to my father. His position in the Navy is largely ornamental. But the information that he gets about what the Navy is doing has enabled him to make investments that otherwise would have been beyond his intellectual capacity."

Eliza must have looked taken aback.

"I am a bastard," said the Marquis.

"I knew he was wealthy, but assumed 'twas all inherited," Eliza said.

"What he *inherited* has been converted inexorably to soft money, in just the manner we spoke of a few minutes ago," d'Ozoir said. "Which amounts to saying that he has slowly over time lost his independent means and become a pensioner of the French Government—which is how *le Roi* likes it. In order for him to preserve any independent means, he has had to make investments. The reason you are not aware of this is that his investments are in the Mediterranean—the Levant, and Northern Africa—whereas your attentions are fixed North and West." And here he reached out and took Eliza firmly by the hand and looked her in the eye. *"Which is where I would like them to stay*—and so let us attend to the matter of Baltic timber, I beg you."

"Very well," Eliza said, "You say that in the early seventies, you had Huguenots doing it in Dutch ships. Then there was a long war against the Dutch, no?"

"Correct. So we substituted English or Swedish ships."

"I am guessing that this worked satisfactorily until four years ago when *le Roi* expelled most of the Huguenots and enslaved the rest?"

"Indeed. Since then, I have been desperately busy, trying to do all of the things that an office full of Huguenots used to do. I have managed to keep a thin stream of timber coming in from the Baltic—enough to mend the old ships and build the occasional new one."

"But now we are at war with the two greatest naval powers in the world," Eliza said. "The demand for ship timber will go up immensely. And as the de la Vegas and I have just finished proving, we cannot get it from France. So you want my help in reëstablishing the *Compagnie du Nord* here, at Dunkerque."

"I should be honored."

"I will do it," she announced, "but first you must answer me one question."

"Only ask it, mademoiselle."

"How long have you been thinking about this? And did you discuss it with your half-brother?"

Jean-Jacques, with an uncanny sense of timing for a six-month-old, began to cry from the next room. D'Ozoir considered it. "My half-brother Étienne wants you for a different reason."

"I know—because I breed true."

"No, mademoiselle. You are a fool if you believe that. There are many pretty young noblewomen who can make healthy babies, and most of them are less trouble than you."

"What other possible reason could he want me?"

"Other than your beauty? The answer is Colbert."

"Colbert is dead."

"But his son lives on: Monsieur le marquis de Seignelay. Secretary of State for the Navy, like his father before him, and my father's boss. Do you have the faintest idea what it is like, for one such as my father—a hereditary Duke of an ancient line, and cousin of the King—to see a commoner's son treated as if he were a peer of the realm? To be *subordinated* to a man whose father was a *merchant?*"

"It must be difficult," Eliza said, without much sympathy.

"Not as difficult for the Duc d'Arcachon as some of the others—for my father is not as arrogant as some. My father is subservient, flexible, adaptable—"

"And in this case," Eliza said, completing the thought—for the Marquis was in danger of losing his nerve— "the way he means to adapt is by marrying Étienne off to the female who most reminds him of Colbert."

"Common origins, good with money, respected by the King," said the Marquis. "And if she is beautiful and breeds true, why, so much the better. You may imagine that you are some sort of outsider to the Court of Versailles, mademoiselle, that you do not belong there at all. But the truth of the matter is thus: Versailles has only existed for seven years. It does not have any ancient traditions. It was made by Colbert, the commoner. It is full of nobles, true; but you fool yourself if you believe that they feel comfortable there—feel as if they belong. No, it is *you*, mademoiselle, who are the perfect courtier of Versailles, you whom the others shall envy, once you go there and establish yourself. My father feels himself slipping down, sees his family losing its wealth, its influence. He throws a rope up, hoping that someone on higher and firmer ground will snatch it out of the air and pull him to safety—and that someone is *you*, mademoiselle."

"It is a heavy charge to lay on a woman who has no money, and who is busy trying to raise an infant," Eliza said. "I hope that your father is not really as desperate as you make him sound."

"He is not desperate *yet*. But when he lies awake at night, he schemes against the possibility that he, or his descendants, may become desperate in the future."

"If what you say is creditable, I have much to do," said Eliza, turning from the window, and smoothing her skirt down with her hands.

"What shall you do first, mademoiselle?"

"I believe I shall write a letter to England, monsieur."

"England! But we are at war with England," the Marquis pointed out, mock-offended.

"What I have in mind is a Natural-Philosophic sort of discourse," Eliza said, "and Philosophy recognizes no boundaries."

"Ah, you will write to one of your friends in the Royal Society?"

"I had in mind a Dr. Waterhouse," Eliza said. "He was cut for the stone recently."

The Marquis got the same aghast, cringing, yet fascinated look that all men did whenever the topic of lithotomy arose in conversation.

"Last I heard, he had lived through it, and was recovering," Eliza continued. "Perhaps he has time on his hands to answer idle inquiries from a French countess."

"Perhaps he does," said the Marquis, "but I cannot understand why the first thing that enters your mind is to write a letter to a sick old Natural Philosopher in London."

"It's only the *first* thing, not the *only* thing, that I'll do," said Eliza. "It's a thing easily done from Dunkerque. I would begin a conversation with him, or with someone, concerning money: soft and hard."

"Why not discuss it with a Spaniard? They know how to make money that people respect all around the world."

"It is precisely because the English coinage is so pathetic that I wish to take up the matter with an Englishman," Eliza returned. "No one here can believe that Englishmen accept those blackened lumps as specie. And yet the trade of England is great, and the country is as prosperous as any. So to me England seems like an enormous Lyon: poor in specie, but rich in credit, and thriving through a system of paper transfers."

"Which will boot them nothing in a war," said the Marquis. "For in war, a king must send his armies abroad, to places where soft money is not accepted. Therefore he must send hard money with them that they may buy fodder and other necessaries. How then can England war against France?"

"The same question might be asked of France! By your leave, monsieur, her money is not as sound as you might like to think,"

"Do you suppose that this Dr. Waterhouse will have answers to such questions?"

"No, but I hope that he will engage in a discourse with me whence answers might emerge."

"I believe that the answer lies in Trade," said the Marquis. "Colbert himself said, 'Trade is the source of finance, and finance is the vital sinews of war.' What our countries cannot pay for with bullion, they will have to get in trade."

"*C'est juste,* monsieur, but do not forget that there is trade not only in tangible stuff like Monsieur Wachsmann's wax, but also in money itself: the stock in trade of Lothar von Hacklheber. Which is a murky and abstruse business, and a fit topic of study for Fellows of the Royal Society."

"I thought they only studied butterflies."

"Some of them, monsieur, study banks and money as well; and I fear they have got a head start on our *French* lepidopterists."

Cap Gris-Nez, France
15 DECEMBER 1689

A DUTCHMAN PAINTING THIS SCAPE would have had little recourse to pigments; a spate of gull-shit on a bench could have served as his palette. The sky was white, and so was the ground. The branches of the trees were black, except where snow had begun sticking to them. The château was half-timbered, therefore plaster-white in most places, webbed with ancient timbers that had turned the color of charcoal as they absorbed snow-damp. The roof was red tile; but this was mostly covered in snow. From place to place the presence of a stove underneath was betrayed by a seeping lake of red. It was not especially grand as châteaux went nowadays: a rectangular court open on the side facing the Channel, with stables to one side, servants' quarters to the other, and the big house holding them together, squarely facing the sea. Before it the ground dropped away sharply, and so the shoreline was not visible: just a distant strip of gray saltwater, which faded into the white atmosphere far short of the Dover shore.

A four-horse carriage and a two-horse baggage-wain were drawn up in the court. Booted footmen and drivers, wrapped in damp wool, were stomping from horse to horse, removing empty feed-bags and cinching harnesses. A large woman, her face lodged at the end of a tunnel of bonnet, emerged from the servants' quarters, tugging a heavy blanket over her shoulders. She got a foot on the step below the carriage door and launched herself into it, making the vehicle list and oscillate on its suspension. A pair of men emerged from the stable, whacking smoky wads from the bowls of their clay pipes. They pulled on heavy gloves and mounted horses; as they swung legs over saddles, their heavy riding-coats parted for a moment, showing that each of these men was rigged like a battleship with an assortment of small cannons, daggers, and cutlasses.

The front door of the main house swung open and color burst forth: a dress in green silk, complicated by ribbons and flounces in many other colors, a pink face, blue eyes, yellow hair held up with diverse jewelled pins and more ribbons. She turned about to bid a last farewell to someone inside, which made the skirt flare out, then turned again and walked into the courtyard. Her attention was fixed on the one person here who had not yet mounted a horse or climbed aboard a vehicle: a man as brief and stout as a mortar, in a long coat and boots that had turned black from damp. His hat—a vast tricornered production rimmed in gold braid and fledged with ostrich-plumes—had toppled from his head and listed on the snow like a beached flagship. The prints made in the snow by his boots, and the furrows carved by the skirts of his coat and the scabbard of his small-sword, proved that he had been eddying about the court for quite a while. His gaze was fixed on a small bundle that was in midair just in front of him.

The woman in the green dress bent down to pick up the forgotten hat, and gave it a shake, releasing a flurry of snow from the ostrich-plume.

The bundle reached an apogee, hung there for a moment a few feet above the man's bare head, and began to accelerate toward the ground. He let it drop freely for a moment, then got his gloved hands underneath it and began gently to slow its descent. The bundle came to a stop only a hand's breadth above the ground, the man bent over like a grave-digger. A scream emerged from the bundle, which made the woman's spine snap straight; but the scream turned out to be nothing more than the prelude to a long, drawn-out cackle of laughter. The woman relaxed and exhaled, then jerked to attention again as the man emitted a long whoop and heaved the bundle high into the air again.

In time she managed to get the man's attention without leading him to drop the baby. Hat was exchanged for infant. She climbed into the coach, handing the baby in before her to a smaller woman who was sitting across from the big one. He—despite being dressed as a gentleman—clambered onto a perch at the back of the coach, normally used by a pair of footmen, but of a comfortable width for one man of his physique. The train of horses and vehicles pulled out onto the frozen road that meandered along the cliff-tops, and turned so that England and the Channel were to the right, France to the left.

A few hundred yards along, they slowed for a few moments so that the woman in the green dress could gaze out the window at some new earthworks that had been thrown up there: a revetment for a pair of mortars. Then they moved on, a thicket of legs and a storm of reins, black against the fresh snow, which muffled the sounds of their passage and swallowed them up, leaving nothing for a painter to depict except a blank canvas, and nothing for a writer to describe except an empty page.

"ONE OF THE OTHER THINGS they have at Versailles is physicians." The voice emerged from a grate in the back of the coach.

"Oh, but we have those in abundance aboard our ships, my lady."

"You have *barbers*. You have consulted them for months, and still cannot sit down! I am speaking of *physicians*."

"It is true that barbers make a specialty of the *other* end of the anatomy from that which concerns *me*," said the man on the perch. "Nature, though, offers her own remedies. I have packed my breeches with snow. At first it was shocking, intolerable." He had to wait now, for some moments.

"You laugh," he went on, "but, my lady, you do not appreciate the relief that this affords me, in more ways than one. For not only does it relieve the pain and swelling aft, but also, a similar but not so unpleasant symptom fore, which any man would complain of who went on a journey of any length in your company . . ."

Two of the women laughed again, but the third was having none of it, and answered him firmly: "The journey is not so long, for those of us who can sit down. The destination is a place where wit is prized, so long as it is discreet and refined, and does not offend the likes of Madame de Maintenon. But these sailorly jests of yours shall be immense *faux pas*, and shall defeat the whole purpose of your coming there."

"What *is* the purpose, my lady? You summoned me, and I reported for duty. I supposed my rôle was to keep my godson amused. But I can see that you disapprove of my methods. In a few years, when Jean-Jacques learns to talk, he will, I'm certain, take my side in the matter, and demand to be flung about; in the meantime, I am dragged along in your wake, purposeless." He gazed curiously out to sea; but the train had turned inland, and the object of his desire was rapidly receding into the white distance. He was hopelessly a-ground.

"You are forever fussing over your ships, Lieutenant Bart, wishing that you had more, or that the ones you have were bigger, or in better repair . . ."

"All the more reason, my lady, for me to jump off of this unnatural conveyance and return to Dunkerque post-haste!"

"And do what? Build a ship with your own hands, out of snow? What is needed is not Jean Bart in Dunkerque. What is needed is Jean Bart at Versailles."

"What purpose can I serve there, my lady? Pilot a row-boat on the King's reflecting-pool?"

"You want resources. You compete for them against many others. Your most formidable competitor is the Army. Do you know why the Army gets all the resources, Lieutenant Bart?"

"Do they? I am shocked to hear this."

"That is because you never see them; but if you did, you would be outraged at how much money they get, compared to the Navy, and how many of the best people. Let us take Étienne de Lavardac as an example."

"The son of the duc d'Arcachon?"

"Do not affect ignorance, Lieutenant Bart. You know who he is, and that he knocked me up. Can you think of any young nobleman with stronger ties to the Navy? And yet when war broke out, what did he do?"

"I've no idea."

"He organized a cavalry regiment and rode off to war on the Rhine."

"Ungrateful pup! I'll work him over with the flat of my cutlass."

"Yes, and when you are finished you can go to Rome and poke the Pope in the eye with a stick!" suggested the smaller of the Countess's two assistants.

"It is a splendid idea, Nicole—I shall do it for you!" Bart returned.

"Do you know *why* Étienne made such a choice?" asked the lady, unamused.

"All I know is, someone needs to teach him some more manners."

"That is *exactly wrong*—someone needs to teach him *less*. For he is generally agreed to be the politest man in France."

"He must have forgot his manners at least *once*," said Jean Bart, pressing his face to the grate and peering at little Jean-Jacques, who had his face buried in his mother's left breast.

"Nay, for even when he impregnated me he did so politely," said the mother. "It is because of this sense of honor, of decorum, that he, and all the other young Court men, prefer the Army to the Navy."

"Hmm!"

"At last I have rendered you speechless, Jean Bart, and so I'll take this rare opportunity to explain further. Every man at Court professes his loyalty to the King, indeed does little else but prate about it from sunup to sundown, which pleases the King well enough in times of peace. But in time of war, each and every man must go out and demonstrate his loyalty with deeds. On a battlefield, a Cavalier may attire himself in magnificent armor and ride forth on a brilliant steed to engage the foe in single combat; and what is better, he does so in full view of many others like him, so that those who survive the day can get together in their tent when it is all over and agree on what happened. But on the sea all is different, for our dashing fop is lumped together with all of the other men on the ship, who are mostly common sailors; he lives with them, and cannot move from place to place, or engage a foe, without their assistance. To order a gang of swabbies, 'charge your cannon and fire it in the general direction of yonder dot on the horizon,' is altogether different from galloping up to a Dutchman on a rampart and swinging your sword-blade at his neck."

"We do not fire at dots on the horizon," huffed Jean Bart, "however, I take your meaning only too well."

"You, because of your recent exploit, are a shining counter-example to this general rule; and if we can get a physician to patch up your arse so that you can sit down at dinner and regale some Court ladies with the story—preferably without resorting to profanity or any other ribald elements—it shall translate directly into more money for the Navy."

"And more Court fops to adorn my decks?"

"That comes unavoidably with money, Jean Bart, it is how the game is played." And then she was banging on the carriage ceiling. "Gaetan! Over there, I see what looks like a new powder-magazine, let's go have a look."

"If my lady wishes to review *all* of his majesty's new coastal fortifications," said Jean Bart, "it is a thing more easily done from the deck of a ship."

"But then I don't get to interview the local *intendants,* and learn the gossip behind the fortifications."

"Is *that* what you were doing?"

"Yes."

"What did you learn?"

"That the chain of interlocking mortar emplacements we viewed this morning was financed by a low-interest loan to His Majesty's Treasury from Monsieur le comte d'Etaples, who melted down a twelfth-century gold punchbowl for it; and at the same time he improved the road from Fruges to Fauquembergues so that it can carry ammunition-carts even during the spring thaw; and in return the King saw to it that an old lawsuit against him was delayed indefinitely, and he got to hold a candle one morning at the King's levée."

"It makes one wonder what fascinations may be connected with yon powder-house! Perhaps some local Sieur cashed in his great-grandpère's ruby-set toenail-clippers to pay for the roof!" exclaimed Jean Bart, to stifled gurgles from Nicole and the large woman inside.

"Next summer, when Baltic timber is stacked to three times your height around the shipyard of Dunkerque, we shall see then if you are still mocking me," said she who was not amused.

"I BEG YOUR PARDON, mademoiselle; but this sound that you are making, 'yoo-hoo! yoo-hoo,' has never been heard before in his majesty's stables, or anywhere else in France that I know of. To the humans who live here, such as myself and my lord, it is devoid of meaning, and to the horses, it is a cause of acute distress. I beg you to stop, and to speak French, lest you cause a general panic."

"It is a common greeting in Qwghlmian, monsieur."

"Ah!" This brought the man to a hard stop for several moments. The stables of Versailles, in December, were not renowned for illumination; but Eliza could hear the gentleman's satins hissing, and his linens creaking, as he bowed. She made curtseying noises in return. This was answered by a short burst of scratching and rasping as the gentleman adjusted his wig. She cleared her throat. He called for a candle, and got a whole silver candelabra: a chevron of flames, bobbing and banking, like a formation of fireflies, through the ambient miasma of horse-breath, manure-gas, and wig-powder.

"I had the honor of being introduced to you a year ago, along the banks of the Meuse," said the gentleman, "when my lord—"

"I remember with fondness and gratitude your hospitality, Monsieur de Mayet," said Eliza, which jerked another quick bow from him, "and the alacrity with which you conducted me into the presence of Monsieur de Lavardac on *that* occasion—"

"He will see you immediately, mademoiselle!" announced de Mayet, though not until after they had watched a second candelabra zoom back and forth a few times between the stall where they were standing, and one that lay even deeper in the penetralia of the stables. "This way, please, around the manure-pile."

"TRULY, MONSIEUR, YOU ARE SECOND to none in piety. Even Father Édouard de Gex is a wastrel compared to you. For in this season of Christmas, when all go to Mass and hear homilies about Him who lived His first days in a stable, Étienne de Lavardac d'Arcachon is the only one who is actually living in the same estate, and sleeping on a pile of hay."

"To *piety* I can make no claims whatever, mademoiselle, though I do aspire, at times, to the lesser virtue of *politeness.*"

They had fetched out a chair for her to sit on, and she had accepted it, only because she knew that if she didn't, Étienne would be too stricken with horror to speak. He was squatting on a low stool used by farriers. The floor of the stall had been strewn with fresh straw, or as fresh as could be had in December.

"So Madame la duchesse d'Arcachon explained to me, when I arrived at La Dunette yester evening, and found that you and your household had moved out of it; not merely out of the *house,* but the entire *estate.*"

"Thank God, we had received notice of your approach."

"But the purpose of my sending that notice was not to drive you out to his majesty's stables."

"No one has been *driven,* mademoiselle. Rather, I am *lured* hither by the prospect of assuring *your* comfort at La Dunette, and preserving *your* reputation."

"That much is understood, monsieur, and deep is my gratitude. But as I am to be lodging in an outlying cottage, which cannot even be seen from the main house, and which is reached by a separate road, your mother is of the view that you may stay at home, even as I lodge at the cottage, without even the most censorious observer perceiving any taint. And I happen to agree with her."

"Ah, but, mademoiselle—"

"So firm is your mother in holding this view that she shall be gravely offended if you do not return home at once! And I have come to deliver the message in person so that you can be under no misapprehensions as to *my* view of the matter."

"Ah, very well," Étienne sighed. "As long as it is understood that I am not being *driven* from here by what *some* perceive as its discomforts and inconveniences—" and here he paused for a moment to glare at several Gentlemen of the Bedchamber and other members of his household, who were fortunate enough to be hidden in darkness "—but, as it were, fleeing in terror of the prospect that my conduct is, in the eyes of my mother, other than perfect."

Which was somehow construed as a direct order by his staff; for suddenly, hay-piles were detonating as liveried servants, who had burrowed into them for warmth, leapt to action. Great doors were dragged open, letting in awful fanfares of blue snow-light, and illuminating a gilded carriage, and diverse baggage-wains, that had been backed into nearby stalls.

Étienne d'Arcachon shielded his eyes with one hand, "Not from the light, which is nothing, but from your beauty, which is almost too great for a mortal man to gaze upon."

"Thank you, monsieur," said Eliza, shielding her own eyes, which were rolling.

"Pray, where is this orphan that some say you rescued from the clutches of the Heretics?"

"He is at La Dunette," said Eliza, "interviewing a prospective wet-nurse."

THE QUILL SWIRLED and lunged over the page in a slow but relentless three-steps-forward, two-steps-back sort of process, and finally came to a full stop in a tiny pool of its own ink. Then Louis Phélypéaux, first comte de Pontchartrain, raised the nib; let it hover for an instant, as if gathering his forces; and hurled it backwards along the sentence, tiptoeing over i's, slashing through t's and x's, nearly tripping over an umlaut, building speed and confidence while veering through a slalom-course of acute and grave accents, pirouetting though cedillas and carving vicious snap-turns through circumflexes. It was like watching the world's greatest fencing-master dispatch twenty opponents with a single continuous series of maneuvers. He drew his hand up with great care, lest his lace cuff drag in the ink; it inflated for a moment as it snatched a handful of air, then flopped down over his hand, covering all but the fingertips that pinched the pen, and giving them an opportunity to warm up. Twin jets of steam unfurled from Pontchartrain's cavernous elliptical nostrils as he re-read the document. Eliza realized she'd stopped breathing, and released her own cloud of steam. As she emptied her lungs, her dress hugged her suddenly around the waist while relaxing its grip on her thorax. Some milk leaked out of her breasts, but she had anticipated this, and swathed herself in cotton. It was most unusual for a virgin, who had merely adopted an orphan, to lactate. She smelled like a dairy. But the room was so cold that no one could smell anything but dust and ice.

"If you would, my lady, verify that I have not erred in setting down the principal." He withdrew his left hand from its warm haven between his thighs and gave the page a one-hundred-and-eighty-degree rotation. Eliza stepped forward, trying not to push a vast front of milk-scent before her, and rested her hands on the marble tabletop, then drew them back, for the stone jerked the warmth from her flesh. Her arms were tired. Walking here through the corridors of the palace, she had had to lift up her skirts—heavy winter stuff—lest they drag in the human turds that littered the marble floors. Most of these were frozen solid, but a few were not, and in the dim galleries she could not see the steam rising from these until it was too late.

Those corridors, and the divided, subdivided, and sub-sub-divided apartments that crowded in on them, were Versailles as it *was*. The wing where Monsieur le comte de Pontchartrain, *contrôleur-général*, had his offices, were Versailles as it was *meant to be,* meaning that the rooms were spacious, the windows many and large, the floors turd-free. Pontchartrain sat at a table with his back to an arched window that looked out over the gardens. His bony ankles, protected only by silk stockings, were crossed, like a pair of sticks being rubbed together. The sun was on his back. His periwig cast an Alp-like shadow across the table, and the document. The amount of money that Jean Bart's corsairs had taken from Eliza, and that she was loaning to the Treasury, was written out on the page, not in numerals but in words; and so large was the amount that, fully expressed to all of its significant digits, it spread across three lines of the document, and had forced the Count to dip his quill twice. It was like a chapter of the Bible; and as she read it, her mind was invaded by any number of memories of the deals she had arranged, the people she had met, the nights she had gone without sleep as she had accumulated this fortune. These recollections, which were of no utility to her now, and which she did not desire, simply leaked out. Milk was leaking out of her breasts, she could feel a leaky period coming on, she'd been suffering loose stools, she needed to urinate, and if she kept thinking about these things any more, tears would leak from her eyes. She had a passing phant'sy that she ought to go round and fetch Jean Bart from whatever salon he was regaling with corsair-tales, and put his nautical mind together with that of some corset-maker, and get them to invent some garment, some system of stays, laces, rigging, lashings, and caulk that would wholly encase body and head, and keep all unwelcome fluids and memories where they belonged.

But it was not available just now. She felt the warmth of the sun on her face; or maybe that was the gaze of the *contrôleur-général.* "The amount is correct," she announced, and hitched up her skirts in the rear with her cold hands and tired arms, and stepped back until her face was protected in shadow.

"Very well," said the Count in a gentle voice, like a kindly physician, and rotated his large brown eyes toward an aide, who for the last several minutes had been edging closer and closer to a fireplace at the other end of the room. Pontchartrain dipped his quill, set it to the page, and executed a lengthy series of evolutions, moving his arm from the shoulder. A vast mazy PONTCHARTRAIN took shape at the base of the page. The aide bent forward and countersigned.

Pontchartrain rose. "I hoped that my lady would consent to join me for some refreshment, while . . ." and he glanced at the aide, who had moved into the Count's place at the table and was busying himself with a panoply of wax-pots, ribbons, seals, and other gear.

"I would gladly do so, or eat rocks, for that matter, if it is to happen near the fireplace."

The Count offered the Countess his arm and together they glided to the pagan spectacle that answered to the name of fireplace here. Two chairs had been set out; both were armchairs, for the guest and the host were of equal rank. He got her settled in one of them, then picked up a log with his own two hands and threw it onto the fire; not a wholly normal thing for a Count to do, and presumably a coded gesture, meant to convey to Eliza that the Count did not mean to stand on ceremony. He dusted his hands together and then polished them with a lace handkerchief as he sat down. A maid shuffled forward on cold and unresponsive feet, worried her hands out of her sleeves, and poured coffee, sending up gales of steam.

"You've been doing a lot of these, my lord?" Eliza asked, looking over at the table, where the sealing process was just entering its opening rounds.

"Rarely for such amounts. Never for such a charming creditor, my lady. But yes, many Persons of Quality have followed the King's example, and lent idle assets to the Treasury, where they may be put to work."

"You will be gratified to know that those assets have been working very hard indeed along the Channel," Eliza said. "Any English Ship of Force that dares sail that way stares up into many new guns, protected by new revetments, fed by powder-houses linked by excellent roads that were only cow-paths when his majesty added those lands to France."

"It pleases me very much to hear this!" exclaimed the Count, crinkling up his eyes and rocking forward in his chair. Eliza was startled to see that he was entirely sincere; then wondered why it was so startling.

The Count's face began to sag as he looked at Eliza's and saw nothing there. "Please forgive me if I am . . . inappropriately subdued," she said, "it is just that I have been traveling for some time. And now that I am finally here, there is so much to do!"

"Soon all that will be behind you, my lady, and you can enjoy the season! You should get some rest. This *soirée* that Madame la duchesse d'Arcachon is hosting tomorrow . . ."

"Yes. I *do* need to conserve my energies, if I am to remain awake for even one-third of *that*."

"I do hope that when you have recovered from the journey, my lady, we shall have more opportunities to converse. As you know, I am rather new to the post of *contrôleur-général*. I accepted the position gladly, of course . . . but now that I have had a few months to settle in, I find that it is far more interesting than I had ever imagined."

"*Everyone* imagines it to be interesting in a *financial* sense," said Eliza.

"Of course," said Pontchartrain, sharing her amusement. "But I did not mean it that way."

"Of course not, monsieur, for you are an intelligent man, not motivated by money—which is one of the reasons his majesty chose you! But now that you are here, you find it fascinating *intellectually*."

"Indeed, my lady. But you are one of the very few at Versailles who can understand this."

"Hence your desire to carry the conversation forward. Yes, I understand."

Pontchartrain dropped his eyelids and inclined his head minutely, then opened his eyes again—they were large and handsome—and smiled at her.

"Do you know Bonaventure Rossignol, my lord?"

The smile faltered. "I know *of* him, my lady, but—"

"He is another fish out of water."

"He does not even live here, does he?"

"He lives at Juvisy. But he will be at La Dunette tomorrow. As will you, I trust?"

"Madame la duchesse has honored us with an invitation. Neither of us would miss it for anything."

"Seek me out there, monsieur. I shall introduce you to Monsieur Rossignol, and we shall found a new *salon*, restricted to people who love numbers more than money."

"AH, HERE COMES OUR CHAPERONE at last!"

"Our *chaperone*!?"

"But of course, Monsieur Rossignol. Madame la duchesse will join us. Otherwise people would talk! And look, Monsieur le comte de Pontchartrain is coming as well! I have wanted to introduce you to him."

This name was sufficient to make Rossignol turn his head, or want to. But the head was encased in a wig that cascaded over his shoulders, over which he had draped a heavy wool blanket, rendering independent movement of head and torso inadvisable. He rose to his feet, triggering small avalanches—for he and Eliza had been waiting in this open sleigh long enough for drifts to form in their laps. As he tottered around to get a view of the garden entrance of La Dunette, he reminded Eliza of a club balanced on a juggler's palm. He had much in common physically with Pontchartrain; but where the Count's eyes were warm and brown, Rossignol's were hot and black. And not hot in a passionate way, unless you counted his passion for his work.

A recorder arpeggio—some fragment of a minuet—leaked out of the doors for a moment as servants pulled them open. Pontchartrain stepped out, looked up, and blinked at the falling snow, then pirouetted towards his hostess, who had fallen behind, and was shooing him forward in violation of all rules of precedence. An aurora of red silk bloomed around her as she drew out a scarf and allowed it to settle atop her wig. With fingers slowed by cold, fat, and arthritis, she knotted it under a chin, then accepted Pontchartrain's proffered arm and stepped out into the frozen garden with more gingerness than was really warranted. The gravel paths near the château had been swept clear of snow; the sleigh was stopped a stone's throw away, on a track that wandered off into the Duke's hunting-park. Party-goers surged to the door and the fogged windows to bid the Duchess farewell, as if she were sailing to Surinam, and not just going on a quarter of an hour's sleigh-ride on her own property.

Rossignol rotated back around to gaze at Eliza. There was no point in sitting, as he'd just have to stand up again when the Duchess and the Count arrived.

"Monsieur Rossignol," said Eliza, "every child knows that the juice of a lime, or a bit of diluted milk, may be used to write secret messages in invisible ink, which may later be made to appear by scorching it before hot coals. When you stare at me in this way, it is as if you phant'sy that some message has been writ upon my face in milk, which you may make visible by the heat of your scrutiny. I beg you remember that more often than not the procedure goes awry, and the paper itself catches fire."

"I cannot help that God made me the way I am."

"Granted; but I beg you. Monsieur le comte d'Avaux, and Father

Édouard de Gex, have given me enough of such glares, in the last few days, to raise blisters on my brow. From you, monsieur, I should be grateful for a *warm,* rather than *hot,* regard."

"It is obvious enough that you are flirting with me."

"Flirtation is *customarily* more or less obvious, monsieur, but you do not have to *mention* it!"

"You invited me on a sleigh-ride, and led me to think it would be you and me alone together—'it shall be never so cold, Bon-bon, and I shall freeze to death if I do not have anyone to share my blanket with'—and then we waited, and waited, and now it is obvious that I shall be sharing my blanket with a Count, or a Dowager. It is a little étude in cruelty. I observe such all the time in people's love-letters. I understand this. But it would be very foolish of you, my lady, to believe that you shall achieve some power over me by playing such girlish games."

Eliza laughed. "Never crossed my mind." She lunged forward, spun around, and took the seat next to Rossignol. He looked down at her, startled. "Why not?" Eliza said, "as long as we are chaperoned."

"Flirting with you without result is more interesting than doing nothing," Rossignol insisted, "but since our adventure, you really have paid me very little attention. I think it is because you got into some trouble you could not get out of by your own wits, and so became indebted to me in a way; which you chafe at."

"We will speak of chafing later," said Eliza, and then actually batted her snow-laden eyelashes at him. She patted the seat next to her.

"I must greet the Count and the—" but he was cut short as Eliza grabbed the back of his breeches and jerked down hard. She had only meant to force him to sit down; but to her shock she all but de-pantsed him, and would have stripped him naked to the knees had he not sat down violently. Like a bullfighter wielding the cape, she heaved the blanket over his lap just in time to hide all from the Count and the Duchess, who looked their way at the sudden movement.

"You must put some meat on your hips, otherwise what is the point of wearing a belt?" she whispered.

"Mademoiselle! I *must stand up* for the Count and the—"

"Dowager, is that what you called her? She is no dowager, her husband is alive and well, and tending to the King's affairs in the South. Don't worry, I shall fix it." She leaned against Rossignol's shoulder and raised her voice: "Madame la duchesse, Monsieur le comte, Monsieur Rossignol is mortified, for he would stand up to greet you; but I won't let him move. For his slender frame makes as much heat as a coal-stove, which is the only thing keeping me alive."

"Sit, sit!" insisted the Duchess of Arcachon. "Monsieur, you are like my son, too polite for your own good!" She had reached sleigh-side. Three stable-hands converged, and helped Pontchartrain help her into the sleigh. She was a big woman, and when she threw her weight on the bench, facing Eliza and Rossignol, the runners broke loose on the snow and the sleigh moved backwards a few inches. All three of the occupants whooped: the Duchess because she was alarmed, Eliza because it was amusing, and Bonaventure Rossignol because Eliza, under the blanket, had shoved her cold hand into his drawers and seized hold of his penis as if it were a lifeline. Presently the Count took a seat next to the Duchess. The horses—a team of two matched albinos—nearly bolted, so cold and impatient were they, and there was harsh language from the driver. But then they settled into a trot. The four passengers waved at the crowd inside, who'd been mopping steam off the windowpanes with their hand-kerchiefs. Eliza waved with one hand only. After an initial shrinkage, Rossignol had come erect so fast that she was worried about his health. He had squirmed and glared, but only until he recognized that the situation was perfectly hopeless; now he sat very still, listen-ing to the Duchess, or pretending to.

She was matronly, decent, and genuinely popular: the living embodiment of the traditional Lavardac virtues of simple sincere loyalty to King and Church, in that order, without all of the schem-ing. In other words, she was just what a hereditary noble was *supposed* to be; which made her both an asset and a liability to the King. By supporting him blindly, and always doing the right thing, she made of her family a bulwark to his reign. But by exhibiting genuine nobil-ity, she was implicitly making a strong case for the entire idea of a hereditary peerage with much power and responsibility, and making the new arrivals—Eliza included—seem like conniving arrivistes by comparison. Sitting in the Duchess's sleigh and firmly massaging the erect penis of the King's cryptanalyst, Eliza had to admit the validity of this point; but she admitted it *to herself*. She had no choice but to make do with what she had—which at the moment was nothing at all, except for a handful of Rossignol. She still did not have more than a few coins to her name.

The sleigh moved briskly on the trail, which had been groomed in advance of the party. In a few moments they passed out of the for-mal garden and into a huddle of buildings that was concealed from view of La Dunette's windows by adroit landscaping. The scent of manure from the hunting-stable of Louis-François de Lavardac d'Ar-cachon was driven away suddenly by a cloud of lavender-scented steam, surging from the open side of a shed where a servant was stir-ring a vat over a great smoky fire.

"You make your own soap here?" Eliza said. "The fragrance is wonderful."

"Of course we do, mademoiselle!" said the Duchess, astonished by the fact that Eliza found this worthy of mention. Then something occurred to her: "You should use it."

"I already impose on your hospitality too much, my lady. Paris is so well-supplied with parfumiers and soap-makers, I am happy to go there and—"

"Oh, no!" exclaimed the Duchess. "You must never buy soap in Paris—from strangers! Especially with the orphan to think of!"

"As you know, my lady, little Jean-Jacques is now in the care of the Jesuit fathers. They make their own soap, probably—"

"As they had better!" said the Duchess. "But you bring clothes to him sometimes. You will have them laundered here, in my soap."

Eliza did not really care, and was happy to give her assent, since the Duchess of Arcachon was so firm on this point; if she hesitated for a moment, it was only because she was a bit nonplussed.

"You should use the Duchess's soap, mademoiselle," said Pontchartrain firmly.

"Indeed!" said Rossignol—who, given the circumstances, would probably be speaking in one-word sentences for a while.

"I accept your soap with all due gratitude, madame," said Eliza.

"*My* laundresses do not wear gloves!" huffed the Duchess, as if she had been challenged on some point. This rather dampened conversation for some moments. They had passed clear of the outbuildings, and circumvented a paddock where the Duke's hunting-mounts were exercised in better weather, and entered now into a wooded game-park, bony and bare under twilight. Pontchartrain opened the shades on a pair of carriage-lanterns that dangled above the corners of the benches, and presently they were gliding along through the dim woods in a little halo of lamplight. In a few moments they came to a stone wall that cut the forest in twain. It was pierced by a gate, which stood open, and which was guarded, in name anyway, by half a dozen musketeers, who were standing around a fire. The wall was twenty-six miles long. The gate was one of twenty-two. Passing through it, they entered the *Grand Parc*, the hunting-grounds of the King.

The Duchess seemed to regret the matter of the soap, and now suddenly worked herself up into a lather of good cheer.

"Mademoiselle la comtesse de la Zeur has said she will start a *salon* at La Dunette! I have told her, I do not know how such a thing is done! For I am just a foolish old hen, and not one for clever discourse! But she has assured me, one need only invite a few men who are as clever as Monsieur Rossignol and Monsieur le comte de Pont-chartrain, and then it just—*happens!*"

Pontchartrain smiled. "Madame la duchesse, you would have me and Monsieur Rossignol believe that when two such ladies as you and the Countess are together in private, you have nothing better to do than talk about *us?*"

The Duchess was taken aback for a moment, then whooped. "Monsieur, you tease me!"

Eliza gave Rossignol an especially hard squeeze, and he shifted uneasily.

"So far, it does not seem to be *happening,* for Monsieur Rossignol is so quiet!" observed the Duchess in a rare *faux pas;* for she should have known that the way to make a quiet person join the conversation is *not* to point out that he is being quiet.

"Before you joined us, madame, he was telling me that he has been wrestling with a most difficult decypherment—a new code, the most difficult yet, that is being used by the Duke of Savoy to communicate with his confederates in the north. He is distracted—in another world."

"On the contrary," said Rossignol, "I am quite capable of talking, as long as you do not ask me to compute square roots in my head, or something."

"I don't know what that is but it sounds frightfully difficult!" exclaimed the Duchess.

"I'll not ask you to do any such thing, monsieur," said Pontchartrain, "but some day when you are *not* so engaged—perhaps at the Countess's *salon*—I should like to speak to you of what I do. You might know that Colbert, some years ago, paid the German savant Leibniz to build a machine that would do arithmetic. He was going to use this machine in the management of the King's finances. Leibniz delivered the machine eventually, but he had in the meantime become distracted by other problems, and now, of course, he serves at the court of Hanover, and so has become an enemy of France. But the precedent is noteworthy: putting mathematical genius to work in the realm of finance."

"Indeed, it is interesting," allowed Rossignol, "though the King keeps me very busy at cyphers."

"What sorts of problems did you have in mind, monsieur?" Eliza asked.

"What I am going to tell you is a secret, and should not leave this sleigh," Pontchartrain began.

"Fear not, monseigneur; is any thought more absurd than that one of us might be a foreign spy?" Rossignol asked, and was rewarded by the sensation of four sharp fingernails closing in around his scrotum.

"Oh, it is not foreign spies I am concerned about in this case, but domestic speculators," said the Count.

"Then it is even more safe; for I've nothing to speculate *with,*" said Eliza.

"I am going to call in all of the gold and silver coins," said Pontchartrain.

"*All* of them? All of them in the entire country!?" exclaimed the Duchess.

"Indeed, my lady. We will mint new gold and silver *louis,* and exchange them for the old."

"Heavens! What is the point of doing it, then?"

"The new ones will be worth more, madame."

"You mean that they will contain more gold, or silver?" Eliza asked.

Pontchartrain gave her a patient smile. "No, mademoiselle. They will have precisely the same amount of gold or silver as the ones we use now—*but they will be worth more,* and so to obtain, say, nine *louis d'or* of the new coin, one will have to pay the Treasury ten of the old."

"How can you say that the *same coin* is now worth *more?*"

"How can we say that it is worth what it is *now?*" Pontchartrain threw up his hands as if to catch snowflakes. "The coins have a face value, fixed by royal decree. A new decree, a new value."

"I understand. But it sounds like a scheme to make something out of nothing—a perpetual motion machine. Somewhere, somehow, in some unfathomable way, it must have repercussions."

"Quite possibly," said Pontchartrain, "but I cannot make out where and how *exactly.* You must understand, the King has asked me to *double* his revenues to pay for the war. Double! The usual taxes and tariffs have already been squeezed dry. I must resort to novel measures."

"Now I understand why you would like the advice of France's greatest *savants,*" said the Duchess. Whereupon all eyes turned to Rossignol. But he had suddenly braced his feet and jerked his head back. For a few moments he stared up at the indigo sky through half-closed eyes, and did not breathe; then he exhaled, and took in a deep draught of the cold air.

"I do believe Monsieur Rossignol has been seized by some sudden mathematical insight," said Pontchartrain in a hushed voice. "It is said that Descartes's great idea came to him in a sort of religious vision. I had been skeptical of it until this moment, for the very thought seemed blasphemous. But the look on Monsieur Rossignol's face, as he cracked that cypher, was unmistakably like that of a saint in a fresco as he is drawn, by the Holy Spirit, into an epiphanic rapture."

"Will we see a lot of this sort of thing, then, at the *salon*?" asked the Duchess, giving Rossignol a very dubious look.

"Only occasionally," Eliza assured her. "But perhaps we ought to change the subject, and give Monsieur Rossignol an opportunity to gather his wits. Let's talk about . . . horses!"

"Horses?"

"*Those* horses," said Eliza, nodding at the two that were drawing the sleigh.

She and Rossignol were facing forward. The Duchess and the Count had to turn around to see what she was looking at. Eliza took advantage of this to wipe her hand on Rossignol's drawers and withdraw it. Rossignol hitched up his breeches weakly.

"Do you fancy them?" asked the Duchess. "Louis-François is inordinately proud of his horses."

"Until now I had only seen them from a distance, and supposed that they were simply white horses. But they are more than that; they are albinos, are they not?"

"Ths distinction is lost on me," the Duchess admitted, "But that is what Louis-François calls them. When he comes back from the south he will be glad to tell you more than you wish to hear!"

"Are they commonly seen? Do many people have them here?" Eliza asked. But they were interrupted by, of all things, a man riding an albino horse: Étienne de Lavardac d'Arcachon, who had ridden out from the château to meet them. "I am mortified to break in on you this way," he said, after greeting each of them individually, in strict order of precedence (Duchess first, then Pontchartrain, Eliza, horses, mathematician, and driver), "but in your absence, Mother, I am the acting host of the party, and must do all in my power to please our guests—one of whom, by the way, happens to be his majesty the King of France—"

"Oooh! When did *le Roi* arrive?"

"Just after you left, Mother."

"Just my luck. What do his majesty and the other guests desire?"

"To see the masque. Which is ready to begin."

ONE END OF THE GRAND ballroom of La Dunette had been converted into the English Channel. Papier-mâché waves with plaster foam, mounted on eccentric bearings so that they cycled about in a more or less convincing churn, had been arranged in many parallel, independently moving ranks, marching toward the back of the room, and raked upwards so that any spectator on the ballroom floor could get a view of the entire width of the "Channel" from "Dunkerque" (a fortified silhouette downstage) to "Dover" (white cliffs and green fields upstage). To stage left was a little pen where a consort sawed away on viols. To stage right was a royal box where King Louis XIV of France sat on a golden chair, with the Marquise de Maintenon at his right hand, dressed more for a funeral than a Christmas party. A retinue was massed behind them. So close to the front of it that he could have put a hand on Maintenon's shoulder was Father Édouard de Gex—this a way of saying that there had better be no salacious bits. Not that Madame la duchesse d'Arcachon would ever even conceive of such a thing; but she had hired artists and comedians to produce it, and one never knew what such people would come up with.

The name of the production was *La Métamorphose*. Leading man and guest of honor was one Lieutenant Jean Bart, who knew as little of what to do on stage, during a masque, as would a comedian in a naval engagement; but never mind, it had all been written around him and his dramaturgickal shortcomings. The opening number took place on the beach at Dunkerque. A mermaid, perched on a rock, looked on as Jean Bart and his men (dancers dressed as Corsairs) attended an impromptu Mass celebrated on the beach. Exit Priest. Jean Bart led his men onto their frigate (which was no larger than a rowboat, but wittily decked out with masts and yards sprouting every which way, and fleur-de-lis banners). The frigate took to the Channel's bobbing waves and headed for England. The mermaid, stranded solus downstage right, sang an aria about her lovesick condition; for she had quite fallen in love with the handsome Lieutenant (in an earlier version, there had been no Mass on the beach; it had opened with Jean Bart spawled on the rock in a state of deshabille and the mermaid feeding grapes to him; but the Duchess had had words with the players, and mended it).

Neptune now arose from the waves and sang a duet with the mermaid, his daughter. He wanted to know why she was so morose. Learning the answer, he became cross with Jean Bart and vowed to take revenge on him in the traditional godly style of subjecting him to an inconvenient metamorphosis.

In the next scene, Jean Bart's frigate did battle with a larger English one, and there was a lot of swinging from ropes and fake swordplay, which Bart did very well. Just as he was about to grasp the laurels of victory, angry Neptune appeared and, with a thrust of his trident and a roar of kettledrums, transformed Bart into a cat (effected by Bart's putting on a mask while everyone was distracted by the histrionics of the sea-god). Because cats cannot give orders and are averse to water, this threw his men into disarray and they were all captured by the English.

The next scene took place far upstage, on the English shore, where the French sailors were pent up in a prison in Plymouth, gazing out barred windows across the Channel and pining, at considerable length, for France. This was by far the dullest part of the production and gave many a Countess an opportunity to powder her nose; but the upshot was that the mermaid, hearing their dirge, and spying the valiant French corsairs imprisoned through no fault of their own, begged her father to undo the spell he had laid on Jean Bart. Which was grudgingly done, though not until Bart, in his smaller, feline form, had slipped out between the bars of his cell and scampered onto the beach. Changed back into a man, he climbed into a rowboat, shoved it off the beach of Plymouth, and rowed to France.

When Jean Bart had achieved this feat for real, a few months ago, it had taken him fifty-two hours. That was compressed into about a quarter of an hour here. The passage of two days, two nights, and four hours was suggested as follows: Apollo, in a golden chariot suspended from an overhead track by wires, appeared low in the east (stage left); traversed the entire stage in a great arc, singing an aria all the while; and set low in the west (stage right) just as his sister Diana was being launched from stage left in a silver chariot. When she set in the west, Apollo reappeared (for his chariot had been unhooked and rushed around the back of the château) at stage left again, and sang through the second day of Jean Bart's epic row. Then Diana sang through the second night. During the first day and night, Apollo and Diana respectively mocked the poor figure below them, refusing to believe at first that anyone would have the stupidity or hubris to row a boat from Plymouth to France. During the second day and night, they literally changed their tunes: Astounded to see that Jean Bart was still alive, and still hauling on those oars, they began to sing his praises and to cheer him on.

It concluded at the end of the second night with Diana setting at stage right, Apollo rising at the left, and Jean Bart center stage, desperately trying to row the last mile or so to freedom. Apollo and Diana sang a duet, urging him on; and finally Neptune (who had perhaps had enough of their caterwauling) popped out of the waves, sang an additional stanza about what a magnificent chap Jean Bart was, and, raising his trident, ordered that the waves of the sea escort this hero safely back to shore. Which they did, in the form of four dancers painted blue and wearing foamy white caps.

Even *this* audience, which included some of the most jaded and cynical persons on the face of the earth, could hardly keep a dry eye as Jean Bart finally staggered up onto the beach where it had all started, accompanied by a flood tide of patriotic music; but just as the party-goers were erupting in an ovation, yet another god descended from the rafters, dressed in gold, brandishing a lightning-bolt, and crowned with a laurel-wreath: yes, Jupiter himself, but all bedizened with French touches to make of him a hybrid of France with the King of the Gods; or rather, to imply that there was no substantive difference. Apollo, Diana, and Neptune were amazed, and did obeisance; the insouciant Jean Bart favored Jupiter with a courtly Versailles bow. Jupiter had come to make his ruling, which was that Jean Bart did indeed deserve to be subjected to a metamorphosis: but of a rather different sort than being turned into a cat. He handed down a package in golden paper, crowned with a laurel wreath, and Mercury took it from his hand, pranced about for a while in a gratuitous solo, and delivered it to Jean Bart, setting the laurel wreath on Bart's head. Lieutenant Bart opened the package. Out tumbled a bolt of red. He held it up, and it unfurled: the long red coat and red breeches of a Captain in the French Navy.

The rigging that held the various Gods and Goddesses in the firmament now went into creaking and groaning movement, pulling those Olympian figures up or away so that Jean Bart was left alone on the stage to receive an ovation from the crowd. He hugged the uniform to his chest, turned stage right, and bowed very low to the King. This caused the laurel wreath to fall from his head. He snatched it just before it struck the floor and everyone in the room said, "Oh!" at once. Then, seized by an idea, he straightened up and tossed the wreath directly at Louis XIV, who did not fail to catch it. Everyone in the room said, "Ah!" The King, not the least bit discomposed, raised the laurel to his lips and kissed it, eliciting a great cheer from the assembled nobles of Versailles. For that moment, everything in France was perfect.

MUCH MORE HAPPENED at the soirée, but it all felt like an afterthought to the masque. Captain Jean Bart lost no time changing into his red uniform; then he danced all night, with every lady in the house. Eliza for once in her life was flummoxed by the intensity of the competition; for in order to dance with Captain Bart, one had to be asked by him, which meant that one had to be able to see, or at least hear him; and at the end of each number the man in red was immediately walled up in a rampart of pretty silk and satin gowns, as all of the hopeful girls—most of whom were taller than Bart—crowded around him, hoping to catch his eye. Eliza was petite and hopelessly shut out. Moreover, she had some obligations as hostess. The Duchess had granted her leave to add some names to the guest list. Eliza had invited four minor courtiers and their wives: all petty nobles of northern France who had loaned money to the Treasury and built fortifications along the Channel coast. They had done so precisely in the hope that it would lead to their being invited to parties such as this one. Now their schemes had come to fruition; but they looked to Eliza to manage some of the details, such as introductions. Each of them had recently had an audience with Pontchartrain and received a loan document similar to Eliza's, albeit with a smaller amount inscribed upon it; each now phant'sied that this would entitle him to spend the entire evening following Pontchartrain around as full and equal participant in any conversation the *contrôleur-général* might become engaged in. In order to remain in the Count's good graces, Eliza had to track them around the château and snatch them away on some pretext or other whenever they started to annoy their betters. This was work enough for a single evening; but, too, it was expected that she would dance at least twice with Étienne, as his titular girlfriend. And since she had jerked him off in the sleigh, it would have been poor form not to dance at least one time with Rossignol.

Rossignol danced like a cryptanalyst: perfectly, but with little self-expression. "You did not understand the soap conversation," he said to her.

"Monsieur, was it that obvious? Please explain it to me!"

"During the time of the poisonings, ten years ago, where do you suppose all of those ambitious courtiers got their arsenic? Not by their own labors certainly, for they are helpless in practical matters. Not from Alchemists, for those style themselves holy men. Who, other than Alchemists, has mortars and pestles, vats, retorts, and ways of getting exotic ingredients?

"Soap-makers!" Eliza exclaimed, and felt herself blushing.

"Some laundresses wore gloves in those days," said Rossignol, "because their mistresses would have them go into Paris and buy soap that was loaded with arsenic. They would wash the husband's clothing in that soap, and he would absorb the poison through his skin. And so for a Duchess to make her own soap, on her own estate, is more than just a quaint tradition. It is a way for her to protect herself and those she loves. When she offers you, mademoiselle, the use of her soap, and of her laundry, it means two things: first, that she has true affection for you, and second, that she fears someone might wish you ill."

Eliza could not speak. She scanned the crowd over Rossignol's shoulder for a glimpse of d'Avaux, and, not finding him, forced Rossignol to spin around so that she could see the other half of the room.

"I beg your pardon, but which one of us is leading, my lady?" asked Rossignol. "Who is it you look for? You think of someone who wishes you ill? Do not be too sure of your first assumptions—that is a common error in cryptanalysis."

"Do you know who—?"

"If I did I should tell you at once, if for no other reason than that I should enjoy another sleigh-ride some day. But no, mademoiselle, I cannot guess who it is that the Duchess is so worried about."

"Excuse me, but may I break in?" said a man's voice behind Eliza.

"We are in the middle of something!" Eliza snapped; for men had been pestering her all night. But Rossignol had stopped dancing. He released his grip on Eliza, backed away one step, and bowed deep.

Eliza spun around to see King Louis XIV acknowledging the bow with a warm look. He loved his codebreaker.

"But of course you are, mademoiselle," said the King of France, "when my two most intelligent subjects put their heads together and converse, why, *pourquoi non,* how could they not be in the middle of something? But your expressions are so grave! It does not befit a Christmas celebration!" He had caught Eliza's hand somehow, and drawn her into the pattern of the dance. Eliza was no more capable of intelligent speech than she had been a minute ago.

"I have much to thank you for," said Louis XIV.

"Oh, no, your majesty, for—"

"Has no one ever told you that to contradict the King is not done?"

"I beg your pardon, your majesty—"

"Monsieur Rossignol has told me that you did a favor for my sister-in-law last autumn," said the King. "Or perhaps it was for the Prince of Orange; this is not clear."

Something now occurred that had only happened to Eliza a few times in her life: She lost consciousness, or close to it. A like thing had happened when she and her mother had been dragged off of the beach in Qwghlm and loaded into the longboat of the Barbary Corsairs. It had happened again, some years later, when she had been taken down to the waterfront of Algiers and traded to the Sultan in Constantinople for a white stallion—taken from her mother without even being given the opportunity to say good-bye. And a third time beneath the Emperor's palace in Vienna, when she'd been queued up with a string of other *odalisques* to be put to the sword. On none of these occasions had she actually crumpled to the ground. Neither did she now. But she might have, if Louis XIV, who was a big man, graceful and strong, had not kept an arm firmly about her waist.

"Come back to me," he was saying—and not, she guessed, for the first time. "There. You are back. I see it in your face. What is it you fear so much? Have you been threatened by someone? Tell me who has done it, then."

"No one in particular, your majesty. The Prince of Orange—"

"Yes? What did he do?"

"I should not tell you what he *did;* but he *said* I must spy for him or he would put me on a ship to Nagasaki, for the amusement of the sailors."

"Ah. You should have told me this immediately."

"That—my failure to be perfectly frank with you—is truly the source of my fear, your majesty, for I am not without guilt."

"I know this. Tell me, mademoiselle. What drives you to make such decisions? What is it you *want?*"

"To find the man who wronged me, and kill him." In truth, Eliza had not thought about this for so long that the idea sounded strange to her ears, even as it came from her lips; but she said it with conviction, and liked the sound of it.

"Certain things you have done have pleased me immensely. The 'Fall of Batavia.' The loan of your fortune. Bringing Jean Bart to Versailles. Your recent efforts for the *Compagnie du Nord.* Others, such as the matter of the spying, displease me—though now I understand better. It is good that we have had this conversation."

Eliza blinked, looked around, and understood that the music had stopped, and everyone was looking at them.

"Thank you, mademoiselle," said the King, and bowed.

Eliza curtseyed.

"Your majesty—" she said, but he was gone, engulfed by the mobile Court, a school of expensively cinched waists and teased wigs.

Eliza went into a corner to get coffee and to think. People were following her—her own little Court of petty nobles and suitors. She did not precisely *ignore,* because she did not really *notice,* them.

What had happened? She needed a personal stenographer, so that she could have the transcript read back to her.

She had inadvertently given the King the wrong idea.

"Do you enjoy the soirée, my lady?"

It was Father Édouard de Gex.

"Indeed, Father, though I confess I do miss that little orphan—he stole my heart in the weeks we were together."

"Then you may have a little piece of your heart back any time you wish to visit. Monsieur le comte d'Avaux was at pains to make certain that the infant was comfortably housed. He predicted that you would be a frequent caller."

"I am indebted to the Count."

"We all are," said de Gex. "Little Jean-Jacques is a splendid boy. I look in on him whenever I have a moment. I hope to complete what you have begun, and d'Avaux has carried forward."

"And that is—what precisely?"

"You snatched the lad from death *physical*—the war—and *spiritual*—the doctrines of the heretics. D'Avaux saw to it he was placed in the best orphanage in France, under the care of the Society of Jesus. To me, it seems that the natural culmination is that I should raise him up into a Jesuit."

"I see, yes . . ." said Eliza dreamily, "so that the little Lavardac bastard does not create further complications by breeding."

"I beg your pardon, my lady?"

"Please forgive me, I am not myself!"

"I should hope not!" De Gex was actually blushing. Which wreaked a great change for the better on his face. He was dark, with prominent bones in the cheeks and nose, and had it in him to be handsome; but usually he was very pale from too many hours spent in dark confessionals listening to the secret sins of the court. With some pink in his cheeks he was suddenly almost fetching.

"Please," Eliza said, "I am still flustered by the memory of dancing with the King."

"Of course, my lady. But when you have gathered your wits, and remembered your manners, my *cousine* would like to renew her acquaintance with you." He leveled his burning gaze at a corner where the duchesse d'Oyonnax was smiling into the eyes of some poor young Viscount who had no idea what he was getting into.

De Gex took his leave.

She had spoken the truth to the King. For on the day she'd been swapped for the albino stallion, and loaded on a galley for Constantinople, she'd made a vow that one day she would find the man who was responsible for her and Mummy being slaves in the first place, and kill him. She had never divulged this to anyone, except Jack Shaftoe; but now, unaccountably, she had blurted it out to the King. She had done so with utmost conviction, for it really was true; and he had seen the look on her face, and believed every word.

"I have much work to do tomorrow, thanks to you, mademoiselle."

It was Pontchartrain, again favoring her with a benign smile.

"How so, monsieur?"

"The King was so moved by the story of Jean Bart's heroism that he has directed me to release funds for the Navy, and for the *Compagnie du Nord*. I am to attend his levée tomorrow, so that we may sort out the details."

"Then I shall not detain you any later, monsieur."

"Good night, mademoiselle."

The King thought she was referring to William of Orange. She had made some reference to William—again, if only she had a transcript!—and a moment later she had changed the subject and said she wanted to find the man who had wronged her, and kill him— and the King had put those two truths together to make a falsehood: his majesty now believed that Eliza's goal in life was to assassinate William! That she had spied on William's behalf only as a ruse so that she could get close to him.

She spun around, hoping to find the King, to get his attention, to explain all—but found herself looking into the face of a man dressed all in red. Jean Bart, putting his corsair skills to use, had hacked his way through a throng of female admirers to reach Eliza. "Mademoiselle," he said, "Madame la duchesse has announced that this is to be the last dance. If I might have the honor?"

She let her hand float up and he took it. "Normally, of course, I should make way for Étienne d'Arcachon in such a case," he explained, in case Eliza had been wondering about this—which she hadn't. "But he is outside, bidding farewell to the King."

"The King's leaving?"

"Is already in his carriage, mademoiselle."

"Oh. I had been hoping to say something to him."

"You and everyone else in France!" They were dancing now. Bart was amused. "You have already danced with his majesty! Mademoiselle, there are women in this room who have sacrificed babies in the Black Mass hoping to conjure up a single word, or a glance, from the King! You should be satisfied—"

"I don't want to hear about such things," Eliza said. "It makes me cross that you would even mention such horrors. You have been drinking, Captain Bart."

"You are right and I am wrong. I shall make it up to you: As it happens, I shall see the King in a few hours—I have been summoned to his levée! We will discuss naval finance. Is there anything you would like me to pass on to his majesty?"

What could she say? *I don't really mean to kill William of Orange* was not the sort of message she could ask Captain Bart to blurt out at the levée; nor was *I don't really know precisely who it is I mean to kill.*

"It is sweet of you to offer and I do forgive you. Does the King talk much at his levées, I wonder?"

"How should I know? Ask me tomorrow. Why?"

"Does he gossip, tell stories? I am curious. For I told him something, just now, that, if it were to get around, would make me very unpopular in England."

"Pfft!" said Jean Bart, and rolled his eyes, dispensing with the entire subject of England.

"Do ask the King one thing for me, please."

"Only name it, mademoiselle."

"The name of a physician who is good down here." She let her hand slide down a few inches and patted him. She did it with exquisite caution. But nonetheless Jean Bart yelped and jumped, his face split open in agony. Eliza gasped and jumped back in horror; but his grimace relaxed into a smile, and he lunged after her and snared her back, for he was only joking.

"I have already been to see such a physician."

"That is good," said Eliza, still laughing, "for I would see you sit down before you go home."

"Fifty-two hours of rowing did its damage, this is true; but this physician has been at my arse with all manner of poultices, and unmentionable procedures, and I am healing well. And this is the best bandage of all!" brushing some lint from the epaulet of his new red coat.

"If only all wounds could be healed by putting on new clothes, monsieur!"

"Don't all women believe this to be true?"

"Sometimes they behave as if they did, Captain Bart. Perhaps I simply have not picked out the right dress yet."

"Then you should go shopping tomorrow!"

"It is a fine thought, Captain. But first I need some money. And as there is none in France, you must go out to sea and capture some gold for me."

"Consider it done! I owe it to you!"

"Try to keep that in mind tomorrow, Jean Bart."

Letter from Daniel Waterhouse to Eliza
JANUARY–FEBUARY 1690

Mademoiselle de la Zeur,

Thank you for yours of December '89. It took some time crossing the Channel, and I daresay this shall fare no better. I was touched by your expression of concern, and amused by the narrative of the timber. I had not appreciated how fortunate England is in this respect, for if we want timber in London, we need only denude some part of Scotland or Ireland where a few trees still stand.

I would be of help to you in your quest to understand money, if for no other reason than that I would understand it myself. But I am perfectly useless. Our money has been wretched for as long as I have been alive. When it is so bad, it is no easy matter to discern when it is getting worse; but hard as it might be to believe, this seems to be occurring. I was bedridden for some months following the removal of my Stone, and did not have to go out and buy things. But when I had recovered sufficiently that I could venture out once again, I found it clearly worse. Or perhaps the long time spent not having to haggle over daily purchases, lifted the scales from my eyes, so that the absurdity of the situation was made clear to me.

I keep running accounts at several coffee-houses, pubs, and a bottle-ale house in my street, so that every small purchase need not be attended by a tedious and irksome transfer of coin. Many who go out more often than I do have formed together into societies, called Clubbs, which facilitate purchase of food, drink, snuff, pipe-tobacco, &c., on credit. When, through some miracle, one comes into possession of coins recognizable as such, one runs out and tries to settle one's more important accounts. The system staggers along. People do not know any better.

Here we have Whigs and Tories now. In essence these are, respectively, Roundheads and Cavaliers, under new guises, and less heavily armed. Tories get their money from the land that they own. To simplify matters greatly, one might say that France is a country consisting entirely of Tories; for all of the money there derives ultimately from the land. You might have had Whigs too, if you'd not expelled the Huguenots. And some of your Atlantic seaports are said to be a bit Whiggish. But as I said, I am over-simplifying to make a point: If you understand how money works in France, then you know everything about our Tories. And if you understand how it works in Amsterdam, then you know our Whigs.

The Royal Society dwindles, and may not last to the end of the century. It no longer enjoys the favor of the King as it did under Charles II. In those days it was a force for *revolution,* in the new meaning of that word; but it succeeded so well that it has become conventional. The sorts of men who, having no other outlet for their ideas, would have devoted their lives to it, had they come of age when I did, may now make careers in the City, the Colonies, or in foreign adventures. We of the Royal Society are generally identified as Whigs. Our President is the Marquis of Ravenscar, a very powerful Whig, and he has been assiduous in finding ways to harness the ingenuity of the Fellows of the Royal Society for practical ends. Some of these, I gad, have to do with money, revenue, banks, stocks, and other subjects that fascinate you. But I must confess I have fallen quite out of touch with such matters.

Isaac Newton was elected to Parliament a year ago, in the wake of our Revolution. He had made a name for himself in Cambridge opposing the former King's efforts to salt the University with Jesuits. He spent much of the last year in London, to the dismay of those of us who would prefer to see him turn out more work in the vein of *Principia Mathematica.* He and your friend Fatio have become the closest of companions, and share lodgings here.

POST-SCRIPT—FEB. 1690

After I wrote the above, but before I could post this, King William and Queen Mary prorogued and dissolved Parliament. There have been new elections and the Tories have won. Isaac Newton is no longer M.P. He divides his time between Cambridge, where he toils on Alchemy, and London, where he and Fatio are reading *Treatise on Light* by our friend and erstwhile dinner-companion Huygens. All of which is to say that I am now even more useless to you than I was a month ago; for I am in a failing Society linked to a Party that has lost power and that has no money, there being none in the kingdom to be had. Our most brilliant Fellow devotes himself to other matters. It were *presumptuous* of me to expect a reply to a letter as devoid of useful content as this one; but it would have been *insolent* of me to have failed to respond to yours; for I am, as always, your humble and obedient servant—

Daniel Waterhouse

Letter from Eliza to Daniel
APRIL 1690

NEWTON would have us believe that Time is stepped out by the ticking of God's pocket-watch, steady, immutable, an absolute measure of all sensible movements. LEIBNIZ inclines toward the view that Time is nothing more nor less than the change of objects' relationships to one another—that movements, observed, enable us to detect Time, and not the other way round. NEWTON has laid out his system to the satisfaction, nay, amazement of the world, and I can find no fault in it; yet the system of LEIBNIZ, though not yet written out, more aptly describes my own subjective experience of Time. Which is to say that during the autumn of last year, when I and all around me were in continual motion, I had the impression that much Time was passing. But once I reached Versailles, and settled into lodgings at my cottage on the domain of La Dunette, on the hill of Satory above Versailles, and got my household affairs in order, and established a routine, suddenly four months flew by.

The purpose for which I was sent to Versailles, early in December, was accomplished before Christmas, and all since then has been tending to details. I should probably return to Dunkerque, where I could be more useful. But I am held here by various ties which only grow stronger with time. Every morning I ride down the hill through a little belt of woods, just to the south of the *Pièce d'eau des Suisses,* that separates the land of the Lavardacs from the royal domain of Versailles. This takes me down into the old hamlet of Versailles, outside the walls of the palace, which is growing up into a village. Diverse monasteries, nunneries, and a parish church have taken root there since the King moved his court to this place some eight years ago, and in one of them, the Convent of Sainte-Genevieve, my little "orphan" boy makes his home. If weather is good, I take him for a perambulation around the King's vegetable-garden: a limb of the gardens of Versailles that is thrust forth into the middle of the town. Being a working garden, whose purpose is to produce food, this is not as formal or as fashion-able as the parterres west of the Château. But there is more here for little eyes to see and little hands to grasp, especially now that spring is coming. The gardeners are forever mend-ing their trellises in expectation that peas and beans will climb up them in a few months; and to judge by the thoughtful way that little Jean-Jacques gazes upon these structures, he will be clambering up them like a little squirrel even before he has learned how to walk. Sometimes too we will go a little farther, into the Orangerie, which is an immense vaulted gallery wrapped around three sides of a rectangular garden, and open to the south so that its glazed walls can capture the warmth of the winter sun, and store it in stone. Tiny orange trees grow here in wooden boxes, waiting for summer to come so that the gardeners can move them out of doors, and Jean-Jacques is fascinated by the green globes that are to be found among their dark leaves.

In due time I bring him back to Ste.-Genevieve's for an appointment with a wet-nurse. You might think that I would then go directly to the Château to immerse myself in Court doings. But more often than not I turn around and ride back up through the Bois de Satory to La Dunette, where I tend to various affairs. In my early months here, these were of a finan-cial, but now they are more of a social, nature. Note, however, that La Dunette is no farther away from the King's great Château than is the Trianon Palace or many other parts of the royal domain, and so it does not feel like a separate place from Versailles, but more of an out-building of the King's estate. This illusion is strengthened by the architecture, which was done by the same fellow who designed the King's Château.

The grounds of La Dunette spread across the Plateau of Satory, a hilltop that extends southwards from the wooded brow of a rise that overlooks the *Pièce d'eau des Suisses* and the south wing of the King's Château. This land is hidden by the woods from direct view of the Dauphin, the Dauphine, and other royals who dwell in the palace's south wing. But once that screen of trees has been penetrated, the domain of the de Lavardacs resembles in every way the much larger Royal gardens down the hill. This means that it is divided up, here and there, by great pompous stone walls, with massive iron grilles set into them from place to place; and those walls terminate in brick cottages, which I suppose are meant to recall guardhouses. In fact they have no practical purpose whatever that I can discern. They are there because they look good, like the knobs on the ends of a banister. The domaine of La Dunette contains four such cottages. Two are unfinished on the inside, and one is having its roof replaced. I live in the fourth. There is just enough room in it for my little household. It is tucked in under the eave of the woods of Satory so that I can duck out the back door and ride down into Versailles whenever I please without having to traverse any of the gravel paths that radiate from the main château of La Dunette. I do so frequently, going down to the palace for a dinner-party or to attend the couchée of some Duchess or Princess. And so my existence here is independent of the de Lavardacs for the most part. However, at least once a week I go to the main residence to have dinner with Étienne under the supervision of Madame la duchesse d'Arcachon.

M. le duc d'Arcachon I have never met. During my earlier life at Versailles, as a governess, I saw him from a distance a few times, surrounded by other big-wigs, but my social standing was so mean that there was no circumstance under which I could have met him. Later my status was elevated; but he was in "the South" tending to business of some nature. He was at Versailles through much of 1689, while I was absent; then he went back into "the South" a few weeks before I came there in December. He was supposed to be back for Christmas; but one thing and then another has kept him away. A few times a week Madame la duchesse receives a letter from Marseille, where M. le duc is looking after the galleys of the Mediterranean fleet; or Lyon, where he is meeting with the King's money-men, and acquiring victuals, powder, &c; or Arcachon, where he is looking after Lavardac family affairs; or Brest, where he is responsible for shipment of men and matériel to the forces in Ireland. Madame la duchesse always replies on the same day, hoping her letter shall catch him before he has moved on to some other port. This has happened often enough that M. le duc has learned a little bit about me and my activities, or lack thereof, here; and lately he has begun writing to me personally at the cottage. It seems that I am to be useful to this family in some way other than as an eligible belle for Étienne. The Duc has recently become involved in some sort of momentous transaction that is in the offing down south, and that he expects to yield a large quantity of hard money when it comes off, which is expected to occur late in the summer. To report any more than this would be indiscreet, but if I am reading his most recent letter correctly, he wishes me to look after certain of the details: a large transfer of metal through Lyon.

So at last I shall have something to do, and can expect the passage of time to slow down again, as I go into violent movement, and change my relations with all around me.

Eliza, Countess de la Zeur

La Dunette
MID-JULY 1690

LA DUNETTE MEANT "POOP DECK," the high place on a ship's stern-castle from which the captain could see everything. The name had come to Louis-François de Lavardac, duc d'Arcachon, some twelve years earlier, as he had stood upon the brow of the hill, peering, between two denuded trees, across the frozen bog that would later become the *Pièce d'eau des Suisses,* at the southern flanks of the stupendous construction site that would shortly become the royal palace of Louis XIV.

The King got things built more quickly than anyone else, partly because he had the Army to help him and partly because he hired all of the qualified builders. And so *La Dunette* was still nothing more than an empty stretch of high ground with a clever name when *le Roi* had given his cousin, the duc d'Arcachon, a personal tour of the palace. They had lingered particularly in the Queen's Apartments: a row of bedchambers, antechambers, and salons that stretched between the Peace drawing-room and the King's guardroom on the upper storey of the palace's southern wing. The King and the Duke had strolled up and down the length of those apartments once, twice, thrice, pausing before each of the high windows to enjoy the view across the *Parterre Sud,* and the Orangerie below it to the rise of the Bois de Satory a mile away. The duc d'Arcachon had, in the fullness of time, perceived what the King had wished him to perceive, which was that any buildings erected on or near the crest of the hill would spoil the Queen's view, and give her the feeling that the de Lavardacs were peering down into her bedroom windows. And so a great pile of expensive architectural drawings had been used to start fires in the Hôtel d'Arcachon in Paris, and the duc had hired the great Hardouin-Mansart and implored him to design a château altogether magnificent—but invisible from the Queen's windows. Mansart had situated it well back from the crest of the hill. Consequently, from the windows of the château of La Dunette proper, the view was limited. But Mansart had laid out a promenade that swung out along a lobe of the garden and led to a gazebo, perched demurely on the brink of the hill, and camouflaged with climbing vines. From there the prospect was superb.

Before dinner was served, the Duke and Duchess of Arcachon invited their guests—twenty-six in all—to stroll out to the gazebo, enjoy the breeze (for the day was warm), and take in the view of the Royal Château of Versailles, its gardens, and its waterways. From this distance it was difficult to make out individuals and impossible to hear voices, but large groups were obvious. Out in the town, beyond the *Place d'Armes,* the Franciscans had lit a bonfire before their monastery and were dancing around it in a circle; from time to time, a few notes of their song would blow past on a slip of breeze. Another revel was underway along the Grand Canal, a mile-long slot of water stretching away from the Château along the central axis of the King's garden. From here, it was a milling mob of wigs. Even the stable-hands out in the *Place d'Armes* had got a bonfire going, which had attracted hundreds of commoners: townspeople, servants of Versailles and nearby villas, and country folk who had seen the pillars of smoke and heard the pealing of bells, and come in to find out what all the excitement was about. Many of these probably had only the haziest of ideas as to who William of Orange was and why it was good that he was dead; but this did not hold them back from lusty celebration.

Étienne d'Arcachon raised his glass, and silenced the little crowd around the gazebo. "To toast the death of the Prince of Orange*

---

* For the French did not recognize William's title as King of England

would be uncouth, even though he was a perfidious and heretickal *usurper* and an enemy of France," he said. This oration, being ambiguous, only threw the guests—who were all standing on tiptoe with glasses poised—into utter confusion. They froze long enough for Étienne to dig himself out of his own rhetorical hole: "But to toast the victory of the French, the free English, and the Irish at the Battle of the Boyne is honorable."

They did so.

"The only event," Étienne continued, "that could make the day more glorious would be a victory at sea, to match the one on land; and *voilà*, God has answered our prayers accordingly. The French Navy, of which my father has the high honor of being Grand Admiral, has routed the English and the Dutch off Beachy Head, and even now menaces the mouth of the River Thames. France is victorious on all fronts: on the sea, in Ireland, in Flanders, and in Savoy. To France!"

Now *that* was a toast. Everyone drank. Then it was "to the King!" and then "to the King of England!" meaning James Stuart, then "to Monsieur le duc!" which le duc had to sit out, since it was bad form to toast oneself. Servants scurried about cradling swaddled magnums and refilled glasses for the next round. Then M. le duc raised his glass: "To the Countess de la Zeur, who has done so much to give the Navy its sinews." Which obliged Eliza to say, "To Captain Jean Bart who, they say, distinguished himself yet again off Beachy Head on his ship *Alcyon*!"

Madame la duchesse, peering down at Versailles through a spectacular Instrument, now initiated a controversy, as follows: "Louis-François, those revelers along the Canal do not celebrate the death of the Prince of Orange, they celebrate *you*!" and she handed her husband a gold and silver caduceus (emblem of Mercury, bringer of information) with lenses cleverly mounted in the eyes of the two snakes that were wound about its central pole. The duc brought it to his face as if expecting the serpents to drive their fangs into his cheeks, and blinked fiercely into the optics. But anyone who had good eyes could see that a few gilded barques had taken to the wavelets of the Grand Canal, and were jerking about in an extemporaneous reënactment of the Battle of Beachy Head. As combatants swung boat-paddles to dash up barrages of spray, blooms of white water appeared here and there, looking from this range much like cannon-smoke. From time to time the musket-like report of an ivory-inlaid paddle smacking the water, or a gilded oar-shaft snapping, would echo up from the vale of Galie. A drunken boarding-party, perhaps still fired by the memory of Jean Bart's visit of a few months past, sprang from one boat to another, swinging like pirates on silken ropes, crashing into the brocade awnings, bucking the ebony and boxwood poles of the pavilions, smashing the velvet furniture. They must have been royal bastards, or Princes of the Blood, to behave so. A smaller boat was capsized; conversation lulled around the gazebo as rescuers paddled to the scene, then welled up into laughter and witticisms as combatants were dragged out of the canal and their bobbing periwigs fished out on the tips of swords.

"Ah, it is a great day," announced the Duke, who looked, in his formal Grand Admiral uniform, like a galleon on legs. He was saying it to his wife; but something occurred to him, and he added, "and it will only get better, for France, and for us. God willing." His eyes turned in their sockets towards Eliza. As his head was covered in a wig, and the wig had an admiral's hat planted athwart it, he did not like to turn his head from side to side if he could avoid it; such complicated maneuvers demanded as much prudent premeditation as tacking a three-masted ship.

Eliza, recognizing as much, sidestepped into the Duke's field of view. "I cannot imagine why you look to *me* when you say this, Monsieur le duc," she said.

"Soon, if I have my way, you shall hear from Étienne a certain *proposition* that shall make it all perfectly clear."

"Is it anything like the proposition you have spoken of in your letters to me?"

The very mention of this made the Duke nervous, and his eyes flicked left and right to see if anyone had heard; but soon enough they returned to Eliza, who was smiling in a way that let him know she had been discreet. The Duke stepped forward in the cautious bent-kneed stride of an African matron with a basket of bananas on her head. "Don't be coy, Étienne's proposal will be of an *entirely different nature!* Though it's true I should like to see *both* of them come together at the same time, in the autumn—say, October. My birthday. What do you say to it?"

Eliza shrugged. "I cannot answer, monseigneur, until I know more of both propositions."

"We'll get that sorted out! The boy is still young in many ways, you know—not too old to benefit from some fatherly advice, especially where affairs of the heart are concerned. I have been away too much, you know? Now that I am back—for a little while, at least—I shall talk to him, guide him, give him some backbone."

"Well, it is good to have you back, even briefly," said Eliza. "It is odd, I feel as if I have met you before. I suppose it comes from seeing your busts and portraits everywhere, and your handsome features echoed in the face of Étienne."

By now the Duke had drawn close to Eliza. He had put on cologne recently, something Levantine, with a lot of citrus. It did not quite mask another odor which put Eliza in mind of rotting flesh. A bird, or some little scurrying creature, must have given up the ghost some days ago under the gazebo, and gone foul in the heat.

"Time for dinner soon," said the Duke. "My time here is short. Meetings with the King, and the Council. Then to the Channel coast to greet the victorious Fleet. But after that I go south. I have already despatched orders to my *jacht*. You and I must talk. After dinner, I think. In the library, while the guests are strolling in the garden."

"The library is where I shall be," said Eliza, "at your service, and waiting for you to explain all of these cryptic statements."

"Ah, I shall not explain all!" said the Duke, amused. "Only enough—just enough. That will suffice."

Eliza's head snapped around to a new azimuth, and her attention settled on a group of guests, mostly men, who had migrated off the marble floor of the gazebo and gathered on the gravel path to smoke. It was rude to break off her conversation with the Duke in such a way. But her movement had not been voluntary. It had been occasioned by a word, spoken loudly, by one of these men. The word was *une esclave*, which signified, a slave—a *female* slave. The speaker was Louis Anglesey, the Earl of Upnor. He was nominally an Englishman. But he had spent so much of his life in France that he was indistinguishable, in his speech, dress, and mannerisms, from a French noble. He had come over with James Stuart following the Revolution in England, and become an important man in the exiled King's court at St.-Germain-en-Laye. This was not the first time Eliza had seen him socially.

It was not unusual to hear the word *esclave* in such company. Many at Versailles made money from the slave trade. But normally the word was used in masculine, plural form, to denote a ship-full of cargo bound for some plantation in the Caribbean. The singular, feminine form was rare enough to have turned Eliza's head.

In the corner of her eye, she saw the pale oval of some woman's face turn around to stare at her. Eliza had reacted so sharply that someone else had taken notice of it. She needed to control her reactions better. She wondered who it was; but to look over and find out would be obvious. She forced herself not to, and tried instead to memorize a few things about this lady who was giving her the eye: tall, and dressed in pink silk.

She looked back at the Duke, ready to apologize to him for having been distracted. But it seemed that he considered his chat with Eliza to be finished. He had caught someone's eye and wanted to go talk to him. He most civilly took his leave from Eliza, and glided away. Eliza tracked him with her eyes for a few moments. As he passed in front of the tall woman in pink silk, Eliza glanced up, just for an instant, to see who it was. The answer was, the Duchess of Oyonnax.

Having settled that, Eliza turned her attention back to Upnor and his circle of admirers.

James Stuart and his French advisors phant'sied that, once they had retaken Ireland, they might move thence to Qwghlm, which could be used as a sort of outlying demilune-work from which to mount an invasion of northern England. This had at least something to do with Eliza's popularity at the two Courts: the French one at Versailles, and the exile-English one at St.-Germain. Consequently she had seen and heard enough of Upnor, in the last half-year, to know the first parts of this story by heart. It was the tale of the day he had made his escape from England.

He had sent his household ahead of him to Castle Upnor, where they had made ready to board ship and sail to France as soon as he arrived. For he had stayed behind in London, supposedly at great risk, to attend to certain matters of stupendous importance. These matters were, however, far too deep and mystical for Upnor to say anything about them in mixed company. This suggested that they had something to do with Alchemy, or at least that he wished as many people as possible to believe so. "I could not allow certain information to fall into the hands of the usurper and those of his lackeys who pretend to know of matters that are, in truth, beyond their ken."

At any rate, after completing his affairs in London, Upnor had mounted a stallion (he was a horse-fancier, and so this part of the anecdote was never related without many details concerning this horse's ancestry, which was more distinguished than that of most human beings) and set off a-gallop for Castle Upnor, accompanied by a pair of squires and a string of spare mounts. They had departed from London around dawn and ridden hard all morning along the south bank of the Thames. From place to place, the river road would cross some tributary of the great river, and there would be a bridge or ford that all traffic must use.

In the middle of one such bridge, out in the countryside, they had spied a lone man on horseback, wearing common clothes, but armed; and it had appeared from his posture that he was waiting.

For the sorts of people the Earl was apt to tell this story to, this last detail sufficed to *classify* the anecdote as if it had been a new botanical sample presented to the Royal Society. It belonged to the genus "Persons of Quality beset by varlets on the road." No type was more popular round French dinner tables, because France was so large and so infested with Vagabonds and highwaymen. The nobles who came together at Versailles must occasionally travel to and fro their fiefdoms, and the perils and tribulations of such journeys were one of the few experiences they shared in common, and so that was what they talked about. Such tales were, in fact, told so frequently that everyone was tired of them; but any new variations were, in consequence, appreciated that much more. Upnor's had two distinctions: It took place in England, and it was embroidered, as it were, on the back-cloth of the Revolution.

"I knew this stretch of road well," Upnor was saying, "and so I dispatched one of my squires—a young chap name of Fenleigh—to ride down a side-track that angled away from the main road and led to a ford half a mile upstream of the bridge." He was scratching out a crude map on the gravel path with the tip of his walking-stick.

"With my other companion, I proceeded deliberately up the main road, keeping a sharp eye for any confederates who might be lurking in hedges near the approaches to the bridge. But there were none—the horseman was alone!" This puzzled or fascinated the listeners. It was another odd twist on the usual rustic-ruffian tale; normally, the shrubs would be infested with club-wielding knaves.

"The horseman must have noted the way in which we were peering about, for he called out: 'Do not waste time, my lord, 'tis not an *ambuscado*. I am alone. You are not. Accordingly, I challenge you to a duel, my blade 'gainst yours, no seconds.' And he drew out a spadroon, which is an abominable sort of implement, just the sort of thing you would expect commoners to invent if you make the mistake of suffering them to bear arms. More brush-cutter than weapon really. Sharpened on one side like a cutlass."

Upnor, of course, was telling the story in French. He gave the ruffian the most vulgar rural accent he could manage. He devoted a minute or two to dilating on the pathetic condition of the knave's horse, which was one step away from the knacker and exhausted to boot.

Upnor was rated one of the finest swordsmen of the Anglo-French nobility. He had slain many men in duels when he had been younger. He did not fight so much any more, as his style was one that relied upon speed and acute vision. Nevertheless, the very notion that such a rustic fellow would challenge Upnor to a duel practically had the French nobles falling down onto the path with tears running down their cheeks.

Upnor was clever enough to tell the story in a deadpan style. "I was . . . more . . . *befuddled* than anything else. I answered: 'You have me at a disadvantage, sirrah—perhaps if you tell me who you are, I'll at least know why you want to kill me.'

" 'I am Bob Shaftoe,' he answered."

This, as it always did, caused a hush to descend over Upnor's listeners.

" 'Any relation to Jacques?' I asked him." (For the same question was on the minds of those who were gathered around Upnor listening.)

"He answered, 'His brother.' To which I said, 'Come away with me to France, Bob Shaftoe, and I shall put you on a galley in the sunny Mediterranean—perhaps you may cross paths with your brother there!' "

Upnor's audience loved to hear this. For they all knew of Jacques Shaftoe, or *L'Emmerdeur* as he was called in these parts. The name did not come up in conversation as frequently as it had a couple of years ago, for nothing had been heard from *L'Emmerdeur* since he had crashed a party at the Hôtel Arcachon and made a disgraceful scene there, in the presence of the King, in the spring of 1685. Precisely what had taken place there on that night was rarely spoken of, at least when members of the de Lavardac family were within earshot. From this, Eliza gathered that it was dreadfully embarrassing to them all. Because Eliza was now linked, in most people's minds, to the family de Lavardac, they extended her the same courtesy of never talking about the events of that evening. Eliza had given up on ever finding out what had really happened there. Jack Shaftoe, who for a time had been a sort of hobgoblin of the French Court, a name to make people jump out of their skins, had dwindled to quasi-legendary status and was rapidly being forgotten altogether. From time to time he would appear as a figure in a picaresque *roman*.

Nevertheless, for Upnor even to mention the name of Shaftoe around La Dunette was more than daring. It was probably a *faux pas*. This might have explained why the Duke had suddenly terminated his conversation with Eliza, and gone off in the opposite direction. It was the sort of thing that led to duels. Some of Upnor's listeners were conspicuously nervous. It was, therefore, quite deft of Upnor to have turned the story around in this manner, by implying that Jack Shaftoe, if he was indeed still alive, was a slave on one of the duc d'Arcachon's galleys. Eliza now risked a glance over at the duc, and saw him red-faced, but grinning at Upnor; he favored Upnor with the tiniest suggestion of a nod (anything more would have undermined the Admiral-hat) and Upnor responded with a deeper bow. The listeners who, a few seconds earlier, had worried about a duel, laughed all the louder.

Upnor continued with the narration. "This Robert Shaftoe said, 'Jack and I have long been estranged, and my errand has naught to do with him.'

"I asked him, 'Why do you bar my progress, then?'

"He said, 'I say that you are about to take out of this country something that does not rightfully belong to you.'

"I said, 'Are you accusing me of being a thief, sirrah?'

"He said, 'Worse. I say you pretend to own a slave: an English girl named Abigail Frome.'

"I said, 'There's no pretense in that, Bob Shaftoe. I own her as absolutely as you own that wretched pair of boots on your feet, and I've the papers to prove it, signed and sealed by my lord Jeffreys.'

"He said, 'Jeffreys is in Tower. Your King is in flight. And if you do not give me Abigail, you shall be in the grave.'

Now Upnor had his audience rapt; not only because it was a good story, but because he had managed to connect the half-forgotten, but still powerful name of Jack Shaftoe to the late upheavals in England. Of course the French nobility were fascinated by the recent tendency of the English to chop off their kings' heads and chase them out of the country. They were helpless in their fascination at the thought that William of Orange and his English allies must somehow be in conspiracy with all the world's Vagabonds.

Dinner had already been announced, and the Earl of Upnor knew that his time was short, and so he put the anecdote to a quick and merciful end as he and the other dinner-guests trooped down the garden path to the big house. In the story, Upnor delivered a sort of homily to Bob Shaftoe, putting him in his place and expounding on the glories of the class system, and then Fenleigh, who had by that time forded the river and come round behind, galloped toward Bob and tried to take him with a sword-thrust from behind. Bob heard him coming at the last instant and whipped his spadroon around to parry the blow. Fenleigh's rapier was deflected into the croup of Bob's miserable horse, which reared up. Bob could not manage his horse because he was busy fending off a second blow from Fenleigh (though also, it was clearly implied, because men of his status did not really belong on horseback in the first place). Bob won the exchange nevertheless by almost severing Fenleigh's right arm above the elbow, but he payed for it by being obliged to fall off his horse (extremely funny to the polished equestrians here). He landed balanced "like a sack of oats" on the stone parapet of the bridge. Upnor and his other companion were galloping toward him with pistols drawn. Shaftoe was so terrified he lost his balance and fell into the river, where (and here the story became suspiciously vague, for they had reached the house, and were deploying to their places at the long dinner-table) he either drowned or was slain by a volley of pistol-balls from Upnor, who stood on the bridge using him for target practice as he floundered along in the current of the river. "And what is a river but a lake that has failed to stay within its ordained limits, and now tumbles helplessly toward the Abyss?"

DINNER WAS DINNER. Dead things cooked, and sauced so that one could not guess how long they had been dead. A few early vegetables; but the winter had run long and the growing season had started late, so not much was ripe yet. Some very heavy and sweet delicacies that the Duke had imported from Egypt.

Eliza was seated across from the duchesse d'Oyonnax and tried to avoid meeting her eye. She was a big woman, but not fat, though middle-aged. She wore a lot of jewels, which was risqué in these times (she really ought to pawn them for the War, or, barring that, hide them), but she carried it off well; in this her size helped. Eliza was irked by this woman: by her physical presence, her wealth, what she had done, but most of all by her confidence. Other women, she knew, disliked Eliza because they envied *her* confidence, and so Eliza was startled to observe a similar reaction in herself to Madame la duchesse d'Oyonnax.

"How is your little orphan?" the Duchess asked Eliza, at one point. To bring this up was either naïve, or rude, and it caused a few heads to twitch their way—like housecats alert to faint fidgeting.

"Oh, I do not think of him as *mine* any more, but *God's*," Eliza returned, "and anyway he is not so little now: a year old—or so we think, as there is no way to be sure precisely when he was born—and walking around already. Creating no end of trouble for the nurses."

This elicited a few chuckles from those who had small children. It was a well-crafted reply on Eliza's part, calculated to place defenses athwart all possible axes of attack from Oyonnax; but the Duchess responded only with an unreadable gaze, seeming almost nonplussed, and dropped the topic.

A young officer—Eliza recognized him as one Pierre de Jonzac, an aide to the Duke—sidestepped into the room carrying a dispatch. The Duke accepted it gratefully, for he was bored. People around him had poked fun at him for not eating any of his food; but the Duke had silenced them with the information that he was on a special diet, "for my digestion," and had eaten previously by himself. He opened the dispatch, glanced at it, slapped the table, and shook for a few moments with suppressed laughter; but all the while he was shaking his head back and forth, as if to deny that there was anything funny.

"What is it?" asked Madame la duchesse d'Arcachon.

"The report was false," he said. "The Franciscans will have to douse their bonfire. William of Orange is not dead."

"But we had reliable news that he was *struck from the saddle by a cannonball*," said the Earl of Upnor—who, being a man of some importance in James Stuart's army, got all the latest intelligence.

"And so he was. But he is not dead."

"How is that possible?" And the table went into an uproar over it, which did not die down for twenty minutes. Eliza found herself thinking of Bob Shaftoe, who must be there at this battle on the Boyne, if he had not died of disease over the winter. Then she happened to glance up, and once again saw the green eyes of the Duchess of Oyonnax gazing at her interestedly.

"Now, as to the transaction," said the Duke, once he had got his pipe lit. The fragrance of the smoke was welcome, for the dead-animal smell Eliza had noticed out at the gazebo seemed to have followed them into the drawing-room. She was of a mind to go and throw the doors open, to admit some rose-scented air from the gardens; but that would have defeated the purpose of a private meeting in this place.

"It's going to involve moving a lot of silver. I want you to go to Lyon and make the arrangements."

"Will the silver actually be passing through Lyon, then, or—"

"Oh yes. You shall see it. This is not just a *Dépôt* sort of manipulation."

"Then why Lyon? It is not the best place."

"I know. But you see, it will come off of my *jacht* at Marseille. From there, Lyon is easy to reach—right up the Rhône, of course."

"It makes sense, then. It is safer than any alternative. Tell me, is it coined?"

"No, mademoiselle."

"Oh. I had assumed it would be pieces of eight."

"No. It is pigs. Good metal, mind you, but not coined."

"It makes more sense to me as we go along. You do not wish to be moving uncoined silver around, any more than you must. You want instead a Bill of Exchange, payable in Paris."

"Yes, that is it precisely."

"Very well. There are several houses in Lyon that can do this."

"Indeed. And normally I would not care which one of them handled it. But in this case, I specifically want you *not* to use the House of Hacklheber. I have reason to believe that the old ogre, Lothar, will be most unhappy with me after the transaction goes through." And the Duke laughed.

"I see. May I guess, from this hint, that it has something to do with piracy?"

Plainly the Duke thought this a stupid question. But he was polished, and handled it in good form. "That is the word that Lothar will attach to it, no doubt, in order to justify any . . . retaliations he may contemplate. But the method is normal, in a war. I am sure you will see nothing unusual in it, mademoiselle, given that you are such a friend of Jean Bart, and that along with the Marquis d'Ozoir you are a direct supporter of his exploits?" He laughed again, with gusto; and she felt his breath on her face, and with some trepidation drew it into her nostrils, and smelled death. It reminded her of something in addition to death, however.

"You look peaked, mademoiselle. Are you all right?"

"The air is stuffy."

"We shall go outside, then! I have nothing further to say, other than that you should plan to be in Lyon no later than the end of August."

"Shall I see you there?"

"It is not known. There is another aspect of this transaction, which has nothing to do with money, and everything to do with the honor of my family. It is a matter of personal revenge, which need not concern you. I must tend to it *myself*, of course—that's the whole point! No telling where or when exactly. Nevertheless, you may count on my being back in Paris, at the Hôtel Arcachon, for my birthday party on the fourteenth of October. It shall be splendid. I am already making the plans. The King will be there, mademoiselle. You and I shall see each other then and there, and if Étienne has done the honorable thing, why, then I shall expect a blessed announcement!"

He turned and offered his arm to Eliza, who took it, trying not to recoil from the smell of him. "I am certain it shall all come to pass just as you say, monsieur," she said. "But as I go outside with you, I should like to change the subject, if I may, to horses."

"Horses! It is a *welcome* change of subject! I am a *great* fancier of them."

"I know, for the evidence has been all around me ever since I came here seven months ago. I noticed quite early that you have some albinos in your stable."

"Indeed!"

"Seeing this, I phant'sied that such horses must be very popular among the Quality here, and that, in consequence, I could expect to see many more of them, in the stables of the King and of the many other nobles who live in these parts. But this has not been the case."

"I should hope not! For the entire point of having them is that they are rare. They are distinctive. They are of Turkish stock."

"May I ask who you bought them from? Is there some breeder hereabouts who has connections in the Levant?"

"Yes, mademoiselle," said the Duke, "and he has the honor of being on your arm at this moment. For it is I who imported the Pasha to France some years ago, from Constantinople, via Algiers, in an unfathomably complex exchange of assets—"

"The Pasha?"

"A stud, mademoiselle, an albino stallion, the father of all the others!"

"He must have been magnificent."

"*Is* magnificent, for he still lives!"

"Really?"

"He is old, and does not venture out of the stables so often, but on a warm evening such as this, you may go down to the paddock and see him stretching his stiff old legs."

"When did you import the Pasha?"

"When? Let me see, it would have been ten years ago."

"Are you certain?"

"No, no, what am I saying!? Time passes so quickly, I quite lose track. It would have been eleven years ago this summer."

"Thank you for satisfying my curiosity, and escorting me out to your beautiful garden, monsieur," said Eliza, bending to one side to bury her nose in a rose—and to hide her reaction from the Duke. "I shall go for a stroll now, by myself, to clear my head. Perhaps I shall go down and pay my respects to the Pasha."

LIKE MOST OTHER PEOPLE, Eliza had never in her life been more than a stone's throw away from an open flame. Wherever she was, there was always *something* burning: a cooking-fire, a candle, a pipe-bowl of tobacco or *bhang,* incense, a torch, a lanthorn. These were tame fires. Everyone knew that fire could go wild. Eliza had seen the aftermath of such fires in Constantinople, in the countryside of Hungary, where much had been burned as it was attacked by Ottomans or defended by Christians, and in Bohemia, which was studded with old forts and castles that had been put to the torch during the Thirty Years' War. But she had never actually seen a fire grow from a tame spark to a feral conflagration until a couple of years ago, in Amsterdam, when a Mobb of Orangist patriots had gathered before the house of a Mr. Sluys, who had lately been exposed as a traitor to the Dutch Republic, and burned the place to the ground. They had done this by hurling torches in through windows. The house had been abandoned a few minutes earlier by Mr. Sluys and his household, who had not had time to board the place up. For several minutes, very little had seemed to happen, and the crowd had only become more agitated—the feeble and steady flickering of the torches, slowly dying on the floors of dark rooms, drove them into a kind of frenzy. But then a sudden sunrise of yellow light shone from an upstairs window, where a curtain or something had caught fire. This had probably saved the lives of several in the Mobb who had been so desperate to see the house come down that they would have jumped in through the shattered windows to attack it with their bare hands. After that, the fire built steadily for a few minutes, spreading from room to room. This was absorbing to watch, but not especially remarkable. It was even tedious, after a while. But at some point the fire had vaulted over some invisible threshold and simply exploded, over the course of a few heartbeats, into a monstrous thing that wore the envelope of the house as a suit of ill-fitting clothes. It sucked in so much air that it howled, and snatched wigs and caps from the heads of bystanders. Burning timbers shot up in the air like meteors. Vortices of white flame formed, fought, joined, and were swallowed. The ground hummed. Rivers of molten lead—for the house was full of it—spilled out onto the street and traced glowing nets in the crevices between the ashlars, fading from yellow to orange to red as they cooled. For a few moments it seemed that the fire might spread to engulf all Amsterdam in another minute, and all of the Dutch Republic the minute after that. But it had been contained between the thick masonry firewalls to either side. Pent up, it was almost more terrible than it would have been free, for all of its intensity was concentrated between those walls, instead of being allowed to spread and dissipate.

Now tears were a watery thing, and so a pedantic schoolman might insist that they were opposite in nature to fire, and could have naught in common with that element. Yet, just as Eliza had never been far from little fires, so she had never been far from the shedding of tears. Children were everywhere, and they cried all the time. Full-grown people did it less often, but they still cried. Especially women. In the *banyolar* of Algiers, the *harim* of the Topkapi Palace, and various European households, Eliza had spent most of her time in the company of women of all ages and stations, and rarely did a single day pass without her seeing at least one person get a little sniffly and moist about the eyes, whether out of pain, anger, sadness, or joy. Eliza often allowed even herself to shed a tear or two in private, and had done so more freely since the birth of Jean-Jacques. But these sheddings of tears were like so many candle-flames or kitchen-fires: elements of domestic life, controlled, unremarkable.

Eliza had seen, on occasion, crying of an altogether different nature: wild, hair-pulling, clothes-rending, spine-warping tear-rage. It had never happened to her, though, and she did not really ken it, until that evening when she walked down to the paddock out behind the stables of the Duc d'Arcachon, on the Plateau of Satory, and found herself standing face to face with Pasha: an albino Arabian stallion whom she had last encountered at dockside in the harbor of Algiers, eleven years ago. She and her mother had been snatched from the beach of Outer Qwghlm by a coastal raiding-galley of the Barbary Corsairs, and taken off into slavery; but presently they had learned that these Corsairs were operating in concert with a Christian ship. For they had spent the entire journey to Algiers being molested in a dark cabin by an uncircumcised man with white skin, who liked to dine on rotten fish. Delivered to Algiers, they had been assigned to a *banyolar* and become assets of some enterprise there, of which it was not possible to know very much, save that it imported certain goods—including slaves—from Christendom, exporting in exchange silks, perfumes, blades, delicacies, spices, and other luxuries of the East. When Eliza had reached puberty, she had been traded to Constantinople in exchange for this stallion—though according to what the Duke had just claimed, the exchange had been much more complicated than that, which only added insult to injury, since it implied that Eliza, by herself, was not worth as much as this horse. She had vowed then and there to find the smelly man in the dark cabin and kill him one day. Christendom being a large place—France alone had twenty millions of souls—she had supposed that finding the villain might take a while.

She had been wrong-footed by the easiness of it. She had only been in Christendom for seven years! And it had only taken her two years to meet her first de Lavardac, and three or four to lay eyes, from a distance, on the duc d'Arcachon himself. Had she been a little more perceptive she might have recognized the duc for what he was, and done him in, a long time ago.

What had she been doing instead? Socializing with Natural

Philosophers. Putting on airs. Making money; all of which was now gone.

The tears that came over her, then, when she let herself into the paddock, and came face to face with Pasha, and saw and knew all, were to normal everyday tears as the burning of Mr. Sluys's house had been to the flame of a candle. It raged up in her so fast that it seemed, for a few moments, as if it might have the power to burst free from the confines of her body and make blades of grass bend double and flood the pasture with salty dew, make Pasha crumple to his arthritic knees, blow the fences down, make the trees sag and groan as in an ice-storm. Which might have been better for Eliza; but as it was, this self-feeding vortex of sorrow, humiliation, and rage could not escape her ribcage, and so it was her ribs that took all the punishment. For once it was a good thing to be wearing a corset, for without that reinforcement she might have broken her own back with these sobs. Like the burning house of Sluys, she howled, she creaked, and the tears coming out of her felt no less hot than streams of molten lead. Fortunate it was for Eliza that all of the guests were gathered some distance away, deafened by their own happy uproar. The only witness was Pasha. A younger horse might have been spooked by the transmogrification of the Countess de la Zeur into a Fury, a Medea. Pasha merely turned sideways, the better to keep Eliza within view, and nuzzled the green grass.

"I have not the *remotest* idea what has come over you, mademoiselle," said a woman's voice. "It is quite the strangest reaction I have ever seen, to a horse."

The Duchess of Oyonnax had timed the intrusion well. A minute before, Eliza wouldn't have been able to stop herself even if the entire guest list had suddenly appeared around her. But the outburst had insensibly faded to a long slow run of sobs, which skidded to a halt when Eliza realized she was being watched.

She straightened up, took a deep breath, shuddered it out, and hiccuped. She must look red-faced and perfectly ridiculous; this she knew. She must look as if she hadn't aged a day, in body or mind, since her first encounter with Pasha. This made her wince a little bit; for on *that* day, she had lost her mother forever; and now, all of a sudden, here she was with a bigger, older, richer and stronger woman, who had materialized just as suddenly and inexplicably as Mum had vanished eleven years ago. This was perilous.

"Say nothing," said Madame la duchesse d'Oyonnax, "you're in no condition to, and I don't desire to know why this horse has such an effect on you. Given who it belongs to, I can only assume it is something unspeakable. The details are probably gross and tedious and in any event they are not important. All that I need to know of *you*, mademoiselle, I have seen on your face before, during and after dinner: that in general you are strangely fascinated by tales of women in a condition of slavery. That in particular you have found yourself in a like predicament; for you do not love Étienne de Lavardac, but will soon be cornered into marrying him. That you loathe his father the Duke. Please do not attempt to deny these things, or I am very much afraid that I shall laugh out loud at you."

And she paused, to give Eliza the opportunity; but Eliza said nothing.

The Duchess continued: "I understand situations of this type as perfectly as Monsieur Bonaventure Rossignol understands cyphers. I phant'sied *my* predicament unique in all the world, until I came to Versailles! It did not take me long to understand that no one need put up with such unfair situations. There are ways to arrange it. No one lives forever, mademoiselle, and many do not deserve to live as long as they do."

"I know what you are talking about," said Eliza. Her voice sounded quite strange at first, as though it belonged to a different Eliza altogether, one who had just been born screaming out of the old. She cleared her burnt throat and swallowed painfully. She could not keep her eyes from straying over to the shack where the Duchess had her soap made.

"I see that you do," said the Duchess.

"There is nothing you could say to me that would change my intentions."

"Of course not, proud girl!"

"My ends are fixed, and have been for many years. But as to *means,* it is possible that I might benefit from advice. For I do not care what happens to me; but if I pursue my ends through means that are obvious, it could lead to the little one in the orphanage being injured."

"Then know that you are in the most tasteful and cultivated society the world has ever seen," said the Duchess, "where there is a refined and subtle way of doing *anything* that a person could conceive a wish for. And it would be disgraceful for one of your quality to go about it in a rude and obvious style."

"I would that you know one thing, which is that this is not about succession. It is not a matter of inheritance. It is a question of honor."

"This is to be expected. You loathe me. I have seen it in the way you look at me. You loathe me because you believe that my late husband's money was the only thing that I cared about. Now, you want my advice; but first you are careful to stipulate that you are better than I, your motives purer. Now, listen to me, Mademoiselle la comtesse. In this world there are very few who would kill for money. To believe that the Court of France is crowded with such rare specimens is folly. There used to be, at court, many practitioners of the Black Mass. Do you really think that all of these people woke up one morning and said, 'Today I shall worship and offer sacrifices to the Prince of Evil?' Of course not. Rather, it was that some girl, desperate to find a husband, so that she would not be sent off to live out the rest of her life in some convent, would hear a rumor that such-and-such person could prepare a love potion. She would save her money and go into Paris and buy a magic powder from some mountebank. Of course it had no effect at all; but she would cozen herself into believing that it had worked a little bit, and so conceive a desperate hope, and a desire for something a little bit stronger: a magic spell, perhaps. One thing would lead to another, and in time she might find herself stealing the consecrated Host from some church, and taking it to a cellar where a Black Mass would be sung over her naked body. Errant foolishness all of it. Foolishness leading to evil. But did she set out to do evil? Did she ever conceive of herself as evil? Of course not."

"So much for lonely hearts, desperate for love," said Eliza. "What of those who were married, and whose husbands dropped dead? Did they act out of love?"

"Do *you* propose to act out of love, mademoiselle? I have not heard the word *love* escape your pretty mouth. I heard something about *honor* instead; which tells me that you and I have more in common than you would like to admit. You are not the only woman in the world who is capable of taking offense at a violation of her honor, and who has the steel to respond. *Tout le monde* knows that Étienne de Lavardac seduced you—"

Eliza snorted. "Do you think it's that? I don't care about that."

"Frankly, mademoiselle, I could not care less why it is that you want your marriage to be brief and your widowhood long."

"Oh, no. It is not Étienne who deserves this."

"The duc d'Arcachon, then? Very well. There is no accounting for taste. But you must understand that refinement is not compatible with haste. If you want the Duke dead *now*, go and stab him. If you want to enjoy his being dead for a little while, and to see your orphan grow up, you will have to be patient."

"I can be patient," Eliza said, "until the fourteenth of October."

The Gulf of Cadiz
5 AUGUST 1690

The Spaniards tho' an indolent Nation, whose
Colonies were really so rich, so great, and so far
extended, as were enough even to glut their utmost
Avarice; yet gave not over, till, as it were, they sat still,
because they had no more Worlds to look for; or till
at least, there were no more Gold or Silver Mines to
discover.

— DANIEL DEFOE,
A Plan of the English Commerce

WITH ONE EYE JACK peered through his oar-lock across the gulf. He
was looking edge-on through a slab of dry heat that lay dead on the
water, as liquefacted glass rides above molten tin in a glass-maker's
pan. On a low flat shore, far away, white cabals of ghosts huddled
and leaped, colossal and formless. None of the slaves quite knew
what to make of it until they crawled in closer to shore, a cockroach
on a skillet, and perceived that this Gulf was lined with vast salt-pans,
and the salt had been raked up into cones and hillocks and step-
pyramids by workers who were invisible from here. When they
understood this, their thirst nearly slew them. They had been rowing
hard for days.

Cadiz was a shiv of rock thrust into the gulf. White buildings had
grown up from it like the reaching fingers of rock crystals. They put
into a quay that extended from the base of its sea-wall, and took on
more fresh water; for one of the ways that the Corsairs kept them on
a leash was by making sure that the boat was always short of it. But
the Spanish harbor-master did not suffer them to stay for very long,
because (as they saw when they came around the point) the lagoon
sheltered in the crook of the city's bony arm was crowded with a fleet
of Ships that Jack would have thought most remarkable, if he had
never seen Amsterdam. They were mostly big slab-sided castle-arsed

ships, checkered with gun-ports. Jack had never seen a Spanish treasure-galleon in good repair before—off Jamaica he had spied the wrack of one slumped over a reef. In any event, he had no trouble recognizing these. "We have not arrived too early," he said, "and so the only question that remains is, have we arrived too late?"

He and Moseh de la Cruz, Vrej Esphahnian, and Gabriel Goto were all looking to one another for answers, and somehow they all ended up looking to Otto van Hoek. "I smell raw cotton," he said. Then he stood up and looked out over the gunwale and up into the city. "And I see *cargadores* toting bales of it into the warehouses of the Genoese. Cotton, being bulky, would be the first cargo to come off the ships. So they cannot have dropped anchor very long ago."

"Still, it is likely we are too late—surely the Viceroy's brig would waste no time in going to Bonanza and unloading?" This from the *raïs* or captain, Nasr al-Ghuráb.

"It depends," van Hoek said. "Of these anchored fleet-ships, only *some* are beginning to unload—*most* have not broken bulk yet. This suggests that the customs inspections are not finished. What do you see to larboard, Caballero?"

Jeronimo was peering towards the anchored fleet through an oar-lock on his side. "Tied up alongside one of the great ships is a barque flying the glorious colors of His Majesty the Deformed, Monstrous Imbecile." Then he paused to mutter a little prayer and cross himself. When Jeronimo attemped to say the words "King Carlos II of Spain," this, or even less flattering expressions, would frequently come out of his mouth. "More than likely, this is the boat used by the tapeworms."

"You mean the customs inspectors?" Moseh inquired.

"Yes, you bloodsucking, scalp-pilfering, half-breed Christ-killer, that is what I meant to say—please forgive my imprecision," answered Jeronimo politely.

"But the Viceroy's brig would not have to clear customs here at Cadiz—it could do so at Sanlúcar de Barrameda, and avoid the wait," Moseh pointed out.

"But as part of his ransackings, the Viceroy would be certain to have cargo of his own loaded on some of these galleons. He would have every reason to linger until the formalities were complete," Jeronimo said.

"Hah! Now I can see up into the Calle Nueva," said van Hoek. "It is gaudy with silks and ostrich-plumes today."

"What is that," Jack asked, "the street of clothes-merchants?"

"No, it is the exchange. Half the *commerçants* of Christendom are gathered there in their French fashions. Last year these men shipped goods to America—now, they have gathered to collect their profits."

"I see her," said Jeronimo, with a frosty calm in his voice that Jack found moderately alarming. "She is hidden behind a galleon, but I see the Viceroy's colors flying from her mast."

"The brig!?" said several of the Ten.

"The brig," said Jeronimo. "Providence—which buggered us all for so many years—has brought us here in time."

"So the thunder that rolled across the Gulf last night was not a storm, but the guns of Cadiz saluting the galleons," Moseh said. "Let us drink fresh water, and take a siesta, and then make for Bonanza."

"It would be useful if we could send someone into the city now, and let him loiter around the House of the Golden Mercury for a while," van Hoek said. Which to Jack would have meant no more than the singing of birds, except that the name jogged a memory.

"There is a house in Leipzig of the same name—it is owned by the Hacklhebers."

Van Hoek said, "As salmon converge from all the wide ocean toward the mouths of swift rivers, Hacklhebers go wherever large amounts of gold and silver are in flux."

"Why should we care about their doings in Cadiz?"

"Because *they* are sure to care about *ours,*" van Hoek said.

"Be that as it may, there's not a single man, free or slave, aboard this galleot who could get through the city-gate. So this discussion is idle," said Moseh.

"You think it will be any different at Sanlúcar de Barrameda?" van Hoek scoffed.

"Oh, I can get us into that town, Cap'n," Jack said.

AFTER THE HEAT of midday had broken, they rowed north, keeping the salt-pans to starboard. Their ship was a galleot or half-galley, driven by two lateen sails (which were of little use today, as the wind was feeble and inconstant) and sixteen pairs of oars. Each of the thirty-two oars was pulled by two men, so the full complement of rowers was sixty-four. Like everything else about the Plan, this was a choice carefully made. A giant war-galley of Barbary, with two dozen oar-banks, and five or six slaves on each oar, and a hundred armed Corsairs crowding the rails, would of course bring down the wrath of the Spanish fleet as soon as she was sighted. Smaller galleys, called bergantines, carried only a third as many oarsmen as the galleot that they were now rowing across the Gulf of Cadiz. But on such a tiny vessel it was infeasible, or at least unprofitable, to maintain oar-slaves, and so the rowers would be freemen; rowing alongside a larger ship they'd snatch up cutlasses and pistols and go into action as Corsairs. A bergantine, for that reason, would arouse more suspicion than this (much larger) galleot; it would be seen as a nimble platform for up to three dozen boarders, whereas the galleot's crew (not counting chained slaves) was much smaller—in this case, only eight Corsairs, pretending to be peaceful traders.

The galleot was shaped like a gunpowder scoop. Beneath the bare feet of the oarsmen there was loose planking, covering a shallow bilge, but other than that there was no decking—the vessel was open on the top along its entire length, save for a quarterdeck at the stern, which in the typical style of these vessels was curved very high out of the water. So any lookout gazing down into the galleot would clearly see a few dozen naked wretches in chains, and cargo packed around and under their benches: rolled carpets, bundles of hides and of linen, barrels of dates and olive oil. A spindly swivel-gun at the bow, and another at the stern, both fouled by lines and cargo, completed the illusion that the galleot was all but helpless. It would take a closer inspection to reveal that the oarsmen were uncommonly strong and fresh: the best that the slave-markets of Algiers had to offer. The ten participants in the Plan were distributed in outboard positions, the better to peer through oarlocks.

"In this calm we'll have at least a night and a day to await the Viceroy's ship," Jack noted.

"Much hangs on the tides," van Hoek said. "We want a low tide in the night-time. And the weather must remain calm, so that we can row away from any pursuers during the hours of darkness. At sunrise the wind will come up, and then anyone who can see us will be able to catch us . . ." His voice trailed off to a mumble as he pondered these and other complications, which had seemed hardly worth mentioning when they had been developing the Plan, and now, like shadows at sunset, stretched out vast, vague, and terrifying.

The brassy light of late afternoon was gleaming in through their larboard oar-locks when the galleot sank slightly lower into the water, and began to quiver and squirm in a current. At first they did not even recognize it—this was the first river of any significance they'd encountered since passing Gibraltar, or for that matter since leaving Algiers. Jack knew in his arms and his back why the Moors who'd roved up this way ages ago had named it al-Wadi al-Kabir, the Great River. When Jeronimo felt it tugging at his oar, he stood up and thrust an arm through his oar-lock to clip the top of a wave with one cupped hand. Slurping up a mouthful of water, he coughed, and then affected a blissful expression. "It is fresh water, the water of

the Guadalquivir, rushing down from the mountains of my ancestors," he announced, and more in that vein. During this ceremony
his oar did not move, which meant that no oars on that side could.

"Speaking personally," Jack said loudly, "I have more experience
of sewers than of mountain streams, and cannot believe we have
come all this distance to row in circles in the run-off of Seville and
Cordoba!"

Jeronimo thrust out his chest and prepared to challenge Jack to a
duel—but then the *nerf du boeuf* came down across the Spaniard's
shoulder blades as their overseer reminded them that they were yet
slaves. Jack wondered how long it would take Jeronimo to get into a
sword-fight after he was allowed to have a sword.

The next few hours provided more reminders of their lowly station in the world as they stroked upstream with the sun clawing at
their faces. Van Hoek cursed almost without letup, and Jack
reflected that, for an officer, nothing could be more humiliating
than to face backwards, and never see where you were headed. But
at some point they began to see tops of masts around them, and
heard the blessed sound of the anchor-chains rumbling through
their hawse-holes, and bent forward over their warm oars to stretch
out the muscles of their backs.

Nasr al-Ghuráb, the *raïs*, was *kul oglari*, meaning the son of a Janissary by a woman native to the territory round Algiers—in any event,
he spoke passable Spanish as well as Sabir. In the latter tongue, he
now said, "Bring out the spare wretches." Planking was pulled up
and four damp oar-slaves climbed out of the bilge and quickly
replaced Jack, Moseh, Jeronimo, and van Hoek. This took place
under cover of a sail that had been spread out above them as if to be
mended, so that any curious sailors who might be looking down
from a yard or maintop of a nearby ship would not witness the ennoblement going on in the aisle of this newly arrived galleot. Meanwhile—in case anyone was counting heads—four of the Corsair crew
retreated beneath the shade of the quarterdeck to take refreshment
and doze. A canvas sack full of old clothes—looted from persons
who were now captives in Algiers—was also brought up, and the four
began to paw through it like children playing dress-up.

"Turbans are advisable for going abovedecks," Jack pointed out,
"as my hair's sandy, and van Hoek's is red, and that of Moseh—"

They all stood and looked dubiously at Moseh until finally he
said, "Get me a dagger and I'll cut off the forelocks—*crypto*-Jews can
expect no better."

"May you become free and rich and grow them until you must
tuck them into your boot-tops," Jack said.

They spent the last hour before sunset up on the towering quarterdeck turbaned, and covered in the long loose garments of Algerines. The town of Sanlúcar de Barrameda rose above them on the south bank where the river flowed into the gulf. It resembled a feeble miniature rendition of Algiers—it was encompassed by a wall, and below it spread a beach of river-sand where some fishermen had spread out their nets to inspect them. Van Hoek gave the town but a glance, then seized a glass from the *raïs,* climbed up the mast, and devoted much time to scanning the water: apparently reading the currents, and fixing in his mind the location of the submerged bar. Moseh's attention was captured by a suburb that spread along the bank upstream of the town, outside the walls: Bonanza. It seemed to consist entirely of large villas, each with its own wall. After a while the avid Jeronimo spied the Viceroy's coat of arms flying from one of these, or so they all assumed from the invective that geysered forth.

Jack, for his part, was looking for a place to land their little rowboat after it got dark. In the interstices between walled places he could easily make out a fungal huddle of Vagabond-shacks, and with some concerted looking it was not difficult to make out a scrap of mucky, useless river-bank where those persons came down to draw water. Jack got a compass bearing to it, though it remained to be seen how this would serve them when it was dark and the current was pushing them downstream.

" 'Twere foolish to go ashore in daylight," Jeronimo said, "and, when night falls, 'twere foolish *not* to. For smuggling and illicit trade are the only reasons for anyone to visit Sanlúcar de Barrameda nowadays. If we don't try to do something illegal the night we arrive—why, the authorities will become suspicious!"

"If someone asks . . . what *kind* of illegal thing should we say we are undertaking?" Jack asked.

"We should say we have a meeting with a certain Spanish gentleman—but that we do not know his real name."

"Spanish gentlemen, as a rule, are insufferably proud of their names—what sort refuses to identify himself?"

"The sort who meets with heretic scum in the middle of the night," Jeronimo returned, "and fortunately for *you,* there are many of that sort in yonder town."

"That schooner is strangely over-crowded with Englishmen and Dutchmen of high rank," van Hoek offered, pointing with his blue eyes at a rakish vessel anchored a few hundred yards downriver.

"Spies," Jeronimo said.

"What is to spy on *here*?" Jack asked.

"If Spain took all of the silver on those treasure-galleons in the harbor of Cadiz, and locked it up, the foreign trade of Christendom would wither," Moseh explained. "Half the trading companies in London and Amsterdam would go bankrupt within the year. William of Orange would declare war on Spain before he allowed such a thing to happen. Those spies are here, and probably in Cadiz as well, to inform William of whether a war will be necessary this year."

"Why would the Spaniards *want* to hoard it?"

"Because Portugal has opened vast new gold mines in Brazil, and—as Dappa can tell you—supplied them with numberless slaves. In the next ten years, the amount of gold in the world will rise extravagantly and its price, compared to that of silver, will naturally decline."

"So the price of silver is certain to rise . . ." Jack said.

"Giving Spaniards every incentive to hoard it now."

Night came over Spain as they stood there and talked, and lights were lit in the windows of Sanlúcar de Barrameda and in the great villas of Bonanza, where dinners were being cooked—Jeronimo had told them of the queer Spanish practice of dining late at night, and they had already made it part of the Plan. The rhythm of the waves, heaving themselves sluggishly against the beach at the foot of the town, underwent some sort of subtle change, or so van Hoek claimed. He spoke words in Dutch that meant "the tide is running out" and climbed down a pilot's ladder into the galleot's tiny skiff, which had been let down into the water. Here he took a kilderkin— a small keg, having a capacity of some eighteen gallons—removed one end, ballasted it with rocks, and planted a few candles in it. After lighting the candles he released it into the Guadalquivir, and then spent the better part of an hour watching it glide slowly out to sea. Jack meanwhile kept his eyes fixed on the landing-place that he had picked out on the river-bank, as slowly it faded and became a black void in a constellation of distant lanthorns.

They doffed their turbans and cloaks and changed into European clothes, of which there was no shortage in the dress-up sack. Then they moved down into the skiff and began rowing across the river's current. Jack directed them towards the spot he'd picked out. Twice van Hoek insisted that they pause in midstream, backing water with the oars, while he threw a sounding-lead overboard to check the depth. Jeronimo spent the voyage winding a long strip of cotton around his head, lashing his jaw shut—a task not made any quicker by his tendency to think out loud. Thinking, for him, amounted to making florid allusions to Classical poetry until everyone around him had fallen into a stupor. In this case he was Odysseus and the mountains of Estremaduras were the Rock of the Sirens and this gag he was putting on himself was akin to the ropes by which Odysseus had bound himself to the mast.

"If the Plan is as leaky as that similitude, we are all as good as dead," Jack muttered, once the gag was finally in place.

The arrival of all four of them would cause a commotion in the Vagabond-camp, or so Jack had managed to convince the other nine. So he waded into shore from a few yards out, then (reckoning no one could see him, and he was safe from mockery) fell to his knees on the strand, like a Conquistador, and kissed the dirt.

Here was the moment when he would simply disappear. He had never traveled down this way, but he had heard of this camp: it was supposed to be small but rich, an entrepôt for the better sort of Vagabond. A few days' travel up the coast, then, a vast Vagabond city clung to the walls of Lisbon—from there, the way north was well-known. He reckoned that he could be in Amsterdam before winter, if he used himself hard. From there, the passage to London had always been easy, even when England and Holland had been at war—and now they were practically a single country.

This had been his secret Plan all along, and he'd spent more time working it out in his mind than he had following the numberless permutations and revisions of the Plan of Moseh. All he need do was walk up into the brush, and keep walking. This might be the doom of Moseh's plan, or not—but (to the extent he'd paid attention at all) he suspected it was doomed anyway. Nothing that relied upon so many people could ever work.

But Jack's feet did not move him thus. After a few moments he stood, and began to move carefully away from the river-bank, pausing every two steps to listen for movement or breathing around him. But he did not simply bolt. Somehow the commands that his mind sent toward his feet were blocked by his heart, or other organs. It might have been because others in the Cabal had shown him mercy and loyalty where Eliza had not. It might have been the smell of this Vagabond-camp and the wretched and loathsome appearance of the first people he spied, which reminded him of how poor and dirty Christendom was in general. Too, he was strangely curious to see how the Plan came out—somewhat like a spectator at a bear-baiting who was willing to pay money just to see whether the bear tore the dogs to bloody shreds, or the other way round.

But what really addled his mind—or clarified it, depending on one's point of view—was his certainty that the Duc d'Arcachon had become involved, somehow. This much had been obvious from the evolutions of the Plan during the nine months since they'd presented it to the Pasha. By hiding the fact that he could understand Turkish, Dappa had learned much.

Now, Jack really had no particular reason to care so much about said Duke—he was an evil rich man, but there were many of those. However, at one point when he'd been stupefied by Eliza, he had volunteered to kill that Duke one day. This was the closest he'd ever come to having a purpose in life (supporting his offspring was tedious and unattainable), and he had rather enjoyed it. D'Arcachon had now been so helpful as to reciprocate by attempting to hunt him down to the ends of the earth. Jack took a certain pride in that, seeing in it what his Parisian friend St.-George would call good form. To slink away now and live like a rat in East London, forever worrying about the Duke's homicidal intentions, would be bad form indeed.

When Jack and his brother Bob, as boys, had done mock-battle in the Regimental mess-hall in Dorset, they had been rewarded for showing flourish and *élan;* and if soldiers threw meat at boys for showing good form, might not the world shower Jack with silver for the same virtue?

Even so, Jack's mind was not entirely made up until he had been ashore for perhaps a quarter of an hour. He had been edging quietly round the nimbus of light cast by a Vagabond campfire, counting the people and judging their mood, straining to overhear snatches of zargon. Suddenly a silhouette rose up between him and the fire, no more than five yards away: a big man with a strangely mummified head, carrying a crossbow, drawn back and ready to shoot. It was Jeronimo—who must have been sent ashore, as part of the Plan, to hunt Jack through the woods and launch a bolt through his heart if he showed any sign of treachery.

This confirmed in Jack's mind that he really must remain faithful to the Plan. Not out of fear—he could easily slip away from Jeronimo—but out of sentimentality of the cheapest and basest sort. For Jeronimo wanted to go back to Estremaduras as badly as any man had ever wanted anything, and yet he was about to turn his back on that place, which was almost within sight, and go off to face (in all likelihood) death. It was the most abysmally poignant thing Jack had ever witnessed outside of a theatre, it made his eyes water, and it settled his mind.

So, slipping away from Jeronimo, he made his way into the firelight and (after calming the Vagabonds down just a bit) told them he was an Irishman who, along with several other Papists, had been press-ganged in Liverpool (this was likely and reasonable-sounding to the point of being banal) and that before setting out for America he and some of the other sailors wanted to pay their respects at Our Lady of Buenos Aires, a mariners' shrine inside the town (this was also very plausible, according to Jeronimo), and there would be a few *reales* in it for anyone who could sneak them into the town. This offer was taken up enthusiastically, and within the hour, Jack, Moseh, van Hoek, and Jeronimo (sans crossbow) were inside Sanlúcar de Barrameda.

Now Jeronimo and van Hoek went off towards a smoky and riotous quarter near the waterfront while Jack and Moseh went to reconnoiter in a finer neighborhood up the hill. Moseh had no particular idea where they were going and so they walked up and down several streets, looking in the windows of the white buildings, before slowing down in front of one that was adorned with a golden figure of Mercury. Remembering Leipzig, Jack instinctively looked up. Though there were no mirrors on sticks here, he did see the red coal of a cigar flaring and then blurring into a cloud of exhaled smoke— a watcher on the rooftop. Moseh saw it, too, and took Jack's arm and hustled him forward. But as they hurried past a window Jack turned his face toward the light and glimpsed a molten vision from his pox-scarred memories: a bald head surmounting wreaths of fat, looming above a table where several men—mostly fair-haired—sat eating and talking.

When they had gotten some distance down the street, Jack said: "I saw Lothar von Hacklheber in there. Or perhaps it was a painting of him, hung on the wall to preside over the table—but no, I'm sure I saw his jaw moving. No painter could've captured that cannonball brow, the furious eyes."

"I don't doubt you," Moseh said. "So van Hoek must have been right. Let us go and find the others." Moseh turned his steps downhill.

"What was the purpose of that reconaissance?"

"Before you make mortal enemies, it is wise to know who they are," Moseh said. "Now we know."

"Lothar von Hacklheber?"

Moseh nodded.

"I should've thought our enemy was the Viceroy."

"Outside of Spain, the Viceroy has no power. The same is hardly true of Lothar."

"Why does the House of Hacklheber have aught to do with it?"

Moseh said, "Suppose you live in a house in Paris. You have a water-carrier who is supposed to come once a day. Usually he does, sometimes he doesn't. Sometimes his buckets are full, sometimes they are half-empty. But your house is a large one and requires water in small amounts all the time."

"That is why such houses have cisterns," Jack said.

"Spain is a large house. It requires money all the time, to purchase goods from other countries, such as quicksilver from the mines of Istria and grain from the north. But its money arrives once a year, when the treasure-fleet drops anchor at Cadiz—or, formerly, here. The treasure-fleet is like the water-carrier. The banks of Genoa and of Austria have, for hundreds of years, served—"

"As money-cisterns, I see," Jack said.

"Yes."

"But Lothar von Hacklheber is not a Genoese name, unless I am mistaken," Jack said.

"About sixty years ago Spain went bankrupt for a time, which amounts to saying that the Genoese bankers did not get paid what was due them, and fell on hard times. Various mergings and marriages of convenience occurred as a result. The center of banking moved northward. That, in a nutshell, is how the Hacklhebers came to have a fine house in Sanlúcar de Barrameda. And, I would guess, a finer one in Cadiz."

"But Lothar is *here,*" Jack said, "meaning—?"

"He probably intends to take delivery of the silver pigs that we are going to steal tomorrow, and pay the Viceroy with something else—gold, perhaps, which would be better for one who wanted to spend much soon."

In a few minutes' nosing around the lower precincts, dodging brawlers and politely declining offers from whores, they located van Hoek and Jeronimo, who were posing, respectively, as a Dutch *commerçant* wanting to smuggle cloth to America on the next outgoing ship (which would have been illegal, because the Dutch were heretics), and his Spanish conspirator, who'd recently had his tongue cut out for some reason. They were in a tavern, conversing with a seamy-looking Spanish gentleman who, oddly enough, spoke good Dutch—a *cargador metedoro* who acted as a Catholic front man for Protestant exporters. Jack and Moseh walked past the table to let it be known that they were here, and then staked out the tavern's exits in case of trouble—which was not really much use, since they were still unarmed, but seemed like good form. There they waited for a while, as van Hoek conversed with the *cargador.* The conversation proceeded fitfully in that this Spaniard appeared to be participating in two card-games at once, and losing money at both. Jack could see he was one of those men who are not right in the head when it comes to gambling, and was tempted to join in and fleece him, but it did not seem meet just now.

Not that propriety had ever shaped Jack's actions in the past. But only now was it coming clear to him that he had forgone his one opportunity to escape, and thereby gambled his life upon the success of the Plan: a Plan that, only an hour ago, he was silently mocking as inconceivably complex, and dependent upon too many persons' exhibiting sundry rare virtues, such as cleverness and bravery, at just the right times. It was, in other words, a Plan that only desperate men would have come up with, a Plan in which it made no sense to participate unless one had no alternatives whatsoever. Jack had only gone along with it, to this point, because he'd always known he could jump ship before the worst parts of it were put into action.

Yet these others were not like John Cole.* Moseh and van Hoek and the others were more in the mold of John Churchill.†

Accordingly, Jack did not gamble, but contented himself with a tankard of *cerveza*—the first liquor that had passed his lips in something like five years—and simply gazing at the whores and barmaids, who were the first human females he had seen (other than the bat-like phantasms of Algiers) since Eliza. And his view of *her* had been obstructed by an incoming harpoon.

Suddenly van Hoek was on his feet, but he was smiling. A few moments later the four were outside on a tavern-street running along the foundations of the wall that faced the water—this looked as if sailors had been trying to undermine it, for hundreds of years, by burrowing tunnels through the stone with their urine.

"It is arranged," van Hoek said. "He believes that my cargo will arrive tomorrow, or possibly the next day, on a *jacht,* and that she will be in a desperate hurry to cross the bar and unload. He says that ships from the north do this all the time, and that he can bribe the soldiers to fire signals during the night-time."

They walked beneath Our Lady of Buenos Aires, which was disappointing: a fleck of stone in a bushel-sized niche. They departed the city the way they had entered into it, through a series of sneakings and petty briberies. An hour later they were in Bonanza, marking a path from the Vagabond-camp to the landward gates of the Viceroy's villa by slashing blazes on tree-trunks. The sky above Spain was just beginning to dissolve the faintest stars when they returned to the galleot. The Corsairs, and the other members of the Cabal, were giddy that they'd actually come back; then excited, knowing that the

---

* The East London mudlark who had succeeded in stealing an anchor only after sacrificing Dick Shaftoe to the Thames, and then passed out drinking so that he was apprehended the next day.

† Who was not especially pleasant to pass the time with, but who had a knack for getting things done.

Plan would actually go forward; then moody and apprehensive. They all tried to get some sleep, and most of them failed.

IN MID-MORNING, van Hoek began sending up spouts of pipe-smoke that swirled up through beams of hot sun and began migrating upriver—evidence of a breeze too faint for Jack to feel on his skin. This pleased everyone (because it suggested the brig could sail up from Cadiz today) except for van Hoek (who took it as a sign that the weather might be changing). The Dutchman spent the day pacing up and down the galleot's central catwalk, just like a slave-driver, save that instead of cracking a whip he was fussing endlessly with his pipe and gazing balefully at the sky. It was senseless, Jack thought, to exert so much grim attention on weather that was not really changing. Then—brushing past van Hoek in the aisle—he came close enough to make out some of his words, and understood that the Dutchman was not cursing the elements, but rather praying. And he was not praying for the success of the Plan, but for his own immortal soul. Van Hoek had rowed as a slave for years because he refused to turn Turk. The Cabal had managed to convince him, through long debates on the roof of the *banyolar,* that the Plan did not really amount to piracy, because the Viceroy's silver pigs were contraband to begin with, and the Viceroy himself a sort of landlubber Corsair. Finally van Hoek had accepted their arguments, or claimed to. But today he seemed to be in fear of hellfire.

Meanwhile, preparations were under way beneath the quarter-deck, and on those parts of the oar-deck that could be concealed under sails. The common slaves were encouraged to eat, drink, and rest. Members of the Cabal mostly unpacked certain strange goods, and organized them. In the rigging above, Corsairs adorned the masts and yards with a whorish gaudy array of banners and streamers.

The only pause in this work occurred in mid-afternoon, when the Viceroy's brig—flying its own gorgeous panoply of banners—came up the coast. At first, Moseh and several other Cabal-men were nearly frantic with anxiety that she would reach the Viceroy's palace with plenty of daylight remaining, and that the treasure would be unloaded this afternoon, before their eyes. But after firing a salute, which was answered by several guns on the city's walls, she paused outside the infamous *barra,* and sent out a longboat to take soundings, and then bided her time for an hour or two, allowing the tide to rise a bit. Then she raised more canvas and rode that tide up into the river. Van Hoek lay flat on the oar-deck, poked his spyglass out through an oar-lock, and gazed upon the brig with the dumb-founded intensity of a stalking cat.

Her progress up the river was no quicker. When she entered the estuary her sails went slack. After maundering about for a while she struck her canvas altogether. Then long sweeps felt their way out through ports in a lower deck. The brig's crew began to pull on them and she crawled towards Bonanza yawing and faltering in the confusion of the river's current and the tide.

This gave the *raïs,* Nasr al-Ghuráb, more than enough time to have the galleot's anchors weighed—a tedious job that involved eight slaves circling a windlass as free crewmen worked the messenger cable. The galleot got under way not long after the brig had passed by, and soon drew abeam of the larger, slower ship, then began to draw in closer as both vessels worked upriver. As soon as they had come within hailing distance, Mr. Foot ascended to the quarterdeck, garbed in a flame-colored silk caftan; raised a polished brass speaking-trumpet to his lips; and launched into a peroration. No one would ever guess he had been rehearsing it for months. His Spanish was so miserable that it actually caused Jeronimo (naked, and pulling on an oar) to flinch and writhe in agony. To the extent that Mr. Foot's words conveyed meaning at all, he was trying to convince the Spaniards on the Viceroy's brig that they really ought to be interested in certain splendiferous goods that he, Mr. Foot, the owner and captain of this galleot, had of late brought out of the Orient— particularly, carpets. He ordered a carpet to be hoisted up from a lug, as if it were a sail.

On the decks of the brig, now, a kind of split developed between labor and management: the ordinary seamen (at least, the ones not pulling on sweeps) seemed to find the ludicrous appearance of the galleot, and the spectacle of the incoherent Mr. Foot, a welcome entertainment. They began shouting rude things to him from various tops and ratlines, trying to provoke him. But the officers, true to form, were not amused, and kept shouting at Mr. Foot to keep his distance. Mr. Foot only cupped one hand to his ear and pretended not to understand, and ordered more and gaudier carpets to be hoisted from all available spars. They had loaded the galleot by making the rounds of the least reputable rug merchants of Algiers and hauling away their most immobile stock.

When only a few fathoms separated the galleot's oar-tips from those of the brig, the Spanish captain finally drew his cutlass and brought it down—which was the signal for some gunners in the forecastle to discharge their swivel-gun across the galleot's bow, showering the forward-most oar-slaves with a welcome spray of river water. Mr. Foot looked flabbergasted (which for him was not difficult) for a count of five, and then turned to his steersman and began waving his arms frantically—which, with the sunset radiant in the fabric of his caftan, made him look like a parrot with clipped wings being chased around a basket by a snake. The galleot fell away, to cheers and applause from the crew of the brig.

Gazing aft from his bench, Jack saw van Hoek at work, hidden beneath the quarterdeck, making sketches of the brig's rigging. These would be useful to Jack later, because he had heard more of these events than he'd seen. As they had drawn close to the brig, though, he had been able to look up into the spyglasses of two Spanish officers who had ascended to the maintop. If the Cabal hadn't already known that the brig was full of treasure, they might have guessed as much from this show of alertness. For their pains, the Spanish officers saw nothing more than a few dozen chained wretches, a very modest number of freemen, and nothing in the way of weaponry. More to the point, they got a good long look at the galleot: enough to fix it in their memories, so that they'd recognize it in an instant when they saw it again.

There was a bit of flailing about—enough to convince the captain of the Viceroy's brig that these rug-pedlars had been scared out of their wits—then the big drum began to thump a brisk tempo and the slaves applied themselves to their work. The galleot sprang upriver, leaving the brig behind. After about half an hour, the drum was silenced and the galleot dropped anchor once more, this time in a place some distance above Bonanza where the river oozed through brackish marshes. Jack was released from his irons immediately and climbed halfway up the mainmast, whence he could gaze back downriver and observe the final quarter-hour of the brig's several-month-long journey from Vera Cruz to Bonanza. At sunset she finally dropped anchor below the Viceroy's villa, and the sound of cheering and celebratory gunfire drifted up the river. A lighter came out from a quay to collect the Viceroy and his wife and take them home.

Later, Dappa, watching through a spyglass, announced that a guard had been posted on the quay: perhaps a dozen musketeers, as well as a swivel-gun for taking pot-shots at anything that came within range looking shootable. But other than a boat-load of what appeared to be luggage, nothing came out of the brig before sundown, which meant nothing would come out of it until sunup.

"Is there anything downriver?" van Hoek asked significantly.

"Sails, glowing like coals, out to sea, headed towards Sanlúcar—a small ship* flying Dutch colors," Dappa announced.

---

* "Ship" in this context meaning anything with three masts, square-rigged.

"Tomorrow, she'll be flying French ones," van Hoek said, "for that must be *Météore*—the Investor's *jacht*."

After dark, the Ten were free to move about, making no pretenses. The remaining slaves were distributed fairly among oars. Al-Ghuráb presented Jack with a long bundle wrapped in black cloth, and Jack was astonished to find it was his Janissary-sword. It was in a new scabbard, and it had been shined and sharpened, but Jack recognized it by the notch that had been made in its edge when it had collided with Brown Bess under Vienna. Apparently the weapon had lodged in some Corsair's treasure-hoard during Jack's captivity. Jack wanted in the worst way to belt it on, but it would only drown him if he tried to swim with it. So instead he put it to use by severing the galleot's anchor cables. This would put them in a most awkward position if ever they wanted to stop the vessel again, for any reason. But after the events of the coming hours, to stop anywhere in Christendom would be suicide. And they could not afford to devote the better part of an hour to toiling with hawsers and cables just now. Having finished this errand, Jack handed the sword to Yevgeny, who was packing a certain bag.

During the winter storm season, this lot of slaves had (weather permitting) spent two hours a day rowing the galleot around the inner harbor of Algiers, learning to pull in unison without the need for a pounding drum. Now they emerged from the marshes without a sound—or so Jack managed to convince himself as he squatted in the bows with Dappa, slathering his naked body with a mixture of ox-grease and lamp-black. The galleot was making excellent time, helped along by the first stirrings of the out-going tide. Up on the splintery foothold that served as the galleot's maintop, Vrej Esphahnian had taken over lookout duty. He claimed that he could now see currents of light flickering through the brush between Sanlúcar de Barrameda and Bonanza: hundreds (they hoped) of torch-carrying Vagabonds feeling their away through the darkness along the trails that the Cabal had marked out the night before, converging on the estate of the Viceroy, drawn by the rumor that, on the night of his return to the Old World, the Viceroy might hand out alms to the poor.

"Can you see anything of *Météore*?" van Hoek demanded.

"Maybe a lanthorn or two, out to sea beyond the bar—it is difficult to say."

"Really it does not matter, as long as she is out there, and was noted by the harbor-master before dark," Moseh said. "Assuming that 'Señor Cargador' is not too drunk to stand, he'll be pacing along the battlements now, wringing his hands over the fate of the cargo in that *jacht* and pestering the night watch."

"Is it time for us to go yet?" Jack asked. "I smell like one of my dear mother's charred rib-roasts, and would fain take a bath."

"This would be a good time, I think," van Hoek said.

"Please do not take it the wrong way," said Mr. Foot, "but once again I wish you Godspeed, and Dappa as well."

"This time I will accept it, or any other blessings sent my way," Jack said.

"We'll see you on the deck of that brig, or not at all," Dappa said. Then he and Jack jumped off into the river.

If Jack had been in his right mind, and if he had known he would one day become involved in a Plan such as this one, he never would have divulged, to his fellow oarsmen, the information that he had grown up a mudlark in East London, and that accordingly he had much experience swimming in estuaries, among anchored ships, in the dark, with a knife in his teeth. But that was all water under London Bridge. The last several months, as other members of the Cabal had refined the Plan or practiced other parts of it, Jack had been renewing his old skills, and imparting them to Dappa. The African had never been a swimmer for the simple reason that rivers in his part of the world were filled with crocodiles and hippopotami. But life had taught him to be adaptable—or as Dappa himself had put it, "I know that there are worse things than being wet, so let us get on with it."

He and Jack now swam down the Guadalquivir, pushing before them a very large barrel, denominated a tun, which had been tarred black and laden with a long piece of heavy chain so that only a hand's breadth extended above the surface. A circle of ox-hide was stretched over the top like a drum-head to prevent water from spilling in and sinking it altogether. Meanwhile the galleot backed water, fighting the river's current, and began to spin round in mid-channel so that it was pointed upstream. But it was consumed in the darkness, from Jack's and Dappa's point of view, before it had half-completed that maneuver.

They swam on, paddling like dogs to keep their heads out of the water, frequently reaching out with one hand to touch the tun, which like them was being swept by the river toward the sea. If the tun happened to ship water and begin sinking, they would want to know sooner rather than later, because it was tethered to each of their wrists by a short length of rope. The only way to judge their position was by gazing up at the lights of Bonanza, where Spaniards who had grown rich from America were just sitting down to dinner. Jack had learned, by now, to recognize the windows of the Viceroy's villa. Tonight every candlestick in the place was blazing, to celebrate the master's return. But Jack was satisfied to see that on the landward side, it was now besieged by a small army of Vagabonds.

They almost missed the brig. At the last minute they had to swim hard across the current to prevent being swept right past her. The combined flow of the great river and of the tide moved them much more quickly than they had appreciated. Jack and Dappa collided with the brig's larboard anchor cable hard enough to leave long rope-burns on their bodies. The tun toddled downstream for a few yards and reached the end of its tethers just short of thudding into the brig's stempost. Its momentum nearly yanked Jack and Dappa off the anchor cable, to which they were clinging like a pair of snails.

Jack hugged the taut anchor cable for a few minutes and simply breathed with his eyes closed, until Dappa lost patience and gave him a nudge. Then Jack let go and swam as hard as he could against the current, edging sideways a few inches at a stroke, until eventually he reached the opposite anchor cable. This slanted into the water about three fathoms away from the one that Dappa had, by now, made himself fast to with a rope around his waist. Jack did the same here, leaving his hands free. He could not see a thing but he guessed that Dappa had already removed his necessaries from the tun. Indeed, when Jack pulled on his wrist-tether the great barrel moved in his direction—though Dappa was maintaining tension on *his* tether, so that the tun remained stretched out in the current between them, staying well clear of the brig's stempost.

Soon the rim of the tun was in his grasp. Groping around atop a jumble of cold rough chain-links, Jack found a rope-end, and drew it out and hitched it around the anchor-cable using a sailor-knot he'd learnt to do with his eyes closed—just as Dappa had presumably done with the other end of the same rope. The brig's twin anchor-cables were now joined by a length of sturdy manila with plenty of slack in it. In the middle of that length was a spliced-in loop, called a cringle, and fixed to that cringle was one end of a chain, somewhat longer than the river was deep here (as they knew from van Hoek's soundings) and several hundred pounds in weight.

Stowed atop the chain were several implements—notably a matched pair of short axe-like tools, packed in oakum to keep them from clanking about "and waking the ducks," as van Hoek liked to phrase it. Jack removed these one by one and hung them about his shoulders on their braided cotton straps. When the only thing remaining in the tun was the chain, Jack tipped it so that the water of the Guadalquivir spilled in over its top. Within a few moments the weight of the chain had driven it down below the surface. Immediately the line he'd lashed round the anchor cable began to take that weight. It tightened, but his knotwork held fast and it did not slip down.

What he feared most, now, was a long wait. But he and Dappa had used up more time than the Plan called for, or else the galleot had moved too hastily, for almost immediately they began to hear shouting from upstream: several voices, mostly in Turkish but a few in Sabir (so that the Spaniards on the brig would overhear, and understand), shouting: "We are adrift!" "Wake up!" "We're dragging the anchor!" "Get the oarsmen to their stations!"

The watch on the brig heard it, too, and responded smartly by clanging a bell and hollering in nautical Spanish. Jack drew a deep breath and dove. Pulling himself hand-under-hand down the anchor cable, he descended until his ears hurt intolerably, which he knew would be a couple of fathoms deep—deeper than the draft of the onrushing galleot, anyway—and then began assaulting the cable with the edge of a dagger. He was working blind now, feeling one greased hand slide over another—a trick he'd worked out to prevent accidentally severing a finger. The blade made an avid seething noise as it severed the cable's innumerable fibers one by one and thousands by thousands.

One of the cable's three fat strands burst under his blade and unscrewed itself—he felt it slacken under his cheek, for he was gripping the cable between his head and shoulder, and felt the other two strands stretch and bleat as they took the load. He had no idea what might be going on twelve feet above. The galleot must be approaching, but it made no appreciable noise. Then there was a stifled thump, felt more than heard. He flinched, thinking it was the sound of the collision, and bubbles erupted from his nostrils. His eyes were still closed in the black water, and he was seeing phantasms: poor Dick Shaftoe being pulled up out of the Thames ankle-first. Was this how Dick's last moments had been? But such thoughts had to be banished. Instead he conjured up van Hoek on the roof of the *banyolar* weeks ago, saying: "When we are some ten fathoms away from the brig I'll strike the big drum once—just before we collide, twice. You'll hear this, and with any luck so will the Vagabonds ashore, so they can make more noise for a few moments—"

Jack sawed viciously at the cable and felt the yarns of the second strand spraying outwards like rays from the sun. He sensed the hull of the galleot over his head all of a sudden and felt real panic knowing it stretched, an impenetrable bulwark, between him and air. At once came two thuds of the drum. He hacked at the cable's one remaining strand and finally felt it explode in his hand like a bursting musket, the crack swallowed up in an incomparably vaster sound: a grinding drawn-out crunch like giants biting down on trees. The cut end of the cable snapped upwards and lashed him across the shoulder. But it did not whip round his neck, as had happened in many nightmares of recent months.

Something hard and smooth was pushing against the skin of Jack's back—the hull-planks of the galleot! He could not tell up from down. But those clinkers were lapped one over the next like shingles, and by reading their edges with one hand he knew instantly which way was down towards the keel, and which was up towards the waterline. Swimming, fighting his own buoyancy that wanted to stick him against the hull, he finally broke the surface and whooped in air, baying like a hound.

Above he heard shouting and panic, but no gunfire. That was good, it meant that the brig's officers had recognized them as the feckless rug-merchants seen earlier today, and not jumped to the conclusion that they were under attack. The Corsairs had lit lanterns up and down the length of the galleot shortly before the collision, so that Spaniards running up from belowdecks, rubbing sleep out of their eyes, would be presented with the reassuring sight of oarsmen who were still safely in chains, and free crew members who were unarmed and disorganized.

The galleot drifted away from Jack, or rather he drifted away from it. He squirmed round in the water to face the hull of the brig, which was onrushing—or rather the current was sweeping Jack toward it. And this was the single most terrifying moment of the Plan. The hull was angled up out of the water at the stem, to ride over waves, but it would ride over swimmers as easily. It was already blotting out the stars. The current would drive him underneath it if he did not gain some sort of purchase on it first. He would in effect be keel-hauled, and might or might not emerge a few minutes later, alive or dead, flayed by the carapace of barnacles that the brig had grown on her hull during her long Atlantic passage.

He had the means to save himself: a pair of boarding axes, taken out of the chain-barrel earlier. These looked like hatchets with long handles and small heads. Projecting out of the back of the head was a sharp curved pick, like a parrot's beak. Jack got a grip on one of these, twisted it round in his hand so it would strike pick-first, and wound up to assault the brig's hull. But the weight of his arm and of the axe drove the rest of him, including his head, under the surface. Drifting blind, he caught the hull on his chest and face. The barnacles dug into his skin like fish-hooks and the current knocked his legs out from under him, plastering his entire body up against the hull below the waterline. As a final, feeble gesture, the pick of his boarding axe might have pecked at the hull, a foot or so above water. But it found no purchase there. After a few moments he slipped down farther, the barnacles scoring his thighs, stomach, chest, and face as the current forced him under.

This was it, then: the exact keel-hauling he had worried about. He slipped again and the boarding axe tried to jerk itself out of his grasp. It must have caught on something—perhaps the edge of a single barnacle, or a caulked gap between planks. He pulled on it and it held for a moment, then started to break loose; its grip on the hull was not firm enough to pull his head up out of the water. But he had a second boarding axe that was trailing on a neck-rope and bumping uselessly against the hull. As Jack had nothing else to occupy the time while he was being flayed and drowned, he pawed water until he got a grip on that boarding axe, then brought it back, fighting that damned current, and drove it into the hull as hard, and as high, as he could. A sharp crunch of barnacle-shells was followed by the sweet thunk of iron driving into wood. Jack pulled with both hands, now, then brought the first axe away and struck with it, and finally managed to get his face up through the roiling crest of the bow-wave. He drew half a breath of air and half of water, but it was enough. Two more vicious strikes with the boarding axes brought his head and chest up out of the water. He wrapped the axes' braided tethers round his wrists and hung there for a minute or two, just breathing.

BREATHING SEEMED INFINITELY MORE FINE and more momentous than anything that could possibly be going on around him, but after a while the novelty wore off and he began to wake up and to take stock of his situation.

The lights along the shore were gone, which meant that they were adrift in the channel as planned. Probably they were still gliding past the no man's land between Bonanza and Sanlúcar de Barrameda. And yet the brig was still pointed upstream and her anchor cables were still stretched taut, because of that heavy chain she was dragging along the river-bottom. A person on the brig, preoccupied with having just been collided with by a rug-galleot, might not notice the drift.

Abovedecks, which might have been a different continent for all it mattered to Jack, some kind of acrid discussion was going on between Mr. Foot and a Spaniard (Jack assumed it was the ranking officer on the brig). The latter seemed to think that he was greatly humiliating Mr. Foot before his crew by lecturing to him on certain elementary facts about how properly to anchor a ship in an estuary. Mr. Foot, far from being embarrassed, was doing his best to elongate the argument by almost but not quite understanding everything that the other said. His ability to misapprehend even the simplest declarations had been driving his acquaintances into frenzies of annoyance for years. Finally he had discovered a practical use for it.

Meanwhile the oarsmen on the galleot were putting on a great show of indolence, *very* gradually getting themselves settled into position to row away from the brig. But certain decorative encrustations on the galleot's high stern had become entangled in supremely functional matters on the brig's bowsprit, such as the martingale (a spar projecting vertically downwards from about the middle of the bowsprit) and the stays that held it in place. The disentanglement of the two vessels took some time, and was noisy, which was good because a few yards away the Cabal was hard at work doing things that, in other circumstances, would have waked the dead.

The brig had a sort of blind spot (or so they hoped) around her stempost. The stempost was nothing more than the foremost part of the keel, where it broke out of the water and slanted up to support the figurehead, the bowsprit, and the railing around the ship's head. This part of the ship was made for dashing against the sea as she fought through weather, and so was devoid of complications such as hatches and ports, which tended to be weak and leaky. Furthermore it was sharply undershot, and difficult to see from the deck above. One could get a clear look at it only by going to the head, kneeling down, and thrusting one's head down and out through the shitehole (which had been deemed unlikely by the architects of the Plan) or by clambering out onto the bowsprit to work the rigging associated with the spritsails. Those sails would not come into use tonight, but this posed a danger nonetheless, as several seamen had gone out there to work on the disentanglement.

But there was nothing Jack could do about that, so he tried to concentrate on matters nearer to hand. There was a veritable crowd down here! Yevgeny, Gabriel, and Nyazi had jumped from the galleot moments before the collision, and had evidently had better luck with their boarding axes than Jack—perhaps because they had not been half-drowned to start out with. They had converged on the stempost, which was one enormously thick piece of solid wood, and after pulling in bags of tools and weapons tethered to their ankles they had driven spikes into that wood with muffled hammers and hung little rope slings from the spikes, just big enough to serve as footholds. Jack let go of one of his axes, flailed out, and grabbed an empty one. With some thrashing around he was able to get a foot into it. Yevgeny, also coated in black grease, was barely visible above, standing in another one of these foot-loops. He offered Jack a hand, and pulled him all the way up out of the water. Jack and Yevgeny were now plastered up against the hull together, just to one side of the stempost. Yevgeny thumped Jack's shoulder five times, meaning "we are five." So on the opposite side of the stempost, Gabriel and Nyazi must have established footholds of their own. Apparently Dappa had avoided the fate of keel-hauling, too.

There followed an hour of something approaching boredom. The general circumstances were anything but boring, of course, yet there was nothing for Jack to do except hang there and await death or deliverance. Yevgeny thrust a sack into Jack's hand. Jack found a pair of breeches inside, and a belt, and the Janissary-sword. The galleot worked itself free and rowed off, driven on a fresh gale of invective from the supremely irritated Spaniards—who almost immediately realized that they were being pushed downriver by the tidal current, and were already more than a mile from the Viceroy's villa. They tried the anchor cables and found them taut, but not taut enough. Then they tried bringing them in, and found them fouled by the mysterious lashings of Jack and Dappa. Shouts and thuds reverberated dimly through the hull-planking as the crew were ordered belowdecks to man the sweeps.

But they had barely begun to row, there in the broad estuary below Sanlúcar de Barrameda, when the galleot—which had been stalking them through the night—shot out of the darkness, moving with a speed that the pudgy, barnacle-fouled brig could only dream of, and came on almost as if making for a head-on collision. It diverted to starboard at the last possible moment (to the relief of Jack and the others, who would have been crushed), folded her oars on that side, and skimmed down the side of the brig, shearing away half of her sweeps, and leaving her there like a bird with one wing shot off.

Now this, of course, was an overt attack, the brig's first inarguable proof that she was under assault by pirates. So her captain moved just as van Hoek had predicted: He ordered that a cannon be run out and fired, as a signal to whomever was keeping watch over the harbor from the battlements of Sanlúcar de Barrameda.

But a single cannon-shot in the night-time is an ambiguous statement, and difficult to interpret—especially when what it is trying to say is something extremely implausible, such as that a Viceroy's treasure-brig is being assaulted by a Corsair-galley in the midst of one of Spain's most important harbors. And no sooner had the brig fired its distress-shot than another ship, a bit farther out to sea, fired *several:* this was *Météore,* the *jacht* that had appeared out of the Gulf towards sunset, flying Dutch colors. In response, a ragged patter of signals were fired from the town's batteries. This had been done at the request of the *cargador metedoro,* who had been talked into believing that he had incoming goods on that *jacht* and did not want to wake up tomorrow morning to discover that she had run aground on the bar.

The Viceroy's brig, spinning helplessly in the swirling currents, was swept out over the bar and into the Gulf of Cadiz without anyone in the town's having a clear idea of what was going on.

There was a half-moon that night, and as they drifted into the Gulf Jack watched it chasing the lost sun towards the western ocean, all aglow on its underside, like a ball of silver heated on one side by the burning radiance of a forge. It was shrouded in ripped and frayed tissues of cloud that stole some of its light: new weather coming in from the ocean, which was bad for them, because it meant that tomorrow their pursuers would have wind.

And tonight their prey were beginning to have it: a chilly breeze coming in straight from the Atlantic. Seamen had already gone to stations on the upperdeck to raise sails and get under way as best they might. Jack sensed that the Spaniards were breathing easier now: The ride down the dark river among anchored ships and over the shallow bar had been dangerous, but now they had a lot of water under their keel, and they had a bit of wind. After a few minutes' preparations they could raise some sails and move out a bit farther from the town, to eliminate the risk of running aground, and wait for daylight.

They were unaware that the galleot, after shearing away their oars, had rowed out into the Gulf and transformed herself into another kind of ship entirely. Stowed in the aisle that ran up her center, between the benches, had been an uncommonly large carpet, rolled up into a bundle some ten yards long. But that carpet (if all had gone according to the Plan) was now jetsam, unrolled and adrift in the Gulf of Cadiz somewhere. Its former contents—a tree-trunk of straight-grained fir from the slopes of the Atlas Mountains, spokeshaved to a smooth needle shape, bolstered with iron hoops, and tipped with a barbed iron spearhead—had been brought forward and mounted on the nose of the galleot, somewhat like a bowsprit, but nearer to the waterline, and not so encumbered with stays and martingales. That iron spearhead should even now be skimming over the waves at a velocity of about ten knots, with fifty tons of galleot behind it, and one Spanish treasure-brig dead ahead.

The general plan was to strike the brig on her quarter, which meant towards the stern, where large cannons were somewhat less plentiful. The only drawback was that this made it impossible for the five boarders who were clinging to the stempost to see the galleot approaching (to the extent they could see *anything* by the flat chalky light of the setting half-moon). But the sudden screaming from the other end of the ship gave them a good clue that the time was now. They waited for a moment, as many footsteps receded, and then finally swung their grapples up and over the rail. Each man pulled on his rope until he felt the flukes catch in something (no way of guessing what, or how sturdy it might be) and after testing it with a few sharp tugs, abandoned his foot-loop and gave himself up to his rope. Because the hull flared out overhead they all swung far away from it, and swept to and fro above the water like pendulums.

Jack's arms nearly gave way, for they had grown stiff in the fresh breeze coming off the ocean, and he slid down a short distance before finally whipping a leg round the rope and trapping it between shins and ankles. After that it was just rope-climbing, which was something he had done far too much of in his life. Consequently he surprised himself by being the first boarder to tumble over the rail and feel the blessing of wood against the soles of his feet.

He was standing in that part of the ship known as the head, gazing down her length. The moonlight was horizontal and so the masts, the rigging, and a few standing figures were columns of silver, but the deck was a black pool, completely invisible. A vast commotion was underway astern. Several pistols were suddenly discharged, making Jack startle. At the same moment he heard a gaseous eruption from very nearby, and turned to discover a Spaniard seated on a bench with his breeches round his ankles, gazing up, moonfaced with astonishment, at Jack. He made as if to stand, but Jack simply fell into him, driving one shoulder into the man's abdomen to prevent him from calling out, shoving his buttocks into the hole he'd been sitting on, and wedging him into place with gleaming knees projecting into the sky. The Spaniard threw out one hand like a grapple on a rope, reaching for his coat, neatly folded on the bench, where a loaded pistol lay. But out came the Janissary-sword. Jack put its point against the Spaniard's belly. "I'll have that, señor," he said, and took the pistol up in his free hand.

The other four boarders were just struggling over the rail. The timing was apt, because now there was a mighty splintering pop from astern. One of the benefits of having been a galley-slave of the Barbary Corsairs for several years was that Jack knew and recognized that sound: It was a large iron spear-head piercing the hull of a European ship. And it was followed a moment later by a crash that made them all hop to keep their balance.

Nyazi had clambered aboard farther astern than anyone else, and was all of a sudden blind-sided by a Spaniard who came at him silently with a dagger. The weapon lunged forward and met only air. Nyazi had somehow sensed the attack and gone elsewhere. Then he was back, swinging his cutlass, and felled his attacker with a frantic back-handed slash.

Then Dappa, Gabriel, Yevgeny, and Jack all moved at once, without discussion. Some parts of the Plan were complicated, but not this one. A brig had but two masts, and each mast had a platform halfway up called a top, reachable by clambering up a ladderlike web of shrouds. At this moment the fore-top was unoccupied. Jack handed the pistol to Dappa, who tucked it into his belt and began climbing. Yevgeny was loading some pistols he had brought with him (it being impractical to keep them loaded, and their powder dry, when they were bumping about in a partly submerged bag). Jack and Gabriel worked their separate ways astern along the larboard and starboard rails respectively, Jack swinging his Janissary-sword and Gabriel a sort of queer two-handed scimitar of Nipponese manufacture, on loan from some Corsair-captain's trophy case. They were severing not heads, but haul-yards: the lines, running in parallel courses through large blocks, that were used to hoist up the yards from which the ship's sails were all suspended.

Finally, then, Jack and Gabriel began to ascend the main shrouds, converging on the maintop where three Spanish sailors had belatedly realized that they were under siege. One of these drew out a pistol and pointed it down at Jack, but was struck in the arm by a pistol-ball from Dappa, shooting from a few yards away on the fore-top. A moment later Yevgeny fired from down on the deck, and apparently missed—assuming he was even trying to hit anything. For the two unhurt sailors on the maintop were dumbfounded to find themselves under fire from the bows of their own ship, only moments after being rammed astern, and it was probably better to have them stunned and indecisive than wounded and angry. Jack and Gabriel gained the maintop at about the same time, disarmed the two unhurt sailors at sword-point, and encouraged them, in the strongest possible terms, to descend to the deck. Yevgeny tossed up a couple of muskets, which were not even loaded yet.

Not that it mattered. For Jeronimo, standing back on the quarterdeck of the galleot, had seen Jack's and Gabriel's exploits. Raising to his lips the same speaking trumpet that Mr. Foot had used, only hours before, to try to sell carpets to the Viceroy, he now delivered a flowery oration in noble Spanish. Jack did not know the language that well, but caught the obligatory reference to Neptune (in whose jurisdiction they now were) and Ulysses (representing the Cabal) who had gone into a certain cave (the estuary of the Guadalquivir) that turned out to contain a Cyclops (the Viceroy and/or his brig) and escaped by poking said Cyclops in the eye with a pointed stick (no metaphor here; they had done it literally). It would have sounded magnificent, booming out of that trumpet and across the water, except that it was commingled with bewildering spates of profanity that made the sailors edge backwards and cross themselves.

Jeronimo identified himself, then, as El Desamparado Returned from Hell—as if he could have been any other. He reminded the brig's captain that he was now adrift in the Gulf with a completely disabled ship and a skeleton crew, that his tops were now commanded by boarders armed with muskets, and, in case anyone was insufficiently scared, he told the lie that ten pounds of gunpowder were encased in the hollow head of the battering-ram now buried deep in the brig's vitals, not far away from the powder magazine, and that it could easily be detonated at the whim of who else but El Desamparado.

Jack had the benefit of watching this performance from an exclusive private loge, as it were, at the back of the theatre. He noticed a sigh run through the brig's crew when the fell sobriquet of El Desamparado first rang from the trumpet. The battle turned at that instant. When the gunpowder was mentioned, pistols and cutlasses began clattering to the deck. Jack judged that the captain, and one or two officers, were willing to fight—but it scarcely mattered, because the crew, exhausted from the passage of the Atlantic, were not keen on giving their lives to make the Viceroy slightly richer, when the taverns and whorehouses of Sanlúcar de Barrameda glowed so warmly from the shore a couple of miles away.

Six Barbary Corsairs—now resplendent in turbans and scimitars—came aboard the brig, along with the other members of the Cabal. Two of the Corsairs remained on the galleot, prowling up and down the aisle with whips and muskets to remind the oar-slaves that they were yet in the power of Algiers. The brig's crew were disarmed and herded up to the poop deck, and several swivel-guns were charged with double loads of buckshot and aimed in their direction, manned by Corsairs or Cabal-members with burning torches. The officers were put in leg-irons and locked into a cabin guarded by a

Corsair. They were joined by Mr. Foot, who made them chocolate; as it was felt by many in the Cabal that the best way to keep several Spanish officers in a helpless stupor was to have Mr. Foot engage them in light conversation.

Jeronimo led Nasr al-Ghuráb, Moseh, Jack, and Dappa belowdecks to the shot-locker, and hacked off a giant padlock, and flung its hatch open. Jack was expecting to see lead cannonballs, or nothing but rat-turds, because life had trained him to expect grievous disappointments and double-crossings at every turn. But the contents of that locker gleamed as only precious metals could—and gleamed yellow.

Jack thought of finding Eliza in the hole beneath Vienna.

"Gold!" Dappa said.

"No, it is a trick of the light," Jeronimo insisted, moving his torch to and fro, experimenting with different positions. "These are silver pigs."

"They are too regular in their shape to be pigs," Jack pointed out. "Those are bars of refined metal."

"Nonetheless—silver it must be, for gold is not produced by the mines of New Spain," said El Desamparado doggedly. Now Jack had a small insight concerning Excellentissimo Domino Jeronimo Alejandro Peñasco de Halcones Quinto: He had a tale worked out in his head, like the tales written in the moldy books of his ancestors. The tale was the only way for him to make sense of his life. It ended with him finding a hoard of silver pigs, tonight, here. To find anything other than silver pigs was to suffer some sort of cruel mockery at the hands of Fate; finding gold was as bad as finding nothing.

But Jack's reflections, and the Caballero's denials, were interrupted by a sharp noise. The *raïs* had taken a coin from his belt-pouch and tossed it onto one of the bars. It spun and buzzed, a disk of silvery white on a slab of yellow. "That is a piece of eight—if you have forgotten the color of silver," said Nasr al-Ghuráb. "What it lies on is gold."

Then, for a long time, none of them uttered a sound. Even Jeronimo's tongue had been silenced.

Moseh cleared his throat. "I think Jews have no word for this," he said, "because we do not expect to get so lucky. But Christians, I believe, call it Grace."

"I would call it blood money," said Dappa.

"It was *always* blood money," Jeronimo said.

"You told us, once, that the silver mines of Guanajuato were worked by free men," Dappa reminded him. "This, being gold, must come from the mines of Brazil—which are worked by slaves taken from Africa."

"I have watched you shoot a Spanish sailor not half an hour ago—where were all your scruples then?" Jack asked.

Dappa glared back at him. "Overcome by a desire not to see my comrade get shot in the face."

Jeronimo said, "The Plan does not allow for finding gold where we expected silver. It means we have thirteen times as much money as we reckoned. Most likely we will all end up killing each other—perhaps this very night!"

"Now your demon is talking," said al-Ghuráb.

"But my demon always speaks the truth."

"We will continue with the Plan as if this were silver," Moseh said nervously.

Jeronimo said, "You are all filthy liars, or imbeciles. Obviously there is no reason to go to Cairo!"

"On the contrary: There is an excellent reason, which is that the Investor expects to meet us there, to claim his rake-off."

"The investor *himself*!? Or did you mean to say, the Investor's *agents*?" Jack said sharply.

Moseh said, "It makes no difference," but exchanged a nervous look with Dappa.

"I heard one of the Pasha's officials joking that the Investor was going to Cairo to hunt for Ali Zaybak!" said the *raïs*, trying to inject a bit of levity. The attempt failed, leaving him bewildered, and Moseh on the verge of blacking out.

"Why do we waste breath speaking of the Frog?" Jeronimo demanded. "Let the whoreson chase phant'sies to the end of the earth for all we care."

"The answer is simple: He has a knife to our throats," said al-Ghuráb.

"What are you talking about?" Jack asked.

"That *jacht* did not sail down here only to provide a diversion," said the Corsair. "He could have dispatched any moldy old tub for that purpose."

"The Turk makes sense," Dappa said to Jack in English. "*Jacht* means 'hunter,' and that is the swiftest-looking vessel I've ever seen. She could sail rings around us—firing broadsides all the while."

"So *Météore* is poised to kill us, if we play any tricks," Jack said, "but how will she know whether or not we need to be killed?"

"Before we row away tonight, we are to sound a certain bugle-call. If we fail—or if we sound the wrong one—she'll fall on the galleot at first light, like a lioness on a crate full of chickens," the Turk answered. "Likewise, we are to give certain signals to the Algerian ships that will escort us along the coast of Barbary, and to the French ones that will accompany us through the eastern Mediterranean."

"And you are the only man who knows these signals, I suppose," Dappa said, finding amusement here, as he did in many odd places.

"Hmph . . . what's the world coming to when a French Duke cannot bring himself to trust a merry crew such as ours?" Jack grumbled.

"I wonder if the Investor knew, all along, that the brig would contain gold?" Dappa said.

"I wonder if he will know *tomorrow*," said Jack, staring into the eyes of the *raïs*.

Al-Ghuráb grinned. "There is no signal for that information."

Moseh, clapping his hands together, now said, "I believe the *larger* point our captain is making is that even if *some* of us . . ." glancing towards Jeronimo, "are inclined to turn this unexpected good fortune into a pretext for intrigues and skullduggery, we'll not even have the opportunity to scheme against; betray; and/or murder one another unless we get the goods off this brig *fast* and commence rowing."

"This is merely a postponement," Jeronimo sighed. Obviously, it would take many days to cheer him up. "The inevitable result will be double-crossings and a general bloodbath." He reached down with both hands and heaved a gold bar off the top of the hoard with a grunt of effort.

"One," said Nasr al-Ghuráb.

Jeronimo began trudging up the stairs.

Moseh stepped forward and wrapped his fingers around a bar; bent his knees; and pulled it up off the stack. "It is not so different from pulling on a wooden oar," he said.

"Two," said the *raïs*.

Dappa hesitated, then forced himself to reach out and put his hands on a bar, as if it were red hot. "White men tell the lie that we are cannibals," he said, "and now I am become one."

"Three."

"Don't be gloomy, Dappa," Jack said. "Recall that I could've run away last night. Instead I listened to the Imp of the Perverse."

"What is your point?" Dappa muttered over his shoulder.

"Four," said al-Ghuráb, watching Jack grab a bar.

Jack began to mount the stairs behind Dappa. "I'm the only one of us who had a *choice*. And—never mind what the Calvinists say—no man is truly damned until he has damned himself. The rest of you are just like trapped animals gnawing your legs off."

> What when we fled amain, pursu'd and strook
> With Heav'ns afflicting Thunder, and besought
> The Deep to shelter us? This Hell then seem'd
> A refuge from those wounds: or when we lay
> Chain'd on the burning Lake? that sure was worse.
> — MILTON,
> *Paradise Lost*

They left the ram embedded in the brig's buttock and rowed off about an hour before dawn as one of the Corsairs played a heathen melody on a bugle. Most of their previous cargo and ballast had been thrown overboard as the gold bars had been passed from hand to hand up out of the brig's shot-locker and across the deck and slid down a plank into the galleot. As sunrise approached, the breeze off the ocean consolidated itself into a steady west wind. First light revealed a colossal wall of red clouds that began somewhere below the western horizon and reached halfway to the stars. It was a sight to make sailors scurry for safe harbor, even if they were not aboard an undecked, anchorless row-boat fleeing from the iniquity of Man and the wrath of God.

The distance to the Strait of Gibraltar was seventy or eighty miles. With no wind to fill their sails that would take longer than a day; in these circumstances, it could be done before nightfall.

Van Hoek payed no attention to those clouds, which were many hours in their future; he was gazing at the waves around them, which began to develop little white hats as the sun and the wind came up. "They will be able to make six knots," he said, referring to the Spanish ships that would be chasing them, "and *that* beauty will be able to make eight," nodding at *Météore*, which was becoming visible a few miles in the distance. Jack and everyone else knew perfectly well that in these circumstances—the hull recently scraped and waxed, and combining the use of sails and oars—the galleot could likewise sustain eight knots.

They might, in other words, have been able to flee from the *jacht* and make a run for freedom on this very day—but first they would have had to fight the Corsairs on board. And at the end of the day they'd have to rely on other Corsairs to protect them from Spanish vengeance. So they adhered to the Plan.

The first several miles, from Sanlúcar de Barrameda to Cadiz, might have been an ordinary morning cruise, no different from their training-voyages around Algiers. But *Météore*—now flying French colors—raised as much sail as she could, and began to shadow them, a mile or two off to the west. Perhaps she only wanted to observe, but perhaps she was waiting for an opportunity to board them, and seize all the proceeds, and send them back into slavery or to David Jones's Locker. So they made as much speed as they could, and were already running scared, and rowing hard, when they came in sight of Cadiz. Two frigates sailed out from there and challenged them with cannon-shots across the bows—evidently messengers had galloped down from Bonanza during the night.

The day then dissolved into a long sickening panic, a slow and stretched-out dying. Jack rowed, and was whipped, and other times he whipped other men who were rowing. He stood above men he loved and saw only livestock, and whipped skin off their backs to make them row infinitesimally harder, and later they did the same to him. The *raïs* himself rowed, and was whipped by his own slaves. Whips wore out and broke. The galleot became an open tray of blood, skin, and hair, a single living body cut open by some pitiless anatomist: the benches ribs, the oars digits, the men gristle, the drum a beating heart, the whips raw dissected nerves that spun and whorled and crackled through the viscera of the hull. This was the first hour of their day, and the last; it quickly became too terrible to imagine, and remained thus without letting up, forever, even though it was only a day—just as a short nightmare can seemingly encompass a century. It passed out of time, in other words, and so there was nothing to tell of it, as it was not a story.

They did not begin to be human again until the sun went down, and then they had no idea where they were. There were not as many men in the galleot as there had been when the sun had come up and they had dipped dry oars into the whitecaps as the bugle played. No one was really sure why. Jack had a vague recollection of seeing bloody bodies going over the gunwales, pushed by many hands, and of an attempt that had been made to throw him overboard, which had come to naught when he had begun thrashing around. Jack assumed that Mr. Foot could not have survived the day, until later he heard ragged breathing from a dark corner of the quarterdeck, and found him huddled under some canvas. The rest of the Cabal had all survived. Or at least they were all present. The meaning of survival was not entirely clear on a day like this. Certainly they would never be the same. Jack's similitude about trapped beasts gnawing their legs off had been intended as a sort of jest, to make Dappa feel less guilty, but today it had come true; even if Moseh, Jeronimo, and the others were still breathing, and still aboard, important pieces of them had been chewed off and left behind. That night, it did not occur to Jack that, for some of them at least, this might amount to an improvement.

Raindrops were coming out of the dark, and they lay on their bellies on the benches letting the water cleanse their wounds. The galleot was bucking in huge pyramidal seas that rushed at her from various directions. Some were afraid they would run aground on the shore of Spain. But van Hoek—once he was able to speak again, and had finished praying to God for forgiveness and redemption—said he was certain he had spied Tarifa off to port, gleaming in the sunlight of late afternoon. This meant that the weather was driving them into the open Mediterranean; that the Corsair-countries were on their starboard; and that they were now a part of Spain's glorious past.

Off Malta
LATE AUGUST 1690

"SINCE BEFORE THE TIME of the Prophet my clan has bred and raised camels on the green foothills of the Mountains of Nuba, in Kordofan, up above the White Nile," said Nyazi, as the galleot drifted languorously through the channel between Malta and Sicily. "When they are come of age, we drive them in great caravans down into Omdurman, where the White and the Blue Nile become one, and thence we follow tracks known only to us, sometimes close to the Nile and sometimes ranging far out into the Sahara, until we reach the Khan el-Khalili in Cairo. That is the greatest market of camels, and of many other things besides, in the world. Sometimes too we have been known to follow the Blue Nile upstream and cross over the mountains of Gonder into Addis Ababa and points beyond, even ranging as far as sea-ports where ivory-boats set their sails for Mocha.

"Unlike my comrade Jeronimo I am not one to tell flowery stories, and so I will merely relate that on one such journey, many of the men in my caravan fell ill and died. Now we are great fighters all. But we were so weakened that, in a mountain pass, we fell prey to a tribe of savages who have never heard the word of the Prophet; or if they have, they have disregarded it, which is worse. At any rate, it was their custom that a young man could not come of age and take a wife until he had castrated an enemy and brought his orchids of maleness to the chief shaman. And so every man of my clan who had not died of the disease was emasculated, except for me. For I had been riding behind the caravan to warn of ambushes from the rear. I was on an excellent stallion. When I heard the fighting, I galloped forward, praying that Allah would let me perish in battle. But by the time I drew near, all I heard was screaming. Some of it was the cries of the men being castrated, but, too, I heard my own brother—who had already suffered—shouting my name. 'Nyazi!' he cried, 'Fly away, and meet us at the Caravanserai of Abu Hashim! For henceforth you must be the husband of our wives, and the father of our children; the Ibrahim of our race.'"

This engendered a respectful silence from each of the Ten, save one. Jack held his cupped hands in front of him like scale-pans, bobbled them, and let one drop. "Beats having your nuts cut off by wild men," he said.

At this Nyazi flew into a rage (which was something Nyazi did very well) and launched himself on Jack more or less like a leopard. Jack fell on his arse, then rolled onto his back—which hurt, because his back was still one large scab. He managed to get his knees up in Nyazi's ribs, then used the strength of his legs to shove him off. Nyazi sprawled flat on *his* back, screamed just as Jack had done, and there was pinned to the deck by Gabriel Goto and Yevgeny. It was several minutes before he could be calmed down.

"I offer you my apologies," he said, with extreme gravity. "I forgot that you have suffered an even worse mutilation."

"Worse? How do you reckon?" asked Jack, still lying flat trying to think of a way to stand up without doing any more damage to his back.

Nyazi copied Jack's gesture of the bobbling scale-pans. "My clansmen could still perform the act—but they did not wish to. You wish to, but cannot."

"Touché," Jack muttered.

"Because of this, I see, now, that you were not accusing me of cowardice, and so I no longer feel obligated to kill you."

"Truly you are a prince among camel-traders, Nyazi, and no man is better suited to be the Ibrahim of his race."

"Alas," Nyazi sighed, "I have not yet been able to impregnate even a single one of my forty wives."

"Forty!" cried several of the Cabal at once.

"Counting the several I already had; ones we had acquired in trade during this trip and sent home via a different route; and those of the men who had been made eunuchs by the savages, the number should come to forty, give or take a few. All waiting for me in the foothills of the mountains of Nuba." Nyazi got a faraway look in his eye, and an impressive swelling down below. "I have been saving myself," he announced, "refusing to practice the sin of Onan, even when *ifrits* and succubi come to tempt me in the night-time. For to spill my seed is to diminish my ferocity, and weaken my resolve."

"You never made it to the Caravanserai of Abu Hashim?"

"On the contrary, I rode there directly, and there waited for my poor clansmen to catch up with me. I understood it might be a long wait, as men who have suffered in this way naturally tend to avoid long camel rides. After I had been there for two nights, a caravan came down out of the upper White Nile laden with ivory. The Arabs of the caravan saw my skill with camels, and asked if I would help them as far as Omdurman, which was three days to the north. I agreed, and left word with Abu Hashim that I would be back to meet my brothers in less than a week.

"But on the first night out, the Arabs fell on me and put a collar around my neck and made me a slave. I believe they intended to keep me forever, as a camel-driver and a butt-boy. But when we got near Omdurman, the Arabs went to a certain oasis and drew up not far from a caravan headed by a Turk. And here the usual sort of negotiation took place: The Arabs took the goods they wished to trade (mostly elephant tusks) and piled them up halfway between the two camps, then withdrew. The Turks then came out and inspected the goods, then made a pile of the stuff they wished to trade (tobacco, cloth, ingots of iron) and withdrew. It went back and forth like this for a long time. Finally I was added to the Arabs' pile. Then the Turks came out and took me away along with the Arabs' other goods, and the cursed Arabs did likewise with the goods of the Turks, and we went our separate ways. Eventually the Turks took me as far as Cairo, and there I tried to escape—for I knew that my clansmen would be at the Khan el-Khalili during a certain time of year, which is late August. Alas, I was caught because of the treachery of a fellow-slave. Later I tore a leg from a stool and beat him to death with it. The Turks could see that I would be trouble as long as I remained in Cairo, and so I was traded to an Algerian corsair-captain who had just rowed into port with a cargo of blonde Carmelite nuns."

Jack sighed. "I am never one to turn down a yarn. But I detect a certain repetitive quality in these galley-slave narrations, which forces me to agree with (speaking of blonde slave-girls) dear Eliza, who took such a dim view of the whole practice."

"But as I recall from *your* narrations—which were not devoid of a certain repetitive quality, by the way—" Dappa said, "she objected on *moral* grounds—not because it led to monotonous storytelling."

"I, too, could probably dream up some highfalutin *grounds* if all I had to pass the time was embroidery and bathing."

"I did not realize that pulling on an oar posed such a challenge to your intellect," Dappa returned.

"Until *la suette anglaise* delivered me from the French Pox, I had no intellect at all. When I'm rich and free, I'll come up with a hundred and one reasons why slavery is bad."

"A single good one would suffice," Dappa said.

Feeling the need for a change of subject, Jack turned towards Vrej Esphahnian, who had been squatting on his haunches smoking a twist of Spanish tobacco and watching the exchange.

"Oh, mine is banal compared with everyone else's," he said. "As you may recall, my brother Artan sent out letters to diverse places, inquiring about the market for ostrich plumes. What came back convinced him that our family's humble estate might be bettered if we established a trading-circuit to Northern Africa. I was dispatched to Marseille to make it so. From there, by buying passage on small coastal vessels, I tried to work my way down the Balearic coast of Spain towards Gibraltar, which I supposed would be a good jumping-off place. But I did not appreciate that the Spanish coast from Valencia downwards is infested with Moorish pirates, whose forefathers once were the lords of al-Andalus. These Corsairs knew the hidden coves and shallows of that coastline as well as—"

"All right, all right, you have said enough to convince me that it is, as you said, the usual galley-slave tale," Jack said, strolling over to the rail and stretching—very carefully. He picked up a bulging skin and squirted a stream of stale water into his mouth, then stood up on the bench to contemplate the rock of Malta, which was drifting by them a few miles to starboard. He had just realized that it was a very small island and that he'd better look at it while he had the chance. "What I meant was: How did you end up on my oar?"

"The ineffable currents of the slave-market drove me to Algiers. My owner learned that I had some skills beyond oar-pulling, and put me to work as a bookkeeper in a market where Corsairs sell and trade their swag. The winter before last, I made the acquaintance of Moseh, who was asking many questions about the market in *tutsaklar* ransom futures. We had several conversations and I began to perceive the general shape of his Plan."

"He told you about Jeronimo, and the Viceroy?"

"No, I learned of that on the same night as you."

"Then what do you mean when you say you understood his plan?"

"I understood his basic principle: that a group of slaves who, taken one by one, were assigned a very low value by the market, might yet be worth much when grouped together cleverly . . ." Vrej rolled up to his feet and grimaced into the sun. "The wording does not come naturally in this bastard language of Sabir, but Moseh's plan was to synergistically leverage the value-added of diverse core competencies into a virtual entity whose whole was more than the sum of its parts . . ."

Jack stared at him blankly.

"It sounds brilliant in Armenian." Vrej sighed.

"How came *you* to be at the bottom of the slave-market?" Jack asked. "I know your family was not the wealthiest, but I should've thought they'd pay anything to ransom you from Algiers."

Vrej's face stopped moving, as if he had spied a Gorgon atop one of Malta's cliffs. Jack gathered that the question was an impolite one, by Armenian standards.

"Never mind," Jack said, "you are right, it makes no difference *why* your family would not, or could not, pay your ransom." Then, after there'd been no word from Vrej in quite a while: "I'll not ask again."

"Thank you," said Vrej, as if forcing the words past a clenched garrotte.

"Nonetheless, it is remarkable that we ended up on the same oar," Jack continued.

"Algiers in wintertime is lousy with wretched slaves, trying to dream their way to freedom," Vrej admitted, in a voice still tight and uneven. But as he continued talking, the anger, or sadness, that had possessed him for a few minutes slowly drained away. "I reckoned Moseh for another one of these at first. As one conversation led to the next, I perceived he was a man of intelligence, and began to think that I should throw in my lot with him. But when I learned that he had acquired a new bench-mate named Jack Shaftoe, I looked on it as a sign from God. For I owe you, Jack."

"*You* owe *me!?*"

"And have, ever since the night you fled Paris. On that night my family and I incurred a debt to you, and if necessary we will travel to the end of the world, and sell our souls, to make good on it."

"You can't be thinking of those damned ostrich plumes?"

"You left them in our trust, Jack, and made us your commission-agents in the matter."

"They were trash—the amount of money is trivial. Please do not consider yourself under any obligation . . ."

"It is a matter of principle," Vrej said. "So I hatched a Plan of my own, every bit as complex as the Plan of Moseh, but not nearly so interesting. I'll spare you the details, and tell you only the result: I was traded to your oar, Jack, and chained to you in *fact*—though chains of iron are nothing compared to the chains of debt and obligation that have fettered us since that night in Paris in 1685."

"That is extremely civil of you," Jack said. "But the only thing in all the world that makes me feel more ill at ease than being obliged, is some other man's feeling obliged to me—so when we reach Cairo I'll accept a few extra pounds of coffee, or something, to cover the proceeds from the sale of those ostrich-plumes, and then you and I can go our separate ways."

AFTER RIDING THE front of a storm through the Strait of Gibraltar, they had spent a couple of days riding out the gale in the Alboran Sea, the anteroom of the Mediterranean. When the weather had settled down they had sailed southeast, steering toward the peaks of the Atlas Mountains, until they'd picked up the Barbary Coast not far from the Corsair-port of Mostaganem. They had not put in there—partly because they had no anchors, and partly because Nasr al-Ghuráb seemed to be under strict instructions not to make contact with the world until they had reached their destination. But a few miles up the coast from Mostaganem, where a river came down off the north slopes of the Atlas and spilled into the sea, al-Ghuráb had caused a certain flag to be run up the mast. Not much later a bergantine had come rowing out of a hidden cove and had drawn alongside them, carefully remaining a bow-shot away. There had been some shouting back and forth in Turkish, and the galleot's skiff had been sent over, carrying two corsairs and Dappa, and collected kegs of fresh water and some other victuals. This bergantine had then shadowed them on the slow progress along the coast to the harbor of Algiers. Slow because they had almost never laid hands on the oars; no one wanted to, most were not fit to, and the *raïs* had not asked them to.

At Algiers most of the regular oar-slaves had been transferred into the Peñon, the squat Spanish fortress in the middle of the harbor, and locked up, for the time being, in places where they could not tell the tale of what they had seen. Empty wooden crates had come back, and the Cabal had busied itself packing the gold bars into them and stuffing straw in between so that they would not clank. Only after the crates had been nailed securely shut had fresh—and ignorant—oar-slaves been brought aboard.

They had also acquired a new drum. For on the day following their deliverance from Spaniard and storm, Jack Shaftoe had made a great ceremony of tossing the old one overboard. It had been a large wooden barrel-half with a cowhide stretched over the top, the hair still on it except where it had been worn away from being pounded. It was mottled white and brown like an unlabelled map, and it had bobbed stubbornly alongside them for a while, a little world loose in the sea, until Jack had stove it in with an oar. Meanwhile, Jeronimo had solemnized it in his own way: looking about at the gore that lined the hull, and the exhausted and half-flayed rowers, he had said, "We are all blood brothers now." Which he had probably intended as some sort of sacrament-like benediction. For his part, Jack could see any number of grave drawbacks to being part of the same family as Jeronimo. But he had kept these misgivings to himself so as not to mar the occasion. Jeronimo had included, among his new brothers, all of the galley-slaves who were not members of the Cabal, and promised that he would use his share of the proceeds to ransom them. This had produced only eye-rolling from those slaves who could understand what he was saying. As days had gone by, his promises had flourished like mushrooms after an autumn rain, until he had laid out a scheme for constructing or buying an actual three-masted ship, manning it with freed slaves, and setting out to found a new country somewhere. But as they had inched across the map towards Algiers, a depression had settled over him, and he'd gone back to predictions of a bloodbath in Egypt—or possibly even Malta.

Accompanied by another, more heavily armed galleot, they had left Algiers behind—they hoped forever. They had rowed briskly eastwards, passing by one small Corsair-port after another until they had traversed the mouth of the Gulf of Tunis and reached the Ras el Tib, a rocky scimitar-tip pointed directly at Sicily, a hundred miles to the northeast. Here they had offloaded all but a dozen of their oar-slaves and then used their sails to take them out into deep water—the first time they'd lost sight of land since the night of their escape from Bonanza. The *raïs* had immediately ordered the galleot's Turkish colors struck, and had raised French ones in their stead.

THUS DISGUISED—if a new flag could be considered a disguise—they now sailed under the guns of various medieval-looking fortresses that had been built, by various occult sects of Papist knights, on crags and ridges looking north across the strait. No cannonballs were fired in their direction, and after a few hours, when they rounded a point and gazed into the Grand Harbor of Malta, they understood why: for a whole French fleet was riding at anchor there beneath the white terraces and flowered walls of Valletta. Not just merchant ships—though there were at least a dozen of those—but men-of-war, too. Three frigates to serve as gun-platforms, and a swarm of tactical galleys.

And—as van Hoek was first to notice—there was also *Météore*. Evidently she had passed through the Strait of Gibraltar behind them and then made directly for Malta, to join up with the fleet, and await the galleot. Jack borrowed a spyglass to have a look at the *jacht,* and was rewarded by a view of a new flag that had been run up her mizzen-mast. It was a banner emblazoned with a coat of arms that he'd last seen carved in bas-relief on the onrushing lintel of a door in the Hôtel Arcachon in Paris. "I would know that arrangement of fleurs-de-lis and Neeger-heads anywhere," he announced. "The Investor is here in person."

"He must have come down via Marseille," van Hoek remarked.

"I *thought* I smelled a fish gone bad," Jack said.

Likewise, their galleot was noticed and identified immediately. Within a few minutes a longboat had been sent out from *Météore,* rowed by half a dozen seamen and carrying a French officer. This fellow clambered aboard the galleot and made a quick inspection—just enough to verify that the crew was orderly and the vessel seaworthy. He handed the *raïs* a sealed letter and then departed.

"I wonder why he just doesn't *take* us," Yevgeny muttered, leaning on the rigging and gazing at all those warships.

"For the same reason that the Pasha did not do so when we were in the harbor of Algiers," Moseh said.

"The Duke's interests in that Corsair-city are deep," Jack added. "He dares not queer his relations with the Pasha by violating the terms of the Plan."

"I would have anticipated a more thorough inspection," said Mr. Foot, arms crossed over his caftan as if he were feeling a chill, and glancing uneasily at a gold-crate.

"He knows we got *something* out of the Viceroy's brig—and that it was valuable enough to make us risk our lives by tarrying in front of Sanlúcar de Barrameda for several hours, transshipping it to the galleot. If we'd found *nothing* we'd have fled without delay," Jack said. "And that is as good as an inspection."

"But does he know *what* it is?" Mr. Foot asked. They were within earshot of their skeleton crew of oar-slaves and so he had to speak obliquely.

"There is no way he *could*," said Jack. "The only communication he's had from this boat is a bugle call, which was a pre-arranged signal, and I doubt that they had a signal meaning *thirteen*." *Thirteen* was a sort of code meaning *twelve or thirteen times as much money as we expected.*

"Still, we know that the Pasha of Algiers sent out messages on faster boats than ours, to all the ports of the Levant, telling the masters of all harbors to deny us entry."

"All except for *one*," Yevgeny corrected him.

"Might he not have sent a message here to Malta, telling about the thirteen?"

Dappa now came strolling along. "You are forgetting to ask a very interesting question, namely: Does the Pasha know?"

Mr. Foot appeared to be scandalized; Yevgeny, profoundly impressed. "I should *imagine* so!" said Mr. Foot.

Dappa said, "But have you noticed that, on every occasion when the *raïs* has parleyed with someone who does not know about the thirteen, he has been at pains to make sure I am present?"

"You, who are the only one of us who understands Turkish," Yevgeny observed.

Jack: "You think al-Ghuráb has kept the matter of the thirteen a secret?"

Yevgeny: "Or wishes us to *think* that he has."

Dappa: "I would say—to *know* that he has."

Mr. Foot: "What possible reason could he have for doing such a thing?"

Dappa: "When Jeronimo gave his 'blood brothers' speech, and all the rest of you were rolling your eyes, I chanced to look at Nasr al-Ghuráb, and saw him blink back a tear."

Mr. Foot: "I say! I say! *Most* fascinating."

Jack: "For the Caballero, who is every inch the gentleman, it was no easy thing to admit what the rest of us have all known in our bones for so long: namely that we have found our natural and rightful place in the world here, among the broken and ruined scum of the earth. Perhaps the *raïs* was merely touched by the brutally pathetic quality of the scene."

Dappa: "The *raïs* is a Corsair of Barbary. His sort enslave Spanish gentlefolk for *sport*. I believe he intends to make common cause with us."

Mr. Foot: "Then why hasn't he come out and said as much?"

Dappa: "Perhaps he has, and we have not been listening."

Yevgeny: "If that is his plan, it depends entirely on what happens here in Malta. Perhaps he waits to announce himself."

Jack: "Then it all pivots on that letter the Frenchman brought—and speaking of that, I believe we are delaying the ceremony."

Nasr al-Ghuráb had retreated to the shade of the quarterdeck with the other members of the Cabal, who were looking toward them impatiently. When Jack and the others had arrived, the *raïs* passed the letter around so that all could inspect the splash of red wax that sealed it. Jack found it to be intact. He had half expected to find the arms of the Duc d'Arcachon mashed into it, but this was some sort of naval insignia. "I cannot read," said Jack.

When the letter had made its way back to the *raïs* he broke the seal and unfolded it. "It is in Roman characters," he complained, and handed it to Moseh, who said, "This is in French." It passed into the hands of Vrej Esphahnian, who said, "This is not French, but Latin," and gave it to Gabriel Goto, who translated it—though Jeronimo hovered over his shoulder cocking his head this way and that, grimacing or nodding according to the quality of Gabriel's work.

"It begins with a description of very great anguish in the houses of the Viceroy and the Hacklhebers on the day following our adventure," said the Jesuit in his curiously accented Sabir; though he was nearly drowned out by Jeronimo, who was laughing raucously at whatever Gabriel had glossed over. Gabriel waited for Jeronimo to calm down, then continued: "He says that his friendship with us is strong, and not to worry that every port in Christendom is now alive with spies and assassins seeking to collect the huge price that has been put on our heads by Lothar von Hacklheber."

Which caused several of them to glance nervously towards the Valletta waterfront, judging whether they might be within musket-, or even cannon-range.

"He is trying to scare us," Yevgeny snorted.

"It is just a formality," Jack put in, "a—what's it called—?"

"Salutation," said Moseh.

Gabriel continued, "He says he has received a message from the Pasha, carried on a faster boat, to the effect that everything has gone exactly as planned."

"Exactly!?" said Moseh, a bit unsettled, and he searched al-Ghuráb's face. The *raïs* gave a little shrug and stared back at him coolly.

"Accordingly, he sees no reason to depart from the Plan now. As agreed, he will lend us four dozen oar-slaves, so that we can keep pace with the fleet on its passage to Alexandria. Victuals will be brought out on a small craft in a few hours. Meanwhile the *jacht* will send out a longboat to collect the *raïs* and the ranking Janissary—these will go to pick out the oar-slaves."

Now all began talking at once. It was some time before their various conversations could be forged into one. Moseh did it by striking the new drum, which silenced them all; they'd been trained to heed it, and it reminded them once more that they were still enrolled as slaves on the books of the *hoca el-pencik* in the Treasury in Algiers.

Moseh: "If the Investor does not learn of the thirteen until Cairo, he'll demand to know why we did not tell him immediately!" (shooting a reproachful look at the *raïs*). "It will be obvious to him that we sought to play out a deception, and later lost our nerve."

Van Hoek: "Why should we care what the bastard thinks of us? It's not as if we intend to do business with him in the future."

Vrej: "This is short-sighted. The power of France in Egypt—especially Alexandria—is very great. He can make it go badly for us there."

Jack: "Who says he's ever going to find out about the thirteen?"

Jeronimo laughed with sick delight. "It begins!"

Moseh: "Jack, he expects his payment in silver pigs. We don't have any!"

Jack: "Why give the son of a bitch anything?"

Van Hoek, grimly amused: "By *continuing to* conceal what the *raïs* has *thus far* concealed, we are already talking about screwing the investor out of twelve-thirteenths of what would otherwise come to him. So why make such scruples about the remaining one-thirteenth?"

Moseh: "I agree that we should either screw the Investor thoroughly, or not at all. But I would argue for completely open dealings. If we simply follow the Plan and give the Investor his due, we will all be free, with money in our purses."

Jeronimo: "Unless *he* decides to screw *us.*"

Moseh: "But that is no more likely *now* than it was before!"

Jack: "I think it was *always* very likely."

Yevgeny: "We cannot tell the Investor of the thirteen *here, now.* For then he will say that we tried to hide it earlier, as part of a plan to screw him, and use it as a pretext to seize the galleot."

Van Hoek: "Yevgeny is an intelligent man."

Jack: "Yevgeny has indeed read the Investor's character shrewdly."

Moseh clamped his head between the palms of his hands, massaging the bare places where forelocks had once grown. For his part, Vrej Esphahnian looked ill at ease to the point of nausea. Jeronimo had gone back to dire predictions, which none of them even heard any more. Finally Dappa said, "Nowhere in the world are we weaker than we are here and now. It is not the time to reveal great secrets."

In this, it seemed, he spoke for the entire Cabal.

"Very well," Moseh said, "we'll tell him in Egypt, and we'll hope he'll be so pleased by unexpected fortune that he'll overlook past deceptions." He paused and heaved a sigh. "Now as for the other matter: Why does he want both the *raïs* and the ranking Janissary to come out in the longboat to collect the slaves?"

"It is a routine formality," said the *raïs*. "For him to do otherwise would be very odd."*

"Remember, we are speaking of a French Duke. He will hew to protocol no matter what," Vrej agreed.

"Only one of us can pass for a Janissary. I will go," Jack said. "Get me a turban and all the rest."

"EVEN IF THAT DUKE STARED me full in the face, I doubt he would recognize me," Jack said. "My face was covered most of the time that I was in his house—otherwise, he never would have mistaken me for Leroy. I only let the scarf fall at the very end—"

"But if there was any truth *whatsoever* in your narration," said Dappa carefully, "it was a moment of high drama, exceeding anything ever staged in a theatre."

"What is your point?"

"In those short moments you may have made a vivid impression in the Duke's memory."

"I should hope so!"

"No, Jack," Moseh said gently, "you should hope *not*."

Only Moseh, Dappa, and Vrej knew that the Investor had for some years been combing every last fen, wadi, and reef of the Mediterranean for the man identified, by Muslims, as Ali Zaybak. Moseh and Dappa had followed Jack to the dress-up sack to fret and wring their hands. Vrej was completely unconcerned, though: "In those days Jack had long hair, and a stubbled face, and was heavier. Now with his head and face shaved, and a turban, and with him so gaunt and weather-tanned, I think there is little chance of his being recognized—provided he keeps his trousers on."

"What possible reason could there be to take them off?" Jack demanded hotly.

THE LONGBOAT CAME OUT. Jack and the *raïs* climbed in. Dappa came, too, as interpreter—for they had agreed that it would be unwise for Jack to let it be known that he spoke Vagabond-French. The longboat took them not to *Météore* after all, but to a part of the harbor

---

* It was the rule, on Corsair-galleys, that the *raïs* was in command of the ship and its crew, while the Agha of the Janissaries was in command of the fighters.

where no fewer than half a dozen war galleys of the French Navy were tied up on either side of a long stone pier. The longboat was tied up at the pier's end by a couple of barefoot French swabbies. The tide was quite low, so Jack, Nasr al-Ghuráb, and Dappa took turns ascending a ladder to the pier's sun-hammered top and there met the same young officer who had earlier brought them the letter. He was a slender fellow with a high nose and an overbite, who bowed slightly, and greeted them without really showing respect. Introductions were made by an aide. The officer was identified as one Pierre de Jonzac.

"Tell Monsieur de Jonzac that he has the smallest nostrils of any human who ever lived," Jack said in the most vulgar Sabir he could muster, "which must serve him well in his dealings with his master."

"The Agha of the Janissaries greets you as one warrior to another," Dappa said vaguely.

"Tell him that I am grateful that he has personally taken responsibility for getting us and our cargo to Egypt," the *raïs* said.

French was exchanged. Pierre de Jonzac stiffened. His pupils widened and his nostrils shrank at the same time, as if they shared a common drawstring. "He understandeth little, and resenteth much," Dappa said out of the side of his mouth.

"If we do not take our time, here, and pick out a good complement of slaves, why, we will fall behind the convoy, and Dutch or Calabrian pirates will end up with our cargo—" began the *raïs*.

"—of whose nature we are ignorant," added Jack.

"—but which the Duke appears to value highly," finished Dappa, who could see for himself how this was going. When he said all of this in French, Pierre de Jonzac flinched, and looked as if he were about to order them flogged. Then he seemed to think better of it.

De Jonzac spun on his heel and led them down the pier. The hulls of the French galleys were low as slippers and narrow as knives and could not even be seen from here, but each one had—as well as a pair of masts—both a fore- and a stern-castle, meant to carry her pay-load of cannons and Marines as high above the foes' as possible. These castles—which were all decorated, gilded, and painted in the finest Barock style—seemed to hover in the air on either side of the pier, bobbing gently in the swell. It was a strangely peaceful scene—until they followed de Jonzac to the edge of the pier and looked down into one of the galleys: a stinking wood-lined gouge in the water, packed with hundreds of naked men, chained by their waists and ankles in groups of five. Many were dozing. But as soon as faces appeared above them, a few began to shout abuse, and woke up all the rest. Then they were all screaming.

"Rag-head! Come down here and take my seat!"

"You have a pretty ass, nigger! Bend over so we can inspect!"

"Where do you want to row today?"

"Take me! My oar-mates snore!"

"Take him! He prays too much!"

And so forth; but they were *all* shouting as loud as they could, and shaking their chains, and stomping the deck-planks so that the hull boomed like a drum.

"*Je vous en prie!*" said Pierre de Jonzac, extending a hand.

It came clear that they were expected to take a few slaves from each galley. A rite soon took shape: They'd cross a gangplank from the pier to the sterncastle and parley with the captain, who would be expecting them, and who would have helpfully culled out a few slaves—always the most miserable tubercular specimens on his boat. Nasr al-Ghuráb would prod them, inspect their teeth, feel their knees, and scoff. This was the signal to begin haggling. Using Dappa as his intermediary, al-Ghuráb had to reject *galériens* one by one, beginning always with the most pitiable, and these would be sent down into the ever-boiling riot of Vagabonds, smugglers, pickpockets, deserters, stranglers, prisoners of war, and Huguenots chained to the benches below. Then it would be necessary to pick out a replacement, which involved more haggling, as well as endless resentful glares, verbal abuse, bluffing, and stalling from the petty officers—called *comités*—who controlled the oar-deck, and tedious un-chaining and re-chaining. The longboat could only ferry ten or so slaves out to the galleot at a time, so five loads, and as many round trips, were needed.

Al-Ghuráb's strategy had been that he would wear the French down by taking his time and choosing carefully; but as the day went on it became obvious that time was on the side of the captains of the galleys, who relaxed in their cabins, and of Pierre de Jonzac, who sipped Champagne under a giant parasol on the pier, while Jack, Dappa, and al-Ghuráb toiled up and down the gangplanks smelling the bodies and enduring the curses of the *galériens*. They picked out perhaps two boat-loads of reasonably good slaves before they began to lose their concentration, and after that they were more concerned with getting to the end of the day with some vestiges of dignity. Jack led many a *galérien* down the aisle that day. Some of them had to be prodded down the entire length of a one-hundred-fifty-foot ship to be offloaded. Each of those who was staying behind felt bound to say *something* to the one who was being taken off:

"I hope the Mohametans bugger you as often as you've whined about your wife and kids in Toulouse!"

"Send us a letter from Algiers, we hear the weather is very nice there!"

"Farewell, Jean-Baptiste, may God go with you!"

"Please don't let the Corsairs ram us, I have nothing against them!"

It was on the very last trip of the day that Jack—standing in the aisle of a galley while the *raïs* argued with a *comité*—was dazzled, for a moment, by a bright light shone into his eye. He blinked and it was gone. Then it was back: bright as the sun, but coming from within this galley. The third time, he held up an arm to shield his eyes, and squinted at it sidelong, and perceived that it was coming from the middle of a bench near the bow, on the starboard side. He began walking towards it—creating a sensation among the *galériens,* who had all noticed the light on his face and were screaming and pounding their benches with amusement.

By the time he'd reached the forward part of the oar-deck, Jack had lost track of the light's source—but then one more flash nicked him again, then faded and shrank to a little polygon of grey glass, held in a man's fingers. Jack had already guessed it would be a hand-mirror, because these were commonly found among the few miserable effects that galley-slaves were allowed to have with them. By thrusting it out of an oar-lock, or raising it high overhead, the owner could see much that would otherwise be out of his view. But it was cheeky for a *galérien* to flash sunlight into the eyes of a free man standing in the aisle, because this was most annoying, and might be punished by breakage or confiscation of the mirror.

Jack looked up into the eyes of the insolent wretch who had been playing tricks on him, and recognized him immediately as Monsieur Arlanc, the Huguenot, whom he had last seen buried in shit in a stable in France.

Jack parted his lips; Monsieur Arlanc raised a finger to his, and shook his head almost imperceptibly. Then he swiveled his eyes in their sockets, leading Jack's gaze over the gunwale and across the choppy black water of the harbor, off in the general direction of Sicily. Jack's attention rolled aimlessly about the harbor, like a loose cannonball on a pitching deck, until it fell into a hole, and stopped. For he could clearly see a sort of heathen half-galley riding the swells at the harbor's entrance, but obliterated, every so often, by a flash of light just like the one that had come from the hand-mirror of Monsieur Arlanc.

The half-galley was none other than the Cabal's galleot.

Jack's first thought was that the new slaves must be staging a mutiny and that his comrades were signalling for help. But the flashes emanated not from the quarterdeck, where the Cabal would make their last stand in a mutiny, but from a point down low and amidships: one of the oar-locks. It must be one of the new *galériens*, probably chained safely to his bench by now, but reaching out with a hand-mirror to flash signals to—whom, exactly?

Jack turned around to face the pier-side, which had fallen into deep shade as the sun had swung around over the high crags and castles of Malta. By blocking the sun's glare with his hand he was able to see a vague spot of bluish light prowling around the pier's shadows. The mirror was held in an unsteady hand on a rocking boat far away, and so the spot of light frequently careered off into the sky or plunged into the waves. But it would always come back, and work its way carefully down the pier, and then dart upwards at the same place. After this had occurred several times, Jack raised his sights to the top of the pier and saw Pierre de Jonzac sitting there at a folding table with a quill in one hand, staring out to sea. Each mirror-flash lit him up with a ghastly light, and after each one he glanced down (his wig moved) and made a mark (his quill wiggled).

"I suppose you think this was all predestined to happen, monsieur," said Jack, "but I like to believe you had some say in the matter, and therefore deserve my thanks."

"There is no time to talk," Arlanc said. "But know that the men they have sent you are very dangerous: murderers, conspiracists, phanatiques, looters of bakeries, outragers of women, and locksmiths gone bad."

"I would rather have a Huguenot or two," Jack mused, scanning the other four members of Monsieur Arlanc's team. The headman, who sat on the aisle, was a Turk.

"It is a noble conception, Jack, but not destined to happen. They will never agree to it—it is not part of their plan."

"What about God? Doesn't He have a plan?"

"I believe only that God preserved me until now so that I could show you what I have showed you," said Monsieur Arlanc, glancing up towards de Jonzac frozen in another pallid flash, "and thereby repay you for your generosity in the stables. What on earth are you doing, by the way?"

"It is a long story," Jack said, taking a step away—for al-Ghuráb had finally picked out the last slave, and was calling to him. "I'll explain it when we reach Egypt."

Monsieur Arlanc smiled like a saint on the gridiron, and shook his head. "This galley will never reach Egypt," he said, "and my mortal body is, as you can see, one with it." He patted the chain locked round his waist.

"What, are you joking? Look at the size of this armada! We'll be fine."

Arlanc closed his eyes, still smiling. "If you see Dutch colors, or English, or—may God forbid it—both combined, make for Africa, and stop not until you have run aground."

"And then what? Go on foot across the Sahara?"

"It would be easier than the journey we begin tomorrow. God bless you and your sons."

"Likewise you and yours. See you at the Sphinx." Jack stormed off down the aisle. For once, the *galériens* did not hound him the whole way. They seemed sober and deflated instead, as if they had all guessed at the subject of Jack's and Monsieur Arlanc's conversation.

THE VOYAGE FROM MALTA to Alexandria was a rhumb-line a thousand miles long. The Dutch hit them halfway, five days into the passage, somewhere to the south of Crete. Jack supposed that if he were God watching the battle from Heaven it might make some kind of sense: the onslaughts of the Dutch capital ships, the stately maneuvers of the French ones, and the slashing zigzags of the galleys would form a coherent picture, and seem less like an interminable string of dreadful accidents. But Jack was just a mote on a galleot that was evidently considered too small to be worth attacking, or defending. *Now* they understood why the shrewd Investor had never insisted on having the loot taken off the galleot and loaded into a man-of-war: He must have suspected that half or more of his capital ships would end up on the bottom of the Mediterranean.

Every time a French frigate was struck by a Dutch broadside, a vast cloud of spinning planks, tumbling spars, and other important materials would come flying out the opposite side and tear up the water for a hundred yards or more. After this had happened several times the ship would stop moving and a galley would be brought in to tow it from the line of battle, somewhat like a servant scurrying into the middle of a lively dance-floor to drag away a fat count who had passed out from drink.

The galleot, for its part, wandered about aimlessly, like a lost lamb searching for its mother in a flock that was being torn apart by wolves. Van Hoek spent the day up on the maintop, cheering for the Dutch, and occasionally shouting explanations—so cryptic and technical as to be useless—of what was going on to the others. Very early the Cabal had met to discuss surrendering to the Dutch forthwith.

But there was much that could go awry with that plan. At the very best it would mean surrendering all of the gold, and many in the Cabal did not share van Hoek's natural affinity for the Dutch side of things anyway.

The galley to which Monsieur Arlanc was chained survived most of the battle without serious damage. Then (according to van Hoek) she was called in to ram a certain Dutch ship. Along the way she came under fire from others, and a bomb apparently went off in her sterncastle, starting a fire that, a few minutes later, detonated her powder magazine and essentially blew open her stern. Very quickly her bow began to point up in the air, her ram sweeping relentlessly upwards like the hand of a clock. The *galériens* in the forward half of the ship—presumably including Monsieur Arlanc—let go their oars and hooked their arms over their benches, though some of them broke loose, so that skeins of slaves dangled and swung like strings of trout hanging before a fishmonger's stall.

"Let us row in that direction," Jack said, "because it is no more dangerous than what we are doing anyway, and because it is good form."

There was profound apprehension on the faces of other members of the Cabal. Vrej Esphahnian opened his mouth as if to lodge an objection but then a large cannonball hummed past, a couple of yards over their heads, confirming Jack's point and sparing them many tedious deliberations. So Nasr al-Ghuráb brought the tiller around and they made for the sinking galley.

Meanwhile Jack went down among the oar-slaves—but not before asking Yevgeny to fetch a certain large hammer, and an anvil.

On the night before their departure from Malta, when most of the fleet's ordinary seamen had been ashore carousing and/or receiving Holy Communion, and most of its officers attending formal dinners, the Cabal had armed themselves with blunderbusses and then worked their way down the aisle, unchaining one pair of slaves at a time and searching them. Turbans, head-rags, and loincloths had been shaken out and groped, jaws and butt-cheeks pried apart, hair combed through or cut off. Jeronimo had scoffed at this—more so after being told it was all because of a warning from a "heretic Frog slave." But he went silent as soon as he saw a complete set of fine lock-picks being drawn out through the anal sphincter of a stocky middle-aged *galérien* named Gerard. And he remained silent as an increasingly astounding variety of hardware was produced, like conjurors' tricks, from diverse orifices and bits of clothing. "If I see a granado coming from some man's nostril I will be no more surprised than I am now," he said. Finally a mirror was found, and then another—confirming Jack's story. Nyazi was uncharacteristically pensive, and said: "Honor dictates that we send the Investor to Hell forthwith, along with as many of his clan as we can get our daggers into." But El Desamparado flew into a rage that did not abate until he had ranted for the better part of an hour and made many trips up and down the length of the galleot flailing away with a *nerf du boeuf.*

Now these *galériens* were no more impressed by Jeronimo's prowess with the whip than they were by his Classical allusions.* At the height of his rage Jeronimo was no more or less prepossessing than any *comité* of the French Navy. It was, rather, the odd comments he made when he calmed down that convinced them all that El Desamparado was a madman, and scared them all into silence and submission.

In any event, the French padlocks that had secured the slaves when they'd been brought over had been tossed into the bilge, and their chains heated up in the galleot's portable brazier and hammered shut, just in case any lock-picks had escaped the search.

Now, as the galleot rowed through the wreckage of the French flotilla with clouds of grapeshot and lengths of smoking chain flying overhead, Jack fished one of those padlocks out of the bilge. As Yevgeny parted the chain of Gerard with a few terrible hammer-blows, Jack worked his way through the giant key-ring that the French had handed over to them, and got that padlock open. Then Jack, Yevgeny, Gerard, and Gabriel Goto got into the skiff and rowed the last few yards to the slowly sinking galley.

Hundreds of chained men had already been pulled below the water, and perhaps two score remained above it. The bench to which Monsieur Arlanc and his four companions were joined by a common chain, and from which they'd all been dangling for the last quarter of an hour, was only a couple of yards above the water now, and their legs were washed by every wave. Jack clambered onto that bench holding one end of the chain that went around Gerard's waist, then wrapped Gerard's chain around Arlanc's and padlocked them together. He threw away the key and, for good measure, smashed the body of the lock with a hammer to make it unpickable.

Gerard's eyes went immediately to the chain that went round the

---

* This galleot was the *Argo,* the Cabal were Argonauts on their way to the Orient in search of the Golden Fleece, and the treacherous slaves were like Ares, fallen into the hands of the Aloadae to be chained up in a bronze vessel for thirteen months

waists of Monsieur Arlanc and his four comrades, and terminated at the end of the bench along the aisle, where it was padlocked to a stout loop of iron.

Jack jumped back into the skiff; handed Gerard his set of lock-picks; and threw him overboard, saying, "Go and redeem thyself."

Of course there was much more to it than that, and when Jack told the tale afterwards he would give the full report, with all due embellishments: the hysterical blubbering of some *galériens,* the pious praying of others, the many strong hands that shot up out of the water to grip the gunwales of their skiff and were cut away by Gabriel's sword. The officers and French Marines still clinging to the galley's forecastle, trying to buy passage on the galleot, or failing that, to fight their way aboard, only to be beaten back by Jeronimo and Nyazi and van Hoek and the others. The banks of powder-smoke drifting by overhead, and the bodies of the drowned *galériens* below: pale blurred forms in strings of five, like pearls.

But at the time Jack took little notice of this *ambience* and concentrated on the matter of the lock and the chain almost as intently as Gerard. At the moment that the galley pulled Gerard under water he still had not got the lock open, and Jack began to think his plan had failed. The Turk who sat in the aisle was pulled under crying "Allahu Akbar!" and then the man who sat next to Monsieur Arlanc went down intoning "Father into your hands I commend my spirit." Then it came to the point where Monsieur Arlanc's face was only visible in the troughs of the waves. But then the head of Gerard re-appeared, followed by that of the Turk; they were clambering uphill, using the galley as a ladder even as it slid deeper. Gerard reached a temporarily secure place, turned around, hefted the opened padlock in one hand, and flung it at Jack's head. Jack ducked it and laughed. "There is your redemption, English!" screamed Gerard, weeping with rage.

Now THEY MADE direct for the Mouths of the Nile, sailing by day and rowing by night. Every few hours they sighted remnant ships of the French fleet, now scattered across fifty miles. Several times they saw *Météore,* which had survived the battle with the amputation of her mizzenmast, and she signalled to them with mirror-flashes.

"A group of two, then a group of three," said Nasr al-Ghuráb.

"According to the Plan, this is a signal that we are to curtail the voyage, and put in at Alexandria instead of going on to Abu Qir," Moseh said.

Al-Ghuráb rolled his eyes. "That would be as good as going direct to Marseille. In *El Iskandariya,* the French are almost more powerful than the Turks."

"There is no point in making it *easy* for the Investor to bugger us," Jeronimo scoffed.

"Then we shall go to Cairo and make it slightly more difficult," said the *raïs*.

"Cairo I like better than Alexandria," Jack said, "but I do not like Cairo *much*. It is a cul-de-sac—the end of the line."

"Not so—we could row up the Nile to Ethiopia!" Dappa said.

Nyazi, viewing Dappa's jest as a challenge to his hospitality, declared that he would gladly sleep naked in the dirt to the end of his days in order to provide the Cabal with comfortable beds—providing they could get as far as the foothills of the Mountains of Nuba.

"The entire point of choosing Cairo was that it is as far East as Mediterranean vessels can go," Moseh reminded them, "and so our cargo should have the highest value there, at the reputedly stupendous bazaar of the Khan el-Khalili, in the very heart of that ancient city, called by some the Mother of the World. And this is as true *now* as it was *before.*"

"But once we go in we cannot come out—the Investor needs only to post ships before the two Mouths of the Nile, at Rosetta and Damietta, and we are bottled up," van Hoek pointed out.

"Nonetheless, this half of the Mediterranean is yet Turkish. Turks control every harbor," said the *raïs*, "and word has gone out, on faster boats than ours, that if a galleot should appear, with a crew of mostly infidels, and such-and-such markings, it is to be impounded at once, and the crew put in irons. Going to Cairo and trading our cargo for a vast array of goods in the Khan el-Khalili is not such a miserable fate compared to the alternatives—"

"One, being buggered by the Investor in Alexandria," said Jeronimo.

"Two, being thrown into a dungeon-pit in some flyblown port in the Levant," said Dappa.

"Three, running the ship aground in some uninhabited place and trudging off into the Sahara bent under the weight of our cargo," said Vrej.

"Ethiopia sounds better every minute," said Dappa.

"I shall distribute my wives equally among the nine of us who still have penises," proclaimed Nyazi, "and Jack can have my finest camel!"

"Jack, fear not," said Monsieur Arlanc, taking him aside. "I know one or two *negociants* in Grand Caire. Through them, I can help you sell your share of the goods, and get a bill of exchange, payable in Amsterdam."

Jack sighed. "I do not predict any of us will sleep easy in Cairo."

So they made no response to messages from the Investor's *jacht,* and used their (now) superior speed to stay well clear of her. And yet they did not attempt to pull away and vanish during the night-times, as there was no advantage in throwing the Investor into a rage.

High sere country, veiled in dust, began to appear off to starboard. The water took on a brown tinge and then became polluted with mud, sticks, and straw, which Nasr al-Ghuráb called *sudd.* He said it had been washed down out of Egypt by the Nile. The river, he said, would be at its fullest now, as it was the month of August.

Then one midday they spied a hill with a single Roman column rising out of its top, and a city jumbled about its base. "It looks as if a movement of the earth has shaken the whole city down into rubble," Jack said, but the *raïs* said that Alexandria always looked that way, and pointed to the fortifications as proof. Indeed a square-sided stone castle rose from the middle of the harbor, at the end of a broad causeway; it seemed orderly and showed no signs of damage. One or two of the faster French ships had already dropped anchor under the shelter of its guns. Gazing for a few moments through a borrowed spyglass, Jack could see men in periwigs going to and fro in longboats, parleying with the customs officials, who here as in Algiers were all black-clad Jews.

"The French pay three percent—merchants of other nations pay twenty," Monsieur Arlanc commented, "probably thanks to the machinations of your Investor, and of other great Frenchmen." Since his being rescued from the galley, he had been accepted as a sort of advisor to the Cabal.

"Once the Turks see how the French fleet was mangled by the Dutch, perhaps they'll change their policy," van Hoek said.

"Not if the Duc d'Arcachon bribes them with a galleot-load of gold bars," Jack put in.

Most of the French fleet, including *Météore,* set their courses direct for the harbor of Alexandria proper. Nasr al-Ghuráb, however, pointed them straight up the coast; raised all the sail he could; and put the *galériens* to work, driving them at a blazing speed of nine knots for two hours. This brought them to a cusp of land called Abu Qir. From here Alexandria was still plainly visible through dust and heat-waves, and presumably the reverse was true; no doubt some French officer had watched every oar-stroke through a spyglass.

There was no city at Abu Qir, other than a few huts of Arab fishermen surrounded by spindly racks where they put fish out to dry in the sun. But there was a solid Turkish fort with many guns, and a customs house below it, having its own pier. Moseh and Dappa went in using the skiff while the *raïs* and the others managed the ticklish job of bringing the galleot alongside the pier. Out of the customs house came the Jew who was in charge of the place, followed by Moseh, Dappa, and a couple of younger Jews—his sons—who carried sticks of red wax, bottles of ink, and other necessaries. The Jew was speaking a queer kind of Spanish to Moseh. He spent a couple of hours going through the hold, putting a customs-seal on each of the wooden crates without actually inspecting them, and without exacting any duties—this, of course, had all been pre-arranged on the Turkish side, by the Pasha working through his contacts in Egypt. This customs house at Abu Qir was the only one in the Ottoman Empire, or the world for that matter, where they could have done it.

The inspector made it clear to everyone within earshot that he was not happy with any part of the arrangement, but he did his part and departed without creating any obstructions or demanding any *baksheesh* above and beyond what he was getting anyway: a purse of pieces of eight, handed to him by Nasr al-Ghuráb after the "inspection" was complete.

This inspector turned out to be a hospitable soul, who importuned Moseh to come in and share an evening meal—making the reasonable assumption that the galleot would remain tied up to his pier all night. And indeed this would have been easiest. But a French sloop-of-war had been dispatched from Alexandria and was halfway to them now, her triangular sail apricot-colored in the late afternoon sun, and no one liked the looks of that. Furthermore, according to this Jew, a fine high-road called the Canopic Way joined Alexandria to Abu Qir, and riders on good horses could easily make the trip in a couple of hours. Having no particular desire to be trapped between the French sloop and a hypothetical squadron of French night-riders, Nasr al-Ghuráb ordered the galleot to put to sea about an hour before sunset. Under other conditions this would have been most unwise. But the current of the Nile would tend to push them away from the land, and according to the weather-glass that van Hoek had improvised from a glass tube and a flask of quicksilver, the skies would be clear for at least another day. So they abandoned themselves to the waves, and spent an uneasy night throwing the sounding-lead over the side and hauling it in again, over and over and over, lest they run aground in the Nile's shifting sands.

When the sun rose upon one tired and irritable Cabal, they found themselves in the center of a vast half-moon-shaped bay, contained between the headland of Abu Qir to the southwest, and a huge sand-spit to the northeast, some twenty miles farther along the coast from Abu Qir. This bay had no distinct shore, but rather smeared away into mud-flats that extended for many miles inland before they became worthy of supporting trees, crops, and buildings. It soon became plain that the galleot had been drifting in a lazy orbit, a vast whorl of current driven by the Nile. For according to the *raïs*, the sand-spit to the northeast had been constructed, one grain of silt at a time, by the Rosetta Mouth, which was bedded in it somewhere. And when the sun bubbled up from the horizon and shone as a red disk through the haze of floury dust sighing down from the Sahara, it silhouetted a skyline of mosque-domes and minarets, deep among those mud-flats, which was the city of Rosetta itself.

The morning's peace was then broken by wailing and sobbing from the head of the galleot. Jack went forward to find Vrej Esphahnian kneeling on the heavy timber that had once supported the ram. The Armenian was now doing some ramming of his own, repeatedly butting his forehead against the timber and clawing at his scalp until blood showed. He did not appear to hear anything Jack said to him. So Jack lingered until he was certain that Vrej did not intend to hurl himself into the bay, and then returned to the quarterdeck, where tactics were being discussed.

As soon as it had grown light enough to see, they had turned the galley northwards and begun rowing out of this bay. Rosetta (or Rashid, as al-Ghuráb called it) had been close enough that they'd heard the city's muezzins wailing at the break of dawn. But the *raïs* explained that to reach the city they would have to go several miles north to the tip of the bar, and find their way in at the river-mouth, then work upriver for an hour or two.

It was not long before the French sloop came into view; she had sailed out into deeper waters for the night and was now patrolling off the Rosetta Mouth. Fortunately a wind came up from the southwest, and by raising some canvas the galleot was able to run before it, overshooting the river-mouth and making excellent speed towards the east—as if she intended to go in at the Damietta Mouth, a hundred miles away, or to break loose altogether and make a run for some other port. The sloop's skipper had no choice but to bite down hard on that bait, and to chase them downwind. When she had drawn abeam of the galleot, and begun to converge toward them, al-Ghuráb struck the canvas, wheeled about, and set the oar-slaves to work rowing upwind. The sloop came about in response. But lacking oars, she could only work upwind by tacking, and so she had no hope of keeping pace with the galleot. The gap between the two vessels was about half a mile to begin with, and grew steadily as they rowed towards the snarl of interlocking and ingrown sand-bars that guarded the Nile's Rosetta Mouth.

These maneuvers took up half the day, which gave Vrej Esphahnian time to calm down. When he seemed capable of speech again, Jack brought him a cup and a wineskin, and sat with him in the bow—now the least foul-smelling part of the ship, as they were working into the wind.

"Forgive my weakness," said Vrej in a hoarse voice. "When I saw Rosetta, I could think only of the tales my father told me, of how he passed through that place with his boat-load of coffee. He had nursed that boat through countless narrow seas and straits, canals and river-courses, and when he passed through customs at Rosetta and sailed down to the river's mouth, suddenly the vast Mediterranean opened up before him: to some, an emblem of terror and harbinger of wild storms, but to him a vista of freedom of opportunity. From there he sailed direct to Marseille and—"

"Yes, I know, introduced coffee to France," said Jack, who knew the rest of the tale at least as well as Vrej himself. "Now excuse me for tacking upwind, as it were, against the general direction of your narration. But according to your brother's version of this story, your father acquired that boat-load of coffee in Mocha."

Vrej, taken aback: "Yes—Mocha is where coffee from Ethiopia, silver from Spain, and spices from India all come together."

"I have seen maps," said Jack impressively, "maps of the whole world, in a library in Hanover. And I seem to recollect that Mocha lies on the Red Sea."

"Yes—as Nyazi can tell you, it lies in Arabia Felix, across the Red Sea from Ethiopia."

"And furthermore I am under the impression that the Red Sea empties into the ocean that extends to Hindoostan."

Vrej said nothing.

"If it is true that Cairo is the end of the line—that no vessel can go farther east than that—then how did your father manage to get his ship from Mocha, on the Red Sea, to *here*?"

Vrej was now sitting with his eyes tightly shut, cursing under his breath.

"There must be a way through!" Jack said, then stood up to shout the news to the others. As he did, he noticed, in the corner of his eye, a movement of Vrej's hand. It was subtle. Yet any man in the world would notice it, and many would step away in response, or even reach across toward his sword-hilt, because Vrej was unmistakably reaching towards the handle of the dagger that was bound in his waist-sash. His hand moved no more than a finger's breadth before he mastered the impulse and moved it back. But Jack noticed it, and faltered, and looked into the eyes of Vrej Esphahnian, red and swollen from weeping. He saw sadness there (of course), but he did

221

not see murderous passions; only a kind of surrender. "That's the spirit, Vrej!" he said, giving him a hearty shoulder-slap, and then Jack stepped away and called the Cabal to council.

That night the peace of the Street of the Wigmakers in the *souk* of Rosetta was wrecked by the sound of a pistol-butt being hammered against an old wooden door. The head of an angry man was thrust out between shutters above, and became much less angry when he saw that two of the three visitors were Turks (or at least dressed that way), and one of those a Janissary. Pieces of eight jangled in a purse improved his mood even more. Door-bolts were removed, the visitors admitted.

The dwelling was clean and well-tended, but it smelt as if the floor-sweepings of every barbershop in the Ottoman Empire had been stuffed into its back room and left to ripen. Tea was brewed and tobacco proffered. After some half an hour of preliminaries, the visitors made a business proposal. Once the owner got over his astonishment, he accepted it. A boy was sent off to the Street of the Barbers at a dead run. While they waited, the wigmaker lit some lamps and displayed his wares. The finished products were big wigs mounted on wooden block-heads, destined for export to Europe; but they looked almost as strange to the European visitors as they did to any Arab, for during the years that they had spent pulling oars, fashions had been changing: wigs were now tall and narrow, no longer flat and broad.

Deeper in the shop were the raw materials, and here choices had to be made. Even the finest Barbary horse-hair was too coarse for tonight's project. At the other end, hanks of fine, lustrous human hair from China were available—but these were the wrong color and it would take too long to dye them.

A bleary-eyed Turkish barber came in and began heating water and stropping razors. The customers settled on some sandy brown goat hair, intermediate in price.

The Janissary's head and face were now shaved clean by the barber, and the fine fuzz on the upper cheeks burned away, dramatically but painlessly, using spirits of wine soaked into wads of Turcoman cotton. The barber was paid off and sent home. The wigmaker then went to work, painting the naked skin with pine gum one tiny patch at a time and stabbing tufts of goat hair into the goo. After two hours, the Janissary smelled overpoweringly of goats and pine-trees, and looked like he hadn't had a shave or haircut in years. And when he was stripped to the waist, revealing a back ridged with whip-scars, anyone would have identified him not as a Janissary but as a wretched oar-slave.

PIERRE DE JONZAC RETURNED to the bank of the Nile an hour after dawn, just as he had promised or threatened to, and he brought with him his entire squadron of dragoons. Yesterday they'd galloped headlong to the very edge of the quay and pulled up just short of charging across the gangplanks, all panting and sweaty and dust-caked from having galloped up and down the Canopic Way for a night and a day trying to follow the maneuvers of the galleot.

Using Monsieur Arlanc as interpreter, Nasr al-Ghuráb compli-mented de Jonzac on the splendid appearance of his self and his troops this morning—for it was obvious that the menials at the French Consulate had been up all night grooming, scrubbing, starching, and polishing. The *raïs* went on to apologize for the con-trastingly dismal state of his ship and crew. Some of them were "enjoying the shade of the vines," which was a poetic way of saying they were in the bazaar (which had a leafy roof of grapevines) buy-ing provisions. Others were "sipping mocha in the Pasha's house." De Jonzac looked on this (as he was meant to) as a crashingly unsub-tle way of claiming that members of the Cabal were inside the stone fort built by the Turks to control the river, showering *baksheesh* upon officialdom. The fort was nearby enough to literally overshadow them, and scores of resplendent Janissaries were peering down from its battlements, casting a cold professional eye on the French dra-goons. The point being that Rosetta was very different from Alexan-dria; *here* the French might have a consulate, and some troops, but (as the saying went) that and a few *reales* would buy them a cup of Mocha.

This point was entirely sound, but al-Ghuráb had spoken only lies so far. The real reason that only a few Cabal members were visible on the galleot's quarterdeck was that four of them (Dappa, Jeronimo, Nyazi, and Vrej) had been riding south, post-haste, all through the night, hoping to cover the hundred and fifty miles to Cairo in two days. And another of them was chained to an oar.

"It was uncommonly humane of you to set free a third of your oar-slaves last night," de Jonzac commented, "but since my master owns part interest in them, we have made arrangements, among our *numerous* and *highly placed* Turkish friends in yonder Fort, to have them all rounded up and sent back to Alexandria."

"I hope that your Navy will be able to find benches for them to sit on," shouted van Hoek.

De Jonzac's face grew red and stormy-looking, but he ignored the cruel words of the Dutchman and continued: "Some of them were eager to talk to us, even before we put thumbscrews on them. So we know that you have been hiding certain metallurgical information from us."

The night before—needing some ready cash to pay wigmakers and horse-traders—they'd broken open a crate, and pulled out a gold bar, in full view of certain oar-slaves who'd later been set free. This had been done in the hope and expectation that they'd later divulge it to de Jonzac.

The *raïs* shrugged. "What of it?"

De Jonzac said, "I've sent a message to Alexandria informing my master that certain numbers mentioned in the Plan must now be multiplied by thirteen."

"Alas! If only the calculation were that simple, your master could relax in the splendor of his Alexandrian villa while you went to Cairo to balance the books. In fact it is much more complicated than that. Our friend in Bonanza turns out to have diversified his portfolio far beyond the usual metal goods. The hoard will require a tedious appraisal before we can reckon its value."

"*That* is a routine matter—you forget my master is well acquainted with the workings of the Corsair trade," de Jonzac sniffed. "He has trusted appraisers who can be dispatched hither—"

"Dispatch them instead to Cairo," said the *raïs*, "for that is where *our* trusted appraisers dwell. And send for your master, too. For there is one treasure here whose value only *he* can weigh."

De Jonzac smiled thinly. "My master is a man of *acumen*—I assure you he leaves appraisals to *experts*, save, sometimes, when it comes to Barbary stallions."

"How about English geldings?" the *raïs* asked, and nodded to Yevgeny and Gabriel Goto.

Down on the oar-deck, Jack began to rattle his chains and to scream in English: "You bloody bastards! Sell me out to the Frog, will you? Motherless wog scum! May God's curse be on your heads!"

Calmly ignoring this and further curses, Yevgeny came up behind Jack, pinioned his elbows together behind his back, and lifted him up off the bench so that de Jonzac could get a good look at him. Gabriel Goto then grabbed Jack's drawers and yanked them down so they hung around the knees.

De Jonzac observed a long moment of silence as a *frisson* ran through his dragoons.

"Perhaps it is Ali Zaybak—perhaps some other English wretch who stood too close to a fire," the *raïs* said drily. "Can *you* recognize Jack Shaftoe?"

"No," de Jonzac admitted.

"Having recognized him, could you place a value on his head?"

"Only my master could do that."

"Then we will see you, and your master, in Cairo, in three days," said Nasr al-Ghuráb.

"That is not enough time!"

"We have been slaves for *years,*" said Moseh, who had been standing quietly, arms folded, the whole time, "and we say that three more days is too long."

LATER THAT DAY they set off upriver, mostly under sail-power. The main channel was a few fathoms deep and perhaps a quarter-mile wide—which meant that they were never more than an eighth of a mile from French dragoons. For de Jonzac had sent out two pairs of riders to shadow them, one pair on each riverbank.

As soon as the galleot got clear of Rosetta—which was a sprawl of mostly humble dwellings with no wall to mark its boundary—Jack was dragged away from his bench and draped about in diverse neck-collars, manacles, and leg-irons, then taken back to the concealment of the quarterdeck where Yevgeny devoted a quarter of an hour to smiting an anvil, rattling chains, and producing other noises meant to convince anyone listening that Jack was being securely fettered. Meanwhile Jack—never one to stint on dramaturgy—screamed and cursed as if Yevgeny were bending red-hot irons directly around his wrists. In fact, the reason for his cries of agony was that he was ripping handfuls of goat-hair from his scalp and head. The skin was left covered with a scaly crust of hardened pine-gum. Various scrubbings with turpentine and lamp-oil got that off, taking several layers of skin and leaving him raw from the collarbones upwards. He wrapped his burning head in a turban, got dressed, belted on his sword, and strolled out into view looking every inch a Janissary; then paused, turned around, and shouted some abuse in Sabir at an imaginary chained wretch behind him.

He dared not look directly at his audience during this performance, but van Hoek was spying on the dragoons through an oar-lock, and reported that they'd witnessed most of it. They did not have much leisure for spying, though. The river was at its highest now, filling its channel and frequently spilling out into surrounding countryside, and so the galleot did not have to work her way around shallows as she would have in other seasons. Yet the current was gentle and she could easily make seven miles an hour upstream. Jack had been expecting a desert, and he could tell one was out there somewhere from the way everything collected a film of yellow dust.

But Egypt, seen from here, was as moist and fertile as Holland. And as crowded. Even in the most remote stretches they were never out of sight of several dwellings. They passed villages a few times an hour, and large towns several times a day. For as far as they could see to both sides of the river, the flat countryside was covered with golden fields of corn and rice, and veined with wandering lines of darker green: the countless water-courses of the Delta, lined, and frequently choked, with reeds and rushes as high as a man's head. Palm trees grew in picket-lines along waterways, and towns were belted with orchards of figs, citrus, and cassia.

All of it was scenery to the Cabal, and an obstacle course to the French riders. They fell behind the galleot when they had to swing wide around river-bends and flooded fields, then caught up when they found a way to cut across one of the river's vast meanders. Fortunately for them they had left Rosetta trailing strings of fresh horses; and Egypt, like most of the Turks' empire, was a settled and orderly country. Traveling along her high-roads was not as easy as in England, but it was easier than in France, and so they were able to keep pace during the day. This gave Moseh, Jack, and the others confidence that the four who'd gone ahead—Nyazi's group—had reached Cairo without difficulty.

At night the wind fell. Rather than attempting to row through the dark, and perhaps run aground or stray into some backwater, the *raïs* simply tied the galleot to a palm tree along the riverbank and then organized the Cabal into watches. The dragoons actually served as an outlying guard-post, as they were not keen to see the galleot's cargo fall into the hands of some local Ali Baba and his forty thieves.

In the middle of the second day, the wind failed and the *raïs* sent a dozen slaves ashore to pull the galleot by ropes—which was why they had not released all of the slaves in Rosetta. In this way they came, late in the afternoon, to the place where the Nile diverged into its two great branches: the one that they had just navigated, and another that ran to Damietta. Here, as night fell on the second day, they tied the galleot up again, and bided during the hours of darkness. Jack stood an early morning watch, then climbed into a hammock on the quarterdeck and fell asleep in the open air.

When he awoke, the sun was rising, the ship was under way, and he could see a strange terrain of angular mountains off to the west. Sitting up for a better look, he recognized them as Pyramids. When he had got his fill of gawking at those—which took a good long while—he turned around to face the rising sun and gazed across the Nile into the Mother of the World.

Now this was like trying to comprehend all the activity of an ant-hill, and read all the words in a book, and feel all the splendor of a cathedral, in one glance. Jack's mind was not equal to the demands that Cairo placed on it, and so for a long while he fixed his attention on small and near matters, as if he were a boy peering through a hollow reed. Fortunately there were many such matters to occupy him: the Nile here was at least as big as the Danube at Vienna, and its course was crowded with boats laden with grain that had been brought down out of Upper Egypt. The captains of those boats had been shooting cataracts and beating back crocodiles for weeks, and were in no particular mood to make way for the unwieldy galleot. Many enemies were made as they worked their way in to the east bank of the river and made the galleot fast to a quay.

Almost immediately they were engulfed in camels, which is never pleasant, and rarely desirable—especially when they are being ridden and led by fierce-looking armed men. Jack thought they were under assault by wild nomads until he began noticing that all of them looked like Nyazi, and many were smiling. Then he heard Jeronimo bellowing in Spanish, "If I had a copper for every fly that swarms on you, beast, I'd buy the Spanish Empire! You smell worse than Vera Cruz in the springtime, and there is more filth clinging to your body than most animals shit in a year. Truly you must have sprung fully formed from a heap of manure, as flies and Popes do— may God have mercy on my soul for saying that! Jack Shaftoe is there smiling at me, thinking that you, camel, and I are well matched for each other—later I'll make him your wife perhaps and you can take him out into the desert and do with him what you will."

Dappa and Vrej were off seeing to other matters, but shortly Jack caught sight of Nyazi. He had had a joyous reunion with his clan-members. Jack was glad he had not been there to endure it.

Nasr al-Ghuráb now unchained all of the galley-slaves at once— some two score of them—and told them that they could go now into Cairo, and never come back; or they could join in with the Cabal, and never leave it; but these were their only two choices. Within moments, all but four of them had vanished. Those who remained were a Nubian eunuch, a Hindoo, the Turk who had been at the head of Monsieur Arlanc's oar, and an Irishman named Padraig Tallow. The first three had somehow made the calculation that their chances were better with the Cabal, while Padraig (Jack suspected) just wanted to see how it would all come out. Monsieur Arlanc was offered the same choice as the others, and to Jack's delight he elected to throw his lot in with the Cabal.

They all got busy pulling the gold-crates out of the galleot and loading them onto the camels, which took no more than half an hour. The *raïs,* accompanied by van Hoek, Jeronimo (who'd had enough of camels), the Turk, the Nubian, and several of Nyazi's clansmen (who wanted to see what it was like to ride on a boat), cast off the galleot's lines and took her downriver, heading for an isle in midstream a few miles distant where boats were bought and sold. The camel-caravan meanwhile formed up and prepared to move out.

SOME OF THOSE GALLEY-SLAVES, as they had considered the choice that they'd been given, had asked searching questions about the Plan. The most frequently heard was: "Why do you not simply ride out of town with your treasure? Why bother waiting for this Investor—who has made obvious his intention to cheat you?" Jack was not unsympathetic to this line of questioning. But in the end he had to agree with Moseh and Nasr al-Ghuráb, who answered by pointing with their chins across the Nile, toward the city that the Turks had built up there, called El Giza. It had mosque-domes, leafy gardens, baths, and houses of pleasure. But, too, it had dungeons, and high walls with iron hooks on them, and a *Champs de Mars* where thousands of Janissaries drilled with muskets and lances. There would be judges in there, too, and some of them would probably be sympathetic to a French Duke who complained that he was being robbed by a rabble of slaves.

The Turkish authorities had already been alerted by a couple of exhausted French dragoons who had galloped up on half-dead horses as the camels were being loaded. So as the caravan left the Nile behind and began winding through the 2,400 wards and quarters of Cairo, it was carefully followed by Janissaries, not to mention hundreds of beggars, Vagabonds, pedlars, courtesans, and curious boys.

Now Cairo was a sort of accomplice in everything that happened there. It was large enough to engulf any army, and wise enough to comprehend any Plan, and old enough to've outlived whole races, nations, and religions. So nothing could really happen there without the city's consent. Nyazi's caravan, three dozen horses and camels strong, armed to the teeth, laden with tons of gold, was nothing here. The train of men and animals was frequently chopped into halves, thirds, and smaller bits by yet stranger processions that burst out from narrow ways and cut across it: gangs of masked women running and ululating, columns of Dervishes in high conical hats pounding on drums, wrapped corpses being paraded around atop stilts, squadrons of Janissaries in green and red. Every so often they would stumble upon a *shavush* in his emerald-green, ankle-length robe, red boots, white leather cap, and stupendous moustache. Then every camel in the procession had to be made to kneel, every man had to dismount, until he had wandered past; and as long as they had stopped, Vagabonds would run up and spray rose-water at them and demand money for it.

Even if Jack had not known, when he'd disembarked from the galleot, that Egypt was the world's oldest country, he'd have figured it out after an hour's slow progress through Cairo's streets. He could see it in the faces of the people, who were a mixture of every race Jack had ever heard about, and some he hadn't. Every face told as many tales as a whole galley full of oar-slaves. Likewise their houses, which were made partly of stone, partly of timbers so old and gnarled they looked petrified, and mostly of bricks, hand-made and rudely baked, some looking as if they might bear the hand-prints of Moses himself. As many buildings were being torn down, as built up; which only stood to reason, as all the space had been claimed, and there was nothing to do but shift the available materi-als from one site to another, much as the Nile continually built and dissolved the sand-bars of the Delta by pushing grains of sand from place to place according to its whim. Even the Pyramids had had a gnawed look about their corners, as if people had been using them for quarries.

After hours of working deeper into the city they reached the Khan el-Khalili: a shambolic market, bigger in itself than all but a few European cities. Nyazi bade Jack take his shoes off and led him into an ancient mosque and up a steep spiral staircase that was dark and cool as a natural cave. Finally they stepped out on the roof and Jack looked out upon the city. The river was too far away to be seen from here and so what he saw was a million dusty flat rooves piled with bales, barrels, bundles, mounds, and household detritus. Each roof had its own peculiar height, and the lower ones seemed in dan-ger of becoming buried.

Cairo was like the bottom of a vast pit whence the inhabitants had been madly trying to escape for thousands of years, and the only way out was to dig up clay, quarry limestone, and tear down empty houses and defenseless monuments, and pile the proceeds ever higher. Who had lately been winning the race could be judged by whose roof was highest. The losers could not keep pace with their neighbors, or even with the drifting dust that assiduously covered anything that failed to move, and so gradually sank from sight. Jack had the phant'sy that he could go into any house in Cairo, descend into the cellar, and find an entire house buried beneath, and yet another house beneath that one, and so on, miles down. Never had the preachers' line "He will come to judge the quick and the dead" been so clear to Jack; for here in this Bible-land, Quick and Dead were the only two categories, and the distinction between them the only Judgment that mattered.

So he drew comfort from being in the Khan el-Khalili, which appeared to be the quickest part of the city. The caravan wound through market-streets devoted to every good imaginable, from slaves to butter to live cobras, and eventually reached a place that, Jack thought, must be the dead center of the entire metropolis. It was a yard, or perhaps an alley: a rectangle of dirt, a bow-shot in length, but not above five yards in width, hemmed in by four- and five-storey buildings. Above, a narrow aperture provided light, but something translucent had been thrown across between the para-pets of the buildings: caravan-tents and tarpaulins, Jack suspected. These formed a continuous roof overhead, letting in dusty light but sealing the place off from eavesdroppers. The surrounding build-ings were astonishingly quiet—the quietest place in Cairo—and they smelled of hay. Ships coming down the Nile had replenished the place with food for the horses and camels that were stabled here.

"This is where it began," remarked Nyazi. "This was the seed."

"What do you mean?" Jack asked.

"A hundred generations ago, some men like me camped here—" stomping the dirt with one sandal "—for the night with their camels, and in time the camp put down roots, and became a caravanserai. The market of Khan el-Khalili grew up around it, and Cairo around *it*. But you see the caravanserai remains, and still we come here to sell our camels."

"It is a good place to meet the Duke," Moseh said. "The Plan was sound all along. For, according to what Nyazi has said, not a single day has gone by in this place, since the very beginning of the world, when silver and gold have not passed from hand to hand here. Its presence was not dictated by any king, nor was it prophesied by any creed; it emerged of its own accord, and endures regardless of what the Sultan in Constantinople or the Sun King in Paris might prefer."

> Friendship is a Vertue oftener found among Thieves
> than other People, for when their Companions are
> in Danger, they venture hardest to relieve them.
> —*Memoirs of the Right Villanous John Hall*

The ground floors of the caravanserai's buildings had high ceil-ings so that without having to duck, or doff their turbans, men could ride camels into them, and that was just what the clan of Nyazi did.

That night, Nasr al-Ghuráb came back with his contingent, and with Dappa and Vrej, whom they hadn't seen since Rosetta.

"Truly the forkings and wanderings of the Nile are as unknowable as the streets of Cairo," said Dappa, blinking his eyes in amazement, "but Vrej found an Armenian coffee-trader, no more than five minutes' walk from this place, who knew all about the way to Mocha. You go downstream to the great fork, and take the Damietta branch, and after a few miles there is a village on the right bank where a water-course strays off eastwards. In time that stream goes all the way to the Red Sea."

"Then much traffic must pass through it!" Moseh exclaimed.

"It is jealously guarded by the head men of the villages that bestride it, and by the Turkish officials," Dappa agreed.

"And for that very reason," said Vrej, picking up the narrative, "other Egyptians, in neighboring precincts, have been at work with picks and shovels, scooping out short-cuts that bypass the larger villages and toll-stations. These look like nothing more than stagnant dead-ends, or reed-choked sewer-ditches, when they are visible at all; and you may be sure that they are guarded by the farmers who dug them, every bit as jealously as the main channel. So we shall not make it through to the Red Sea without crossing the palms of innumerable peasants with *baksheesh*—the total expense will be dumbfounding, I fear."

"But we will have a boat-load of gold," said Yevgeny.

"And we will be running for our lives," added Jack, "which always makes spending money not quite so painful."

"And those farmers will want to keep it all a secret from their Turkish overlords just as badly as we will," predicted Jeronimo.

"Not quite as badly," Moseh demurred, "but badly enough."

"Very good then," said Surendranath, the Hindoo galley slave who had chosen to throw in his lot with them. "You have shown extreme wisdom in establishing your *batna*."

"Avast! We are all People of the Book here, and have no use for your idolatrous claptrap," said Jeronimo.

"Steady there, Caballero," said Jack, "I know from personal experience that Books of India contain much of interest. What else can you tell us about this *batna*, Surendranath?"

"I learnt it from English traders in Surat," said the befuddled Surendranath, "It stands for Best Alternative To a Negotiated Agreement."

A recess, now, as the phrase was translated into diverse languages.

Moseh said, "Be it English or Hindoo, there's still wisdom in it.

Our friend, born and raised a *banyan,* understands that escaping over the flooded fields and through the wadis to the Red Sea is an *alternate* plan—a *contingency* and nothing more." As Moseh was saying these words, he gazed deliberately into the eyes of those members of the Cabal he deemed most impetuous. But he began and ended with his eyes locked on Jack's. Moseh concluded, "To have a *batna* is good and wise, as Surendranath has pointed out. But the *Negotiated Agreement* is much better than this *Best Alternative.*"

"Moseh, you have sat next to me for years and heard all of my stories, and so you know that I only love one thing in the world, even in spite of this," said Jack, pulling up the loose sleeve of his garment to display the track of the harpoon in his arm. "There should be no doubt in your mind that I would rather be on a ship bound for Christendom tomorrow, than fleeing for my life towards the Red Sea, like some miserable Hebrew of yore. But like those Hebrews I'll not be a slave any longer."

"We are all in accord *there,*" said Dappa.

"Then, as I have been chosen to represent the Cabal in our final negotiation with the Investor, I must ask you all to do one thing. I am a Vagabond, and was never one for swearing pompous oaths and prating about honor. But this undertaking is no longer a Vagabondish sort of enterprise—so every man among you must now swear, by whatever he considers holiest, that you are with me tomorrow. That, whatsoever happens in my dealings with the Duke—whether I show foolishness or wisdom—whether I remain collected, or lose my temper, or piss my breeches—whether or not the Imp of the Perverse comes to pay me a visit—you are with me, and will accept my decision, and live or die with me."

Here Jack had been expecting a long, awkward pause, or even laughter. But the sword of Gabriel Goto was out of its sheath before Jack's words had stopped echoing round the narrow yard. The newcomers flinched. In a simple swift movement Gabriel reversed his sword and presented its hilt to Jack, and in the light of the fire the blade shimmered like a swift stream of clear water beneath the rising sun. "I am samurai," he said simply.

Padraig, the big Irishman, stepped forward and spat into the fire. "We've a saying," he said to Jack in English. "Is this a private fight, or can anyone join in? Well, I'm in, which ought to suffice. But if you want me to swear by something, then I do swear on my mother's grave above the sea in Kilmacthomas, and damn you if you think that's not as good as being a samurai."

Moseh took the scrap of Indian bead-work from around his neck, kissed it, and tossed it to Jack. "Throw that into the fire if I fail you," he said, "and let it become part of the dust of the Khan el-Khalili."

Vrej said, "I have followed you thus far, Jack, seeking to make good on the debt that my family owes you. I swear on my family that I will pay you back."

Monsieur Arlanc said, "I do not believe in swearing oaths. But I do believe that I am destined to see the matter through to its proper end."

Van Hoek said, "I swear by my right arm that I'll never be taken by pirates again. And this Investor is a pirate in the eyes of God."

"But cap'n, you are left-handed!" Jack said, trying to lighten the mood, which he was beginning to find oppressive.

"To make good on the oath, I must use my strong left hand to cut off the right," said van Hoek, missing the humor altogether. Indeed, the jest had put him into a more emotional state than any of his fellow-slaves had ever seen. Suddenly he drew his cutlass out; lay his right fist on a bench with only the little finger extended; and brought the cutlass down on it. The last joint of the pinky flew off into the dust. Van Hoek thrust his weapon back into its scabbard, then went out and retrieved the severed digit and held it up in the fire-light. "There is your oath!" he growled, and flung it into the fire. Then he sagged to his knees, and passed out in the dirt.

Some uneasiness, now, as the others wondered whether they would be expected to cut off pieces of themselves. But Nyazi withdrew from the folds of his cloak a red Koran, and he and Nasr al-Ghuráb and the Turk from Arlanc's galley gathered around it and said holy words in Arabic, and for good measure, announced that they would make the *haj* if they survived. Likewise Yevgeny, Surendranath, and the Nubian swore fearsome oaths to their respective gods. Mr. Foot, who had been lurking round the edges of the fire-light looking vaguely indignant, announced that it would be superfluous for him to swear loyalty since "the whole enterprise" had been his idea (apparently referring to the ill-starred cowrie shell voyage of many years back) and that in any case it "would never do" to show anything other than loyalty to his comrades and that it was "bizarre" and "shocking" and "unseemly" and "inconceivable" for Jack to even suggest that he, Mr. Foot, would do otherwise.

"I swear by my country—the country of free men," said Dappa, "which at the moment has only sixteen or so citizens, and no territory. But it is the only country I have and so by it do I swear."

Jeronimo stepped forward, piously wringing his hands, and began to mumble some words in Latin; but then his demon took over and he shouted, "Fuck! I do not even believe in God! I swear by all of you Vagabonds, Niggers, Heretics, Kikes, and Camel-Jockeys, for you are the only friends I have ever had."

THE DUC D'ARCACHON had disembarked from his gilded river-barge, and was riding towards the Khan el-Khalili on a white horse, accompanied by several aides, a Turkish official or two, and a mixed company of rented Janissaries and crack French dragoons. Behind them rumbled several empty wagons of very heavy construction, such as were used to carry blocks of dressed stone through the streets. This much was known to the Cabal half an hour in advance—word had been brought by the messenger-boys who moved through the streets of Cairo like scirocco winds.

Every master jeweler in the city had been hired by the Duc d'Arcachon—or, failing that, had been bribed not to do any work for the Cabal—and were now converging on a certain gate of the Khan el-Khalili to await the Duke. This was common knowledge to every Jew in the city, including Moseh.

A flat-bottomed, shallow-draft river-boat waited at the terminus of a canal that wandered through the city and eventually communicated with the Nile. It was only half a mile from the caravanserai, down a certain street, and the people who dwelled along that street had carried their chairs and hookahs indoors and rounded up their chickens and were keeping their doors bolted and windows shuttered today, because of certain rumors that had begun to circulate the night before.

It was mid-afternoon before the clatter and rumble of the Investor's entourage penetrated the still courtyard where Jack stood in the lambent glow of the stretched canvas above. He took a deep whiff of air into his nostrils. It smelt of hay, dust, and camel-dung. He ought to be scared, or at least excited. Instead he felt peace. For this alley was the womb at the center of the Mother of the World, the place where it had all started. The *Messe* of Linz and the House of the Golden Mercury in Leipzig and the Damplatz of Amsterdam were its young impetuous grandchildren. Like the eye of a hurricane, the alley was dead calm; but around it, he knew, revolved the global maelstrom of liquid silver. Here, there were no Dukes and no Vagabonds; every man was the same, as in the moment before he was born.

The challenges and salutations were barely audible through the stable's haystacks; Jack could not even make out the language. Then he heard horseshoes pocking over the stone floor, coming closer.

Jack rested his hand on the pommel of his sword and recited a poem he'd been taught long ago, standing in the bend of a creek in Bohemia:

> *Watered steel-blade, the world perfection calls,*
> *Drunk with the viper poison foes appals.*
> *Cuts lively, burns the blood whene'er it falls;*
> *And picks up gems from pave of marble halls.*

"That is he!?" said a voice in French. Jack realized his eyes were closed, and opened them to see a man on a white, pink-eyed *cheval de parade*. His wig was perfect, an Admiral's hat was perched atop it, and four little black patches were glued to his white face. He was staring in some alarm at Jack, and Jack almost reached for one of the pistols in his waist-sash, fearing he had already been recognized. But another *chevalier*, riding knee to knee with the Duke to his left side, leaned askew in his saddle and answered, "Yes, your grace, that is the Agha of the Janissaries." Jack recognized this rider as Pierre de Jonzac.

"He must be a Balkan," remarked the Duke, apparently because of Jack's European coloration.

A third French *chevalier* rode on the Duke's right. He cleared his throat significantly as Monsieur Arlanc emerged from the stables and fell in beside Jack, on his left hand. Evidently this was to warn the Duke that they were now in the presence of a man who could understand French. Moseh now emerged and stood on Jack's right to even the count, three facing three.

The Frenchmen—wishing to command the field—rode forward all the way to the center of the alley. Likewise Jack strolled forward until he was drawing uncomfortably close to the Duke. Finally the Duke reined in his white horse and held up one hand in a signal for everyone to halt. De Jonzac and the other *chevalier* stopped immediately, their horses' noses even with the Duke's saddle. But Jack took another step forward, and then another, until de Jonzac reached down and drew a pistol halfway from a saddle-holster, and the other aide spurred his horse forward to cut Jack off.

Behind the Duke and his men, it was possible to hear a considerable number of French soldiers and Janissaries infiltrating the caravanserai, and before long Jack began to see musket-barrels gleaming in windows of the uppermost storeys. Likewise, men of Nyazi's clan had taken up positions on both sides of the alley to Jack's rear, and the burning punks of their matchlocks glowed in dark archways like demons' eyes. Jack stopped where he was: perhaps eight feet from the glabrous muzzle of the Duke's horse. But he chose a place where his sight-line to the Duke's face was blocked by the aide who had ridden forward. The Duke said something *sotto voce* and this man backed his mount out of the way, returning to his former position guarding the Duke's right flank.

"I comprehend your plan," said the Duke, dispensing with formalities altogether—which was probably meant to be some kind of insult. "It is essentially suicidal."

Jack pretended not to understand until Monsieur Arlanc had translated this into Sabir.

"We had to make it *seem* that way," answered Jack, "or you would have been afraid to show up."

The Duke smiled as if at some very dry dinner-table witticism. "Very well—it is like a dance, or a duel, beginning with formal steps: I try to frighten you, you try to impress me. We proceed now. Show me *L'Emmerdeur!*"

"He is very near by," said Jack. "First we must settle larger matters—the gold."

"I am a man of *honor,* not a *slave,* and so to *me,* the gold is *nothing.* But if *you* are so concerned about it, tell me what you propose."

"First, send your jewelers away—there are no jewels, and no silver. Only gold."

"It is done."

"This caravanserai is vast, as you have seen, and full of hay at the moment. The gold bars have been buried in the haystacks. We know where they are. You do not. As soon as you have given us the documents declaring us free men, and set us on the road, or the river, with our share of the money in our pockets—in the form of pieces of eight—we will tell you where to find the gold."

"That cannot be your entire plan," said the Duke. "There is not so much hay here that we cannot simply arrest you, and then search it all at our leisure."

"While we were going through the stables, hiding the gold, we spilled quite a bit of lamp-oil on the floor, and buried a few powder-kegs in haystacks for good measure," Jack said.

Pierre de Jonzac shouted a command to a junior officer back in the stables.

"You threaten to burn the caravanserai, then," said the Duke, as if everything Jack said had to be translated into childish language.

"The gold will melt and run into the drains. You will recover some of it, but you will lose more than you would by simply paying us our share and setting us free."

An officer came out on foot and whispered something to de Jonzac, who relayed it to the Duke.

"Very well," said the Duke.

"I beg your pardon?"

"My men have found the puddles of lamp-oil, your story seems to be correct, your proposal is accepted," said the Duke. He turned and nodded to his other aide, who opened up his saddle-bags and began to take out a series of identical-looking documents, formally sealed and beribboned in the style of the Ottoman bureaucracy.

Jack turned and beckoned toward the doorway where Nasr al-Ghuráb had been lurking. The *raïs* came out, laid down his arms, and approached the Duke's aide, who allowed him to inspect one of the documents. "It is a cancellation of a slave-deed," he said. "It is inscribed with the name of Jeronimo, and it declares him to be a free man."

"Read the others," Jack said.

"Now for the *important* matter, mentioned earlier," said the Duke, "which is the only reason I made the journey from Alexandria."

"Dappa," read al-Ghuráb from another scroll. "Nyazi."

A cart rattled out from behind the French lines, causing Jack to flinch; but it carried only a lock-box. "Your pieces of eight," the Duke explained, amused by Jack's nervousness.

"Yevgeny—and here is Gabriel Goto's," the *raïs* continued.

"Assuming that the wretch you displayed in Alexandria really was *L'Emmerdeur,* how much do you want for him?" the Duke inquired.

"As we are all free men now, or so it appears, we will *likewise* do the honorable thing, and let you have him for free—or not at all," said Jack.

"Here is that of van Hoek," said the *raïs,* "and here, a discharge for me."

Another tolerant smile from the Duke. "I cannot recommend strongly enough that you give him to me. Without *L'Emmerdeur* there is no transaction."

"Vrej Esphahnian—Padraig Tallow—Mr. Foot—"

"And despite your brave words," the Duke continued, "the fact remains that you are surrounded by my dragoons, musketeers, and Janissaries. The gold is mine, as surely as if it were locked up in my vault in Paris."

"This one has a blank space where the name should go," said Nasr al-Ghuráb, holding up the last document.

"That is only because we were not given *this* one's name," explained Pierre de Jonzac, pointing at Jack.

"Your vault in Paris," Jack said, echoing the Duke's words. He now spoke directly to the Duke, in the best French he could muster. "I am guessing that would be somewhere underneath the suite of bedchambers in the west wing, there, where you have that god-awful green marble statue of King Looie all tarted up as Neptune."

A Silence, now, almost as long as the one Jack had experienced, once, in the grand ballroom of the Hôtel Arcachon. But all things considered, the Duke recovered quickly—which meant either that he'd known all along, or that he was more adaptable than he looked. De Jonzac and the other aide were dumbfounded. The Duke moved his horse a couple of steps nearer, the better to peer down at Jack's face. Jack stepped forward, close enough to feel the breath from the horse's nostrils, and pulled the turban from his head.

"This need not alter the terms of the transaction, Jack," said the Duke. "Your comrades can all be free and rich, with a single word from you."

Jack stood there and considered it—genuinely—for a minute or two, as horses snorted and punks smoldered in the dark vaults of the caravanserai all around him. One small gesture of Christlike self-abnegation and he could give his comrades the wealth and freedom they deserved. At any earlier part of his life he would have scoffed at the idea. Now, it strangely tempted him.

For a few moments, anyway.

"Alas, you are a day too late," he said at last, "for last night my comrades swore any number of mickle oaths to me, and I intend to hold them to account. 'Twere bad form, otherwise."

And then in a single motion he drew out his Janissary-sword and plunged it all the way to the hilt into the neck of the Duke's horse, aiming for the heart. When he hit it, the immense muscle clenched like a fist around the wide head of the blade, then went limp as the watered steel cleaved it in twain.

The blade came out driven on a jet of blood as thick as his wrist. The horse reared up, the Duke's jeweled spurs flailing in the air. Jack stepped to one side, drawing a pistol from his waistband with his free hand, and fired a ball through the head of the aide who had brought the documents. The Duke just avoided falling off his horse, but managed to hold on as it bolted forward a couple of paces and then fell over sideways, pinning one of the Duke's legs and (as Jack could hear) breaking it.

Jack looked up to see Pierre de Jonzac aiming a pistol at him from no more than two yards away. Moseh had meanwhile stuck his tongue out, and gone into motion. A flying hatchet lodged in de Jonzac's shoulder, causing him to drop the weapon. A moment later his horse collapsed, shot through the head, and de Jonzac was thrown to the ground practically at Jack's feet. Jack snatched the fallen pistol; aimed it at the head of de Jonzac; then moved the barrel slightly to one side and fired into the ground.

"My men think you are dead now, and won't waste balls on you," Jack said. "In fact I have let you live, but for one purpose only: so that you can make your way back to Paris and tell them the following: that the deed you are about to witness was done for a woman, whose name I will not say, for she knows who she is; and that it was done by 'Half-Cocked' Jack Shaftoe, *L'Emmerdeur,* the King of the Vagabonds, Ali Zaybak: Quicksilver!"

As he said these words he was stepping over to the Duc d'Arcachon, who had dragged himself out from under his horse and was lying there, hatless and wigless, propped up on one elbow, with the jagged ends of his leg-bones poking out through the bloody tissues of his silk stockings.

"Here I am supposed to give you a full account and explanation of your sins, and why you deserve this," Jack announced, "but there is no time. Suffice it to say that I am thinking of a mother and daughter you once abducted, and disgraced, and sold into slavery."

The Duke pondered this for a moment, looking bewildered, and then said: "Which ones?"

Then Jack brought the bright blade of the Janissary-sword down like a thunderbolt, and the head of Louis-François de Lavardac, duc d'Arcachon, bounced and spun in the dirt of Khan el-Khalili in the center of the Mother of the World, and the dust of the Sahara began to cloud the lenses of his eyes.

Now Jack got the idea that it was raining, because of the spurts of dust erupting from the ground all around him. Frenchmen, Janissaries, or both were firing at him from above—feeling free to do so now that Jack had apparently slain all three of the Frenchmen in the alley. Monsieur Arlanc and Nasr al-Ghuráb had made themselves scarce. Jack ran into the stables, which had become the scene of a strange sort of indoor battle. Nyazi's men, and the Cabal, were outnumbered. But they'd had plenty of time to ready positions among the haystacks and watering-troughs of the stable, and to string tripwires between pillars. They could have held the French and Turks off all day, if not for the fact that the stables had been set on fire—possibly on purpose, but more likely by the muzzle-flash of a weapon. Jack vaulted into a trough, drenching himself and his clothes, and then scurried back through an apparently random hail of musket-balls to where Yevgeny, Padraig, Jeronimo, Gabriel Goto, the Nubian eunuch, and several of Nyazi's clan were frantically rifling haystacks for gold bars and piling them into heavy wagons. These were drawn by nervous horses with grain-sacks over their heads to keep them from seeing the flames—a cheap subterfuge that was already wearing thin. At a glance Jack estimated that somewhat more than half of the gold had been recovered.

Moseh, Vrej, and Surendranath, with their merchants' aptitude for figures, knew where every last bar was hid, and were making sure that none went missing. That was a job best done by calm men. As men were more intelligent than horses, one could not keep them calm by putting sacks over their heads; some kind of real security had to be provided, from fire, smoke, Janissaries, dragoons, and—what else had the Duke mentioned?

"Have you seen any French musketeers?" Jack inquired, when he had located Nyazi. As long as they remained in the stables, Nyazi was their general.

It was easier to talk now than it had been a few minutes ago. Smoke had rendered muskets useless, and flames the possession of gunpowder extremely dangerous. The thuds of musket-fire had died away and were being supplanted by the ring of blade against blade, and the shouting of men trying to shift their burdens of fear to their foes.

"What is a musketeer?"

"The Duke claimed he had some," Jack said, which did not answer Nyazi's question. But there was no time to explain the distinction between dragoons and musketeers now.

A horn had begun to blow from the back of the stables, giving the signal that the gold wagons were ready to depart. Nyazi began to holler orders to his clansmen, who were distributed around the smoke in some way that was clear only to him, and they began falling back toward the wagons. This was their attempt at an orderly retreat under fire, which as Jack knew was no easy thing to manage even with regular troops under good conditions. In fact it was almost as chaotic as the advance of the Janissaries, who had overrun at least part of Nyazi's defensive line and were now stumbling forward, gasping and gagging, tripping over rakes and slamming into pillars, charging toward the sound of the trumpet call—not so much because the enemy and the gold were there, as because one could not blow a bugle without drawing breath, and so it proved that air was to be had ahead.

Jack got as far as a place where the smoke was diluted by a current of fresh air, then was nearly spitted by a bayonet-thrust coming in from his left rear, aimed at his kidney. Jack spun almost entirely around to the right, so the tip of the blade snagged in the muscle of his back but was deflected, cutting and tearing the flesh but not piercing his organs. At the same time he was delivering a back-handed cut to the head of the bayonet's owner. So the fight was over before Jack knew it had started. But it led immediately to a real sword-fight with a Frenchman—an officer who had a small-sword, and knew how to use it. Jack, fighting with a heavier and slower weapon, knew he would have to end this on the first or second exchange of blows, or else his opponent could simply stand off at a distance and poke holes through him until he bled to death.

Jack's first attack was abortive, though, and his second was nicely parried by the Frenchman—who backed into a pitchfork that was lying on the floor, and tripped over its handle, sprawling back onto his arse. Jack snatched up the pitchfork and flung it like a trident at his opponent just as he was scrambling to his feet. It did no damage, but in knocking it aside, the Frenchman left himself open for a moment and Jack leapt forward swinging. His opponent tried to block the blow with the middle of his small-sword, but this weapon—designed for twitchy finger-fighting and balletic lunges—was feeble shelter against Jack's blade of watered steel. The Janissary-blade knocked the rapier clean out of the French officer's hand and went on to cut his body nearly in half.

There was a clamor of voices and blades and whinnying horses off to his right. Jack desperately wanted to get over there, because he suspected he was alone and surrounded.

Then one of the powder-kegs exploded. At least that was the easiest way to explain the crushing sound, the horizontal storm of barrel-staves, pebbles, nails, horseshoes, and body parts that came and went through the smoke, and the sudden moaning and popping of timbers as sections of floor collapsed. Jack's ears stopped working. But his skull ended up pressed against the stone floor, which conducted, directly into his brain, the sound of horseshoes flailing, iron-rimmed cartwheels grinding and screeching, and—sad to say—at least one cart-load of gold bars overturning as panicked horses took it round a corner too fast. Each bar radiated a blinding noise as it struck the pavement.

Lying flat on his back gave him the useful insight that there was a layer of clear air riding just above the floor. He pulled his soaked tunic off, tied it over his mouth and nose, and began crawling on his naked belly. The place was a maze of haystacks and corpses, but light was shining in through a huge stone arch-way. He dragged himself through it, and out into the open—and into battle.

Monsieur Arlanc got his attention by pelting him in the head with a small rock, and beckoned him to safety behind an overturned cart.

Jack lay amid scattered gold bars for a while, just breathing. Meanwhile Monsieur Arlanc was crawling to and fro on his belly, gathering the bullion together and stacking it up to make a rampart. The occasional musket-ball whacked into it, but most of the fire was passing over their heads.

Rolling over onto his belly and peering out through a gun-slit that the Huguenot had prudently left between gold bars, Jack could see the large floppy hats characteristic of French musketeers. They had formed up in several parallel ranks, completely blocking the street that ran down to the canal where the Cabal's means of escape was waiting. These ranks took turns kneeling, loading, standing, aiming, and firing, keeping up a steady barrage of musket-balls that made it impossible for the men of the Cabal to advance, or even to stand up. This human road-block was only about forty yards away, and was completely exposed. But it worked because the Cabal's forces did not have enough muskets, powder, and balls left to return fire. And it would continue working for as long as those musketeers were supplied with ammunition.

Meanwhile the stable continued to burn, and occasionally explode, behind them. The situation could not possibly be as dire as it *seemed* or they would all be dead. Between volleys of musketeer-fire Jack heard the whinny of horses and the rattling bray of camels. He looked to the left and saw a stable-yard, surrounded by a low stone wall, where several of Nyazi's men had gotten their camels to kneel and their horses to lie down on their sides. So they had a sort of reserve, anyway, that could be used to pull the carts down to the boat—but not as long as those carts were forty yards in front of a company of musketeers.

"We have to outflank those bastards," Jack said. Which was obvious—so others must have thought of it already—which would explain the fact that only a few members of the Cabal were in evidence here. The left flank, once he looked beyond that embattled stable-yard, looked like a cul-de-sac; movement that way was blocked by a high stone wall that looked as if it might have been part of Cairo's fortifications in some past æon, and was now a jumbled stone-quarry.

So Jack crawled to the right, working his way along the line of gold-ramparts and immobilized carts, and spied a side-street leading off into the maze of the Khan el-Khalili. At the entrance of this street, a Janissary was pinned to a wooden door by an eight-foot-long spear, which Jack looked on as proving that Yevgeny had passed by there recently. A hookah jetted arcs of brown water from several musket wounds. Once he had entered the street, and gotten out of view of the musketeers, Jack got to his feet and threw his weight against a green wooden door. But it was solider than it looked, and well-barred from the inside. The same presumably went for every door and window that fronted on this street; there was no way to go but forward.

He rounded a tight curve and came to a wee square, the sort of thing that in Paris might have, planted in its center, a life-size statue of Leroy leading his regiments across the Rhine, or something. In place of which stood Yevgeny, feet planted wide, arms up in the air, manipulating a half-pike that he had evidently ripped from the hands of a foe. Yevgeny was holding it near its balance-point and whirling it round and round so fast that he, and the pike, taken together, seemed and sounded like a monstrous hummingbird. Three Janissaries stood round about him at a respectful distance; two, who'd ventured within the fatal radius, lay spreadeagled in the dust bleeding freely from giant lacerations of the head.

One dropped to his knees and tried to come in under Yevgeny's pike, but the Russian, who was turning slowly round and round even as he spun the weapon, canted the plane of its movement in such a way that its sharpened end swept the fellow's cap off, and might have scalped him had he been an inch closer. He collapsed to his belly and crept back away—which was not possible to do quickly.

All this presented itself to Jack's eyes in the first moment that he came into this tiny plaza. His first thought was that Yevgeny would be defenseless against anyone who came upon the scene with a projectile weapon. Scarcely had this entered his mind when one of the two standing Janissaries backed into a door-nook, withdrew a discharged pistol from his waist-sash, and set about loading it. Jack picked up a fist-sized stone and flung it at this man. Yevgeny stopped his pike in mid-whirl, swung the butt high into the air, and drove the point into the body of the man who'd dropped to his stomach. The third, construing this as an opening, gathered his feet under him so as to spring at Yevgeny. Noting this, Jack let out a scream that astonished the man and made him have second thoughts and go all tangle-footed. He turned towards Jack and, distracted as he was by Yevgeny on his flank, parried an imagined attack from Jack, and mounted a weak one of his own. Yevgeny meanwhile chucked the pike at the pistol-loader, who had dropped his weapon into the dirt when Jack's rock had caught him amidships (which was understandable) and gone down on both knees to retrieve it (a fatal mistake, as it had turned him into a stationary target).

The one who was fighting with Jack swooped his blade wildly from side to side. This was not a good technique, but its sheer recklessness set Jack back on his heels long enough for him to turn and run away. Yevgeny noted this, and pursued him hotly.

Three ways joined together in this little space. Jack had entered along one of them. That poor unnerved Janissary, and Yevgeny, had exited along the way that led off to Jack's left. This was the way Jack needed to probe if there was to be any hope of outflanking the musketeers. It led imperceptibly downhill, away from the caravanserai and towards the canal. To Jack's right, then, was a needle's eye, which is to say a very narrow arch built to admit humans while preventing camels from passing out of the stables. Peering through that, he saw that beyond it the alley broadened and ran straight for about ten yards to a side entrance of the caravanserai, which was sucking in a palpable draft of air to feed the howling and cackling flames. A squad of some eight or ten French soldiers were just emerging from the smoke. They had prudently cast off their muskets and powderhorns, but otherwise looked none the worse for wear—they must have found some way to circumvent the fire.

But Jack's view of these was suddenly blocked by a figure in a black ankle-length robe: Gabriel Goto, who stepped out from the shelter of a doorway and took up a position blocking the eye of the needle. At the moment he appeared to be unarmed; but he stopped the Frenchmen in their tracks anyway, by raising up his right hand and uttering some solemn words in Latin. Jack was no Papist, but he'd been in enough battles and poorhouses to recognize the rite of extreme unction, the last sacrament given to men who were about to die.

Hearing musket-fire from the opposite way out—the way Yevgeny had gone—Jack turned to look, and saw a somewhat wider street that wound off in the direction of where those musketeers had established their road-block. Ten or twelve yards away, just where it curved out of view, a corpse lay sprawled on its back.

Jack turned round again to look at Gabriel Goto, who had planted himself just on this side of the needle's eye and was standing in a prayerful attitude as the Frenchmen came towards him. The samurai waited until they were no more than two yards away. Then he reached under his cloak and drew out his two-handed saber, gliding forward in the same movement, like a snake over grass, and tracing a compound diagram in the air with his sword-tip. Then he drew back, and Jack noticed that the head, neck, and right arm of one Frenchman were missing—removed by a single diagonal cut.

As Gabriel Goto seemed to have matters well in hand at the needle's eye, Jack went the other way, slowing as he approached the corpse that lay in the street. It was the Turk from Monsieur Arlanc's oar. He had been shot in the head with a musket, which was a polite way of saying that a lead ball three-quarters of an inch in diameter had hit him between the eyes traveling at several hundred miles an hour and turned much of his skull into a steaming crater. This gave Jack the idea of looking up, which was fortunate, as he saw a French musketeer kneeling on a rooftop above, aiming a musket directly at him. Smoke squirted from the pan. Jack darted sideways. A musket-ball slammed into a stone corner just above him, driving a shower of flakes into his face but not doing any real harm. Jack jumped back out and looked up to see Nasr al-Ghuráb up on that rooftop, lunging at the musketeer with a dagger. The *raïs* won that struggle in a few moments. But then he was struck in the leg by a musket-ball fired, from only a few yards' distance, by a Janissary posted directly across the way. He fell, clutching his leg, and looking in astonishment and horror at the fellow who'd shot him, and shouted a few words in Turkish.

Jack meanwhile ran ahead, rounded a curve, and was confronted by a Y. The left fork led to a point in the main street, directly in front of the musketeers' position; anyone who did so much as poke his head out of there would get it blown off in an instant. The right fork led to a point *behind* the musketeers, and so that was the one they wanted; but the French had had the good sense to throw up a barricade consisting of a wagon rolled over onto its side. Two muskets were immediately fired at Jack, who without thinking dove headlong into the deep gutter that ran down the center of the street. This had no more than a trickle of sewage in the bottom; it was lined with stone and (because of the slight curve in the street) protected him from musket-fire.

He rolled onto his back and looked straight up to see the sniper who had shot al-Ghuráb having his throat cut by Nyazi, who had somehow gotten to the roof. But rather than advancing, Nyazi was obliged to throw himself down to avoid fire from a few other Janissaries who were on the adjoining rooftop. Though he could not understand much Turkish or Arabic, Jack could tell the two languages apart by their sounds, and he was certain that several other Arabic-speaking men—Nyazi's clansmen—were up there, too. So it was going to be camel-traders versus Janissaries on the rooftops.

Levering himself up on his elbows and surveying the street, Jack could now see Yevgeny, Padraig, and the Nubian backed into doorways, safe for now, but unable to advance toward the musketeers' barricade.

Jack retreated up the gutter, squirming like an eel, until he was out of the line of fire, then got to his feet and ran back to the front of the stables, where the wagon-train was pinned down. There he could see into the stable-yard, where Jeronimo was saddling an Arab horse, apparently getting ready to do something.

From one of their supply-wagons Jack secured a powder-keg and an earthenware jar of lamp-oil. Then he turned round and went back, at first crawling on his belly and pushing these items before him, later hugging the keg to his belly and running. A rightward glance at the T intersection told him that Gabriel Goto was still embroiled at the needle's eye, French body parts continuing to thud down every few seconds. The sword whirling through the air tracing Barock figures, like the pen of a royal calligrapher.

Jack paused near the Turk's body to pry the wax-sealed bung from the jar of lamp-oil. He poured about half the contents over the powder-keg, dribbling it on slowly so that it soaked into the dry wood rather than running off. Then he came round the curve into the Y intersection and dove once more into the gutter: a trough with vertical sides and a rounded bottom, like a U, wide enough that the keg, laid sideways, could fit into it, remaining mostly below street level. But the round ends of the keg, bound by iron hoops, rolled like cartwheels along the sloping sides of the U.

Pushing the reeking keg in front of him, he inched forward until he began to draw direct fire from the musketeers manning the barricade, no more than ten yards away. Then he gave the keg a panicky shove and backed away. His intention had been to pour the remainder of the lamp-oil into the gutter and use it as a sort of liquid fuse. But here events overtook him. For Yevgeny had come up with the idea of trying to set fire to the barricade, and had fashioned a sort of burning lance from a spear and an oily rag. As Jack watched from the gutter, Yevgeny fired a pistol alongside this contrivance, igniting it; then he stepped out into the street and immediately took a musket-ball in the ribs. He paused, stepped farther into the street, and took another in the thigh. But these wounds apparently did not even qualify as painful by Russian standards, and so with perfect aplomb he hefted the flaming harpoon, judged the distance, then hopped forward three times on his good leg and hurled it towards the powder-keg. Another musket-ball hit him in the left wrist and spun him around. He fell like a toppled oak towards the street. At the same moment Jack rolled up out of the gutter and found himself standing in the middle of the Y with his back to the barricade.

There was a sudden bright light. It cast a long shadow behind Gabriel Goto, who was walking down the street painting the ashlars with a long streak of blood that drizzled from the hem of his black robe. He appeared to be perfectly unharmed.

Jack turned around to see planks fluttering down all over the neighborhood, and stray wagon-wheels bounding along the street. The right fork of the Y, where the barricade had once stood, was just a smoky mess. Above it, on the rooftop, Nasr al-Ghuráb had dragged himself into position despite a flayed and butchered thigh. He whipped out a cutlass, threw his good leg over the parapet, shouted "Allahu Akbar!" and fell into the inferno, landing on two musketeers, crushing one and cutting the other in half.

At the same moment, Jack saw movement down the left fork of the Y, which had not figured much into the battle as it led to a place directly in front of the musketeers. But all of a sudden a lone man on horseback was galloping across that space: It was Excellentissimo Domino Jeronimo Alejandro Peñasco de Halcones Quinto, mounting a one-man cavalry charge on his Arab steed. He almost reached the enemy without suffering any injuries, for he had timed his charge carefully, and none of the musketeers were in position to fire. But as he galloped the last few yards, screaming "Estremaduras!" a shower of blood erupted from his back; some officer, perhaps, had shot him with a pistol. The horse was hit, too, and went down on its knees. This would have pitched any other man out of the saddle, but Jeronimo seemed to be ready for it. As he flew out of the saddle he shoved off with both feet, pitching his hindquarters upwards; tucked his head under; landed hard on one shoulder, and rolled completely over in a somersault. In the same continuous movement he sprang up to his feet, drew his rapier, and drove it all the way through the body of the officer who had shot him. "How do you like that, eh? El Torbellino made me practice that one until I pissed blood; and then he made me practice it some more until I got it right!" He pulled out the rapier and slashed its edge through the throat of another Frenchman who was coming up from one side. "Now you will learn that a man of Estremaduras can fight better when he is bleeding to death than a Frenchman in the pink of health! I judge that I have sixty seconds to live, which—" plunging his rapier into a a musketeer's neck "—should give me more than enough time to—" cutting another musketeer's throat "—kill a dozen of you—four so far—" he now revealed a dagger in the other hand, and stabbed a fleeing musketeer in the back "—make it five!"

But then several musketeers finally converged on El Desamparado, realizing that there was no escape from the man unless they killed him, and plunged their bayonets into his body.

"Yevgeny!" Jack shouted, for the Russian was only a few yards away from him, lying on his back in the street as if asleep. "We will be back with the heavy carts in a minute to get you."

Then Jack, Padraig, the Nubian, and Gabriel Goto charged the barricade four abreast, and got through what was left of it with no difficulty. Padraig stayed behind to batter the surviving musketeers into submission with a quarter-staff, and to pick over their bodies for better weapons. Above them, several of Nyazi's clansmen were charging across the rooftops, having overcome the Janissaries up there.

They came into the rear of the formation of musketeers that had been blocking the main street. At a glance Jack could not tell whether El Desamparado had slain his full quota of a dozen; but it was obvious that he would not slay any more. The rest were milling around, out of formation, and so Jack and his comrades simply discharged all of their remaining loaded firearms into their midst and then fell upon them with swords. The ones who survived all of this stumbled back over the bodies of El Desamparado and his victims and retreated into the side-street that had formed the left fork of the Y, where the men of Nyazi's clan were able to rain stones and a few musket-balls on their heads.

Finally, now, the clansmen of Nyazi were able to bring the horses out of the stable-yard and hitch them to the gold-wagons, though various dragoons, musketeers, and Janissaries continued to harass them from all around; and now the thieves of Cairo were beginning to make their presence known, too. Flocks of them began to coalesce in doorways and corners, hidden by the greedy shadows of late afternoon, and made occasional sorties into the light in the hope of fetching some gold. In spite of this, within a quarter of an hour they were able to drive away from the stables—a cyclone of flame now—with four of the original six gold-carts.

Jack and Gabriel Goto were riding on the last of these, supposedly to act as a rear-guard. But both of them had another errand in mind as well. When they came abreast of the side-street where the barricade had been exploded, they reined in the cart-horse, jumped off, and ran up to recover Yevgeny.

Because of the smoldering debris that half-choked the street, they could not see the place where he had fallen until they were almost upon it. But then they found nothing except a wide smear of gore. Yevgeny's blood had outlined the paving-stones in narrow red lines as it trickled between them, seeking the gutter. But Yevgeny himself was nowhere to be seen. The only other traces of him that remained were his left hand, which had been shot off, and a few rude characters drawn in blood on the pavement. An uneven line of bloody footsteps meandered up the street toward the stables, and disappeared into dust and smoke.

"Can you read it?" Jack asked Gabriel.

"It says, 'Go the long way round,'" Gabriel answered.

"What the hell does that mean?"

"Specifically? I do not know. Generally? It suggests that he will go some *other* way."

"Spoken like a Jesuit."

"He has gone *that* way," said Gabriel, pointing toward the caravanserai, "and we must go *this*." Pointing back towards the gold-carts.

"We are needed there anyway," Jack said, breaking into a run. For their cart had already come under attack from a mixed mob of thieves, Vagabonds, Janissaries, and French soldiers. The appearance of Jack and Gabriel on their flank, bloody sabers held high, got rid of most of them. But looters better armed and more determined were close behind them, and so Jack and Gabriel and a few of Nyazi's men rattled the half-mile down to the canal hotly pursued, though at a prudent distance, by a sort of wolf-pack.

At the foot of the street where it gave way to the canal, Mr. Foot, Vrej, Surendranath, and van Hoek were waiting—looking as if they had been through some adventures of their own this afternoon. They had thrown a heavy platform across the gap between the quay and the river-boat, and the other three gold-carts had already rumbled across it, spilling many of their contents on the deck.

Parked to one side of the street was a humble-looking hay-wain, harnessed to a camel. As the last cart, carrying Jack and Gabriel, jounced past it, a whip cracked and this vehicle bolted out into the middle of the street. By this point nothing could have prevented the gold-cart from reaching the platform, so Jack vaulted off of it, and turned round to face the hay-wain, anticipating some sort of attack. But by the time he had recovered his balance, the hay-wain had stopped in the middle of the street, directly in the path of the pursuing horde. The driver (Nyazi!) and another man (Moseh!) jumped off and chocked its wheels there, and at the same time the pile of hay on the cart's back seemed to come alive; most of the load showered into the street. Revealed were a long tubular black object (a cannon!) and, clambering to his feet next to it, a black man (Dappa!).

Now in a way this was not surprising, for it was all a part of the plan—they'd spent all of yesterday buying the damned piece. In another way it *was*, for it was supposed to have been set up at dockside, loaded, aimed, and ready to be fired. Instead of which it had just gotten here—*in the nick of time,* Jack thought, *if it had been loaded.* But Dappa, rather than jamming a torch against its touchhole, now began to rummage through a clanking assortment of implements strewn about his feet, while from time to time casting a glance up the length of the street to (at first) count, and (presently) estimate the number of heavily armed, screaming men sprinting their way.

"I have not done this before," he announced, fishing out, and inspecting, a long, rusty pick, "but have had it all explained to me, by men who have."

"Men who have lost sea-battles and been taken as galley-slaves," Jack added.

Dappa brushed hay from the butt of the cannon and shoved the pick into the touch-hole.

"Help load the boat!" Jack screamed at Moseh and Nyazi. To Dappa he suggested, "For Christ's sake, don't worry about clearing the bloody touch-hole!"

Dappa returned, "If you'd be so good as to get the tampion out of my way?"

Jack scurried around to the muzzle-side of the wagon, turned his back to the on-rushing horde—which was not a thing that came naturally to him—reached up, and yanked out a round wooden bung that had been stuffed into the gun's muzzle. It was shot out of his hand by a pistol-ball.

Dappa had an arrow through his sleeve, though not, apparently, through his arm. He was regarding a long-handled scoop. "As you are in such a hurry today," he announced, "we shall dispense with the customary procedure of swabbing out the barrel." As he spoke he shoved the scoop into some crunchy-sounding receptacle, which was hidden from Jack's view by the side of the wagon, and raised it up heaped with coarse black powder. Balancing this in one hand he produced a copper-bladed spatula in the other, and leveled the powder-charge; then, moving with utmost deliberation so as not to spill any, he turned the scoop end-for-end and introduced it to the cannon's muzzle, then, slowly at first, but quicker as he went along, hand-over-handed it until the entirety of its long handle had been swallowed by the barrel. He then gave it a half rotation to disgorge its load, and began gingerly to extract it.

Jack had until now been caught between a desire to make sure that Dappa didn't do it wrong, and a natural concern for what was approaching. To describe the foremost of the attackers as *irregulars* would have been to give far too high an estimate of their discipline, motives, armaments, and appearance; they were thieves, avaricious bystanders, micro-ethnic-groups, and a few Janissaries who had broken ranks when they had caught sight of gold bars. Most of these had faltered when they had caught sight of the cannon. But awareness had now propagated up the street that it was still in the process of being loaded. Meanwhile the French platoons had re-formed and begun marching in good order down the hill, reaming the street clear in a manner very like what the gun-swab would have done to the barrel of the cannon, had Dappa not elected to omit that step. The emboldened rabble swarming out from their places of conceal-ment mingled together with the not-so-emboldened ones being rammed down the street by this piston of French troops and all joined together into—

"An avalanche, or so 'tis claimed by certain *Alpine galériens* I have rowed with, may be triggered by the sound of cannon-fire." Dappa had torn off his shirt, wadded it up, and stuffed it down the barrel, and was now feeding in double handfuls of shot. He followed that with his turban, and finally took up his long rammer. "I wonder if we may *halt* an avalanche thus." His long dreadlocks, freed from the imprisonment of the head-wrap, fell about his face as he bent for-ward to get the pad of the rammer into the muzzle.

"Don't bother taking the rammer out—at this range 'twill serve as a javelin," was Jack's last advice to Dappa, as he turned his back and began to stalk up the hill towards the Mobb. For there were one or two fleet-footed scimitar-swingers, far ahead of the pack, who might arrive soon enough to interfere with the final steps of the rite.

"Where did that horn of priming-powder get to?" Dappa won-dered.

Jack feinted *left* long enough to convince the *hashishin* on the *right* that he had a clear path to Dappa; then Jack lashed out with a foot and tripped him as he ran by. Moseh emerged from nearer to the quay. He had located another boarding axe, his tongue was com-ing out, he had an eye on the man who'd just planted his face in the street, and he was followed by Nyazi and Gabriel Goto, who had been watching all of these developments with interest and decided to leave off ship-loading work.

A scimitar slashed downward from the left; Jack angled it off the back of his blade. A tapping sound from behind suggested that Dappa had found his priming-powder and was getting it into the touch-hole.

"Has anyone got a light?" Dappa said.

Jack butt-stroked his opponent across the jaw with the guard of his sword and yanked a discharged pistol out of the fellow's waist-band, then turned round and underhanded it across five or six yards of empty space to Dappa. Which might have got him killed, as it entailed turning his back on his opponent; but the latter knew what was good for him, and prudently flung himself down.

As did Jack; and (as he saw now, turning his head to look up the hill) as did nearly everyone else. A small number of utterly unhinged maniacs kept running toward them. Jack got to his feet, making sure he was well out of the way of the cannon's muzzle, and backed up to the wagon. Nyazi, Moseh, and Gabriel Goto closed ranks around him.

There followed a bit of a standoff. Crazed *hashishin* aside, no one in the street could move as long as Dappa had them under his gun. But as soon as Dappa fired it, he'd be defenseless, and they'd be swarmed under. Pot-shots whistled their way from a few doorways up the street; Dappa squatted down, but held his ground at the cannon's breech.

It bought them the time they needed, anyway. "All aboard!" called van Hoek—a bit late, as the boat had already cast off lines, and the gap between it and the quay was beginning to widen. "Now!" called Dappa. Jack, Nyazi, Gabriel Goto, and Moseh all turned and ran for it. Dappa stayed behind. The French regulars leapt to their feet and made for him double-time. Dappa cocked the pistol, held its pan above the small powder-filled depression that surrounded the orifice of the cannon's touch-hole, and pulled the trigger. Sparks showered and, like stars going behind clouds, were swallowed in a plume of smoke. A spurt of flame two fathoms long shot from the cannon's muzzle, driving the ram-rod, some pounds of buckshot, and half of Dappa's clothing up the length of the street. The riot that came his way a moment later suggested that none of it had been very effective. But by the time the Mobb engulfed the cannon, Dappa was sprinting down the quay. He jumped for it, caromed off the gunwale, and fell into the Nile; but scarcely had time to get wet before oars had been thrust into the water for him to grab onto. They pulled him aboard. Everyone went flat on the decks as the French soldiers discharged their muskets, once, in their general direction. Then they passed out of sight and out of range.

"What went awry?" van Hoek asked.

"Our escape-route was blocked by a company of French musketeers," Jack said.

"Fancy that," van Hoek muttered.

"Jeronimo and both of our Turks are dead."

"The *raïs?*"

"You heard me—he is dead, and now you are our Captain," Jack said.

"Yevgeny?"

"He dragged himself away to die. I suspect he did not want to be a burden on the rest of us," Jack said.

"That is hard news," van Hoek said, gripping his bandaged hand and squeezing it.

"It is noteworthy that both of the Turks were killed," said Vrej Esphahnian, who had overheard most of this. "More than likely one of them betrayed us; the Pasha in Algiers probably planned the whole thing, from the beginning, as a way to screw the Investor out of his share."

"The *raïs* seemed very surprised when he was shot by a Janissary," Jack allowed.

"It must have been part of the Turks' plan," said Vrej. "They would want to slay the traitor first of all, so that he would not tell the tale."

Upstream, a Turkish war-galley had been dispatched from Giza to pursue them. But it had feeble hope of catching them, for the Nile was not a wide river even at this time of the year, and such width as it had was choked by a jam of slow-moving grain barges.

Night fell as they were approaching the great fork of the Nile. They took the Rosetta branch to throw off their landward pursuers, then cut east across the Delta, following small canals, and got across to the Damietta Fork by poling the boat over an expanse of flooded fields several miles wide. By the time the sun rose the following morning, they had struck their masts, and anything else that projected more than six feet above the waterline, and were surrounded by tall reeds in the marshy expanses to the east.

At the end of that day they made rendezvous with a small caravan of Nyazi's people, and there a share of the gold was loaded onto their camels. Nyazi and the Nubian both said their farewells to the Cabal at this point and struck out for the south, Nyazi visibly excited at the thought of a reunion with his forty wives, and the Nubian trusting to fortune to get him back to the country from which he had been abducted.

Eastwards on the boat continued Jack, Mr. Foot, Dappa, Monsieur Arlanc, Padraig Tallow, Vrej Esphahnian, Surendranath, and Gabriel Goto, with van Hoek as their captain and Moseh as their designated Prophet. It was a role in which he seemed uncomfortable until one day, after many wanderings and lesser adventures, they came to a place where the reeds parted into something that could only be the Red Sea.

There Moseh stood in the bow of the boat, lit up by the rising sun, and spoke a few momentous words in half-remembered

Hebrew—prompting Jack to say, "Before you part the waters, there, please keep in mind that we're on a boat, and have nothing to gain from being left high and dry."

Van Hoek ordered the masts stepped and the sails raised, and they set a course for Mocha and the Orient, free men all.

BOOK 5

the Juncto

Eliza to Leibniz
LATE SEPTEMBER 1690

Doctor,

I have been a few days in Juvisy, a town on the left bank of the Seine, south of Paris, where Monsieur Rossignol has a château. This is a natural stopping-place for one who has come up from the south. I have been in Lyon for almost a month tending to some business, and am just now returning to Île-de-France. Juvisy is a sort of fork in the road; thence one may follow the river into Paris, or else strike cross-country westwards toward Versailles. Monsieur Rossignol placed his stables and staff at my disposal so that my little household, and our brief train of horses and carriages, could refresh themselves while they waited for me to make up my mind. Jean-Jacques is at Versailles, and I have not seen him since I departed for Lyon, and so my heart told me to go that way; but there is much to be done in Paris, and so my head bid me go thither. I am going to Paris.

When I woke up this morning, the estate was strangely quiet. I drew a blanket over my shoulders and went to the windows, where I beheld a grotesque scene: during the night the garden had become matted with unsightly lumps of damp straw. The gardeners, sensing an unseasonable drop in temperature yester evening, had been out late into the night packing straw around the smaller and more delicate plants, like nurses tucking their babies in under duvets. All was now dusted with silver. Taller plants, such as the roses, had frozen through. The little pools around the fountains were glazed, and the statues had picked up a frosty patina that gave keen definition to their rippling muscles and flowing garments. The place was quiet as a graveyard, for the workmen, having toiled half the night to erect ramparts of straw against the invading cold, were all sleeping late.

It was quite beautiful, especially when the sun came up over the hills beyond the Seine and suffused all of that frost with a cool peach-colored light. But of course for such cold to strike France in September is monstrous—it is like a comet or a two-headed baby. Spring was late in coming this year. France's hopes for an adequate harvest depended on a long, warm autumn. As much as I admired the beauty of those frosted roses, I knew that grain, apples, vines, and vegetables all over France must have suffered the same fate. I sent word to my staff to prepare for an early departure, then tarried in M. Rossignol's bedchamber only long enough to bid him a memorable farewell. Now—as you will have discerned from my wretched penmanship—we are in the carriage, rattling up the Left Bank into Paris.

During my earlier life here, I'd have been beside myself, for this early frost would have sent the commodities markets into violent motion, and it would have been of the highest importance for me to get instructions to Amsterdam. As matters stand, my responsibilities are more profound, but less immediate. Money surges and courses through this realm in the most inscrutable ways. I suppose one could construct some sort of strained analogy—Paris is the heart, and Lyons the lungs, or something—but in any event, the system does not work, and money does not flow, unless people *make* it work, and I have become one of those people. At first I worked mostly for the *Compagnie du Nord,* which imports Baltic timber to Dunkerque. Through this I came to know more than I should care to about how *le Roi* finances the war. Lately I have also become embroiled in some scheme of M. le duc d'Arcachon whose details remain vague. It was the latter that took me down to Lyon; for I traveled down there in August in the company of the Duke himself. He installed me in a *pied-à-terre* that he maintains in that city, then journeyed onwards to Marseille where he planned to embark on his *jacht* for points south.

We are coming up on the University already, we move too fast, the streets are empty as if the whole city mourns for the lost harvest. All is frozen except for we who move quickly so as not to freeze. Soon we shall cross the river and reach the *hôtel particulier* of Arcachon, and I have not got to the main points of my letter yet. Quickly then:

§ What do you hear from Sophie concerning Liselotte, or, as she is addressed here, Madame? For a few weeks, two years ago, she and I were close. Indeed I was prepared to jump in bed with her if she gave me the sign; but contrary to many steamy rumors, it never happened—she wanted my services as a spy, not as a lover. Since I returned to Versailles, she and I have had no contact at all.

She is a lonely woman. Her husband the King's brother is a homosexual, and she is a lesbian. So far, so good; but where Monsieur gets to indulge in as many lovers as he pleases, Madame must find love furtively. Monsieur, even though he does not desire Madame, is jealous of her, and persecutes and sends away her lovers.

If Court gossip has any truth in it, Madame had become close, in recent years, to the Dauphine. This is not to say that they were lovers, for the Dauphine had been having an affair with her maid, a Piedmontese woman, and was said to be quite faithful to her. But as birds of a feather flock together, Madame and the Dauphine, the maid, and a few other like-minded women had formed a little clique centered upon the Private Cabinet of the Dauphine's Apartment, just next to the Dauphin's quaint little library on the ground floor of the south wing.

I was aware of this two years ago, though I never saw the place with my own eyes. For I was engaged in those days as a tutor of the niece of M. la duchesse d'Oyonnax, who was lady-in-waiting to the Dauphine. By no means was the Duchess ever part of this little circle of *clitoristes,* for she is clearly an admirer of young men. But she knew of it, and was in and out of the Private Cabinet all the time, waiting on these people, attending their levées and couchées and so on.

Now as you must have heard, a few months ago the Dauphine died suddenly. Of course, whenever anyone dies suddenly here, foul play is suspected, especially if the decedent was close to M. la duchesse d'Oyonnax. Over the summer, everyone was expecting the Dauphin to marry Oyonnax, which would have made her the next Queen of France; but instead he has secretly married his former mistress—the maid-of-honor of his half-brother. Not a very prestigious match!

So nothing is clear. Those who cannot rid their minds of the conviction that the Dauphine must have been poisoned by Oyonnax, have had to develop ever more fanciful hypotheses: that there is some secret understanding between her and the Dauphin, for example, that will bring her a Prince of the Blood as her husband, &c., &c.

Personally, while harboring no illusions as to the moral character of Oyonnax, I doubt that she murdered the Dauphine, because she is too clever to do anything so obvious, and because it has deprived her of one of the most prestigious stations at Court: lady-in-waiting to the next Queen. But I cannot help but wonder as to the state of mind of poor Liselotte, who has seen her most intimate social circle exploded, and no longer has a comfortable haven within the Palace. I believe that Oyonnax may have positioned herself so as to be drawn into that vacuum. I wonder if Madame writes to Sophie about this. I could simply ask M. Rossignol, who reads all her letters, but I don't wish to abuse my position as his mistress—not yet, anyway!

§ Speaking of M. Rossignol:

Though my stay at Château Juvisy was cut short by the frost, I was able to notice several books on his library table, written in a queer alphabet that I recognized dimly from my time in Constantinople but could not quite place. I asked him about it, and he said it was Armenian. This struck me as funny since I had supposed that he would have his hands quite full with all of the cyphers in French, Spanish, Latin, German, &c., without having to look so far afield.

He explained that M. le duc d'Arcachon, prior to his departure for Marseille in August, had made an unusual request of the *Cabinet Noir:* namely, that they examine with particular care any letters originating from a Spanish town called Sanlúcar de Barrameda during the first week of August. The *Cabinet* had assented readily, knowing that letters came into France from that part of the world only rarely, and that most were grubby notes from homesick sailors.

But oddly enough, a letter had come across M. Rossignol's desk, apparently postmarked from Sanlúcar de Barrameda around the fifth day of August. A strange heathenish-looking thing it had been, apparently penned and sealed in some Mahometan place and transported none too gently across the sea to Sanlúcar. It was written in Armenian, and it was addressed to an Armenian family in Paris. The address given was the Bastille.

As bizarre, as striking as this was, even I might have let it pass without further notice had it not been for the fact that on the sixth of August a remarkable act of piracy is said to have taken place off Sanlúcar: as you may have heard, a band of Barbary Corsairs, disguised as galley-slaves, boarded a ship recently returned from New Spain and made off with some silver. I am certain that M. le duc d'Arcachon is somehow implicated.

[Written later in a more legible hand]

We have reached the Paris dwelling of the de Lavardacs, the Hôtel d'Arcachon, and I am now at a proper writing-desk, as you can see.

To finish that matter of the Armenian letter: I know that you, Doctor, have an interest in strange systems of writing, and that you are in charge of a great library. If you have anything on the Armenian language, I invite you to correspond with M. Rossignol. For though he is fascinated by this letter, he can do very little with it. He had one of his clerks make an accurate copy of the thing, then re-sealed it, and has been trying to track down any surviving addressees, in hopes that he may deliver it to them. If they are alive, and they choose to write back, M. Rossignol will inspect their letter and try to glean more clews as to the nature of the cypher (if any) they are using.

§ Speaking of letters, I must get this one posted today, and so let me raise one more matter. This concerns Sophie's banker, Lothar von Hacklheber.

I saw Lothar recently in Lyon. I did not *wish* to see him, but he was difficult to evade. Both of us had been invited to dinner at the home of a prominent member of the *Dépôt*. For various reasons I could not refuse the invitation; I suspect that Lothar orchestrated the whole affair.

To shorten this account somewhat, I shall tell you now what I only divined later. For as my driver and footmen would be tarrying in the stables for some hours with Lothar's, I had given instructions to *mine* that they should find out all that they could from *his*. It had become obvious that Lothar was trying to dig up information concerning me, and I reckoned that turnabout was fair play. Of course his grooms and drivers could know nothing of what Lothar had been thinking or doing, but they would at least know where he had gone and when.

Through this channel, I learned that Lothar had set out from Leipzig in July with a large train, including a prætorian guard of mercenaries, and made his way down to Cadiz, where he had transacted certain business; but then he had withdrawn up the coast to Sanlúcar de Barrameda, where he had apparently expected some momentous transaction to come off during the first week of August. But something had gone wrong. He had flown into a rage and made a tremendous commotion, despatching runners and spies in all directions. After a few days he had given orders for the whole train to ride up to Arcachon, which is a long hard journey over land; but they had done it. Lothar meanwhile accomplished the same journey in a hired barque, so that he was waiting for them when they arrived at Arcachon late in August. Immediately he announced that they would turn around and make for Marseille. Which they did, at the cost of several horses and one man; but they reached the place a few days too late—late for *what*, these informants knew not—and so they withdrew up the Rhône to Lyon, which is a place where Lothar is much more comfortable. Of course I was already in Lyon, having been dropped off there by M. le duc d'Arcachon a week earlier; from which it was easy enough to guess that the person Lothar had hoped, but failed, to intercept in Marseille had been M. le duc. Now perhaps it was his intention to tarry in Lyon, and wait for the return of d'Arcachon. I was going to add "like a spider in his web" or some such expression, but it struck me as absurd, given that Lothar is a mere baron, and a foreigner from a country with which we are at war, while the duc d'Arcachon is a Peer, and one of the most important men in France. I stayed my quill, as it would seem ludicrous to liken this obscure and outlandish Baron to a spider, and the duc d'Arcachon to a fly. And yet *in person* Lothar is much more formidable than the duc. At the House of Huygens I have seen a spider through a magnifying-glass, and Lothar, with his round abdomen and his ghastly pox-marked face, looked more like it than any other human I have beheld. Spider-like was he in the way that he dominated the dinner-table, for it seemed that every other person in the room was noosed to a silken cord whose end was gripped in his dirty ink-stained mitt, so that when he wanted some answer from someone he need only give them a jerk. He was absurd in his determination to find out from me precisely *when* M. le duc would be returning from his Mediterranean cruise. Every time I beat back one of his forays he would retreat, scamper around, and attack from a new quarter. Truly it was like wrestling with an eight-legged monster. It demanded all of my wits not to divulge anything, or to tumble into one of his verbal traps. I was tired, having spent the day meeting with one of Lothar's competitors discussing certain very complicated arrangements. I had gone to this dinner naïvely expecting persiflage. Instead I was being grilled by this ruthless and relentless man, who was like some Jesuit of the Inquisition in his acute perception of any evasions or contradictions in my answers. It is a good thing I had come alone, or else whatever gentleman had escorted me should have been honor-bound to challenge Lothar to a duel. As it was, our host *almost* did, so shocked was he by the way that Lothar was ruining his dinner-party. But I believe that even this was a sort of message that Lothar intended to send to me, and through me to the duc: that so angry was he over what had occurred off Sanlúcar de Barrameda that he considered himself in a state akin to war, in which normal standards of behavior were cast aside.

You are probably terrified, Doctor, that I am about to demand a formal apology of Lothar, and that I have designated you as the luckless messenger. Not so, for as I have told you, it is obvious that Lothar has no intention of apologizing for anything. Whatever M. le duc d'Arcachon took from him is more important than his reputation or even his honor. He was announcing as much by his behavior at dinner, and I doubt not that word of it has already gone out among all of the members of the *Dépôt*. The bankers I was dealing with there suddenly lost their nerve, and broke off negotiations with me—all except one, a Genoan with a very tough reputation, who is demanding a large rake-off "to cover the extraordinary precautions," and who insisted that a peculiar clause be inserted into the agreement: namely, that he would accept *silver,* but never *gold.*

I fear that in the end I failed utterly to keep Lothar at bay. *How long will Mademoiselle be staying in Lyon?* I have no fixed plans, mein Herr. *But is it not true, mademoiselle, that a soirée is planned at the Hôtel d'Arcachon on the fourteenth of October?* How did you know of this, mein Herr? *How I know of it is none of your concern, mademoiselle—but that is a fixed plan, is it not? And so it is not truthful, is it, to assert, as you have just done, that you have no fixed plans?* And so on. Lothar knew more than he should have known, for he must have spies at Versailles or in Paris; and whenever he divulged some morsel of information he had thus acquired, it was as if he had punched me in the stomach. I could not hold my own against him. He must have known, by the end of the dinner, that le duc would be passing through Lyon at some time during the first or second week of October. He is down there now, I am certain, waiting; and I have sent word, every way I know how, to the naval authorities in Marseille, that when le duc returns he must take great care.

Thus forewarned, le duc ought to be perfectly safe; for how much power can one Saxon baron wield, in Lyon? Yet Lothar's bizarre confidence jangled my nerves.

It was not until later, during my third round of negotiations with the said Genoan banker, that I began to get some inkling of what motivated Lothar, and how he knew so much. This banker—after a lengthy discussion of silver vs. gold—rolled his eyes and made some disparaging reference to Alchemists.

Now, during that dreadful dinner, Lothar had, more than once, made some dismissive comment about M. le duc, along the lines of "He does not know what he has blundered into."

On the admittedly fragile basis of these two remarks, I have developed a hypothesis—a vague one—that the ship that was looted off Sanlúcar de Barrameda contained something of great importance to those—and I now number Lothar among them—who put stock in Alchemy. It appears that M. le duc d'Arcachon, in concert with his Turkish friends, has stolen that cargo—but perhaps they do not comprehend what it is. Now, all of the Alchemists are up in arms about it. This would explain how Lothar has come to be so well-informed as to what is happening in Versailles and in Paris, for many members of the Esoteric Brotherhood are to be found in both places, and perhaps Lothar has been getting despatches from them.

I have seen you, Doctor, standing next to Lothar on the balcony of the House of the Golden Mercury in Leipzig. And it is well known that Lothar is banker to Sophie and Ernst August, your patrons. What can you tell me of this man and what motivates him? For most Alchemists are ninehammers and dilettantes; but if my hypothesis is correct, *he* takes it seriously.

That is all for now. Members of this household are queued up six deep outside the door of this chamber, waiting for me to finish so that they can importune me to make this or that decision concerning the party planned for the fourteenth. Between now and then, I shall be absurdly busy. You shall not hear from me until it is all over, and then everything is going to be different; for on that evening, many dramatic changes may be expected. I can say no more now. When you read this, wish me luck.

Eliza

Leibniz to Eliza

EARLY OCTOBER 1690

Mademoiselle,

Please accept my apologies on behalf of all German barons.

I have already told you the tale of how, when I was five years old, following my father's death, I went into his library and began to educate myself. This alarmed my teachers at the Nikolaischule, who prevailed upon my mother to lock me out. A local nobleman became aware of this, and paid a call on my mother, and in the most gentlemanly way possible, yet with utmost gravity and firmness, made her see that the teachers in this case were fools. She unlocked the library.

That nobleman was Egon von Hacklheber. The year must have been 1651 or 1652—memory fades. I recall him as a silver-haired gentleman, a sort of long-lost, peregrine uncle of that family, who had spent most of his life in Bohemia, but who had turned up in Leipzig around 1630—driven there, one presumes, by the fortunes of what we now call the Thirty Years' War, but what in those days just seemed like an endless and mindless succession of atrocities.

Shortly after he caused the library to be unlocked for me, Egon departed on a journey to the west, which was expected to last for several months, and to take him as far as England; but on a road in the Harz Mountains he was waylaid by robbers, and died. By the time his remains were found, they were nothing more than a skeleton, picked clean by ravens and ants, still clad in his cloak.

Lothar had been born in 1630, the third son of that family. None of those boys had attended school. They had been raised within the household, and educated by tutors—some hired, others simply members of the family who possessed knowledge, and a willingness to impart it. Egon von Hacklheber, a man of exceptional erudition, who had traveled widely, had devoted an hour or two each day to educating the three von Hacklheber boys. Lothar had been his brightest pupil; for, being the youngest, he had to work hardest to keep up with his brothers.

If you have done the arithmetic, you'll know that Lothar was in his early twenties when Egon departed on his fatal journey. By that time, dark days had fallen on that family, for smallpox had burned through Leipzig, taken the lives of the two older boys, and left Lothar—now the scion—mutilated as you have seen him. The death of his uncle Egon perfected Lothar's misery.

Much later—rather recently, in fact—I became aware that Lothar maintains some peculiar notions as to what "really" happened. Lothar believes that Egon knew Alchemy—that he was, in fact, an adept of such power that he could heal the gravest illnesses, and even raise the dead. Yet he would not, or could not, save the lives of Lothar's two brothers, whom he loved almost as if they were his own sons. Egon had departed from Leipzig with a broken heart, with no intention of ever coming back. His death in the Harz might have been suicide. Or—again this is all according to the eccentric notions of Lothar—it might have been faked, to hide his own unnatural longevity.

I believe that Lothar is simply out of his mind concerning this. The death of his brothers made him crazy in certain respects. Be that as it may, he believes in Alchemy, and phant'sies that if Egon had stayed in Leipzig a few years longer he might have imparted to Lothar the secrets of Creation. Lothar has not ceased to pursue those secrets himself, by his own methods, in the thirty-some years since.

Now, as to the infamous Duchess of Oyonnax—

"I LEFT INSTRUCTIONS NOT to be disturbed."

"Please forgive me, mademoiselle," said the big Dutchwoman, in passable French, "but it is Madame la duchesse d'Oyonnax, and she will not be put off."

"Then I *do* forgive you, Brigitte, for she is a difficult case; I shall meet her presently and finish reading this letter later."

"By your leave, you shall have to finish it *tomorrow*, mademoiselle; for the guests arrive in a few hours, and we have not even begun with your hair yet."

"Very well—tomorrow then."

"Where shall I invite Madame la duchesse to wait for you?"

"The *Petit Salon*. Unless—"

"Madame la duchesse d'Arcachon is entertaining her *cousine*, the big one, in there."

"The library then."

"Monsieur Rossignol is toiling over some eldritch Documents in the library, my lady."

Eliza took a deep breath, then let it out slowly. "Tell me, then, Brigitte, where there might be a room in the Hôtel Arcachon that is not crowded with early-arriving party-guests."

"Could you meet her in . . . the chapel?"

"Done! Give me a minute. And, Brigitte?"

"Yes, my lady?"

"Is there any word of Monsieur le duc yet?"

"Not since the last time you asked, mademoiselle."

"The *jacht* of the duc d'Arcachon was sighted approaching Marseille on the sixth of October. It was flying signal-flags ordering that fast horses and a coach must be made ready at dockside for immediate departure. That much we know from a messenger who was sent north immediately when everything I have just described to you was perceived, through a prospective-glass, from a steeple in Marseille," Eliza said. "This news came to us early this morning. We can only assume that *le duc* himself is a few hours behind, and will show up at any moment; but it is not to be expected that anyone in this household could know any more than that."

"Monsieur le comte de Pontchartrain will be disappointed," said the Duchess of Oyonnax in a bemused way. She nodded at a page, who bowed, backed out of the chapel, then pivoted on the ball of one foot and bolted. Eliza, comtesse de la Zeur, and Marie-Adelaide de Crépy, duchesse d'Oyonnax, were now alone in the private chapel of the de Lavardacs. Though Oyonnax, never one to leave anything to chance, took the precaution of opening the doors of the little confessional in the back, to verify that it was empty.

The chapel occupied a corner of the property. Public streets ran along the front, or altar end, and along one of the sides. That side had several stained-glass windows, tall and narrow to fetch a bit of light from the sky. These had small casements down below, which were normally closed to block the noise and smell of the street beyond; but Oyonnax opened two of them. Cold air came in, which scarcely mattered considering the tonnage of clothing that each of these women was wearing. A lot of noise came in, too. Eliza supposed that this was a further precaution against their being overheard by any eavesdroppers who might be pressing ears against doors. But if Oyonnax was the sort to worry about such things, then this chapel was a comfortable place for her. It contained no furniture—no pews—just a rough stone floor, and she had already verified that there was no one crouching behind the little altar. The chapel was hundreds of years older than any other part of the compound. It was unfashionably Gothick, dim, and gloomy, and probably would have been knocked down long ago and replaced with something Barock were it not for the windows and the altar-piece (which were said to be priceless treasures) and the fourth left metatarsal bone of Saint Louis (which was embedded in a golden reliquary cemented into the wall).

"Pontchartrain sent no fewer than three messages here this morning, requesting the latest news," said Eliza, "but I did not know the *contrôleur-général* had *also* contacted *you,* my lady."

"His curiosity on the matter presumably reflects that of the King."

"It does not surprise me that the King should be so keen to know the whereabouts of his Grand Admiral. But would it not be more proper for such inquiries to be routed through the Secretary of State for the Navy?"

The Duchess of Oyonnax had paused by one of the open casements and levered it mostly closed, making of it a sort of horizontal gun-slit through which she could peer at the street. But she turned away from it now and peered at Eliza for a few moments, then announced: "I am sorry. I supposed you might have known. Monsieur le marquis de Seignelay has cancer. He is very ill of it, and no longer able to fulfill his obligations to his majesty's Navy."

"No wonder the King is so intent on this, then—for they say that the Duke of Marlborough has landed in force in the South of Ireland."

"Your news is stale. Marlborough has already taken Cork, and Kinsale is expected to fall at any moment. All of this while de Seignelay is too ill to work, and d'Arcachon is off in the south on some confusing adventure of his own."

From out in the courtyard, beyond the rear doors of the chapel, Eliza heard a muffled burst of feminine laughter: the Duchess of Arcachon and her friends. It *was* curious. A few paces in one direction, the most exalted persons in France were donning ribbons and perfume and swapping gossip, getting ready for a Duke's birthday party. Beyond the confines of the Arcachon compound, France was getting ready for nine months' starvation, as the harvest had been destroyed by frost. French and Irish garrisons were falling to the onslaught of Marlborough in chilly Ireland, and the Secretary of

State for the Navy was being gnawed to death by cancer. Eliza decided that this dim, chilly, empty room, cluttered with gruesome effigies of our scourged and crucified and impaled Lord, was not such a bad place after all to have a meeting with Oyonnax. Certainly Oyonnax seemed more in her element here than in a gilded and ruffled drawing-room. She said: "I wonder if it is even *necessary* for you to kill Monsieur le duc. The King might do it for you."

"Do not talk about it this way, if you please!" Eliza snapped.

"It was merely an observation."

"When le duc planned tonight, it was summer, and everything seemed to be going perfectly. I know what he was thinking: the King needs money for the war, and I shall bring him money!"

"You sound as though you are defending him."

"I believe it is useful to know the mind of the enemy."

"Does le duc know *your* mind, mademoiselle?"

"Obviously not. He does not rate me an enemy."

"Who *does*?"

"I beg your pardon?"

"*Someone* wishes to know your mind, for you are being watched."

"I am well aware of it. Monsieur Rossignol—"

"Ah, yes—the King's Argus—*he* knows *all*."

"He has noticed that my name crops up frequently, of late, in letters written by those at Court who style themselves Alchemists."

"Why are the chymists watching you?"

"I believe it has to do with what Monsieur le duc d'Arcachon has been up to in the south," said Eliza. "Assuming that *you* have been discreet, that is."

Oyonnax laughed. "You and I associate with two entirely different sorts of chymists! Even if I were indiscreet—which I most certainly am not—it is inconceivable that a brewer of poison, working in a cellar in Paris, should have any contact with a noble practitioner of the Art, such as Upnor or de Gex."

"I did not know that Father Édouard was an Alchemist as well!"

"Of course. Indeed, my divine cousin perfectly illustrates the point I am making. Can you phant'sy such a man associating with Satanists?"

"I cannot even phant'sy *myself* doing so."

"You aren't."

"What are *you* then, if I may inquire?"

Oyonnax, in a strangely girlish gesture, put a gloved hand to her lips, suppressing a laugh. "You still do not understand. Versailles is like this window." She swept her arm out, directing Eliza's eye to a scene in stained glass. "Beautiful, but thin, and brittle." She opened the casement below to reveal the street beyond: a wood-carrier, looking like a wild man, had dropped his load to have a fist-fight with a young Vagabond who had taken offense because the wood-carrier had bumped into a whore that the Vagabond was escorting into an alley. A man blinded by smallpox was squatting against a wall releasing a bloody phlux from his bowels. "Beneath the lovely glaze, a sea of desperation. When people are desperate, and praying to God has failed, they begin to look elsewhere. The famous Satanists that Maintenon is so worried about wouldn't recognize the Prince of Darkness if they went down to Hell and held a candle at his levée! Those necromancers are just like the mountebanks on the Pont-Neuf. You can't make a living as a mountebank by offering to trim people's fingernails, because the clientele is not desperate enough. But you *can* make a living as a tooth-puller. Have you ever had a tooth go bad, mademoiselle?"

"I am aware that it hurts."

"There are people at Court who suffer from aches of heart and spirit that are every bit as intolerable as a toothache. Those who prey on them, are no different from tooth-pullers. The emblems of the devil are no different from the pliers brandished by tooth-pullers: visual proof that these people are equipped to ply their trade, and satisfy their customers."

"You are so dark! Is there anything you believe in?"

Oyonnax closed the casement. The gruesome images outside were gone. "I believe in beauty," she said. "I believe in the beauty of Versailles, and in the King who created it. I believe in your beauty, mademoiselle, and in mine. The darkness beyond has power to break through, just as those people out there could throw rocks through this window. But behold, the window has stood for centuries. No one has thrown a rock through it."

"Why not?"

"Because there is a balance of powers in the world, which can only be perceived by continual attention, and can only be preserved by—"

"By the unceasing and subtile machinations of persons such as you," Eliza said; and the look in the green eyes of Oyonnax told her that her guess was true. "Is that why you have involved yourself in my vendetta against the Duke?"

"I am *certainly* not doing so out of any affection for you! Nor out of sympathy. I don't know, and don't wish to, why you hate him so, but the stories told about him make it easy to guess. If le duc were a great hero of France—a Jean Bart, for example—I should poison *you* before suffering *you* to harm *him*. But as matters stand, Monsieur le duc is a poltroon, absent for months when he is most needed. Wise was *le Roi* in subordinating him to Monsieur le marquis de Seignelay. But now that de Seignelay is dying, the duc d'Arcachon will try to re-assert his former eminence, which shall prove a disaster to the Navy and to France."

"So you see yourself as doing the King's work."

"I see myself as serving the King's ends." Madame la duchesse d'Oyonnax removed from her waistband a pale-green cylinder, scarcely bigger than a child's finger, and displayed it on the palm of her gloved hand. She was standing several paces away, which forced Eliza to approach her. Eliza did so in spite of a sudden horripilation that had spread over her scalp like a slick of burning oil. Her hands were clasped together in front of her stomach, in part to keep them warm—but in part to keep them close to a slim dagger that she was in the habit of hiding at the waist of her dress. Which was a queer thing to be thinking about, here and now; but she would not put anything past the Duchess, and wanted to be ready in the event that Oyonnax tried to throw something in her face or jab her with a poi-soned needle.

"You'll never appreciate how easy this is going to be compared to a typical poisoning," said Oyonnax in a light conversational tone, as if this would set Eliza at ease. Eliza had now drawn close enough to see the green thing: a tiny phial such as might be used for perfume, carved out of jade, bound in bands of silver, with a silver stopper on a fragile chain. "Don't dab this behind your ears," said the Duchess.

"Is it one of those that is absorbed through the skin?"

"No, but it smells bad."

"Then *le duc* will certainly notice it in a drink."

"Yes—but not in his food. You know of his peculiar tastes?"

"I know more than I should care to of that."

"This is what I mean when I say it is going to be easy for you. Nor-mally an ingested poison must be tasteless, and such are frequently ineffective. This stuff is as deadly as it is foul—yet *le duc* will never notice it when it is mixed with a meal of rotten fish. All that *you* need to do is to find some way of getting into the private kitchen where his dreadful repast is prepared. This will not be a trivial matter—yet it will be much easier than the machinations most people must go through."

"Most *poisoners*, you mean . . ."

Oyonnax did not respond to—perhaps did not even *understand*—the correction. "Take it, or don't," she said, "I'll not stand here like this any longer."

Eliza reached out to pluck the phial from Oyonnax's palm. As she did so, the other's larger hand closed around hers, and then Oyonnax brought her other hand over and clamped it on top, so that Eliza's fist, clenched around the green phial, was swallowed up between the Duchess's hands. Eliza was staring fixedly at this, having no desire whatever to see the Duchess's face, now so close to hers. But Oyonnax would not let go; and so finally Eliza turned her head that way, and, with some effort, raised her eyes to gaze directly into those of Oyonnax. She could not bear to do so for more than a moment; but it seemed that this was enough for the Duchess to be satisfied. Satisfied of *what,* Eliza did not know. But Oyonnax gave Eliza's fist one last squeeze and pushed it towards Eliza's breast, then released her. "It is done," said the Duchess. "You shall accomplish it tonight, then?"

"It is already too late—I must get ready."

"Soon, then."

"It can never be soon enough for me."

"People will talk, after it happens," said the Duchess. "Pay them no mind, and have patience. It is not whether this or that person believes you to be a murderer, or even can prove it, but whether they have the dignity necessary to level such an accusation."

BRITTLE DISJOINTED HOURS FOLLOWED. Monsieur le comte de Pontchartrain, and later the King himself, did not leave off sending messengers around to inquire as to the whereabouts of the duc d'Arcachon. For some reason these all wanted to speak to Eliza—as if she were expected to know things that the Duchess of Arcachon did not. This in no way simplified preparations for the soirée. Eliza had to get coiffed and dressed while holding at bay these inquisitive messengers, who, as the afternoon wore on, were of progressively higher rank. Finally, near dusk, a coach and four rattled into the court, and Eliza called out "Hallelujah!" She could not run to the window because a pair of engineers were braiding extensions into her hair; but someone else did, and disappointed them all by reporting that it was merely Étienne d'Arcachon.

"He'll do," said, Eliza, "now they'll pester *him* instead of *me.*"

But presently, word filtered up that Étienne had literally called out the cavalry—despatched riders of his own personal regiment, on the swiftest mounts, to probe southwards along the roads that his father was most likely to take north, with instructions to wheel round and gallop back to the Hôtel Arcachon the moment they saw the Duke's distinctive white carriage. This would give at least a few minutes' warning of the Duke's arrival—which was of the highest importance to Étienne, the Politest Man in France, as it would have been a grave embarrassment for the King to attend a Duke's birthday-party only to be snubbed, in the end, by the guest of honor. This way, the King could continue to bide his time in the Royal *Palais du Louvre*—which was only a few minutes' ride away—and come to the Hôtel Arcachon (which was in the Marais, not far off the Pont d'Arcole) only when positive word had been received that the Duke was on his way.

So Eliza was pestered no further by messengers; but now Étienne d'Arcachon wished to have a private audience with her. And so did Monsieur le comte d'Avaux. And so did Father Édouard de Gex. She told her hairdressers to work faster, and to forget about the last tier in the ziggurat of counter-rotating braids that was rising into the heavens above her pate.

"MADEMOISELLE, ALLOW ME THE HONOR of being the first to compliment your beauty—"

"I would prefer it if you were as keen to *get out of my way* as to hurl flattery at me, Monsieur le comte," said Eliza, brushing past d'Avaux. "I am on my way to speak with Étienne de Lavardac in the chapel."

"I shall escort you," d'Avaux announced.

Such had been the vehemence of Eliza's passage that her skirts had bullwhipped around d'Avaux's ankles and his sword, and nearly upended him, but he had more aplomb than any ten other French diplomats, and so presently appeared on her arm, looking as perfectly composed as an embalmed corpse.

They were hurrying down a gallery that had been obstructed by servants balancing food-trays and carrying party-decorations; but when these saw the onrushing Count and Countess, they took shelter in the lees of pilasters or ducked into niches.

"I would be remiss if I failed to express to you, mademoiselle, my concern over the choices you have lately been making as to social contacts."

"What!? Who!? The de Lavardac family? Pontchartrain? Monsieur Rossignol?"

"It is precisely because you are so frequently seen in the company of these fine persons, that you must reconsider your decision to associate with the likes of Madame la duchesse d'Oyonnax."

Now Eliza's free hand strayed to her waistband, for she had a sudden terror that the green phial would fall out and shatter on the floor and fill the gallery with a smell as foul as her intentions. It was such an obvious gesture that d'Avaux would have seen it, had he been facing her; but he was looking in another direction.

"Like it or not, monsieur, she is a fixture of Court, and I cannot pretend she doesn't exist."

"Yes, but to have private meetings with such a woman, as you have done three times in the last two months—"

"Who has been counting, monsieur?"

"*Everyone,* mademoiselle. That is my point. Even though you may be pure as snow—"

"Your sarcasm is rude."

"This is a rude conversation, being a hurried one. As I was saying, you might be as upright as de Maintenon herself. But if and when Monsieur le duc d'Arcachon dies—"

"How can you speak of this, on his birthday!?"

"One year closer to death, mademoiselle. And even if the manner of his death is as innocent as falling from a horse, or going down on a sinking ship, people will say *you* had something to do with it, if you continue to tryst in dark places with Oyonnax."

"Anyone can bandy accusations. Few have the dignity to make them count."

"Is that what Oyonnax told you?"

This left Eliza speechless for a turn; so d'Avaux continued: "I was *born* a count, you were *made* a countess; I am one of those few who can accuse you."

"You really are hideous."

"I accused you before, after you spied for the Prince of Orange; but you escaped trouble, because you were doing it for Madame, and because you paid. Now you are alone, and you have no money. I do not know who it is precisely that you mean to poison: perhaps the Duke, perhaps Étienne, perhaps one and then the other. I am strongly tempted to wait and to watch as you do these crimes, and then destroy you—for to see you chained to a stone wall in the Bastille would be most satisfying to me. But I cannot allow a Duke and Peer of the Realm to suffer murder, merely to slake my own base cravings. And so I warn you, mademoiselle, not to—"

"Kill me," said a voice from ahead of them.

D'Avaux and Eliza, still clamped together side by side, arm in arm, had reached the ancient double doors at the back of the chapel, and gone through. It looked entirely different now. Eliza half supposed they had come into the wrong room. The sun had gone down, so no light came through the windows; but hundreds of candles were now burning on scores of silver candelabras. Their light gleamed on the polished backs of many gilded chairs, which in lieu of pews had been arranged on the stone floor—no, on a Persian carpet laid over the floor. The altar was covered in a white silk cloth encrusted with gold brocade, though this was difficult to see, as the front half of the chapel had been turned into a fragrant jungle of white flowers. Eliza's first thought, oddly, was, *Where the hell did those come from at this time of the year?* but the answer must have been some nobleman's stifling Orangerie.

Étienne de Lavardac d'Arcachon, attired in full-dress cavalry colonel's uniform, was sprawled on the carpet at the base of the altar, posed like an artist's model. Resting on the carpet before him, at the head of the aisle, were two shiny objects: a serpentine dagger, and a golden ring.

D'Avaux had stiffened up so violently that Eliza half hoped he was undergoing a stroke. But his grip on her arm slackened, and he began to retreat.

Étienne was having none of that; he jumped to his feet. "Stay! If you please, Monsieur le comte. Your presence here is fortuitous and most welcome. For it were improper for me to meet with Mademoiselle la comtesse without some chaperon; which, as I have lain here awaiting her, has been troubling me more than words have power to express."

"I am at your service, monseigneur," said d'Avaux, watching beneath a creviced brow as the nimble young Arcachon collapsed to the floor, and resumed his former pose.

"Kill me, mademoiselle!"

"I beg your pardon, monsieur?"

"My suffering is unendurable. Please end it by taking up yon flamboyant dagger, and plunging it into my breast."

"But I have no *wish* to kill you, Monsieur de Lavardac," said Eliza, and threw d'Avaux a vicious glare; but d'Avaux was far too profoundly taken aback to notice.

"Then there is only one other way in which my suffering can be ended; but it is too much to hope for," said Étienne. And his eyes fell on the band of gold.

"Your discourse is fascinating—but strangely clouded," said Eliza. She was moving cautiously up the aisle toward Étienne. D'Avaux, trapped, stood at attention in the back.

"I would be more direct, but such a magnificent being are you, and such a base Vagabond am I, that even to give voice to my desire is unforgivably rude."

"I have comments. First, you may be over-praising me, but I forgive you. Second, I know something of Vagabonds, and you are not one. Third, if you must be rude in order to say what is on your mind, then please be rude. For considering what it is that you appear to be asking—"

The chapel door whacked open and in stormed an officer, dressed in the same regimental colors as Étienne, but of less plumage. He stopped in the aisle and turned white as a freshly picked orchid, and was unable to speak.

But everyone knew what he was going to say. Eliza came out with it first. "Monsieur, you have news of Monsieur le duc?"

"Forgive me, mademoiselle—yes—if you please—his carriage has been sighted, coming on at great velocity—he shall be here in an hour."

"Has word of this been sent to the *Palais du Louvre*?" asked Étienne.

"Just as you directed, monsieur."

"Very well. You are dismissed."

The officer was more than glad to be dismissed. He took a last beady look around, then bowed, and backed down the aisle. As he was going arse-first out the door, he rammed someone who was attempting to come in. There was an exchange of abject apologies back in the shadows; then in stalked a robed and hooded figure, looking like Death without the scythe. He pulled back the hood to reveal the pale face, the dark eyes, and the carefully managed facial hair of Father Édouard de Gex; and the look on his face proved that he was as surprised, not to say alarmed, by all of this as anyone else.

"I say, was this all *planned*?" demanded Eliza.

"I received an anonymous note suggesting that I should be ready to perform the sacrament of marriage on short notice," said de Gex, "but—"

"You had better be ready to perform the sacrament of extreme unction, if the young Arcachon does not untie his tongue, or hide that dagger," said Eliza, "and as to short notice—well—a lady requires a little more time!" And she stomped out of the chapel.

"My lady!" called de Gex several times as he pursued her down a gallery; but she had not the slightest intention of being called back in there, and so she ignored him until she was a safe distance removed from the chapel, and had reached a more frequented part of the house. By that point, de Gex had caught up with her. "My lady!"

"I'm not going back."

"It is not my design to coax you back. *You* are the person I wished to see. For when Monsieur Rossignol and I made inquiries as to your whereabouts, they said you had gone to the chapel. It was never my intention to interrupt a—"

"You interrupted *nothing*. Why were you with Monsieur Rossignol?"

"He has got some new messages from the Esphahnians."

"The who?"

"The Armenians. Come. Please. I pray you. It's important."

FATHER ÉDOUARD DE GEX ESCORTED Eliza to the library as fast as *he* could walk, which meant that he kept edging ahead. The most direct route took them through the grand ballroom of the Hôtel Arca-chon. Here, though, he faltered, and fell behind. Eliza wheeled about. De Gex was gazing up at the ceiling. This was understandable, for the de Lavardacs had hired Le Brun himself to paint it, and he had only recently finished. It was a colossal tableau featuring Apollo (always a stand-in for Louis XIV) gathering the Virtues about him in the bright center while exiling the Vices to the gloomy corners. The Virtues were not sufficiently numerous to fill the space, and so the Muses were there, too, singing songs, composing poetry, &c. about how great the Virtues were. Along the edges of the piece, diverse earthly humans (courtiers on one side, peasants on the next, then soldiers, then churchmen) listened adoringly to, or gazed raptur-ously at, the Virtue-promoting works of the Muses whilst generally turning their backs to, or aiming scornful glares at, all of those Vices crowded into the corners. Just to make it sporting, though, you might see, if you looked carefully enough, a Soldier succumbing to Cow-ardice, a Priest to Gluttony, a Courtier to Lust, or a Peasant to Sloth.

So *everyone* who came in here looked at the ceiling; but the expression on the face of de Gex was most peculiar. Rather than being dazzled by the splendour of the work, he looked as if he were expecting the ceiling to fall in on them.

He finally directed his dark eyes at Eliza. "Do you know what hap-pened here, mademoiselle?"

"A fabulously expensive remodeling campaign that took forever and is only just finished."

"But do you know why?"

"Le Brun is always engaged at Versailles, except when *le Roi* leaves off building it so that he can go fight a war. And so only since war broke out has any progress been made here."

"No. I meant, do you know why they remodelled?"

"From the looks of it I should say it was de Maintenon."

"*De Maintenon?!*" De Gex's reaction told Eliza that her answer had been emphatically wrong.

"Yes," she said, "she came along in 1685, did she not? Which is when this remodel got under way . . . and the subject matter of the painting is so markedly Maintenon-esque."

"Correlation is not causation," de Gex said. "They *had* to remodel, because of a disastrous Incident that took place in that year."

And then De Gex seemed to remember that they were in a hurry, and once again began striding toward the library. Eliza stomped along beside, and a little behind him.

"You *do* know what happened here—?" he continued, and glanced back at her.

"*Something* grievously embarrassing—*so* embarrassing that no one will tell me what it was."

"Ah. To the library, then." They departed the ballroom and entered a gallery.

"What was that you said earlier, about being asked to perform a marriage on short notice?"

"I received a note to that effect. I suspect it was from your beau. Never mind; obviously he was deluding himself."

"It is a bit sad," said Eliza, remembering the chairs carefully arranged in the little chapel, never to be sat on, and the precious flowers, never to be seen or smelled before they were hauled out to a midden. "Perhaps he had in mind a sort of elopement—but being so polite, wished to arrange it so that it would enjoy the sanctions of Family and Church."

"That is between you and him," said de Gex a bit coldly, and hauled upon the library door for Eliza. "If you please, mademoiselle."

"I PHANT'SIED YOU MIGHT FIND this interesting in more than one way," said Bonaventure Rossignol. He sat with his back to the arched window of the library, which, though dark, afforded a view over the torch-lit courtyard of the Hôtel Arcachon. Eliza was shocked to observe occasional snowflakes spiraling down—so intemperate and remorseless was this winter, they might as well be living in Stockholm.

Before Rossignol was a broad table on which he had spread out a panoply of letters, books, and notes. Many bore the Armenian script.

"I mentioned to you before that the *Cabinet Noir* had intercepted a remarkable letter, posted during the first week of August from Sanlúcar de Barrameda, and addressed to the family Esphahnian, who were said to be dwelling in the Bastille."

"You had not mentioned the family name to me," said Eliza, "but it scarcely matters, and it is almost certainly an assumed name anyway—"

"Why do you say that?" said de Gex.

"Esphahnian simply means 'of Esphahan,' which is a city where a vast number of Armenians dwell," Eliza explained. "It is as if you went to live among the Turks and they called you 'Édouard the Frank.'"

Rossignol nodded. "I agree it is probably not the true name of this family, but it is the name we shall use, lacking any other. At any rate, I inquired after them, and learned that some Armenians had indeed been put in the Bastille in 1685 and kept there for a year or so: a mother and a large brood of sons. One of them died there. The matriarch was released soonest, then the brothers. Some went to debtors' prisons.

"It took me some time to track them all down, for more have died in the meantime, and it was difficult to establish who is the eldest of the brothers. I found him—Artan Esphahnian—in a wretched *entresol* not far from here, and caused the letter from Sanlúcar to be delivered to him.

"A few days later, Artan mailed a letter addressed to one Vrej Esphahnian *in Cairo.* I had an exact copy of it made, then sent it on its way. At the time, I held no particular opinion as to who this Vrej fellow might be—like you, mademoiselle, I suspected that the name Esphahnian was a meaningless ruse, or perhaps even a vector of hidden information, which, if true, might mean that Vrej was not even related to Artan.

"Nothing further happened until yesterday, when a letter came in addressed to Artan, posted from Rosetta, at the mouth of the Nile— and *written in the same hand as the one from Sanlúcar de Barrameda.* Now this was remarkable, for I had translated the Sanlúcar letter into French, and it had said *nothing* about Egypt. It was full of family chitchat. The fellow who wrote it—who I now believe to be Vrej Esphahnian—had been out of contact with Artan for a long time. He had said nothing whatever about what he was doing in Sanlúcar or whither he might be going next. And yet Artan, upon receiving this document, had known, somehow, that he must post his reply to Vrej *in Cairo.* Not long afterwards, this Vrej had appeared at Rosetta—which is *en route* to Cairo—long enough to despatch yet another letter filled with banal chitchat."

"And so it is obvious to you that encrypted messages are contained in these letters," Eliza continued; for she had spent enough time listening to the discourse of Natural Philosophers to recognize when one of them was developing a hypothesis. "This I understand well enough, and I compliment you on your prowess. But why do you deem it so important to tell *me* about it?"

Rossignol was not willing to attempt an answer, and looked at de Gex. From which Eliza collected that it must be a delicate matter; for de Gex, as de Maintenon's favorite churchman, was allowed to speak bluntly in a way that was unusual in a place where insults were commonly answered with rapier-thrusts. "We who love and admire the family de Lavardac," he said, "are terribly concerned that Monsieur le duc d'Arcachon, acting out of the most noble motives, and exhibiting marvelous ingenuity and strength of will, has made a mistake. We would assist him in mending his error before it leads to embarrassment. It were best to mend it this evening, before the ramifications spread any further. To bring it before Madame la duchesse d'Arcachon, or Étienne, might not be as productive as to bring it before *you*, mademoiselle."

"Very well. Does the mistake have something to do with Alchemy?"

The briefest of pauses. Then: "Indeed, mademoiselle. Monsieur le duc participated in an act of piracy, which, as you know, is a usual thing in war, and wholly honourable. However, I am sorry to report that he was misinformed by persons who were ignorant, or perhaps malicious. Monsieur le duc *supposed* that the prize was silver pigs. In fact it was gold. And not just any gold, but gold imbued with miraculous—even divine—qualities."

"I see," said Eliza. "And needless to say, the Esoteric Brotherhood takes a proprietary interest in it?"

"I should prefer to say *custodial*, not *proprietary*. This material is not for just anyone to possess. In the wrong hands it could do the Devil's work."

"Hmm. Would Lothar von Hacklheber's be the wrong hands?"

"No, mademoiselle. Lothar is a difficult man, but one knows where he lives, and one can reason with him. A boat-load of Vagabonds at large in the Mediterranean, bound for Egypt—*that* is the wrong hands."

"Well, you may set your mind at ease, Father Édouard. The gold you seek was to have come ashore along with Monsieur le duc. He planned to drop it off in Lyon. It should now locked in the strong-box of a certain banker there, who values it only as gold. I shall be pleased to supply you with his name. He has no awareness of, or interest in, its supernatural characteristics. Presumably he will be pleased to exchange it for an equal or larger weight of *mundane* gold."

"We should be in your debt, mademoiselle."

"You may consider the debt discharged, if you tell me one thing."

"Name it, mademoiselle."

"The Bastille is a prison for enemies of the Realm. Why were the Esphahnians thrown into it?"

"Because they were thought to be connected to what happened here in 1685."

"And—since I will be the last person in France to know—*what happened here in 1685*!?"

"You may have heard, on the lips of servants or other vulgar persons, tales concerning a man called *L'Emmerdeur*. By your leave, mademoiselle! For even his epithet is almost too vulgar to speak aloud."

"I have heard of him," said Eliza, though in her ears, the sound of her own voice was nearly drowned out by the *stomp, stomp, stomp* of her heart. "I did hear a story once that he showed up uninvited at some grand soirée in Paris and made a bloody mess of it—"

"That was here."

"In this house!?"

"In this house. He cut Étienne's hand off, and completely destroyed the ballroom."

"How can one Vagabond, vastly outnumbered by armed noblemen, single-handedly destroy a Duke's ballroom?"

"Never mind. But to make matters worse, all of these things happened in the presence of the King. Most embarrassing."

"I can imagine!"

"The King of the Vagabonds, as he was styled, made his escape. But the Lieutenant of Police was able to determine that he had been dwelling in a certain apartment not far from here—and the Esphahnians were living directly below him. He had befriended them, and drawn them somehow into his schemes. But since *he* was long gone, retribution fell instead on the Esphahnians. Off they were taken to the Bastille. Their business was destroyed, their health suffered grievously. Now those who survived dwell as paupers in Paris."

Through the windows came the clatter and rasp of many horseshoes and iron wheel-rims on cobblestones. All turned to see the white carriage of the duc d'Arcachon—wrought to look like a giant sea-shell borne on the foam of an incoming tide—being drawn, by a team of six mismatched and exhausted horses, into the courtyard. It passed below them, out of their view, and pulled up before the entrance of the ballroom.

But the noise did not let up, but doubled and redoubled, as into the open gates of the Court rode a vanguard of Swiss mercenaries, and a squadron of noble officers, and finally the gilded carriage of Louis XIV, lighting up the court as the Chariot of Apollo.

ÉTIENNE, WHEREVER HE WAS (presumably, at the door of the ballroom), could finally relax, for much that must have been troubling him had been resolved in these few moments. His father had come home. No more would embarrassing questions be asked about where the Grand Admiral of France was during this time of need. Almost as important, this party now had a guest of honor; and so the many guests who had come would not go home disappointed. Most important of all, the King had arrived, and had arrived *last.*

Eliza, by contrast, had so many things to fret about that she almost could not keep track of them. She left de Gex and Rossignol far behind as she threaded her way among servants and courtiers toward the ballroom.

She hated herself for having a phial of poison in her waistband. Stupid! Stupid! She could not even use it now, without drawing fire from d'Avaux! So it was worse than worthless. It had never occurred to her that she would have to carry the damned thing on her person all the time. It could not be left in a drawer for fear that someone would happen upon it, by chance or because snooping. The phial had only been in her waistband for a few hours, but she'd gladly have traded it for a back-load of firewood. It seemed to burn her stomach, and she had developed a nervous habit of patting it every few seconds. And for this useless burthen, she had put herself, in some unspecified way, into the power of the Duchess of Oyonnax.

But in its power to cause trouble for Eliza, this matter of the poison might be as nothing compared to what she had heard concerning the exploits of Jack Shaftoe in this house—nay, this very *room* (for she had entered the ballroom now) five years ago.

When the carriages of *le duc* and *le Roi* had entered the courtyard moments ago, Eliza had darted out of the library before de Gex or Rossignol could offer her his arm. She had done this because she required a few moments by herself to think—to recall all that had happened since she had met Jack below Vienna in 1683, and to ask herself who might know that she had once been associated with *L'Emmerdeur?*

Leibniz knew, but he was discreet. The same could be said of Enoch Root. Around Leipzig, Jack and Eliza had been seen together by several people, none of whom was likely to be rated as credible by the French nobility. The most high and mighty person who had seen them together—and, as she recalled this, Eliza felt the heat rising into her face like steam from a cauldron when the lid is lifted off—was Lothar von Hacklheber, who had gazed down on her from the balcony of the House of the Golden Mercury in Leipzig. Jack had been right next to her, posing as a manservant, a porter. Unlikely that even Lothar would connect such a figure with *L'Emmerdeur.*

After that, they had traveled to Amsterdam. A few Dutch people had seen them together. But again, there was no reason for these people to suppose that the ruffian sometimes seen in Eliza's company was the legendary Vagabond King. Before long, Jack had gone down to Paris. Only then had he truly become famous to these people. He had ridden a horse into this room and wrecked the duc d'Arcachon's party, fled Paris, and eventually found his way back to Amsterdam—where he had tracked Eliza down in her favorite coffeehouse. They had spent all of an hour together—an hour that had culminated in an unpleasant scene, whose details Eliza did not care to recall to mind, beneath the Herring-Packers' Tower, just as Jack had set sail on the slave-trading voyage from which he could never return. By now, of course, he'd been dead any number of years. But *that* was not the question. The question was: Had anyone seen Jack and Eliza together during that hour in Amsterdam?

The answer was *of course they had,* for as she'd later found out, she'd been tailed, the whole time, by two spies in the employ of d'Avaux. D'Avaux! Who even at this moment was glaring at her from across the ballroom, as if reading minds were as easy for him as reading codes was to Rossignol. D'Avaux's two spies had later been killed by the hand of William of Orange himself. But d'Avaux was alive, *and he knew.*

All this time the Duke's carriage had been sitting in the courtyard, like an egg in a stone sarcophagus. Its door was open, and one of the footmen had thrust his head and upper body into the dark interior, and lit a few candles. His arm shook from time to time, as if he were trying again and again to get a tired passenger to wake up. The delay was perfectly convenient for those inside—close to a hundred of the titled nobility of France—as it afforded them the opportunity to arrange themselves in a long receiving-line that coiled and undulated around the ballroom. Outside the double doors, servants had rolled out a carpet so that the Duke, and later King, could tread on red wool instead of gray snow. An honor guard had formed up to either side of that road of scarlet: members of Étienne's cavalry regiment to one side, and, facing them, a detachment of marines. Étienne stood just inside the doors, waiting, with his mother on his arm.

Finally something was happening. The cavalry and the marines drew sabers and cutlasses respectively, and raised them up to form an arch of steel above the red carpet. Étienne nodded to a pair of servants, who drew open the ballroom's immense doors, letting in a blast of snowy air; Étienne screwed up his face and stepped back half a pace; his mother the duchess bowed her head and reached up with her free hand to prevent her lace headdress from being sheared off. Outside, the mud-spattered buttocks of the footman could be seen emerging from the door of the white carriage, straining and jolting, as he seemed to be helping someone out who required much help.

Eliza's view of these proceedings got better and better, for she was being impelled toward the head of the receiving-line by a kind of social peristalsis. Even Dukes and Duchesses, in this circumstance, gave precedence to Eliza, who had come to be seen as an honorary de Lavardac. No one would admit her to the line, but all insisted that she move ahead. And so she kept advancing towards the open doors, and got a very clear view of what came out of that carriage.

It was not a Duke. The word "wretch" came to mind, for this man could barely stand up, and if he owned a periwig, he'd lost it, or forgotten it in the coach. His thinning hair was short and dark, and shellacked with sweat and grease, and his face beneath it was so pale it looked almost green. He could not stand or walk without assistance, and yet he would on no account let go of some great burdensome item of luggage: a sort of strong-box. It had a handle on either end. One of the footmen supported the wretch on his right side. The wretch, then, kept his left hand clenched around one of the strong-box's handles. The other footman had grabbed the box's opposite handle just in time to keep it from falling out of the carriage door. And so they formed up three abreast: footman, wretch, footman, and began an ungainly progress along the red carpet.

Eliza had now come close enough to the doors that she could hear Étienne saying to his mother, "Is that Pierre de Jonzac?" Instantly she saw that the wretch was none other. For the filthy, torn, and stained clothes that he was wearing had once been a naval officer's uniform. And if in her mind's eye she cleaned the wretch up, mended his clothes, and endowed him with thirty pounds more weight, a few pints of blood, and a decent periwig, the result was very like Monsieur de Jonzac.

Seeing this, Eliza developed in her mind a theory of what was going on here, which was wrong; but it was not too unlike everyone else's theories, which would govern their actions until they knew more. The theory was that the duc d'Arcachon was still inside the white carriage, getting freshened up for the party, and that he had sent his aide de Jonzac out ahead of him bearing a treasure-chest full of booty, justly and valiantly won during some dire and exhausting combat in the Mediterranean, which was about to be presented to the King of France. It even occurred to Eliza that the Duke, finding himself unexpectedly in possession of a small mass of enchanted gold, rather than a large amount of silver pigs, had galloped straight through Lyon without stopping, and brought it here directly. Risky—but fantastically dashing, and almost enough to make her admire the man. She turned round to catch the eye of Father Édouard de Gex, who was not far away; and he had come to a similar phant'sy, and his gaze was already fixed on that strong-box. Someone next to him *was*, however, looking back at Eliza; she glanced up to find herself spiked on the unreadable glare of Louis Anglesey, Earl of Upnor.

De Jonzac, the footmen, and the chest had covered two-thirds of the distance to the door. As they drew closer to the light, they looked more and more pitiable. The footmen had been standing on the back of the carriage for a week and their faces and livery were coated with road-grime. Beneath the gray dirt, *their* flesh was ruddy from cold; but de Jonzac was gray through and through. His lips had disappeared, being of the same hue as the surrounding flesh, and they moved unceasingly, as if he were trying to say something. But if any sound came forth, Eliza could not hear it from this distance. Étienne greeted de Jonzac, but got no recognition or answer. He and the duchess moved out of the way so that this unwieldy parade could fit through the door. No doubt remained in Eliza's mind now that something was terribly awry; but most of the others in the room were still working on the wrong theory. This included even poor Étienne, who sensed that something was desperately the matter, but was nailed to his post by etiquette. He turned towards the white carriage to greet his father, who should emerge next; but the door, hanging open, revealed that the vehicle was empty. A stable-hand slammed it shut and pounded on it twice, and the driver cracked his little whip, compelling the half-dead horses to make one last, brief journey to the stable-yard.

"Father Édouard!" Eliza said, raising her voice to be heard above the murmur of astonishment running through the guests. "Please tend to Monsieur de Jonzac; he is grievously wounded." Eliza's nose had confirmed this, for de Jonzac and the footmen had shuffled past her by now, leaving in their wake a scent of rotting flesh. De Jonzac had gangrene. The footmen, half deranged from exhaustion, only wanted some place to lay de Jonzac out on the floor; instead they had staggered into the midst of a formal Court ball. They were dumbfounded, lost.

De Gex had got a whiff of it, too. He stepped out briskly and got in front of the footmen. "Let him down. It is all right. Gently down—" (To the majordomo:) "Monsieur! Bring blankets, and a couch, or something that can be used as a litter. Have someone else summon a surgeon." (To de Jonzac, now lying on the polished floor, his head on the palm of de Gex's hand:) "What is that you say? I cannot hear you, Monsieur—pray save your strength, it can wait."

De Gex seemed to have matters so well in hand that Eliza decided to go and inform Étienne (whose view of de Gex and de Jonzac had been blocked by a moving wall of inquisitive courtiers) as to what was going on. She found him still paralyzed by an unsolvable conun-drum of etiquette; for the moment the Duke's white carriage had moved out of the way, the King's golden one had rattled forward to take its place, and even now the door was being opened. For none of the members of the King's entourage had the slightest idea, yet, that things had gone all wrong. And it was too late to tell them now, for Louis XIV was standing at the head of the carpet, and the Marquise de Maintenon was on his arm.

Eliza spun around and said "The King!," which was the one word that could have dispersed the crowd around de Jonzac and de Gex. The receiving line re-formed, though it made a wide detour around the stricken man on the floor, and the two who were occu-pied near him: de Gex, who was kneeling on the floor and bending close to hear de Jonzac, and the Earl of Upnor, who kept undoing latches on the strong-box, only to find that there was always another.

All of this became obvious to the King in an instant as the crowd melted away from his line of sight like frost in a sun-beam. He was the only person in the Hôtel Arcachon who had the freedom to behave normally. For in the presence of the King, no one other than the King could be acknowledged. Hence, for example, the unnatural posture of Étienne d'Arcachon, who stood fixedly with his back to the scene within, as if nothing at all was happening. The King, though, had eyes only for de Jonzac. He got half a pace ahead of de Main-tenon, then turned to her and said a few private words, taking his leave of her with utmost courtesy. Then he strode forward, turning to Étienne and the Duchess as he went by, and exchanging a word with each: *monsieur; madame.* Into the ballroom he came, sweeping his cape from his shoulders, and in the same motion he whirled it down to cover the shivering body of Pierre de Jonzac. The King then took a step back and posed there, body erect, one foot slightly ahead of the other, toe pointed and slightly turned out, head inclined toward his injured subject, and inquired of de Gex: "What does he say?"

"If you please, your majesty," said de Gex. For some time he had been holding up a hand for quiet. But the arrival of the King had silenced the room as nothing else could have. De Gex now bent very close, so that de Jonzac's lips were practically nuzzling his ear, and repeated what he heard:

"The deed . . . you are about to witness . . . was done for the love of a woman . . . whose name . . . I will not say . . . for she knows who she is . . . and it was done by . . . 'Half-Cocked' Jack Shaftoe, *L'Em-merdeur,* the King of the Vagabonds, Ali Zaybak: Quicksilver!"

"What on earth is he talking about?" asked the King. "What

deed?" And it was well that he said *something,* as everyone else was struck dumb, so mortified were they by the mention of the forbidden name in this, of all places!

Upnor had continued to worry at the hasps of the strong-box the whole time—somewhat improperly, but then, he was merely an Englishman. Finally he got it open. He flipped the lid back with a thud and a clatter, practically thrusting his face into the cavity in his eagerness to get at the treasure within. But in the next moment he recoiled as if a cobra had leapt out of the box. He actually let out a long, incoherent yell. A few people nearby screamed, and looked away.

"Ladies, and persons of a sensitive disposition, will avert their eyes," said the King, who retreated a few steps.

Étienne de Lavardac, Madame la duchesse d'Arcachon, Madame la duchesse d'Oyonnax, Monsieur le comte d'Avaux, and a few others drew closer to see what it was. De Gex, who was closest, leaned over the top of the chest and reached into it with his right hand, making the sign of the cross, and muttering a sentence in Latin. Then he rose to his feet and hauled out a severed human head.

"Louis-François de Lavardac, duc d'Arcachon, has come home," he announced. "May he rest in peace."

Now, AT THIS MOMENT Eliza was far from clear-headed; yet she was the most clear-headed person in the room, with the possible exception of the late duke. Though she was still in a lot of trouble—much more trouble than three minutes ago, in fact—she knew two things absolutely. One was that the duc d'Arcachon was dead. Her mission in life had, therefore, been accomplished. The other was that Jack Shaftoe was alive, had redeemed himself, and loved her. Best of all, he loved her from a tremendous distance, which made being loved by him ever so much less inconvenient. And so even as people were still gasping and screaming and fainting all around her, Eliza was moving toward the duchesse d'Oyonnax, who, aside from Eliza, was the coolest person in the room. She looked almost amused. Eliza fished the little green phial out of her waistband. She approached Oyonnax from the side, reached out with her left hand, grasped that of Oyonnax, and drew it towards her, twisting it palm up. With her right hand Eliza pressed the phial down on Oyonnax's palm. The Duchess's fingers curled about it involuntarily, before she knew what it was, and Eliza got clear.

Her attention—and that of almost everyone else in the room— turned to d'Avaux, who had approached the King, and received permission to speak. It was a wonder he had sought permission, for he was in such a rage that he was almost slavering. He kept looking back at Eliza, which gave Eliza the idea that it might be best for her to draw closer and listen in.

"Your majesty!" cried d'Avaux. "By your majesty's leave, I say that while the *perpetrator* of this atrocious crime may be far away, the *first cause and inspiration* of it is close by, yea, within the reach of your majesty's sword almost, so that your majesty may have satisfaction presently—for she, the woman in whose name *L'Emmerdeur* committed this murder, is none other than—" and he raised his hand before his face, index finger extended, like a pistol-duellist in the moment before he levels the weapon at his foe. His gaze was rapt on Eliza. The fatal finger began to descend toward her heart. She reached up and caught that digit, however, while it was still directed toward the magnificent Le Brun ceiling, and bent it back sharply enough to make d'Avaux inhale sharply—which meant he could not finish his sentence. *"Merci beaucoup, monsieur,"* she whispered, and executed a full three-hundred-sixty-degree pirouette that brought her face to face with the King while relegating d'Avaux to the background. Her hand was behind the small of her back now, still gripping d'Avaux's finger. She had carried it off—or so she hoped—in such a manner that an observer, still in shock over the appearance of the severed head of the birthday boy, might think that d'Avaux had courteously offered her his hand, and she had gratefully accepted it.

"By your leave, your majesty, I have heard it said that the rules of etiquette dictate ladies before gentlemen; was I deceived?"

"In no way, mademoiselle," said the King.

"I tell you, it was—" began d'Avaux; but the King silenced him with a flick of the eyes, and Eliza reinforced the message with some torque on the finger.

"Moreover, it is said that the laws of Heaven place love before hate, and peace before war; is it true?"

"Pourquoi non, mademoiselle?"

"Then as a lady who stands before your majesty on an errand of love, I beg precedence over this gentleman, my dear friend and mentor, Monsieur le comte d'Avaux, whose red and angry visage tells me he is on some errand of hateful retribution."

"So terrible is the news to-night that it would bring me, if not *pleasure,* then perhaps a few moments' *diversion* from what is so *unpleasant,* to grant you precedence over Monsieur d'Avaux; provided that *his* errand is not of an urgent nature."

"Oh, not at all, your majesty, what I have to say will be every bit as useful to you in a few minutes' time as it is now. I insist that Mademoiselle la comtesse de la Zeur go ahead." D'Avaux finally worried his finger free and backed off a step.

"Your majesty," said Eliza, "I grieve for *le duc*. I trust he has gone to his reward. I pray that *L'Emmerdeur* will get what he deserves for what he has done. But I cannot, I will not, allow the so-called King of the Vagabonds the additional satisfaction of disrupting the peaceful conduct of your majesty's household, that is to say *La France;* and so, notwithstanding my feelings of shock and grief at this moment, I beg your leave to accept the proposal of marriage that was tendered to me earlier this evening by Étienne de Lavardac—now, duc d'Arcachon."

"Then marry him with all the blessings a King can bestow," the King answered.

And in this moment Eliza was startled by a most unexpected rush of sound from all about her. In any other circumstance she'd have recognized it instantly. But here, given all that had happened, she had to look about and verify it with her eyes: the guests were applauding. It was not, of course, a raucous ovation. Half of them were openly weeping. Many of the ladies had fled the room. Madame la duchesse d'Arcachon was being carried out unconscious, and Eliza's unwitting fiancé only remained in the room because someone was obliged to greet Madame la marquise de Maintenon. But for all that, the remaining guests produced a spontaneous patter of applause. It was not that they had forgotten the Duke's head—*that* was unlikely— but that they found something stirring in how this scene of shock and horror had been adroitly reversed. The applause was an expression of defiance. Eliza, understanding this belatedly, acknowledged it with a diffident curtsey. Presently Étienne drifted to her side—someone had explained matters to him—and took her hand, and then the applause welled up again, for just a moment. Then it died abruptly and was replaced by altogether more fitting sounds of sobbing, wailing, and praying. Eliza was distracted for a moment by a glimpse of a rider out in the courtyard wheeling his mount around with great panache, and galloping out into Paris. It was the Earl of Upnor.

Then she attended to the King, who was speaking: "Father Édouard. We came together here for a small celebration. But the only celebration that is fitting, on an evening such as this one, is that of the Mass."

"Of course, sire."

"We will observe a funeral Mass for Monsieur le duc d'Arcachon. Following that, a wedding for the new duc and Mademoiselle la comtesse de la Zeur."

"Yes, sire," said de Gex. "By your majesty's leave, the family chapel has already been made ready for a wedding; shall we perform the funeral here, where there is more room, and move to the chapel thereafter?"

King Louis XIV made a tiny nod of assent, and then turned his gaze on d'Avaux, who had not yet been dismissed. "Monsieur le comte," said the King, "you were about to voice an opinion as to the identity of the woman who inspired the heinous murder of my cousin?"

"By your majesty's leave," d'Avaux said, "If we interpret *L'Emmerdeur*'s statement *literally*, it will only amount to something banal. I have no doubt that he was merely trying to impress some *whore* he met once in Paris." And he could not prevent his eyes from flicking at Eliza for just a moment as he said this; but then he returned his attention to the King. "I was, rather, attempting to make a more *general* statement about *all* the enemies of France, and what moves them." He backed away one step, turned, and swept his arm up and out towards a corner of the painted ceiling, where Pandora was opening up her Box (in— come to think of it—an odd reminder of the box-opening scene that had just played out on the ballroom floor) to release a flood of demonic Vices. Pandora had been painted, as everyone knew, to resemble Mary, the usurper Queen of England. The foremost of the Vices rushing out of her box was green-eyed Envy, who had been made to resemble Sophie of Hanover. It was to Envy that d'Avaux now drew the King's attention. "That, your majesty, is the lady love, not only of *L'Emmerdeur*—who is after all a nobody—but also of all the Dutch and English. Envy is what inspires their *chivalrous* acts."

"You powers of observation are as keen as ever, monsieur," said the King, "and I have never been more pleased to number you among my subjects."

At this d'Avaux bowed very deeply. Eliza could not help but think that, for all the frustration and defeat d'Avaux had suffered here, this immense compliment from *le Roi* was more than compensation enough. It made her wonder: *Did the King know everything?*

The King continued: "Monsieur le comte d'Avaux has, as usual, spoken wisely. It follows that if we are to baffle Envy's devotees, we should celebrate all that is magnificent in this Realm: with funerals, the magnificence that has passed, and with weddings, the magnificence that is yet to come. Let it be so."

And it *was* so.

Most of the guests went home following the funeral in the ballroom, but enough remained to fill the chapel for the wedding. After that, they went directly into a *second* funerary mass; for Madame la duchesse d'Arcachon had not recovered from the sight of her husband's head pulled from the box. What everyone had taken for a swoon, had in fact been a stroke. One side of her body had already gone lifeless by the time they had carried her to her bedchamber, and during the subsequent hours, the paralysis had spread to engulf the other side as well, and finally the heart had stopped. And so, by the time the newlyweds emerged from the doors of the Hôtel Arcachon, around midnight, and climbed into a borrowed carriage (for the white seashell-coach was both fouled and broken), both of Étienne's parents were dead, and being made ready for shipment to consecrated ground at La Dunette. Étienne was duc, and Eliza was duchesse, d'Arcachon.

The new Duke and Duchess consummated their union under many blankets in a carriage en route to Versailles, and arrived at La Dunette in the darkest and coldest hours before dawn. Fresh hoofprints in the snow on La Dunette's gravel paths told them that they were not the first to come this way since the snow had ceased to fall. When they reached the château, they found the servants already awake and dressed, and red around the eyes. The doyenne of the maidservants took Eliza to one side, and let her know that she must go down to the Convent of Ste.-Genevieve immediately, for there was dreadful news. Eliza, unwilling to wait for preparations to be made, straddled the first horse she could get to—it was an albino mare—and rode it bareback down to the little convent full of weeping and praying nuns. She went directly to the room where Jean-Jacques slept. She knew already what she would see there, for she had seen it before in nightmares, as every parent does: the shattered window, curtains riven, muddy bootprints on the sill, and the empty cradle. The blankets had been taken; that was a comfort to her, as it suggested that wherever Jean-Jacques might be, he was at least not freezing to death. Left in the little bed was a note, addressed to the Countess de la Zeur; for whoever had penned it had not got the news of her new rank and title. It read:

Fräulein!
You and your Vagabond have something of mine. I have
something of yours.

—*L*

Schloß Wolfenbüttel, Lower Saxony
DECEMBER 1690

It seems to us indeed that this block of marble
brought from Genoa would have been exactly the
same if it had been left there, because our senses
make us judge only superficially, but at bottom
because of the connection of things the whole universe with all of its parts would be entirely different,
and would have been another from the beginning,
if the least thing in it went otherwise than it does.
— LEIBNIZ

THE FORMAL INTRODUCTIONS HAD PLAYED against the backdrop of a
fireplace large enough to burn a small village. For half an hour or so,
Nicolas Fatio de Duillier and Gottfried Wilhelm Leibniz had inched
towards each other as if conjoined by an invisible spring stretched
through the middle of the muttering swarm of Freiherren and
Freifrauen. When finally they drew within hailing distance of each
other they switched over to French and launched into an easy chat
about involutes, evolutes, and radial curves. Leibniz moved on into a
tutorial about a new notion he had been toying with in his spare time,
called parallel curves, which he illustrated by drawing invisible lines on
the hearth with the toe of his boot. Petty nobles of Lower Saxony who
trespassed on these were politely asked to move, so that Fatio could
draw several invisible lines and curves of his own. Then he managed,
in a single grammatically correct sentence, to make reference to Apol-
lonius of Perga, the Folium of Descartes, and the Limaçon of Pascal.

The walls of the room were decorated with impossibly optimistic
paintings, two to three fathoms on a side, of sowers, reapers, and
gleaners plying their respective trades in sun-gilded fields. Fickle
light was shed on these by flames burning in bronze baskets carried
on the heads of naked, muscle-bound, bronze blackamoors planted
on ten-ton pedestals in the corners.

Fatio looked significantly at his watch. "The sun rose—what—two hours ago? At this latitude, we have—say—two hours of daylight remaining?"

"A bit more, sir, by your leave," answered Leibniz with a wink, or perhaps a cinder had flown into his eye. But that was all that needed to be said. Both men turned their backs to the fire for a last helping of warmth, then marched towards the room's exit, groping through darkness and smoke for the door.

They were blinded by powerful bluish light. The Schloß's galleries—which served not only as connecting passages, but also as a sort of perimeter defense against the climate—ran around its exterior wall, and had plenty of windows. The low light of the heavy winter sun ricocheted off the ice-crusted snow that covered the dead gardens, filling these corridors with chilly brilliance. An indignant servant slammed the doors behind them to keep the heat in. Leibniz and Fatio began to match each other's pace down the length of the gallery, moving just short of a sprint. The cold seemed to have dissolved their stockings. It was imperative to keep the knees and calves working.

"Some family," Fatio ventured. "One *hears* of them but does not *meet* them."

"They grow into the interstices left between *other* families," Leibniz admitted. "You would find the Hanover crowd more interesting."

"They *do* seem *impossibly* fecund," Fatio said. "The Winter Queen left children strewn all over the place, and Sophie, at one time or another, has given birth to nearly *everyone*."

"Sophie married in to *this* lot," Leibniz said, glancing back.

"And that is how you became her librarian?"

"Privy Councillor," Leibniz corrected him.

"Sir! I beg you to accept my apologies and my congratulations!" announced Fatio, faltering and reaching for his hat so that he could bow; but Leibniz caught his elbow and pulled him along.

"Never mind, it happened quite recently. In brief, the family of Dukes whose ancestral home is this Schloß put on a tremendous spate of baby-making round the time of the Thirty Years' War, probably because they were besieged here for æons by Danes, Swedes, and God knows who else, and had nothing to do but fuck. Four brothers were born in an interval of eight years! All survived!"

"Calamity!"

"Indeed. Through the 1650s the lads ran riot through the courts of Christendom, trying to mitigate the unnatural surplus of virgins that had built up during the War. All of them wanted Sophie. One of them was too fat and, in any event, Catholic. One was too drunk and impotent. One was famously syphilitic. But the youngest—Ernst August—was, as the Færy Tale has it, *just right!* Sophie married him."

"But my dear Doctor, how did the youngest brother end up in the best position?"

They came to a corner of the Schloß and turned into another endless gallery.

"In 1665 the drunk one died. Ernst August and Georg Wilhelm—the syphilitic—were off sowing their wild oats. So John Frederick—"

"By process of elimination, he would be the obese Catholic?"

"Yes. He appropriated the Duchy and raised an army to defend it. By the time news of this *coup de main* had made its way to the Venetian brothel where Ernst August and Georg Wilhelm had set up their head-quarters, 'twas a *fait accompli.* Later, like good brothers, they worked out a settlement. John Frederick got the great prize, and was made Duke of Hanover. Georg Wilhelm became Duke of Celle. Ernst August—despite being a Protestant—remained the Bishop of Osnabrück. The odds and ends of the clan ended up here in Wolfenbüttel—you have just met them. Now, Ernst August and Sophie had already resolved to make their little fiefdom into a Parnassus, a kingdom of Reason—"

"So they hired you, naturally."

"No, actually, there was a *lot* of that going round at the time. John Frederick wanted to do the same at Hanover."

"It must have been a good time to be a savant."

"Indeed, one could name one's price. John Frederick had more money and a vast library."

"Right, now I am starting to remember it. Huygens told me that after he taught you everything he knew concerning mathematics—which would have been round about the early 1670s—you had to leave Paris and take a job in some cold bleak place." Fatio looked significantly out the window.

" 'Twas Hanover actually—a distinction without a difference, as to you it would seem very like Wolfenbüttel."

Leibniz ushered Fatio into an entrance hall dominated by frighteningly massive staircases.

Sounding a bit perplexed, Fatio said, "Rather a lot of people must have died then, for Ernst August to become Duke of Hanover—"

"John Frederick died in '79. Georg Wilhelm still lives. But it was Ernst August who became Duke of Hanover, by dint of this or that sub-clause in the agreement made between him and his brothers—I'll spare you details."

"So Sophie got to merge *her* Parnassus with John Frederick's—of which you were the crowning glory—"

"Really you do flatter, sir."

"But why did I have to come down *here* to meet you? I'd expected to find you at Hanover."

"The Library!" Leibniz answered, surging past the younger man and hurling himself against an immense door. There was a bit of preliminary cracking and tinkling as ice shattered and fell from its hinges. Then it yawned open to afford Fatio a view across several hundred yards of flat snow-covered ground to a dark uneven mountainous structure that was a-building there.

"No fair making comparisons with the one Wren's building at Trinity College," Leibniz said cheerfully. "*His* will be an ornament—not that there is anything wrong with that—*mine* will be a tool, an engine of knowledge."

"Engine?" Fatio, who was well-shod, pranced out into the snow in pursuit of Leibniz, who had given up any hope of preserving his boots and shifted to a sort of plodding, stomping gait.

"Our use of knowledge progresses through successively higher levels of abstraction as we perfect civilization and draw nearer to the mentality of God," Leibniz said, as if making an off-handed comment about the weather. "Adam named the beasts; meaning, that from casual observations of particular specimens, he moved to the recognition of species, and then devised abstract names for them—a sort of code, if you will. Indeed, if he had not done so, Noah's task would have been inconceivable. Later, a system of writing was developed: spoken words were abstracted into chains of characters. This became the basis for the Law—it is how God communicated His intentions to Man. The Book was written. Then other books. At Alexandria the many books were brought together into the first Library. More recently came the invention of Gutenberg: a cornucopia that spills books out into specialized markets in Frankfurt and Leipzig. The merchants there have been completely unreceptive to my proposals! There are too many books in the world now for any one mind to comprehend. What does Man do, Fatio, when he is faced with a task that exceeds the physical limits of his body?"

"Harnesses beasts, or makes a tool. And beasts are of no use in a Library. So—"

"So we want tools. Behold!" Leibniz proclaimed, taking his hands from his coat-pockets just long enough to direct a sort of shoveling gesture at the looming Pile. "It must be obvious to you that this was a stable* until quite recently. I will stipulate that this is a mean begin-

---

* In this context meaning a *cavalry* stable, a large structure situated near a palace, and serving as home and headquarters for a military organization, as opposed to a barn for keeping beasts out of the rain.

ning for a library and that you will be able to elicit howls of laughter from the Royal Society and from any *salon* at Versailles by describing it to them . . ."

"On the contrary, Doctor! When I bid you *adieu* I shall go straight back to the Hague to resume my studies with Mr. Huygens. 'Twill be a year or more before I address the Royal Society on *any* matter. Wren's library remains half-built for want of funds."

"Very well, then," Leibniz muttered, and led Fatio through a temporary door of rough planks and into the stable. It was unheated, but it got their faces out of the wind, and their feet out of the snow. The foundation and ground-floor walls were made of large blocks of undressed stone. Everything above those was built of timbers. So far, the temporary scaffolding was more substantial than the structure itself, which was only sketched in with a few posts and beams. Fatio was baffled, and soon turned his huge eyes downwards to the several tables arrayed in the center of the main floor.

"One day we shall haul out these rude workbenches and replace them with polished desks where scholars will go to their work, illuminated by sky-light from a high fair cupola above," Leibniz said, craning his head back so that his wig shifted, and thrusting his index finger up through the cloud of vapor that had veiled his words.

"The cupola is a fine innovation, Doctor. Getting adequate light is ever a problem in libraries. Sometimes I am tempted to burn one page to shed light on the next."

"It is but one instance of the principle."

"Which principle?"

"I told you I am trying to build a tool, an engine." Leibniz sighed out a vast cloud of steam.

The tabletops supported divers forms of industry. Each was a gelid still-life unto itself. About half were given over to the library-building project (drawings weighed down with stones and wood-scraps, ragged quills projecting from frozen ink-wells, half-completed ledgers, clamped timbers surrounded by knee-high piles of wood-shavings) and half to whatever the Doctor was interested in at the moment. Fatio drew up short in front of a table strewn with what appeared to be stones; but as he did not fail to note, each stone was impressed with the skeleton of a leaf, insect, fish, or beast—some of them utterly unfamiliar.

"What—"

"I have laid off of *Dynamics* for the time being and am trying to finish another book *Proto-gaea,* whose subject matter you may know from the title. But let us refrain from digressions," said Leibniz, shuffling carefully across the cluttered room. He paused to regard a colossal piece of furniture. "You see I am not the first to contemplate the making of a knowledge engine."

Fatio closed his eyes, which was the only way to pry his attention from the outlandish skeletons, and stepped back, then maneuvered over to join Leibniz.

"Behold, the Bücherrad!"* Leibniz said.

Viewed end-on, the Bücherrad was hexagonal, and nearly as tall as Fatio. When he worked his way round to the front, he saw that it consisted mostly of six massive shelves, each one a couple of fathoms long, bridging the interval between hexagonal end-caps that were mounted on axles so that the whole apparatus could be revolved. But each of the six shelves was free to revolve on an axis of its own. As the Bücherrad spun, each of those shelves counter-rotated in such a way that it maintained a fixed angle with respect to the floor, and did not spill its load of books.

Going round to the other end, Fatio was able to see how it worked: a system of planetary gears, carven from hard wood, spun about the central axle-tree like Ptolemaic epicycles.

Then Fatio turned his attention to the books themselves: curious folio volumes, hand-written, all in the same hand, all in Latin.

"These were written out personally by one Duke August, a forerunner of that lot you just met. He lived to a great age and died some twenty-five years ago. It was he who assembled most of this collection," Leibniz explained.

Fatio bent slightly at the waist to read one of the pages. It consisted of a series of paragraphs each preceded by a title and a long Roman numeral. "It is a *description* of a book," he concluded.

"The process of abstraction continues," Leibniz said. "Duke August could not keep the contents of his library in his memory, so he wrote out catalogs. And when there were too many catalogs for him to use them conveniently, he had woodwrights make Bücherrads—engines to facilitate the use and maintenance of the catalogs."

"It is very ingenious."

"Yes—and it is threescore years old," Leibniz returned. "If you do the arithmetick, as I have, you may easily demonstrate that to hold all the catalogs needed to list all the world's books would require so many Bücherrads that we would need some Bücherrad-rads to spin them around, and a Bücherrad-rad-rad to hold all of them—"

"German is a convenient language that way," Fatio said diplomatically.

---

* Wheel of Books.

"And so on with no end in sight! There are not enough wood-wrights to carve all of the gears. New sorts of knowledge-engines will be demanded."

"I confess you have lost me, Doctor."

"Observe—each book is identified by a number. The numbers are arbitrary, meaningless—a kind of code, like the names Adam gave to the beasts. Duke August was of the old school, and used Roman numerals, which makes it that much more cryptickal."

Leibniz led Fatio away from the center of the floor toward the rugged stone walls, which were mostly barricaded by high thick ramparts covered in canvas tarpaulins. He peeled up the edge of one and flung it back to reveal that the rampart was a stack of books, thousands of them. All of them had been bound in the same style, in pigskin (for like many noble bibliophiles Duke August had bought all his books as masses of loose signatures and had them bound in his own bindery, by his own servants). The newest ones (say, less than half a century old) were still white. More ancient ones had turned cream, beige, tan, brown, and tar-colored. Many bore scars of long-forgotten encounters between pigs and swineherds' cudgels. The titles, and those long Roman numerals, had been inscribed on them in what Fatio now recognized as Duke August's hand.

"Now they are in a heap, later they shall be on shelves—either way, how do you find what you want?" Leibniz asked.

"I believe you are now questioning me in a Socratic mode."

"And you may answer in any mode you like, Monsieur Fatio, provided that you do answer."

"I suppose one would go by the numbers. Supposing that they were shelved in numerical order."

"Suppose they *were*. The numbers merely denote the order in which the Duke acquired, or at least cataloged, the volumes. They say nothing of the contents."

"Re-number them, then."

"According to what scheme? By name of author?"

"I believe it would be better to use something like Wilkins's philosophical language. For any conceivable subject, there would be a unique number. Write that number on the spine of the book and shelve them in order. Then you can go directly to the right part of the library and find all books on a given subject together."

"But suppose I am making a study of Aristotle. Aristotle is my subject. May I expect to find all Aristotle-books shelved together? Or would his works on geometry be shelved in one section, and his works on physics elsewhere?"

"If you look at it that way, the problem is most difficult."

Leibniz stepped over to an empty bookcase and drew his finger down the length of one shelf from left to right. "A shelf is akin to a Cartesian number-line. The position of a book on that shelf is associated with a number. But only *one* number! Like a number-line, it is one-dimensional. In analytic geometry we may cross two or three number-lines at right angles to create a multi-dimensional space. Not so with bookshelves. The problem of the librarian is that books are multi-dimensional in their subject matter but must be ordered on one-dimensional shelves."

"I perceive that clearly now, Doctor," Fatio said. "Indeed, I am beginning to feel like the character of Simplicio in one of Galileo's dialogs. So let me play that rôle to the hilt, and ask you how you intend to solve the problem."

"Well played, sir. Consider the following: Suppose we assign the number three to Aristotle, and four to turtles. Now we must decide where to shelve a book by Aristotle on the subject of turtles. We multiply three by four to obtain twelve, and then shelve the book in position twelve."

"Excellent! By a simple multiplication you have combined several subject-numbers into one—collapsed the multi-dimensional space into a uni-dimensional number-line."

"I am pleased that you favor my proposal thus far, Fatio, but now consider the following: suppose we assign the number two to Plato, and six to trees. And suppose we acquire a book by Plato on the subject of trees. Where does it belong?"

"The product of two and six is twelve—so it goes next to Aristotle's book on turtles."

"Indeed. And a scholar seeking the latter book may instead find himself with the former—clearly a failure of the cataloging system."

"Then let me step once again into the rôle of Simplicio and ask you whether you have solved *this* problem."

"Suppose we use *this* coding instead," quoth the Doctor, reaching behind the bookcase and pulling out a slate on which the following table had been chalked—thereby as much as admitting that the conversation, to this point, had been a scripted *demo'*.

2	Plato
3	Aristotle
5	Trees
7	Turtles
$2 \times 5 = 10$	Plato on Trees

$3 \times 7 = 21$	Aristotle on Turtles
$2 \times 7 = 14$	Plato on Turtles
$3 \times 5 = 15$	Aristotle on Trees
[etc.]	

"Two, three, five, and seven—all prime numbers," remarked Fatio after giving it a brief study. "The shelf-numbers are composites, the products of prime factors. Excellent, Doctor! By making this small improvement—assigning prime numbers, instead of counting numbers, to the various subjects—you have eliminated the problem. The shelf position of any book may be found by multiplying the subject-numbers—and you may be assured it will be *unique*."

"It is a pleasure to explain it to one who grasps the principle so readily," Leibniz said. "Huygens and the Bernoullis have both spoken highly of you, Fatio, and I can see that they were by no means insincere."

"I am humbled to hear my name mentioned in the same sentence with theirs," Fatio returned, "but since you have been kind enough to so favor me, perhaps you will indulge me in a question?"

"It would be my privilege."

"Your scheme is a fine way to *build* a library. For the correct position of any book may be found by taking the product of the several primes that correspond to its subjects. Even when those numbers grow to several digits, that presents no great difficulty; and in any event it is well known that you have invented a machine capable of multiplying numbers with great facility, which I now perceive is just one element of the immense knowledge engine you have proposed to build."

"Indeed, all of these are of a piece, and may be considered aspects of my *Ars Combinatorica*. Did you have a question?"

"I fear that your library, once built, will be difficult to *understand*. You are seeking the help of the Emperor in Vienna, are you not?"

"It cannot be accomplished without the resources of a great kingdom," Leibniz said vaguely.

"Very well, perhaps you are in communication with some other great prince. At any rate, it would seem, then, that you wish to make your Knowledge Engine on a colossal scale."

"Marshalling resources is a continuing problem," the Doctor said, still treading gingerly.

"I predict that you will find success, Doctor Leibniz, and that one day there will rise up, in Berlin, Vienna, or even Moscow, a Knowledge Engine on a titanic scale. The shelves will extend for countless leagues and will be crowded with books all arranged according to the rules of your system. But I fear that I could very easily become lost in the bowels of that place. Looking at a shelf I might see some number, eight or nine digits long. I would know this to be a composite number, the product of two or more primes. But to decompose such a number into its prime factors is a notoriously difficult and tedious problem. There is a curious *asymmetry* about this approach, in other words, lying in the fact that *to its creator* the structure and organization of the great library will be clear as glass—but to a solitary visitor it will seem a murky maze of impenetrable numbers."

"I do not deny it," Leibniz answered without hesitation, "but I find in this a sort of beauty, a reflection of the structure of the universe. The situation of the solitary visitor, as you have described it, is one with which I am familiar."

"That is odd, for I conceive of you as the creator who stands with his hand on the Bücherrad and comprehends all."

"You should know this about me. My father was a learned man who owned one of the finest libraries in Leipzig. He died when I was very small. Consequently I knew him only as a jumble of childish perceptions—between us there were *feelings* but never any rational connection, perhaps somewhat like the relationship that you or I have with God."

And he related a story about how he had, for a time, been locked out of his father's library, but later re-admitted.

"So I ventured into that library which had been closed up since the death of my father and still smelled like him. It might seem funny for me to speak of the smell, but that was the only connection I could draw at the time. For the books were all written in Latin or Greek, languages I did not know, and they treated of subjects with which I was completely unfamiliar, and they were arranged upon the shelves according to some scheme that must have been clear to my father, but to me was unknown, and would have been beyond my ken even if someone had been there to explain it to me.

"Now in the end, Monsieur Fatio, I mastered that library, but in order to do it I first had to learn Greek and Latin, and then read the books. Only when I had done these things was I finally able to do the most difficult thing of all, namely to understand the organizing principle by which my father had arranged the books on the shelves."

Fatio said: "So you are not troubled by the plight of my hypothetical scholar, a-mazed in the penetralia of your Knowledge Engine. But Doctor Leibniz, how many persons, dropped into a library of books written in unknown languages, could do what you did?"

"The question is more than just rhetorical. The situation is not merely hypothetical," Leibniz answered. "For every human being who is born into this universe is like a child who has been given a key to an infinite Library, written in cyphers that are more or less obscure, arranged by a scheme—of which we can at first know nothing, other than that there does appear to be *some* scheme—pervaded by a vapor, a spirit, a fragrance that reminds us that it was the work of our Father. Which does us no good whatever, other than to remind us, when we despair, that there *is* an underlying logic about it, that was understood once and can be understood again."

"But what if it can only be understood by a mind as great as God's? What if we can only find what we want by factoring twenty-digit numbers?"

"Let us understand what we may, and extend our reach, insofar as we can, by the making of engines, and content ourselves with that much," Leibniz answered. "It will suffice to keep us busy for a while. We cannot perform *all* of the calculations needed without turning every atom in the Universe into a cog in an Arithmetickal Engine; and then it would be God—"

"I think you are coming close to words that could get you burnt at the stake, Doctor—meanwhile, I turn to ice. Is there a place where we could strike a balance between those two extremes?"

THE DOCTOR HAD CAUSED a large shed to be scabbed onto the outer wall of the stable and filled with the books and papers most important to him. In one corner stood a black stove having the general size and shape of the biblical Tower of Babel. When they arrived it was merely warm, but Leibniz wrenched open several doors, rammed home half a cord or so of wood, and clanged them to. Within seconds, ears began to pop as the mickle Appliance sucked the air from the room. The iron tower began to emit an ominous rumbling and whooshing noise, and Leibniz and Fatio spent the rest of the conversation nervously edging away from it, trying to find the radius where (to paraphrase Fatio) being burnt alive was no more likely than freezing to death. This zone proved surprisingly narrow. As Leibniz fussed with the stove, which had taken up a kind of eerie keening, Fatio stepped back a pace, and let his eye fall on a sheet of paper—the topmost of several that were sticking out of a book. A few lines of printing were visible at the top of the page, written in Leibniz's hand:

DOCTOR

THE RECENT EVENTS IN THE BALLROOM OF THE HÔTEL ARCACHON WERE OF SUCH A DRAMAT-ICK NATURE THAT I CANNOT BUT THINK YOU HAVE

ALREADY HAD ACCOUNTS OF THEM FROM DIVERSE
SOURCES HOWEVER MY VERSION FOLLOWS . . .

Beyond that point all was swallowed up between the pages of the
enclosing book, which was expensively bound in red leather,
ornately gilded with both Roman and Chinese characters.

"Any possibility of tea?" Fatio inquired, spying a kettle that had
been left on one of the steps of the flaming ziggurat. Shielding his
face in the crook of one arm, Leibniz ventured closer, seized a poker,
and lunged like a fencing-master at the kettle to see whether it contained any water. Meanwhile Fatio peeled back the topmost sheet
to reveal a letter written on different paper, in a different hand:
Eliza's!

> To G. W. Leibniz from Eliza, the Marrying Maiden
> Doctor,
>   You will want to know everything about the dress I was mar-
> ried in. The stomacher is made of Turkish watered silk deco-
> rated with several thousand of the tiny pearls that come from
> Bandar-Kongo on the Persian Gulf . . .

Leibniz had been rummaging in a drawer. He pulled up a black
slab about the size of a folio book, impressed with a single huge Chinese character, and snapped off a corner. "Caravan tea," he
explained. "Unlike your English and Dutch tea, which comes loose
off of ships, this stuff was brought overland, via Russia—it is a million
dried leaves pressed together into a brick."

Fatio did not seem to be as fascinated by this as Leibniz had
hoped. Leibniz tried another gambit: "Huygens wrote to me
recently, and mentioned you had come over from London."

"Monsieur Newton and I devoted the month of March to reading Mr. Huygens's *Treatise on Light* and were so taken with it that we
agreed to divide forces for the year—I have been studying with
Huygens—"

"And Newton toils at his Alchemy."

"Alchemy, theology, philosophy—call it what you will," Fatio said
coolly, "he is close to an achievement that will dwarf the *Principia*."

"I don't suppose it has anything to do with gold?" asked Leibniz.

Fatio—generally so birdlike-quick in his answers—allowed some
moments to pass. "Your question is a bit vague. Gold is important to
Alchemists," he allowed, "as comets are to astronomers. But there
are some, of a vulgar turn of mind, who suppose that Alchemists are
interested in gold only in the same sense as *bankers* are."

"*C'est juste.* Though there is a troublesome banker, not far from here, who seems to value it in *both* the monetary and the Alchemical sense." Leibniz, who until this point in the conversation had been the embodiment of good cheer, deflated as he was saying these words, as if he had been reminded of something very grave, and his eye strayed over to the outlandish red-leather book. This topic had had the same effect on his spirits as a handful of earth tossed into a fire. Again, Fatio allowed some moments to pass before he responded; for he was studying Leibniz carefully.

"I think I know who you mean," Fatio said finally.

"It is most curious," Leibniz said. "Perhaps you have heard some of the same stories concerning this as I have. The entire controversy, as I understand it, revolves around a belief that there is a particular sample of gold, whose precise whereabouts are unknown, but that possesses some properties that make it more valuable, to Alchemists, than ordinary gold. I would expect a *banker* to know better!"

"Do not make the error of believing that all gold is the same, Doctor."

"I thought Natural Philosophy had proved at least *that* much."

"Why, *some* would say it has proved the *opposite!*"

"Perhaps you have read something new in London or Paris that I have not seen yet?"

"Actually, Doctor, I was thinking of Isaac's *Principia.*"

"I have read it," Leibniz said drily, "and do not recollect seeing anything about gold."

"And yet it is clear enough that two planets of equal size and composition will describe *different* trajectories through the heavens, depending on their distances from the sun."

"Of course—that is necessarily true, by the inverse-square law."

"Since the two planets *themselves* are equal in every way, how can this difference in their trajectories be accounted for, unless you enlarge your scope of observations to include the difference in their situations vis-à-vis the sun?"

"Monsieur Fatio, a cornerstone of *my* philosophy is the identity of indiscernibles. Simply put, if A cannot be discerned from B, then A and B are the same object. In the situation you have described, the two planets are indiscernible from each other, which means that they ought to be identical. This includes having identical trajectories. Since they are obviously *not* identical, in that their trajectories differ, it follows that they must in *some* way be discernible from each other. Newton discerns them by assigning them differing positions in space, and then presuming that space is somehow pervaded by a mysterious presence that accounts for the inverse-square force. That is, he discerns one from the other by appealing to a sort of mysterious external quality of space . . ."

"You sound like Huygens!" Fatio snapped, suddenly annoyed. "I might as well have stayed in the Hague."

"I am sorry if the tendency of me and Huygens to agree causes you grief."

"You may agree with each other all you like. But why will you not agree with Isaac? Can you not perceive the magnificence of what he has achieved?"

"*Any* sentient man can perceive that," Leibniz returned. "*Almost all* will be so blinded by its brilliance that they will be unable to perceive its flaws. There are only a few of us who can do that."

"It is very easy to carp."

"Actually it is rather difficult, in that it leads to discussions such as this one."

"Unless you can propose an alternative theory that mends these supposed flaws, I believe you should temper your criticisms of the *Principia*."

"I am still developing my theory, Monsieur Fatio, and it may be a long time before it is capable of making testable predictions."

"What conceivable theory could explain the discernibility of those two planets, without making reference to their positions in absolute space?"

THIS LED TO AN INTERLUDE in the snow outside. Doctor Leibniz packed two handfuls of snow together between his hands, watched warily by Fatio. "Don't worry, Monsieur Fatio, I'm not going to throw it at you. If you would be so helpful as to make two more, about the size of melons, as like to each other as possible."

Fatio was not quick to warm to such a task, but eventually he squatted down and began to roll a pair of balls, stopping every couple of paces to pound away the rough edges.

"They are as close to indiscernible as I can make them under these conditions—which is to say, in twilight with frozen hands," shouted Fatio towards Leibniz, who was a stone's throw off, wrestling with a snowball that weighed more than he did. When no response came back, he muttered, "I shall go in and warm my hands if that is acceptable."

But by the time Nicolas Fatio de Duillier had got back to Leibniz's office, his hands were warm enough to do a few things. He took another look at the papers stuck into the Chinese book. The letter from Eliza was inordinately long, and appeared to consist entirely of gaseous chatter about what everyone was wearing. Yet on top of it was the other document, addressed *to* the Doctor but written *in* the Doctor's hand. A mystery. Perhaps the book was a clue? It was called *I Ching*. Fatio had seen it once before, in the library of Gresham's College, where Daniel Waterhouse had fallen asleep over it. The sheaf of papers had been used to mark a particular chapter entitled: *54. Kuei Mei: The Marrying Maiden*. The chapter itself was a bucket of claptrap and mystickal gibberish.

He put it back where he'd found it, and went over to the shed's single tiny window. Leibniz now had his back pressed against an immense snowball and was trying to topple it over by thrusting with both legs. Fatio strolled once around the room, pausing to riffle through any prominent stacks of papers that presented themselves to his big pale eyes. Of which there were several: letters from Huygens, from Arnauld, from the Bernoullis, the late Spinoza, Daniel Waterhouse, and everyone else in Christendom who had a flicker of sense. But one of the larger stacks consisted of letters from Eliza. Fatio reached into the middle, grabbed half a dozen leaves between his thumb and index finger, and snapped them out. He folded them and stuffed them into his breast pocket. Then he ventured back outside.

"Are your hands warm, Monsieur Fatio?"

"Exceeding warm, Doctor Leibniz."

The Doctor had arranged the three snowballs—one giant one and the two small indiscernibles—on the field between the stable, the Schloß, and the nearby Arsenal. The triangle defined by these balls was nothing special, being neither equilateral nor isosceles.

"Isn't this how Sir Francis Bacon died?"

"Descartes, too—froze to death in Sweden," the Doctor returned cheerfully, "and if Leibniz and Fatio can go down in the annals next to Bacon and Descartes our lives will have been well concluded. Now, if you would be so good as to go to that one and tell me of your perceptions." The Doctor pointed to a small snowball a few paces in front of Fatio.

"I see the field, the Schloß, Arsenal, and Library-to-be. I see you, Doctor, standing by a great snowball, and over there to the right, not so far away, a lesser one."

"Now pray do the same from the other snowball that you made."

A few moments later Fatio was able to report: "The same."

"Exactly the same?"

"Well, of course there are slight differences. Now, Doctor, you and the large snowball are to my right, and closer than before, and the small snowball is to my left."

Leibniz now deserted his post and began stomping towards Fatio. "Newton would have it that this field possesses a reality of its own, which governs the balls, and makes them discernible. But I say the field is not necessary! Forget about it, and consider only the balls' *perceptions*."

"Perceptions?"

"You said yourself that when you stood *there* you perceived a large snowball on the left, far away, and a small one on the right. *Here* you perceive a large one on the right, near at hand, and a small one on the left. So even though the balls might be indiscernible, and hence identical, in terms of their external properties such as size, shape, and weight, when we consider their *internal* properties—such as their *perceptions* of one another—we see that they are different. So they *are* discernible! And what is more, they may be discerned without reference to some sort of fixed, absolute space."

By now they had, without discussion, begun trudging back towards the Schloß, which looked deceptively warm and inviting as twilight deepened.

"You seem to be granting every object in the Universe the power to perceive, and to record its perceptions," Fatio ventured.

"If you are going to venture down this road of subdividing objects into smaller and smaller bits, you must *somewhere* stop, and stick your neck out by saying, '*This* is the fundamental unit of reality, and *thus* are its properties, on which all other phænomena are built,'" said the Doctor. "*Some* think it makes sense that these are like billiard balls, which interact by colliding."

"I was just about to say," said Fatio, "what could be simpler than that? A hard wee bit of indivisible matter. That is the most reasonable hypothesis of what an atom is."

"I disagree! *Matter* is complicated stuff. Collisions between pieces of matter are more complicated yet. Consider: If these atoms are infinitely small, why, then, is it not true that the likelihood of one atom colliding with another is essentially zero?"

"You have a point," said Fatio, "but I hardly think it is somehow *simpler* to endow these atoms, instead, with the ability to perceive and to think."

"Perception and thought are properties of souls. It is no worse to posit that the fundamental building-block of the Universe is *souls* than to say it is wee bits of hard stuff, moving about in an empty space that is pervaded by mystickal Fields."

"Somehow a planet's perception of the sun and all the other planets, then, causes it to behave exactly as if it were in such a 'mystickal Field,' to an uncanny degree of precision."

"I know it sounds difficult, Monsieur Fatio, but 'twill work out better in the long run."

"Physics, then, becomes a sort of vast record-keeping exercise. Every object in the Universe is distinguished from every other object by the uniqueness of its perceptions of all the other objects."

"If you think on it long enough you will see it is the only way to distinguish them."

"Why, it is as if every atom or particle—"

"I call them monads."

"Monad, then, is a sort of Knowledge Engine unto itself, a Bücherrad-rad-rad-rad . . ."

Leibniz summoned a weak smile.

"Its gears grind away like the ones in your Arithmetickal Engine, and it decides what to do of its own accord. You knew Spinoza, did you not?"

Leibniz held up a warning hand. "Yes. But pray do not put me in with him."

"If I may just return to the topic that got us started, Doctor, it seems to me that *your* theory allows for a possibility you scoffed at— namely, that two lumps of gold might be different from each other."

"Any two such lumps *are* different, but it is because, being differently situated, they have different perceptions. I am afraid that *you* want to assign mystickal properties to some gold and not other."

"Afraid why?"

"Because the next thing you'll do is melt it down to extract that mystery and put it in a phial."

Fatio sighed. "In truth, *all* these theories have their problems."

"Agreed."

"Why not admit it, then? Why this stubborn refusal to consider Newton's system, when yours is just as fraught with difficulties?"

Leibniz drew to a halt before the front stoop of the Schloß, as if he'd rather freeze than continue the discussion where it might be overheard. "Your question is dressed up in the guise of Reason, to make it appear innocent. Perhaps it is. Perhaps not."

"Even if you do not think me innocent, pray believe that my confusion is genuine."

"Isaac and I had this conversation long ago, when we were young, and matters stood quite differently."

"How odd. You are the only person, other than Daniel Waterhouse, who has ever called him by his Christian name."

The look of uncertainty on Leibniz's face now hardened into open disbelief. "What do *you* call him, when the two of you are alone together in your London house?"

"I stand corrected, Doctor. There are *three* of us who have known him thusly."

"That is a very clever sentence you just uttered," Leibniz exclaimed, sounding genuinely impressed. "Like a silken cord turned in on itself and knotted into a snare. I commend you for it, but I will not put my foot in it. And I will thank you to keep Daniel out of it as well."

Fatio had turned red. "The only thing I wish to snare is a clearer understanding of what has passed between you and Isaac."

"You want to know if you have a rival."

Fatio said nothing.

"The answer is: you do not."

"That is well."

"You do not have a rival, Fatio. But Isaac Newton does."

Ireland
1690–1691

THE KING'S OWN BLACK TORRENT Guards had been founded by a man King William did not like very much (John Churchill), and as a sort of punishment for that, the regiment had now been exiled in Ireland for almost two years. Bob Shaftoe had learned many things about this island during that time: For example, that it was commonly divided into four pieces, which were variously styled Kingdoms or Duchies or Presidencies or Counties depending on whom you were talking to and what peculiar notions they held concerning the true nature and meaning of Irish history. Connaught was one, and the others were Ulster, Leinster, and Munster.

Bob heard about Connaught first, but saw it last. Nevertheless, he felt he knew something of it. He had heard endless discourse of it during the last thirteen years from his Irish "out-laws," the kin-folk of the late Mary Dolores, most of whom bore the surname of Partry.

Until of late, the Partry clan and their swine, kine, assorted free-ranging poultry, and one bewildered sheep had teemed in a bit of shed in Rotherhithe, which lay across the Thames from Wapping, about a mile downstream of the Tower of London. Teague Partry—

one of three Partrys who had, at one time or another, enlisted in the Black Torrent Guards—had often volunteered to stand watch on Develin Tower, the extreme southeastern vertex of the citadel, in spite of the fact that it was sorely exposed to raw weather coming up the River, and detested by all of the other soldiers. The cold wet winds, he claimed, reminded him of Connaught, and from his Develin vantage point he could see all the way downriver to Rother-hithe and keep an eye on his four-legged assets. Teague rhapsodized about Connaught all the time, and did it so convincingly that half the regiment was ready to move there. Bob had taken it with a grain of salt because he knew that Teague had never in his life ventured more than five miles' distance from London Bridge, and was merely repeating tales told to him by his folk. From which Bob had collected, very early, something that it would have benefited the Partrys to know, namely that Ireland was a mentality, and not a physical place.

After the Revolution the Partrys had slaughtered all their livestock, deserted their Regiment, gathered up what money they could, and escaped to Dublin. Several months later, Bob had been shipped to Belfast with the rest of his regiment, and with the Dutch colonel who'd been put in command of it. Now, King William found John Churchill hard enough to trust when he was inside London Wall. He could not possibly bring himself to trust Marlborough (or any other English commander) with an elite regiment on Irish soil, especially when Churchill's former master, James, was only a few marches south, in Dublin. So it was under a Colonel de Zwolle that the King's Own Black Torrent Guards voyaged to Belfast, and under him that they tarried on that island over two winters. When Bob next saw Churchill, he would assure his old chief that he had not missed a thing.

From their point of disembarkation the regiment had marched south for a few days, and then wintered over in a camp at Dundalk, which lay near the border between the part of Ireland called Ulster and the one called Leinster. Out of a full strength of 806 men they suffered casualties of thirty-one dead, thirty-two so disabled that they had to be retired, and many hundreds who were laid low for a time but later got better. Most of these casualties were put down to disease or hunger, a few to accidents and brawls—zero to combat, of which there was none. This was an exceptionally good record.

They were encamped near a Dutch regiment commanded by one of Colonel de Zwolle's old drinking- and hunting-buddies. The Dutch soldiers suffered very little from disease, though they were every bit as cold and hungry. They kept their camp so clean that it was mocked as "the Nunnery" by certain men in Bob's regiment, who espoused a more temperate approach to hygiene. But when English soldiers began dying at a rate of several per day, the Black Torrent Guards finally began to pay some attention to de Zwolle's nagging and to emulate some of the practices of their Dutch neighbors. Coincidentally or not, the number of men sick in bed began to drop not long afterwards. When spring came and the rolls were called, it was found that they had suffered much lighter casualties than other English regiments.

In June 1690, then, William of Orange finally arrived in Ulster as only a King could, viz. with three hundred ships, fifteen thousand troops, hundreds of thousands of pounds sterling, more Princes, Dukes, and Bishops than a boat-load of playing-cards and chess-sets, and a lot of Dutch artillery. He marched south, pausing at Dundalk long enough to collect the regiments that had wintered over there, and then invaded Leinster at the head of thirty-six thousand men. He made straight for Dublin, where James Stuart had established his rebel Parliament. King William had a wooden house, designed by one Christopher Wren—that same bloke who was building the new St. Paul's in London. It was ingeniously made so that it could be taken down in sections at a few minutes' notice, transported on wagons, and put back up again wherever William decided to establish his headquarters. Normally he erected it in the midst of his army, which was not at all usual for a campaigning King, and made a good impression on his soldiers.

James Stuart had been spoiling for a fight for a year and a half. He marched north from Dublin at the head of twenty-five thousand men and, after some preliminary maneuvering, set up a position on the south bank of the river called Boyne.

The next day, William was reconnoitering the north bank in person, looking for crossing-places, when a Jacobite cannonball hit him on the shoulder and knocked him off his horse. Jacobites on the opposite bank saw it happen, and saw a vaguely king-shaped object being carried away in haste by agitated Protestants.

What they could not see, from that side of the Boyne, was that the cannonball was a spent ricochet that had glanced off William's shoulder and dealt him no serious harm. They made the wholly reasonable assumption that William the Usurper was dead and reported as much up the chain of command.

The next day William launched a diversionary attack across the Boyne not far from where he had been hit. He waited for James to move his main force that way, then crossed the river in force elsewhere. The first to mount this main attack were William's best and favorite soldiers, the Dutch Blue Guards. But they were followed closely by several companies of the King's Own Black Torrent

Guards, a plum job that never would have been afforded them if they'd been under the command of Marlborough. De Zwolle had spent the winter plying his superiors with brandy and sending letters to London; that probably explained how Bob and his men were given such a splendid opportunity to have their heads hacked off in a bog. They crossed the Boyne, at any rate, and formed up on the south bank, and withstood several Jacobite cavalry charges. This was not an easy thing to do. They did it in direct view of King William, who had found a vantage point on the north bank from which to observe his beloved Blues.

The captain of Bob's company was killed very early and so Bob had to assume effective command of threescore men for the rest of the day. This had very little effect on anything. Whether or not their captain was alive, Bob's job was to get his men to believe that they really were safer standing together as a unit, as opposed to throwing their muskets down and diving into the river. Far be it from Bob to think about his company's or his regiment's reputation at Court.

If he had thought about it, he might have counseled his men to break and run instead.

That night the King came to their camp to tell them what fine fellows he thought they were. Now the Irish Army had simply vanished; the only evidence they'd been present at the Boyne was the thousands of pikes and muskets they had thrown down on the ground, the better to outrun their pursuers. King William's host had climbed up out of the river-valley and spread out across churned and trampled pastures between the hamlet of Donore and the village of Duleek—places that, like færies, were spoken of, by Irishmen, as if they really existed, but that could not actually be seen. As they went they harvested the dropped weapons, hugging bristly faggots of them to their chests and finally letting them drop in clanking heaps when they decided to set up camp.

As their baggage had not caught up with them, they spent the night in the open, and as there were no trees hereabouts they used the captured weapons for firewood. They were not worth keeping as weapons—a fact that was obvious to Bob, but tended to be ignored by those who espoused the view that the Irish had thrown them down out of cowardice. Bob found flintlocks without flint, muskets with cracked barrels, pikes that could be snapped over the knee.

A few hours after nightfall, anyway, they received their King. He had suffered an asthma attack while fording the river and was still wheezing piteously—which evidently hurt, because of the cannonball injury—so he tended to speak in very short sentences. He was sitting askew on a tired horse. He spoke in Dutch to de Zwolle and then in English to the company captains and to Bob. He did not look at them, however; he was very close to falling asleep in the saddle, and could not tear his eyes away from the musket-bonfires.

What he said was that, with regiments such as his own Black Torrent Guards, he could not only take Ireland but Flanders, too, and fight all the way to Paris.

Bob stayed up late gazing into the fire, which was slowly devolving into a red tangle of melted gun-barrels, and pondered some of the longer-term implications of the King's statement. Overall, the notion was somewhat troubling. On the other hand, an invasion of France might afford him an opportunity to seek out Miss Abigail Frome.

The next day they left the field pimpled with smoking twists of blackened iron and marched south to Dublin. James Stuart had already run off to France. Protestants were running wild, looting Catholic homes. Bob ventured into a certain quarter where Protestants were more apt to behave themselves, if indeed they went there at all. He found Teague Partry sitting on a stoop smoking a clay pipe and gravely observing the bums of passing milk-maids, as if nothing much had happened recently. But the right side of his face was flushed red, as if sunburnt, and pocked with recent wounds that all appeared to have radiated from a common center.

Teague bought him a mug of beer (it being Teague's turn to do this) and explained to him that James's foreign cavalry regiments had panicked first, finding their escape route blocked by the Irish infantry, had opened fire on them to clear the way. He put it to Bob that Irishmen had it in them to fight effectively when they were not being massacred by Continental cavaliers who were supposed to be on their side, and (pointing significantly to his face) when they were provided with guns that projected musket-balls instead of blowing up in their faces. Bob agreed that it was so.

Later the bulk of William's army marched west across the island, out of Leinster and into the southern realm of Munster. They laid siege to Limerick, which was one of the few places in Ireland that had proper fortifications, and could serve as the venue for a proper military engagement. Unfortunately, the Irish had little use for proper military engagements. William's Dutch cannons blasted a hole in the city wall; Bob rushed in at the head of his company and got conked in the head by a bottle hurled at him from the top of a ruin by a massive hag in a wimple, screaming something at him in Gaelic. Bob, who knew nothing about his father, or his mother's father, had long been preoccupied by the suspicion that he might be partly, or even largely, Irish, and while he lay unconscious on the rubble of the shattered wall of Limerick, he had a strange dream concerning the nun who had thrown the bottle—the import of it was that she was his great-aunt or something, scolding him for everything bad he had ever done.

His skull was merely dented, but his scalp was nearly taken off, and had to be sewed back on by a barber-surgeon who advised him to grow his hair back again as soon as he could; "And for god's sake get a wife before you go bald, or women and children will run away from you screaming!" He was only trying to be cheerful, but Bob growled at him that he had already found his true love, and that scars on his pate were the least of his concerns.

The Earl of Marlborough finally got leave from the distracted King to sail across to Munster. He took the cities of Cork and Kinsale, but he did it without the help of his Black Torrent Guards. Then he went home to spent a comfortable winter in London while Bob and the regiment remained encamped outside of Limerick, fending off occasional sorties by the Irish cavalry, and keeping up a running, sporadic battle with bands of armed peasants who styled themselves "rapparees."

The rapparees actually *did* have firearms that worked, and had learned to strip them down into their parts in seconds. The locks they kept in their pockets, the barrels they corked shut and hid in sloughs or streams, the stocks they thrust into wood-piles, or anywhere else a bare stick might go unnoticed. So what appeared to be a crew of half-naked peat-cutters or a congregation strolling to Mass could scatter into the waste at a word or a gesture, and reconstitute itself an hour later as a band of heavily armed marauders.

Because of the rapparees there were few places on the island, outside of Ulster, where Englishmen could feel safe in groups of less than an infantry company. But one of those places was the south bank of the river Shannon just downstream of Limerick. As the winter eased, and the hair grew back over his wound, Bob began to go there by himself and sit under a solitary tree overlooking the river and smoke his pipe and brood. The reading of books was not available to him. He'd lost his interest in whoring. He had heard his men's stories, jokes, and songs so many times he could not suffer them any more. Drink made him feel poorly, and card-playing was pointless. He suffered, in other words, from a want of things that he could do to pass the time.

So he sat under his brooding-tree and gazed across the wide river Shannon. Like all the other rivers of the British Isles, it had a long estuary leading in from the sea to a port (Limerick in this case) that had been built where the river first became narrow enough to be bridged. The Shannon was the boundary between Munster and Connaught, and so by looking across it Bob could gaze into that land of legend so highly spoken of by the Partrys. From here Connaught looked like the rest of Ireland. But what did he know?

When King William had come over before the Battle of the Boyne he had brought fresh recruits to replace the ones who had sickened and died over the winter, but not enough of the sort Bob favored. Bob had however managed to recruit half a dozen English Protestants who had never actually been to England. They had grown up on various farms in Ireland that their fathers or grandfathers, who had been Cromwell-soldiers, had taken away from Gaelic Catholics. But the various revolutions of the last decades had turned their families into Vagabonds of an extraordinarily hard and dour cast, roaming around Eire in search of organized violence. Bob knew how to talk to men like that, and so they had spread the word among themselves and gravitated toward the King's Own Black Torrent Guards, and continued to gravitate still.

After the Battle of the Boyne, a Protestant wool-merchant of Dublin (who had grown wealthy from the fact that the Irish were not allowed to sell their wool overseas except through England) had donated some portion of his lootings to buy these new recruits weapons and uniforms, and they had formed a company. So the Black Torrent Guards were now a slightly oversized regiment, with 14 companies instead of 13, and a nominal strength of 868 men.

One day Bob reached his brooding-tree and turned around to discover that he had been followed out by Tom Allgreave and Oliver Good, two of the original Phanatiques he'd recruited last year in Dundalk. They were a quarter of a mile behind him, exchanging the lead position every few steps, as if egging each other on. Each of them had a sword dangling from his belt, part of the motley collection of brought and stolen weaponry that had been showered upon the Fourteenth Company by that wool-merchant.

To give great long blades to such boys was dangerous. Fortunately the boys knew it, or anyway had found out as much, over the course of the winter, by slashing each other in what were meant to be playful exchanges. By the time Tom and Oliver drew within hailing-distance of Bob, he had guessed why they had come: They required instruction in sword-fighting. Normally this was considered a pastime of effete courtiers, a pointless, useless, out-moded affectation; in a word, idle. But among common folk, especially older ones who remembered Cromwell, the lore of the spadroon continued to circulate. Word had apparently got round to Tom and Oliver that Bob knew something of the practice. Those boys were unreconstructed

Puritans who had nothing to do all winter long, as drinking, gambling, and whoring were ruled out on religious grounds. One could pray for only so many hours a day. It was not possible to practice marksmanship because powder and balls were strictly rationed. So it was not clear to Bob whether they had decided to take up the practice of sword-fighting because they genuinely cared about it, or because there was literally nothing else for them to do.

It did not matter either way, as Bob was idle, too. And so as Tom and Oliver got to within a horseshoe-throw of his brooding-tree, Bob knocked the ashes out of his pipe, stood up, reached around himself, and drew out his spadroon. The Puritans were thrilled. "You'll want to stand sideways, as you make a narrower target that way, and it gets your sword-arm that much closer to the other bloke," Bob said. He raised the sword up until its guard was touching his nose, the blade pointing vertically into the air. "This is a sort of salute, and do not on any account mistake it for some foppish affectation, as it says to any man who stands before you, 'I mean to engage in swordplay with you, do not just stand there and be hit, but either defend yourself, or else retire.'"

Tom and Oliver now nearly killed themselves getting their weapons unsheathed, and then nearly killed each other getting them into the salute position. "Oliver, what you have in your hand is a rapier, and I do not know the method of its use as well as I do that of the spadroon," Bob said, "but anyway we shall try to make shift with the tools at hand."

Thus did Bob open up a new defencing academy on the south bank of the river Shannon. It became popular very quickly and then just as quickly collapsed to some half a dozen men who were genuinely interested in the subject. After a month they were joined by Monsieur LaMotte, a Huguenot cavalry captain who happened to spy them as he was riding by one day. He was expert with a cavalry saber, which was a somewhat similar weapon to the spadroon, but he had also studied the rapier, and so he was at last able to give Oliver some instruction in what to do with his weapon. In general, cavalry officers (who tended to be Persons of Quality) would never fraternize thusly with common foot-soldiers, but the Huguenots were an exceeding queer lot. Many were common Frenchmen whose families had grown wealthy in trade and then been kicked out of France. Now they were in Ireland, gaining some small revenge by teaching the defencing tricks of the Continental nobility to savage Anglo-Irish Puritans.

OLIVER GOOD'S GRANDFATHER had dwelt for a dozen years on a farm between Athlone and Tullamore, which placed it in Leinster. But it lay not far from the Connaught frontier, which was regarded by Protestants as the utmost boundary of civilization. He had obtained title to the land by driving off its Catholic inhabitants, the Ferbanes, who had driven their cattle west across a ford of the Shannon and thereby vanished from ken. Good's justification, if he needed any, was that those Ferbanes had taken part in the Rebellion of 1641 and expanded their farm at the expense of some neighboring Protestants who had come over from England in Elizabethan times. But he had to stop using that justification after he was confronted by several ragged men who appeared on the property one day claiming to be the descendants and rightful heirs of those same Elizabethan Protestants! After that, if anyone dared question his claim to the land, he said it was his by right of conquest, and because he had a piece of paper that said so.

He and his children toiled on the land as only Puritans could toil on the land, and made many improvements, few of which were obvious, none of which produced results quickly. They bore arms all their days and often rode the countryside hunting down "disorderly elements." They did not see those ragged Protestants any more, and forgot about them altogether, except for their surname, which could be read from the odd gravestone: Crackington.

After Charles II restored the monarchy, however, it was learned that the Crackingtons had somehow found their way back to England and made themselves pests and parasites on their relations, who went to the new Parliament (along with thousands of other Anglo-Irish landholders who had been displaced by other Cromwellian soldiers) and demanded that the Phanatiques be cast out of Ireland. As one of the new King's first acts had been to put Cromwell's head up on a stick, their chances of success seemed reasonable enough. In the end, they got only part of what they wanted. Some of the Cromwellian settlers were kicked off their land and some were not. The Goods managed to hang on to theirs, but only because of some obscure and contingent political happenstance at Westminster.

They were not, however, free to practice their religion any more, and that was what drove them off the land in the end, and sent half of them to Massachusetts. The Crackingtons came back and took over the farm, with all of its improvements, and began to prosper, and even paid for the reconstruction of the local Anglican church (which the Goods had made useful as a barn). This had occurred not long after the birth of Oliver Good, with the result that he had only ill-formed childish memories of the farmstead that he intended to re-occupy one day.

Then when James II became King, he re-Catholicized Ireland. The Crackingtons awoke one morning to find breaches in their fences, and wild Connaught kine grazing in their enclosures, guarded closely by red-haired men who spoke no English and carried French muskets. It was not possible to persuade them to leave because the new Catholic government in Dublin had confiscated the weapons of the English gentry. After not very long the Crackingtons judged it prudent to leave until a judge could rule on the title to the land—or the titles to the lands, rather, as by this point the farm comprised half a dozen contiguous patches of dirt, each of which had an equally complex story. The Ferbanes, it turned out, had been carrying on boundary-feuds with their neighbors for five hundred years—some were mere interlopers who'd been driven inland by the Vikings.

At any rate the Crackingtons packed up what household effects they could, rounded up a few horses (the Ferbanes had driven most of them off), and set out for Dublin, where they kept a town-house. Along the way they were set upon by rapparees. But just when it looked as if all were lost, they were saved by a Protestant militia band that came on in a grand, noisy rush and drove the rapparees away. The Crackington patriarch thanked these mangy-looking Protestants again and again, and promised to reward them in golden guineas if they would sent a representative to call on him at his town-house in Dublin—"my name," he said, "is Mr. Crackington and anyone in Dublin—" (by which he meant any Anglican English gentleman) "—will be able to direct you to my house."

"Did you say *Crackington*?" said one of the militia. "My name is *Good*. Do you know me?"

After this certain unpleasantries, which Oliver Good declined to speak much of, had been visited upon the Crackingtons, and it was unclear whether any of them had made it as far as Dublin—but if they had, they'd have found their town-house looted, and occupied by Catholics, anyway. But the point was that all of Ulster, Leinster, and Munster were like that farm between Athlone and Tullamore.

England was divided into parcels of land whose ownership was clearly established. It was like a wall made of bricks, each brick an integral thing surrounded by a clear boundary of white mortar. Ireland was like a daub-wall. Every generation came around with a fresh hod and troweled a new layer of mud atop all of the previous ones, which instantly hardened and became brittle. The land was not merely encumbered; it was the sum of its encumbrances.

Connaught was supposedly different because it had not succumbed to the incursions of the English. But it had troubles of its own because those Irish who declined to be conquered fled there in times of trouble and squatted on the land of the Irish who had always lived there.

DEFENCING-PRACTICE WENT ON MUCH LONGER than anyone really wanted. The war was not quick to resume in the spring of 1691. King William's supreme commander in Ireland was now Baron Godard de Ginkel, another Dutchman. His objective was obviously Connaught, which was guarded by the Shannon and by the fortified cities of Limerick, Athlone, and Sligo. Irish diggers bossed around by French engineers had devoted the whole winter to building up those cities' earth-works. Therefore Ginkel wanted boats and pontoons for crossing the river, and guns for knocking down the fortifications. Those cost money. Parliament had very little of it, and had become surly about handing it over to their Dutch king, whom they were already sick of. Nothing was forthcoming until the end of May, which convinced Bob and all the rest that they were truly lost and forgotten in Ireland, and destined to be stranded here, and to become the next players in stories of the Ferbane-Crackington-Good type.

For his part, King Louis XIV of France did little to disabuse the combatants of the feeling that they had dropped off the map of Christendom. The Battle of the Boyne had been *the* battle for Ireland, or so everyone in Christendom believed, according to a letter Bob had got from Eliza. They believed it not because it had any particular military weight but because there had been a King on each side of a river and one had crossed over it and the other had turned his backside to it and run away, and not stopped running until he'd reached France.

During the battle that had given the Black Torrent Guards their name, their commander, Feversham, had been asleep. Even when he was awake he was daft, because of his brain injury. John Churchill had been the real commander and Bob and the other foot-soldiers had done the fighting. Yet Feversham had got the credit for all. Why? Because it made a good story, Bob supposed, and people could only make sense of complicated matters through stories. Likewise the war for Ireland, which had ceased to be a good story when the Kings had left the stage.

Thus Bob in a very bleak mood all through April. On the 9th of May, a flock of sails appeared in the Shannon estuary, and sword-practice came to a halt, and the pupils of Bob's fencing-academy gathered silent under the shade of the brooding-tree to watch a French convoy coming up the river towards Limerick. The ships were cheered by small crowds gathered in tiny raucous clumps on the Connaught side, and saluted by guns on the walls of Limerick. It was noted by all of the men around Bob that the cannon-salutes were returned in full measure (they had no lack of powder), but the cheers were not (these were supply-, not troop-ships).

Monsieur LaMotte took a spyglass from his saddle-bag, climbed halfway up the tree, and made observations. "I see the colors of a field-marshal; the big ship, there, third from the lead, she is carrying the new French commander . . ." then all the air went out of him in a long sigh, like bagpipes collapsing, and he said nothing for a minute or so, not because he had nothing to say but because he was the sort of fellow who did not like to utter as much as a word until he had made himself master of his emotions. "It is the butcher of Savoy," he said in French to another Huguenot who was standing under the tree.

"De Catinat?"

"No, the other."

"De Gex?"

"This is a field-marshal, not a priest."

"Ah." The other Huguenot ran to his horse and galloped away.

In English, La Motte explained: "I have recognized the coat of arms of the new French commander. His name is St. Ruth. A nobody. Our victory is assured."

The muttering of the men resumed, and there were sporadic outbreaks of laughter. LaMotte climbed down out of the tree wearing an expression as if he'd just seen his mother being keel-hauled under St. Ruth's flagship. He handed his spyglass to Bob, then went to his horse without a word and cantered away, stiff-backed.

Bob was glad to have the loan of the spyglass, for one of the smaller ships, farther back in the line, had familiar lines. His eyes unaided could not make out the colors flying from her mizzen-mast. With a bit of fiddling and focusing, and steadying the spyglass against the bole of the tree, he was able to see the coat of arms he had been looking for: for St. Ruth had brought a pair of lieutenant-generals with him, and one of them bore the title Earl of Upnor.

BOB HAD SAT AND WATCHED marvels during his idle spring: a butterfly forcing its way out of a cocoon, and an apple-blossom burgeoning from a sticky green pod. Those two unfoldings had much in common with each other, and with something that happened in Bob's soul during the next hours. The behavior of the Huguenot cavalrymen served as a model and source of inspiration. Not that Bob generally wanted such things, but his time in Ireland had left him pressed together and folded up inside a stiff dry husk that protected him but imprisoned him, too. The same was true of all the others. But the knowledge that St. Ruth was here had sent a dread-thrill running through the camp of the Huguenots and shocked them all alive. Bob had no idea who St. Ruth was or what he had done in Savoy, but it did not matter; the effect of it was that the Huguenots now suddenly perceived themselves as being in the thick of a story. It was not a King-story and might never be written down, but it was a good story to *them*.

Years ago Bob had gone deaf in one ear, and had put it down to standing close to guns. But then one day a barber had reached into that ear with a wee hook and wrenched out a bung of brown wax, hard as pine-wood, and just like that Bob could hear again—he could hear so well it almost hurt, and could sense things going on all round him with such definition that for the next day he had difficulty keeping his balance. On the 9th of May 1691, all of Bob's senses came alive thusly, and his lungs filled with air for the first time since he had waded across the Boyne with Jacobite musket-balls taking bites out of his hat.

They struck camp and withdrew from Limerick altogether during the next fortnight, and marched with the sun on their backs to Mullingar, in the center of the island, where all of King William's host was assembling. A few days after they arrived the trains of wagons began to come from Dublin in their clouds of dust and noise, bringing the great cannons and mortars that had been sent from the Tower of London.

On June 8th they marched west to Ballymore and easily took a little out-post there, and made prisoners of one of the best Irish regiments, which had been left exposed in the middle of nowhere for no reason.

On June 19th they reached Athlone, which bestrode the Shannon. It consisted of an English town on the Leinster side—which the Jacobites abandoned almost immediately—and an Irish city on the Connaught side—which they retreated into, and defended with unnerving ferocity for two weeks. Scouts were sent across the Shannon; most did not come back. The ones that did brought news that cascaded down the chain of command to Bob: General St. Ruth had brought his whole army to a camp west of the Irish town, just out of range of Ginkel's Dutch cannon.

The battle of Athlone was straightforward and bloody: Ginkel's artillerymen fired a cannonball a minute for ten days, and an avalanche of bombs and mortar-stones, across the river into the Irish town and completely destroyed it. Meanwhile his foot-soldiers tried again and again to force a crossing on the stone bridge joining the English to the Irish town. This was the only way of reaching the Connaught side of the Shannon, and everyone knew it. The Irish had destroyed one segment of the bridge. The gap would have to be closed with timbers. Under hellish covering fire of artillery, Ginkel's troops would go there at night and try to throw beams across the gap while Irish snipers hidden in the ruins of Athlone pierced them with musket-balls. Then Irish troops would show equal bravery in going down and setting the timbers afire, or casting them into the Shannon.

The Irish won the battle of the bridge, but lost that of Athlone when two thousand of Ginkel's troops forded the Shannon down-stream on June 30th and forced their way into the Irish town.

St. Ruth thereby lost Athlone, and all of his troops who were trapped inside of its walls. The rules of Continental siege warfare were in effect, meaning that towns could hope for easy treatment if they surrendered but that resistance was to be punished by massacre. Bob's chief worry, then, was that he would be given a direct order to go into Athlone and massacre someone. The only thing that would be worse would be if the victims turned out to be Mr. McCarthy's company of foot-soldiers from Baron Youghal's regiment. Mr. McCarthy was a Dublin candle-maker who had spent all of his money to raise and outfit a company, and made himself its captain. Along the way he had recruited Teague Partry, who had in turn recruited several other of Bob's out-laws. Jack Shaftoe's sons—Bob's nephews—had gotten swept up in Regimental life, much as Jack and Bob had done at the same age. For all Bob knew, the boys might be carrying muskets now. So it was not out of all possibility that Bob might be obliged to swing a spadroon into the necks of his nephews during the mopping-up of Athlone. It was the sort of dilemma that might make a fellow anxious. Fortunately Bob had (as was his habit) imag-ined and anticipated the worst, and made up his mind in advance what he should do if it came to pass: He would excuse himself, declare himself Irish (easily enough done, as 'twas only a state of mind anyway), make the sign of the cross over his red-coated breast, and go running off into Connaught with the Partrys. He even had a sort of excuse worked out: He'd declare that the hag who'd brained him with the bottle in Limerick was his long-lost great-aunt. This scheme had the added advantage of getting him closer to Upnor. After the Jacobites had lost the war, he'd sign up with an Irish mer-cenary regiment and go campaigning on the Continent. If he picked the right time and place to desert, he could then simply *walk* to wherever Abigail was.

This plan actually seemed more attractive to him the more he con-sidered it, and the more phantastickal refinements he added onto it.

By the time he crossed that half-wrecked bridge into what had been the Irish side of Athlone, he was almost looking forward to finding whatever was left of Mr. McCarthy's company, and surrendering to it.

What he did *not* want was to find them dead, or to see them being hunted down in the streets by the Danish horsemen, who had reverted to the ways of the Vikings. So his fondest hope and worst nightmare were separated by an infinitesimally slender distance.

But he found nothing in Athlone save dead or dying Irishmen buried in settling piles of rubble. Fortunately a good part of the civilian population of Athlone had already fled into Connaught. A small Irish garrison was trapped near the bridge and enthusiastically butchered by the Danish cavalry. However, the great bulk of St. Ruth's force never even saw fighting, and remained safe in its camp. Ginkel spent several days getting his army across the river, which meant that St. Ruth could stage a leisurely and orderly retreat of his whole army toward the interior of Connaught, or indeed all the way to the port of Galway if he chose.

So Bob found himself in the fabled land of Connaught. No, it couldn't be; this part was connected to Leinster and the rest of the damned island by that bridge, it was an excrescence of the bad, ruined Ireland into the good. And fortunately it was surrounded by a wall to prevent the contagions of the world from spreading. Irish Athlone was just a buboe, holding the plague pent up inside.

When they got the order to march out of its western gate, then they would enter the true Connaught that Teague Partry had sung of during his long raw watches on the Develin Tower.

"It is Sunday, the twelfth of July, *Anno Domini* sixteen hundred and ninety-one," said Captain Barnes helpfully, shaking Bob's shoulder. "The train has arrived; we expect a long march."

Very faint pink light gleamed in jackets of dew that had formed on the cold pale stones all around. Bob exerted all his will not to close his eyes and go back to sleep.

They were still in Athlone, sleeping in a half-wrecked wool warehouse that stood on the road uphill from the bridge. Wheels were grinding on the ashlars of that road, drawn by hundreds of patient hooves that beat a lulling tattoo on the stones.

Ginkel's army had marched out a day ago and left them behind to await a train of wagons from Dublin, and to make sure it got across the bridge safely. Today they would have to catch up with the army and, if that army was on the move, accomplish a second march as well.

When someone was trying to kill him and his men (which was not really all that often), Bob's chief professional obligation was to think about that. At all other times he thought about food. Treading carefully among sleeping men, he came to a place where he could look out through a bomb-hole and see orange flames fondling the bum of Black Betty, the company's prize kettle, out in the court. There would be a sort of gruel boiling in it, with shreds of mutton flashing to the top occasionally, and an inch of grease floating on it. In other weathers a cloud of steam would be roiling from Black Betty's mouth, but today she was surrounded and hemmed in by æons of fog proceeding out of the west, seemingly drawn by the feeble promise of the pink gloaming over Leinster. If any steam was coming out of Black Betty, it was like a fart in a whirlwind.

By the time Bob had groped his way to the coffee-pot and burnt his hands and lips on a tin cup of Mocha's finest, the pink light that had greeted him earlier had been snuffed out by the progress of this fog. When he went about nudging men awake, they were all certain it must be midnight, and not dawn as Bob earnestly claimed.

Connaught would not let go of her mysteries easily, then. By the time they fell in with the regiment, chasing the customary, hideous screams of sergeants through the gloom, a kind of profound blue-gray light had begun to emanate from the fog: light without warmth or even the colors that made men remember warmth. There was a lot of bumping into other companies in rubble-congested streets, and standing still for no discernible reason, and then at last a gate materialized around them and they understood that the regiment was forcing its way through a bottleneck. They marched out of Athlone and left its unburied dead to the flies—for only flies could reach the ones who lay in the cellars of the fallen-in buildings.

Immediately the road began to fork and fork again, offering passages to Roscommon, Tuam, Athleag, or Killimor. Bob gazed down every one of those tracks with frank longing. But young officers on horseback were posted at every turning to ensure that the regiment, and the wagon-train, did not stray in the fog.

They marched on the high road, the road west toward Galway. Everything about the conduct of the operation said to Bob that it would be a long trudge with no objective other than to put distance behind them, and no prospect of actual fighting. But late in the morning—or so he guessed from the color of the fog, which had taken on a brassy shimmer, like a counterfeit guinea—he heard musket-fire far off.

It could not be *his* regiment. It must be some other battalion of Ginkel's main army. So Ginkel had not marched on ahead of them at all. He had done a day's march and then stopped. And from the sound of those muskets it was clear *why:* St. Ruth had only retreated a few miles down the road from Athlone.

They joined in with another column, marched for a mile, and crossed a river at a place called Ballinasloe. Immediately the rope of men and beasts raveled and frayed into a wide mess, each strand pursuing a different course. This would only occur if they had butted up against the army of St. Ruth, and were spreading out to form a battle-front.

Lone cavaliers dashed from left to right and right to left, wearing the colors of Brandenburgish, Danish, Huguenot, or Dutch cavalry regiments; these were engaged in the supremely important tasks of finding the ends of the line. The great bodies of soldiers were still proceeding towards the front, occasionally crossing over each other's paths, but more and more often moving along parallel courses. The fog shone more brightly to their left, which suggested that they were going generally westwards. Bob's left knee was hurting rather more than his right one—not only were they moving down-slope, but the ground on the right, toward the Ballinasloe road, was higher.

They'd seen no sign of the Jacobite army other than a few Irish-men hanged by the necks from tree-limbs along the road, presum-ably for desertion. But as they worked their way down from the road they did come upon a dead horse from Patrick Sarsfield's Irish cav-alry regiment, which was still warm and steaming. It was in a field, or rather, an expanse of disturbed soil. Every patch of dirt in Ireland bore the marks of desperate soldiers who had pawed through it in search of potatoes that might've been overlooked by other, slightly less desperate fellows. This horse had broken its leg stepping into a hole where some lucky man had struck a jackpot. Its rider had put it down with a pistol-ball to the brain and limped away on a pair of French-style boots in good repair. Bob followed the boot-prints, and his men followed him, until a mounted Dutch officer—one of de Zwolle's aides—coalesced out of the fog, ordered them to abandon this pursuit, and signalled that they should form up into a line. And a good thing, too, as the ground had been getting soupier, and they were very nearly down in a bog by this point.

Now that all burdens had been thrown down and the commotion of the march had ceased, Bob found that he could hear for a great distance. In fact, he was convinced that they had mistakenly set up only a stone's throw from the enemy. But the sound came and went with the sluggish convolutions of the fog, telling him that it was only a trick played on his ears by the queerness of the air, and further evi-dence that Connaught was a realm of mischievous færies.

Setting aside eldritch deceptions, and listening patiently whilst smoking his way through three pipe-bowls of tobacco, and (above all) thanking that barber for having drawn the wax out of his ear, Bob collected the following:

That there was a bog before them, much broader than he had supposed at first, perhaps half a mile from this side to the other. That water stood, rather than ran, at its bottom. That it was occupied by the enemy, but not heavily; it was not a position to be held, but an obstacle to slow down the onslaught of the Protestant legions. Beyond it, however, the ground rose up again, in some places to heights that would command the whole battlefield. The great bulk of the Jacobites were there, working with picks and shovels in reasonably dry ground (the implements bit rather than splashed). When a breeze finally came up, it became possible to hear canvas flapping. They had not taken their tents down yet; they had no thought of retreating. To the north and the south—that is to say, on the wings—were the cavalry. By process of elimination, infantry was in the center.

The Irish foot did not have the equipment or the training to form itself up into pike-squares and so were defenseless against horse. Therefore St. Ruth would only put them where cavalry could not go. It followed that the bog must be a formidable barrier, for St. Ruth was trusting it to preserve his infantry from a frontal charge. The Butcher of Savoy, as the Huguenots called him, had, however, felt obliged to put his cavalry at the ends, to prevent the infantry from being flanked and destroyed; so there must be easier ways of getting across the bog in those places.

In this section of the line—which seemed to be towards Ginkel's right, or north flank—all was orderly and quiet. But at the left or southern flank, which might be as much as two miles away, they were having great difficulty forming up into line because of some skirmishes—most likely Sarsfield's enterprising and high-spirited cavalry. Sporadic cackles of fire came from that direction and occasionally swelled into abrupt throat-clearings, but never developed into a proper engagement.

As this was Sunday, the French and Irish regiments were taking turns at Mass; Bob could track the gradual progress of two or perhaps three different priests along the Jacobite line of battle, stopping every so often to deliver a warlike homily and celebrate a truncated version of the sacrament. He only knew *un peu de français* and a wee bit o' Gaelic, but after hearing several repetitions of these homilies, and the synchronized cheering of the congregants, he thought he had a clear enough notion of what was being said.

The breeze became dependable and the fog finally began to dissolve.

He strolled to the left and exchanged gossip with Greer, the sergeant of the fourteenth company. Then he strolled to the right and discovered an English cavalry regiment and chatted with one of its sergeants for a time. By now it was possible to understand where the Black Torrent Guards were situated. Ginkel's army, like St. Ruth's, had been arranged with infantry in the center and cavalry on the wings. Bob's regiment was farther to the right than any of the other foot, and his company farther right than any other company; from their location northwards to the road, it was nothing but horse all the way.

The fog had lifted to the point where he could see his own regimental colors, about a musket-shot away, slightly uphill of the line established by the soldiers. He walked toward them and arrived just in time to see a conference breaking up: Colonel de Zwolle had served brandy and given orders to all of his company commanders. Bob about-faced and fell into step beside Captain Barnes, who was returning to the company.

"*Ne pas faire de quartier,*" ' Bob said. "That's what the priests are saying across the bog."

Captain Barnes had a degree from Oxford. "After what happened in Athlone, it is to be expected."

"Is it the same for us, then? No quarter?"

"Sergeant, your aversion to killing Irishmen is the talk of the regiment. Do not embarrass me today by turning suddenly into a paragon of mercy."

Captain Barnes was the fifth son of a modestly important Bristol family, and had a quick mind. It had been expected of him that he would become a vicar. Instead he had discomposed his family by deciding to become an infantry officer. He was not yet twenty-five and still seemed more the student of divinity. He liked commanding troops in battle, and did a surprisingly good job of it, as long as they hewed to the tactics and maneuvers of conventional warfare, against similar opponents. Which might sound like damning with faint praise, but very few men could actually do this. He grew uncertain, and began to make bad decisions, when asked to do anything that was not explicitly covered by the rules of war. At such moments other rules must of necessity come into play, and the rules he was wont to fall back on were the sort that were taught in church. And he was bright enough to see that this was, in a war, ridiculous.

"You want a brute for a sergeant, so that he can go do the mopping-up while you wring your hands and disavow his unchivalrous deeds," Bob said. "For that type of sergeant you must look in a common regiment. But we were organized by Churchill—"

"The Earl of Marlborough, to you!"

"In truth, to me he is *John*. But whatever he is called, he has odd tastes in sergeants, and though *he* has been replaced by de Zwolle, *you* are stuck with *me*—unless you would care to promote another from the ranks."

"You'll do, Sergeant Shaftoe."

Finally the fog had lifted so that they could see as far as they pleased, though things more distant were wrapped in shimmering auras, bristling with iridescent needles. All was more or less as Bob had seen it with his ears. Across a bog they faced a hill whose near slope was exceeding well trenched, the trenches filled with Irish musketeers in gray coats. They would be armed with good new French muskets, not the trash that had served as firewood after the Battle of the Boyne. Far to the south the Jacobite line curved around the flank of the hill into some trees, and thus out of Bob's view. Directly in front lay what appeared to be the worst part of the bog, where three water-filled ruts twined together in the heart of a morass. The main Athlone-Galway road was no more than a few hundred paces off to the right. It sported first a bridge and then a long, strait causeway over the boggy ground.

A mass of English and Huguenot cavalry were deployed in a clump around the road. Bob could see several regimental standards at a glance, meaning that this was probably styled a division, thus probably commanded by a major-general. Most likely the Huguenot Henri de Massue, who, though he'd never see France again, still went by his French title, the marquis de Ruvigny. Ruvigny was one of three generals King William had sent out to Ireland in the spring to replace ones who had exasperated him with their slowness. Another was a Scotsman, Hugh MacKay, who was commanding the division of infantry—Bob's division, for the nonce—that was now looking out over the bog.

The bridge and the causeway could be reached by a short advance, which raised the question of why this cavalry division had not already taken it. The answer lay half a mile farther down the road, where an old castle rose up above the western end of the causeway. It was little more than a wreck: just four mossy stone walls, with mounds at the corners suggesting towers. But the tops of the walls were furry with musket-barrels, and the surrounding hamlet had been fortified with earth-works. Several roads then radiated westwards from the village. Various Jacobite regiments had positioned themselves short distances up those roads so that they could converge on any force that made it over the causeway and into the killing-zone around the castle.

Bob spent more time than was good for him searching out the standards of the Irish foot regiments and trying to identify Baron Youghal's colors. That would tell him approximately where Mr. McCarthy the candlemaker was situated with the Partrys' company. But he was unable to see matters clearly, as most of these regiments were dug in on the hill farther south and across the bog, two miles or more away, and their colors had not been particularly large or glorious to begin with.

"This is an excellent position," Bob said admiringly. "It could not be better—for the Irish."

Captain Barnes gave him a sharp look, but softened when he understood that Bob was merely stating facts, and according a sort of gentlemanly respect to the foe. "Today we will be dragoons, until we are told otherwise."

"Where are our horses, then?"

"We must imagine them."

"Imaginary horses are much slower than the other kind."

"We need never mount up. Dragoons are supposed to ride *into* battle, then *dismount* and fight as infantrymen," Barnes reminded him. "We *walked* here, that much is true. But that's in the past. Now it's as if we have all just climbed out of our saddles."

"That is why they have placed us here, hard up against the cavalry—we are to support them," Bob supposed, looking into Barnes's eyes. Barnes showed no sign of disagreement. Bob turned away from General MacKay's part of the field—the bog in the center— and toward General Ruvigny's—the road, the causeway, and the village. At first glance this latter seemed the harder assignment, but he felt unaccountably relieved that they would not have to harry thousands of Irishmen out of the maze of ditches that they had cut into the peat.

Bob continued, "We are meant to advance along the road, I take it." He then turned his attention to the castle, and tried to count the colors on its walls and in the surrounding village.

"It is a better assignment than to advance across that bog," Barnes observed.

"Anything would be better than that, Captain," Bob said. "When I am hit I want to fall with sun in my eyes. Not mud in my lungs."

BOB, NORMALLY AN IN-THE-THICK-OF-THINGS kind of soldier, now had the unfamiliar opportunity of sitting still and watching the battle unfold, just like a General. This came about because the cavalry to which they were attached was not ordered to do anything for the first few hours; no General in his right mind would send his regiments across that causeway in the face of those defenses. In fact, very early on most of Ruvigny's cavalry were detached and sent miles down the line toward the left wing, leaving only a regiment or so to guard the road. If the Black Torrent Guards had been real dragoons (with horses) they probably would have gone, too. As it was, they were stuck in the least active part of the battlefield.

But every other part of the line attacked. The only part Bob could see was the foot in the center, but from distant rumblings of thousands of hooves, and movements of reinforcing horse across the Irish rear, he could tell that a large cavalry engagement was under way at the opposite end.

MacKay's infantry spent the first few hours of the battle failing against their Irish counterparts. Though 'twere more just to say that Ginkel had failed by ordering them even to try. The Irish had cut successive lines with protected passages from one to the next. The walls of the ditches were graded to afford protection against an attack from the east while leaving their occupants naked to fire from the west. So as soon as MacKay's men fought their way across the sucking mud into *one* ditch, they would find that their foes had all vanished like wills-o'-the-wisp and reappeared in the *next* ditch uphill, whence they could fire musket-balls into the attackers at their pleasure. A small number of English actually managed to get through all of the ditches and hedgerows, but by the time they had done so, they were more a smattering of refugees than an army; and when they finally staggered out into open country along the base of the hill, they were confronted by an Irish battle-line that looked as if it had drawn itself up on a parade ground. The Irish charged with a roar that reached Bob's ears a few seconds after he saw them leap forward, and the surviving English fell back all the way to where they had started an hour before. By the time any semblance of order had been reëstablished among MacKay's battalions, the Irish had reoccupied the very same positions, in the forward-most ditch, as they'd been in when the fog had first lifted. The field looked the same as it had before, save that dead Englishmen were strewn all over it. Farther south it was the same except that the dead were Danish, Dutch, Hessians, and Huguenots.

While respecting Irishmen as individuals, Bob had always viewed their regiments primarily as a source of comic relief. He was fascinated to see them chasing Hessian storm-troopers across a bog. It was the first time in his knowledge that their ferocity and love of country had come into alignment with military competence. At the same time he was apprehensive, for the Partrys' sake, of what might happen next, because the cavalry fight at the far end sounded more ferocious than any he had ever heard. He could not believe that the French and Irish could withstand such an assault for long. But nothing happened; the Protestant cavalry never broke through. The battle was a stalemate.

Bob watched two more attacks across the bog. Both failed in the same way as the first; the Irish not only stopped them cold, but threw them back, and not only threw them back but overran some of their positions and spiked some of their field-pieces. Captain Barnes: " 'Tis worse even than a Pyrrhic victory; 'tis a Pyrrhic defeat."

General MacKay was as wet, cold, and furious as a cat in a rainbarrel. He had led the failed attacks personally. As the afternoon turned into evening he had worked his way north up the line. It was plain that the center could not be forced, and he had no real choice but to probe that part of the bog around the piles of the causeway. For the fourth attack, therefore, he got permission from Ginkel to lead the Black Torrent Guards—who had done nothing so far—on a thrust parallel to and just a bit south of the road.

This attack failed like the others. Bob and his men had learned from the mistakes of the fellows they had been watching, and so they took fewer casualties. But it failed nonetheless, partly because of the ditches, and partly because of the plunging musket-fire that came down from the parapets of the ruined castle when they advanced within range. It was demoralizing to see a large building such as Aughrim Castle vanish behind a cloud of gray smoke as hundreds of muskets were discharged at once.

But they all suspected that they might have succeeded with more men. Bob mentioned to Captain Barnes, who reported to de Zwolle, who told General MacKay, that before the battle he'd spied a pair of regimental standards in the bog just by the causeway, where it entered Aughrim village. During one of the earlier attacks he had watched those colors move far south to the center of the line, where the fighting had been fiercest. They had not returned since. So the village's defenses were not what they had once been.

MacKay rode the line, having a look at the Black Torrent Guards, and pronounced them not half so wet, muddy, and exhausted as the men who'd attacked in the center; which he looked on as proving that this was not such a very boggy part of the bog, and that cavalry might get across it. He was being trailed by a motley string of European and English cavaliers who, because they had not done any fighting yet, were spotless and jittery. At one point MacKay got into a dispute with them, which he ended by wheeling his horse and charging directly toward Aughrim Castle just to show that it could be done. His horse took a header over a wall and stopped hard in muck on the other side, and MacKay flew off and ended up wetter, dirtier, and angrier than he had been before. Most of the cavaliers were convinced it could be done, and the others were now too ashamed to speak their minds.

The Black Torrent Guards were ordered to advance as far and as fast toward the castle as they could, and then throw themselves down in the bog and shoot at any Irish heads that showed above the parapet. It was hoped that this would lessen the damage inflicted on Ruvigny's skeletal division of cavalry as they galloped across and alongside the causeway. For every other route along which Ginkel's army might advance had been blocked; Ruvigny's squadrons were the only fresh troops he had; and the only way to avoid total defeat was to mount a charge along that causeway.

The Black Torrent Guards were sent across the bog first, in full view of the castle, to draw off some fire, but the Irish seemed to recognize that tactic for what it was and saved their loads for the cavalry, which came thundering down the road a few moments later.

Only ragged firing sounded from Aughrim Castle as the first squadrons rode directly past it. They galloped into the village with almost no casualties and found that it had been left nearly undefended, as Bob had predicted.

Bob got up on one knee to fire his musket at a head silhouetted against the evening sky, and was hit in the chest by something that made a strange zooming noise. He dropped his weapon and fell flat on his back.

When he woke up a couple of his men had ripped his coat open to examine the wound, which was in a bad spot, near where his left collarbone joined his breastbone. And yet Bob was still alive, and not coughing up blood. Not feeling bad at all, really.

He was being looked after by one Hamilton, a big bloke, infamous for uncouth qualities. Hamilton had planted a knee on Bob's shoulder to pin him in a more convenient attitude, and was picking curiously at a hard object embedded in Bob's flesh. Bob found this extremely annoying and said so more than once. "Oh, fuck it!" Hamilton decreed, and dived into Bob's chest, planting his lips over the wound. After a quick suck and a bite he popped up again with something yellow in his teeth, and spat it out for examination.

" 'Tis a pretty brass button," he announced, "a bit dented by the ram-rod, but 'twill suffice to replace the ones we tore off your coat just now."

"Or we may fire it back to its owner," said one Roberts, who always did what Hamilton did, but not as well. He had a knee on Bob's *other* shoulder. "If *we* should run out of ammunition, I mean."

Not more than ten minutes had passed while Bob lay on his back on the ground, but when he got up again it was a new battle. All of Ruvigny's horse had now crossed over, and more was on the way, galloping up from the opposite wing where they'd been balked all afternoon. The gates of Aughrim Castle were open, and a lot of screaming and hasty praying could be heard within its walls as the unlucky garrison was put to the sword (*vide* Rules of Continental Siege Warfare). The squadrons not participating in this massacre had positioned themselves around the edge of the village and made ready to be attacked by the Irish and French battalions not far away, but such an attack never came; something had gone wrong in St. Ruth's chain of command, orders to counter-attack had not been issued or else were not getting through, and his generals were unwilling to do it on their own initiative.

Bob wrapped his coat around himself to cover the wound, which was bleeding, but not hissing or spurting. He strolled uphill a short distance and climbed up onto one of the earthen ramparts that the Irish had thrown up to defend Aughrim village.

He could see some Irish dragoons retreating off to his right. In the overall scheme this was amazingly stupid, and probably fatal, but they had no way of knowing.

"Sergeant!"

Bob looked down into the face of Captain Barnes, which was in the middle of a transition from intense anxiety to giddy relief; for the nonce it looked more quizzical than anything. "I was given to understand you had suffered a dire injury!"

"I was shot in the chest," Bob said guardedly. "One of those musketeers drilled me about here, from perhaps fifty yards." Bob glanced towards the corner of the castle from which the button had been fired. A French standard was being cut down by trophy-hunting cavaliers.

"Then you should be taking your rest! We have been ordered to garrison the castle," said Barnes.

"Has my bedchamber been made ready?"

"Alas, there are no chambers of any kind, only roofless cells," Barnes answered deadpan. "We could make you a bed from ammunition cases."

"I thought they had none."

"They have thousands of musket-balls in there," Barnes said.

"Then why did they not use them?"

"Because they are made for English muskets—ever so slightly larger than the barrels of their French muskets."

Hamilton had ambled to within earshot of this conversation, and responded, "Haw! I always knew we Englishmen had bigger balls than the French!" Indeed, all of the private soldiers found it hilarious. But sergeants and captains—who were actually responsible for getting musket-balls to the troops—could only wince at such a story, even when it had befallen the enemy.

Bob looked off to the south and saw a series of English and Huguenot cavalry squadrons slipping like a knife-blade into a gap between the Irish infantry, and the stunned cavalry to its rear. They were swinging round behind the Irish foot, getting into position to charge them, panic them, and mow them down like hay.

"Captain Barnes," Bob said, "you have said it yourself. I have been shot in the chest and am plainly a casualty of war, *hors de combat,* and for now my duties must be assumed by another sergeant. . . . Fortunately your company's assignment is trivial. There will be no counter-attack made against yonder castle this afternoon." Bob turned his back on Barnes and strode down the slope of the rampart, muttering, "Or this month, this year, this century."

ONCE THE DANES and the Huguenots over-ran the field like flocks of starlings scouring the earth for worms, Bob's red Guards uniform would not help him; this side of the bog, any man on foot was under a death sentence. Because the French/Irish phant'sied themselves the army of the true King (James II), many of their regiments wore the same red uniforms, and the only way to tell them apart was by looking for small badges or devices thrust into their hats: sprigs of green for King William's forces, scraps of white paper for James Stuart's. These were difficult to see even in good light. Bob's hat had been lost in the bog anyway.

Fortunately the battle had long ago got to that stage where riderless horses were wandering about, instinctively forming up into little herds, looking for quiet places to graze. They were being pursued by men under orders to round them up. Bob ventured into a sort of no-man's-land that had opened up between the village and some Irish battalions retreating from it, and pretended that he had been given such orders. For the available horses, he was striving against two men who were younger and quicker than he was; but being older and wiser and (today) luckier, he had the satisfaction of being able to rest, crouching alongside a fragment of stone wall, while they chased a saddled horse directly towards him. He vaulted up onto the wall, grabbed the mount's dragging reins, and swung a leg over its saddle before it even knew he was about. He inferred that it had been ridden by a member of Ruvigny's cavalry who'd fallen or been shot out of the saddle, but that it had followed its squadron across the causeway just to be sociable. At any case it was a good horse and fresh. Bob pulled its nose round southward and whacked it lightly with the flat of his spadroon.

He galloped into the heart of the battle while it still deserved that name, before it turned into a rout and massacre. Ruvigny's cavalry had by now broken through the Irish flank altogether and were charging south, traversing the hill. To their left and downhill lay the entrenchments crowded with Irish foot-soldiers in their gray coats. To their right and uphill were the white tents of the Jacobite encampment. In front of them was nothing but a flimsy barrier of cavalry: not above three squadrons of what looked like an English Catholic regiment.

Bob had begun by galloping in the wake of this charge, but soon caught up and found himself in the middle of it—close enough that he could see the faces of those English Papists, Persons of Quality all, and watch them think as the attack bore down on them. Some seemed ready to die for their faith and rode forward with a certain look of calm ferocity that Bob admired very much. Some stood their ground—not, Bob thought, out of courage but out of terror, as rabbits freeze when the hawk flies overhead. Some wheeled and ran. But a contingent of three riders, who had been situated toward the rear, turned away and rode south in a way that looked purposeful to Bob.

Bob knew what they were doing: first, preserving their regimental standard (one of the three riders was the standard-bearer). This would enable them to erect the colors on a high place later, so that the scattered squadrons and stragglers could converge on it and re-form into an effective battalion. Without that scrap of cloth they could never amount to anything but lost Vagabonds. Second, they were going to the other wing where Sarsfield was commanding the bulk of the Jacobite cavalry, and apparently doing a very good job of it; in a few minutes they would come back at the head of several regiments.

Bob out-stripped Ruvigny's cavalry in an instant when they galloped into the Catholic squadrons and stopped to duel it out with pistols and sabers. French Protestants fighting for the King of England crossed blades with English Catholics fighting for the King of France. Bob, having no personal interest in their quarrel, rode

through them all like a cannonball through a bank of smoke and discovered himself in open country pursuing the three riders.

The standard-bearer was moving slowest, and gradually falling
behind. Bob almost had him when the fellow chanced to look back;
then he let out a yell and spurred his horse forward. The two officers
in front, perhaps eight lengths ahead of him, looked back to see
their standard-bearer in trouble; he could not defend himself without dropping the colors. As this happened Bob got a direct view of
their faces and realized for the first time that one of the two was
Upnor.

After a brief exchange of words, Upnor drew back hard on one
rein to wheel his mount around, while the other officer shot ahead
to get the message out to Sarsfield. Bob—who had a lot to keep track
of—heard a loud crack and assumed a pistol had gone off. The
standard-bearer, four lengths ahead of Bob, faltered. Bob looked
again for Upnor, but he had vanished! Then in the corner of his eye
he saw the standard-bearer coming up fast—having brought his
mount nearly to a stand-still while Bob was still at a gallop. Bob had
no time to do anything but stick his spadroon out. The blade struck
something hard and the weapon was wrenched out of his grasp, and
he was nearly thrown back onto the horse's croup. What saved him
was that this had all occurred just short of a declivity in the hillside, a
little water-course running straight down into the bog, therefore
straight across their path. Both Bob's horse and that of the standard-
bearer had seen it coming, and in the absence of orders to the contrary, slowed down.

Bob recovered his equilibrium just shy of this gulley and shook
his hand frantically in the air a few times. It felt as if it had been
stung by a bee. Lacking another blade, he drew out his pistol, which
he had put out of his thoughts until this moment because it was useless while galloping. But now he was standing still, as was the
standard-bearer, no more than four yards away from him.

The standard was hung from one end of a full-length pike so that
it would rise to thrice the height of a man and be visible above a
teeming battlefield. While galloping, the bearer had held it nearly
horizontal, like a jousting-lance, in his left hand, while using his
right to hold the reins. Bob had overtaken him on the left and he
had reflexively raised up the pike-staff to parry Bob's blow; Bob's
spadroon had cut into it at an angle about a third of the way from
the top and come to a stop, wedged into the wood.

The standard-bearer now raised the pole to vertical and planted
it, leaving Bob's spadroon high in the air and out of reach. Hug-

ging the pike against himself and his horse's ribs to steady himself, he drew out a pistol of his own. He was a beautiful blond English boy of about eighteen and Bob shot him in the head. He was wearing a steel cuirass to protect his torso and so it was the head or nothing.

A light misty rain had commenced and the late afternoon sun had gone out like a snuffed candle, leaving gray twilight. Bob looked down the gulley, drawn by an anguished noise, and saw Upnor's horse thrashing around with a broken leg. Then he saw Upnor clambering up out of the gulley intact. The crack he had heard before must have been Upnor's horse breaking its leg when it tried to stop and wheel around in the wrong place.

Bob had discharged his only pistol and there was no time to reload. The standard-bearer had squeezed his trigger involuntarily and fired *his* pistol into the air. Bob dismounted, staggered on cramped legs over to the standard, and threw it down. He glanced over at Upnor, who had got himself up above his horse on the brink of the watercourse and pulled out a pair of pistols, one in each hand. He aimed one at his horse and pulled the trigger; Bob saw the white sparks from the flint, but it did not fire—the pan had gotten wet.

Upnor now gave Bob a sort of appraising look. Bob planted his foot on the pike at the place where his spadroon was lodged in it, and pulled up on the end until it snapped; then he came up with the weapon in his hand. The Earl of Upnor took one look at it and then, with no hesitation, aimed his other pistol down into the ditch and put his charger out of its misery. He dropped both of his pistols, turned to face Bob, and drew out his rapier. For being something of a traditionalist in these matters, he had not yet adopted the more fashionable small-sword.

"Sergeant Shaftoe," he said, "since we last met, your brother has achieved even greater infamy than he had *then*. Now the Battle of Aughrim has been lost. I am not likely to see the sun rise again. But I can at least thank Providence that she has placed you in my power, that I may salvage something of the day by sending the brother of *L'Emmerdeur* to Hell."

"I phant'sied 'twas *you* who were in *my* power," Bob muttered.

Upnor cast off his cloak to reveal a shining steel cuirass underneath, with a vest of light mail under that.

"Not at all chivalrous," Bob observed.

"On the contrary, nothing is more characteristic of the chivalric classes than to put on armor and go round ridding the country of rebellious Vagabonds—as your own cavalry is demonstrating!"

With a wry tilt of the head, Upnor pointed toward the lower slopes of the hill where King William's cavalry was hunting Irishmen, frantic to kill as many as they could before they lost the daylight altogether. The Earl was a sophisticated man who enjoyed this irony, and wanted Bob to share it with him.

"Enough talking," Bob said, raising his guard to his face. "I did not come here to make friends with you." And he snapped the blade down and away, completing the salute. Upnor took half a step forward, raising the rapier to a guard position, then made a little show of remembering his manners and acted out the faintest memory of a salute. He was so dexterous with a sword that he could convey certain qualities, such as sarcasm, simply through nuances in his movements. Bob now stepped towards Upnor, hoping to back him up against the brink of the gulley; this also situated Bob on slightly higher ground.

"It's about the girl, isn't it? Abigail, my pretty slave," Upnor exclaimed. "I had forgotten."

"No, you hadn't."

"Tell me, do you believe that killing me will help you repossess her?"

"Not really. She'll pass to your heirs and assigns, and I will kill *them.*"

Upnor did not like this very well. "It is revenge, then," he concluded. He spun on the ball of one foot, ran down the bank for several yards to build up speed, then leapt across to the opposite brink. "In that case you are obligated to pursue me—so *I* am entitled to choose the ground. Come over here, Sergeant!"

Bob backed up for a few paces to get a running start, but by the time he was ready to make his leap, Upnor had moved back up to stand directly across from him, rapier aimed out into the space above the stream, positioned to impale Bob in mid-jump. "You hesitate a second time! You could have cut me down before I jumped across," Upnor said reproachfully.

Bob did not see fit to dignify this with a reply. He sidestepped up the bank; Upnor tracked him until he stopped. Then the Earl turned his head sideways and cupped his hand to his ear like a bad actor. "Hark! Patrick Sarsfield's cavalry is approaching, I do believe!"

"Those sound like Danish hooves to me."

Upnor made a sound like *heh-heh,* a completely unconvincing simulation of a laugh.

"Why are you playing message-boy, my lord? Why is not St. Ruth doing his job?"

"Because his head was carried off by a cannonball," Upnor responded. He brought the back of his hand to his mouth, pretending to cover a yawn. "It is a dull sword-fight so far," he complained.

"Let me across and it will become exciting soon enough."

"No, it is that you lack passion! A Frenchman would have leaped over by now. Perhaps it would help if I told you that I have fucked your sweet Abigail."

"I assumed as much," Bob said levelly.

"And you . . . *haven't?*"

"It is none of your business."

"It is all of my business, as she is my property, and I broke her maidenhead with *this* rapier, just as I am about to break *yours* with this one! So do not be coy, Sergeant, I know you have not enjoyed Abigail. Perhaps you shall, one day. But be sure to bring some sheepgut. I am afraid that I, or one of my friends, have given her a nasty social disease."

Bob jumped over the ditch at this time. Upnor backed away and let him land safely, but then closed in on him quickly, twitching the rapier with his right hand and now drawing a dagger with his left.

"Don't look at the poniard, silly man," Upnor chided him. "You must fix your gaze upon your opponent's eyes—just as Abigail Frome stares into mine when I am pleasuring her."

Bob, reckoning that this was enough, wrapped his right arm across his body, drawing the blade back in position to let go a haymaker. Part of the plan was to convince Upnor that his predictable taunts had actually made Bob angry. So Bob let out a bellow as he launched himself toward Upnor while letting go a mighty backhanded swing.

This was something he had practiced for a whole month with Monsieur LaMotte. Upnor's light blade could never stand up to a scything attack by the heavier spadroon, and so he had little choice but to drop his blade and step back to let it whoosh by. But Bob's forward rush would bring him into dagger range. So Upnor drew his right foot (which had been foremost) back, while pivoting on his left, turning sideways to let Bob charge past him. At the same time he raised his left hand so that he could plunge the dagger into Bob's ribs as he went by.

All of which went according to plan except for the last bit. For instead of rushing by standing up, Bob had planted his feet and dived forwards, so that his trunk was too low to receive Upnor's dagger. The back-handed cut had flung his body into a twisting movement from his left to his right, and so as he hurtled past he was spinning to face his opponent's legs. Bob's left arm and shoulder went through first, extended to take his impact on the ground. Then his head, and the right arm and spadroon trailing along his body. As soon as his left elbow struck the peat he curled that arm around and caught Upnor's right leg, trapping it against his body.

Upnor needed that leg to take his weight as he moved backwards, and thus had no choice but to fall down, even as Bob was getting his own knees under him. Upnor knew that to fall on his stomach was death, so he spun and landed on his arse and rolled up onto his back, his legs going straight up in the air. If this were a Parisian *Salle d'Armes* he might have turned it into a backwards somersault and come up fighting, but this was nearly impossible in a stiff cuirass. So Upnor's legs and arse reached apogee and then came down again. He was going to come up forwards. He planted his right elbow to push off against the ground but kept his guard up with the left, keeping that dagger pointed in the air. Bob had now got up on one knee and managed to take a swing at it. He fully intended to take Upnor's hand off at the wrist, but either his aim was bad or Upnor reacted with exceptional speed, because instead the blow struck the dagger's handle just behind the guard, right where Upnor's thumb and index finger gripped it, and ripped it loose from Upnor's hand. It whirred off and vanished in gloom and mist.

Upnor did a sideways roll away from Bob and came up angry. "You are a cold, cold, cold-blooded knave!" he exclaimed. "I think you do not care about Abigail at all!"

"I care enough to win this."

"You have been practicing against someone who knows the rapier," Upnor said. "Tell me, did he show you this?"

Bob liked to sit in a meadow and throw bits of bread to the birds. He had done this once with a flock of some hundred pigeons who had, once they'd gotten the general idea, surrounded him and waited patiently for him to throw out each scrap. But presently a sparrow had come along and begun to collect evey last crumb that Bob tossed, even though it had been one against a hundred. Even if Bob lured the sparrow to one side, then threw the morsel to the other, the little bird would come across like a flash of light from a signal-mirror and wend its way among the stumbling pigeons and pluck the bread right out from under their open beaks, which would snap together on thin air.

Bob now learned that he was a pigeon and Upnor a sparrow. One moment he was certain that his spadroon was about to take Upnor's leg off at the knee, and the next, the Earl was somewhere else, and the point of the rapier was headed for Bob's heart. In desperation he pawed at it with his left hand and diverted it so that it got him just under the ribs on the right side and passed out his back. As Bob fell back, his flailing left hand struck the guard of the rapier, a swirl of silvery bars, and his fingers closed around it. This would prevent Upnor from drawing it out and stabbing Bob again and again as he lay on the ground. Bob landed flat on his back, preceded by that part of the rapier that had gone all the way through him, and found himself pinned, nailed like Jesus. Upnor was pulled forward and ended up staring down into Bob's face from not far away.

"Lung?" Upnor guessed.

"Liver," Bob said, "or else I could never do this." He inhaled and then spat at Upnor's face, but it came out as a feckless spray.

" 'Twill be a slow-festering wound then," Upnor said. "I will gladly supply you with a quicker death if you will be so good as to let go my weapon." He glanced up for a moment, distracted by the sound of hurtling cavalry. "Sarsfield," he pronounced. "Let us finish, I must go to them."

Bob turned his head sideways, just to get Upnor's visage out of his sight. He saw a queer thing silhouetted against the deepening gray sky above the hill: a fellow in a gray coat perched on a pole above a ditch, not far away. No, he was not perched, but swinging across it, a matted ponytail trailing behind him like a profusion of battle-streamers from a regimental flag. It was an Irish infantryman, pole-vaulting across the ditch. Coming to the aid of Upnor, his English overlord. He would probably have a dirk or something to finish Bob off with.

"When you go to the next world," Upnor said, "tell the angels and demons that we know everything about your infamous cabal, and that we will have the gold of Solomon!"

"What the bloody hell are you talking about!?" Bob exclaimed. But before answering, Upnor peeled Bob's hand off the guard, pinky first. He planted his foot in Bob's stomach and stood up, yanking the blade out.

"You know perfectly well," he said indignantly, "Now go and do as I have instructed you!" He aimed a death-blow at Bob's heart. Bob put his hands up to slap it aside. Then a large object hurtled across the sky and smashed into the rapier's guard, crumpling the bars and sending it spinning away.

Upnor staggered back, gripping a damaged hand. Bob looked up to see a bulky figure in a ragged muddy gray coat, gripping eight feet or so of pike-staff: the same bit that Bob had broken off the cavalry standard.

Bob levered himself up on his elbow and rose to a seated position to find the cool, level gaze of Teague Partry directed his way. Teague had a head like a cube of limestone, and brown hair pulled back tight against his skull, though many strands had come loose during the day's fighting and been plastered back with mud. His blue-gray eyes were set close together, redoubling the intensity of his glare.

"What d'you think y'are, a *character* in a friggin' *novel*, Bob? Can you not perceive that the gentleman is wearin' *armor*, and knows more concernin' swordsmanship than you ever will?"

"I perceive it well enough now, Teague."

Upnor had, during Teague's scolding of Bob, gone over and retrieved his rapier. He held it now in his left hand, advancing crabwise toward Teague.

"Look out, Teague, he's as dangerous with his left as he is with his right—"

"Bob! You make too much and too little of him at the same time. As a 'fencer he's a caution, 'tis plain enough to see, but in the larger scheme, Bob, what is he but a friggin' tosser wavin' a poker around in the dark." By this time Upnor had advanced to within about eight feet and so Teague gave his stave a toss upward, gripped it with both hands at the end, and with a grunt, swung it round in a long arc parallel to the ground, catching Upnor in the side and flattening him. Upnor made a grab at the end of the staff, which had ended up hovering over his face, but his movements were cramped by his steel cuirass, which now sported a huge dent jabbing deep into his side. Teague withdrew the stave, shifted his grip so that he was holding it in the middle, raised it up above his head, and began to execute a series of brisk stabbing motions, with the occasional mighty swing. These were accompanied by metallic bashing sounds and screams from Upnor's end of the stick.

Between these efforts he sent the following, loosely connected string of comments and observations Bob's way:

"You have responsibilities now, Bob. You must lose this naïve understanding of violence! You are *embarrassin'* me in front of the lads! You can't play by their rules or they'll win unfailingly! You don't engage in courtly play-fightin' with one such as this. You get a great friggin' tree-branch and keep hittin' him with it until he dies. Like *that*. D'you see, boys?"

"Aye, Uncle Teague," came back two voices in unison.

Bob looked to the other side of the ditch and saw a pair of blond lads there, each holding the reins of a horse. One of them—it looked like Jimmy—had the horse Bob had rode in on, and the other—by process of elimination, Danny—had the standard-bearer's.

"There," Teague said. "Now get you over the ditch and be gone with the lads."

"I've been run through the liver."

"All the more reason to stop your lollygaggin'. You'll bleed to death shortly or heal up in a few weeks—the liver has a miraculous power of regeneration, while the body lives. Take it from an Irishman."

Bob slumped forward on his hands, then got his knees under him. He could hear blood dripping onto the ground. But it was only dripping, not coming in a continuous stream, or (worse) a series of spurts. If he had seen a private soldier with such a wound, he'd have guessed that the fellow would live, once the wound was packed with something to stop the bleeding. Upnor had been right; if Bob died of this, it would be because it festered in the days to come.

"I'm not askin' you to *walk*. You may ride one horse and the boys may share the other."

"And you, Teague?"

"Oh, it's into the ditch with me, Bob, into the bog. I'll collect a musket from one of the Englishmen I killed today, and go a-rappareein'." Teague's eyes now turned into running pools, and he tilted his head back and sniffled. "Get you gone, none of us has a moment to waste."

"I'll raise a monument in London," Bob promised, and got up slowly. He did not pass out.

"To me? They wouldn't have it!"

"To Upnor," Bob said, staggering past the Earl's smashed corpse, and kicking the rapier aside into the watercourse. "A fine statue of him, looking just as he does now, and an inscription: 'In Memoriam, Louis Anglesey, Earl of Upnor, finest swordsman in England, beaten to death with a stick by an Irishman.'"

Teague considered it for a moment, then nodded. "In Connaught," he added.

"In Connaught," Bob agreed, then eyed the ditch. It looked as wide as the Shannon. But the boys were waiting on the other side: Jack's boys, and now Bob's. For under the circumstances they were likely the only children Bob would ever have. Teague gave him a mighty shove in the arse as he flew back over the water. By the time Bob got up from a rough, agonizing tumble on the far side and turned to thank him, Teague Partry was gone.

A Hay-rick, St.-Malo, France
9 APRIL 1692

The mind is its own place, and in it self
Can make a Heav'n of Hell, a Hell of Heav'n.
— MILTON,
Paradise Lost

"THIS MUST BE how syphilis spreads: blokes like me, hopping from place to place."

"Why, Bob! I don't believe anyone's ever said anything quite so romantick to me."

"I can't guess what you were expecting when you roger an old sergeant in hay."

"Come, lace me back up."

"Would you hold your hair up out of the way? There, that's better . . ."

" . . ."

" . . . tedious work, ain't it?"

"Oh, stop complaining."

"I've no complaints. But we could have left this bit on, you know."

"Yes, and the stockings as well, and we could have done it standing up, and you with your boots and breeches on. But for me to *enjoy* it, Bob, I require a sense of abandon, of freedom, that only comes with removal of clothes."

"This tight enough?"

"It is fine . . . for the same reason, Bob, I could do without your idle ruminations on syphilis, and how it spreads."

"*I* don't have it, mind you. Haven't rogered anyone in years."

"Nor do I. And neither have I."

"What d'you mean, you told me you've a baby boy, six months old—"

"*Last* time we met. Now, *seven* months."

"Be that as it may, how can you say you haven't rogered anyone in years?"

"Sex with my husband I leave out of the reckoning altogether."

"Strikes me as a large omission."

"It would not, if you had ever had sex with Étienne de Lavardac, duc d'Arcachon."

"Can't say as I have, Madame."

"Unless you did, and forgot about it. At any rate—he has been doing it to me again lately."

"*Lately* . . . ah. You are saying that there was a cessation, round about the time of the birth of number two, and now he is trying for three."

"In *his* mind they are One and Two respectively. For the first, being a bastard, is a zero; which means a nullity, something that does not exist."

"That—the bastard I mean—is the one you had round about the time I shipped out to Dundalk, and you got marooned in Dunkerque?"

"Yes. Why?"

"Just refreshing my memory, my lady, no need to be getting all stiff in the spine—cor! It's gone loose, I shall have to re-lace from the beginning."

"It is not necessary. Just get to work buttoning up the bodice."

"Got ripped a bit, I'm afraid."

"I'll have it mended. Come, I am apprehensive that someone will happen along and discover us."

"Ah, but not to worry—I'm naked!"

"How is it better to be naked?"

"As long as I keep my mouth shut, I'll be indistinguishable from one of your French nobility. They'll run away in terror."

"Especially when they see your scars. Very impressive."

"You would never think so, if you had any notion of the pain that comes with these scars, the weakness, the helplessness—draining pus for months—not knowing from one moment to the next whether you shall live or die—"

"You forget that I have given birth twice."

"Touché. Ah, but now you've brought me back round to my topic."

"What is your topic?"

"You never talk about the bastard."

"Perhaps, from that, you should collect that I do not wish to speak of him."

"I was merely asking as a routine courtesy, as is common among parents."

"How are Jack's boys?"

"Jimmy and Danny are Regimental boys like their father and nuncle. If they're doing as they ought to—which is unlikely—they are, at this moment, peeling potatoes at our camp outside of Cherbourg."

"Do they have any inkling that you are acting as a spy for Marlborough?"

"Why, what an impolite question, Madame la duchesse! I am in no way certain that I *am* a spy. Haven't made up my mind yet. Haven't sent any information his way."

"Well, when you decide to do so, you may send it through me."

"*If* I decide to do so."

"You will. An invasion of England is planned, is it not?"

"When French and Irish regiments march up to the tip of the Cotentin Peninsula and form great camps in the spring-time, it does make one tend to think 'long those lines, don't it?"

"In the end you'll not suffer England to be invaded. You'll inform Marlborough."

"Marlborough's in disgrace. He and his meddlesome wife got on the wrong side of William and Mary. He had to sell his offices, his commissions. He is nothing now."

"Yes, it is the talk of every *salon* in Versailles. But if England is invaded, he will be un-disgraced very rapidly, and put at the head of some regiments. And you will rally to him."

"As you seem so certain of these things, I deem all your questions answered, madame—so I turn them round. Does the Duke of Arcachon have any inkling that *you* are a spy?"

"Your supposition is mistaken. I spied for England *once*. Now I do it for myself."

"Ah. So, if we are to cross the Channel, you should like to know of it for your own purposes."

"You say this—'for your own purposes'—as if I am the only one in the world who *had* purposes."

"Very well, very well . . . damned lot of buttons, ain't it?"

"You did not seem to mind so much when you were undoing them ten minutes ago."

"*Twenty* minutes, by your leave, madame, do allow me *some* pride. Ten minutes! Am I really so perfunctory?"

"Perhaps *I* am."

"Hmm, now, that is an unusual turning of the tables . . . it is supposed to be *he* who is perfunctory and selfish, and *she* who wants to stretch it out."

"Ah, but I *did* stretch it out, Sergeant, when I was inspecting it for signs of the French Pox. And a long stretch it was."

"You try to change the subject, and to distract me with flattery—but this methodical inspection of my yard is further proof of the businesslike nature of the transaction just concluded, is it not?"

"Very well . . . I hope that Number Three, as you count them, or Two, as Étienne does, will be half-Shaftoe rather than half-Lavardac, and, in consequence, altogether fitter, handsomer, and cleverer than Number Two/One, bless his poor little heart."

"I . . . I . . . I am shocked!"

"*Why* so shocked, you who've been in battles and seen, and done, the worst that men can do?"

"P'raps that is not so terrible, set against the worst that *women* can do."

"You protest too much. You are not serious. Though 'tis true there are terrible women in the world, I am not one of them."

"Why, to *use* a man in such a way . . . am I to have no knowledge of my own offspring!?"

"Why did you not ask such penetrating questions *prior* to fucking me in a haystack, Sergeant Shaftoe? Were you not aware, until now, that fucking leads to babies?"

"Very well, very well . . . *that* is not why I am shocked."

"*Why* then, Bob?"

"Of course, I know you don't really fancy me. So, 'tis not that I have been let down on that score."

"Just as *I* know *you* do not really fancy *me*."

"Of course not. Though you are fetching, a bit."

"Just as are you in your own mottled way, Bob."

"But I always assumed that you had me simply because you couldn't have Jack."

"Just as you have me because you can't have Abigail?"

"Just so, madame. But it did never enter my head that it was, at root, a baby-making proposition . . . what is wrong with Number Two/One?"

"Lucien is, to use an English expression, a funny-looking kid. 'Tis common among Lavardacs. Moreover, he is listless and slow to thrive."

"What of Number One/Null?"

"The most beautiful child who ever lived. Bright, happy, vigorous, altogether radiant."

"What's his name?"

"He was *baptized* Jean-Jacques."

"I can guess where the Jacques is from."

"Yes, and the Jean is from Jean Bart."

"You named your firstborn after a pirate and a Vagabond?"

"Don't be so haughty. One of them is your brother, after all."

"But why this careful phrasing: 'He was *baptized* Jean-Jacques'?"

"He answers to Johann."

"How's that again?"

"Johann. Johann von Hacklheber."

"Peculiar name that, for the bastard of a French duchess."

"He has been . . . *visiting* in Leipzig for a few days short of eighteen months. When he went there, he was not quite a year and a half old. I have got reports of him from friends who dwell in that part of the world, and they inform me that he is called by the name Johann von Hacklheber there."

"Now, anything with a 'von' in it is a noble name—like 'de' here, am I right?"

"Oh yes. He dwells in the household of a German baron."

"I know nothing of the ways of Continental nobility, but it strikes me as an unusual sort of arrangement."

"You have no idea."

"You may not know it, Madame, but you have got a sort of burning glow about the face and eyes now, a bit like during sex, but different."

"It is another form of desire, that's all."

"You want the boy back. You are not happy with the arrangement . . . oh, Jesus!"

"Go ahead and say it."

"He was *taken from you*!?"

"Yes."

"Jesus. *Why!?*"

"Never mind. My purpose is to get to him who took my boy, and . . ."

"Get your boy back, I assume?"

" . . ."

"Or, to judge from the look on your face, perhaps I should not make assumptions."

"Let me tell you what is truly evil about what was done to me eighteen months ago."

"I am listening."

"You are probably phant'sying parallels, similitudes, between what was done to your Abigail and what was done to my Jean-Jacques. But put such thoughts out of your mind. Abigail is a slave, held against her will, misused. A prisoner. This is no longer true of my Jean-Jacques. He is better off as Johann in Leipzig than he was as Jean-Jacques in Versailles. The captors of Abigail are imbeciles—guilty of a failure of imagination. By keeping her in a miserable estate, they make *you* miserable, 'tis true—but your path is clear: It is the path so familiar from myths and legends, the path of righteous fury, revenge, retribution, rescue. Lothar von Hacklheber has done something infinitely more cruel. He has made my boy *happy*. If I were able, somehow, to go to Leipzig and steal him back, the child would be terrified and miserable. And perhaps justly so, for when I got back I should have no choice but to deposit him in some Church orphanage outside of Versailles to be raised by nuns and made over into a Jesuit priest."

"Hoosh. I am glad for my own sake, madame, that I was not anywhere near you at the moment when you first came to understand this . . ."

"\. . ."

"Why are you staring at me thus? It makes me think I had better put my clothes back on—perhaps arm myself as well."

"\. . ."

"Are you only just understanding it *now!*?"

"If an idea is terrible enough, the mind is unwilling to swallow it in one go, but regurgitates and chews it like cud many times before it goes down for good. This is one that I have been chewing on for more than a year. It took me several weeks, after Jean-Jacques was abducted, for me to establish his whereabouts. By the time I could formulate even a hasty and ill-conceived plan to go fetch him back, I was pregnant with Lucien. It is only now that Lucien has been born, and I have recovered from it, that I can consider taking any steps in the matter of Jean-Jacques. And now it is too late. There. Done. I have swallowed it."

"All right. I could see this coming. Put your head there on my breastbone, madame, I'll hold you in my arms, so you don't collapse, or come undone. Sob all you want, I have you, no one's looking, we have time."

"\. . ."

"\. . ."

"\. . ."

"Now that you mention it, my lady, to have the love of my life enslaved and raped by a syphilitic lord does seem quite mild by comparison."

"I cannot tell if you are being sarcastic."

"Neither can I, madame, I honestly cannot. But tell me this: If you cannot get your boy back without destroying his welfare, then what *do* you intend?"

"In pondering this very question I have hesitated, and in hesitating I have only made matters worse. Soon I shall act."

"And what is the end you have fixed on?"

"I mean to end up, in some sense, with my boot on the neck of Lothar von Hacklheber, and him looking up helpless into my eyes."

"Well. Well! Let me just say that the last bloke who had *me* in such a fix was the Earl of Upnor, and—"

"My powers of organization exceed those of the late Upnor by a significant margin, and so I intend to arrange matters so that I will not end up being beaten to death with a stick by an Irishman."

"Ah. *That* is good news."

"Tell me everything about what is being prepared around Cherbourg, Sergeant Shaftoe, whether you intend for it to be relayed to Marlborough, or not."

"Very well. But how will this intelligence be of any help to you in your machinations against—oh, never mind. You're glowering at me."

"You speak so knowingly of my machinations, as if I were some ridiculous figure in an Italian opera, who does naught but machinate; yet if you could follow me about, you would observe a tired mother who follows her husband from Versailles to St.-Malo, and suckles her infant, and occasionally throws a dinner party, and perhaps once or twice a year fucks a cryptologist in a carriage, or a sergeant in a haystack."

"*How* will this lead to your boot on Lothar's throat again? Never mind, never mind. I'm certain I'd never understand it anyway."

"You are in good company. If I do it right, not even Lothar will understand it."

Château d'Arcachon, St.-Malo, France
11 APRIL 1692

"THE ENGLISH HAVE DEVISED an extraordinary scheme for the military defense of their homeland, which is that *they have no money*," said Monsieur le comte de Pontchartrain, *contrôleur-général* of France and (now) Secretary of State for the Navy.

This curious gambit was meant for Eliza, for Pontchartrain was gazing directly into her eyes when he came out with it. But others were privy to the conversation. Five were seated around the basset-table in the *Petit Salon:* besides Eliza and Pontchartrain, there were Étienne d'Arcachon, who was serving as dealer; a Madame de Bearsul, who was the very young wife of a captain of a frigate; and a Monsieur le chevalier d'Erquy, who was from just down the coast. These latter two were, of course, unique souls, precious in the eyes of God, endowed with any number of more or less interesting personal quirks, virtues, vices, &c., but Eliza could scarcely tell them apart from all of the other people who were at this moment seated around card-tables in her *Petit Salon*, playing at billiards or backgammon in her *Grand Salon*, bowling outside on her damp lawn, or noodling around on her harpsichord.

This was St.-Malo in the spring of '92. An invasion force was massing. It would quite obviously be departing from Cherbourg, which was only half as far from the shore of England as was St.-Malo; but facilities there, at the tip of the peninsula, were not adequate to sustain so many ships and regiments during the weeks it would take for them to gather and draw up into a coherent force. The regiments—ten thousand French and as many Irish, the latter evacuated from Limerick—were obviously not as mobile as the ships, and so they had first claim to the territory, food, fuel, whores, and other military musts in the immediate vicinity of Cherbourg. By process of elimination, then, the ships of the Channel fleet, and the galleys of the Mediterranean fleet that had lately passed the Gates of Hercules and voyaged north to take part in the invasion, were stationed in Channel ports within striking distance: most important, Le Havre and St.-Malo. Of those, Le Havre was twice as close to Paris, and a hundred times easier to reach from there, since the Seine joined them. So, much larger and more fashionable parties must, at this moment, be going on in noble châteaux around Le Havre. St.-Malo, by contrast, was hardly connected to France at all. A doughty pedestrian like Sergeant Bob Shaftoe could get to it, but such a journey was not recommended for normal people; everyone came to St.-Malo by sea. The family de Lavardac had for a long time maintained a château, which looked out over the harbor to one side, and had farms and an excellent *potagerie* out back. As the fortunes of that family had waxed, this had become the grandest house in St.-Malo, and the former duc d'Arcachon had loved to come here and pace to and fro on the terrace with a golden prospective-glass gazing down upon his privateer-fleet. Eliza had heard much of the place. Having spent most of her married life pregnant at La Dunette, she'd never laid eyes on it until a month ago. But she'd loved it immediately and now wished she could live here year-round.

The astonishing appearance of Bob Shaftoe—who, along with his regiment of Irish mercenaries, had marched right past, en route to Cherbourg from their winter quarters above Brest—had enlivened her first week's stay at the place. His return visit last week had forced her to put her rusty scheming-and-intriguing skills to use again, there being no proper, sanctioned way for a French Duchess and nursing mother to meet with an English sergeant and probable spy who just happened to be the brother of the most infamous villain in Christendom.

Eliza and Étienne, the infant Lucien, and their household had reached St.-Malo a fortnight in advance of the Mediterranean Fleet. More recently, other Ships of Force had come in from Brest, Lorient, and St.-Nazaire. All of these galleys and ships had officers, who quite often were of noble rank. The social obligations placed upon *le duc* and *la duchesse* d'Arcachon were correspondingly immense. Another duchesse would have welcomed those obligations in the same way as generals welcomed wars, or architects cathedral-commissions. Eliza delegated all of the work to women who actually enjoyed such things (she had inherited a large household staff from the previous duchesse d'Arcachon). Her old trusted aides, such as Brigitte and Nicole, and a few retired privateers deeded to her by Jean Bart, she kept close. The retinue of social climbers that had arrived in the wake of her marriage to Étienne, she put to work arranging parties, which kept them busy and, though it did not make them happy, infused them with feelings that they were wont to confuse with happiness.

Eliza, then, merely had to get dressed, show up, try not to forget people's names, and make conversation. When she became insufferably bored, she would claim she could hear Lucien bawling, and flit off to the private apartments in the other wing of the château.

And so the only thing the least bit novel about her situation at this moment—viz. seated at a basset-table watching her husband deal out cards to idle nobles—was that the fellow seated directly across the table from her was of titanic importance. At any other of the parties that the Arcachons had hosted in the few weeks just past, it would have been the captain of some Ship of the Line, cringing and servile in the presence of his master, the Grand Admiral of France (for Étienne had inherited the title). Today, though, it was Pontchartrain who, technically, ranked Étienne d'Arcachon! Étienne was under no obligation to toady, however, as he and Pontchartrain were both of such lofty stature as to be essentially equals. Pontchartrain had turned up unexpectedly this morning on a *jacht* that had sailed in from Cherbourg. He had spent all of dinner trying to catch Eliza's eye, and *not* because he wanted to flirt with her. She had invited the count to join her and Étienne at basset. Then, to prevent the gentlemen from crossing swords, or the ladies from poisoning each other, for the other seats at the table, Eliza had picked out this Madame de Bearsul and this Monsieur d'Erquy, precisely because they were nobodies who would not interfere too much in the conversation. Or such had been her phant'sy. Of course each of them had turned out (as mentioned) to be fully autonomous souls possessed of free will, intelligence, and an agenda. D'Erquy had heard, through the grapevine, that Eliza had been buying up bad loans from petty nobles like him who had been foolish enough to lend money to the government. De Bearsul was angling for a position in the household of some higher and mightier Court personage. To Pontchartrain, who was accustomed to meeting with the King of France almost every day, they might as well have been ants or lice. And so, about five hands into this basset-game, he had locked his brown eyes on Eliza's and made this curious remark about the English and their lack of specie.

Basset was simple, which was why Eliza had chosen it. Each player was dealt thirteen cards face up on the table, and placed money on any or all of them. The dealer then dealt cards from the bottom and the top of the deck alternately, gaining or losing wagers on all cards of matching ranks. As turns went on, the wagers escalated by a factor of as much as sixty. The dealer was kept very busy. Étienne had had to strap on his basset-dealing prosthesis: a cupped hand with spring-loaded fingers, made to grip a deck of cards. The players could be busy or not, depending on how many of their cards they elected to put money on. Eliza and Pontchartrain had laid only token wagers, which was a way of saying that they were more interested in conversation than in gambling. D'Erquy and de Bearsul were more heavily engaged in the game, and their squeals, moans, stifled curses, sudden outbursts of laughter, &c., provided a ragged, bursty continuo-line for this duet between the other two.

"My English friends have been complaining of this lack of coin for years—especially since the onset of war," said Eliza, "but only you, monsieur, would have the penetration to see it as a defensive strategy."

"That is just the difficulty—I did *not* penetrate it until rather late," said Pontchartrain. "When one is planning an invasion, one naturally makes plans to pay the soldiers. It is as important as arming, feeding, and housing them—perhaps *more* so, as soldiers, paid, can shift for themselves when arms, food, and shelter are wanting. But they must be paid in *local* money—which is to say the coin of the realm in whatever place is being invaded. It's easy in the Spanish Netherlands—"

"Because they are Spanish," said Eliza, "and so you can pay them in Pieces of Eight—"

"Which we can get anywhere in the world," said Pontchartrain. "But English pennies can only be gotten in England. *Supposedly* they are minted—"

"At the Tower of London. I know," said Eliza, "but why do you say *supposedly?*"

Pontchartrain threw up his hands. "No one ever sees these coins. They come out of the Mint and they vanish."

"But is it not the case that *anyone* may bring silver bullion to the Tower of London and have it minted into pennies?"

Pontchartrain was nonplussed for a moment. Then a smile spread over his face and he burst out in laughter and slapped the table hard enough to make money jump and buzz atop the playing-cards. It was a rare outburst for one of Pontchartrain's dignity, and it stopped the game for a few moments.

"Monsieur, what an honour and a privilege it is for us to bring you a few moments' diversion from your cares!" exclaimed Étienne. But this only brought an echo of the first laugh from Pontchartrain.

"It is precisely of my cares that your magnificent wife is speaking, monsieur," said Pontchartrain, "and I believe she is getting ready to suggest something cheeky."

Étienne's face pinkened. "I pray it shall not be so cheeky as to create an embarrassment for our guests—"

"On the contrary, monsieur, 'tis meant to embarrass the English!"

"Oh, well, *that* is all right then."

"Pray continue, madame!"

"I shall, monsieur," said Eliza, "but first you must indulge me as I speculate."

"Consider yourself indulged."

"The *jacht* on which you arrived is under conspicuously heavy guard. I speculate that it is laden with specie that is meant to cross the Channel with the invasion force and be used to pay the French and Irish soldiers during their campaign in England."

Pontchartrain smiled weakly and shook his head. "So much for my efforts at secrecy. It is said of some that he or she has a nose for money; but I truly believe, madame, that you can smell silver a mile away."

"Do not be silly, monsieur, it is, as you said, an obvious necessity of a foreign invasion."

For some reason she glanced, for a moment, at D'Erquy, and then regretted it. The poor chevalier was so transfixed that it took all her discipline not to laugh aloud. This poor fellow had melted down the family plate and loaned it to the King in hopes that it would get him invited to a few parties at Versailles. The interest payments had at first been delayed, then insufficient, later nonexistent. The man with the power to make those payments, or not, was seated less than arm's length away—and now it had been revealed that he had sailed into St.-Malo on top of a king's ransom in silver, which was locked up on a *jacht* a few hundred yards down the hill. A word, a flick of the pen, from Pontchartrain would pay back the loan, or at least pay the interest on it—and not just in the form of a written promise to pay, but in actual metal. This was the only thing D'Erquy could think about. And yet there was not a single word he could say, because to do so would have been impolite. Etiquette had rendered him helpless as effectively as the iron collar around a slave's neck. All he could do was watch and listen.

"Want of silver is not your difficulty, then," Eliza continued. "Very well. You must needs translate it across the Channel—very risky. For in the annals of military history, no tale is more tediously familiar than that of the train of pay-wagons, bringing specie to the troops at the front, that is ambushed and lost en route, with disastrous consequences to the campaign."

"We have been reading the same books," Pontchartrain concluded. "Even so, as we laid plans for this operation during the winter, I am afraid I paid more attention to my rôle as Secretary of State for the Navy, than that of *contrôleur-général*. Which is to say that I placed more emphasis on preparations of a purely military nature than on the attendant financial arrangements. Not until I reached Cherbourg the other day, and was confronted with the invasion in all of its complexity and scale, did I really grasp the difficulty of getting this specie to England. To send it across in an obvious and straightforward manner seems madness. I have considered breaking it up into small shipments and sending them over in the boats of those who smuggle wine and salt to remote ports of Cornwall."

"That would distribute the risk, but multiply the difficulties," said Eliza. "And even if it succeeded, it would not address the great difficulty, which is that if the silver is not accepted on the local—which is to say, English—market, then the troops will not deem themselves to have been paid."

"Naturally we should like to pay them in English silver pennies," said Pontchartrain, "but matters being what they are, we may have to use French coins."

"This brings us back to the conversation we had in the sleigh at La Dunette two years and some months ago," Eliza said; and the answering look on Pontchartrain's face told her that she had struck home.

But here Madame Bearsul threw a quizzical look in the direction of the Politest Man in France, who intervened. "On behalf of those of our guests who were not in that sleigh," Étienne said, "I beg permission to interrupt, so we may hear—"

"I speak of the recoinage, when all of the old coins were called in and replaced with new," said Eliza. "By royal decree, the new had the same value, and so to those of us who live in France, it made no difference. But they contained less silver or gold."

"Madame la duchesse, who in those days was Mademoiselle la comtesse, said to me, then, that it must have consequences difficult to foretell," said Pontchartrain.

"Before Monsieur le comte says a word against himself," said Eliza, "I would have the honor of being the first to rush to his defense. The *favorable* consequences of the recoinage were immense: for it raised a fortune for the war."

"But Madame la duchesse was a true Cassandra that evening in the sleigh," said Pontchartrain, "for there have been consequences that I did not foretell, and one of them is that French coins are not likely to be accepted at full value in English market-places."

"Monsieur, have you given any thought to minting invasion coin?" asked d'Erquy.

"Yes, monsieur, and to using Pieces of Eight. But before we take such measures, I am eager to hear more from our hostess concerning the English Mint."

"I am simply pointing out to you, monsieur," said Eliza, "that there already exists a mechanism for importing silver bullion to England, at no risk to France; having it made into good English coin in London; and transferring the coin into the hands of trusted French agents there."

"What is this mechanism, madame?" inquired d'Erquy, suspicious that Eliza was having them on.

"France's chief connection to the international money market is not here in St.-Malo, or even in Paris, but rather down in Lyon. The King's moneylender is of course Monsieur Samuel Bernard, and he works hand-in-glove with a Monsieur Castan. I know Castan; he is a pillar of the *Dépôt*. He can deliver money to any of several merchant banking houses who maintain agencies in Lyon, and get negotiable Bills of Exchange which can be endorsed to French agents who can transport them to London in advance of the invasion. These may be presented well in advance of the expiry of their usance to bankers in London who, upon accepting them, will make whatever arrangements may be necessary to have the coin ready on the date the bills come due—which may mean that they shall have to ship bullion over from Amsterdam or Antwerp and have it minted at the Tower. But that is their concern, not ours, and their risk. The coin shall be delivered to our agents, who need merely transport it to the front to pay the troops."

Early in this discourse, the mouth of Madame de Bearsul fell open, as if she might more easily take in these difficult words and notions through her *mouth* than her ears; and as Eliza went on, similar transformations came over the faces of all her other auditors, including some at adjacent tables; and by the time she reached the terminal phrase *pay the troops*, they had all begun glancing at each other, trying to build solidarity in their confusion. And so before anyone could give voice to his amazement, Eliza, with unfeigned, uncharacteristic ardor for her role as entertainer to the bored nobility of France, had got to her feet (obliging Étienne, Pontchartrain, and d'Erquy to stand) and begun to arrange a new parlor-game. "We are going to put on a little masque," she announced, "and all of you must sit, sit, sit!" And she called to a servant to bring quills, ink, and paper.

"But, Eliza, how can gentlemen sit in the presence of a lady who stands?" asked Étienne.

"The answer is simple: In the masque, I am no lady, but a God: Mercury, messenger of Olympus, and patron deity of Commerce. You must phant'sy wings on my ankles."

The mere mention of ankles caused a little intake of breath from Étienne, and a few eyes flicked nervously his way. But Eliza forged on: "You, Monsieur de Pontchartrain, must sit. You are the Deliverer: the *contrôleur-général* of France."

"That should be an easy rôle for me to play, Mercury," said the *contrôleur-général*, and, with a little bow to Eliza, sat down.

Now—since the ranking man in the room had done it—all others were eager to join in.

"First we enact the simple Bill of Exchange," said Eliza, "which requires only four, plus Mercury. Later we will find rôles for the rest of you." For several had gravitated over from different tables to see what the commotion was about. "This table is Lyon."

"But, Mercury, already I cannot suspend my disbelief, for the *contrôleur-général* does not go to Lyon," said Pontchartrain.

"We will remedy that in a few minutes, but for now you are in Lyon. Sitting across from you will be Étienne, playing the rôle of Lothar the Banker."

"Why must I have such a ridiculous name?" demanded Étienne.

"It is an excellent name among bankers—Lothar is *Ditta di Borsa* in Lyon, Bruges, and many other places."

"That means he has impeccable credit among other bankers," said Pontchartrain.

"Very well. As long as the fellow is as well-reputed as you say, I shall accept the rôle," said Étienne, and sat down across the table from Pontchartrain.

"You have money," said Eliza, and used one hand as a rake to sweep a pile of coins across the table so that it ended up piled before Pontchartrain. "And you wish to get it—here!" She strode through the double doors to the *Grand Salon* where a backgammon game had been abandoned. "Madame de Bearsul, you are a merchant banker in London—this table is London."

Madame de Bearsul approached London with a show of cringing, blushing, and hand-wringing that made Eliza want to slap her. "But, madame, I know nothing of such occupations!"

"Of course not, for you are so well-bred; but just as Kings may play Vagabonds in masques, you are now a merchant banker named Signore Punchinello. Here, Signore Punchinello, is your strong-box." Mercury clapped the backgammon-set closed, imprisoning the game pieces, and handed it to de Bearsul, who with much hair-patting and skirt-smoothing took a seat at London. Monsieur le chevalier d'Erquy pulled her chair out for her, for, anticipating Eliza's next command, he had followed them into the *Grand Salon.*

"Monsieur, you are Pierre Dubois, a Frenchman in London."

"Miserable fate! Must I be?" complained d'Erquy, to general amusement.

"You must. But you need not sit down yet, for you have not yet made the acquaintance of Signore Punchinello. Instead, you wander about the city like a lost soul, trying to find a decent loaf of bread. Now! Places, everyone!" and she walked back into the *Petit Salon,* where the Lyon table had been supplied with quills, ink, and paper.

"Monsieur *le contrôleur-général,* give your silver—which is to say, *France's* silver—to Lothar the Banker."

"*Monsieur, s'il vous plaît,*" said Pontchartrain, shoving the pile across the table.

"*Merci beaucoup, monsieur,*" said Étienne, a bit uncertainly.

"You must give him more than polite words! Write out the amount, and the word '*Londres,*' and a time, say five minutes in the future."

Étienne dutifully took up his quill and did as he was told, putting down "half past three," as the clock in the corner was currently reading twenty-five minutes past. "To the *contrôleur-général* give it," said Eliza. "And now you, *contrôleur-général,* write an address on the back, thus: 'To Monsieur Pierre Dubois, London.' Meanwhile you, Lothar, must write an *avisa* addressed to Signore Punchinello in London, containing the same information as is in the Bill."

"The Bill?"

"The document you have given to the *contrôleur-général* is a Bill of Exchange."

Pontchartrain had finished addressing the Bill, and so Mercury snatched it out of his hand and pranced out of the room and gave it to "Pierre Dubois," who had been watching, bemused, from the doorway. Then she returned to "Lothar," who was writing out the *avisa* with a good deal more formality than was called for. Mercury jerked it out from under the quill.

"Good heavens, I haven't even finished the Apology yet."

"You must learn better to inhabit the rôle of Lothar. He would not be so discursive," said Mercury, and wafted the *avisa* out of the room to "Signore Punchinello." "In truth, there would be two or even three copies of the Bill and the *avisa* both, sent by separate couriers," said Mercury, "but to prevent the masque from becoming tedious we shall only use one. Signore Punchinello! You said earlier you did not know how to play your rôle; but I tell you now that you need only know how to read, and be capable of recognizing Lothar's handwriting. Do you? (The correct answer is 'Yes, Mercury.')"

"Yes, Mercury."

"Monsieur Dubois, I think you can guess what to do."

Indeed, "Pierre Dubois" now helped himself to a seat at the London table across from "Signore Punchinello," and presented the bill.

"Now, signore," said Eliza to Madame de Bearsul, "you must compare what is written on Monsieur Dubois's Bill to what is in the *avisa*."

"They are the same," answered "Punchinello."

"Do they appear to have been written in the same hand?"

"Indeed, Mercury, the hands are indistinguishable."

"What time is it?"

"By yonder clock, twenty-eight minutes past the hour of three."

"Then take up yonder quill and write 'accepted' across the face of the Bill, and sign your name to it."

Madame de Bearsul did so, and then, getting into the spirit of the thing, opened up her backgammon-set and began to count out pieces.

"Not yet!" said Mercury. "That is, it's fine for you to count them out, and make sure you have enough. But good banker that you are, you'll not give them to Monsieur Dubois until the Bill has come due."

But they only had to wait for a few more seconds before the clock bonged twice, signifying half past three; then the backgammon pieces were pushed across the table into the waiting hands of "Pierre Dubois."

"*Voilà!*" announced Mercury to the audience, which by this point numbered above twenty party-guests. "The first act of our masque draws to a happy ending. Monsieur *le contrôleur-général* has transferred silver from Lyon to London at no risk, and even converted it to English silver pennies along the way, with practically no effort! All by invoking the supernatural powers of Mercury." And Eliza took a little curtsey, and basked for a few moments in the applause of her guests.

ENTR'ACTE

"I am the *contrôleur-général* of France, madame; I know what a Bill of Exchange is." This from Pontchartrain, who had maneuvered her into a niche and was muttering out the side of his mouth with uncharacteristic harshness.

"And I know your title and your powers, monsieur," said Eliza.

"Then if you have more to say concerning the Mint, I would fain hear it—"

"In good time, monsieur!"

Madame de Bearsul was pitching a minor scene at "London." Petulance was something she did well. "I have given up my coins to Monsieur Dubois—in exchange for *what*!?"

"Bills written in the hand of a banker who is *Ditta di Borsa*—as good as money."

"But *they are not money!*"

"But Signore Punchinello, you may turn them into money, or other things of value, by taking them to an office of Lothar's concern."

"But he is in Lyon, and I am stuck in London!"

"Actually he is in Leipzig—but never mind, for he maintains an office in London. After the Usurper took the throne, any number of bankers from Amsterdam crossed the sea and established themselves there—"

"Wait! First Lothar was in Lyon—then Leipzig—then Amsterdam—now London?"

"It is all one thing, for Mercury touches all of these places on his rounds." And Eliza thrust an arm into a boozy-smelling phalanx of young men and dragged forth a young Lavardac cousin and bade him sit down near the backgammon table. "This is Lothar's factor in London." She grabbed a second young man who had been snickering at the fate of the first, and stationed him in the short gallery that joined the two salons, calling this Amsterdam.

"I must register an objection! (Pardon me for speaking directly,

but I am trying to inhabit the rôle of an uncouth Saxon banker),"
said Eliza's husband.

"And you are doing splendidly, my love," said Eliza. "What is your
objection?"

"Unless these chaps of mine in Amsterdam and London are titled
nobility, which I'm led to believe is generally *not* the case—"

"Indeed not, Étienne."

"Well, if they are not of independent means, it would seem to suggest that—" and here Étienne colored slightly again, "forgive me, but
must I—" and he balked until both Eliza and Pontchartrain had made
encouraging faces at him, "well, *pay* them—" he half-swallowed the
dreadful word—"I don't know, so that they could—*buy*—food and
whatnot, presuming that's how they get it? For I don't phant'sy they
would have their own farms, living as they do in cities."

"You must pay them!" Eliza said loud and clear.

Étienne winced. "Well, it hardly seems worth all the *bother* for me
to be taking in silver here, and sending Bills to one place, and *avisas*
to another, all so that I can end up handing the silver over to Signore
Punchinello in the end." He scanned nearby faces uncertainly, taking a sort of poll—but everyone was nodding profoundly, as if the
duc d'Arcachon had made a telling point. All of those faces now
turned towards Eliza.

"You get to keep some of the money," Eliza said.

Everyone gasped as if she had jerked the veil from a statue of
solid gold.

"Oh, well, that puts it in a whole new light!" exclaimed Étienne.

"The amount collected by Pierre Dubois in London was not quite
as large as what I gave to you," said Pontchartrain. He then turned to
look at Eliza. "But, madame, I live in Paris."

Eliza went into the opposite corner of the *Petit Salon* and patted a
gilded harpsichord. Pontchartrain excused himself from Lyon and sat
before it. Then, to amuse himself and to provide incidental music for
the second act of the masque, he began to pick out an air by Rameau.

Eliza beckoned to a middle-aged Count dressed in the uniform of
a galley-captain. Until recently, he and a friend had been playing at
billiards. "You are Monsieur Samuel Bernard, moneylender to *le Roi*."

"I am to portray a *Jew*!?" said the dismayed Count.

The music faltered. "He is an excellent fellow, the King speaks
highly of him, monsieur," said Pontchartrain, and resumed playing.

"But now there is no one in Lyon!" said Étienne.

"On the contrary, there is Monsieur Castan, an old *confrère* of Monsieur Bernard," said Eliza, and dragged the Count's erstwhile billiards-
opponent over to occupy the chair warmed by Pontchartrain.

Lately the room had become a good bit louder, for the galley-captain playing Samuel Bernard had adopted a hunchbacked posture and begun rolling his eyes, leering at the ladies, and stroking his chin. Meanwhile the "Amsterdam" and "London" crowd, which consisted mostly of younger people, had become restive, and begun to engage in all sorts of unauthorized Transactions.

"Fetch me a bowl of dough," Eliza said to a maid.

"Dough, madame?"

"Dough from the kitchen! And an empty fruit-bowl or something. Hurry!" The servant hustled out. "Places, everyone! Act the Second begins. Monsieur le comte de Pontchartrain, pray continue playing your beautiful music, it is entirely fitting." Indeed, some of the guests who had not been assigned specific rôles had begun dancing to it, so that "Paris" had already become a center of beauty, culture, and romance.

"I am your servant, madame," said Pontchartrain.

"No, I am Mercury. And I say you have dough!"

"Dough, Mercury?" Pontchartrain looked about curiously but continued to play.

"You rarely *see* it, of course, and you never handle it. *Pourquoi non,* for you are a member of the *Conseil d'en-Haut* and a trusted confidant of *le Roi Soleil.* But you know that you have dough!"

"How do I know it, Mercury?"

"Because I have whispered it into your ear. You have a thousand kitchens in which it is being prepared, all the time. Now, call Monsieur Bernard to your side, and let him know."

Monsieur Bernard did not need to be summoned. Using his billiard-cue as cane, he staggered over—for he had perfected his Jew act—and bent close to Pontchartrain, rubbing his hands together.

"Monsieur Bernard! I have dough."

"I believe it, monseigneur."

"I should like to see, oh, a hundred pieces of dough transferred safely and swiftly to the hands of Monsieur Dubois in London."

"Hold!" commanded Mercury, "you do not yet know the identity of your payee in London."

"Very well—make the Bill endorsable to one of my agents, to be determined later."

"It shall be done, my lord!" announced "Bernard," who then leered up at Eliza for his cue.

"Go and tell your friend," Eliza said.

"Don't I *get* anything?"

"Monsieur! You have *got* the word of the *contrôleur-général* of France! What more could you possibly ask for?"

"I was just asking," said "Bernard" a little bit resentfully, and then crab-walked across the *Petit Salon* to "Lyon," where his billiards-partner awaited. "*Mon vieux, bonjour.* Monsieur le comte de Pontchartrain has dough and wants a hundred pieces of it in London."

"Very well," said "Castan" after some *sotto voce* prompting from Mercury. "Lothar, if you would get a hundred pieces of dough to our man in London, I shall give you a hundred and ten pieces of dough here."

"Heavens! Where is this dough?" Étienne demanded—a bit confused, for in the first run-through, he had been given actual silver.

"I don't have any just now," said "Castan," who had been a bit quicker than Étienne to see where this was going, "but my friend Monsieur Bernard has heard from Monsieur le comte de Pontchartrain who has heard from Mercury himself that there is dough a-plenty, and so, in the sight of all these good Lyonnaise—"

"We call them *le Dépôt*," put in Eliza, indicating several persons who had gathered round the basset-table to watch.

"—I say that I shall pay you a hundred and ten pieces of dough any day now."

"Very well," said "Lothar," after looking up at Eliza for permission. Now some time was spent in draughting the necessary papers. Meanwhile Eliza had thrust her hands into a great warm ellipsoid of bread-dough that had been fetched out of the kitchens by a cook, and torn it apart into two pieces, a small and a large. The small she placed in an empty fruit-bowl, which she took into the *Grand Salon* and slammed down on a gilded sideboard near the backgammon-table, astonishing Madame de Bearsul. "Tear this in half, and continue tearing the halves in half, until you have thirty-two pieces of dough," decreed "Mercury," then stormed away before de Bearsul could pout or fret. Eliza fetched the great bowl containing the larger amount of dough, and set it into the arms of the young banker she had posted in "Amsterdam." Three younger guests, eight to twelve years of age, had already converged on the sideboard, overturned the fruit-bowl, and begun tearing the dough into bits. "Very good, you are the English Mint, and that is the Tower of London," Eliza informed them. Then, because they were being a bit too enthusiastic, she cautioned them: "Remember, I desire only thirty or so."

"We thought a hundred!" said the oldest of the children.

"Yes; but there is not enough dough in London to make so many."

By now the paperwork had been settled in "Lyon." A new wrinkle had been added: this time, "Lothar" made the Bill out, not to "Dubois" but to "Castan," who was sitting across the table from him. "Castan" then had to flip it over and write on the back that he was transferring the Bill to Monsieur Dubois. It was due in fifteen minutes. "Castan," handed it to "Dubois" on the outskirts of "Lyon" at 4:12 and "Dubois," after a detour for a thimble of cognac, arrived in "London" at 4:14 and handed it to "Punchinello," who compared it as before to the *avisa,* and checked the time. She was just about to write "accepted" across it when ever-diligent "Mercury" stayed her hand.

"Stop! Think. Your solvency, your credit hang in the balance. How many pieces of dough do you have?"

The eyes of "Punchinello" strayed towards the "Tower of London," where thirty-two dough-balls were arrayed eight by four.

"Those don't belong to you," said Mercury. She scooped them into the fruit-bowl and handed it to the Lavardac cousin who was pretending to be Lothar's factor in London.

Madame de Bearsul was starting to get it. "I'm going to be needing those—I've a note from your uncle, right here, says you owe me a hundred."

"I don't have a hundred!" complained the young banker.

"Mercury comes to the rescue, as usual!" announced Eliza. "Does anyone else here in London have dough?"

"I've got a great bowl of it," said an adolescent voice from the next room.

"You're not in London!" answered "Mercury." And she turned to the "London" nephew and gave him an expectant look.

"Cousin! Come in here and bring me some of the family dough!" he called.

The young man with the dough-bowl staggered into the room. Whereupon Eliza gave the nod to a pair of six-year-old boys who had been crouching in a corner with wooden swords. They rushed out and began to batter the dough-bearer about the shins and ankles. "Augh!" he cried.

"Pirate attack in the North Sea!" Eliza announced.

The dough-carrier was hindered badly by his inability to see the little boca-neers, for the bowl blocked his view. Nevertheless, after having been chased several times around the entirety of Britain, he arrived in port some minutes later (4:20) listing badly to starboard, and upended the bowl, dumping out the dough-load at the Tower of London. "Hurry!" said Eliza, "only five minutes remaining until the Bill expires!"

And it was a near thing; but working feverishly, and with some help from Eliza, the Coiners were able to get the balance of Lothar's London correspondent up above one hundred dough-pieces by 4:23. This was slammed down triumphantly before "Signore Punchinello," who disgustedly shoved it across the table into the embrace of "Pierre Dubois." It was 4:27 exactly. The entire crowd, players, audience, and servants alike, now burst into applause, thinking that the play was over. The only exceptions were Monsieur le chevalier d'Erquy, who had been left holding the dough, and the twin six-year-old pirates who—not satisfied with the amount of sword-play, swash-buckling, and derring-do in the play thus far—had begun trying to sever his hamstrings and Achilles tendons with blunt force trauma.

"In all seriousness, Mercury," complained d'Erquy, "how are the coins to be transported from London to the front? For if half of what is said of England is true, the place is full of runagates, Vagabonds, highwaymen, and varlets of all stripes."

"Never fear," said Eliza, "if you only wait a few days, the front will come to you, and French and Irish troops will march in good order to your doorstep in the Strand to receive their pay!" Which prompted a patriotic cheer and a standing ovation, and even a couple of tossed bouquets, from the crowd.

"But if I may once again play the rôle of the uncouth banker," said Étienne—who had abandoned his post in "Lyon" to watch the denouement—"why on earth should the English Mint strike coins whose purpose is to finance a foreign invasion of England?"

This quieted the crowd so profoundly that Étienne felt rather bad about it, and began to formulate what showed every sign of being a lengthy and comprehensive apology. But Eliza was having none of it. "You don't know England!" she said, "But I do, for I am Mercury. England has factions. The one that rules now is called the Tories, and they make no secret that they loathe the Usurper, and want him out. Indeed, our invasion plans are predicated, are they not, on the assumption that the English Navy will look the other way as our fleets cross the Channel, and that the common folk of England, and much of the Army, will joyfully throw off the yoke of the Dutchman and welcome our French and Irish soldiers with open arms. If we grant all of these assumptions, why, there is no difficulty in supposing that the Tory masters of the Mint will strike a few coins for the House of Hacklheber—"

"Or whichever bank we elect to deal with," put in Pontchartrain.

"—without asking too many awkward questions as to where those coins are intended to end up."

"Yes—I see the whole thing now as if you have painted a picture," said Étienne. At which most of the party-guests attempted to get faraway looks in their eyes, as though gazing raptly at the same picture that Étienne was viewing in his mind's eye.

Though there were exceptions: "Samuel Bernard," unable or

unwilling to let go of the scheming-Jew impersonation that had garnered him so many laughs and so much attention, was still back in
the *Petit Salon,* storming to and fro between "Paris" and "Lyon," waving his stick around and demanding to know when *he* was going to
see some of this dough that Monsieur le comte de Pontchartrain had
spoken of so convincingly; and "Castan," his partner in billiards,
finance, and (now) drinking (for they had got control of a decanter
of something brown), was also beginning to make himself heard on
the matter. "What are they on about?" inquired Étienne.

"Don't worry, 'Lothar the Banker,'" said Eliza. "You will be paid
back."

Étienne's brow furrowed. "That's right—I quite forgot! I haven't
seen any dough! Is that what those two are so upset about?"

Pontchartrain intervened, sharing a warm private look with Eliza.
"Those two, monsieur, have just discovered something called liquid-
ity risk."

"It sounds dreadful!"

"Never mind, Monsieur le duc. It is a phantom. We do not have
such things in France."

"That's fortunate," said the duc d'Arcachon. "They were starting
to make me a bit anxious—and I'm not even a banker!"

Eliza to Lothar von Hacklheber
12 APRIL 1692

Mein Herr,

PRIDE is a vice to which a woman is no less susceptible
than a man, and I, perhaps, more than other women. PRIDE,
like other vices, is arrogant of what room it can claim in the
human breast, and jealous of that occupied by the Virtues,
which it ever seeks to trample on or drive out.

When I rushed to little Johann's nursery eighteen months
ago to discover his cradle empty, a war began within my soul.
On one side was the Virtue of Love: a mother's natural love for
her child. On the other was the Vice of Pride: pride wounded,

aggrieved, and humiliated. It was not merely that I had been bested, but that it had happened while I was far away attending a fashionable soirée, rather than staying at home and tending to my duties as a mother. Pride, therefore, was urged on by Shame; and together their legions charged across the field and swept Love's feebler forces before them. All that I have done since then, where Johann is concerned, has been dictated by Pride. Love's counsel has rarely been heard, and when I have heard it, I have wilfully ignored it.

But the soul harbors its own tides. Much has changed in eighteen months. I have a new little boy now. Impetuous Pride, I have learned, is better at seizing ground than holding it. Love's inroads have insensibly made up all the ground that she lost, and more. This letter may be considered the instrument of Pride's surrender, and Love's victory. It only remains for terms to be negotiated.

Of course you have already dictated the terms; you laid them out with admirable clarity in the note that was left in Johann's crib. You seek the return of the gold that was seized off Bonanza in August of 1690 and that is believed to be in the hands of the band of thieves and pirates led by the villain Jack Shaftoe. You phant'sy that I had something to do with the theft and that I know where Jack is to be found.

In truth I had nothing to do with it and I have no idea where he is. But this is a prideful response, which brings me no closer to seeing my little boy again. The *loving* response is to give you, sir, what you want, to appease your anger and balm your wounds, though it be never so humiliating to me, your humble and obedient servant.

So: though I cannot return the gold, and do not know where Jack is, I shall protest no more, but do all in my power to give you what I can in compensation.

As to the whereabouts of Jack Shaftoe: no one knows this, though Father Édouard de Gex and Monsieur Bonaventure Rossignol have devised a scheme to ferret him out. One of the members of his pirate-band writes letters, from time to time, to his family in France. These letters are intercepted and read by Monsieur Rossignol, who, however, is unable to extract all of their meaning, as they are written in an impenetrable code. He makes copies of them and passes them on to the family.

The family are coffee merchants who until recently lived as paupers in Paris. Then they were discovered by Madame la duchesse d'Oyonnax, who as you may know is the *cousine* of de

Gex. She began to serve their coffee exclusively at her *salon*, and soon enough de Maintenon herself, at her levée, was heard to ask for coffee of this marque, and in no time at all, this family had established a coffeehouse in the village of Versailles, where they serve a steady walk-in trade as well as purveying beans to the royal château and the other estates that abound in this area.

Obviously de Gex is behind this. For where previously the family in question were dispersed among various prisons and poorhouses around Paris, now they are all dwelling together in one house in Versailles where the *Cabinet Noir* can easily keep an eye on them. As I have mentioned, all of the letters that are sent to France by their brother who is a member of Jack Shaftoe's pirate-band are passed on to them, in the hopes that they will write back to him, and in so doing, divulge something to M. Rossignol. So far this has not been productive of useful information. The family do not write back. This appears to be because they have nowhere to write back *to*. For the ship of *L'Emmerdeur* and his band is wandering all over the Red Sea and the Persian Gulf, so that trying to intercept it with a letter posted from Paris is akin to trying to strike a horsefly with a round fired from a siege-mortar. Nevertheless, the scheme that M. Rossignol and Fr. de Gex have devised to trace Jack's movements is well-conceived and likely to bear fruit sooner or later. When it does, I shall be in a position to know about it, and will pass the information on to you.

As to the gold you lost: since I cannot satisfy you where this is concerned, I have resolved to compensate you, inasmuch as that is possible, by other means. I am well aware that the gold taken off Bonanza possesses special properties, the loss of which no amount of mundane silver and gold can make good. But until such time as the thieves are tracked down, there is nothing I can do but try to make up your losses in the only way I know how. I lost all of my personal assets shortly after Johann was born, and so have no money of my own that I could send you. The property of my new family, the Lavardacs, is not at my disposal. I can dwell in the family residences, but not sell them. I can eat off the family plate, but not melt it down. However, my position does afford me a matchless vantage-point on the workings of French government finance. I frequently become aware of opportunities in this field from which a man in your position could reap considerable gains with little effort or risk. As a sort of down-payment or, if you will, interest on the lost gold of Bonanza—which I have every intention of repaying in full when it becomes possible—I present you, now, with such an opportunity—the first in what I hope will grow into a long series of profitable liaisons.

Your agent in Lyon, Gerhard Mann, will presently be able to tell you more concerning this, but here it is in a nutshell: The French government needs to transfer silver to England to pay the French and Irish troops who will invade that country from around Cherbourg in late May. They were going to ship the silver over directly, but recently I have convinced them that it will be more efficient to make use of the existing commercial channels, viz. a Bill issued in Lyon against the credit of M. Castan (backed, it goes without saying, by France) and payable in silver coin in London. The Bill would need to be issued early in May and payable in late May or early June, and it would have to be transferable, since the identity of the French payee in London might not be known until later, and in any case, for obvious reasons, would need to be kept secret.

Because this is being arranged at the last minute, during wartime, you could probably demand a very high fee, as these things go.

Moreover, the transaction would involve relatively little risk for you. You may laugh at this, for it must sound absurd to claim that shipping silver to England in wartime is not risky; but it is true, for the reason that *the invasion probably will never happen.* And if it does, it will fail. The entire plan is predicated on the assumption that the common people of England will *welcome* an invasion by French and Irish troops come to place a Catholic on the throne. Nothing more absurd can be imagined. You may easily verify this through your own excellent sources. So by far the most likely outcome is that the Bills you issue in Lyon will never reach England, and never be presented for payment; the transaction will be cancelled, and you shall get to keep the fee and the float on the funds transferred in Lyon. The *worst* possible outcome, then, is that the Bills *are* presented and accepted; but this would be nothing more than a routine, albeit large, transaction for the House of Hacklheber.

I have done all in my power to predispose M. le comte de Pontchartrain, M. Bernard, and M. Castan to select the House of Hacklheber as its bank for this transaction. They show signs of favoring the idea; yet as you know, there is much competition in Lyon, and I do not have the power to compel them to deal with you. I shall continue to work discreetly on your behalf unless you write back requesting that I desist.

In return I ask nothing, save that you might show me more favor than in the past, and consider allowing me to pay a brief visit (chaperoned if you wish) to little Johann, if I can find some way of getting to Leipzig.

I am, mein Herr, your humble and obedient servant

Eliza, duchesse d'Arcachon, comtesse de la Zeur

Eliza to King William III of England
12 APRIL 1692

Majesty,

By now you must have heard from a hundred different sources that an invasion of your Realm is being readied on the Cotentin Peninsula. You may even know that it is to set sail from Cherbourg during the third or fourth week in May. I shall not waste your time, then, belaboring these facts. I write to you, not as a spy for England, but as a champion of France. This invasion must never be allowed to go forward. It is a ruinously stupid plan. Its defeat will neither improve the security of England (since it is doomed in any case) nor bring England glory (since it is so feeble and ill-conceived). The French have convinced themselves otherwise. Somehow they have made themselves believe that all England is against your majesty, and that your majesty's Army and Navy are so riddled with secret Jacobites that they will declare their allegiance to James Stuart as soon as the signal is given; that the Royal Navy will suffer the French to cross the Channel in force, English regiments will make themselves scarce while a French beachhead is established in Wessex, and English people will welcome French and Irish invaders on their territory. Perhaps all of this is true; but to my ear it sounds absurd. I suspect that your spies and emissaries in France have been making a pretense of hostility to your majesty and whispering, into the ears of their French counterparts, all sorts of flattering and seductive nonsense about how England is poised for a Jacobite rebellion. If so, your majesty, the deception has worked all too well, and made the French so cocksure that they have laid plans, devised stratagems, and formulated resolves that seem to your humble and obedient servant like utter lunacy.

I pray that you will write a letter, or send an emissary, to King Louis XIV; announce that you know of the invasion plans; and make *le Roi* understand that the project is doomed. If French troops and sailors must be sacrificed on the fields of Mars, then let it happen in fair and honourable clashes of arms. It is more than I can bear to see them go down to David Jones's Locker in pursuit of a folly.

Eliza, Duchess of Qwghlm, Duchess of Arcachon

P.S. I have sent three copies of this letter in the holds of three different smugglers' boats. If you have received redundant copies, please accept my apologies for so making a pest of myself; but the matter is important to me.

Eliza to Monsieur le Chevalier d'Erquy
13 APRIL 1692

Monsieur,

Thank you for your assistance in despatching those letters to England. I could never have made the necessary contacts without the assistance of one such as you, a Breton born and bred, who knows his way around the little coves and harbors of the Golfe de St.-Malo. I pray that you will forgive me for having laughed at the look on your face. It was entirely proper and prudent for you to open and examine those letters before you became complicit in sending them across the Channel, for who knows what they might have contained. Many times it has happened that a woman, well-meaning but foolish, allowed herself to be duped, by some conniving wretch of more wit and less virtue, into carrying letters that contain damaging information. Far from being angry with you, I am indebted to you for having had the prudence to examine the letters before turning them over to those smugglers. In return, I pray you will forgive me for the way I laughed out loud when you were confronted with page after page of gibberish. As you must have collected by now, I dabble in the stocks that are traded at the bourses of London and Amsterdam. Because of the state of war that now exists between France and Holland/England, it is difficult for me to communicate with my brokers there through the channels that are customary in peacetime. *That* is why I put you to so much bother in sending those letters. But such communications, by their nature, consist predominantly of numbers and financial jargon. You should not be surprised that you were unable to make any sense of them.

This brings my subject around to business. You should know that my resources are limited and, for the most part, illiquid. However, many of the assets of the Lavardac family naturally produce revenue. Farms, for example, generate rents, which are delivered to our coffers. Those coffers are also drained by countless expenses, but if the affairs of the family are well managed, some surplus may from time to time result. It then becomes my responsibility to see to it that the surplus is put to productive use. Many opportunities for investment present themselves to me every day; I try to distribute the available capital among these in a rational way.

So the rumors that you have evidently been hearing are correct. I have, on several occasions, purchased distressed loans from persons who have lent money to the King's treasury and who have found that the interest payments on those loans are insufficient for their needs.

Like all proper transactions in a market, these must be of benefit to both parties. To the original lender (which would be you, in this case) the benefit is that you receive hard money, where before you had only a piece of paper signed by the *contrôleur-général* promising to make interest payments. For me, the benefit is somewhat more difficult to explain. It is a service I perform for the King. Suffice it to say that by consolidating a large number of such loans into a single instrument, representing a very large amount of government debt, I may help to bring some simplicity and clarity to what would otherwise be a most complex and tedious welter of affairs. In this way the œconomy of France may be better regulated and altogether more efficient.

At this point it is necessary to bring up the awkward and distasteful subject of terms. Specifically, we must decide what is to be the discount at which your loan is to be sold—i.e., for each hundred *livres tournoises* of principal that you originally loaned to his majesty's treasury, how many *livres tournoises* are you to receive from the buyer now? Such discussions are naturally repellent to Persons of Quality. Fortunately, we may refer the matter to an impartial judge: the market. For if you were the only man in France who had ever tried to sell such a loan, why, we should have to work out terms without any reference to established customs or precedents. Endless discussion would be entailed, every word of it beneath our dignity as nobility of France. But as it happens there are many hundreds of recent precedents. I myself have purchased no fewer than eighty-six loans. At the moment, you are one of seven men who is offering me such an opportunity. When the number of participants is so large, a price emerges, as if by magic. And so I can tell you that the price of one hundred *livres tournoises* of French government debt, three years ago, was eighty-one *livres tournoises*. Two years ago it was sixty-five, a year ago it was holding steady around forty, and today it is twenty-one. Which is to say that for every hundred you loaned the Treasury, I will pay you twenty-one today. Tomorrow the price may rise again, in which case it would benefit you to hold on to the loan, and sell it later; on the other hand, it might decline further, in which case you may wish you had sold it today. It is regrettably not possible for me to offer you advice in the matter.

My attorney at Versailles is M. Ladon and I have let him know that he may hear from you on this. He is quite proficient in such transactions, having, as I mentioned, carried out more than four score of them. If you elect to proceed, he shall see to it that all of the requisite papers, &c., are drawn up correctly.

In closing, I thank you again for your assistance in sending the letters to England. I shall probably need to send more in the near future; but now that you have shown me where to go, and introduced me to the right men, my staff, some of whom are old Marines from around Dunkerque, should know what to do.

Eliza, duchesse d'Arcachon

Café Esphahan, Rue de l'Orangerie, Versailles
26 APRIL 1692

"YOU WERE EXPECTING SOMEONE DIFFERENT? It is all right, madame. So was I."

This was how Samuel Bernard introduced himself to Eliza, lobbing the words across the coffee-house as he cut toward her table.

By arranging the meeting in a coffee-house in the town, as opposed to a salon in a château, Eliza had already obviated several days' invitation-passing and preliminary maneuvers. Not satisfied even with this level of efficiency, Bernard had now lopped off half an hour's introductory persiflage by jumping into the middle of the conversation before he had even reached her table. He came on as if he meant to place her under arrest. Heads turned towards him, froze, and then turned away; those who wished to gawk, looked out the windows and gawked at his carriage and his squadron of musket-brandishing bodyguards.

Bernard scooped up Eliza's hand as if it were a thrown gauntlet. He thrust out a leg to steady himself, bowed low, planted a firm dry smack on her knuckles, and gleamed. Gleamed because threads of gold were worked into the dark fabric of his vest. "You thought I was a Jew," he said, and sat down.

"And what did you think *I* was, monsieur?"

"Oh, come now! You already know the answer. You just aren't thinking! I shall assist you. *Why* did you phant'sy I was a Jew?"

"Because everyone says so."

"But *why*?"

"They are mistaken."

"But when otherwise well-informed persons are mistaken it is because they *wish to be* mistaken, no?"

"I suppose that's logical."

"Why would they *wish to be* mistaken about me—or *you*?"

"Monsieur Bernard, it has been so long since I began a conversation so briskly! Allow me a moment to catch my breath. Would you care to order something? Not that you are in need of further stimulation."

"I shall have coffee!" Bernard called out to an Armenian boy with a peach-fuzz moustache, dressed like a Turk, who had been edging toward them, impelled by significant glares and subtle finger-flicks from the proprietor, Christopher Esphahnian, but intimidated by Bernard. The garçon sped into the back, relieved to have been given orders. Bernard glanced about the coffee-house. "I could almost believe I was in Amsterdam," he remarked.

"From the lips of a *financier,* that is flattery," Eliza said. "But I believe that the intent of the decorator was to make you believe you were in Turkey."

Bernard snorted. "Does it work for *you,* madame?"

"No, for I have been in the coffee-houses of Amsterdam, and I share your opinion."

"You do not say that you have been in Turkey."

"Do I *need* to? Or have others been saying it *for* me?"

Bernard smiled. "We return to our subject! People say of *me* that I am a Jew, and of you that you are an *odalisque,* sent here by the Grand Turk as a spy—"

"They do!?"

"Yes. Why?"

The good thing about Bernard was that when he said something jarring he would quickly move on to something else. Eliza decided 'twere better to keep pace with him than to dwell on this matter of her and the Grand Turk. "The only thing I can think of that you and I have in common, monsieur, is a predilection for finance."

Bernard let it be seen that he was not fully satisfied with this attempt. He had a long, complicated French nose, close-set eyes, and a mouth turned up tight, like a recurved bow, at the corners. The look on his face might have been one of frustration, or intense concentration; perhaps both. He was trying to get her to see something. "Why do I wear cloth of gold? Because I am some kind of a fop? No! I dress well, but I am not a fop. I wear this to remind me of something."

"I supposed it was to remind *others* that—"

"That I am the richest man in France? Is that what you were going to say?"

"No, but it is what I was *thinking.*"

"Another rumor—like that I am a Jew. No, madame, I wear this because it used to be my trade."

"Did you say *trade*!?"

"My family were Huguenots. I was baptized in the Protestant church of Charenton. You can't see it any more, it was pulled down by a Catholic mob a few years ago. My grandfather was a painter of portraits for the Court. My father, a miniaturist and an engraver. But God did not bestow on me any artistic talent, and so I was apprenticed to a seller of cloth-of-gold."

"Did you serve out your whole apprenticeship, monsieur?"

"*Pourquoi non*, madame, for then as now, I always fulfill my contracts. My formal *métier* is *maître mercier grossiste pour draps d'or, d'argent, et de soie de Paris.*"

"I think I finally begin to understand your point, Monsieur Bernard. You are saying that you and I have in common that we do not belong."

"We make no sense!" Bernard exclaimed, throwing up both hands and raising his eyebrows in dismay, mocking a certain type of courtier. "To these people—" and he shoveled his hands across the Rue de l'Orangerie at Versailles—"we are what meteors, comets, sunspots are to astronomers: monstrous deviations, fell portents of undesired change, proof that something is wrong in a system that was supposedly framed by the hand of God."

"I have heard some in this vein, too, from Monsieur le marquis d'Ozoir—"

Bernard would not allow such a foolish sentence to be finished; he spewed air and rolled his eyes. "*Him!* What would he know of *us*? *He* is the epitome of who I mean—son of a Duke! A bastard, I'll grant you, and enterprising, in his way; yet still wholly typical of the established order."

Eliza now judged it best to stop talking, for Bernard had led her off into some wild territory—as if enlisting her, a Duchess, in some sort of insurgency. Bernard saw her discomfort, and physically drew back. The Armenian boy whispered up on slippered feet, bearing on a gaudy salver a tiny beaker of coffee clenched in a writhen silver zarf. Eliza gazed out the windows for a few moments, letting Bernard enjoy the first few sips. His guards had long since set up a perimeter defense around the Café Esphahan. But if she looked beyond that, cater-corner across the Rue de l'Orangerie, she could see deep into a vast rectangular plot embraced on three sides by a vaulted gallery-cum-retaining wall that supported the southern wing of the King's palace. This garden was open to the south so that during the winter it could gather in the feeble offerings of the sun. The King's orange trees, which lived in portable boxes of dirt, were still cowering back inside the warm gallery, for the last few nights had been clear and cold. But the garden was crowded with palm trees; and it was the sight of their blowing fronds, and not the faux-Turkish decor inside the café, that made it possible for her to phant'sy that she was sitting along some walled garden of the Topkapi Palace.

Bernard had settled down a bit. "Never fear, madame, for my father and I both converted to Catholicism after the revocation of the Edict of Nantes. Just as you have married a hereditary Duke."

"I don't really see what those two have to do with each other."

"They were, if you will, sacraments that we undertook to show that we were submitting to the established order of this country— the same order that we undermine by pursuing what you so aptly described as our predilection for finance."

"I don't know that I agree with that, monsieur."

Bernard ignored Eliza's weak protest. "Sooner or later the King will probably make me a Count or some such, and people will pretend to forget that I once served an apprenticeship. But do not be fooled. To them, you and I are as noble; as French; and as Catholic; as *him*!" and Bernard shot out one hand as if hurling a dagger. The target was a painting on the ceiling that depicted an immense, shirtless, muscle-bound, ochre-skinned *hashishin* with a red turban and a handlebar moustache raising a scimitar above his head. "And that is why they say I am a Jew; for this amounts to saying, an inexplicable monster."

"As long as it's just us inexplicable monsters here," said Eliza (as indeed it was; for most of the other patrons had bolted) "shall we—"

"Indeed, yes. Let us review the figures," said Bernard, and blinked twice. "The number of invasion troops is some twenty thousand. Each receives five *sols* per day; so that is five thousand *livres* a day. The number of sergeants is, in round numbers, a tenth of the number of troops, but they receive twice the pay; add another thousand *livres* a day. Lieutenants receive a *livre* a day, captains get two and a half; at any rate, when you add it all up, reckoning dragoons, cavalry, *et cetera*, it comes to some eight thousand a day—"

"I have made it ten thousand, to allow for other expenses," said Eliza.

"*C'est juste.* So why do you ask for half a million *livres* in London?"

"Monsieur, England is not so large as France, 'tis true; and yet it is much larger than some scraps of land in the Netherlands that have been fought over for months. Years."

"Those places you speak of in the Low Countries are fortified. England is not."

"The point is well taken, but the distance between the landing-sites in Devon and London is considerable. It took William of Orange a month and a half to cover the same interval, when *he* invaded."

"Very well, I grant you that fifty days' pay—almost two months—for this army comes to half a million *livres*. But why must every last penny of it be minted in advance, in London? Surely if the campaign progresses beyond a beach-head there will be opportunities to ship specie to the island later."

"Perhaps and perhaps not, monsieur. I only know of this one opportunity, and seek to make the most of it. You make this more complicated than it is. I have been asked to tender advice on how the troops might be paid. You and I seem to agree that half a million *livres* is a reasonable, though perhaps generous, estimate of the amount that will be required. This is not too large an amount for the normal channels of commerce. I ask for as much as I think shall be needed. If half that amount is actually coined at the Tower of London, then I shall consider the transaction to have come off passing well."

"The matter becomes complicated when the entire transaction is made to pass through Lyon," said Bernard. "It is a large bolus for the *Dépôt* to swallow. If we could instead transfer it through a *public* market where there were proper banks . . ."

"Monsieur Bernard. You tempt me. For nothing would afford me such fascination as to sit here with you all morning and afternoon drinking coffee and discoursing of the peculiarities of Lyon and the *Dépôt*. Quite possibly we might have similar views on it. But as matters stand, Lyon is, by long tradition, France's connexion to the financial system of the world, and it is through Lyon that we must send all of this money. It may be a bit quaint, a bit odd; but fortunately there are sophisticated houses there, such as the Hacklhebers, who have ready access to public markets in other cities."

"I understand, madame," said Bernard. "But the carrying capacity of the *Dépôt* is limited. France fights on more than one front. There are other demands on the credit of her treasury."

"I have seen the silver with my own eyes, Monsieur Bernard. It was stacked in the hold of Monsieur le comte de Pontchartrain's *jacht* in St.-Malo. This is merely an alternate, more prudent means of getting it to London."

"And I do not question that, madame. But during wartime, the temptation will be strong to use that silver elsewhere—to spend it twice."

"*Now* I perceive why it is that you are shunned by Court fops, monsieur. For you to suggest that Monsieur le comte de Pontchartrain would do anything of the sort is most rude."

"Ah, madame, but I said nothing of that noble man. It is not *he* who matters in this case—for, last I heard, Monsieur le comte de Pontchartrain was not the King of France."

"Then you are being even more impertinent!"

"Not at all. For the King is the King, and it is his prerogative to spend his money twice, or even three times, if that is his pleasure, and neither I nor any other Frenchman will say a word against him! It might, however, make a difference to the *Dépôt*."

"Suppose the *Dépôt* was asked to adapt to these trying new circumstances, and it was found wanting, and in consequence, France had to get a modern banking system? Would that not be better for France, and for you, monsieur?"

"For me, perhaps—as well as for you. For France, there might be grave disruptions."

"That is beyond my scope. I am like a housewife shopping for turnips in the market. If I go to my old traditional turnip-sellers and they ask too high a price for turnips of poor quality, and not enough of them, why, I shall go and buy my turnips elsewhere."

"Very well," said Bernard, "I depart for Lyon this afternoon to meet with Monsieur Castan. I might relay your challenge to the *Dépôt* and we might see if they have got enough turnips for you."

"Monsieur, what is this word *might* doing in the sentence? You do not strike me as a flirtatious man, in general."

"You have a house in St.-Malo, madame."

"Indeed, monsieur."

"It is said you are quite fond of the place—more so than La Dunette." Bernard glanced in that general direction, for La Dunette was only a couple of musket-shots up the hill from the Rue de l'Orangerie. But all he could see in that quarter was another gaudy painting of wild Turks in action.

"You would like it, too, for St.-Malo is a place where Commerce rules."

"I understand. For that is where the ships of the *Compagnie des Indes* call, or have I been misinformed?"

"*Many* ships call there; but if India is a particular interest of yours, monsieur, then that is what we shall speak of."

"How can it *not* be of interest to *us*, madame? Have you any notion of the profits made in that part of the world by the V.O.C. and the British East India Company?"

"Of course, monsieur. They are proverbial. As is the perpetual failure and reincarnation of the *Compagnie des Indes*. You need only ask Monsieur le marquis d'Ozoir—"

"The history is all too well known. I am more concerned with the future."

"Then truly you *are* a shameless flirt, Monsieur Bernard, for I can scarcely contain my curiosity any longer—what are you thinking?"

"I don't know."

"Nonsense!"

"It is quite true. All I know is that I look at the *Compagnie des Indes* and see—nothing! Nothing is happening. Something *should* be happening. It is curious."

"You have scented an opportunity."

"As have *you*, madame."

"Oh—you refer to the silver in London?"

"Now *you* flirt with *me*. Madame, it is within my power to make this happen. I may have been re-baptized as a Catholic, but this has not prevented my maintaining any number of contacts with Huguenots who elected to leave. They have gone to places like London and prospered. You know this perfectly well, for you have filled the void that was created in the *Compagnie du Nord* by their departure. You buy timber from them in Sweden and Rostock all the time. So yes. I can see to it that your silver is transferred, and I shall. But it shall not be profitable. It shall not be especially convenient. Monsieur Castan's credit with the *Dépôt* shall be over-extended for a time. I shall have to twist his arm. And I hate dealing with Lothar."

"Very well. What could I do, monsieur, to show my gratitude for your undertaking so many travails?"

"You could direct your intelligence upon the strange case of the *Compagnie des Indes* in faraway St.-Malo. *You*, I take it, have no interest in this?"

"None whatsover, monsieur; the *Compagnie du Nord* is my sole concern."

"That is well. You will supply me with your thoughts and observations, then, concerning the other?"

"It will be a joy to converse with you on the topic, monsieur."

"Very well." Bernard got to his feet. "I am off to Lyon, then. *Au revoir.*"

"Bon voyage."

And Samuel Bernard exited the Café Esphahan as abruptly as he had come in.

His gilded chair was still warm when Bonaventure Rossignol sat down in it.

"I have seen Kings travel with a smaller guard," Eliza remarked; for both she and Rossignol devoted some time now to enjoying the spectacle of the departure of Bernard's carriage, his train of lesser vehicles, his out-riders, spare horses, grooms, *et cetera* from the Rue de l'Orangerie.

"Many Kings have less to fear," Rossignol remarked.

"Oh? I did not know Monsieur Bernard had so many enemies."

"It is not that he has enemies as a King does," Rossignol corrected her, "which is to say, identifiable souls who wish him ill, and are willing and able to act on those wishes. Rather, it is that from time to time a sort of frenzy will come over certain Frenchmen, which only abates when a financier or two has been hanged from a tree-limb or set on fire."

"He was trying to warn me about such things," Eliza said, "but his squadron of mercenaries conveys it much more effectively than words."

"It is curious," said Rossignol, turning his attention to Eliza. "I know that you are married to a Duke, and share his bed, and bear his children. Yet this causes me not the least bit of jealousy! But when I see you talking to this Samuel Bernard—"

"Put it out of your head," Eliza said. "You have no idea."

"What does this mean, I have no idea? I may be a mathematician, but yet I know what passes between a man and a woman."

"Indeed; but you are not a *commerçant*, and you haven't the faintest idea what passes between the likes of me and Bernard. Don't worry. If you were a *commerçant*, I shouldn't be attracted to you—just as I'm not attracted to Bernard."

"But it looked for all the world as if you were flirting."

"As indeed we were—but the intercourse to which this flirting will lead is not sexual."

"I am perfectly confused now—you are playing with me."

"Come now, Bon-bon! Let us review matters. Out of all the men in Germany, which did I choose for a friend?"

"Leibniz."

"And what is he?"

"A mathematician."

"Holland?"

"Huygens . . . a mathematician."

"England?"

"Daniel Waterhouse. A Natural Philosopher."

"France?"

" . . ."

"Come now! When I came to Versailles for the first time, and got invited to Court soirées, and was pursued by any number of randy Dukes, to whom did I give my affections?"

"You gave them to . . . a mathematician."

"What was that mathematician's name?" asked Eliza, cupping a hand to her ear.

"It was Bonaventure Rossignol," said Bonaventure Rossignol, and flicked his black eyes to and fro to see if anyone was listening.

"Now, when I got myself into a big mess of trouble outside of St.-Diziers, who was the first to learn of it?"

"That fellow who was reading everyone's mail. Bonaventure Rossignol."

"And who came galloping to my rescue across half of France, and journeyed north with me to Nijmegen, and put me on a boat?"

"Bon—"

"Stop. The name is beautiful and distinguished. But I prefer to call him Bon-bon."

"Very well, then, it was Bon-bon."

"Who made love to me along the banks of the Meuse?"

"Étienne de Lavardac."

"Who else?"

"Bon-bon."

"And who helped me concoct a plan to get out of my terrible mess of trouble?"

"Bon-bon."

"Who helped me cover my traces, and forged documents, and lied to the King and to d'Avaux?"

"Bon-bon."

"And who is the father of my first-born?"

"I've no idea."

"Only because you avoided looking at him, when you had the opportunity. But I tell you Jean-Jacques looks very much like Bon-bon—there is no trace in him of the tainted blood of the Lavardacs. You are the father, Bon-bon."

"What is your point?"

"Only that it is absurd for you to be jealous of this Samuel Bernard. Whatever may pass between him and me in the way of business is nothing compared to the adventure that you and I had, and the son that we share."

The attention of "Bon-bon" had strayed to a painting of a fabulous, many-domed mosque that adorned a wall behind Eliza. "You remind me of things I would forget. I could have done a better job."

"Nonsense!"

"I could have exonerated you entirely from charges of spying."

"In retrospect, perhaps. But I do believe it worked out for the best."

"What . . . you married to a man you do not love, and Jean-Jacques held captive by a demented Saxon banker?"

"But that is not the end of the story, Bon-bon. We have met here today to further the story along."

"Yes. And it is an interesting choice of venue," Rossignol said, leaning far over the table and lowering his voice so much that Eliza nearly had to touch her forehead against his in order to hear him. "I have read every scrap of these people's mail for two years, you know, but never seen their faces, and certainly never sipped their coffee."

"Do you fancy it?"

"It is a cut above the usual swill, to be sure," said Rossignol, "but on its merits as a beverage, it would never be so chic if you and Madame la duchesse d'Oyonnax were not forever singing its praises."

"You see? There is nothing I would not do in the service of cryptology," said Eliza with a smile, and spread out her hands, inviting Rossignol to take in the magnificence of the Café Esphahan. "Have you learned anything recently?"

"This is not the place or the time to speak of it! But no," said Rossignol. "I have been much more preoccupied with reading *your* mail."

"Does it make for interesting reading?"

"A bit *too* interesting. To Lothar you say, 'The invasion of England will surely be called off,' while to some *financier* in Lyon you are saying, 'The invasion will happen soon and we must pay the troops!'"

"You don't know the half of it."

"It makes me worry that you are about to get in trouble again and I shall have to go back to galloping hither and yon, forging documents, and lying to important people . . . all of which I would gladly do!" he added hastily, as the beginnings of a pout had appeared on Eliza's face. "But I think it a miracle that you were forgiven, by the powers that be, for the previous go-round of spying and lying. If you do it again—"

"Your misinterpretation is total," Eliza said. "There was no forgiving, but an œconomic transaction. And I did not get off scot-free, as you seem to phant'sy, but paid a price so terrible I do not think you'll ever fathom it. To you, perhaps, it seems that I am plunging once more into a sea of intrigue from which I was absent for a couple of years—restful years for you, Bon-bon!—but to me it seems I have been submerged in it the whole time, and am only now getting my head above water where I can see and breathe again. I mean to keep clawing away until I have dragged myself out."

"You'll never be out," said Rossignol, "but if it is in your nature to claw, then claw away. Speaking of which, my back has healed since the last time—"

"I have three more engagements to-day, but perhaps I could append a fourth," said Eliza. She reached across the table and set a packet of letters in front of Rossignol. "My out-going mail," she explained. "I was going to post it, but then I thought, why not give it directly to Bon-bon?"

"I shall decrypt them while I await your fourth social engagement," said Rossignol. "Here is your incoming." And he handed Eliza a packet.

"Thank you, Bon-bon. Anything interesting?"

"Compared to most of what I have to read? Madame, you have no idea."

Daniel Waterhouse to Eliza
19 APRIL 1692

I am in receipt of your recent note urgently requesting information concerning the Mint and the men who run it. I cannot fathom why you desire to know such things, so hastily. I can assure you that I am the wrong chap. The right chap is the Marquis of Ravenscar. I have taken the liberty of forwarding your questions to him. You may be assured of his discretion. I hope that everything is well with you; for I am, as always, &c., Daniel Waterhouse.

Roger Comstock, Marquis of Ravenscar, to Eliza
20 APRIL 1692

A LETTER

To Her Grace, ELIZA, Duchess of Arcachon and (though 'tis not recognized in France) Qwghlm

Madame,

Most humbly do I set before you this Offering, and do pray that Your

Grace may deem it a satisfactory Answer to those Inquiries lately despatch'd to my wise Friend and Colleague, Dr. Daniel Waterhouse, F.R.S.

APOLOGY

Olympus' Court no fairer Visage housed
Than that of Helen. Goddesses were roused
To ENVY: which though *petty Vice* on Earth
When spent on High where all's of greater Worth
Loosed Havock down below. Fleets sailed, Gods vied,
For Helen cities fell and heroes died.
ELIZA's Fame on Rumour's wing hath come
To *Albion's* shores. French flatterers, struck dumb,
Have kept her beauty hid 'til now, it seems;
But as a light beneath a Bushel gleams
Thro' any Chink, ELIZA's Charms are out,
And putting *Goddesses* to rout.
A-tremble, Men gaze up, and shall be glad
Not to be Players in her Iliad.

MY LADY,

You who are accustom'd to that incomparable Palace of Versailles would find little in London worthy of casting your eye over, and least of all my habitation near Red Lyon Square, which is yet but a pile of loose stones and timbers. Its sole Glory, at this time, is its Architect, Dr. Daniel Waterhouse, Secretary of the Royal Society, who being a diligent man is oft to be seen in its Precincts surveying, measuring, drawing, &c. Today I chanc'd to meet Dr. Waterhouse about the Property and, upon supplying him with certain Libations, learnt from him that his letter-box had been graced by a missive from the incomparable Duchess of Arcachon and of Qwghlm, who is the subject of some debate among Persons of Quality in this Country; for while some would have it that her Wit is exceeded only by her Beauty, others would have it the other way round. I confess myself incompetent to have an opinion on the matter, for while your letter to Dr. Waterhouse leaves me confounded and dazzled by your Wit, I cannot but suppose that were I to have the honour of encountering you in Person I should be as a-maz'd by your Beauty. Setting aside, then, this Question, which I cannot answer for lack of sufficient Data (though not, I assure you, for want of Curiosity), I shall apply myself to the Question that you put to Dr. Water-house in your recent Missive, viz.: who is in charge of the Mint at the Tower of London, and is it reasonable to assume that he is a good Tory?

The answers, respectively, are Sir Thomas Neale, and yes, it were reasonable to make such an assumption—but WRONG. Reasonable, because, as you have obviously heard, our Government has fallen under the Sway of the Tories since the election of '90. Wrong because this is England, and Offices and Privileges of the Realm are not managed according to REASON but BECAUSE WE HAVE ALWAYS DONE IT THUS. Accordingly, Sir Thomas Neale, Master of the Mint, has his post, not because he is a Tory (for to the extent he holds fixed views on anything, they are Whiggish views, and to the extent he has friends, they are Whigs), but rather because James II gave him the position immediately upon his succession to the throne in February of 1685. Prior to that date, Sir Thomas had served as Groom-Porter of the Court of Charles II. The duties of the Groom-Porter are ill-defined and not susceptible of accurate translation into the language and the customs of *La France*. Nominally the Groom-Porter is in charge of the Sovereign's furniture. Since this, however, rarely changes, it does not occupy very much of his time; consequently he devotes a larger moiety of his energies to furnishings smaller, more mutable and perishable: viz. dice and cards. Whatever other personal shortcomings Sir Thomas might possess, even his most obstreperous detractors would readily agree that never were man and job so perfectly match'd as Sir Thomas Neale, and Dice-Keeper Royal.

Master of the Mint would seem to be a different sort of job entirely and so those of a *Skeptickal* turn of mind might argue, that it would seem to call for a different sort of chap. But no one seems to have offered up any such argument before James II; or if they did, perhaps his majesty did not understand it. Indeed, his appointment of Sir Thomas to run the Mint was construed by some as more evidence (as if more were wanted) tending to shew, that a certain Malady had got the better of the King's Brain. Those of us of a more charitable habit of mind, might perceive a certain kind of Sense in the appointment. For Sir Thomas had become link'd, in the riddled mind of James, with dice and cards, which were associated with Money; hence Sir Thomas was the best chap in the land to coin Money, Q.E.D.

I know Sir Thomas well, for he has been extraordinarily

keen to maintain friendly relations with me, ever since he got it in his head that I am a possible Supplier of Capital. You too, my lady, may so arrange it that you shall hear from him frequently, and even discover him loitering in front of your House several times a Week, merely by giving him some cause to phant'sy that you are in control of some bored Capital that wants an Adventure. For where some *hommes d'affaires* come into the world of Commerce from Shipping, and others from the 'Varsity, Sir Thomas came at it by way of Gambling, and not just of the penny-ante sort, but on the Royal plane. And so where another *commerçant* might employ a Ship-Voyage as his over-arching *Metaphor* for what a business-venture is, Sir Thomas sees all such Projects as Rolls of Dice. And where a Venturer of Ship frame of mind would have a care to raise profits, and reduce risk, by caulking his Ship well, hiring good seamen, keeping an eye on the weather-glass, &c., Sir Thomas's notion of a well-structured Enterprise is one in which the dice are loaded, the cards marked, and the deck stacked, to the utmost extent possible. Indeed, this is why I have not ejected him from my Circle of Friends; for while I'd never risk any of my Capital on one of his Ventures, I very much enjoy having them explained to me, much as I might derive pleasurable diversion from reading a vivid *roman* about some Picaroons.

I might add in passing that James II's equation of Gambling with the Making of Money is not the syphilitic madness that it first seemed. For during the period of forced Idleness that has succeeded the disastrous Election of '90, I have had leisure to consider diverse Schemes to raise money for the Government, which feels a want of Specie chargeable to the War. We contemplate a great national Lottery. To explain the scheme at any more length than that would be tedious, to point out Sir Thomas's aptness for such a Project were to insult your intelligence. We meet from time to time with Mathematickal *Savants* of the Royal Society to explore its statistical penetralia.

In conclusion, I say to you that if you desire to have silver minted here as part of some Adventure (whose details I do not need or wish to know); and if the Adventure enures to the advantage of the Tories (which I hope it does not; but this is none of my business); and if you have phant'sied that our Tory government has some power over the Mint, so that the Mint's interests, and yours, are naturally aligned; then you are mistaken. For the Mint is, I am happy to report, firmly in the grip of a Whig. This need not, however, militate against your Project. For if I read correctly between the lines of your letter, all you really need is a cooperative, not to say compliant, friend in the Mint; and you may make Thomas Neale just that, by meditating upon the Character I have given him in this Missive, and devising your approach to the man accordingly.

I pray that the question you sent to Dr. Waterhouse has been addressed, to your satisfaction, by the foregoing. If I have failed to satisfy, or (may God forbid it) given offense, I beg you to write back telling me as much, so that I may bend every effort to make it good. For it is my very great honour and pleasure to be your humble and obedient servant,

RAVENSCAR

P.S. If your intention is to mint French silver into English coin to pay the French and Irish troops that have been preparing to invade England from around Cherbourg in the third week of May, then I congratulate you on your ingenuity. Delivery of the coins from Mint to Front shall pose a not inconsiderable logistical challenge, and so I make you the following offer: If Admiral Tourville's invasion-fleet makes it across the Channel without being sunk by the Royal Navy, and if the Papist legion establishes a beachhead on English soil without being destroyed by the Army or torn to bits by an enraged Mobb of English rurals, then I shall personally carry every single one of your coins from the Tower of London to the front in my arse-hole, and Deposit them in some Place where they may be easily Picked Up.

Leibniz to Eliza
21 APRIL 1692

Eliza,

You asked—some might say, *commanded*—me to be on the alert for any news out of Leipzig touching on Lothar von Hacklheber in general, and Jean-Jacques—or, as they call him, Johann—in particular. This is not made any easier by the fact that Lothar knows, in a vague way, that I am linked to you. Moreover, I must confess that I am torn between a desire to give you what you have asked me for, and a reluctance to pass on information that is sure to tear open this wound that Lothar inflicted on you a year and a half ago.

So I have avoided going to Leipzig. But yesterday Leipzig came to me, here in Hanover. As you must have heard, my patrons, Ernst August and Sophie, who until recently have been titled the Duke and Duchess of Hanover, have for some time been campaigning in Vienna to have their dignity raised to that of Elector and Electress. France has been opposed to it, and held them in check by diverse political counter-maneuvers whose particulars would fill book after tedious book. To make a long story short, the war, and in particular the recent developments along the Savoy front, has put the Emperor into a state of mind where he will do anything to spite Louis XIV; accordingly, Ernst August and Sophie are, as of a couple of weeks ago, the Elector and the Electress of Hanover, an eyelash below a King and Queen as these things are measured. This has set into motion a whole train of ramifications and realignments, &c., &c., that will give the courtiers along the Leine Strasse things to natter about for years to come. Some of the ramifications are, of course, financial, and so bankers from all over the Empire have come to call on Sophie and Ernst August, to offer their felicitations and to see if they might be of service in the new Electorate. It is all about as interesting to me, as *physics* is to *them;* except that one of these visitors has been Lothar. Sophie and Ernst August invited him to dine with them at the Palace of Herrenhausen outside of Hanover. In filling out the guest list, the chamberlain added my name, which must have seemed logical, as I am a Leipziger and my family has certain ties to that of von Hacklheber. They had no way of knowing about my link to you or the awkwardness that would arise from the matter of Jean-Jacques. Indeed, Sophie is so civilized, and exerts such a civilizing influence on Ernst August, that it would never enter their minds that one of their dinner-guests could be guilty of such an atrocity as baby-snatching. So, quite innocently, they invited me and Lothar to the same dinner, and seated us across the table from each other!

I cannot describe what it is like to sit across from such a man through a long dinner, without spoiling your appetite for a whole fortnight. I'll limit my report to the conversation.

Much of this concerned the war, and was more or less interesting; but you must hear of nothing else there, and so I shall move on to what concerns you personally.

Lothar, you must remember, was there for one purpose, which was to impress Sophie and Ernst August with his intelligence, his foresight, and his many connexions in the world; and so, at a certain point in the evening, after a certain amount of drink had been taken, he hazarded a prediction about the spring campaign. For how better for a banker to impress a potential client than to predict the future, and get it right?

France, he predicted, would soon suffer a humiliation in the northwest—he used the word *Fehlschlag*, which is difficult to translate but means a failed attempt, a miscarriage. He implied clearly that it would take place on or near English soil.

Of course Sophie is not easily impressed by such theatrics. She said, "If you are so sure of this prediction, Baron von Hacklheber, why are you not putting your money where your mouth is? For your mouth may be large, but we all know that your purse is larger yet." This fetched a laugh, even from Lothar. When the commotion had died down, he announced that he would place just such a bet very soon—i.e., that he intended to so dispose his bank's resources that he would gain money if the *Fehlschlag* took place as he had foretold. And to bolster his claim further, he vowed that he would donate a certain sum to any charity Sophie named, and that the money would come out of his profits on the bet, if it paid off, but out of his own purse if he were proved wrong.

Asked by Sophie how he could be so certain about this, he turned an eye in my direction and said that he knew persons in France, of considerable wealth and power, who had in the past been insolent to him, but more recently had been brought to heel—he actually employed the term *bei Fuß!* which is a dog-training command. You see now, Eliza, why I am so reluctant to act as a conduit for this sort of information. Even those at the table who did not know who Lothar was talking about found it a little disgusting.

That is my news, just as you requested it. Frankly, I pine for the days when my letters to you were filled with Natural Philosophy. Perhaps we can resume such discussions in happier times to come. Until then, I have the honor to be, &c.,

Leibniz

P.S. You also requested news of your friend Princess Eleanor and her daughter Princess Caroline. I have met them in Berlin; little Caroline is just as charming as you claimed, and just as intelligent. Eleanor has been betrothed to the Elector of Saxony, who is an ogre straight out of a færy-tale, and who has a mistress reputed to be even worse. The best place to send letters to them will probably be the Electoral court at Dresden.

Eliza to Samuel de la Vega
5 MAY 1692

Here is how peculiar France is: They are calling people Jews who have no trace of Jewishness. It is a long story, of which I'll tell you more if we ever see each other again. It put me in mind of Amsterdam, where there are to be found Jews who really are Jews—a much more logical arrangement!

That is not my only reason for writing to you. For some years I have made little effort to follow the commodities markets in Amsterdam, as, from the remove of Versailles, it it impossible to do this competently. Lately, however, I have taken a position in silver. The details are unimportant. Suffice it to say that I must needs be alert to any moves in the silver market that may occur in the first half of June. My sources of information are not what they once were, and so I am reduced to the estate of a little girl with her nose pressed against the glass; I must judge the trends in the market by observing the behavior of larger and better-informed players.

Though the House of Hacklheber is not the largest, it is probably the best-informed concern in metals. Accordingly, I have resolved to take my cues from them. It would be of great significance to me if the Hacklhebers were suddenly to remove a large quantity (a few tons) of silver from their Amsterdam warehouse. You know where it is. If my guess is correct, the bullion would be transferred directly to a ship on the Ijssel-meer.

Can you spare someone to keep an eye on the Hacklhe-bers' warehouse? As time draws nearer, I shall supply more precise information as to the exact time at which the transfer might occur. The information that I shall require is as follows: the name of the ship carrying the bullion and a complete description of her sail plan, &c., so that she may be identified from a distance, as well as the date and time of her departure from Amsterdam.

In coming weeks, I'll be moving around quite a bit, and so there is little point in your trying to guess my whereabouts. Rather, you should send the particulars to me in care of my good friend and confidant, Captain Jean Bart, of Dunkerque. Captain Bart is a trustworthy fellow; there is no need (and there shall be no time!) to encrypt the message. You know more than I about getting messages out fast, so I'll hold my tongue where that is concerned; but I am guessing you'll want to send riders out from Amsterdam to Scheveningen and there transfer the message to a fast boat, Dunkerque-bound. There should be plenty of time to arrange this; but if you want help setting up the boat, just inform Captain Bart.

I think I have given you enough information now that you shall be able to place bets of your own in the silver market, which are likely to profit you; but if, when all is said and done, you have spent more than you have gained, forward your complaints to me in St.-Malo and they'll not fall on deaf ears.

Eliza

Eliza to the Marquis of Ravenscar
15 MAY 1692

Your Grace's recent letter to me was so courteous as to put the lucubrations of these French flatterers to shame. I must warn you, however, that en route it must have fallen into the hands of some mischievous boy, who added a very rude post-script.

It was most considerate of you to answer all of my silly questions about the Mint. As you must have surmised, I do have in mind taking part in a transaction that will only profit me if the price of silver should happen to rise late in the month of May. I only hope and pray that all of the silver in London is not bought up in the meantime! I tell you this in confidence, my lord, not wishing that you, who have been so forward in assisting me, should suffer any reverses in consequence of what I am about to do. Know, then, that to be in possession of a large quantity of silver, in London, late in the month of May, would be no bad thing. But do you make your purchases discreetly, lest you touch off a buying panic that would drive up the price to absurd heights. For if people see that the Marquis of Ravenscar is selling gold to buy silver, they will assume he is privy to something, and flock to Threadneedle Street to follow his example. While you might admittedly profit from such a speculative bubble by selling into it at the peak (by no means later than the middle of June), it would cause any amount of disturbance and trouble to the current Government; which I am certain you, a good English patriot, should prefer to avoid, even if you are a Whig and that government be run by the Tories.

Eliza

Eliza to Samuel Bernard
18 MAY 1692

Monsieur Bernard,

I am en route from St.-Malo to Cherbourg aboard the *jacht* of my husband. In Cherbourg I'll post this on to Le Havre; I pray it reaches you soon in Paris. I shall tarry in Cherbourg until the invasion is launched.

In St.-Malo this morning I received your despatch of the 12th instant stating that you have the Bills of Exchange in your pocket and want only instructions as to whom they should be endorsed.

This amounts to asking me for the names of the agents who shall be sent across the Channel to present the Bills for payment in London. I regret to inform you that the names of these agents are not known to me yet (though I have some ideas as to who they shall be). Even if they were, I should be chary of sending them to you in a letter during wartime; for the enemy has spies everywhere, and consider what disaster would ensue if our agents' names became known. For most of them are Englishmen secretly loyal to James Stuart—and if they were caught in England with these Bills in their pockets, they should suffer the penalty for High Treason, which is to be half-hanged, drawn, and quartered at Tyburn Cross.

A safer expedient would be for you to endorse the bills to a trusted intermediary who is resident here at Cherbourg, and who shall not be setting foot outside of France until after the invasion. That intermediary can then hold the Bills until the last moment and then endorse them to the several agents just before they cross the Channel. In this way the identity of the agents shall never be exposed to any risk of discovery.

To serve in this role of intermediary, several candidates come to mind, for Cherbourg is crowded just now with notable personages. But all of them are busy and distracted. I, meanwhile, have nothing to do save gaze out the window of my cabin in the sterncastle of this *jacht*, and watch the preparations. As odd as it might sound, I may be the safest person to choose for this rôle, since there is obviously no likelihood whatever of my crossing the Channel and falling into the hands of enemy interrogators; this alone should be a great comfort to the agents whose names I shall write across the backs of those bills before they set forth on their perilous missions. So, unless you object very strongly, simply endorse the Bills to me and send them to me at Cherbourg.

I don't know how Lothar is sending the *avisas* to London, but presumably his channels are swifter than ours, and his payers in England will be ready and waiting for our payees whensoever they arrive.

Eliza

P.S. I look forward to continuing our conversation about St.-Malo. The merchants of the *Compagnie des Indes,* who on a normal day swagger about that town as if they owned it, have been displaced, and quite out-classed, by the captains and admirals of our invasion fleet. As a result they are almost pathetically eager to talk to anyone about anything—including the state of our commerce with India. My head is full of more information than it can hold, and all of it useless to me. After the invasion, we must meet again at the Café Esphahan, and I'll tell you all that I know.

Samuel Bernard to Eliza
23 MAY 1692

Madame la comtesse,

Five Bills should be enclosed, each in the amount of one hundred thousand *livres tournoises* and each endorsed, for the time being, to you. These are drawn ultimately on the credit of the French treasury as personified by M. le comte de Pontchartrain. If you see him, perhaps you could think of a polite way of reminding him that the chain of credit passes through yours truly; my friend Monsieur Castan; and diverse members of the *Dépôt* of Lyon.

It is a good thing that I went to Lyon, for in the end it was necessary for me to involve myself in the negotiations with Lothar (he was obviously present in Lyon, but we were never in the same room together; his factor Gerhard Mann mediated all of our discussions).

Monsieur Castan is cunning and assiduous, but when presented with something outside his scope he does not respond well, and is apt to become flustered and then irritable. This happened very early in our talks with the House of Hacklheber. It took some time for me to understand why: Lothar believes that the invasion will never actually happen; or that if it does, it will be snuffed out within a few hours. In consequence, our negotiations over the terms of these Bills were strangely duplicitous. The nominal purpose was to pay troops in England, and so we had to settle terms in such a way that we—meaning France—could get silver coin in England, while allowing Lothar to realize some profit. In that sense I got what we wanted, viz. wholly legitimate, negotiable Bills which you now have in your hand. But Lothar's true purpose, as I eventually came to understand, was to reap a large windfall at very little risk by expressing a willingness to forward silver for an invasion that would never materialize. In effect he was selling us insurance against the contingency that our invasion fails to fail. It was this subtext that M. Castan had not understood, with the result that he was bewildered by what he saw as erratic demands made by the House of Hacklheber.

At the beginning we proposed that the five Bills' dates of expiry should be at one-week intervals. We envisioned, in other words, that, beginning shortly after the invasion, our agents would present Bills in London approximately once a week for a period of five weeks, as our army fought its way across southern England toward London. We presumed that Lothar would prefer it thus, as it would spread out the transaction over a long period of time and simplify the logistics of buying or shipping the silver and having it minted. This was when we were still naïve enough to believe that Lothar construed payment of the bills as an *opportunity*. Later, as I have mentioned, I perceived that Lothar actually sees the possible consummation of this transaction as a *risk* to be hemmed in and mitigated as strictly as possible. Accordingly, he hated the idea of staggering the Bills' dates, because it would mean committing himself to be at risk (risk of having to pay silver to some unknown person in London) over a period of almost two months. For the first Bill would become payable, in theory, about two weeks following the date that Lothar wrote it in Lyon, i.e., in mid-May. The last one would remain payable in theory as late as the middle of July. It was in his interest to limit our freedom in the matter by having the Bills all payable only during a narrow interval of time shortly after the scheduled date of the invasion. That way, if the invasion came off as scheduled and a stable beach-head were established on English soil, we should have only a few days in which to present the Bill in London and demand that *all* of the silver be supplied *at once*. The deal became, in other words, an all-or-nothing proposition to be resolved, one way or the other, quite early. Indeed, Lothar wanted to issue one single Bill for half a million *livres* rather than breaking it up into several smaller ones—this struck me as too risky and I persuaded him to relent. So there are five separate Bills. Four of them bear the same dates—they are 45-day Bills—and the other is a 30-day Bill. All of them were written by Lothar himself; for only he has authority to write Bills of this size. He wrote them in Lyon on the 6th day of May, the Year of our Lord 1692. Postal time from Lyon to London is generally reckoned at about two weeks, so they could be presented there as early as 20 May (by the French calendar). The 30-day Bill is payable on 5 June, the other four on 20 June.

It is generally to the advantage of the payer (Lothar's factor in London) if the payee (whomever you endorse these Bills to) presents the Bills well in advance of the expiration of their usance, as this will give the payer more time to make arrangements to deliver the specie. That is particularly true in this case, when the acceptance of these Bills in London may trigger purchase or shipment of silver by Lothar.

We have have no reason to present these Bills for payment in London until a successful invasion has occurred, which ought to be no later than the last day of May. The 30-day Bill would then come due almost immediately, which suggests that Lothar will have to have 100,000 *livres'* worth of silver on hand in London. Thus we may be assured of paying our troops the first installment of their salary shortly after their arrival on English soil. The other four bills, as I have mentioned, are not payable until 20 June; and obviously it will be in our best interests to present these at the same time as the 30-day Bill so that Lothar will have two or three weeks' time in which to get an additional 400,000 *livres'* worth of silver to the Tower of London to be minted.

That amount, in British coin, is some 20,000 pounds sterling, which represents two days' produce for the Mint at the Tower; so Lothar's factor will have to deliver some three tons of bullion to the Tower mint no later than the 17th of June. This will present something of a challenge even to a man of Lothar's resources, and so he has been careful to insert a proviso on the four 45-day bills stating that they must be presented to the House of the Golden Mercury, Change Alley, London, no later than fifteen days before the date of expiry, i.e., the stroke of midnight, 5 June.

I remind you that the English use a calendar that long ago was abandoned by the rest of the civilized world. It is ten days behind ours, and falling further behind with each tick of the clock. All of the dates I have mentioned in this letter are in the modern (French) system of reckoning; you must subtract ten days to get their English equivalents.

In all other respects this transaction is wholly normal and self-explanatory and should present no particular difficulties for you or your agents.

It has been my honor and privilege to be of service to France in this matter. I look forward to renewing our acquaintance at the Café Esphahan after the tumult of invasion has subsided.

Your humble &c.

Samuel Bernard

Cabin of Météore, *off Cherbourg, France*
2 JUNE 1692

FOR THREE DAYS *Météore* had been swinging about her anchor in a languid circle like the shadow on a sundial, driven by the comings and goings of the tides. Eliza lived in a great cabin at the stern. Had this been a warship or a merchantman, this would have been the private domain of the captain. One of its walls consisted of an arc of windows, as broad as the whole ship, staring abaft. When Eliza's view through those windows consisted of the town of Cherbourg, it meant that the tide was flooding in from the Channel, pushing *Météore* east-southeast at the end of her cable. When the tide ebbed, then, and *Météore* swung round the other way, she ought to have enjoyed a view out to sea. Instead, for three days she had seen nothing but fog: a murk into which all her carefully laid plans had been slowly dissolving. Very occasionally, loud booming noises would come out of it as gunners on the lost ships would take aim and fire at dark patches that were making suspicious noises. But for the most part it was a source of cacophonous music: sailors blowing trumpets and whistles, beating drums, and calling out in English, Dutch, or French and rattling chains as they raised or lowered anchors, depending on whether they judged it less hazardous to drift with the tide or stay in one place.

The two fleets—to the west, forty-five French ships under Admiral de Tourville, and to the east, ninety-nine Dutch and English ships under Admiral Russell—had collided in plain view of Cherbourg on the 29th, and joined battle. Tourville had driven hard into the center of Russell's line, so careless of the risk of being flanked that he had flanked himself. Standing on *Météore*'s maintop watching the battle through a perspective-glass, Eliza had almost phant'sied she could read Tourville's mind: He believed that the great ships in Russell's center were under command of Jacobites who would strike their colors and run up Stuart flags when he bore in close. Instead of which they had opened fire, and it had developed into a full engagement.

On behalf of Jean Bart, Eliza had of late campaigned in the *salons* of Versailles to persuade young courtiers that the navy was as gallant as the army. Few had taken the bait. For one glorious hour in the Channel off Cherbourg, a battle had played out that, if only Versailles could have seen it, would have left the army denuded of talent for years to come. Never again would Eliza have had to use words to convey the glamour of naval combat, for it was all there plainly to be seen. The flagship of Admiral Tourville was *Soleil Royal*, new, with a hundred guns; as fine a ship as any afloat, for French shipwrights had caught up with and even surpassed the Dutch in recent years. Admiral Russell's flagship was *Britannia*, also with a hundred guns. These two vessels went after each other like fighting cocks. There was no standing off to watch the battle from a remove, no tedious maneuver and counter-maneuver of the line of battle. The worst of the fighting was not delegated to lesser ships and lower ranks. Like two medieval kings jousting in the lists, *Soleil Royal* and *Britannia* went at each other full-bore, each giving as good as it got. Before long they had crippled each other. Only then did Admiral Tourville seem to comprehend that none of the English ships would be coming over to his side—which meant he was outnumbered by more than two to one. New signals went up on the half-ruined *Soleil Royal.* The French fleet suspended the attack and drew off in good order. They had engaged a force double their size, rendered the opposing flagship useless, and stood down, all without losing a single vessel. More importantly to Eliza, the twenty thousand French and Irish soldiers camped outside of Cherbourg—mostly around La Hougue, ten or fifteen miles away—were still safe on terra firma. James Stuart, who had been King of England, and phant'sied he still was, had come out from his pretend Court at St.-Germain to head up the invasion; presumably he had watched this battle from some high place nearby. He had just suffered one more rude shock in a life that had been full of them: Not a single one of the British ships—*his* ships—had shown the slightest inclination to take his part in the dispute. It had to be obvious, even to him, that there would be no invasion.

Eliza would never have been so fatuous as to have said that the day had gone perfectly. For aboard those ships scuttling about on the water were men, and every bloom of powder-smoke meant balls of metal flying through the air and sometimes carrying away legs, or lives. But not a single ship had gone down; it was no longer possible to take seriously the possibility of an invasion; and Eliza's plan was ticking along like a watch.

Then the wind had died, and the brassy haze that had lain on the water for most of that day had congealed into fog. It had come down like a grey velvet curtain terminating the first act of an opera, which was well enough; except that then it had got stuck, and there had been no second, third, fourth, or fifth Acts; only endless, sporadic noises off as the fleets had drifted to and fro, firing at phantoms. The rest of the 29th, fog; the 30th, fog; the 31st, fog; the 1st of June, fog! From time to time some intrepid sailors would reach shore in a long-boat and grope their way along the coast until they found Cherbourg, and they would bring news. In this way they learned, for example, that some French ships (anchored) and some English ones (drifting) had become tangled together in the murk on the second day, and had at each other with cutlasses until the tide had drawn them apart. But really very little happened. On the first day Eliza had wished that all of Versailles could have witnessed the duel of the flagships; every hour since then, she had thanked Providence that no courtiers were anywhere nearby to see this travesty; or (what would was worse) to *not* see it. She did not envy Pontchartrain and Étienne, who would have to approach the King soon and request more money for the navy. She could not guess what the King might *say,* for he was unfailingly civil;

but she knew what he would be *thinking: Why should I scrape my Treasury floor to build wooden tubs so that men may bump into one another in fog?*

She had all but given up hope for her plan when the sun had gone down behind the fog last night. "If I see the sun rise tomorrow morning," she had said, "then perhaps there is a way; if not, the work of the last two months is wasted, and I shall begin all over again."

At first light today she had gazed into the eastern sky half hoping to see nothing but a cliff of fog, for then her plan would have been unequivocally dead, which would have been altogether simpler and easier. Instead she had seen the disk of the sun, as crisp, and about as bright, as a copper coin resting on a bed of ashes.

She closed her eyes; invoked the Devil and the Heavenly Father in the same sentence, in case either of them was listening; and closed the shutters on three of the cabin windows, while leaving the others open. As *Météore* swung round on the morning tide, and exposed her gilded backside to the town, this signal would become visible to those who had been watching for it.

She began to pack some goods into a bag: first, five Bills of Exchange, which she wrapped up in a wallet of skins, oiled to baffle moisture. Then a rolled blanket. Scarves. A comb and some pins, clips, and ribbons for suppressing her hair. Some silver coins, mostly Pieces of Eight chopped into wedge-shaped bits, certain to astonish the English.

The rooves of Cherbourg were glowing, seemingly not with the reflected light of the sun, but rather from within, like hot irons pulled from the forge. A boom sounded from far off, then another, then a ripple of them.

Then someone knocked on her door and her skeleton practically jumped free of her skin; for she phant'sied somehow it was a handful of wayward grapeshot striking *Météore*. She dropped her bag on the floor and kicked it under her bed, then went to the door and unlatched it. It was Brigitte, her lady-in-waiting.

"It is Monsieur d'Ascot to call on you, my lady."

"Bit early."

"Nevertheless, he is here."

"A few minutes while I make myself presentable."

"Shall I help you?"

"No, for I am not really going to make myself presentable. I make him wait because I can, and because it is expected, and because he deserves to be punished for coming so early."

"PARDON ME, MADAME, for having disturbed your morning," said William, Viscount Ascot, in French that sounded as if he'd practiced it while he'd been waiting. Eliza thought of asking him to speak English; but he'd probably take it as an insult. "I was asked to keep you apprised of any news concerning the invasion."

This meant several things. First of all, in spite of the fact that James Stuart had showed up, there must be someone competent still in charge and making information wash up and down the chain of command. Second, this man, Ascot, must be one of the agents who were supposed to carry the Bills of Exchange to London. Third, nothing was going to happen; for if Ascot and the other four agents were going to do it today, all five would have showed up at dawn, and they'd already be fanning out across the Channel in separate boats, each with a Bill of Exchange in his breast pocket.

"Time is drawing very short," Eliza remarked. "The Bills must be presented in London three days from now. They must be sent on their way this morning, or else I might as well tear them up."

"Yes, madame," said Ascot. "The King and Council are aware of it." He meant James Stuart and his claque. As if to emphasize this, he gazed out the window into Cherbourg. Somewhere in the town, on some church-steeple, there must be signalmen poised to raise flags as messages came in from the headquarters at La Hougue. "The fog is lifting!" he exclaimed. "When I was strolling on the upperdeck just now, madame, I was able to see one or two miles out into the Channel."

"And what did you observe, monsieur?"

"Boats coming in, madame."

"Under sail or—"

"No, for the wind is only just coming up. They are longboats, with sailors pulling lustily at the oars. Some of them are towing a damaged ship—a big one."

"Do you think it might be the *Soleil Royal?*"

"Quite possibly, madame. Or"—Ascot smiled—"perhaps what is left of *Britannia.*"

This made Eliza dislike Ascot somehow; for he was after all an Englishman. He was straining visibly to say things he guessed she would like to hear; and his guesses were not very interesting. She was silent for a moment, out of sheer hopelessness. Into that silence Ascot put the words "On those longboats will be information, madame; the information that the King of England shall require to make his decision."

Eliza nodded as if she accepted this; but what she was thinking was, first, *How could even a syphilitic be so insane as to phant'sy that the invasion might still happen* and, second, *If he doesn't cancel it soon I shall have a grave problem on my hands.* She glanced involuntarily at the cabin windows, and the three closed shutters. They'd been visible from Cherbourg for at least half an hour now. Things were in motion that she could no longer control.

For a minute or two it had been possible to hear shouting abovedecks, which aboard ship was a wholly usual thing; more so when longboats were coming in from the Channel bearing news. Eliza had paid no attention to it. Now, though, they heard a thunking splash. A man, or something as big as a man, going overboard.

"Madame, I beg your leave to investigate—" began Ascot.

"Go, go!" said Eliza in English; which startled Ascot so much that he reverted to it as he opened the cabin door.

"I can't imagine what this is all about—what on earth—"

Eliza followed him out the hatch into a dark and somewhat cluttered space sheltered beneath the poop deck. But in a few strides they had emerged onto the open upperdeck of *Météore*. From here they enjoyed a clear view forward, which meant, out of the harbor and into the waters of the Channel. As Ascot had mentioned, many longboats were coming in. *Too* many, to Eliza's suspicious eye; for how many were really needed, to carry a few bits of news? Bright patches shone out here and there in the fog on the Channel: sunlight illuminating squares of canvas that had been strung up to catch the freshening breeze.

As Ascot had mentioned, *one* ship—a big one—was a good deal closer. It was not so much being towed by longboats as being washed into the harbor by the tide. It had somehow caught a sunbeam that had pierced a loop-hole in the fog. Or so Eliza thought when she first caught sight of it out the corner of her eye. When she looked at it full on, though, she realized it was making its own light. It was burning. It was, or had been, *Soleil Royal.*

Her attention was diverted by another *thunk-splash,* then another. It could no longer be denied that men were jumping off the ship.

Several of the sailors on the upperdeck were men she had never laid eyes on before. And to judge from the curious way they were gazing about, they were new to *Météore.*

Just ahead of them a man vaulted over the upperdeck railing *on to* the ship. This was *not* supposed to happen. There was nothing *out there*—it was like a stranger jumping into a second-storey window.

"I say!" exclaimed Ascot, still stuck in English. "I *do* say!"

The newcomer turned to face Ascot. His answer was as follows: "Fucking whoreson Jacobite traitor!" He was raising one arm as he delivered this remark, and punctuated the sentence by turning Ascot's head into a pink spout. The thing in his hand was a blunderbuss.

Eliza went back into the dark space beneath the poop deck and began pulling doors open. The doors led to cabins where Brigitte, Nicole, and a maidservant were lodged. "Into my cabin *now*, no questions!"

She got them all into the big cabin: four women in all. Brigitte was of a mind to heave furniture against the door. But that did not work as well here as it would have ashore, since the significant furniture was bolted down. Some trunks, a chair, and a mattress were all that they could shift for in the way of a barricade. Eliza urged them all to bend their efforts to this task, even though she knew it was absurd. A glance out the windows told her that *Météore* was moving. The English had cut her anchor cable, made her fast to a longboat or two, and were towing her out into the Channel. Better for them to attend to barricade-making than to think too hard about what this portended.

A most unsettling noise radiated through the air all round, and made their breakfasts quiver in their stomachs. Eliza went to a window and saw one of Cherbourg's shore-batteries obnubilated by powder-smoke. The artillerymen had opened fire; she guessed they were hoping to sink *Soleil Royal* before she drifted into the anchorage and set fire to other ships, or exploded. She explained as much to her companions. Fortunately none of them was swift enough to ask how long it might be before the same batteries opened up on *Météore*.

They had been ignored, for a time, by those who had taken the ship—which made perfect sense once Eliza understood that their intention was to take the entire vessel. But now that *Météore* was under way, albeit slowly, English marines had begun to pound desultorily on the door of the cabin. Hammers and prybars were mined from tool-lockers. Splinters began to fly out of *the wall*—rather than waste effort on the barricaded door, they were simply smashing their way through a bulkhead.

Such was the noise that Eliza might almost have overlooked the sudden arrival of the immense one-armed man in her cabin. *Almost;* for he entered through a window, swinging in on the end of a rope, and a chunk of glass hit her in the ear. And the maidservant must have seen him hurtling toward the glass, for she began screaming an instant before the implosion, and kept it up for a few moments after; long enough for the intruder to catch her about the waist by his one proper arm, pick her up, and throw her out of the ship. In the end, the scream was terminated only by her impact with the water. A few seconds later it resumed, sounding a bit gurgly. The large man had big pale blue eyes and seemed distracted; so much to take in, so many things to do. He looked around the cabin, making a quick count of the number of women who had not yet been thrown out (three). He turned and looked back at the ruined window. It was partly blocked by a skein of crazed glass, shredded wood, and caulking, which had complicated the defenestration of the maidservant. The man shrugged and one of his arms tripled in length. For it had been severed below the elbow and replaced with a three-part flail, segments made of some sort of dark, heavy-looking wood, bound and capped with iron, and joined one to the next by short segments of chain. He turned toward the window, judged the distance, and went into a curious shrugging and shivering movement that propagated down the length of the flail and sent its distal segment ripping through what was left of the window-frame like chainshot launched from a cannon. That and a few kicks sufficed to make a clean rectangular aperture through which he presently hurled a screaming Nicole.

Before he could pursue this wench-flinging project any further, he was distracted by the rude irruption into the cabin of a man's arm. The English boarders had made a hole, and one of them was reaching in to see what he might grab. At the top of his list was the brass bolt holding the cabin door closed.

The ramshackle and skeletal arm of the flail rattled across the cabin, a strangely unfolding train of dire consequences, and struck the new intruder round about the elbow with a splintery sort of noise. The arm was withdrawn, leaving a dark cavity through which the one-armed man flung a dagger that had appeared in his hand from nowhere. "Shoot him!" someone screamed, from the other side of the bulkhead; but Brigitte had the presence of mind to topple Eliza's mattress—which had been propped against the cabin door—so that it obscured the rift in the bulkhead. The men on the other side could reach through the hole and thrust it away, but it only flopped back again; which, if Eliza had had more time for reflection, she might have taken as some sort of lesson in how soft defenses could be more effective than hard ones.

Eliza had gone to the missing window. Below was a two-oared skiff. A line ran from it straight up to a grapple snared in the rigging of *Météore*'s mizzen-mast, above; this was how the one-armed man had gotten aboard, though, being one-armed, it seemed he had had to make use of some ingenious block-and-tackle arrangement, much too complicated for Eliza to work out under these circumstances.

The two women who had been flung out earlier were bobbing like lilies on the water, for their skirts had inflated as they had dropped. Eventually they would become waterlogged and sink, but they had both got hold of the little boat's gunwale and seemed fine for now. Which was the very least that Eliza looked for, from her personal staff. Indeed she made a mental note to ask this question of all prospective employees she interviewed in future: You are on your mistress's *jacht* preparing for her *petit levée* when the vessel is taken by English marines and towed out to sea under fire from shore batteries. Barricaded in a cabin, waiting for a fate worse than death, you are picked up and hurled into the sea by a mysterious one-armed giant who has swung into a window on a rope. Do you (a) struggle bootlessly until you sink and drown, (b) scream until someone rescues you, or (c) dog-paddle to the nearest floating object and wait calmly for your mistress to resolve the difficulty?

Eliza had suspected very early that the one-armed man might be some sort of a godsend, and was now convinced of it. She hitched up her skirt, snaked a leg under her bed, caught her bag-handle on the point of her slipper, and jerked it out. Turning to the open window, she paused for a few moments to time her breathing, and the rolling of the seas; then she tossed out the bag, and it landed square in the middle of the rowboat. Then she turned around. Flail-arm, it seemed, had fastened his gaze upon Brigitte with a look that seemed to say, "I mean to throw *you* out next, mademoiselle," and she had declined the honor. Now he was trying to get one arm about her waist (a factitious narrowing of Brigitte's midsection, owed to laces and whalebones). Few men were big, strong, and reckless enough to pick up Brigitte and toss her, when she was not of a mind to be. This fellow *had been*, prior to the loss of his arm. As matters stood, they were evenly matched, unless he elected to beat her senseless with the terrible flail first. And this he was not of a mind to do; though he was plainly enough tempted, Eliza thought she could see a tenderness about his eyes. And so a dire, ungainly, loud struggle, destructive of property and of the dignity of the participants, ranged all across the cabin.

"Brigitte!" Eliza called, at a moment when the one-armed man had tripped over his flail and was slow getting up. Brigitte raised her hot gaze from the intruder and looked up to see Eliza framed in the window. "You may stay and flirt with him all you want, or take him to bed for all I care! But I am departing and shall await you below." And then she vanished from Brigitte's sight.

In spite of herself she let out a yell just before she hit the water. Then she was speechless for a moment, it was so cold; but before more than a few moments had passed, she began paddling toward the wee boat, as best she could. She did this partly out of a thought to the Interview Question, and partly out of fear that Brigitte and

Monsieur Flail-arm might hurtle down atop her at any moment. Heavy splashes behind her confirmed that she'd made the correct choice.

To get four sopping *femmes* aboard so small a boat was no simple thing. Flail-arm, as soon as he'd gone into the water, had prestidigitated another sharp object and severed the line linking the rowboat to *Météore,* and the gap between them had begun to widen. Eliza glanced up at her stolen *jacht* only once. She saw English marines at the poop-deck rail, and English marines in the windows of her cabin (for they had finally got past Brigitte's improvisations). One of them had the bad manners to aim a pistol down at Flail-arm. But just then a boom sounded from not far away, and something whined over their heads and ripped two pounds of oak out of the railing. The marines jumped back, and some flung themselves to the deck. Eliza followed Flail-arm's startled gaze across the water and spied a boat coming on rapidly, under full sail.

Eliza was no great aficionado of ship-types, and made a practice of quitting any conversation in which the men drifted off into, and got stuck on, ship-prattle. But at a glance she guessed this one was eighty feet long. It had no transom and no superstructure, had two masts, was lug-rigged. In Holland it might have gone under the name of *galjoot.* In any case, it was a coastal trading-ship, adequate to cross the Channel, and it was obviously armed with at least one swivel-gun. The shot they had fired at the English marines had been mostly for effect. Never could this little smuggler's craft have challenged *Météore,* had *Météore* been under sail, and properly manned; but as matters stood, the *galjoot* had enough sting in her swivel-guns to give the English second thoughts about standing in plain view and taking pot-shots at Men Overboard. Eliza had spied the boat a few minutes ago, and hoped it might be the one she had hired; this confirmed as much. It made no effort to pursue *Météore,* but wore around so as to make itself a barrier between *Météore* and the rowboat, and then released the air from its sails. *Arbalète* (for that was the name painted on her bows) approached with a curious mixture of charity and hostility, on the one hand flinging out lines for the ladies to snatch from the air, or rake up out of the water, on the other hand keeping loaded muskets at the ready. The only part of this morning's proceedings that they had been led to expect was that they might be collecting an anonymous passenger from the vicinity of *Météore.* All else—the assault of the English longboats, the apparition of the flaming *Soleil Royal,* and Flail-arm with his rowboat—had been unexpected. Eliza was already dreading the re-negotiation of the deal that probably lay ahead with the captain of *Arbalète.* That it had even ventured *this* far into the melee could probably be attributed solely to a bloke standing amidships holding a musket: Bob Shaftoe.

"All is well, Sergeant Bob. No, I don't know who he is. He is a mute, or something. But he seems well-intentioned. The worst I can say of him is that he is more forthright in his methods than would be considered proper at Versailles."

"I have noted him about the waterfront, spying on *Météore*," was Bob's answer.

"Come to mention it, so have I," said Eliza, "but lacking your penetration, sir, I could not make out whether he was *spying*, or merely satisfying his curiosity."

"Perhaps lovely Duchesses are more accustomed to being stared at for hours at a time than mangled Sergeants," Bob said. "To me it looked like spying."

"As perhaps it was, Sergeant Bob; but this morning he has been of service to a boat-load of women."

"Is it to be you alone, or the entire boat-load?" demanded the incredulous Monsieur Rigaud, Captain of *Arbalète*. Until this point, he had been preoccupied by the spectre—even more terrifying to a ship-captain than to any other sort of person—of the *Soleil Royal* drifting past them with gouts of flame spurting from her hundred gun-ports. Rigaud seemed at last to have convinced himself that the English, before setting fire to her, had extracted her stores of gunpowder—i.e., that they wanted her to burn for a long time, make a memorable spectacle for the citizenry of Cherbourg, and perhaps set fire to a few other ships—not simply blow up. If he was right, then the danger to *Arbalète* was past, for the flagship had unequivocally drifted beyond them. He had, accordingly, turned his mind to a threat almost as dire: an onslaught of female passengers.

"Only I," said Eliza, and slung her bag at Rigaud's head.

This was news to the other women, and caused a little flurry of gasps and outcries. Eliza considered trying to explain matters. *Mommy must run off to England and steal three tons of silver.* Instead she reached up—for the rowboat was grinding against *Arbalète's* side—and let Bob seize one of her hands, and a French sailor the other. The weight came off of her feet. She was hoisted aboard *Arbalète* like a bale of silk. "Lovely Brigitte," she called, "I hope that one day you will forgive me for now pressing you in to service as *galérienne*. But you must get in to shore before matters get any worse; and this man, I am afraid—"

"Rows in circles. The same had occurred to me, my lady." Brigitte seized the oars.

"We shall keep our swivel-guns charged, and watch you in to the shore," volunteered Monsieur Rigaud, who had become considerably more pliant now that the rowboat full of women was working *away* from *Arbalète*.

"Send a despatch to Captain Bart in Dunkerque," Eliza called.

"Saying what, Madame?"

"That it is going to happen after all."

"AMPUTATIONS ARE DICEY THINGS," remarked Bob Shaftoe some hours later. For a while, he had had that look on his face that warned Eliza he was pondering something, and likely to blurt out just such a ghoulish observation as soon as he took a whim to speak. "One strives to preserve the elbow, or the knee, at all costs, for that additional degree of articulation in the stump makes all the difference. In a below-the-elbow amputation, the hand is gone, and with it the ability to sense, to grasp, to caress. But yet there is the elbow, and the sinews to make it act. To turn the arm into a flail—a whole train of articulations, unfeeling, ungrasping, yet capable of action—yes, to put a flail on a stump is wholly fitting in a way."

"Remind me to ask you later for your thoughts on disembowelment," said Eliza, then regretted it, for she was already queasy. They were out on the Channel now, the wind had come up, and she was robed, hooded, and swaddled in blankets like a woman out of a desert land—a very cold desert land.

Bob squinted at her. "I've had any number of such thoughts this morning, and have held them back from you." He was alluding to the scenes that they had all beheld from the deck of *Arbalète* as they had sailed east-northeast along the tip of the Cotentin—that stump of an arm that France thrust out toward England. For the first hour or so, their view had been of Cherbourg, and of the waters north of it, which had gradually been unveiled as the last traces of the four-day fog had dissolved into plain air. A goodly part of the Anglo-Dutch fleet was there. The burning of *Soleil Royal* and the invasion of Cherbourg Harbor by longboats were only aspects of a larger action, which they came better to understand as they drew back from it. The English and Dutch had cut a few ships from the French fleet and were going about the tedious and ungallant work of mopping them up: trying to get enough cannonballs into their hulls to sink or ruin them before they could scurry in under the protection of the shore batteries. By the time that Cherbourg had receded from *Arbalète*'s view, that issue was no longer in much doubt: This remnant of the French fleet, if it reached Cherbourg at all, would never sail again. Not long after, *Arbalète* had rounded the Point of Barfleur, which had brought them in view of a vast bay, fifteen miles broad and five deep, pressed like a thumbprint into the eastern side of the Cotentin. It was there, in the shelter of the peninsula, that the bulk of the invasion-transports had gathered to receive soldiers and matériel from the great camps around La Hougue. And it was there, they now discovered, that Admiral Tourville had sought refuge with perhaps two dozen of his ships. Now that the fog had lifted, the bulk of the Anglo-Dutch fleet had formed up off La Hougue and were boring in to finish Tourville off; and since the anchorage proper was protected by shore batteries, this meant longboat-work again. What had happened to *Météore* this morning was, in other words, to be the pattern for what would be done to Tourville's fleet today. Eliza, though she knew little of Naval tactics, could see the logic of it as plainly as if it had been writ out on a page by Leibniz: The English could bring their ships no nearer shore than a certain point because of the shore-batteries. Tourville could not sail what was left of the French fleet—now outnumbered three or four to one—out of the anchorage. And so there was a no-man's-land between the English and French, which soon developed a dark infestation of longboats issuing from all the Anglo-Dutch ships. Unable to maneuver or even to weigh anchor in the jammed anchorage, the crews of the French ships could only stand on the decks and wait to repel boarders.

Arbalète, which under these circumstances could be overlooked as an insignificant smuggler's boat, now made her course due north, threaded her way between a pair of laggardly English men-of-war, and began a sprint for Portsmouth. Before the anchorage of La Hougue was lost to view astern, they noted a spark of light drifting out of it, trying to catch up with its own column of smoke. The burning of the French fleet had begun. Those aboard *Arbalète* could at least turn their backs on the scene, and run away from it. Not so fortunate, as Eliza knew, was James Stuart, who was camped in a royal tent on a hill above La Hougue. He'd have to watch the whole thing. For all that she despised the man and his reign, Eliza couldn't but feel sorry for him: chased out of England once in girl's clothes, during the Commonwealth, and a second time with a bloody nose during the Glorious Revolution; loser of the Battle of the Boyne; chased out of Ireland; and now this. It was while she was mulling over these cheerful matters that Bob Shaftoe unexpectedly piped up with his ruminations on the topic of stumps; which gives a fair portrait of the mood aboard *Arbalète* during her passage to England.

"I HAVE SEEN altogether too many men in my day, living as I have in Vagabond-camps and Regimental quarters. And so it could be that my memory has been overfilled and is now playing tricks on me. But I think that I have seen that man before," Bob said.

"Flail-arm? You mentioned you'd noticed him in Cherbourg, spying or gawking."

"Aye, but even the *first* time I saw him there, I phant'sied I'd seen his face elsewhere."

"If he was spying on me there, perhaps he had been doing the same in St.-Malo, and you'd noticed him on one of your visits," said Eliza, and was immediately sorry that she had raised this topic; for her bowels were in an uproar, she'd spent more time at the head than all others on the boat summed, and Bob had conspicuously refrained from saying anything about it, but only squinted at her knowingly. It was late afternoon. The sun was slicing down across the northwestern sky, making England into a rubble of black lumps in the foreground, and casting golden light on Bob's face.

"I phant'sied I'd make the return voyage, you know."

"You mean, back to Normandy tomorrow? But are you not absent without leave from your Irish regiment? Would you not be flogged for it, or something?"

"I got leave, on a pretext. It is still not too late."

"But it sounds as though you are having second thoughts."

"The closer we draw to England, the better she suits me. I went to France for diverse reasons, none of which have turned out to be any good."

"You hoped it would bring you within reach of Abigail."

"Aye. But instead I was marooned in Brest nigh on half a year, then Cherbourg for three months. And so serving France has brought me no nearer to Paris than if I'd been posted in London. Who knows where they'll have us go next?"

"If what I have heard means anything," Eliza said, "the fighting will be very hot in the Spanish Netherlands this summer. They are probably laying siege to Namur as we speak. That is most likely where Count Sheerness is—"

"And so probably Abigail as well," said Bob, "for if he means to spend the whole summer in those parts, he has brought his household with him. Very well. My most expedient way of reaching that part of the world shall be to re-join the Black Torrent Guards and be shipped thither at King William's expense."

"Don't you suppose your nine months' absence will have been noted? What kind of flogging will they award you for *that*!?"

"I was conducting military espionage in the enemy camp for the Earl of Marlborough," Bob retorted; though the look on his face, and the lilt in his voice, suggested that this had only just come into his head.

"The Earl of Marlborough has been dismissed from all offices, stripped of command. His colonelcy of the Black Torrent Guards will have been sold off to some Tory hack."

"But nine months ago when my mission of espionage began, none of that was true."

"Your idea still seems risky to me," said Eliza, eager to draw the exchange to a curt finish because the rioting had started up in her belly once more.

"Then I shall test the waters first, with Marlborough, before presenting myself to the Regiment," Bob said. "You're going to London! I don't suppose you'd be willing to bring him a private note from me—?"

"Since you cannot read or write, I suppose you'd like me to *pen* the note as well?" said Eliza, and turned her back on Bob, the better to search for a convenient scupper. She did not feel as though she would have time to trudge all the way to the head; besides which, a French sailor was already sitting up there, taking a lengthy shit into the English Channel and singing.

"Your offer is well received," Bob returned. "And as I am unfit to frame a proper letter to an Earl, perhaps I could interest you in *composing* it as well—?"

"I'll just *talk* to him," said Eliza, dropping to her hands and knees. The next thing that emerged from her mouth, however, was altogether unfit for presentation to an Earl; a fact Bob was discreet enough not to point out.

London

4 JUNE (N.S.) / 25 MAY (O.S.), 1692

Where men build on false grounds, the more they build, the greater is the ruin.

—HOBBES,
Leviathan

ELIZA FRETTED, AND BELABORED HERSELF for being too late and too little organized, until the moment that she gazed out the carriage window and saw the waters of the Thames below her, all crammed with shipping. This was too strange to believe for a moment. Then it came to her that this street must be London Bridge, and the carriage must be traversing one of the firebreaks, where it was possible to get a view. The sight of the River triggered a curious reversal in her mood. It was midafternoon of the day nominated, by the French and most of the rest of Christendom, June 4th, and by the English May 25th. Whichever calendar was used, the fact of the matter was that the Bills of Exchange would not expire until the end of the day *tomorrow;* she had, in other words, reached London with more than twenty-four hours to spare. This in spite of the fact that for the last week—since the day that Tourville had assaulted Russell in the Channel, and the fog had closed in—she had been certain she was too late and that the entire enterprise was doomed. From that moment until this, London had seemed infinitely far away, and impossible to reach. Now, having reached it, she wondered what all the fuss had been about. For London was after all a great city and people went there all the time—the number of masts thrust into the air above the Pool spoke to this. Perhaps Eliza had nursed an exaggerated view of its remoteness because of the difficulty she'd had in escaping to it almost three years ago, when her ship had been waylaid by Jean Bart.

At any rate she was across the Bridge and in the City before she had reached the end of these ruminations. The horses irritably dragged the carriage up Fish Street Hill as the coachman irritably popped his whip about their ears. It occurred to Eliza that she had not given the driver a destination, other than London. She had no destination in mind. But the driver had. Presently he turned off to the left, into a slit between new (brick, flat-fronted, post-Fire) buildings. The slit broadened and developed into a rambling composition of chambers and orifices, like the stomachs of a cow. It all seemed to be wrapped around the backside of a big structure that looked somehow like church, but somehow not. Tired Eliza remembered, then, that she had found her way to a country where there was more than just one church. She reckoned that this must be a meeting house of Quakers or some other such sect. At any rate they came, after certain turns, reversals, and squeezings, to a doorway adorned with a sign shaped like the head of an indifferent-looking brown horse. A porter exploded out of the doorway and vied with a footman for the honor of ripping the carriage door open. For painted on the outside of the carriage were the arms of the Marquis of Ravenscar, who Eliza gathered must be a valued regular of this inn or tavern, the Brown Horse or the Old Gelding or whatever they called it—

"Welcome to Nag's Head Court, my lady," said Roger Comstock, the Marquis of Ravenscar, emerging from the door, and bowing as deeply as a man of his maturity and dignity could without peeling a hamstring or lobbing his wig into the gutter. Eliza by now had thrust her head and shoulders out the door (about all she wanted to reveal, given that she had lost contact with her wardrobe some days ago). She ought to have given her undivided attention to Ravenscar; but she could not restrain the urge to look this way and that up the length of Nag's Head Court.

"No, madame, your senses have not misled you, it is just as mean, narrow, and squalid as you feared, and no apology from me shall balance the offense I have done you, by bringing you to it; but it was a suitable place for me to wait, and behold, it is nigh to the mysteries and delights of the 'Change."

Eliza followed his gaze down the alley. It rambled on in the same vein for a stone's throw and discharged into a proper street, which seemed to be crowded with an inordinate number of well-to-do-chaps who were all in a frightful hurry. She knew what it was just that quickly. If she had been wearing Versailles court-makeup, it would have cracked and fallen to the ground like ice from a warming roof. For her face had done something she never allowed it to do at Versailles, namely, opened up into a broad grin. She directed this at Ravenscar, who all but swooned. "On the contrary, my lord, in all London there's no place I'd rather be than the 'Change, and there is no place I am so well suited for, in my present state, than a dark doorway in Nag's Head Court—so—"

Ravenscar was aghast, and quick-stepped to the base of the wee Barock staircase that the footmen had arranged beneath the carriage-door. This was to help her down, if she insisted; but really he was throwing his body across her path as a barrier. "I would not *dream* of escorting a *Duchess* into *that* place! I had hoped that the lady might suffer me to join her in the carriage while we proceeded to some destination worthy to be graced by one of her dignity."

"It is, after all, *your* carriage, monsieur—"

"Nay, madame, *yours*, for as long as you choose to remain on our Isle, and I, your servant."

"Get in the damned carriage, then. And pray lower the shades, for I am not fit to stop light."

Ravenscar did as he was told. The carriage began to move. "Obviously, my driver was able to find you in Portsmouth—?"

"*We* found *him*. The skipper of our boat would not go to Portsmouth, or any other proper port-town, but only to certain coves he knew of. Thence we hired a waggon."

Ravenscar was looking curiously about the interior of the carriage, as if someone were missing. "We?"

"I was with an Englishman."

"A Person of Quality, or—"

"A Person of Usefulness. But somewhat bull-headed. He had set his mind to looking up his whilom Captain. When we reached Portsmouth he began to make inquiries about the fellow—name of Churchill."

Ravenscar winced. "Eeeyuh, the Earl of Marlborough has been clapped in the Tower of London!"

"So you tell me *now*, but, isolated as I'd been, I'd not heard that news. Otherwise I'd have warned my companion not to mention the name."

"They put your man in irons, did they?"

"They did. For I gather that the charge on which Marlborough is being held is that of being a Jacobite spy—?"

"It is *so* ludicrous that I am too embarrassed even to repeat it to you. But a moiety of the English race are the *more* inclined to credit an accusation, the more fanciful it becomes; and whoever it was that arrested your man in Portsmouth—"

"Was of that sort, and, seeing a man just off a boat from Cherbourg, asking the whereabouts of Marlborough, assumed the worst."

"Have they hanged him yet?"

"No, nor will they soon, for haply your carriage came along. *I*, to them, was just a wench in a wet dress; but when *this* fine vehicle made the scene, with your arms on the door, and your driver started in with 'la duchesse' this and 'the Duchess' that—"

"Matters changed."

"Matters changed, and I was able to let those in charge know that hanging my companion would not be in their best interests. But now that I'm here, I would visit Marlborough."

"Many would, my lady. The queue of carriages at the Tower is long. You rank most of them, and should be able to go directly to its head. But if I might, first—?"

"Yes?"

They had been driving around a triangular circuit of Cornhill, Threadneedle, and Bishopsgate, enclosing some twenty acres of ground that contained more money than the rest of the British Isles. It was remarkable that they had been able to converse for even *this* long without the topic having arisen.

"It is frightfully indecent of me to mention this, I know," said

Ravenscar, "but I am, at present, the owner of rather a lot of silver. Rather a lot. They tell me 'tis worth ever so much more *now* than 'twas three weeks ago, when I bought it; but if news were to arrive, say from Portsmouth, that the French invasion had miscarried—"

"It would suddenly be worth ever so much *less*. Yes, I know. Well, the invasion *has* failed."

Ravenscar's pelvis actually rose off the bench as if someone had shoved a dagger into his kidney. His voice vaulted to a higher register: "If we could, then, pay a brief call upon a certain gentleman, now, before you go spreading the news about—"

"I've no intention of doing *that,* as the news shall get here soon enough on its own," said Eliza, which little comforted Ravenscar. "But before *you* spread the news, by selling all of your silver, I have a small transaction that I must conduct at the House of Hacklheber— do you know it?"

"That? It is a hole in the wall, a niche, a dovecote—if you require pocket money in London, madame, I can convey you to the *banca* of Sir Richard Apthorp himself, who will be pleased to extend you credit—"

"That is most courteous of you," said Eliza, rummaging in her pathetic bag, and drawing out a slimy bundle of skins, "but I prefer to get my pocket-money from my own banker, and that is the House of Hacklheber."

"Very well," said the Marquis of Ravenscar, and boomed on the ceiling with the head of his walking-stick. "To the Golden Mercury in 'Change Alley!"

"I CONFESS THAT I was observing through the window—and only out of a gentlemanly concern for your safety," said the Marquis of Ravenscar, "and only after some half an hour had elapsed—for it struck me as rather a lengthy transaction."

Eliza had only just returned to the carriage and was still smoothing her skirts down. She'd been in there for an hour and twelve minutes. *Ten* minutes' waiting would have made Ravenscar impatient; *twenty,* apoplectic. *Seventy-two* had put him through the full gamut of emotional states known to mortal man, as well as a few normally reserved for angels and devils. Now, he was spent, drained. Though perhaps just a bit apprehensive that she would want to go on some *other* errand next.

"Yes, my lord?"

"The fellow had—well, I don't know, a bit of a startled look about him. Perhaps 'twas just my imagination."

"Mind your toes!" This warning came simultaneously from Eliza, and from one of Ravenscar's footmen, who had carried a box up the wee stairs behind Eliza and thrust it inside; its weight overbore his strength, and it crashed onto the floor, making the carriage rock and bounce up and down for a while on its springs. One of the horses whinnied in protest. "Where shall I place the others, madame?" he inquired.

"There are *more*!?" exclaimed Ravenscar.

"Ten more, yes."

"What are we—pardon me, *you*—going to do with so much, er . . . did you say *ten*? Please tell me it is copper."

Eliza flipped the lid open with her toe to reveal more freshly minted silver pennies than the Marquis of Ravenscar had seen in one place in years. He responded in the only way fitting: with absolute silence. Meanwhile his driver answered the question for him.

"*Not* load it on this coach, guv'nor, the suspension won't hold." The driver was struggling to settle the exhausted horses, who had sensed that the carriage was rapidly getting heavier. Another crash sounded from the shelf in the back, causing the vehicle to pitch nose up, and then another on the roof, which began to bulge downward and emit ominous ticks.

"Summon a hackney!" commanded the Marquis, and then swiveled his eyes back to Eliza, imploring her to answer his question.

"What am I going to do with it?"

"Yes."

"Sell it, I suppose, at the same time as you are selling yours. It is rather more pocket-money than I shall be requiring during my stay in your city. Though I should very much like to go to the West End later, and go—what is the word they use for it now?"

"I believe the word you are looking for is 'shopping,' madame."

"Yes, shopping. The money, of course, belongs to the King of France. But, gentleman that he is, he would never begrudge me the loan of a few pounds sterling so that I might change into a new dress."

"Nor would I, madame," said Ravenscar, "if it came to that—but *le Roi*, it goes without saying, has precedence." Ravenscar swallowed. "It is a remarkable coincidence."

"What coincidence, my lord?"

More jingling crashes came to their ears from just behind, where a hackney had pulled up, and was being laden with more strong-boxes. The sound was enormously distracting to Ravenscar, who struggled to keep stringing words together. "Our route to the lovely shops of the West End shall take us past Apthorp's, where—"

"Oh, that's right. You wish to put your silver on the market. Not yet."

"Not yet!?"

"Think of a ship's captain, sailing into battle, guns charged and ready to let go a broadside. If he loses his nerve, and fires too soon, the balls fall short of their target, and splash into the water, and he looks a fool. Worse, he is not afforded the opportunity to re-load. It is like that now."

Ravenscar did not seem convinced.

"After our epistolary flirtation, which I did enjoy so much," Eliza tried, "I should be crestfallen if I journeyed all the way to London only to find that you were a premature ejaculator."

"*Really!* Madame! I do not know how the ladies discourse in France, but here in England—"

"Oh, stop it. 'Twas a figure of speech, nothing more."

"And not a very accurate one, by your leave; for more is at stake here than you seem to know!"

"I know *precisely* what's at stake, my lord." Here Eliza was distracted by some activity without. A man had emerged from the door of the House of Hacklheber, dressed as if about to embark on a voyage, and was signalling for a hackney. There was no lack of these, as word seemed to have spread that coins were falling from the sky hereabouts. Within moments the fellow was on his way.

"Was that one of the shouting Germans?" Ravenscar inquired.

Eliza met his eye. "You could hear them all the way out here?" Then she tilted her head out the window to watch.

"Madame, I could have heard them from Wales. What were they on about?"

Eliza was crooking her finger at someone outside, then nodding as if to say, yes, I mean *you*, sirrah! Presently a face appeared in the window: a hackney-driver, hat in hands. "Follow yonder German until he gets on a boat. Watch the boat until you can't see it any more. Go to—what did you call your Den of Iniquity, my lord?"

"The Nag's Head."

"Go to the Nag's Head and leave word for the Marquis that his ship has come in. Someone there will then give you more of these." Eliza blindly scooped some coins out of her strong-box and slapped them into the driver's hat.

"Right you are, milady!"

"It shall probably be the Gravesend Ferry, but you might have to trail him all the way to Ipswich or something," Eliza added, partly to explain the amount; for she got the idea, from the way Ravenscar had just swallowed his own tongue, that she had overpaid.

The hackney driver was *so* gone, 'twas as if he'd been launched from a siege-mortar. Eliza looked back to Ravenscar. "You asked, what were the Germans shouting about?"

"Yes. I was afraid I should have to venture within and run them through." Ravenscar slapped the scabbard of his small-sword.

"They were full of impertinent questions about what I meant to do with all that silver."

"And you told them—?"

"I affected a noble diffidence, and pretended not to understand any language other than the high French of Versailles."

"Right. So *they* believe that the invasion has begun!"

"I cannot read their minds, my lord; and if I could, I should not wish to."

"And they have in consequence despatched a runner to the Continent. You mentioned Ipswich—implying that his destination is Holland—and his mission is, what?"

Eliza shrugged. "To fetch the rest, I'd suppose."

"The rest of *the Germans*!?"

"No, no, the rest of the *silver*—the remaining four-fifths of it."

An observer standing without the carriage would have seen it buck and rock. Some sort of nervous catastrophe had caused all of the Marquis of Ravenscar's muscles to contract at once. He was a few moments getting his faculties back. When he spoke again, it was from a sprawling, semi-prone position. "What the hell are you going to do with so much silver?"

"Most likely, convert it into Bills of Exchange that can be taken back to France."

"Where the money came from in the first place. Why bother at all?"

"Now it is *you* who asks impertinent questions," Eliza said. "All that need concern you for now is that the Hacklhebers believe the invasion has been launched. They are probably trying to buy silver on the London market *now*. Which shall lead *all* to believe in the invasion, until positive news arrives to the contrary. Your silver has only gone *up* in value."

"In truth there is one other matter that doth concern me," said Ravenscar, "which is that we are sitting out in the street with a king's ransom in silver; pray, could we get it now behind walls, locks, and guns?"

"Wherever you consider it shall be safest, monsieur."

"The Tower of London!" commanded Ravenscar, and the carriage moved, setting off small tinkly avalanches in all the strong-boxes.

"Ah," said Eliza with evident satisfaction, "no want of walls and guns *there,* I suppose; and I shall have an opportunity to pay a call on my lord Marlborough."

"I exist to please you, madame."

Gresham's College
10/20 JUNE 1692

Even *Solomon* had wanted Gold to adorn the Temple, unless he had been supply'd by Miracles.
— DANIEL DEFOE,
A Plan of the English Commerce

"MY *DELIGHT* AT seeing Monsieur Fatio again is joined by *wonder* at the company he keeps!" Feeble as it was, this was the best that Eliza could muster when Fatio walked into the library accompanied by a man with long silver hair—a man who could not be anyone but Isaac Newton.

Even by the standards of savants, this had been a socially awkward morning. Eliza had been in London for a fortnight. The first few days had gone to buying clothes, finding lodgings, sleeping, and vomiting; for obviously she was pregnant. Then she had sent notes out to a few London acquaintances. Most had responded within a day. Fatio's message had not arrived until this morning—it had been shot under her door as she knelt over a chamber-pot. Given the lengthy delay, she might have expected it to be a flawlessly composed letter, the utmost of many drafts; but it had been scratched out in haste on a page torn from a waste-book, and it had asked that Eliza come to Gresham's right away. This Eliza had done, not without much discomfort and inconvenience; then she had waited in the library for an hour. Now Fatio was at last here, looking flushed and wild, as if he had just galloped in from some battlefield. And he had this silver-haired gentleman in tow.

For a few moments he had stood between them, calculating the etiquette; then he remembered his manners, and bowed to Eliza, and spoke in French: "My lady. Our exploit at Scheveningen is never far from my mind. I think of it every day. Which may give some measure of my joy in seeing you again." This had been rehearsed, and he delivered it in too much haste for it to seem perfectly sincere; but the situation was, after all, complicated. Before Eliza could respond, Fatio stepped aside and thrust a hand at his companion. "I present to you Isaac Newton," he announced. Then, switching to English: "Isaac, it is my honor to give you Eliza de Lavardac, Duchess of Arcachon and of Qwghlm."

Fatio scarcely took his eyes from Eliza's face as he spoke these words, and as Eliza and Isaac curtseyed or bowed and said polite things to each other.

Eliza liked Fatio but remembered, now, why the man had always made her a bit uneasy. Nicolas Fatio de Duillier was forever an Actor in an Italian Opera that existed in his own mind. Today's scene at the Library of Gresham's was meant to be some kind of a set-piece. The Duchess, summoned in haste by a mysterious note, fumes impatiently for an hour—dramatick tension mounts—finally, just when she is about to storm out, Fatio saves the day by rushing in, aglow from superhuman efforts, and turns disaster to triumph by bringing in the Master himself. And it *was* dramatick, after a fashion; but whatever genuine emotions Eliza might have had she kept to herself, for no reason other than that Fatio was studying her as a starving man studies a closed oyster.

Newton had been dragged here; this was plain enough. But once he saw Eliza in the flesh, and she became something concrete to him, his reluctance was forgotten. Then it was a simple matter of remembering why he had been brought here.

They sat around a table, like students, all in the same sorts of chairs, with no thought given to rank. Newton fixed his gaze on a small burn-mark on the tabletop, and collected his thoughts for a minute or two. Eliza and Fatio filled the silence with chit-chat. But each kept an eye on Newton. Finally Newton's eyes flicked up to a nearby window, and he got a look on his face as if he were ready to unburden his mind of something. Fatio broke off in mid-sentence and half turned toward him.

"I shall speak as if everything Nicolas has said of your wit and erudition is true," Newton began, "which means that I shall not limp along with half-truths, nor circle back to proffer tedious explanations, as I might do when speaking to certain other Duchesses."

"Then I shall strive to be worthy of Fatio's compliments and of your respect, sir," Eliza answered.

Which seemed to be just the sort of thing Newton had been hoping to hear, for he gave a little nod, and almost smiled, before going on. "I would address in a straightforward way the question of Alchemy, and why I esteem it. For you will think me addled in the mind, that I devote so much time to it. You will think this because all of the Alchemists you have talked to are mountebanks or their fools.

This will have given you a low opinion of the Art and its practitioners.

"You are a friend of Daniel Waterhouse, who does not love Alchemy, and who looks on my time spent in the laboratory as time lost to Natural Philosophy. You know, he went so far as to set fire to my laboratory in 1677. I have forgiven him. He has not, however, forgiven *me* for continuing to study Alchemy. Perhaps he has, by words or gestures, communicated his views to you, my lady.

"You are also a friend of Leibniz. Now, there are those who would have me believe that Leibniz is, to me, some sort of adversary. I do not think so." Newton's eyes strayed towards Fatio as he said this. Fatio turned red, and would not meet his gaze. "I say that the product of mass and velocity is conserved; Leibniz says that the product of mass and *the square of* velocity is conserved; it seems that both of us are correct, and that by applying both of these principles we may build a science of Dynamics—to borrow Leibniz's term—that is more than the sum of these two parts. So in this Leibniz has not detracted from my work, but added to it.

"Likewise, he would not detract from *Principia Mathematica* but rather add to it what is plainly wanting: namely, an account of the seats and causes of Force. In this, Leibniz and I are comrades-in-arms. I, too, would unlock the riddle of Force: Force at a distance, such as joins gravitating bodies, and Forces in and among bodies, as when they collide. Or as here."

Newton extended one hand, palm up, and Eliza supposed for a moment that he was directing her attention to the window set into the wall above this table. But Newton waved his hand around in the air as if trying to catch a moth, and finally steadied it. His palm, which was as pale as parchment, was striped with a little rainbow, projected by some bevel or irregularity in the windowpane. Eliza turned her attention to it. The swath of colors was steady as a gyroscope on a stand, even though Newton's hand never stopped moving. This was a *trompe l'oeil* to best anything daubed on a wall by a mischievous painter at Versailles. Eliza acted without thinking: she reached out with both hands, cupping them together beneath Newton's, and cradled his wayward hand in hers, steadying it. "I see that you are unwell," she said, "for this is not the tremor of a coffee-enthusiast, but the shivering of a man with a fever." Yet Newton's hand felt cold.

"We are all unwell, if it comes to that," Newton returned, "for if some Plague were to take us all, why, these little spectra would still crawl about the room until the End of Days, neither knowing nor caring whether living hands were held up to catch them. Our flesh stops the light. The flesh is weak, yes, but the spirit is strong, and by applying our minds to the contemplation of what has been interrupted by our fleshly organs of sense, we may make our minds wiser and our spirits better, even though flesh decays. Now! I do not have a fever, my lady." He took his hand back, and gripped the arm of his chair to stop its shivering. The little rainbow now fell on Eliza's cupped hands. "But I am mortal and would fain do all that I could, in the time allotted to me, to penetrate this mystery of Force. Now consider this light that you are catching in your hands. It has traveled a hundred million miles from the Sun without being affected in any wise by the Cœlestial Æther. In its passage through the atmosphere it has been subjected to only slight distortions. And yet in traversing a quarter of an inch of window-glass, its course is bent, and it is riven into several colors. It is such an everyday thing that we do not mark it; yet pray consider for a moment just how remarkable it is! During its hundred-million-mile passage, is it not acted upon by the gravity of the Sun, which is powerful enough to hold even mighty Jupiter in its grasp, though at a much greater remove? And is it not acted upon as well by the gravity of the Earth and Moon, and all the other planets? And yet it seems perfectly insensitive to thse mighty forces. Yet there is embedded within this shard of glass some hidden Force that bends it and splits it with no effort. It's as if a cannonball, hurled at infinite speed from some gun of inconceivable might, and passing through ramparts and bulwarks as if they were shadows, were deflected and shivered into bits by a child holding up a feather. What could be concealed within an ordinary piece of window-glass that harbors such potency, and yet affects you and me not at all? Or consider the action of acids, which can in a few moments dissolve stones that have stood unmarked by Time and the elements since the world was formed. What has the power to annihilate a stone God made, a stone that could support a Pyramid, stop fire, or turn aside musket-balls? Some force of immense power must be latent in acids, to destroy what is so strong. And is it so inconceivable that this force might be akin to, or the same as, what bends the light as it passes through the window? Are these not perfectly suitable questions to be asked by those who style themselves Natural Philosophers?"

"If only others who study Alchemy would form their questions so well, and state them so lucidly!" Eliza said.

"The traditions of the Art are ancient and strange. Alchemists, when they say aught, say it in murky similitudes. This is not for me to remedy, save by pursuing the Work to its proper conclusion and thereby making plain what has been occulted for so many centuries.

And it is concerning that Work that I should like to say something to you concerning the gold that Jack Shaftoe stole in Bonanza."

This was such an unexpected turn in the conversation that Eliza flopped back hard in her chair, like a doll tossed into a box. Fatio turned his face toward her and stared avidly. Newton seemed ever so drily amused by her astonishment. "I do not know the nature of your involvement with this, my lady, and it is neither my place, nor my desire, to quarry the truth out of you. It suffices that you are *believed*, by diverse members of the Esoteric Brotherhood, to know something about the matter; and as long as that is true, why, it is in your interest to know *why* Alchemists care so much about this gold. *Do* you know, my lady?"

"I know, or suspect, only what I have inferred from the words and deeds of certain men who desire it. Those men believe that this particular gold has some supernatural properties exceeding normal gold."

"I do not know what the word *supernatural* means, really," said Isaac, bemused. "But you are not far wrong."

"I do not wish to be *at all* wrong. So pray correct me, sir."

"King Solomon the Wise, builder of the Temple, was the forefather of all Alchemists," Isaac said. "Set upon the throne, a young man, fearing himself unequal to the task, he made a thousand burnt offerings to the LORD; who then came to him in a dream and said, 'Ask what I shall give thee.' And Solomon asked not for wealth or power but for an understanding heart. And it pleased the LORD 'so well that Solomon had desired this thing, that he gave him an understanding heart 'so that there hath been none like thee before thee, neither after thee shall arise the like unto thee.' First Kings, Chapter Three, Verse 12. Thus Solomon's name became a byword for wisdom: *Sophia*. What is the name we give to those who love wisdom? Philosophers. I am a philosopher; and though I can never equal the wisdom of Solomon—for it says quite plainly in the chapter and verse I have quoted, that no man who came after Solomon would achieve like wisdom—I can strive to discover some of what is today hidden but was once in plain view in the Temple of Wisdom that Solomon built.

"Now it says, too, that the LORD gave Solomon riches, even though Solomon had not asked for them. Solomon had gold, and moreover he had an understanding heart, so that the secrets hidden within matter—such as I have discoursed of in window-glass and acids—could scarcely have been hidden from his gaze for long. The lucubrations of latter-day Alchemists such as I must be little more than crude mockery of the Great Work that Solomon the Wise undertook in his Temple. For thousands of years, Alchemists have sought to re-discover what fell into obscurity when Solomon came to the end of his years in Jerusalem. Most of their efforts have been unavailing; yet a few of the great ones—Hermes Trismegistus, Sendigovius, the Black Monk, Didier, Artephius—came to similar, if not identical, conclusions as to the process that must be followed to achieve the Great Work. I am very close now—" And here Newton faltered for the first time in several minutes, and took his gaze away from Eliza, and with a little nod and the faintest trace of a smile gathered Fatio once more into the discourse. "*We* are very close now to achieving this thing. I am told, my lady, that there are those who hold my *Principia Mathematica* in some high regard; but I say to you that it shall be nothing but a preface to what I shall bring forth next, provided I can only move the Work a short step further.

"It would be of immense help to us in this if we had even a small sample of the original gold given to Solomon by the LORD."

"Now I understand it at last," Eliza said. "That gold that was taken by Jack Shaftoe and his pirates from Bonanza is believed, by you and other Alchemists, to have been a sample of King Solomon's gold, somehow preserved down through the ages. It is somehow different from the gold that the slaves of the Portuguese dig from the earth in Brazil—"

"The theory of *how* it differs has been developed in more detail than you might care to listen to, particularly if you hold Alchemy to be nonsensical," said Fatio. "It has to do with how the particles— the atoms—of gold are composed, one to the next, to form networks, and networks of networks, *et cetera, et cetera,* and what occupies, or may pass into, the holes in the said nets. Suffice it to say that the Solomonic Gold, though it looks the same, is slightly heavier than mundane gold. And so even those who know nothing of the Art may recognize a sample of this Gold as extraordinary merely by weighing it, and computing its density. A large trove of such gold was found in Mexico some years ago and brought back to Spain by the ex-Viceroy, who intended to sell it to Lothar von Hacklheber, but—"

"I know the rest. But what do you phant'sy was King Solomon's Gold doing in New Spain?"

"There is a tradition that Solomon did not perish, but rather went into the East," said Newton. "You may credit it, or not; but what is beyond dispute is that the Viceroy was in possession of gold that was heavier than the ordinary."

"And you are so certain of this because—?"

"Lothar von Hacklheber sent three assayers across the ocean to New Spain to verify it beyond any shadow of doubt."

"Hmm. No wonder he was so vexed when Jack snatched it from under his nose!"

"May I inquire, my lady, whether you have heard from this Jack Shaftoe recently?"

"He sent me a present in a box, a year and a half ago, but it had quite spoiled in transit, and was buried. Mr. Newton, you may be assured that I, and certain acquaintances of mine in France, are bending all efforts to establish Jack's whereabouts, but this is well-nigh impossible, as he seems to be flitting all about Araby trading. When I learn anything definite, I shall—"

But here Eliza broke off, for she'd been interrupted. Not by any utterance, for both Fatio and Newton were silent, but rather by the expressions that had come over the faces of Newton and Fatio, and the wild looks that were passing between them. Newton in particular seemed too preoccupied to speak.

Fatio, coming alive to the fact that the room had been silent for rather a long while, explained: "It would be a grievous misfortune if these pirates, ignorant of what they had, *coined* the Solomonic Gold and *spent* it. For then it would be dispersed all over the world, and melted down—con-fused—and commingled with ordinary gold, and dispersed to the four winds." Fatio turned his eager gaze back on Newton. His face collapsed, and he launched himself out of his chair, alighting on a knee next to the savant. Newton had raised one trembling hand and clapped it over his eyes. He was shifting about in his chair without letup, almost writhing. Sweat had beaded up on his brow, and a vein in his temple was throbbing at a tempo twice or thrice Eliza's pulse. In all, it seemed Newton was devoting every ounce of will to restraining his body's wild urge to break out into a frenzy. For the moment, his will prevailed, but only just, and he could attend to nothing else.

Eliza might have supposed that Newton was suffering a stroke; but the way Fatio perched next to him, stroking his hand, suggested that this was not the first time it had happened.

Eliza stood. "Shall I summon a physician?"

"*I* am his physician," was Fatio's answer. Odd that, from a mathematician. But perhaps he'd been reading medicine-books.

To oblige the patient and his physician to rise and bid her a courtly farewell did not seem the wisest course. Eliza curtseyed and walked out of the room.

HALF AN HOUR LATER, she was in the House of the Golden Mercury. The office was full of English lawyers—not stacked lock-boxes containing three tons of silver, as she had every right to expect. Indeed, the lawyers out-numbered their clients: four (presumably German) bankers. Of these she had met three before, when she had stopped by with the Marquis of Ravenscar to present the Bills. The fourth was unfamiliar, and older. Eliza supposed that he had come in from Amsterdam.

"Is this a trading-house, or an art gallery?" Eliza inquired, if only to break the silence that had been her only greeting. "For I expected to see silver pennies stacked to the ceiling. Instead of which I am confronted by a Still Life such as has not been seen since the heyday of the Dutch Masters."

No one was particularly amused. But it *did* look like a group portrait. This office was scarcely large enough to serve as a muffin-shop. It contained two heavy desks, or *bancas*, and diverse shelves where ledgers and rolled documents were stored. A strong-box on the floor served as a small reserve of cash; but this was not the sort of place that customarily dealt in large volumes of specie. Such would normally be handled through one of the larger goldsmith's shops, or Apthorp's Bank. A narrow door in the back gave way to a staircase that executed an immediate fierce turn and then shot diagonally upwards through the middle of the office, reducing its volume by one quarter; it was on these stairs that two weeks ago the strong-boxes containing the first installment of the silver had been stacked. But no strong-boxes were there now. Rather, the first stair was claimed by the old banker, who was using it as a sort of dais from which to glower at the entire contents of the London branch of the House of Hacklheber. The old banker was stout, and his bulk entirely filled the width of the stairway, so that as he stood there, just on the far side of the narrow doorway, it looked as if he had been chivvied and tamped into a coffin standing vertically on end with its lid swung open. His jowls bulged like flour-sacks, forming profound vertical crevices to either end of his upper lip, which was as high, white, and sheer as the Cliffs of Dover.

Even if Eliza had not already met the London factor and his two assistants, she would have been able to pick them out amid the crowd by their postures. For they all stood with backs exposed to the old banker, hunched forward, frozen in mid-shrug, as if with his blue eyes he were boring slow holes into their spines.

The lawyers were five strong. To judge from their ages, the quality of their periwigs, and their posture, she guessed two full-fledged barristers and three clerks. The barristers were shoulder-to-shoulder with their clients, the clerks packed like oakum into spaces beneath the stair and among *bancas* that were not, for the most part, shaped at all like human beings. It was well that Eliza's morning sickness had abated, for the smell of coffee, snuff, decaying teeth, unwashed men, and colognes used to overpower same would else have sent her right back out into 'Change Alley, where she'd have gone into a fit as bad as Isaac Newton's. As it was, she had no lack of incentive to make the conversation brief and momentous.

"With so many gentlemen here, there is no room for silver," she remarked. "May I assume that it has all been delivered to the Mint to be coined?"

"My lady," began the London factor. He was literally reading from a prepared script. "The two weeks since you presented the Bills of Exchange at these premises have been eventful ones. Allow me to give you a brief account. You arrived on a day when news of a French invasion was looked for at any moment. The price of silver was high; its availability, nonexistent. You presented five Bills. One was payable immediately, and we paid it. The other four were payable on the tenth of June, by English calendar; that is, today. As no silver was to be had in London we despatched a message, post-haste, to our factory in Amsterdam. Less than twelve hours after its arrival in that city, a ship was underway on the Ijsselmeer laden with silver sufficient to pay the four outstanding Bills. Under normal circumstances she would have reached London and called at Tower Dock in more than enough time for the said bullion to have been minted into English coins before the date of expiry of the said Bills. During her passage across the Narrow Seas, however, she was waylaid, and overhauled by Ships of Force flying the flag of the French Navy. The silver and the ship were taken to Dunkerque, *where they remain*. Because this piracy was carried out by ships flying the fleur-de-lis, it is nominated, by our Dutch insurers, as an Act of War, expressly not covered by our policy; in consequence, the cargo is a total loss."

"Have you tried to buy silver on the local market?" Eliza asked. "There must be a glut of it now that everyone knows that the French invasion has failed. Why, I have heard that the Marquis of Ravenscar sold his holdings two weeks ago."

"News of the piracy did not reach my clients until yesterday," returned a barrister—a feline man not much bigger than Eliza. "Needless to say, my client has bent all efforts, in the short time since, to acquire local silver; but my client's ability to make such purchases is founded upon the credit of his House, not, mind you, as it really is, or ought to be, but as that is *perceived* by other bankers of the City—" and here he could not prevent his eyes from straying toward the window; for a few of those bankers, or their messengers, had begun to gather without.

"And that has suffered a blow, hasn't it," Eliza returned, in a voice suffused with childlike wonder, as if this had only just occurred to her, "because of the pirates and the insurers and whatnot."

"As to your speculations, my client has no comment," announced the barrister, "however I must correct you on a matter of lexicography. You said *pirates*. A pirate owes allegiance to no sovereign. The correct word, in his instance, would be *privateer*. Do you ken the distinction, my lady?"

"Why, yes—a privateer flies the flag of some country or other, and is in effect a part of its Navy."

"Your clarity, where this distinction is concerned, may perhaps reflect your status as the wife of the Grand Admiral of France—the superior of Captain Jean Bart, who confiscated my client's silver."

"That man is incorrigible! Why, only three years ago the rascal confiscated every last penny that I owned! I am relieved to be informed that the House of Hacklheber escaped with comparatively small losses."

"*That* remains to be seen," said the barrister. "A lady's wealth consists of the contents of her jewellery-box, but that of a banking-house consists largely in its credit. Direct losses such as the shipment of silver may be written off, and perhaps recovered. By contrast, when a Person of Quality erects an elaborate complot to destroy the good name of a banking-house—"

"It would be terrible, I could not agree more!" exclaimed Eliza; which shut them all up for a bit, as it was not quite the sort of response they had readied themselves for. "Though, by your leave, you are wrong about a lady's wealth being confined to her jewellery-box. Of far greater value is her honour, which is to a noblewoman what credit is to a banking-house. What I lost to Jean Bart three years ago meant nothing to me. Much more to be feared would be the damage that my good name should incur if persons, whether malicious or simply ill-informed, were to go about spreading a rumor that I had connived to swindle an honest German bank! Does your client not agree, sir?"

"Er . . . my client is not as fluent in the English language as you or I. Before I can speak on his behalf as to whether he agrees or disagrees with your assertion, I shall have to meet with him privily and see to it that our words are translated into German. Pray carry on, my lady; but first, know that nothing in my or my clients' previous statements can or should be construed to imply that I or my client is directly or indirectly accusing you of participating in a swindle."

"That is ever so reassuring. In any case, it is precisely to forestall any such damage to my name that I have rushed here this morning."

"It is?"

"Why, yes! For I had received word that the House of Hacklheber had suffered a reversal of its fortunes. Lothar von Hacklheber is reputed to be a vindictive and unprincipled man. My first thought was that he might try to soften the blow to *his* reputation, by deflecting it onto *me;* which would be most unfair, given that he entered into this transaction of his own free will, and on his own terms, well knowing the risks. Be that as it may, the fact of the matter is that I am here in London, alone, defenseless, with no assets other than my title as Duchess of Qwghlm, which was bestowed on me by King William."

"We are aware of your titles, my lady—English as well as French— as well as how you came by them."

"And so I am here to offer a solution."

"And what is your proposal, my lady?"

"The purpose for which the silver was intended no longer exists. But the Bills have been presented, and accepted, and must be paid in London before day's end, if the reputation of the House of Hacklheber is to survive. I propose that we convert the transaction into another form of payment. France no longer has need of the silver, but she does have a perpetual need of timber—more so than ever, now that so much of her fleet has been burned in the harbors of Cherbourg and La Hougue. She purchases Baltic timber through the *Compagnie du Nord,* which deals with a net-work of Huguenot merchants in the north. Those same houses maintain bureaus within a stone's throw of where we stand; indeed, as I was on my way here just now, I chanced to meet Monsieur Durand, who is the local factor of such a concern. I fetched him along with me." Eliza waved her hand in the window. Instantly the door opened, and the last remaining volume in the House of the Golden Mercury was claimed by a big-nosed, wigless, white-haired gentleman. "I present Monsieur Durand of Durand et fils of London, Stockholm, Rostock, and Riga," Eliza announced. "I have told him all about what has happened— though like most of 'Change Alley he had already heard much of the story. Monsieur Durand has let me know, in the most eloquent French, that, as a result of his many connexions and his long expertise in the north, he has developed a respect for the House of Hacklheber that cannot be shaken by one unfortunate incident of piracy. As such, he is willing to arrange shipment of timber to the *Compagnie du Nord* provided that the four outstanding Bills of Exchange are transferred to him today. He will, in other words, accept the *credit* of your House in lieu of actual delivery of silver bullion. The House of Hacklheber's obligations shall be discharged in full by day's end, and no damage to anyone's repute shall ensue; Lothar von Hacklheber shall be *Ditta di Borsa* tomorrow just as yesterday, and this momentary lapse in his reputation, which has led to the abrupt hiring of so many members of the legal profession, shall be remembered—if it is remembered at all—as one of those brief irrational panics to which markets are everywhere prone."

All of this now had to be explained to the big German at the back of the room. Eliza suspected, from this man's age, his bearing, and the way the others deferred to him, that he must report to Lothar von Hacklheber personally. Clearly he spoke little English; which might have been more help than hindrance to him until now, as he had been gauging the mood of the room, and observing the struggle of wills and the balance of power among the participants. He had seen Eliza walk into a room in which the prevailing mood had been like that in a ravelin under siege. Yet she had astonished the beleaguered defenders by not pressing her advantage when she might have, and instead proffering a way out. Astonishment had developed into relief as Monsieur Durand made his entrance. All of these things the old banker perceived, without knowing any of the particulars; and the more hopeful his underlings allowed themselves to become, the more suspicious he waxed. Now they had to sell him the proposal, in German; but he was not of a mind to buy.

"Are we to understand," said the London factor, translating for him, "that *La France* is to receive—in addition to the hundred thousand *livres* in silver we have already delivered to you—four hundred thousand *livres* worth of silver as booty in Dunkerque *as well as* four hundred thousand *livres* worth of Baltic timber, in exchange for nothing more than five hundred thousand *livres* in French government obligations in Lyon?"

"I recommend you moderate your tone," said Eliza. "Voices carry out into the street; and lurking there in 'Change Alley are any number of City men who have heard all the rumors about the insolvency of the Hacklhebers. When I step out that door, I shall be interrogated like a prisoner on the Inquisition's rack. They will know whether the Hacklhebers have been able to honour their obligations, or not. Through the generous intercession of Monsieur Durand, it will be possible for me to answer in the affirmative." Eliza half-turned toward the door and rested a gloved hand on the latch. The room grew perceptibly darker as a Mobb of 'Change-men on the street outside noted her gesture, and drew closer to the windows, blocking out the light. Eliza continued: "This talk of yours about four hundred thousand *livres* here or there is quite lost on me; I am a mere housewife with no head for numbers." She flexed her wrist and the door-latch made a clicking noise, a bit like the cocking of a flintlock. A volcanic up-welling of German sounded from the rear of the shop; Eliza could not quite follow what was being said, but suddenly the barrister spun to face her and announced: "My client is pleased to accept the proposal, pending resolution of the terms in detail."

"Then pray resolve them with Monsieur Durand," said Eliza, "I am going out for a bit of air."

"And—?"

"And to let the City of London know that the House of Hacklheber is *Ditta di Borsa,* as ever," Eliza added.

"WHAT WAS THAT BIT you hollered into the back, just as you were coming out the door?" asked Bob Shaftoe. "I could not make out your French."

" 'Twas nothing," said Eliza, "only polite leave-taking. I complimented the old fellow on how adroitly he and his colleagues had managed the transaction, and expressed my hope that in future we might work together again thusly."

"And what said he to that?"

"Naught, but only stared into my eyes—overcome with fond emotions, I should say."

"You said before, in St.-Malo, when we—" Bob began, and got lost in his thoughts as his gaze slipped down toward her belly.

"When we were together."

"Yes, you said you wanted your boot on Lothar's neck. And it seems to me you had that, just as you phant'sied. But you let him go?"

"Never," said Eliza, "never. For do not forget that every transaction has two ends, and this is only one of them."

"Very well. I shall not forget it. But I do not *understand* it."

"Neither does Lothar."

"Will you return to France?"

"To Dunkerque," Eliza said, "to pay my compliments to Captain Bart, and to inform the Marquis d'Ozoir that he has got his timber. What of you, Sergeant Bob?"

"I shall remain here for the present time. I've been to visit Mr. Churchill a time or two in the Tower, you know. He shan't be there very much longer, mark my words."

"The judicial proceedings against him have become a farce, such as appeals to the English sense of humor, but all grow weary of it."

"And meanwhile King Louis himself is laying siege to Namur, isn't he? And folks are asking, why does King William keep our best commander locked up on a ridiculous pretext, when a great campaign is under way on the other side of the Narrow Seas? No, my lady, if I were to go back to Normandy, I'd have some explaining to do, and might even be hanged for desertion. That Irish regiment'll be sent

God only knows where—for all I know, they'll wind up in the South, on the Savoy front, a million miles from where I have been trying to go. But soon enough Churchill shall be at the head of an army, and I shall go with that army to Flanders. We shall face the French across some narrow strip of ground. I'll scan the colors on the opposing side, until I spy those of Count Sheerness—"

"And then?"

"Why, then, I shall devise some means of ending up with *my* boot on *his* throat. And we shall enter into a discussion concerning Abigail."

"You attempted that with his brother—Abigail's *previous* owner. He almost killed you, and you did not get Abigail."

"I do not claim 'tis a likely plan, but 'tis *my* plan, and it gives me something to do."

"Can I not simply *buy* the girl from Sheerness?"

"It would raise questions. Why should you care about one English slave?"

"That is my business."

"And Abigail is mine—"

"Would Abigail agree? Or would she prefer that plan that is most likely to lead to her freedom?"

This made Bob a bit stormy-looking. He strove with his temper for a bit. Then he chuckled. "What's the point of flapping my jaw when you'll go and do just what you please, no matter what I say? Be off to Dunkerque, then. But if my wishes have any gravity, you'll tend to yourself and not to me. For I ween you are in a delicate way just now. That is all."

"I am *ever* in a delicate way," said Eliza, "but men pick and choose the time to take notice of it, as it suits their purposes." At this Bob chuckled again, which provoked her. "Let us speak plainly," she said, "for this is where our ways part—you must to the Tower to attend your master in his prison-cell, I must to dockside to arrange passage to Dunkerque." They had arrived at the cross where Grace Church Street changed its name to Fish Street, and plunged down to the Bridge. From their right entered Great Eastcheap; under the name of Little Eastcheap it then wended its way off in the direction of the Tower. A stone's throw down the hill, a lone, stupendous column jutted up from the city, casting a finger of shadow down the length of the street. They'd come nigh to the place where the Fire of London had been kindled a quarter-century before. The column was the Monument that Wren and Hooke had put up to it.

"When you promise to speak plainly, I know to brace myself," said Bob, and then he did literally, leaning back against a brick wall.

"You have seen me sick, and suppose that I am pregnant. This has wrought powerfully on your mind, for you know that Abigail was given syphilis by Upnor and may not be able to give you children, even if you do pry her free from the clutches of Count Sheerness. You have stopped thinking of me as 'Eliza the woman I roger from time to time' and begun to think of me as 'Eliza the expectant mother of my only child.' This has queered your judgment and led you to consider schemes that are not likely to produce Abigail's freedom. Know then that the fœtus—which might have been yours, or my husband's, or any of several other men's—miscarried the night before last. It is with the angels. I would still produce a competent heir for my husband, but must begin a new pregnancy once I have reached France. Perhaps I shall seduce Jean Bart, perhaps the Marquis d'Ozoir, perhaps a Marine who catches my fancy on the street. In any case you must give up hope that any progeny of yours shall come from here—" and Eliza rested her hand on the front of her bodice "—for I am done with being the other woman in the life of Bob Shaftoe and Abigail Frome. Done with being the poppy-elixir that makes you forget your pain, and leads you to dream stratagems that shall never avail you or her a thing. Abigail may be waiting for you, Bob. I am not. Get thee to thy projects, then."

She was gone from Bob's sight before the words penetrated all the way to his heart, for she was a small woman, quick, and dissolved into the traffic down Fish Street Hill like a mote of sugar in a stream of boiling water. Bob did not move, but let the brick wall hold him up for some while, until the proprietor—an insurance-man—thrust his head out the window and gave him that look that Gentlemen give to Vagabonds when it is time for them to be moving on. Bob had a soldier's knack for moving when he did not wish to. He levered himself away from the wall, rounded the corner, and marched down Little Eastcheap toward the Tower, where his Captain would be waiting for him with orders.

BOOK 4

Bonanza

Ahmadabad, the Mogul Empire

SEPTEMBER 1693

When Men fly from danger, it is natural for them to
run farther than they need.
> —*The Mischiefs that ought justly to be appre-*
> *hended from a Whig-government,*
> ANONYMOUS (ATTRIBUTED TO
> BERNARD MANDEVILLE), 1714

EVERY MORNING A MOB OF angry Hindoos convened outside the hospital hoping to have a conversation with Jack on his way in, and so
every day Jack came a little earlier, stealing in through a back door
where manure was carried out and food brought in. Because of that
latter function it was the correct entrance for him to use anyway. He
walked across an enclosed stable-yard, holding one hand before his
face as a sort of visor, to break a trail through the horseflies. At least,
he *hoped* that they were horseflies.

His passage was noticed and commented upon by insomniacal
horses and camels, standing on splinted and bandaged limbs, or
dangling from formidable slings, in stalls all round the yard. A tiger
was here, too, being treated for an abscessed tooth, but she was kept
in a cage in an out-building. Otherwise her fragrance, and the nearly
inaudible sound she made when she yawned, would drive the horses
and camels into frenzies. A horse supporting itself on two legs, and
kicking with the remaining two, was dangerous enough; a horse in a
sling, kicking with all four legs at once, was as dangerous as a cart-
load of Afghans.

The insect situation did not improve when he went inside. In
part, this was because the distinction between inside and outside was
not closely observed in this part of the world; space was divided up
by walls and screens, yes. But they all had great bloody holes in them
(ornately shaped holes painstakingly carved by master craftsmen,
yes, but none the less holes) to let in air and light and (or so Jack

supposed in his more peevish moments) to keep buildings from bursting and falling down when the inmates got to farting—for these people ate beans, or, at any rate, a plethora of mysterious bean-like foodstuffs, as if they were all starving—which, come to think of it, they *were*.

At any rate, the result was that the gallery into which Jack had now entered was thick with flies, zinging through the darkness like spent grapeshot on the fringes of a battle, and crunching into his shaved head and raising welts. They had been drawn here, from all over the Indies, by the smell of diverse sick or injured creatures and their feed and their manure; for this hospital with all its stone screens and lattice-works was like a giant censer dispensing such fragrances into the air of Ahmadabad.

Past the mongoose with the suppurating eye, the jackal with mange, the half-paralyzed king cobra, the stunningly odoriferous civet-cat-with-bone-cancer, the mouse deer with the javelin wound did Jack proceed, and then entered a room filled with bird-cages of bent bamboo, where diverse broken-winged avians were on the mend. A peacock with an arrow stuck sideways all the way through his neck shuffled around, bumping into things and getting hung up on the cages and squawking in outrage. Jack gave him a wide berth, not wanting to get lockjaw off that arrowhead if the peacock should happen to execute a sharp turn in the vicinity of his knees.

Through a rickety door was a room piled floor to ceiling with even smaller cages housing sick or injured mice and rats, some of which sounded distinctly rabid. The less time spent here the better, and so Jack forged on to another room, and down some stone steps.

The smell here transcended mere badness. It was not a smell of mammals or even reptiles, but of an entirely different order of Creation. It was *thrilling*. For quite some time Jack had been breathing through his nose, but now he threw one arm over his face and sucked in air through the crook of his elbow. For the air in this, the deepest and innermost part of the hospital, was (he estimated) fifty percent insects by volume, a sort of writhing meat-cloud that continually hummed, as if he had climbed into an organ pipe. And if even one of those bugs got into a nostril and injured itself trying to struggle free of Jack's nose-hairs, the caretakers would be sure to notice, and then Jack would be out of a job. For the same reason, he had altered his gait, and now shuffled along on bare feet, plowing carefully through the drifts and flurries of bugs on the floor, hoping there weren't any scorpions there just now.

"Jack Shaftoe reporting for duty!" he hollered. The chief bug-doctor, and his diverse hierarchies and sub-hierarchies of assistants, had all been sleeping under gauzy bug-nets suspended from the ceiling. These huddled in the corners of the bug-ward like claques of pointy-headed ghosts. They now began to bobble and twitch as sleepy Hindoos emerged from them. Jack stripped down to the thong that he used to protect what remained of his privities, and handed his clothes to someone (he wasn't sure *whom*, and didn't care; this was Hindoostan, there were a lot of people here, and if you held something out and looked expectant, someone would soon enough take it).

A boy brought him the usual concoction, holding the coconut shell to Jack's lips while others bound Jack's hands together behind his back with a strip of cloth. Out of habit, Jack put his ankles together so that those could likewise be bound. When he had finished gulping down that draught (which was supposed to nourish and replenish the blood), he allowed himself to fall forward, and was caught by many small warm hands and gently lowered onto the floor—though not before it had been gently swept clear of any insects. His bound ankles were brought up to meet his hands, and all were tied together above his bare buttocks. Meanwhile a swathe of gauze was being tied about his head, screening his mouth, nose, and eyes.

Above, he could hear a boom of timber—what sailors would call a yard—being swung around until one end of it was above him. From a pulley on its tip, a stout rope was now brought down and tied to the web of bonds that joined his wrists and ankles, with a couple of turns around his waist to carry most of his weight.

Deeper voices spoke now—the pulley squeaked, the rope tensed, the yard began to tick and groan, and then Jack was airborne. They swung the yard around, Jack skimming along just a hand's breadth above the floor, escorted by giggling and shuffling Hindoo boys. But these suddenly peeled away as the stone floor dropped out from under him and he swung out over a pit: a stone-lined silo perhaps four yards across and somewhat less in depth. They let him hang above the middle of it for a few seconds, prodding him artfully with bamboo poles until he stopped swinging; then the rope was let out and Jack descended. Many torches had been lit for this the most critical part of the operation. The gauze over his eyes strained their light from the air and clouded his vision, which was just as well. They took utmost care not to let his full weight down onto the sandy floor of the pit until they were absolutely certain that no living creature was underneath him. But they or their ancestors had done this many times a day since the beginning of Time and were good at their work. Jack came to rest on the pit-floor without crushing a thing.

Then from small holes and arches and burrows, tanks, puddles,

sumps, rotten logs, decomposing fruit, hives, and sand-heaps all
around, out they came: foot-long centipedes, clouds of fleas, worms
of various descriptions, all manner of flying insects—in short, all
sorts of creatures whatever that subsisted on blood. He felt a bat land
on the back of his neck, and tried to relax.

"That iridescent beetle feasting on your left buttock does not
appear to be injured or sick in the slightest degree!" said a curiously
familiar voice, speaking English with a musical accent. "I think it
should be discharged forthwith, Jack."

"Wouldn't surprise me—the whole country is infested with idlers
and freebooters—like that rabble out front."

"That rabble, as you call them, are the men of the Swapak *mahajan*," said Surendranath—for by this point Jack had recognized him
as none other.

"So they keep telling me—what of it?"

"You must understand that the Swapaks are a very ancient subcaste of the Shudra Ahir—the herdsmen of the Vinkhala tribe—
which is one of the sixteen branches of the Seventh Division of the
Fire Races."

"And?"

"They are divided into two great classes, the noble and the ignoble, the former being divided into thirty-seven subtribes and the latter into ninety-three. The Shudra Ahir were formerly one of the
thirty-seven, until after the Third Incarnation of Lord Kalpa, when
they came up from Anhalwara by way of Lower Oond, and intermarried with a tribe of degenerated Mulgrassias."

"So?"

"Jack, just to put that in context, you must understand that those
people are regarded as Dhangs of the lower subcaste (yet considerably above the Dhoms!) by the Virda, whom they nonetheless abhor.
To give you an idea of just how degenerate they were, these Dhangs,
in an earlier age, had intermarried with the Kalpa Salkh of Kalapur,
of whom almost nothing is known save that not even the ape-men of
Hari would allow themselves to be overshadowed by them."

"I am waiting for your point to arrive."

"The point is that the Shudra Ahir have been herdsmen and feeders of livestock since before the breaking of the Three Jade Eggs,
and the Swapak, for almost as long, have been—"

"Feeders of bloodsucking insects in animal hospitals that are
operated by some other *mahajan* of some other caste—yes, I know,
it's all been tediously explained to me," said Jack, flinching as a cen-
tipede bit through the flesh of his inner thigh and tapped into an
artery. "But those Swapak have been assured of jobs for so many

thousands of years that they have become indolent. They make unreasonable demands of the Brahmins who run this place, and lounge around out front all day and night, pestering passers-by."

"You sound like a rich Frank complaining about Vagabonds."

"If I were not having my blood sucked out by thousands of vermin, I might take offense—as it is, your japes and witticisms strike me as more of the same."

Surendranath laughed. "You must forgive me. When I learned that you were earning your keep in this way, I rashly assumed that you had become a *desperate wretch*. Now I appreciate that you take pride in your work."

"Compared to those layabouts who are encamped in front, Padraig and I—ouch!—are willing to do this work for a more competitive rate, and comport ourselves as professionals."

"I very much fear that you will be comporting yourselves as dead men if you do not get out of Ahmadabad," said Surendranath.

Above, Jack heard commands uttered in Gujarati, then the welcome creak of the pulley. The rope came tight and raised him a few inches off the ground. He writhed and shook himself, trying to shed as many of the creatures as he could. "What are you talking about? They don't even step on *bugs*. What're they going to do to a couple of *men*?"

"Oh, it is not difficult for such people to come to an understanding, Jack, with members of castes that specialize in mayhem."

Jack was now raised up out of the pit and swung round over the floor again. The bug-doctors converged on him with brooms, gently sweeping away the engorged ticks and leeches. Then they let him down and began untying the bonds. As soon as he could, Jack reached up and pulled off the gauze face-mask. Now he was able to get a good look at Surendranath for the first time.

When they'd parted company, outside the customs-house of Surat, more than a year ago, Surendranath, like Jack, had been a shivering wretch, dressed in rags, and still walking slightly bowlegged on account of the thoroughgoing search that was meted out to all who entered the Mogul's realms there, to make sure that they were not secreting Persian Gulf pearls in their rectal orifices.

Today, of course, Jack looked much the same, save that he was covered with bug bites and lying on his belly. But in front of his nose was a pair of fine leather slippers covered with red velvet brocade, and above them, a pair of orange-and-yellow-striped silk breeches, and hanging over those, a long shirt of excellent linen. This was surmounted by the head of Surendranath. He had grown his moustache out but otherwise had a professional shave—which must have cost him dearly, so early in the morning—and he had a sizeable gold ring in his nose, and wore a snow-white turban with an overwrap of wine-colored silk edged in gold.

"It's not *my* fault I'm stuck in this fucking country with no money," Jack said. "Blame it on those pirates."

Surendranath snorted. "Jack, when I lose a single rupee I lie awake all night, cursing myself and the man who took it from me. You do not need to urge me to hate the pirates who took our gold!"

"Very well, then."

"But does this mean that other Hindoostanis, belonging to a different caste, speaking a different language, residing at the other end of the subcontinent, must suffer?"

"I have to eat."

"There are other ways for a Frank to make a living in Hind."

"I see those rich Dutchmen in the streets every day. Bully for them. But I can't make a living from trade when I've nothing to my name. Besides—for Christ's sake, you Banyans make even Jews and Armenians seem like *nuns* in the bazaar."

"Thank you," Surendranath said modestly.

"Besides, in Surat and all the other treaty ports, there is an astronomical price on my head."

"It is true that, as the result of your dealings with the Viceroy, the House of Hacklheber, and the Duc d'Arcachon, all of Spain, Germany, and France now wish to kill you," Surendranath admitted, helping Jack to his feet.

"You left out the Ottoman Empire."

"But Hind is another world! You have seen only a narrow strip along the coast. There are many opportunities in the interior—"

"Oh, one bug-pit is the same as the next, I'm sure."

"—for a Frank who knows how to use the saber and the musket."

"I'm listening," Jack said. "Fucking bugs!" and then—distracted, as he was, by the peculiar nature of Surendranath's discourse, he slapped a mosquito that had landed on the side of his neck. It was only noticed by Surendranath—who made a sound as if he were regurgitating his own gallbladder—and the boy who was standing next to Jack, holding out his neatly folded clothes. Jack met the boy's eye for a moment; then both looked down at the palm of Jack's hand, where the mosquito lay crumpled in a spot of Jack's, or someone's, blood.

"This lad thinks I've murdered his grandmother now," Jack said. "Could you ask him to shut up?"

But the boy was already saying something, in a bewildered—yet piping and clearly audible—voice. The senior bug-doctor hustled over shouting. Then they *all* converged, and to Jack they suddenly all looked every bit as determined and bloodthirsty as their patients. He snatched his clothes.

Surendranath did not even try to argue the matter, but grabbed Jack's arm and led him out of the room in a brisk walk that soon turned into a run. For news of Jack's crime had spread, faster than thought, through the echoing galleries of the hospital and out its innumerable holes to the front, and (to guess from the sounds that came back) a hundred or more unemployed Swapaks had taken it as a signal to force their way in and launch a furious manhunt.

The monkeys, birds, lizards, and beasts sensed that something was happening, and began to make noise, which worked in Jack and Surendranath's favor. The Banyan got lost in the darkness of the intestinal-parasite ward almost immediately, but Jack—who'd been skulking in and out of the place for weeks—surged into the fore, and soon enough got them pointed towards an exit; they staged an orderly retreat through the monkey room, opening all of the cage-doors on their way through, which (to put it mildly) created a diversion. It was a diversion that fed on itself, for the monkeys were clever enough to do some cage-opening of their own. Once all of the primates had been set free, they spread out into surrounding wards and began to give less intelligent creatures their freedom.

Meanwhile Jack and Surendranath fell back, taking a little-used route past the tiger's cage. Jack tarried for a moment to scoop up a couple of the big cat's turds.

Then they were out into Ahmadabad's main avenue. This was wider than most European streets were long. Its vastness, combined with blood loss, always gave Jack a momentary fit of disorientation; had he found his way back into the city, or gotten lost in some remote wasteland? The monsoon rains were finished, and this part of Hindoostan had turned into a sort of gutter for draining chalk-dry air out of the middle of Asia. On its way down from Tibet, today's shipment of wind had made a tour of the scenic Thar Desert, and availed itself of a heavy load of souvenir dirt, and elevated its temperature to somewhere between that of a camel's breath and that of a tandoori oven. Now it was coming down Ahmadabad's main street like a yak stampede, leaving no doubt as to why Shah Jahan had named the place Guerdabad: The Habitation of Dust.

This place had been conquered by Shah Jahan's crowd—the Moguls—a while ago, and the Moguls were Mohametans who did not especially care whether Jack killed a mosquito. Disturbing the peace was another matter, and if rioting Swapaks did not qualify as disturbing the peace, then dozens of monkeys pouring out into the streets, some with their arms in slings, others hobbling on crutches, certainly did—especially when they caught wind of a market up the street and began to make for it. They were mostly Hanuman mon-keys—flailing, whiptailed ectomorphs who acted as if they owned the place—which, according to Hindoos, they did. But there was an admixture of other primates (notably, an orang-utan recovering from pneumonia) who refused to accord the Hanumans the respect they deserved, and so as they all fought their way upwind toward the market, variously scampering on all fours, waddling on all twos, knuckle-dragging, hopping on lamed feet, swinging from limbs of stately mango-trees, and stampeding over rooftops, they were acting out a sort of running Punch-and-Judy show, flinging coconuts and brandishing sticks at one another. Bringing up the rear: a four-horned antelope that had been born with six horns, a baby one-horned rhinoceros, and a Bhalu, or honey bear, blind and deaf, but drawn by the scent of sweet things in the market.

A pair of *rowzinders*—Mogul cavalrymen—came riding up, all tur-baned and scimitared, black studded shields dangling from their brawny arms, to see what was the matter. Immediately they were engulfed in angry Swapaks telling their side of the story and demanding that the *kotwal* and his retinue of whip-, cudgel-, and mace-brandishing goons be summoned to favor Jack with a *basti-nado*, or worse. The Swapaks' protests got them nowhere, as they spoke only Gujarati and the *rowzinders* spoke only Persian. But these Moguls, like conquerors everywhere, had a keen sense of how to profit from local controversies, and their dark eyes were wide open, following the stabbing fingers of the Swapaks, examining the guilty parties. Surendranath was obviously a Banyan, which was to say that he and his lineage had had more or less condemned by God to engage in foreign trade and make vast amounts of money all their lives. Jack, on the other hand, was a Frank wearing a snatch of leather held on by a crusty thong wedged up his butt-crack. The numerous scars on his back testified to his having been in trouble before—a nearly inconceivable amount of trouble. The *rowzinders* sized the Banyan up as a likely source of *baksheesh*, and made gestures at him indicating that he had better stay put for now. Jack they beck-oned over.

Jack unfastened his gaze, with reluctance, from the thickening drama in the street. Industrious monkeys had evidently been open-ing up bird-cages. The entire Flamingo Ward emerged at once. It looked as if a hogshead of fuchsia paint had been spilled down the steps of the hospital. Most of them were in for broken wings, so all they could do was mill around until one of them appointed himself leader and led them away on a random migration into the Habitation of Dust, pursued or accompanied by a couple of Japalura lizards making eerie booming noises. This hospital had recently admitted a small colony of bearded vultures who were all suffering from avian cholera, and these now gained the rooftop; wiggled their imposing chin-bristles in the gritty breeze; and deployed their wings, which rumbled and snapped like rugs being shaken. They had been well-fed on a sort of carrion slurry made from patients that had died of natural causes, and so as they took to the air they jetted long spates of meaty diarrhea that fell like shafts of light across the backs of fleeing beasts: a praying mantis the size of a crossbow bolt, a spotted deer with a boa constrictor entwined in its antlers, and a nilgai antelope being pursued by the hospital's world-famous two-legged dog, which, miraculously, could not only run, but had been known to outpace many three-legged dogs.

Jack approached the *rowzinders* from downwind. The crowd of Swapaks parted to make room for him, though a few spat on him as he went by. Others had already forgotten about Jack and were running towards the animals. Jack got into position between the heads of the two *rowzinders'* horses and then began to protest his innocence in English whilst surreptitiously crumbling a tiger-turd in each hand. A distinctive fragrance made the horses extremely nervous all of a sudden. "There now, settle down, you two," Jack said to them, and stroked each on the nose, one with each hand—smearing streaks of tiger shit from their brows all the way down to their flaring nostrils.

Then he had to step back to save his own life. Both horses reared up and began slashing at the air with their front hooves, and it was all the *rowzinders* could do to stay in their saddles. They galloped off screaming in opposite directions. One charged straight through the middle of a crowd of Hanuman monkeys who were carrying hairy arm-loads of coconut-meat, figs, mangoes, jamboleiras, papayas, yellow pears, green bilimbins, red cashews, and prickly jack-fruit from the dissolving market, pursued by enraged bazaaris who were in turn pursued by a toothless cheetah. A huge Indian bison, as high at the shoulder as Jack was tall, burst out through a rickety wall, shoving a heap of wrecked tables before him, and shambled into the street with a durian fruit dangling from one of his scimitar-like horns.

A formation of running men veered around the bison and headed straight for Jack and Surendranath. Jack mastered the impulse to turn and flee from them. There were four men in all, a pair supporting each end of a giant spar of bamboo, thick as a mast and four fathoms long. Suspended from the middle of the bamboo was a sort of mobile balcony, a lacquered platform surrounded by a low gilded balustrade and artfully strewn with embroidered cushions. The device had four legs of carven ebony, which dangled an arm's length above the pavement. When these palanquin-bearers drew near, they broke stride and began to negotiate with each other.

"What tongue is that?" Jack asked.

"Marathi."

"Your palanquin is carried by *rebels*?"

"Think of it as a merchant-ship. In the parts of Hindoostan where we will be going, they will be her insurance policy."

The bearers were maneuvering the ends of the bamboo so as to bring the palanquin up alongside Surendranath. When they were finished, they set it down on its ebon legs, so close that their master had only to swivel his arse a compass-point to starboard, and sit down. He busied himself for a few moments arranging some glorious floral cushions against a polished backrest in the stern, then scooted back against them.

"If *they* are the insurance policy, what am *I*?"

"You, and any of your Frank comrades you may be able to round up, are the Marines on the quarterdeck."

"Marines are paid at a flat rate—when they are paid at all," Jack observed. "The *last* time our merry crew were together, we each had a share."

"How much is your share worth now?"

Jack was not, in general, a sigher of sighs, but now he sighed.

"Take inventory of your BATNA," Surendranath suggested, eyeing Jack's naked and lumpy form, "and meet me in an hour's time at the Caravanserai." And then he uttered words in the Marathi tongue, and the four Marathas (as Marathi-speakers were called) got their shoulders under the bamboo and hoisted the palanquin into the air. They spun the conveyance end-for-end in the middle of the vast street and trotted away.

Jack scratched a bug-bite, then another half an inch to the left, then forced himself to stop, before it got out of hand.

The clouded leopard emerged from the hospital, quiet as fog, and curled up in the middle of the street to blink at goings-on; her enormous protruding fangs shone like twin stars in the firmament of swirling dust.

Bearded vultures were raiding a butcher's shop in the market. One of them pounded up into the air with all the grace of a porter lugging a side of beef up a staircase.

Jack trudged upwind, headed for the Triple Gate: a set of three arches at the end of the street. Behind him he heard a rustling commotion, approaching fast. By the time he could turn round to look, it had already overtaken him: a trio of bustards—long-legged black and white birds—disputing possession of some dripping morsel. They reminded Jack of the ostrich in Vienna. Tears came to his eyes, which astonished and annoyed him. He slapped himself in the face, swung wide around a huge waddling porcupine, and headed briskly for the Tin Darwaza, as the Triple Gate was called hereabouts.

THE TIN DARWAZA formed one end of the central square of "The House of Hell" (as Jahangir, the father of Shah Jahan, affectionately referred to Ahmadabad). This square—the Maidan Shah—ran for perhaps a quarter of a mile to the opposite end, which was walled off by a clutter of towers, balconies, pillars, arches, and toy fortifications: the Palace of the local King, whose name was Terror of the Idolaters. The middle of the square was mostly open so that *rowzinders* could practice their horsemanship and archery there, and parade for the amusement of Terror of the Idolaters and his wives. There were a few low undistinguished buildings where the *kotwals* held their tribunals and inflicted the *bastinado* on anyone who did not measure up to their standards of conduct. Jack avoided these.

Several Hindoo pagodas had once stood around the Maidan Shah, and they still did; but they were mosques now. Jack's knowledge of local history was limited to what he'd picked up by talking to Dutch, French, and English traders. But he gathered that this Shah Jahan fellow had spawned a boy named Aurangzeb and despised him so thoroughly that he had made him King of Gujarat, which meant that he had had to come and reside in "the abode of sickness" (another one of Jahangir's pet names for Ahmadabad) and continually do battle against the Marathas. Later Aurangzeb had returned the favor by forcibly overthrowing his father and tossing him into a prison cell in Agra. But in the meantime he'd had many years to kill in The Abode of Sickness and to hone his already keen dislike of all things Hindoo. So he had slaughtered a cow in the middle of the main Hindoo pagoda, defiling it forever, and then gone round with a sledgehammer and knocked the noses off all the idols for good measure. Now it was a mosque. Jack gazed into it as he walked by and saw the usual crowd of *fakirs*—perhaps two hundred of them—sitting on the marble pavement with their arms crossed behind their heads. Of these, some were mere novices. Other had been doing it for long enough that their joints had frozen that way. These had begging-bowls in front of them, never without a few rupees, and from time to time junior *fakirs* would bring them water or food.

Some *fakirs* were Hindoos. As their temples had been desecrated, these had no central place to congregate. Instead they were scattered around the Maidan Shah, under trees or in the lee of walls, performing various penances, some of which were more bizarre and some less bizarre than those of the Mohametan *fakirs*. The common objective of all *fakirs* was to get money out of people, and by that definition, Jack and Padraig were *fakirs* themselves.

After a few minutes' search Jack found his partner seated between the two rows of trees that lined the Maidan Shah. Coincidentally, Padraig had chosen a spot along the south side of the square, beneath one of the jutting balconies of the Caravanserai. Or perhaps it was no coincidence. This was one of the more beautiful buildings in the city. It attracted the wealthy men who made Ahmadabad work, just as the Damplatz did in Amsterdam. Neither its beauty nor its wealth meant much to Jack and Padraig in their current estate. But when they loitered here they could watch caravans coming in from Lahore, Kabul, Kandahar, Agra, and places even farther distant: Chinamen who had brought their silks down from Kashgar over the wastes of Leh, and Armenians who had sallied far to the east from their ghetto in Isfahan, and Turkomans from Bokhara, looking like poorer and shorter versions of the mighty Turks who held sway over Algiers. The Caravanserai reminded them, in other words, that it was possible, at least in theory, to escape "The Thorn Bed" (as Jahangir had referred to Ahmadabad in his *Memoirs*).

Padraig was sitting crosslegged on a snatch of rug (or, to be precise, the coarse weavings that rugs came wrapped in). He had a captured mouse, a rock, and a bowl. When he saw an approaching pedestrian who looked like a Brahmin, he would pin the mouse down on the ground and then raise the rock as if he intended to smash it. Of course he never actually *did* smash the mouse, and neither did Jack, when Jack took his turn. If they smashed the mouse they would not get money from the Brahmin, and they would have to spend valuable time searching for a replacement mouse. But by assiduously *threatening* to smash the mouse all day long, they could collect a few *paisas* in ransom money.

"We've been presented—assuming I am reading the signs correctly—with an opportunity to get ourselves killed for money," Jack announced.

Padraig looked up alertly.

A bloody ox femur fell out of the sky and smashed into the pavement, where it shattered. Two bearded vultures plunged down after it and began to squabble over the marrow.

"Here, or somewhere else?" Padraig inquired, watching the vultures coolly.

"Somewhere else."

Padraig let the mouse run away.

THE CARAVANSERAI SPRAWLED along the southern side of the Maidan Shah, and had many balconies and lodges, all surrounded by delicately carved stone screens, but you got into it through an octagonal porch that was topped with an onion-dome. Four sides of the porch were open to the street and four were archways giving entry to the building itself, or to the yard in the middle, where queues of horses and camels were assembled or dispersed, and loaded or unloaded. It was in that yard that they found the palanquin of Surendranath. The Banyan himself was negotiating with a one-eyed Pathan for a couple of horses, and when he saw Jack's and Padraig's condition he decided to acquire some clothing for them, too. This turned out to be long tunics over loose breeches, and turbans to protect their heads.

"Now that we are out of the bug-feeding business we shall have to let our hair grow back," Jack mused as they rode out of town along the Kathiawar Road, which is to say that they were going a little south of west.

"I could have gotten you European clothes with a little effort, but I did not want to spend any longer than was absolutely necessary in the Place of the Simoom," hollered Surendranath, clutching the balusters of his palanquin as it was slugged by another wind-blast. Leaves of exotic trees, curled and spiked like the shells of sea-creatures, whipped past their heads and cartwheeled madly down the road. Jack and Padraig, on horses, were flanking Surendranath's palanquin, and three of the Banyan's aides were following behind on foot, leading a couple of asses laden with baggage.

"With our backs to the wind it is not so bad," said Padraig; but only because he prided himself on making the best of bad situations. Indeed, the street to the Kathiawar Gate was lined with much that would have been scenic, if not for the dust in their eyes: vast gardens of wealthy Banyans and Moguls, mosques, pagodas, reservoirs, and wells.

"With our backs to Ahmadabad it will be better," said Surendranath. "Kathiawar is reasonably settled, and we can make do with the usual *Charan* escort. But when we begin the journey to the northeast, you will have to dress as Europeans, to cow the Marathas."

"Northeast . . . so our destination is Shahjahanabad?" Jack inquired.

"He would prefer to say Delhi," Padraig put in, after Surendranath failed to answer.

"Of course, because he is a Hindoo, and Shahjahanabad is the Mogul name," Jack said. "Leave it to an Irishman."

"The English have given our cities any number of inventive names," Padraig allowed.

"The monsoon season has brought much valuable cargo from the West this year, but all of it lies piled up in warehouses in Surat," said Surendranath. "Shambhaji and his rebels have made the passage to Delhi a dangerous one. Now I have heard, from mariners who have sailed far to the south, that there are strange birds in those regions who live on ice floes, and that when these birds become hungry they will congregate on the edge of the floe, desiring the small fish that swim in the water below, but fearing the ravenous predators that lurk in that same water. The hunters are subtle, so there is no way for these birds to know whether one is lying in wait for them. Instead they wait for one bird, who might be exceptionally bold, or exceptionally stupid, to jump in alone. If that bird returns with a belly full of fish, they all jump in. If that bird never comes back, they wait."

"The similitude is clear," Jack said. "The merchants of Surat are like the birds on the ice floe, waiting to see who will be bold, or stupid, enough to attempt the passage to Delhi first."

"That merchant will reap incomparably higher profits than the others," Surendranath said encouragingly.

"Assuming his caravan actually makes it to Delhi, that is," said Padraig.

SHORTLY THEY PASSED out through the gate and proceeded southwestwards into Kathiawar, which was a peninsula, a couple of hundred miles square, that projected into the Arabian Sea between the Mouths of the Indus on the west, and the Indian subcontinent on the east. The city of Ahmadabad bestrode a river called Sabarmati that flowed south from there for a few miles and spilled into the Gulf of Cambaye—a long, slender inlet that lay along the east coast of this Kathiawar.

The weather rapidly calmed down as they climbed up out of the valley of the Sabarmati and entered into the hilly, sporadically forested country that would eventually become the Kathiawar Peninsula. They stopped for a night in one of the open roadside camps that tended to form spontaneously all over Hindoostan, whenever shadows began to stretch and travelers' stomachs began to growl. These reminded Jack of gypsy camps in Christendom, and indeed the people looked a good deal like gypsies and spoke a similar language. The difference was that in Christendom they were wretched Vagabonds, but here they were running the place. Wandering from one part of the camp to the next, Jack could see not only penniless wanderers and *fakirs* but also rich Banyans like Surendranath, as well as various Mogul officials.

But both of these types—the Banyans and the Moguls—eyed Jack in a way that made him uneasy, and tried to beckon him over. It was just like being in Amsterdam or Liverpool, where solitary males who did not keep their wits about them were liable to be press-ganged. When Jack understood this he disappeared, which was something he had become good at, and made his way back to Surendranath's little camp.

"There are quite a few people hereabouts who look as if they'd like to administer the Intelligence Test to us," he said to Padraig.

Padraig accepted this news with a tiny nod of the head. But Surendranath had overheard them. He had retreated into his palanquin and drawn red curtains around it for privacy, and it was easy to forget he was there.

"What is the Intelligence Test?" he demanded to know, and swept the curtain aside.

"A private joke," said the annoyed Padraig.

But Jack saw good reasons to explain it, and so he said, "Cast your memory back to when Fortune had set us ashore in Surat—"

"I remember it every day," said Surendranath.

"You stayed there to pursue your career. We fled inland to get away from the diverse European assassins who infested that town, and who were all looking for us. Soon enough, we came upon a Mogul road-block. Hindoos and Mohametans were allowed to pass through with only minor harassment and taking of *baksheesh*, but when it became known that we were Franks, they took us aside and made us sit in a tent together. One by one, each of us was taken out alone, and conducted to a field nearby, and handed a musket—which was unloaded—and a powder-horn, and pouch of balls."

"What did you do?" Surendranath demanded.

"Gaped at it like a farmer."

"I likewise," said Padraig.

"So you failed the Intelligence Test?"

"I would rather say that we *passed* it. Van Hoek did the same as we. Mr. Foot tried to load the musket, but got the procedure backwards—put the ball in first, then the powder. But Vrej Esphahnian and Monsieur Arlanc loaded the weapon and discharged it in the general direction of a Hindoo idol that the Moguls had been using for target practice."

"They were inducted," said Surendranath.

"As far as we know, they have been serving in the armed forces of the local king ever since that day." Jack said.

"This happened north of Surat?"

"Yes. Not far from the Habitation of Dust."

"So, were you in the realm of Terror of the Idolaters?"

"No," said Padraig, "this road-block was at a border crossing. The Moguls who gave us the Intelligence Test, and who press-ganged our friends, were in the pay of—"

"Dispenser of Mayhem!" cried Surendranath.

"The very same," said Jack.

"That is an unexpected boon for us," said the Banyan. "For as you know, the realm of Dispenser of Mayhem lies squarely astride the road to Delhi."

"That amounts to saying that Dispenser of Mayhem has been doing a miserable job of controlling the Marathas," Jack said.

"Which means that if we can find Vrej Esphahnian and Monsieur Arlanc, they will have much useful intelligence for us!"

Jack reckoned that this was as good a moment as any to spring the trap. "Indeed, it seems as if the Cabal—wretched and scattered though we are—may be very useful to you, Surendranath. Or to whichever merchant ends up hiring us, and making the run to Delhi first."

A sort of brisk whooshing noise now, as Surendranath yanked the curtain closed around his palanquin. Then silence—though Jack thought he could hear a curious throbbing, as if Surendranath were trying to stifle agonized laughter.

The next morning they got under way early and traveled for a few miles to a border, where they crossed into the realm of Shatterer of Worlds.

"Shatterer of Worlds has extirpated the local Marathas, but there are ragged bandit gangs all over the place," Surendranath said.

"Reminds me of France," Jack mused.

"The comparison is apt," Surendranath said. "As a matter of fact, it is not even a comparison. Shatterer of Worlds is a Frenchman."

"Those damned Frogs are everywhere!" Jack exclaimed. "Does the Great Mogul have any other kings from Christendom?"

"I believe that Bringer of Thunder is a Neapolitan artilleryman. He owns a piece of Rajasthan."

"Would you like us to round up some Frankish clothes, then? To scare away the highwaymen?" Padraig inquired.

"No need—in Kathiawar, they still observe the ancient customs," said Surendranath, and alighted from his palanquin to parley with some Hindoos who were squatting by the side of the road. In a few minutes, one of them arose and took up a position in the front of the tiny caravan.

A STICK WAS JABBED into the salty concrete that passed for soil hereabouts. A yard away was another stick. A third stick had been lashed across the tops of the first two, and a fourth across the bottom. Miles of vermilion thread had been run back and forth between the top and bottom stick. A woman in an orange sari squatted before this contrivance maneuvering a smaller stick through the vertical threads, drawing another thread behind it. A couple of yards away was the same thing again, except that the sticks, the colors, and the woman were different; and this woman was chatting with a third woman who had also managed to round up four sticks and some thread.

The same was repeated all the way to the horizon on both sides of the road. Some of the weavers were working with coarse undyed thread, but most of their work was in vivid colors that burned in the light of the sun. In some places there would be an irregular patch of green, or blue, or yellow, where some group of weavers were filling a large order. In other zones, each weaver worked with a different thread and so there might be an acre or two in which no two frames were of the same color. The only people who were standing were a few boys carrying water; a smattering of bony wretches bent under racks of thread that were strapped to their backs; and a two-wheeled ox-cart meandering about and collecting finished bits of cloth. A rutted road cut through the middle of it all, headed off in the general direction of Diu: a Portuguese enclave at the tip of Kathiawar. This was the third day of their journey from Ahmadabad. The *Charan* continued to plod along ahead of them, humming to himself, occasionally eating a handful of something from a bag slung over his shoulder.

Out of all the thousands of Pieces of India stretched out for viewing, one caught Jack's eye, like a familiar face in a crowd: a square of blue Calicoe just like one of Eliza's dresses. He decided that he had better get some conversation going.

"Your narration puts me in mind of a question I have been meaning to ask of the first Hindoo I met who had the faintest idea what the hell I was saying," he said.

Down in the palanquin, Surendranath startled awake.

Padraig sat up straighter in his saddle and blinked. "But no one has said a word these last two hours, Jack."

Surendranath was game. "There is much in Hindoostan that cries out, to the Western mind, for explanation," he said agreeably.

"Until we washed ashore near Surat, I fancied I had my thumb on the 'stan' phenomenon," Jack said. "Turks live in Turkestan. Balochs live in Balochistan. Tajiks live in Tajikistan. Of course none of 'em ever stay put in their respective 'stans, which causes the world no end of trouble, but in principle it is all admirably clear. But now here we are in Hindoostan. And I gather that it soon comes to an end, if we go that way." Jack waved his right arm, which, since they were going south, meant that he was gesturing towards the west. "But—" (now sweeping his left arm through a full eight points of the compass, from due south to due east) "—in those directions it goes on practically *forever*. And every person speaks a different language, has skin a different color, and worships a different graven image; it is as variegated as *this*" (indicating a pied hillside of weavers). "Leading to the question, what is the basis for 'stanhood or 'stanitude? To lump so many into one 'stan implies you have *something* in common."

Surendranath leaned forward in his palanquin and looked as if he were just about to answer, then settled back into his cushions with a faint smile under the twin spirals of his waxed moustachio. "It is a mystery of the Orient," he said gravely.

"For Christ's sake, you people need to get organized," Jack said. "You don't even have a common government—it's Moguls up here, and from what you are telling me, if we went south we would soon enough run afoul of those Marathas, and farther south yet, it's those fiends in human form, who've got Moseh and Dappa and the others—"

"Your memories of that day have run together like cheaply dyed textiles in the monsoon rain," Surendranath said.

"Excuse me, I was trying not to drown at the time."

"So was I."

"If they weren't fiends in human form, why did *you* jump overboard?" Padraig asked.

"Because I wanted to get to Surat, and those pirates, whoever or whatever they were, they would have taken us the opposite direction," said Surendranath.

"Why do you suppose *we* jumped out, then?"

"You feared that they were Balochi pirates," Surendranath said.

Padraig: "Those are the ones who cut their captives' Achilles tendons to prevent them escaping?"

Surendranath: "Yes."

Jack: "But wait! If they are Balochis, it follows that they are from Balochistan! If only they would stay put, that is."

Surendranath: "Of course."

Jack: "But Balochistan is that hellish bit that went by to port—the country that vomited hot dust on us for three weeks."

Surendranath: "The description is cruel but fair."

Jack: "That would be a Mahometan country if ever there was one."

Surendranath: "Balochis are Muslims."

Padraig: "It's all coming back to me. We *thought* they were Balochi pirates *at first* because they came after us in a Balochi-looking *ship*. Which, if true, would have been good for all of us save Dappa and you, Surendranath, because we were all Christians or Jews, hence People of the Book. *Our* Achilles tendons were safe."

Surendranath: "I must correct you: it wasn't all right for van Hoek."

Jack: "True, but only because he'd made that asinine vow, when we were in Cairo, that he'd cut his hand off if he were ever taken by pirates again. Consequently he, you, and Dappa were making ready to jump ship."

Padraig: "*My* recollection is that van Hoek meant to stay and fight."

Jack: "The Irishman speaks the truth. The cap'n took us between two islands, in the Gulf of Cambaye over yonder—whereupon we were beset by the *second* pirate ship, which was obviously acting in concert with the first."

Padraig: "But *this* one was much closer and was manned by—how do you say—"

Surendranath: "Sangano pirates. Hindoos who steal, but do not kidnap, enslave, maim, or torture, except insofar as they have to in order to steal."

Jack: "And who had apparently taken that first ship from some luckless Balochi pirates, which is why we mistook them for Balochis at first."

Surendranath: "To this point, you are speaking the truth, as I recollect it."

Padraig: "No wonder—this is the point when you jumped out!"

Surendranath: "It made sense for me to jump out, because it was obvious that we were going to lose all of the gold to the Sangano pirates. But van Hoek was preparing to fight to the death."

Jack: "I must not have heard the splash, Surendranath, as my mind was occupied with other concerns. Van Hoek, as you say, was steering a course for open water in the middle of the Gulf, probably with the intention of fighting it out to the end. But we hadn't gone more than a mile when we stumbled directly into the path of a raiding-flotilla, whereupon *all* of the boats—ours, and our pursuers'—were fair game for this new group."

Padraig: "Darkies, but not Africans."

Jack: "Hindoos, but not Hindoostanis, precisely."

Padraig: "Only pirate-ships I've ever heard of commanded by *women*."

Jack: "There are rumored to be some in the Caribbean—but—none the less—it was a queer group indeed."

Surendranath: "You are describing Malabar pirates, then."

Jack: "As I said—fiends in human form!"

Surendranath: "They do things differently in Malabar."

Padraig: "At any rate, even van Hoek could now see it was hopeless, and so he jumped, which was preferable to cutting his hand off."

Surendranath: "Why did *you* jump, Padraig?"

Padraig: "I fled from Ireland, in the first place, specifically to get away from matriarchal oppression. Why did *you* jump, Jack?"

Jack: "Rumors had begun to circulate that the Malabar pirates were even more cruel to Christians than the Balochi pirates were to Hindoos."

Surendranath: "Nonsense! You were misinformed. The *Mohametan* Malabar pirates are that way, to be sure. But if the ships you saw were commanded by women, then they must have been *Hindoo* Malabar pirates."

Padraig: "They are *rich* female Hindoo Malabar pirates now."

Jack: "Mr. Foot had run to the head, either to take a shite (which is what he normally does at such times) or to wave a white flag. But he tripped on a loose gold bar and pitched overboard. I went after him, knowing he couldn't swim. The water turned out to be less than two fathoms deep—I nearly broke my leg hitting the bottom. Accordingly, our ship ran aground at nearly the same moment. The rest is a blur."

Padraig: "It's not *such* a blur. You and I, Monsieur Arlanc, Mr. Foot, van Hoek, and Vrej waded, bobbed, and dog-paddled across those endless shallows for a day or two. At some point we re-encountered Surendranath. Finally we washed up near Surat. The Armenian and the Frenchman later failed the Intelligence Test and wound up in the army of Dispenser of Mayhem."

Surendranath: "Concerning those two, by the way, I have sent out some messages to my cousin in Udaipur—he will make inquiries."

They came over the top of a gentle rise and saw new country ahead. A mile or two distant, the road crossed a small river that ran from right to left towards the Gulf of Cambaye, which was barely visible as a grayish fuzz on the eastern horizon. The river crossing was commanded by a mud-brick fort, and around the fort was a meager walled town. Jack already knew what they would find there: a landing for boats coming up the river from the Gulf, and a marketplace where Pieces of India were peddled to Banyans or European buyers.

Jack said, "It will be good to see Vrej and Arlanc again, assuming they are still alive, and I will enjoy listening to their war-stories. But I already know what they would tell us, if they were here."

This announcement seemed to startle Padraig and Surendranath, and so Jack explained, "There must be some advantage to growing old, or else why would we put up with it?"

"You're not old," Padraig said, "you can't be forty yet."

"Stay. I have lived through more than most old men. Letters I have not learned, nor numbers, and so I cannot read a book, nor navigate a ship, nor calculate the proper angle for an artillery-piece. But people I know well—better than I should like to—and so the situation of Hindoostan is all too clear to me. It is clear when I watch you, Surendranath, speaking of the Moguls, and you, Padraig, speaking of the English."

"Will you share your wisdom with us then, O Jack?" Padraig asked.

"If Vrej Esphahnian and Monsieur Arlanc were here, they would tell us that the Marathas are angry, well-organized, and not afraid to die, and that the Moguls are orgulous and corrupt—that the rulers of this Empire live better while besieging some Maratha fortress than the Hindoos do when they are at peace. They would tell us, in other words, that this rebellion is a serious matter, and that we cannot get the caravan of Surendranath from Surat to Delhi by dint of charm or bribery."

"You seem to be telling me that it is impossible," Surendranath said. "Perhaps we should turn around and go back to the Habitation of Dust."

"Surendranath, which would you rather be: the first bird to jump off the ice floe, or the first bird to climb back onto it with a belly full of fish?"

"The question answers itself," Surendranath said.

"If you listen to my advice, you will not be the former, but you will be the latter."

"You think other caravans will leave Surat first, and fall prey to the rebels," Surendranath translated.

"I believe that any caravan headed to Delhi will have to face the Maratha army at some point," Jack said. "The first such caravan to drive the Marathas from the field shall be the first to reach its destination."

"I cannot hire an army," Surendranath said.

"I did not say you need to hire an army. I said you need to drive the Marathas from the field."

"You speak like a *fakir*," Surendranath said darkly.

THE *MAIDAN* OF THIS KATHIAWAR river-town sported a more or less typical assortment of *fakirs* both Hindoo and Mahometan. Several were content with the old arms-crossed-behind-the-head trick. A Hindoo one was swallowing fire, a red-skirted Dervish was whirling around, another Hindoo was standing on his head covered with red dust. And yet most of them had empty begging-bowls and were going ignored by the townspeople. A score of idlers, barefoot boys, passersby, strolling pedlars and river-traders had gathered around one spectacle at the end of the *maidan*.

They were crowded so closely together that if Jack had not been mounted he wouldn't have been able to see the object of their attention: a gray-haired European man dressed up in clothes that had been out-moded, in England, before Jack had been born. He wore a black frock coat and a broad-brimmed black Pilgrim-hat and a frayed shirt that made him look like a wandering Puritan bible-pounder. And indeed there was an old worm-eaten Bible in view, resting on a low table—actually a plank, just barely spanning the gap between a couple of improvised sawbucks, with a stained and torn cloth thrown over it. Next to the Bible was another tome that Jack recognized as a hymn-book, and next to the hymnal, a little place setting: a china plate flanked by a rusty knife and fork.

Jack seemed to have arrived during a lull, which soon came to an end as an excited young Hindoo came running in from the market nearby, a dripping object held in his cupped hands. The crowd parted for him. He scampered up and deposited it in the center of the *fakir*'s plate: a metal-gray giblet leaking blood and clear juice. Then he jumped back as if his hands had been burned, and ran over to wipe his hands on a nearby patch of grass.

The *fakir* sat for a few moments regarding the kidney with extreme solemnity, waiting for the buzz of the crowd to die away. Only when complete silence had fallen over the *maidan* did he reach for the knife and fork. He gripped one in each hand and held them poised over the organ for a few agonizing moments. The crowd underwent a sort of convulsion as every onlooker shifted to a better viewing angle.

The *fakir* appeared to lose his nerve, and set the utensils down. A sigh of mixed relief and disappointment ran through the onlookers. Someone darted up and tossed a *paisa* onto the table. The *fakir* put his hands together in a prayerful attitude and muttered indistinctly for a while, then reached for his Bible, opened it up, and read a paragraph or two, faltering as he came to bits that had been elided by book-worms. But this was something from the Old Testament with many "begats" and so it scarcely mattered.

Again he took up the knife and fork and struggled with himself for a while, and again lost his nerve and set them down. Mounting excitement in the crowd, now. More and larger coins rang on the plank. The *fakir* took up the hymnal, rose to his feet, and bellowed out a few verses of that old Puritan favorite:

> *If God thou send'st me straight to Hell*
> *When I have breath'd my Last,*
> *Just like a Stone flung in a Well*
> *I'll go down meek and Fast . . .*
> *For even though I've done my Best*
> *T'obey thy Law Divine,*
> *Who am I, thee to contest?*
> *The Fault must all be Mine!*

. . . and so on in that vein until the fire-eater and the Dervish were screaming at him to shut up.

Pretending to ignore their protests, the Christian *fakir* closed up the hymnal, took up knife and fork for the third time, and—having finally mustered the spiritual power to proceed—pierced the kidney. A jet of urine lunged out and nearly spattered an audacious boy, who jumped back screaming. The *fakir* took a good long time sawing off a piece of the organ. The crowd crept inwards again, not because anyone really wanted to get any closer, but because people kept blocking one another's view. The *fakir* impaled the morsel on the tines of the fork and raised it on high so that even the groundlings in the back row could get a clear view. Then in one quick movement he popped it into his mouth and began to chew it up.

Several fled wailing. Coins began to zero in on the *fakir* from diverse points of the compass. But after his Adam's apple moved up and down, and he opened his mouth wide to show it empty, and curled his tongue back to show he wasn't hiding anything, a barrage of *paisas* and even *rupees* came down on him.

"A stirring performance, Mr. Foot," said Jack, half an hour later, as they were all riding out of town together. "Lo these many months I have been worried sick about you, wondering how you were getting along—unfoundedly, as it turns out."

"Very considerate of you, then, to show up *unasked-for* to share your poverty with me," said Mr. Foot waspishly. Jack had extracted him from the *maidan* suddenly and none too gently, even to the point of leaving half the kidney sitting on the plate uneaten.

"I regret I missed the show," said Padraig.

"Nothing you haven't seen before in a thousand pubs," Jack answered mildly.

"E'en so," said Padraig," it had to've been better than what I've been doing the last hour: sneaking round peering at idolaters' piss-pots."

"What learned you?"

"Same as in the last village—they do it in pots. Untouchables come round once a day to empty them," Padraig answered.

"Are the piss and shit always mixed together or—"

"Oh, for Christ's sake!"

"First kidney-eating and now chamber-pots!" exclaimed Surendranath from his palanquin. "Why this keen curiosity concerning all matters related to urine?"

"Maybe we will have better luck in Diu," Jack said enigmatically.

That river-crossing marked the beginning of a long, slow climb up into some dark hills to the south. Surendranath assured them that it was possible to circumvent the Gir Hills simply by following the coastal roads, but Jack insisted that they go right through the middle. At one point he led them off into a dense stand of trees, and spent a while tromping around in the undergrowth hefting various branches and snapping them over his knee to judge their dryness. This was the only part of the trip when they were in anything like danger, for (a) Jack surprised a cobra and (b) half a dozen bandits came out brandishing crude, but adequate, weapons. The Hindoo whom Surendranath had hired finally did something useful: viz. pulled a small dagger, hardly more than a paring-knife really, from his cummerbund and held it up to his own neck and then stood there adamantly threatening to cut his own throat.

The effect on the bandits was as if this fellow had summoned forth a whole artillery-regiment and surrounded them with loaded cannons. They dropped their armaments and held forth their hands beseechingly and pleaded with him in Gujarati for a while. After lengthy negotiations, fraught with unexpected twists and alarming setbacks, the *Charan* finally consented not to hurt himself, the bandits fled, and the party moved on.

Within the hour they had passed over the final crest of the Hills of Gir and come to a height-of-land whence they could look straight down a south-flowing river valley to the coast: the end of the Kathiawar Peninsula. At the point where the river emptied into the sea was a white speck; beyond it, the Arabian Sea stretched away forever.

As they traveled down that valley over the next day, the white speck gradually took on definition and resolved itself into a town with a European fort in the middle. Several East Indiamen, and

smaller ships, sheltered beneath the fort's guns in a little harbor.
The road became broader as they neared Diu. They were jostled
together with caravans bringing bolts of cloth and bundles of spices
towards the waiting ships, and began to meet Portuguese traders
journeying up-country to trade.

They stopped short of the city wall, and made no effort to go in
through those gates, guarded as they were by Portuguese soldiers.
The *Charan* said his farewell and hunkered down by the side of the
road to await some northbound caravan that might be in need of his
protection. Jack, Padraig, Mr. Foot, Surendranath, and their small
retinue began to wander through the jumbled suburbs, scattering
peacocks and diverting around sacred cows, stopping frequently to
ask for directions. After a while Jack caught a whiff of malt and yeast
on the breeze, and from that point onwards they were able to follow
their noses.

Finally they arrived at a little compound piled high with faggots
of spindly wood and round baskets of grain. A giant kettle was dangling over a fire, and a short red-headed man was standing over it
gazing at his own reflection: not because he was a narcissist, but
because this was how brewers judged the temperature of their wort.
Behind him, a couple of Hindoo workers were straining to heave a
barrel of beer up into a two-wheeled cart: bound, no doubt, for a
Portuguese garrison inside the walls.

"It is all as tidy and prosperous as anything in Hindoostan could
be," Jack announced, riding slowly into the middle of it. "A little corner of Amsterdam here at the butt-end of Kathiawar."

The redhead's blue eyes swivelled up one notch, and gazed at
Jack levelly through a rising cataract of steam.

"But it was never meant to last," Jack continued, "and you know
that as well as I do, Otto van Hoek."

"It has lasted as well as anything that is of this earth."

"But when you make your delivery-rounds, to the garrisons and
the wharves, you must look at those beautiful ships."

"Then of ships speak to me," said van Hoek, "or else go away."

"Tap us a keg and dump out that kettle," Jack said, "so we can put
it to *alchemical* uses. I have just ridden down out of the Hills of Gir,
and firewood is plentiful there. And as long as you keep peddling
your merchandise to the good people of Diu, the other thing we
need will be plentiful *here*."

The Surat-Broach Road, Hindoostan
A MONTH LATER (OCTOBER 1693)

> For the works of the Egyptian sorcerers, though not
> so great as those of Moses, yet were great miracles.
> —HOBBES,
> *Leviathan*

"LORD HELP ME," said Jack, "I have begun thinking like an Alchemist." He snapped an aloe-branch in half and dabbed its weeping stump against a crusted black patch on his forearm. He and certain others of the Cabal were reclining in the shade of some outlandish tree on the coastal plain north of Surat. Strung out along the road nearby was a caravan of bullocks and camels.

"Half of Diu believes you *are* one, now," said Otto van Hoek, squinting west across the fiery silver horizon of the Gulf of Cambaye. Diu lay safely on the opposite side of it. Van Hoek had been busy unwinding a long, stinking strip of linen from his left hand, but the pain of forcing out these words through his roasted voice-box forced him to stop for a few moments and prosecute a fit of coughing and nose-wiping.

"If we had stayed any longer the Inquisition would have come for us," said Monsieur Arlanc in a similarly hoarse and burnt voice.

"Yes—if for no other reason than the stench," put in Vrej Esphahnian. Of all of them, he had taken the most precautions—viz. wearing leather gloves that could be shaken off when his hands burst into flame spontaneously. So he was in a better state than the others.

"It is well that we had Mr. Foot with us," said Surendranath, "to bamboozle the Inquisitors into thinking that we pursued some sacred errand!" Surendranath had not spent all that much time among Christians, and his incredulous glee struck them all as just a bit unseemly.

"I'll take a share of the credit for that," said Padraig Tallow, who had lost his dominant eye, and all the hair on one side of his head.

"For 'twas I who supplied Mr. Foot with all of his churchly clap-trap; he only spoke lines that I wrote."

"No one denies it," said Surendranath, "but even you must admit that the inexhaustible fount and ever-bubbling wellspring of non-sense, gibberish, and fraud was Ali Zaybak!"

"I cede the point gladly," said Padraig, and both men turned to see if Jack would respond to their baiting. But Jack had been dis-tracted by an odor foul enough to register even on his raspy and inflamed olfactory. Van Hoek had got the bandage off his right hand. The tips of his three remaining fingers were swollen and weeping.

"I told you," said Jack, "you should have used this stuff." He ges-tured to the aloe-plant, or rather the stump of it, as Jack had just snapped off the last remaining branch. It was growing in a pot of damp dirt, which was carried on its own wee palanquin: a plank sup-ported at each end by a boy. "The Portuguese brought it out of Africa," Jack explained.

"Truly you *are* thinking like an Alchemist, then," muttered van Hoek, staring morosely at his rotting digits. "Everyone knows that the only treatment for burns is butter. It is proof of how far gone you are in outlandish ways, that you would rather use some occult potion out of Africa!"

"When do you think you'll amputate?" Jack inquired.

"This evening," said van Hoek. "That way I shall have twenty-four hours to recuperate before the battle." He looked to Surendranath for confirmation.

"If our objective were to make time, and to cross the Narmada by day, we could do it tomorrow," said Surendranath. "But as our true purpose is to 'fall behind schedule,' and reach the crossing too late, and be trapped against the river by the fall of night, we may proceed at a leisurely pace. This evening's camp would be a fine time and place to carry out a minor amputation. I shall make inquiries about getting you some syrup of poppies."

"More *chymistry!*" van Hoek scoffed, and dipped his hand into a pot of ghee. But he did not object to Surendranath's proposal. "I could have been a *brewer*," he mused. "In fact, I *was!*"

VAN HOEK HAD SURRENDERED his brewing-coppers to Jack and gone down to the harbor of Diu to see about hiring a dhow or something like it. Jack, spending Surendranath's capital, had set some local smiths to work beating the copper tuns into new shapes—shapes that Jack chalked out for them from his memories of Enoch Root's strange works in the Harz Mountains. Surendranath had sent messengers north to the kingdom of Dispenser of Mayhem, along with money to buy the freedom of Vrej Esphahnian and Monsieur Arlanc. Then the Banyan, somewhat against his better instincts, had set about turning himself into a urine mogul.

Some simple deals struck with the caste of night-soil-collectors and chamber-pot-emptiers caused jugs, barrels, and hogsheads of piss to come trundling into van Hoek's brewery-compound every morning. By and large these had been covered, to keep the stink down, but Jack insisted that the lids be taken off and the piss be allowed to stand open under the sun. Complaints from the neighbors—consisting largely of religious orders—had not been long in coming. And it was then that Mr. Foot had come into his own; for he'd been at work with needle and thread, converting his black Puritan get-up into a sort of Wizard's robe. His line of patter consisted half of Alchemy—which Jack had dictated—and half of Popery, which Padraig Tallow could and did rattle off in his sleep.

What Jack knew of Alchemy-talk came partly from the mountebanks who would stand along the Pont-Neuf peddling bits of the Philosopher's Stone; partly from Enoch Root; and partly from tales that he had been told, more recently, by Nyazi, who knew nothing of chymistry but was the last word on all matters to do with camels.

"*Amon,* or Amon-Ra, was the great god of the ancient peoples of al-Khem.* And just as al-Khem gave its name to Alchemy, so did the god Amon serve as namesake of a magickal substance well known to practitioners of that Art. For behold, when the Romans made al-Khem a part of their empire, they perceived in this Amon a manifestation of Jupiter, and dubbed him Jupiter-Ammon, and made idols depicting him as a mighty King with ram's horns sprouting from his temples. To him they raised up a great temple at the Oasis of Siwa, which lies in the desert far to the west of Alexandria. As well as being a great caravanserai, long has that place been a center of mystickal powers and emanations; lo, an oracle of Amon was there from the time of the Pharaohs, and the Roman temple of Jupiter-Ammon was erected upon the same site. It was, and is, a very hotbed of Alchemy, and has become renowned for the production of a pungent salt, which is prepared from the dung of the thousands of camels that pass through the place. The secret of its preparation is known to but a few; but the Salt of Ammon, or *sal ammoniac,* is taken by the caravans to Alexandria and the other trading-centers of North Africa, whence it is distributed the world over by the infinitely various channels of Commerce. Thus have its extraordinary, and some would say

---

* Egypt

magical, powers become known throughout the world. Now, if ignorant pagans could make so much out of what was literally a heap of shit, consider how much more Christians, who know the Bible, and who have access to the writings of Paracelsus, &c., might accomplish! What is present in camel shit, may also be found in the urine of humans, for Aristotle would say that both of these substances are of the same essential nature. Though Plato would observe that the latter is as much more refined and closer to the Ideal as human beings are compared to camels . . ."

All of this was, of course, a long-winded way of letting the neighbors know that Jack and company were about to stink the place up to a degree that no one who had not been near a mountain of fermenting camel shit could even imagine; but Mr. Foot delivered the terrible news at such numbing length and so laden down with homiletical baggage as to beat his auditors into submission before the essential point of what he was saying had even penetrated their minds.

As was ever true of any work that entailed the bending and beating of metal, the conversion of the tuns took longer than anticipated. What Jack was after was a single great round-bottomed wide-mouthed boiler, and a means to suspend it over a "bloody enormous" fire. This was simple enough. But at a later, critical stage of the operation he needed to clamp a sort of hat down over the maw of the kettle, and channel the vapors along a tube to another, smaller vessel where they could be bubbled through water. For the most practical of reasons, it was preferable that this latter vessel be made of glass. But it had proved difficult to get a glass container so large, and so they made do with copper. This explained what happened to Padraig; for against Jack's express instructions, he had, while they were making a trial batch, lifted the lid to peer inside, and been greeted by a jet of white flame.

Around the time of this mishap, managerial acumen arrived in the person of Monsieur Arlanc, and, in Vrej Esphahnian, entrepreneurial legerdemain. Arlanc pointed out that it would be difficult to hire good people, or to maintain their reputation as proficient Alchemists, if the principals were forever torching off body parts, and making the Kathiawar Peninsula ring with screams of agony. Vrej, for his part, had proffered the observation that they would soon need to procure a large number of glass vessels *anyway*, and so it was high time to begin investigating the local market in such wares.

The results were none too encouraging. In Diu there was no Worshipful Company of Glass Sellers, as in London. Indeed, it seemed that glass-making was one of the few arts and crafts that Christians did better than anyone else. There had, according to Vrej, been many brilliant glassworkers in Damascus three hundred years ago, but then Tamerlane had sacked the place and carried them all off to Samarkand, and they had not been heard from since. There was no time just now to send a delegation to Samarkand and make inquiries. So they had to make do with what glass could be collected from the diverse Portuguese chapter-houses, factories, and fortifications around Diu. For the bubbling-vessel, Vrej procured a single windowpane about a hand-span on a side. Jack put his coppersmiths to work letting a hole into the side of the vessel, and van Hoek used his caulking acumen to seal the pane into place so that not too much water would leak out around the edges. All of which took a while. But it required upwards of a fortnight for a given bucket of piss to reach the point where it was ready to be used, and so the hurry was not great. And Arlanc had been kept busy for some while procuring charcoal from the wooded hills in the north. This had to be prepared by locals making countless small batches in countless tandoors, then collected and gathered and shipped. Capital ran low. Vessels came across from Surat bearing news, or at least rumors, that this or that Banyan was readying a caravan and a puissant force of mercenaries to punch through the Maratha blockade along the Narmada; and each such message sent Surendranath into an ecstasy of rage, and caused him to run about the compound (weaving carefully between urine-receptacles) flinging his turban on the ground and then picking it up so that he could fling it down again, while wondering aloud to the gods why he had ever chosen to take up with all of these crazy *ferangs*. For a week, it seemed that all they had to show for their efforts was a sea of putrescent urine; a lot of copper, beaten to outlandish shapes and stuck together with solder and with tar; and a few patches of dirt where dusk seemed to linger even after black night had covered the rest of Hindoostan.

But then finally a cart-train came down out of the north laden with charcoal and with firewood, and Vrej Esphahnian unveiled a wooden crate containing a gross of glass bottles (smoky brown, striated, and bubbly, but more or less transparent), and they were ready to go. Jack had mentioned to them, and Padraig had demonstrated beyond all question, that the apparatus would destroy itself in a spitting storm of white fire shortly after they were finished using it; they had, in other words, one and only one chance.

At last one morning Jack and van Hoek and some local representatives of the chamber-pot-handling caste wrapped cloths around their mouths and noses and set about lugging the vast motley collection of kegs, urns, and pots of fœtid urine up to the great kettle and dumping them in. At the same time, the largest and hottest possible bonfire was kindled beneath. It took some time for the fire to take hold, for the piss had grown chilly sitting out overnight. But when it did, all fled the compound, and many fled the neighborhood. They *would* have fled *screaming*, if they'd had the power to draw breath. Not that they were any strangers to the stench of old piss, by this point; but what the kettle exhaled was of an altogether different order. The broad rim of that kettle might as well have been the maw of Jupiter-Ammon himself, striking mortals dead, not with thunder-bolts from on high, but with burning exhalations drawn up from Hell. It made the air shiver as it came on, and made birds fold their wings and smack their little heads into the ground. Men could do nothing but hide their eyes in the crooks of their arms, plug their noses, and bump into one another until they found a way out. When they had escaped to a radius where it was possible to draw breath, they turned inwards and watched the kettle through sheets of burn-ing tears. From time to time someone would draw in a deep breath and hold it while he sprinted back to the hell-mouth to shove a few more pieces of cord-wood into the fire.

After a while the stench dissipated, and not long after that, steam began to rise. Presently the kettle came to a galloping boil, and they found that they could approach. The Breath of Ammon had all been expelled. But this was not the last time they smelled it, for the kettle had not been capacious enough to hold all the urine they had col-lected, and much remained strewn about the compound in diverse small containers. As the level of the boiling brew fell, they dumped in more urine to top it off again, and each time they did, it let off another scream of Ammon-breath. This went on for much of the day; but finally the last chamber-pot had been emptied and tossed into the street. A few minutes later the stench of sal ammoniac abated for good. There followed an interlude of some hours during which the kettle merely boiled, and threw off a column of steam that rose high over Diu and drifted away into the blue sky over the sea. Jack, peering in over the kettle's rim, saw it boiled down to a small fraction of its former volume, and glimpsed just beneath the foam-ing surface a churning mass of solid yellow-brown stuff. From time to time he reached into it with a paddle, checking its consistency as he had seen Enoch Root do. When it became difficult to stir, he called for charcoal. The mass was stained with black as sacks of the stuff, ground up to the consistency of meal, were dumped in. Jack stirred until the mix was gray, and so dry and thick that the paddle nearly became lodged in it. Moisture was still condensing on his brow, but he knew all the water was nearly gone now, and they must work quickly. The others knew as much as Jack did, having been in on the trial batch that had taken Padraig's eye. So when Jack jumped back from the kettle's rim they did not need to be told what to do: pulling on lines and pushing with sticks, they maneuvered over the kettle's rim an upside-down funnel of the same diameter, and set it down so that the two were joined in an open-mouth kiss, and packed oakum and dribbled tar around the junction so that no fume could escape. All of the vapors emanating from the hot gray mass in the bottom of the kettle were now channeled up into the copper dunce-cap, which had but one outlet: a copper chimney that bent round to the side and developed into a snergly tube, terminated by a U-bend that led into the bottom of the smaller vessel—the bubbler—with the glass port-hole in its side. This was filled with water, as anyone who looked at the window could see. It was two fathoms above the ground, and they had erected a scaffold and a platform of bamboo so that they could work there.

When Jack was satisfied with the progress of the caulking and sealing of the great dunce-cap, he ascended the platform—a tinker's shop and an apothecary-store of ladles, funnels, bottles, and terra-cotta vessels of clove-oil—and was pleased to observe a slight rise in the water-level, followed by a blurp and a collapse as some residual steam forced its way through the water-trap in the U-bend. This happened several more times in the next few minutes as the very last of the moisture was exhaled from the humid cake in the kettle, but then it stopped. There was then an interlude, which grew awkward the longer it went on; but Jack bid them keep stoking the fire and have faith. He was viewing the water level with respect to a wee bubble trapped in the glass pane, and for a while it did not move at all. But then it rose up distinctly, and a moment later a little belch of vapor shimmered up through the water and broke out the top. "It begins!" he announced.

Contrary to claims lately issued by Mr. Foot to the good people of Diu, Jack did not have the power to command the wheeling of the heavens. It was wholly fortuitous that the sun went down a few minutes later. The window in the side of the bubbler gleamed in the light of the sunset, as shiny objects were wont to do. But after the sun had gone down it continued to glow for a length of time that was odd, then remarkable, and, finally, unnatural. For it only got brighter as the night grew darker. Had it not been square, it might have been mistaken for a full moon. It grew so bright that if Jack stared at it full-on he became dazzled, and then could see nothing else. He assigned to Monsieur Arlanc the duty of monitoring the level of the water and adding more as needed to keep it from boiling dry; which had been the error that had led to Padraig's injury. Jack then turned his back on the window and let his eyes adjust. From the platform, he saw, as if he were an actor on a stage, a lake of faces, all turned his way, many with mouths open in wonder, all lit up by the blue-green radiance of the *kaltes Feuer,* the cold fire, of Phosphorus: light-bearer. They were all out of doors, of course, and the cold fire confined to a small vessel of beaten copper; but that was not how it *seemed.* It *seemed* that these people were all walled up inside some black dungeon, which had only a single square window, high up in the wall, through which light shone in from another world.

"This will all be smoking ruins by break of day," he announced, "let us gather what we may of the *kaltes Feuer* and preserve it from the air, and ourselves from fiery death!"

They went about that in two ways. First, someone would from time to time dip a ladle into the top of the bubbler and scoop out portions of the water, and along with it, flecks and flakes of cold fire that swirled through it like sparks above a campfire. This they decanted through funnels into the bottles that Vrej had procured. The glowing bottles were handed down to others on the ground, who stopped them with rags to prevent air from getting in. These were then placed into a tray of simmering water that was going over a bed of coals. Gradually, over a period of hours, the level of water within these bottles declined as it escaped through the rag stoppers. But the amount of light escaping from them did not diminish, for the waxy phosphorus was trapped inside, and tended to cling to the walls, so that each bottle over time acquired a blotchy lining of weird light. When these bottles were nearly dry, they were plucked out and plunged neck-first into a tar-pot, to seal them against infiltration of air.

Second, they dumped ladles of the stuff into clay pots each of which contained a small amount of clove oil. The water fell through the oil and found the bottom of the pot, shedding some of its burden of phosphorus along the way. These pots were then subjected to a similar process of gentle heating, so that the water trapped beneath the oil was driven out as steam. When these pots stopped blurping and steaming, it meant that all the water was gone, and nothing was left but phosphorus suspended in oil. The oil coated the tiny particules of phosphorus and prevented air from touching them, which rendered the stuff safe.

This anyway was the general plan of action. For the most part it actually went this way; but what made it interesting were the mishaps. Every splash and spill remained visible as a pool, burst, or dribbling trail of cold fire. Jack got some splashed on a forearm and did not notice it until he went and stood by the bottle-simmering place for a few minutes; the warmth shining from the bed of coals dried the damp place on his arm, leaving a fine layer of phosphorus that burst into unquenchable flame. Many had similar stories. Presently most of them were naked, having frantically stripped off clothing when it was pointed out to them by excited spectators that they were glowing. Ladles were spilled on the scaffolding by burnt and nervous hands, obliging Monsieur Arlanc to stand his ground with more than human courage as he implored someone to come up and wash away the spill with buckets of fresh water before it dried out. The caulking around the windowpane weeped, then seeped, then began to dribble a steady stream of cold fire. They made shift to catch what they could of this, and confine it to bottles or oil-pots; but matters deteriorated as more and more of the scaffold, the ground beneath it, and the men working on it became tinged with the fire, which could have only one consequence when it dried. Finally Jack ordered Monsieur Arlanc to abandon ship. The Huguenot vaulted down with spryness odd in a man of his age, rending his garments even as he hit the ground; men converged on him with buckets of sea-water and sluiced him off until he was dark. Then all ran away, for the leak around the windowpane had opened wide, and the fire was raining down in a blinding cataract. The water all came out. Air found its way in through the empty bubbler to the chimney, which had become thickly lined with condensed phosphorus. White fire shrieked out of it. The sun rose. What a moment ago had been glowing pools of spilled fire on the black velvet ground, were revealed as damp patches on khaki dirt. The bubbler ripped loose, hurtled away, and impacted on the roof of a monastery half a mile downrange. The chimney and dunce-cap shot into the air, spiraling and pinwheeling through the night sky as if the Big Dipper had scooped up a load of the sun's own fire. It landed somewhere out to sea. Left in the vicinity of the scaffold was a metropolis of small sputtering conflagrations that erupted here and there without warning over the next several hours. Fortunately they had had the wisdom to establish the double-boilers for the bottles and the clove-oil pots at a respectful distance. So they abandoned the center and toiled at the periphery until daybreak. This was not without some dangers of its own; sometimes a bottle would crack from the heat, and then some intrepid person would have to pluck it out with tongs and fling it away, lest in burning and exploding it would detonate the others. This led to the burning-down of the house where they had all been dwelling. In other circumstances, the loss of their domicile would have been rated a grave setback; as it was, they knew they were going to be kicked out of town anyway. A formation of Portuguese pike-men came for them at daybreak. Working amid the smoldering ruins of what had, a month earlier, been a perfectly respectable brewery, Jack and the others had already loaded the bottles (packed very carefully in straw) and the pots of oil into crates, and the crates onto those wagons that remained unburnt, and harnessed these to the few domesticated beasts that had not run away or simply dropped dead of terror during the night-time. They were escorted, not to say pursued, by the pikemen down to the quay where they boarded their hired boat with the phosphorus and what few possessions they still had. Winds favored them; pirates, who had witnessed strange appari-tions in the night sky above Diu, avoided them; and a day and half a later they were in Surat, taking up their position near the head of a great armed trade-caravan, and beginning the long march north and east to Shahjahanabad.

"YOU WILL BE AMUSED to know that where I come from, swords are straight," Jack said. "Some are broader, and indeed, being a plain-spoken people, we call those broadswords. Some are of intermediate size, as rapiers, others whisker-thin, as the small-swords that are lately in vogue. Oh, admittedly one sees a few blades with a bit of a curve to them, as in your cutlass or saber. But compared to these, they're all straight as a line, as are the style and tactics of their usage. Compared to which . . ." Jack extended a hand towards a Mobb of warriors that they had picked up in Surat. There were *Yavanas*—which was to say, Muslims—who had come across the water from the lands to the west, or down out of Afghanistan, Balochistan, or this or that Khanate. And there were Hindoos of diverse martial castes who for whatever reason had elected to throw in their lot with the Moguls. But even within the smallest discernible sub-sub-subtribe each warrior had a weapon—or at least, a dangerous-looking object—completely different from the next bloke's.

Among the personal effects of the Doctor, Jack had once seen books, filled not with letters but with depictions of curves. These he had leafed through in times of boredom; for though he could not read, he could stare at a strange curve as well as any other man. Eliza had sat next to him and pronounced their names: the Limaçon of Pascal, the Kampyle of Eudoxus, the Conchoid of de Sluze, the Quadratrix of Hippias, the Epitrochoid, Tractrix, and the Cassinian Ovals. At the onset of the recitation Jack had wondered how geometers could be so inventive as to produce so many types and families of curves. Later he had come to perceive that of curves there was no end, and the true miracle was that poets, or writers, or whoever it was that was in charge of devising new words, could keep pace with those hectic geometers, and slap names on all the whorls and snarls in the pages of the Doctor's geometry-books. Now, though, he understood that geometers and word-wrights alike were nothing more than degraded and by-passed off-shoots of the South Asian weapons industry. There was not a straight blade in all of Hindoostan. Some weapons had grips at one end and were sharpened elsewhere; these might be classed as swords. Others consisted mostly of handle, with a dangerous bit at one end; these Jack conceived of as axes or spears, depending on whether they looked like they were meant to be swung, or shoved. Still others had strings, and seemed capable of projecting arrows. Jack put these down as bows. But of the sword-like ones, some were bent all the way round to form hooks; some curved first one way, then thought better of it and veered back the other; some had a different curve on either edge, so that they became broad as shovels in parts; some quivered back and forth like wriggling snakes; some forked, or spun off hooks, beaks, barbs, lobes, prongs, or even spirals. There were swords shaped like feathers, horseshoes, goat-horns, estuaries, penises, fish-hooks, eyebrows, hair-combs, Signs of the Zodiac, half-moons, elm-leaves, dinner-forks, Persian slippers, baker's paddles, pelican's beaks, dog's legs, and Corinthian columns. This did not take into account the truly outlandish contraptions that seemed to have been made by piling two or more such weapons atop each other, heating, and beating. Of long-handled swinging-weapons (axes, maces, hammers, halberds, and weaponized farm-implements, viz. war-sickles, combat-flails, assault-shovels, and tactical adzes) there was a similar variety. Most troublesome to Jack's mind, for some reason, were the bows which instead of the good old crescent of English yew, here seemed to've been made from the legs of giant spiders; they were black, sinewy, glossy, spindly things that curved this way and that, and were sometimes longer on one end than the other, so that Jack could not even make out which end was up; which part was the handle; or which side was supposed to face the enemy. For each of these weapon-styles, he knew, there must be a six-thousand-year-old martial art with its own set of unfathomable rites, lingo, exercises, and secrets that could only be mastered through a lifetime of miserable study.

"I suppose you're going to tell me it is all quite mundane compared to the weaponry of our adversaries," Jack muttered.

"In truth you have waxed so peevish that I have avoided that, and all other topics of conversation, these last few hours," said Surendranath.

The Banyan was in his palanquin. Jack rode a horse. This helped explain the peevishness, for the former reclined in the shade of a roof while the latter was protected only by a turban.

"Verily this must be the kingdom of Gordy himself," said Jack.

"Who or what is Gordy?"

"Some bloke who had a Knot once, so tangled that the only way to get it undone was to chop it in twain. The story is proverbial among *ferangs*. It is what we are about to do at the crossing of the Narmada. Rather than see all of these blokes cross scimitars, kitars, khandas, jamdhars, tranchangs, *et cetera* with the Marathas, we are going to cut the Gordian Knot."

"To you it may be a proverb of great significance but to me it is meaningless," said Surendranath, "and I would fain have something like an actual plan of battle before we meet the foe, which will probably occur this very night."

Here Surendranath was only pointing out something that had been weighing on Jack's mind anyway, which was that they had been so preoccupied with making the phosphorus, and recovering from having made it, that they'd not thought much about what to do with it. So Padraig, Vrej, Monsieur Arlanc, and Mr. Foot were sent for, and presently rode up to join Jack and Surendranath. Van Hoek had chopped off the tips of his fingers the night before and, still woozy from shock and opium, was being carried behind on another palanquin.

"This country that we have been traveling through," said the Banyan, "is hardly the type of scene to make any of you write awe-struck letters home, but it is the most dangerous and unsettled part of Hindoostan."

They had made landfall at the port of Surat, which was at the mouth of the river Tapti, and since then had been heading north, following a caravan-road that ran parallel to the sea-coast, a few miles inland. From time to time they would cross some smaller stream that, like the Tapti, meandered down out of the country to their right on its way to the Gulf of Cambaye, to their left. All knew that the biggest such river was called the Narmada and that they would come to it today, but so flat was the landscape that it afforded no hints as to how near or far the great river might be. This coastal plain reminded Jack a little bit of the Nile Delta, which was to say that it was well-watered, populated with many villages, and presented to the traveler a mixed prospect of marshes, farms, and groves of diverse kinds of trees that were cultivated (or at least allowed to stay alive) because they provided fruit or oil or fiber. "We shall see wilder and stranger landscapes farther north," Surendranath promised them, "but by then we shall be out of danger.

"If you think of Hindoostan as a great diamond, then the valley of the Narmada, which we are about to cross, is like a flaw that runs through the heart of it. Hindoostan has ever been divided among several kingdoms. Their names change, and so do their borders—with one exception, and that is the Narmada, which is a natural boundary between the north and the south. North of it, invaders come and go, and control of the cities and strongholds passes from one dynasty to another. To the south, it is a different story. You cannot see them from here, but there is a line of mountains cutting across Hindoostan from east to west called the Satpura Range. The Narmada drains their northern slopes, flowing along the mountains' northern flank through a straight deep gorge for many days' journey. The westernmost extremity of this range is called the Rajpipla Hills, and if the air were not so hazy we would be able to see them off to our right. A day's journey thataway, the Rajpipla Hills draw back away from the Narmada, which, thus freed from the constraints of the gorge, adopts a meandering habit, and snakes across this plain, and broadens to an estuary much like that of the Tapti which we have just put behind us.

"The Moguls have proved little different from other martial races that controlled the north in millennia past, which is to say that the weapons and tactics that served them well in the plains and deserts proved ineffective in breaching the mountain-wall of Satpura. But unlike some who have been content simply to make the Narmada their southern border, they have nursed the ambition of making all Hindoostan a part of the *dar al-Islam* and so probed southwards via the only route that is passable: which happens to be the very road that we are treading on now. Coastal cities such as Broach on the Narmada and Surat on the Tapti they have conquered with ease, and, with a great deal of difficulty, retained. But south of Surat, the interior of Hindoostan is guarded from the western sea by a formidable range of mountains, the Ghats, which are ever a refuge into which the Hindoo resistance—the Marathas—may withdraw when they desire not to meet the Moguls in pitched battle in the plain. Likewise the Satpura Range is mottled with strongholds of the Marathas, even as far west as the Rajpipla Hills. From time to time the Moguls will venture up there and expel them, for those Hills, because of their situation, are like a blade against the throat of the Moguls' commerce; all Western trade, as you know, comes in to the ports of Daman, Surat, and Broach, and the Maratha chieftains well know that they may sever those ports' links to the north by issuing from their forts in the Rajpipla Hills and descending the Ravines of Dhāroli to the Broach Plain—which is where we are now—and catching the caravans when they are backed against the River Narmada. Surat is infested with their sympathizers, and you may be assured that their spies saw us mustering there, and preceded us along this road and have already sent them word of our movements."

"Can we rely on them to attack us *at night?*" Jack asked.

"Only if we are so foolish as to reach the south bank of the Narmada at dusk and attempt a night crossing."

"So be it then," Jack said. "Clever stratagems are quite beyond my powers, but if it is rank foolishness you require, I have no end of it."

JACK RODE AHEAD to view the battle-field in daylight, and to put the mercenaries where he wanted them. With help from a hired guide, he found a suitable place to feign a crossing. A few miles inland of where the Narmada broadened to an estuary, it described a Z, swept around in an oxbow, described an S, and resumed its westward course. In the center of the SZ was a mushroom-shaped head of gravel and sand bulging northwards into the oxbow, and connected at its southern end by the neck of land pinched between the opposing river-bends. In each of these bends, the river's flow had undercut the banks, which rose above the water to no more than the height of a man, but were steep, and covered with scrub. Anyone coming to the river from the south would be funneled through a quarter-mile-wide gap between these bends. Beyond that narrow pass, the neck broadened and flattened, sloping imperceptibly down to the inner bank of the oxbow. The river was broad and shallow there, and seemed an inviting place for a ford; but this was of course the inner or concave surface of the oxbow-bend, and anyone who knew rivers would expect the opposite bank—the oxbow's outer or convex face—to be steeper. Looking across, Jack saw that this was likely the case, though it was obscured by reeds. His local guide assured him that camels, horses, and bullocks could ascend the far bank, and thereby cross over into the North of India, but only if they attempted it in certain places known to him, which he would divulge for a fee. Beasts of burden attempting to ford the river in the wrong places would, however, face slow going through the reeds, only to find their way barred by a bank too steep to scale.

"I'll pay you the amount you have named," Jack promised him, "and I'll double it if you allow me to strike you a few times with this riding-crop."

This required lengthy and difficult translation; but the result in the end was that a *ferang* on a horse could be seen chasing the poor guide all the way out of the oxbow, flailing at him wildly, and cursing the wretch for his greed. Having done which, he wheeled his mount, rode back to the ford, and began pointing out, to his mercenaries, those places that to him seemed best for a crossing.

An unexpected but desirable effect of this reconnaissance was that the mercenaries sorted themselves out. For *they* were scouting Jack, and what they understood to be Jack's plan. They began clumping together, the better to conduct arguments, and presently whole bands of them turned their backs on the enterprise and bolted down-river, headed for Anklesvar or Broach. Though Jack put on a great show of outrage at this, he was in truth pleased with it. The loss of so many mercenaries would make them seem all the more vulnerable in the eyes of the Maratha scouts who, as he knew perfectly well, were observing his every move; and the ones who had remained probably could be depended on. As soon as the deserters were out of earshot, Jack called the remaining ones together.

The Cabal had gone out of their way to recruit men who were proficient in the use of that ancient and simple weapon, the sling. They had rounded up approximately two score of them. Almost none of these had deserted—for they were the lowest-paid and most desperate of all mercenaries. Jack divided them into two platoons and bade them make themselves comfortable on the mushroom-shaped peninsula: one platoon on the western or downstream lobe, the other on the eastern or upstream lobe.

Of the remaining mercenaries, some were edged-weapons men; he set these to work digging a line of fox-holes across the narrowest part of the neck. But he made certain that they could fall back somewhere; and he put those idle slingers to work scooping out some trenches for just that purpose. Others of the mercenaries were archers, and he arranged these in the center of the peninsula so that they could fire volleys over the heads of the men defending the neck.

A vanguard of the caravan arrived bringing a great rolled-up Turkish sort of tent and its single tree-sized pole, its ropes, stakes, &c., as well as some strange cargo packed in straw. The tent they pitched in the center of the peninsula, and the cargo they dragged inside of it to be unpacked. Some of this was distributed to the platoons of slingers. As dusk fell, these could be seen creeping away from the positions where they had spent the afternoon and descending to the river's bank. In ones and twos they worked their way south, converging on the neck: but rather than occupying its open center, they were wading in the stream, sheltering behind the undercut banks, concealed from view by the scrubby vegetation and by darkness. It was just as well that they were on the move, for the caravan had now arrived in force, and horses, camels, bullocks, and even two elephants were crowding through the gap, dividing round the tent, and gathering along the inner bank of the oxbow. Jack had identified those parts of the opposite bank most difficult to climb, and now ordered that it be attempted by those creatures most likely to fail: bullocks drawing wagons.

Even from his less than ideal vantage-point, viz. standing in a tent slathering himself with strange-smelling oil, Jack could picture everything that went wrong just from the bellowing, the immense splashes, futile whip-cracks, curses in diverse tongues, and snapping of spokes and axles.

Even this tumult, however, did not suffice to drown out the sound of the Maratha onslaught. Crafty and subtle these rebels might be when filtering down out of the hills, but on the attack they were as loud as any other army, and perhaps louder than some, as they were fond of drums, cymbals, and other means of terrifying the enemy's critters at a distance. Jack put his eye to a hole in the tent to behold their approach. He had been told over and over again about the Marathas' generous use of elephants in combat, but had scoffed. For all of the strange places Jack had been, there was in him enough of the East London mudlark that he could not believe such a thing was actually done in this world. And yet, on they came: moving battle-towers, lit with torches and agleam with metal, shingled all over with armor, swinging tusks a-bristle with scythe-blades of watered steel. Five abreast these creatures came on to the neck of land, and about their knees swarmed a moving carpet of infantry, their wicked blades gleaming by moonlight, a geometry-lesson from Hell. The air puckered with the peculiar sound made by many arrows: some out-bound from the archers who stood around the tent, but many incoming. A few snicked in through the roof of the tent.

"Bang!" suggested Jack, and a moment later a musket was fired outside by Vrej, as a signal.

Their plan was extremely simple, and so many events were triggered by the firing of this one shot. On the northern bank of the oxbow, local guides kindled bonfires; these shone out across the river as beacons marking the places where the bank was easiest to scale. The caravan-drivers, trapped between the river and the Maratha onslaught, needed no further incentive to make for those lights. Soon the river was striped in four places by columns of sloshing beasts.

The line of sword-wielding mercenaries barring the neck had already begun to desert their earthworks and to fall back, for the elephants were only a few yards away. When the musket sounded, those who had held their ground jumped out, to a man, and split into two groups, occupying the trenches that the slingers had prepared along the flanks of the expected Maratha advance. The archers fired a last volley of arrows. This, and the trenches, and some trip-ropes that had been pounded into place before them, and the congestion caused by the Marathas' entire battle-front being compressed into the narrow pass, caused the onslaught to slow, just on the threshold. A few impetuous Marathas ventured across the line of fox-holes, or even jumped obstacles on horseback; but these were easy marks for the archers and for the few musketeers they had managed to round up.

All of which, wild and memorable though it was, remained well within the normal limits of what one saw in warfare. Night battles were unusual, and (to Jack anyway) ones involving elephants were outlandish; but for all that, it was just a battle. Until a hundred glowing bottles of phosphorus were lobbed out of the scrub to either side of the neck, and dropped out of the sky like falling stars, and burst upon the ground among the attackers. They came in a few ragged volleys, and by the time the last one had fallen, most of the ground that stretched before the Maratha vanguard was glowing. And as if that were not enough, some of it was bursting into flame.

One of the elephants made known his intention to turn around and go back. Jack could not discern, from this range, whether his driver was of the same mind, or not; but it did not matter, for the elephant was leaving. And perhaps he was some sort of a leader among pachyderms, for the idea spread to the others fast and unquenchable as phosphorus-fire. When several elephants with razor-sharp blades all over their tusks decide to pirouette in the midst of a tightly packed mob, there is apt to be disorder, and such was the case now; Jack could not really see through the arch of radiance, but could infer as much from the vocalizations of the Marathas, which sounded like every Italian opera ever written being sung at once.

As the phosphorus on the ground dried out, it burnt. This went on fitfully for longer than was really convenient. Jack and all of the others in the oxbow could not do anything, because they could not see. To their backs, the convoy dribbled across the fords like streams of molasses running down a chilly plate. It would be hours before they were all across. And Jack had been warned not to underestimate the Marathas. It was one thing to spook their beasts, another thing altogether to break the will of their men. For these were not just peasants with sticks, but veterans belonging to castes such as the *Mahar* and the *Mang* whose whole purpose was military service. Such warnings he had been slow to heed, for there was nothing in England that corresponded to it; but Surendranath had drawn a loose analogy between these castes and the Janissaries of the Turks, which began to give Jack the idea. He had accordingly ordered the slingers to hold a few of their bottles in reserve, and when the last of the phosphorus-fires burnt out, he insisted that the mercenaries move up again, and take up their former positions. The archers he moved to the flanks to join the slingers, so that they could fire from behind the protection of the riverbank. All of these measures were soon put to the test by attacks of *Mahar* and *Mang* infantry; and so it was that, as much as he had wanted to avoid it, Jack was finally obliged to ride out from the concealment of the tent, flanked by Mr. Foot on one side and Monsieur Arlanc on the other, and to sally across the neck and drive the die-hard Marathas back screaming all the way to the Ravines of Dhāroli. For Jack, Foot, Arlanc, and their horses were all glowing in the dark. No one even had the temerity to shoot an arrow at them.

"Mr. Foot!" Jack called out to a fiery blob hurtling to and fro in pursuit of demoralized foe-men, "turn thee around and let's to the river. Nothing but dust now lies between us and the Court of the Great Mogul in Shahjahanabad; and he had damn well better be grateful, lest we boil up some urine in *his* town."

the **Juncto** BOOK 5

Mrs. Bligh's Coffee-house, London
SEPTEMBER 1693

"ROGER, YOU ARE a great man now, and worth more than the Great Mogul."

"So I have heard, Daniel—but it is perfectly all right—I do not mind hearing it again."

"You are also educated, after a fashion."

" 'Tis better to be *educable*—but pray continue in your flattery, which is so very unlike you."

"So then. What metaphysical significance do you attach to the fact that you are unable to pay for a cup of coffee?"

"Why, Daniel, I say that I just *did* pay, not for *one*, but *two*—unless that object on the table before you is a *mirage*."

"But you didn't, really, my lord. Coffee was brought forth and you incurred a debt, pricked down on Mrs. Bligh's ledger."

"Are you questioning my *solvency*, Daniel?"

"I am questioning the whole *country's* solvency! Empty out your coin-purse. Right there on the table. Let's have a look."

"Don't be vulgar, Daniel."

"Oh, now 'tis *I* who am vulgar."

"Ever since you had the stone cut out, you have seemingly regressed in age."

"I will bet you the whole contents of *my* purse that *yours* contains not a single piece of metal that could be exchanged for a bucket of cods' heads at Billingsgate."

"If your purse's contents were worth so much, you'd be Massachusetts-bound. Everyone knows that."

"You see? You are afraid to accept the wager."

"Why do you belabor *me* about the fact that England has no money?"

"Because you are a momentous fellow now, rumors career about you like gulls round a herring-boat, and I want you to *do* something about it, so that I can go to America . . . right. Very well, my lord, I shall give you a few minutes to bring your mirth under control. If you can hear what I am saying, wave at me—oh, very good. Roger Comstock, I say 'tis well enough for *you* that you have credit, and can buy cups of coffee, or houses, by simply *asking* for them. Many other men of power enjoy the same privilege—including our King, who appears to be financing his war through some kind of *alchemy.* But some of us are required actually to *pay* for what we buy, and we have nothing to pay *with* at the moment. They say that America is *awash* in Pieces of Eight, and that is a sight I would fain see—alas, ships' captains do not dispense credit, at least, not to Natural Philosophers. . . . Oh yes, my lord, *do* be entertained. I am here in Mrs. Bligh's coffeehouse, in pied rags, solely as a Court Jester to Creditable Men, and request only that you throw a silver coin at me for every giggle and a gold one for each guffaw. Fresh out? What, no coins in the bank? Does your purse hang as flaccid as a gelding's scrotum? 'Tis a common condition, Roger, and this brings me round to *another* subject 'pon which I will briefly discourse while you blow your nose, and wipe the tears from your eyes, and that is: What if all debts, public and private, were to be called in? What if Mrs. Bligh were to march over to this cozy corner with her accompt-book resting open on her bosom like a Bible on a Lectern and say, Roger Comstock, you owe me your own weight in rubies, pay up straightaway!"

"But, Daniel, that never happens. Mrs. Bligh, if she wants coffeebeans, can go down to the docks and shew her book—or her Lectern, in a pinch—to a merchant and say, 'Behold, every powerful man in London is in debt to me, I have collateral, lend me a ton of Mocha and you'll never be sorry!'"

"Roger, what is Mrs. Bligh's bloody book—by your leave, Mrs. Bligh!—but squiggles of ink? I have ink, Roger, a firkin of it, and can molest a goose to obtain quills, and make ink-squiggles all night and all day. But they are just *forms* on a page. What does it say of us that our commerce is built 'pon forms and figments while that of Spain is built 'pon *silver?*"

"Some would say it speaks to our *advancement.*"

"I am not one of those hard cases who believes credit is Satan's work, do not put me in that poke, Roger. I say only that ink, once dried on the page, is a brittle commodity, and an œconomy made of ink is likewise brittle, and may for all we know be *craz'd* and in a state to crumble at a touch. Whereas silver and gold are ductile, malleable, capable of fluid movement—"

"Some say it is because their atoms, their *particules* are bathed in a lubricating medium of quicksilver—"

"Stop it."

"You asked me to wax metaphysical, just a minute ago."

"You are baiting me, Roger. Oh, it is all right. By all means, amuse yourself."

"Daniel. Do you really want to go to Massachusetts, and leave all this behind?"

"*All this* is more amusing, not to mention profitable, to *you* than 'tis to *me*. I want to put distractions behind, go to the wilderness, and work."

"What, in a wigwam? Or do you have a cave picked out?"

"There are plenty of trees remaining."

"You're going to live in a tree?"

"No! Cut them down, make a house."

"I fear you are unused to such labor, Daniel."

"Oh but I am *educable*."

"One really would do better to have an *institution* on which to rely. You could be a vicar of some Puritan church."

"Puritan churches tend not to *have* vicars."

"Oh, that's right . . . then perhaps Harvard College would have you."

"Then again, perhaps not."

"Here, Daniel, is my metaphysical reading of your circumstance:"

"I am braced."

"England is not finished with you yet!"

"Merciful God! What more can England possibly ask of me?"

"I shall come to that momentarily, Daniel. First, I propose a transaction."

"Is this transaction to conclude with *silver* changing hands? Or ink-squiggles?"

"It is to conclude with a sinecure for Daniel Waterhouse. In Massachusetts Bay Colony."

"Damn me, and here am I, on the wrong side of the ocean!"

"The sinecure is attended with certain *perquisites* including a one-way trans-oceanic voyage."

"Are you saying, England wants from me something *so dreadful* that when I have done it, she won't want me around any more?"

"You read too much into it. *You* are the one who has been bawling about Massachusetts for all these years."

"But then why do you specify it has to be one-way?"

"You can come back if you think it would be in your best interests," Roger said innocently. "As long as the Juncto remains in power, you shall have protectors."

"Your voice has the most annoying way of fading just when you are on the verge of saying something interesting. Do you do that for effect?"

"Juncto . . . *juncto* . . . JUNCTO!"

"What on earth is a junk-toe? Some new type of gout?"

"More like a new type of gov't."

"I am quite serious."

"A scholar might say it Latin-style: *yuncto*. Or, a Spaniard thus: *hoonta!*"

"Why don't you just say 'joint,' which is what it means?"

"I know what it means. But then people would suppose we were discoursing of knees or elbows."

"But isn't the *idea* to be mysterious?"

"Then we would call it a *cabal*."

"Oh, that's right. So, you are in a juncto?"

"I am in *the* juncto."

"And your role in *the* juncto is to be—?"

"Chancellor of the Exchequer . . . Daniel, it is childish to make coffee shoot out of your nostrils. You know of someone *better* qualified?"

"What about Apthorp?"

"Sir Richard, as he is called by *polite* men, will run the bank."

"But do you not think he would gladly set aside his duties at Apthorp's Bank to become Chancellor of the Exchequer?"

"No, no, no, no, *no*. I am not speaking of Apthorp's bank. I refer to the Bank of England."

"No such institution exists."

"And no institution exists in Massachusetts Bay Colony that will put a roof over your head and give you a sinecure. But institutions can be *made*, Daniel. That is what an institution *is:* something that has been *instituted*."

"Oh."

"Ah, finally light dawns! You *are* educable, Daniel, very much so!"

"The Bank of England . . . the Bank of England. It sounds, I don't know, *big*."

"That is the point."

"You shall amass some sort of capital, and lend out money."

"This is the timeless function of a *banca*."

"I can only perceive two drawbacks to what is otherwise an excellent plan, my lord . . ."

"Don't say it. We have no capital . . . and no money."

"Just so, my lord."

"Is it not *admirable*, how simple things are in the beginning? Oh, how I love to begin things."

"Let's take them in order . . . what is the capital to be?"

"England."

"Ah, very well, I should have guessed from the name, 'Bank of England.' Now, how about the money?"

"The Bank will issue some paper. But you are right. We need coinage. To be specific, we need *recoinage.*"

A silence now fell over this snuggery in the corner of Mrs. Bligh's coffee-house. Roger had spent enough man-years orating in Parliament that he knew when a Pause for Effect was called for. And Daniel for his part was strangely affected, and lost all interest in speaking for a short time. The notion of recoinage made him strangely *sad,* and he was desirous of figuring out *why.* It would mean calling in all old coins—as well as the plate, candlesticks, bullion, *et cetera*—and melting them in the great crucibles of the Tower. Crucibles that purified and separated the genuine metal from the dross of the counterfeiters but thereby melted all those discrete objects together, destroying their individual characters.

Daniel had in his purse a pound coin stamped with a picture of Queen Elizabeth. He knew this because such coins were rarer than flawless diamonds now, and he was holding it back in case he had to ransom his life somehow. The Golden Comstocks—Roger's ancestors—had imported the metal from Spain and Thomas Gresham had caused the coin to be minted at such-and-such a weight, and had used some of his rake-off to build Gresham's College. The coin had been passing from hand to hand and purse to purse for more than a hundred years, and probably had more tales to tell than a ship full of Irish sailors—yet it was just a single mote in the dust-pile that was the English money supply. In a certain way to take that dust and shovel it into the maw of the crucibles was monstrous, like burning a library.

But imagine the glowing rivers that would spring from the lips of those crucibles when all of that tarnished silver was made clean, and made quick, and con-fused, and all of its old stories driven off as clouds of smoke that the river wind would carry away. Imagine the shining coins in purses everywhere—Mrs. Bligh striking out the debts from her ledger-book, her strong-box becoming a catch-basin for the new money, overflowing and spilling out gleaming rivulets down the street to the bankside coffee-merchants, and thence down the Thames into the wide.

"We've no choice," Daniel understood.

"We've no choice. The Pope has all the gold, all the silver, all the men, and the rich lands where the sun shines. We cannot long stand against Spain, France, the Empire, the Church. Not as long as power is like a scale, with our riches on one pan, and our adversaries' on the other. What are we to do, then? Daniel, you know that I think Alchemy is nonsense! Yet there is something in the *idea* of Alchemy; the conceit that we may cause gold to appear where 'twas not, by dint of artfulness and machinations up here." He pressed the tip of one index finger delicately to his forehead. "We have no mines, no El Dorado. If we want gold and silver we must look not to treasure-fleets from America. Yet if we conduct commerce here, and build the Bank of England, why, gold and silver will appear in our coffers as if by magic—or Alchemy if you prefer."

A pause to sip cold coffee. Then Daniel remarked, "You'll want to take a page from Gresham's book. 'Bad money drives out good.' If the new coin is good, 'twill drive away the bad, not only from this island but everywhere. Everyone will desire English guineas, as they desire Pieces of Eight now. The demand will cause ever more gold and silver to wash up on our shores to be coined in the Tower, just as you prophesy."

Roger was nodding patiently, as if he and the Juncto had figured it all out long ago—which might or might not have been the case—but Daniel found it strangely reassuring all the same, and continued: "At the risk of sounding like a Royal Society partisan—"

"It is not much of a risk. Half of the Juncto are Fellows. And all are partisans of *something.*"

"Very well, then, I submit that you want a Natural Philosopher running the Mint—not the usual corrupt, drunken, time-serving political hack."

This drew a brisk turn of the head from a gentleman who had been standing a short distance behind Roger, talking to another gent, or pretending to. Daniel realized he had spoken too loudly.

The gentleman was glaring at Daniel from beneath a copper-colored wig, one of the new model, narrow, with long ringlets trailing far down the back. The wig said that he had money and rank, yet was no admirer of the French. He would be High Church, Old Money, a reflexive backer of Monarchy—a Tory, as they were called nowadays. Odd that he should be passing the time of day in here—Mrs. Bligh's was a Whig haunt. For that reason Daniel rated it as unlikely that this fellow would challenge him to a duel.

Roger had noticed Daniel noticing all of these things, and had the good instincts not to look back. But his eyes flicked slightly upwards to a windowpane just above Daniel's head, and he scanned the reflections interestedly for a moment. Which in no way prevented his talking at the same time. "Indeed, Daniel, any man plucked from this coffee-house—with one or two exceptions—would be preferable to the fellows running our mint now, who are *tapeworms.*"

Daniel was staring fixedly into Roger's eyes, but in the background he could see the Tory turning away. The Tory planted himself with his back toward Roger, set his coffee-cup down on a sideboard, rested a hand idly on the hilt of his small-sword, and seemed to survey the crowd of merry Whigs filling the house.

"It follows that any Fellow of the Royal Society would be excellent—but merely excellent is not quite good enough, Daniel. Normally it takes me *hours* to explain why this is true. You, thank God, have perceived it instantly. The fate of Britain and of Christendom hinge upon the power of the new good Pound Sterling to drive out the bad—to sweep all opposition from the field and bring gold and silver to our shores from every corner of the earth. The quality of money is only partly due to the purity of its metal—which any Natural Philosopher could see to. It is also a matter of *trust,* of prestige."

Daniel had now realized what was coming, and slid down in his chair, and put his hands over his face. "You don't want *me* to enlist him, Roger! I no longer have his ear. You want Fatio, Fatio, Fatio!"

"Everyone knows he is in-Fatio-ated—but passions are fleeting. You have known him longer than anyone, Daniel. You are the man for it. England needs you! Your Massachusetts sinecure awaits!"

Daniel had parted his fingers now and was peering out through slits in between. Unable to look Roger in the face, he was surveying the distant background. Andrew Ellis—a compact young man with a blond ponytail, an enjoyable, harmless young Parliamentarian—was coming over with a glass of claret in each hand, intent on breaking into the conversation and sharing his enjoyableness with Roger. If Daniel had hopes of weaseling out, he had to do it now. To Roger Comstock, silence implied not merely consent, but a blood oath.

"You cannot know what you are proposing, ensconcing such a man at the Tower, giving him control of our money. He has strange ideas, dark secrets—"

"I know all about the beastliness."

"No, that's not what I mean."

"Alchemy is an even more common vice."

"That's not it, either. He is a heretic, Roger."

"Look who's talking!"

"I mean, he does not even believe in the Trinity!"

Roger got a glazed-over look, as he always did when abstract theological matters were dragged into the conversation. Unlike ordinary men, who required several minutes to become fully glazed over, Roger could do it in an instant, as if a window-sash had dropped in front of him from a great height. Daniel parted his fingers more to observe this phenomenon. But instead his attention was drawn to something even odder: an expensive copper-colored wig hanging in midair behind Roger's chair. Its owner had ducked and darted out from under it as fast as a striking cobra and simply left it behind. It fell to the floor, of course. By that time the owner—who had red hair in a close Caesar crop—was whispering something into Andrew Ellis's ear. It must have been something extremely shocking, to judge from the look of astonishment—nay, horror—that had come over the normally beaming face of Mr. Ellis.

Daniel pushed himself up in his chair to get a better look and perceived that the red-headed gent was now drawing away from Ellis—but Ellis was moving with him, as if they were joined together. Ellis gave out a little whimper.

Daniel could not credit what he was seeing. "Roger, I could almost swear that Mr. Ellis is having his ear bitten."

Roger now took notice for the first time. He stood up, turned around, and quickly verified it. This prolonged ear-biting had drawn very little notice thus far because Ellis had been too astonished to speak and the biter, of course, could not really talk, either—though he did seem to be mumbling something in a low, grinding voice: "So you want to have the ear of Roger Comstock? Then *I* shall have *yours.*"

Oddly, it was Roger's standing up that drew everyone's attention. Then awareness splashed across the room.

"In the name of God, sir!" Ellis cried, and slumped against the paneled wall. The red-head stayed with him, of course, maintaining his bite like a bulldog, working his jaw slowly to gnaw through the cartilage. He planted a hand on the wall to either side of Ellis's head, bracketing him in position. Several of the Whigs in the main room finally moved forward to intervene—but the gentleman who had been talking to the biter earlier whirled to face them, and drew his sword half out of his scabbard. That drove them back like a firecracker.

Roger stepped toward the biter and the bitee, and raised his arm that was nearer the wall, causing his cape to spread open and block Daniel's view of the whole proceedings. He seemed to slap the back of the biter's hand where it was planted on the wall. "Mr. White," he said, in an indulgent tone, "do wipe your chin when you are quite finished." Then Roger skirted around the pair and walked out of the coffee-house. Andrew Ellis collapsed to the floor with a scream and pressed both of his hands to the side of his head. Mr. White came up with a triumphant toss of his head, like a country boy who has just won at apple-bobbing. Something like a dried apricot was lodged in his smile. He plucked it out with one hand to admire it. Andrew Ellis was lying against Mr. White's shins and knees, forcing them back, and so White had to keep his other hand braced against the paneling lest he topple forward. Anyway, he pocketed Ellis's ear and flashed a bloody grin at Daniel.

"Welcome to politics, Mr. Waterhouse," he announced. "This is the world you have made. Rejoice and be glad in it—for you shall not be allowed to leave."

"I am freer to leave than *you* are, Mr. White," Daniel said on his way out, nodding in the direction of the hand that Mr. White was bracing against the wall.

Mr. White now seemed to notice for the first time that a dagger had been shoved all the way through that hand, between the metacarpals and out through the palm, and lodged deep in the wooden wall. Worked into the dagger's pommel, in silver letters, as a sort of calling-card, were the initials *R.C.*

WHEN DANIEL MADE IT out to the street he discovered that his hand had gone into his pocket and got ahold of the Pearl of Great Price and squeezed it so hard, for so long, that his fingers had got tired. The Stone had a sort of devil's-head shape, with two stubby hornlets that had once been lodged in his ureters. He had a habit of gripping it so that those wee knobs stuck out between his knuckles—it fitted his hand almost as well as his bladder.

Riding north across Hertfordshire in a borrowed carriage the next day, he found his hand had gone to it once again, as he reviewed the ear-biting scene in the theatre of his memory. Daniel was meditating on Cowardice. He knew a lot of cowards and saw cowardice everywhere, but just as Mr. Flamsteed's observations of the stars were frequently obnubilated by weather, so Daniel's of Cowardice by Extenuating Circumstances. Viz. a man might explain cowardliness by saying that he had a family to support, or, failing that, with the simple argument that it just was not fair for a young man to give up life or limb. But Daniel had no wife or children of his own, and brother Sterling was doing a fine job of supporting the extended family. And not only was Daniel old (forty-seven), but he ought to've been dead by now, and owed his remaining years solely to Mr. Hooke's pitiless blade-work. So in Daniel Waterhouse, an observer could see cowardliness in its pure form, and perhaps learn something of its nature.

A note from Roger Comstock was on the bench next to Daniel; it had been waiting for him in the carriage this morning. *Dear Daniel,* it read,

> Forgive me my precipitous leave-taking from Mrs. Bligh's yester-eve. As I am sure you have perceived by now, the whole event was a masque, a trifle. Do not allow Mr. White's vulgarities to prey upon your good judgment.
>
> Your coachman is Mr. John Hammond and I have charged him to convey you anywhere you desire, until your errand is accomplished; but I have led him to believe that most of your perambulations shall be confined to the triangle formed by London, Cambridge, and Mr. Apthorp's country house. If you conceive a need to hie to John O'Groats or Land's End, do break the news to him gently.
>
> Yours very sternly,
>
> (signed with a flourish, two inches high)
>
> *Ravenscar*
>
> P.S. I seem to have lost my poniard—have you seen it?

Roger was completely free of any taint of cowardice. Craven he might be, but a coward? Never. *A trifle.* Roger was sincere when he called it that.

It was impossible for Daniel to read in the dim, rocking vehicle, and he had no one to talk to, so sleeping and thinking were the only ways to pass the long drive through the rain up to Cambridge. As he contrasted his fear of Mr. White (which was very much akin to the fear he had previously had of Jeffreys) with how he had once felt about this rock that was now in his pocket, a new hypothesis of cowardice came into his head. The Stone had made him sad, reluctant to die, and anxious—but his fear of it had been as nothing compared to his fear of Jeffreys, and now of White. Yet those men had only spoken threatening words to him. Even when Hooke had reached up between his thighs with the scalpel, Daniel had been gripped by a sort of animal fear, but nothing like the dread of Mr. White, which had kept him awake all last night.

The only difference he could think of was that Hooke *liked* Daniel and White *hated* him. Could it be, then, that Daniel's true cowardice lay in that he could not stand for people to think poorly of him?

That would be a strange shape for cowardice to take. But it tallied well with Daniel's experiences to date. It was Daniel's biography in a sentence. Further, perhaps it was the case that there were certain men, such as Jeffreys and White, who were adept at detecting this particular type of fear, and who had learned to cultivate it and use it against their enemies. Mr. John Hammond, the driver, had a long coachman's whip and used it frequently, but never actually struck the horses with it. Rather, he made it crack in the air around the heads of his team, and used their own fear to drive them.

When Daniel had sent Jeffreys to the Tower and to his scaffold-top meeting with Jack Ketch, he'd phant'sied that he had slain a dragon, and put an end to that part of his life. Yet now Mr. White had appeared out of nowhere. An alarming chap! But much more alarming was what this all implied, namely that the world had more than one dragon—that it was infested with them—and that a fellow who was afraid of dragons must perforce spend all his days worrying about one or another.

This was all very much of the essence, because when Daniel tracked Isaac down, wherever he was, he would not be able to do what needed to be done without first mastering this fear.

As it turned out, he had no occasion to master it in Cambridge. He arrived at Trinity College in time to have a wash and a cat-nap in one of the guest chambers. Then, when the bell rang, he threw on a robe and went to the dining hall and took a place at the high table. Rather close to the head of that table, as it turned out. For between apoplexy and smallpox, Daniel was becoming more senior with every passing month. He was shown respect and even affection. He understood now why men afflicted with his particular brand of cow-ardice would gravitate to stations like this one, even though the Col-lege had fallen on very hard times, and was dishing up thin gruel little different from what was served in the poor-house.

When he inquired after Newton and Fatio, heads turned toward a young man seated near the foot of the table—too far away for Daniel to converse with him—who was called Dominic Masham. This sug-gested much to Daniel, for he knew that the family Masham were close friends and patrons of John Locke. Locke had been living on their estate at Oates since he'd come back from exile in Holland round the time of the Glorious Revolution. Daniel presumed that Locke had established some sort of alchemical laboratory there, for Newton and Fatio had frequently gone there for lengthy stays, as had Robert Boyle until his death a year or two ago. The Mashams had many children and Daniel guessed that this Dominic was one of them, and that he was here as a protégé of Newton.

It was explained to him that Newton, Fatio, and Locke had all been staying in Newton's (and formerly Waterhouse's) chambers here until yesterday morning, when they'd all gone away, leaving Masham behind to tie up some loose ends. Newton and Fatio had gone off together bound for Oates. Locke had gone off by himself down the Barton Road, which led generally southeastwards. But he had declined to state his destination.

"I went right by them," Daniel remarked. For the Mashams' estate lay just off the London-Cambridge road, some twenty miles north of the capital. "What were those fellows up to?" For they also collaborated on theological projects.

It made the men at High Table nervous that Daniel had even asked.

"That is to say, what sorts of stimulating conversations have I missed by being so long absent from this table? Surely, three such men did not sit here in silence."

Everyone sat in silence for a few moments. But then, fortuitously, dinner was over. They all stood up and chanted in Latin, and filed out. Daniel tracked Dominic Masham across the Great Court, and caught up with him beyond the main gate as he was unlocking the portal to Newton's private courtyard. Masham had a distracted and hurried look about him, which suited Daniel's purposes well enough. Daniel had a lanthorn, which he used to illuminate Masham's face.

"Going home soon, Mr. Masham?"

"Tomorrow, Dr. Waterhouse, or as soon as I can gather up certain . . ."

Daniel let Masham's pause dangle embarrassingly for a while before saying, quietly, "You offend me with this affected coyness. I am not a *lass* to *flirt* with, Mr. Masham."

This had the same effect on the younger man as a whip-crack by a horse's ear. He froze and began trying to frame a suitably glorious apology, but Daniel cut him off. "You are charged with gathering together the necessaries for the continuation of the Great Work that Misters Newton, Locke, and Fatio are undertaking at Oates. These may be *books* or *chemicals* or *glassware*—it does not matter to me— what matters is that you are going to Oates in the morning, and you may convey this packet to Mr. Newton with my compliments. It came to me the other day in London. It was sent to Newton by Leibniz."

The mention of the name *Leibniz* threw a look into Dominic Masham's wide green eyes.

"It consists of a letter, and a book. The letter is unique, and more important. The book, as you can see, is the first printing of Leibniz's *Protogaea,* and you may feel free to peruse it during your trip; it will teach you things you have never dreamed of."

"And the letter—?"

"Think of it as an overture, an attempt to mend the breach that occurred in these chambers in 1677."

"*Sir!* You know what happened in 1677!?" Masham exclaimed, in a tone of voice that was somewhat wistful, which seemed to say that he *didn't.*

"I was *here* then."

"Very well, Dr. Waterhouse, I shall not let it out of my sight until it is in Mr. Newton's hands."

"The future of Natural Philosophy revolves around it," Daniel said. "Please tell those three gentlemen that I shall call on them in two days."

"By your leave, sir, there are only the *two* of them there now. Mr. Locke has gone to . . . another place."

"Again you do me a disservice. I know perfectly well that Mr. Locke has gone to Apthorp House."

"Sir!"

SIR RICHARD APTHORP'S COUNTRY dwelling was situated about mid-way between Cambridge and Oxford, not far off the high road that ran from London northwest in the direction of Birmingham. The nearest town of any size was called Bletchley, and Daniel had to stop to ask for directions there, because Sir Richard had in no way made his house an obvious one. This bland countryside seemed oddly well suited for the hiding of secrets in plain sight. In any case, Daniel did not have to utter a word, only slide his window open and watch three Bletchley stable-boys jumping up and down in the street vying with one another to tell him the way to Apthorp House. Meanwhile an older fellow struck up a cheerful exchange with John Hammond. He let Daniel's driver know that the stables at Apthorp House had long since gone full up, and that Sir Richard, as a courtesy to his guests, had retained this man to look after the overflow at his livery stable, which was just round the corner.

Indeed, the lane that meandered between low hills to Apthorp House was nearly paved with horse manure, and when Hammond drew his team up in front of the main building—yet another Barock neo-classical compound fraught with pagan-god-statues—Daniel's eyes were treated to the sight of the finest fleet of carriages he had ever seen, outside of a royal palace. The coats of arms told him who was inside the house. The Earl of Marlborough, Sterling Waterhouse, Roger Comstock, Apthorp, Pepys, Locke, and Christopher Wren were all personal acquaintances of Daniel's. Also well represented was a cat-egory Daniel thought of as "men like Sterling," meaning sons or grandsons of the great Puritan trader/smuggler/firebrands of the Cromwell era, including particularly several Quaker magnates with large holdings in America. There were men with French surnames and others with Spanish: respectively, Huguenots and Amsterdam-Jews who had established themselves in England during the last ten or so years. There were a few nobles of high rank, notably the Prince of Denmark, who was married to Princess Anne. However, Persons of Quality were quite under-represented here, considering the amount of wealth. The nobles who had shown up were what Daniel thought of as "men like Boyle," meaning sons of great lords who were not especially interested in being great according to the ancient feudal definition of that word, and who instead devoted their lives to hanging around the Royal Society or sailing across oceans to trade or to explore.

"This is the world you have made," Mr. White had said to Daniel—blaming him somehow for the Glorious Revolution. But Daniel saw it rather differently. This was the world *Drake* had made, a world where power came of thrift and cleverness and industry, not of birthright, and certainly not of Divine Right. This was the Whig World, and though Drake would have abhorred everything about most of these people, he would have had to admit that he had in a way caused this Juncto.

None of these people really had time to talk to Daniel and so his conversations had a meted-out feeling to them. For all that, they were pleased to see him, and interested in what he had to say, which was soothing for a man equipped with Daniel's particular form of cowardice.

"My Lord Marlborough, if I may just pursue you down this gallery—"

"I am pleased to see you are in a condition to do so."

"Thank you, my lord. On the night that James II fled, you spoke to me on the Tower causeway and voiced grave concern as to the motives and machinations of *Alchemists*."

"You do not need to remind me, Mr. Waterhouse, I am not the sort who ever forgets."

"Pray, where stand you now on such matters?"

"I must admit they seem very quaint and queer to me today, where once they seemed occult and menacing. Yet the Marquis of Ravenscar is very forward in saying that one of the Esoteric Brotherhood ought to be put in charge of our Mint. And I do confess I am loath to throw my money in with this new Bank, and my lot in with this Juncto, when our money is to be recoined by a savant whose ideas are recondite, and whose motives are a source of endless puzzlement to me."

"That will never change, my lord. But if some way could be devised for the motives of this alchemist to be *aligned* with yours, so that you agreed on the *means* whilst perhaps differing as to the *ends*, would that satisfy you?"

"Such alignments of interest are a staple of politics and of war. They may serve for a time. But in the end is always a divergence, and a catastrophe."

"That is a Janus-like utterance, my lord, and for now I will prefer to look only upon its smiling face."

"My lord Ravenscar, tomorrow morning I am off to Oates to tender a version of your proposal to Mr. Newton, unless you say to me beforehand that you have changed your mind."

"Why on earth should I change my mind?"

"Perhaps you would prefer a Mint-master who, insofar as his motives were more intelligible, would prove more manageable."

"I am sure I have no idea what you mean, Daniel."

"I am sure you *lie* like a *dog* in the *sun*. A time-serving hack—a tapeworm—is easy to understand. He will run your mint for you because he receives a stipend, a place to live, influence and prestige. But you must get it very clear in your mind, Roger, that Newton wants none of this. He will benefit from a steady income, it is true. But if I am to interest him in this job, I must hold out enticements. And I say to you that he has the hard, bare soul of a Lincolnshire Puritan, a type of soul I understand well, and the usual incentives are less than nothing to him. If he does it, he shall do it in the name of ideals, and in the pursuit of goals, you may find incomprehensible. And inasmuch as you shall be unable to comprehend his ends, you shall be unable to control, or even influence him."

"That's perfectly all right, Daniel, I can always write you a letter in Boston and ask you to explain what he's on about."

"May I assist you carrying one of those *tomes*, Mr. Halley?"

"Daniel! An unexpected pleasure! I can manage, thank you, but you may assist by telling me in which of these rooms I might find Mr. Pepys."

"Follow me. He is meeting with one Cabal or other at the end of the opposite wing."

"Ah, then wait with me while I rest my arms."

"Are these for his book collection?"

"These are *money*."

"On the pages I see *numbers*. Rumor has had it, Mr. Halley, that you have hired up every computer on this island, and set them to a great work. Now I see the rumors were true."

"These are only the first fruits of their lucubrations—I have brought them up, at the request of Mr. Pepys, to show them as a sort of demo'."

"Why do you say that they are money? To me they could be sines and cosines."

"These are *actuarial* tables, a sort of *extract* or *distillation* from the records of births and deaths of every parish in England. Supplied with these *data* the Exchequer can raise capital by selling annuities to the general public; and if they sell enough of them, why, the law of averages dictates that they will make a profit without fail!"

"What, by *gambling* that their customers will *die*?"

"That is no gamble, Dr. Waterhouse."

"SAFE JOURNEY TO OATES; I shall see you there on the morrow, Mr. Locke."

"You may expect nothing but the warmest hospitality from the Mashams. From Newton you may expect—"

"You forget I have known him for thirty years."

"Right."

". . ."

"I can only guess what machinations you are about, Mr. Waterhouse. But I admit that I shall look forward to your arrival and that I shall feel a weight lifted when you arrive."

"Why, Mr. Locke, what weighs 'pon you?"

"Newton is unwell."

"Love-sick?"

"That is the least of his ailments."

"I shall be there soon, Mr. Locke, with what feeble medicine I may proffer."

"MR. WATERHOUSE, MY SCHEDULE IS a *monolith*, seamless and unbroken. Except for piss-breaks. Shall we?"

"As I need hardly explain to you of all men, Mr. Pepys, nothing now gives me greater satisfaction than pissing—but to piss with you, sir, would be to compound *honor* with *pleasure*."

"Let us then leave the company of these fellows who know not what it signifies, and go piss in each other's company."

"If it would please you to turn to your right out this door, Mr. Pepys, you shall come in view of a garden wall that, earlier, I was sizing up as—"

"Say no more, Mr. Waterhouse, 'tis a magnificent wall, well-proportioned, secluded, admirably made for our usage."

". . ."

"I say, Mr. Waterhouse, have you been buying your breeches from Turks?"

"I am a man of almost fifty, sir, and am permitted a small repertoire of *eccentricities*. As pissing gives me so much pleasure I will brook no interference from my clothing—I'll have my yard out smartly and be finished with my work while you are still fumbling with buttons and clasps."

"Not so, sir, I am only moments behind you."

". . ."

"Makes you want to sing hymns, eh?"

"I *do*, sometimes."

"Word has reached me that you are off to visit Newton tomorrow. I wonder if he has an answer for me on my lottery question."

"Another way of raising money?"

"Think of it rather as a way for ordinary men to enrich themselves at the (trifling) expense of vast numbers of other ordinary men. Of course the Exchequer will have to collect a small rake-off for overhead."

"Of course. Mr. Pepys, when we got the Royal Society going, never did I dream you would find such uses for the knowledge it would generate."

"That is the rub—the lottery is a game of chance, and will founder unless we get the mathematicks just so. I have brought in Newton as a consultant."

"No harm in going straight to the top."

"But he seems to be up to too many other things, Mr. Waterhouse, for he rarely answers my letters, and when he does, he does not discourse on probability but rather accuses me of being in league with Jesuits, or of setting fire to his laboratory . . ."

"Stay. Everyone who has spoken to me concerning Newton in the last few days has employed euphemisms and circumlocutions meant to suggest that he has gone clean out of his mind."

"I always thought *Hooke* was our Lunatick in Residence, but lately Newton . . ."

"Enough. I shall try to get to the bottom of it."

"Right. Now, on your knees, Mr. Waterhouse!"

"I beg your pardon!?"

"Never fear, I shall be joining you in moments . . . my knees being older work slower . . . er . . . ah! . . . owf. There. Now, let us pray."

"You always say a prayer after you piss?"

"Only after a really first-rate one, or when communing with a fellow sufferer, as now. Lord of the Universe, Your humble servants

Samuel Pepys and Daniel Waterhouse pray that You shall bless and keep the soul of the late Bishop of Chester, John Wilkins, who, wanting no further purification in the Kidney of the World, went to Your keeping twenty years since. And we give praise and thanks to You for having given us the rational faculties by which the procedure of *lithotomy* was invented, enabling us, who are further from perfection, to endure longer in this world, urinating freely as the occasion warrants. Let our urine-streams, gleaming and scintillating in the sun's radiance as they pursue their parabolic trajectories earthward, be as an outward and visible sign of Your Grace, even as the knobby stones hidden in our coat-pockets remind us that we are all earth, and that we are sinners. Do you have anything to add, Mr. Waterhouse?"

"Only, Amen!"

"Amen. Damn me, I am late for my next conspiracy! Godspeed, Daniel."

> For the *understanding* is by the flame of the passions,
> never enlightened, but dazzled.
>
> —HOBBES,
> *Leviathan*

Daniel's first emotion, unexpectedly, was a pang of sympathy for young Dominic Masham. Daniel, too, would have been amazed by what John Locke, Nicolas Fatio de Duillier, and Isaac Newton were up to at Oates, if he had not been at Epsom during the Plague Year. As it was, the laboratory that those three lonely hereticks had set up on the Masham estate seemed a masque of what Wilkins and Hooke had done as guests of John Comstock.

He had to admit it was a good deal more civilized, though. No dogs were being disembowelled in Lady Masham's out-buildings. Epsom (in retrospect) had grown up, as if by spontaneous generation, out of earth saturated with blood and manured with gunpowder; it had been dominated by elements of earth and water. Oates was like a potted lily brought over from France; it was made of fire and air. And it was all about the search for the fifth element, the quintessence, star-stuff, God's presence on earth. When Dominic Masham took Daniel round the place, the sun was shining on the white-plastered Barock buildings, the roses of late summer were still a-bloom, windows flung open to let fresh air infiltrate the galleries and drawing-rooms, and Daniel could very easily comprehend why a young fellow who knew no better might convince himself that there *was* a quintessence, that it was everywhere, and especially here, and that men as brilliant as these might reach out and take some of it.

They encountered Fatio posed in the middle of a windowed library, surrounded by Bibles in diverse languages and alphabets. *Protogaea* had been quarantined on a table in the corner. Fatio was putting on a great show of thinking very hard on something and of not noticing that Daniel had entered the room—in effect daring Daniel to interrupt him, so that he could put on a further show of not minding at all. Daniel had no stomach for the game and so with a silent gesture to Masham he ducked out of the room. For about Fatio was a queer aura of fragility; he seemed stiff and scared as a glass figurine perched too close to an edge.

Masham led him on to a study that was obviously Locke's. He had published his *Essay Concerning Human Understanding* four years before. To judge from the storm of letters on his desk, angry criticism was still rushing in, and Locke was at work on a sort of apologia for the next edition: ". . . searches after truth are a sort of hawking and hunting, wherein the very pursuit makes a great part of the pleasure."

Locke's study had French doors that led out into a little rose-garden. The wind blew up now for a few moments and got under the edge of one of those doors, which was hanging ajar, and blew it open, letting cool air curl into the room and blow Locke's papers around. It felt and smelt of autumn. Masham scurried around chasing the blown pages, which was amusing because they had been in utmost disorder to being with. Daniel stepped to the open door to get out of Masham's way and to hide the smile on his face. The gust waned and Daniel heard Locke's voice from the garden, saying things long-winded and soothing and reasonable, interrupted by sharp objections from Isaac Newton.

Daniel stepped out into the garden just in time to be wrapped up in another wind-gust. This weather was stripping browned and withered petals from thousands of shaggy rose-blossoms that dangled like bruised apples from bowers and trellises all around, and they were storming down to earth and scuttling round the place in whorls.

Isaac had not failed to notice him. He was seated in a garden-chaise with his feet up, and he was wrapped in blankets, which did not prevent him from shivering all the time, though the day was only beginning to turn cool. He looked near death: even gaunter than usual, and sunk in on himself, and so devoid of color that one might suppose the blood had been drawn out of his veins and replaced with quicksilver.

"Daniel, it is well that your friend and mine Mr. John Locke foretold your coming, or I should take it the wrong way."

"How so, Isaac?"

"I have got into an odd turn of mind of late. The world seemeth benign enough, as I sit here in a bright garden among friends. But when night falls, as it does earlier and earlier, darkness stretches over my mind, and I phant'sy long menacing shadows cast by everyone and everything I saw during the day-time, which shades are interconnected in plots and conspiracies."

"Everyone, save mad-men in Bedlam, has a Plot. Everyone belongs to a conspiracy or two. What is the Royal Society, besides a conspiracy? I shall not claim I am innocent. But the conspiracy I represent wants only good things for you."

"I shall be the judge of that! How could you possibly know what is good for me?"

"If you could see yourself as I see you, Isaac, you would confess in an instant that I know much more of it than you do. How long has it been since you have slept?"

"Five nights I have sat up by the fire, tending a work."

"The Great Work?"

"You have known me almost as long as I have known myself, Daniel, why do you waste breath asking? For you know that I will not answer you straight out. And you already know the answer. So your question is idle twice over."

"Five nights . . . then I have come haply on this day, as I may be a match for you, Isaac, if you have gone a week without sleep beforehand."

"In what wise do you seek to be my match, Daniel?"

Behind him Masham started to say something and was quickly shushed. Daniel turned halfway round and discovered that Fatio had followed him as far as Locke's study; having now been discovered, he emerged into the garden, moving in an odd diagonal gait like a startled dog, acknowledging Daniel with a little bow. But he would not look Daniel in the eye.

"In what wise? Not as Fatio would be—this was settled between you and me on Whitsunday of the year 1662, unless I read the signs wrong." A slow assenting blink of Newton's bloodshot eyes told him he hadn't. "And certainly not as Leibniz seeks to be."

Fatio scoffed. "We have read Mr. Leibniz's letter—which is nothing more than a butcherous attack on my theory of gravitation!"

"If Leibniz cuts down your theory of gravitation, Monsieur Fatio, it only means he has the courage and forthrightness to set down in ink what Huygens and Halley and Hooke and Wren have all said amongst themselves ever since you presented it to the Royal Society. And I mean to emulate Leibniz now. Stay, Fatio, no show of indignation, please, I cannot abide it. I see three faces in this garden: Fatio, who has just been attacked, and is ready to respond very hotly; Newton, who is strangely ambivalent, as if he agrees with me in secret; Locke, who perhaps wishes I had never come to disturb your colloquium. But disturb it I have, and now I shall disturb it some more. For as I reflect on my career I believe I could have accomplished more if I had not cared so much what people thought of me. Natural Philosophy cannot advance without attacking theories that are old, and beating back new ones that are wrong, neither of which may be accomplished without doing some injury to their professors. I have been a mediocre Natural Philosopher not because I was stupid but because I was, after a fashion, cowardly. Today I shall try boldness for once, and be a better Natural Philosopher for it, and probably get you all hating me by the time I am done. Then it's off to Boston on the next boat. Therefore, Fatio, do not defend your theory or attack that of Leibniz with some tedious outburst, but, prithee, shut up and hate me instead. Isaac, this is what I mean when I say that I shall try to be a match for you today. If you hate me when I leave, then let that be a measure of my success."

"This is a harsh method," Isaac reflected, shivering even more violently now. "But I cannot deny that in my career scientific disputes have always been coupled with the most intense personal enmity. And I am not of a mood to be tender and conciliatory just now. So, have at it. I may understand you better as an enemy than as a friend."

"When I saw you here in this rain of dead petals I was put in mind of the spring of 1666 when I came up to Woolsthorpe and saw you in a flurry of apple-blossoms. Do you recollect that day?"

"Of course."

"I had just ridden up from Epsom where Hooke and Wilkins and I had been holding a colloquium much like this one. The overriding subject of it could be called 'Life: what it is, and is not.' Now I come here and find you studying what I will summarize as 'God: what godhead is and is not.' Have I said it well?"

"This way of saying it is very easily misunderstood," Locke demurred.

"Stay, John," Newton commanded, "Daniel misunderstands nothing."

"Thank you, Isaac," Daniel said. "If what you say is true, 'tis so only in that I have strived for so many years to follow your tortuous windings through these matters. It has been no easy task. Bible-stuff has always been intermingled with your philosophical work, and I could never understand why, in our chambers, star-catalogs were so

promiscuously thrown together with Hebraic scriptures, occult trea-
tises on the philosophic mercury interleaved with diagrams of new tel-
escopes, *et cetera*. But at last I came to understand that I was making it
too complicated. For you, this is no mingling at all; for you the Book
of Revelation, the ramblings of Hermes Trismegistus, and *Principia
Mathematica* are all signatures torn from the same immense Book."

"Why is it, Daniel, that you understand all of these matters with
such clarity, and yet will not join with us? It seems to me as if some
friend of Galileo had looked through his telescope and seen the
moons of Jupiter making their circuits and yet refused to believe his
own eyes, and taken the dead view of the Papists instead."

"Isaac, I have done nothing but ask myself that for sixteen years."

"You refer to what happened in 1677."

"What *did* happen in 1677, anyway?" Fatio inquired. "Everyone
wants to know."

"Leibniz made his second visit to England. He went incognito to
Cambridge, for no purpose other than to have a conversation with
Isaac. Which did occur. But as they punted down the Cam, discoursing, I came upon papers in our chambers proving that Isaac had
fallen into Arianism, which I saw as an unspeakable heresy. I burned
those papers, and with them many of Isaac's alchemical notes and
books—for to me they were all of a piece. To which crime I now confess freely, and offer my repentance, and ask for forgiveness."

"You speak as if you never expect to see me again!" Newton
exclaimed, with tears in his eyes. "I perceived your shame, and knew
your heart, and forgave you long ago, Daniel."

"I know it."

"Most of what you burned anyway was twaddle. You'll see none of
it *here*. Yet *here* I am infinitely closer to the Grand Magisterium."

"I know you have torn Alchemy down to its foundations, and built
it back up, and are recording it in a book called *Praxis,* which will be
to Alchemy what *Principia Mathematica* was to physics. And perhaps
'tis hoped that in combination with some new reading of scriptures
from Fatio, here, and new philosophy from Locke, there, and a
reworking of Christianity on Arian principles from your disciples
scattered round England, it shall all come together in some grand
unifying discourse, a kind of scientific apocalypse in which the whole
universe, and all history, shall be made clear as distilled water."

"You mock us, by making it simple."

"It is not simple, then? 'Twill not all happen at once, in a flash?"

"It is not for us to say in advance the manner of how it might
happen."

"Yet you have been awake five nights tending some work that

you'll not entrust to any assistant. You suffer obvious ill effects of quicksilver poisoning. You will not admit it is the Great Work, but what else could it be? And I cannot read your mind, Isaac, or ask you to divulge secrets, but I can see plainly enough that it *failed*. And if it was meant to combine with Fatio's theory of gravity, then that has failed as well."

"Before you mock our work, sir, prithee tell us in what way Leibniz's has *succeeded*," Fatio demanded.

"His differs from yours in that it does not need to succeed—only not to fail. And I take that to be a more sound way of doing science than your approach, which is all-or-nothing. For as I grow older and see new men coming into the Royal Society I perceive that though Natural Philosophy may have begun with our generation, it need not end with us. Nor am I alone in thinking so." Daniel now lifted up a sheet he had taken from Locke's study, and read: "It is of great use to the sailor to know the length of his line, though he cannot with it fathom all the depths of the ocean. It is well he knows that it is long enough to reach the bottom, at such places as are necessary to direct his voyage, and caution him against running upon shoals that may ruin him."

"What sniveling fool penned that nonsense?" Fatio demanded.

"Mr. John Locke. And the ink is still damp on it," Daniel replied.

"I am quite sure he did not mean it to apply to Isaac Newton!" Fatio returned, jarred, but recovering quickly.

"I believe what you really mean to say is, 'Newton and Fatio,'" Daniel said.

Newton and Fatio looked at each other, and Daniel looked at them. Fatio had a kind of tender, insinuating look on his face, and Daniel got the idea it was very far from the first time he had shown that sort of face to Newton, and that Fatio was used to seeing a tender and loving face looking back his way. But not today. Newton was staring at Fatio not with love, but with avid curiosity, as if suddenly perceiving what had escaped his notice before. Daniel had no love for Fatio, but this made him so uneasy that he lost the courage he'd maintained up until now.

"I wish to tell you a story about Robert Hooke," he announced.

This was one of the few things that could get Isaac's attention away from his minute, penetrating study of Nicolas Fatio de Duillier. He turned his eyes toward Daniel, who went on: "Before I came up to Woolsthorpe, Isaac, I did an experiment with him. We set up a scale above a well, and weighed the same object at the level of the ground, and again three hundred feet below it, to see if there was a difference. For you see, Hooke had an inkling of the inverse-square law."

Isaac did a little calculation in his head and said, "There was no observable difference."

"Just so. Hooke was let down, of course, but as we drove home he conceived a refinement of the experiment, which has never been carried out. But the point of the story is that our colloquium at Epsom *succeeded* at much, but *failed* in that, its most ambitious effort. Did it mean the end of Natural Philosophy? No. The end of Hooke's career, or Wilkins's, or mine? By no means. On the contrary, it led straight on to a *flourishing* of all those things. Which has led me to mistrust apocalyptic readings of Science or of Society. I have not been quick to learn that lesson, either. For example, I phant'sied that the Glorious Revolution would change all, but now I see that Cavaliers and Roundheads have only been replaced by Tories and Whigs, and the war goes on."

"Am I to gather that you intend to draw some parallel between the failures of Hooke, and the prospects for our collaboration?" Fatio said, with forced hilarity. "I supposed you were here as a cat's paw for Leibniz! He at least is a worthy opponent! He came out with calculus after Isaac and I did so, but at least he knows what it is! Hooke is nothing more than a sooty, bloody empiricist!"

"I am here as a cat's paw for Isaac Newton, my friend of thirty years. I fear for him because I perceive that he has an idea of what Natural Philosophy is, and of what he is, that is false. He is so far above all of the rest of us that he has come to believe that he carries the burden of some millennial destiny, and that he must bring Natural Philosophy to some ultimate omega-point or be a failure. He has been encouraged to believe this by certain sycophantic admirers."

"You want him back! You want Isaac to revoke the decision he made on Whitsunday of 1662!"

"No. I want him to *repeat* the same decision in respect of *you*, Fatio. He withdrew from *me* in '62. From Leibniz in '77. Now it is '93, and your card has been dealt."

"I know all about what happened in '62 and '77. Isaac told me. But with us it is a different case. With us there is a real, lasting, mutual affection."

"Nicolas, that much is true," Isaac said. "But you misunderstand. Daniel is working his way round towards another matter."

"What could Mr. Waterhouse possibly say that would be of interest? He is an *amanuensis*, a *secretary*."

"Do not make any more such offending statements about Daniel," Isaac commanded. "He has done us the favor, Nicolas, of thinking about our future. Which is a matter we did not consider at all, so confident were we. But Daniel is right. We have failed. Our line was not long enough to fathom the depths on which we had ventured. It will be necessary to regroup, to start over again. We shall require time and money and leisure."

"Isaac," Daniel said, "two or three years ago, before you set out on the Great Work that has just come to an end, you made inquiries, with Pepys and Roger Comstock and others, concerning the possibility of a position in London. Since then Trinity College has only become more impoverished—your need of a reliable income cannot have been met from that quarter. Now I have come to offer you the Mint."

Everyone now observed a prayerful silence for a minute or two as Isaac Newton considered it.

"In normal circumstances the position would be without interest," he said, "but Comstock has sent adumbrations my way concerning a great Recoinage."

"It is intended that Recoinage would be your Great Work. Which I do not say in jest. For perhaps that is indeed the only way that the Philosophic Mercury could ever be recovered."

"Why do you say that?"

"Hooke could not find the inverse-square law in a well because there was too little of what he was looking for, for his equipment to find it. You could not extract the Philosophic Mercury from gold, perhaps for a like reason."

"You hypothesize that my methods are sound but that there is too little of it in my sample. I disprove your hypothesis by reminding you that my methods are those of the ancients, who, as I believe, did not fail to get what they sought."

"Would you number King Solomon among them?"

"You know as well as I do that he is regarded as the father of Alchemists."

"If King Solomon had been in command of the Grand Magisterium, he would have used it. His wealth was fabled. He must have gathered together a moiety of the world's supply of gold, and extracted the Philosophic Mercury from it."

"Many adepts believe that he did just that."

"It would follow that *ordinary* gold, such as you employ in your Great Work, was *depleted*, while King Solomon's gold was *enriched*, in the quintessence."

"Again, this supposition is commonplace."

"Comes now word that King Solomon's Gold was found by a Viceroy of Mexico who then lost it to the King of the Vagabonds—who absconded with it to India, and there dispersed it, commingling it with the ordinary gold that circulates all over the world as money."

"That is what we are told."

"Short of conquering the whole Orient and collecting all its riches by tyrannical confiscations, there is then no way to recover what the Vagabond King has pissed away—unless you could, by some magical incantation, cause the gold to come from every corner of the earth to London, and pass through the crucibles of the Tower."

Fatio stepped forward, almost blocking the sight-line between Daniel and Isaac. "Now that you have got down to business, you offer up a most reasonable and attractive proposition," he proclaimed. "Prithee explain what you meant earlier."

"*I* shall explain it, Nicolas," Isaac said. "Daniel has done all the explaining we may justly require of him. He means—but is unwilling to say—that your theory of gravity is nonsense and that it has weakened my position vis-à-vis Leibniz. He probably refers also to your claim to be a co-inventor of the calculus, which is, I am sorry to say, perfectly false. Perhaps he has also in mind your pretensions of becoming a medical doctor and curing thousands with a new patent-medicine, and your fanciful interpretations of the Bible, and strange prophecies drawn therefrom."

"But he knows nothing of these!"

"But I do, Fatio."

"What are you saying? I confess the Bible is easier to interpret than you, Isaac."

"On the contrary, I feel that I am all too transparent, for Daniel, and God only knows how many others, have seen through me."

"Not that many—*yet*," Daniel said quietly.

"The nub of it is this: I have let my affection for you cloud my judgment," Isaac said. "I have given much greater credit to your work, Nicolas, than I ever should have, and it has led me down a cul-de-sac and caused me to waste years, and ruin my health. Thank you, Daniel, for telling me this forthrightly. Mr. Locke, you have worked in a gentle way to bring about this epiphany, and I apologize for thinking poorly of you and accusing you of plotting against me. Nicolas, come to London and share lodgings with me and be my help-meet as I move forward in the Great Work."

"I am not willing to be less than your equal partner."

"But you cannot ever be my equal partner. Only Leibniz—"

"Then go and make love to Leibniz!" Fatio cried. He stood poised where he was for a few moments as if he could not believe he'd said it—waiting, Daniel thought, for Newton to retract everything he'd said. But Isaac Newton was long past being able to change his mind. Fatio was left with only one thing he could possibly do: He ran away.

Once Fatio had passed out of view, Daniel began to hear a distant moaning or wailing. He assumed that he was hearing Fatio crying out in grief. But it grew louder. He feared for a moment that Fatio might be coming back toward him with a weapon drawn.

"Daniel!" said Locke sharply.

Locke had gotten to his feet and was standing over Newton, blocking Daniel's view. Locke had begun his career as a physician and seemed to have reverted to his old form now; with one hand he was throwing off the mass of blankets in which Newton had been wrapped up this whole while, with the other, he was reaching for Newton's throat to check his pulse. Daniel rushed toward them, fearing that Isaac had suffered a stroke, or an apoplectic fit. But Newton knocked Locke's hand away from his neck with a shout of "Murder! Murder!"

Locke took half a step back. Daniel drew up on Newton's other side to find him flailing all of his limbs, like a man who was drowning in air. The violence of his movements seemed to levitate his whole body out of his chair for an instant. He fell hard onto the stone patio, yelped, and went stiff, his entire body trembling like a plucked twist of catgut. Daniel dropped to a knee and placed a hand on one of Newton's bony shoulders. What meager flesh he had was hard and thrumming. Newton started away as if Daniel had touched him with a hot iron and rolled blindly against the chair leg, which caught him in the midsection. In a heartbeat he contracted into a fœtal position, wrapping his whole body round the leg of the chair like a toddler who grips his mother's leg with his whole being because he does not want her to walk away. "Murder, murder!" he repeated, more quietly now, as if dreaming of it, though it might have been *Mother, mother.*

Locke spoke from between his hands, which he had clapped over his face like the covers of a book. "The greatest mentality of the world—demented. Oh, God have mercy."

Daniel sat down crosslegged next to Isaac. "Mr. Locke, if you would be so good as to have one of the servants bring me a cup of coffee. I am going to do something I have not done in three decades: sit up all night worrying about Isaac Newton."

"What you have done was necessary and in no way do I fault you for it," Locke said, "but gravely I fear that he shall never be the same."

"You are right. He will be merely the most successful Natural Philosopher in all of history. Which is a better thing to be than a false Messiah. It will take him years to get used to his new station in the world. By the time he is himself again, I'll be out of his reach, in Boston, Massachusetts."

Bonaventure Rossignol to Eliza

MARCH 1694

My lady,

I pray this intercepts you in Hamburg, but I worry that it shall never catch up with you. I am a mortal, earthbound, attempting to get a message to a Goddess who travels in a flying chariot.

Of late I wonder: Do you really ken the devastation of Trade? You might scoff at such a question, as you do naught *but* trade. But to us earthbound mortals, it seems that you float about in a golden nimbus of prosperity, like the halo about a saint. And the company you keep can only enhance this illusion. Besides you, the only people in France who are not prostrate from Famine and Want of Money are your friends Jean Bart and Samuel Bernard. Bernard because he has taken over St.-Malo, driven out what was left of the old *Compagnie des Indes,* and fitted out his own fleet. Bart because the Navy ran out of money and had to be sold off to private investors. What does it say about our commerce, when the most attractive investment in France is a fleet of buccaneers preying on the commerce of *other* Realms?

And so I have every confidence that Captain Bart has conveyed you in safety, and even in comfort, to Hamburg; for what Navy in Christendom could stand against a fleet so well financed, so richly supplied with Baltic timber, and so brilliantly led? (Though I do hope he hurries back, as the British Navy is bombarding Dieppe.) I worry, though, that the posts will fail somewhere between Paris and Hamburg. For all is bankrupt. The spring breezes are redolent, not of tilled earth and burgeoning wildflowers, but the rotting flesh of all the livestock that froze to death during the winter. Rice—*rice!*—is coming in to Marseille from Alexandria, but no one has the means to buy it, for the wellsprings of our coinage have quite dried up. Our Army's commanders slouch despondently around Versailles, wishing they'd had the foresight to join the Navy—as, owing to a want of specie, and even of credit, they cannot fight this year, but only squat in their fortresses, succumbing to disease, and beating back whatever assaults the English may mount against them, supposing that England has two pennies to rub together.

At any rate, my lady, do let me know if this has reached you, and of your itinerary. I know you would be informed of the latest exchanges between Vrej Esphahnian and his family. It will take me a long time to encrypt the report. If my late father's map collection is to be credited, three hundred miles of winding Elbe lie between you and your destination; this should give you time sufficient to accomplish the decipherment. Perhaps I can arrange for it to catch up with your river-boat at Hitzacker or Schnackenburg or Fischbeck or one of the other euphoniously named villages that, according to my father's maps, are soon to be adorned with the grace and beauty of the duchesse d'Arcachon and her baby girl Adelaide.

Bon. Ross.

Eliza to Rossignol
MARCH 1694

Bon-bon,

Yours reached me in Hamburg, where we have been interviewing river-captains and buying provisions for the journey inland. What a grim petulant mood you were in when you let this dribble from your quill! A few remarks:

—Adelaide is no baby, but a toddler of fourteen months, careering around the deck pursued by a squadron of stooping and waddling nurses who are all terrified she'll go over the side.

—Hitzacker is said to be a perfectly lovely village; I'm sorry you don't favor the name of it.

—The parlous condition of Trade is well known to me; who do you suppose arranged for the rice to be shipped from Egypt? Do you think it is a *bad* thing that there shall be no great battles this year? And have you forgotten that my son Lucien sickened and died over the winter just past? Where was my golden halo of prosperity when the Angel of Death came for him in St.-Malo? Really, you quite forget yourself.

But I forgive you. The grimness of your discourse tells me much that is useful of the mood among the Quality of Paris and Versailles. If it eases your mind, know that the confusion of which you complain is the death-throes of an old system— as when a man's heart stops beating but his limbs continue to twitch for some time afterwards. The English, being a small and disorderly country, understood this a few years earlier than the French. Or perhaps that is giving them too much credit. They did not understand, but sensed, it. The tide of quicksilver that rose up in that country around the time of Plague and Fire produced a generation of more than normally acute minds—some, such as Newton, almost too tight-strung to endure the world. These men had power before, but knew not what to do with it, and lost it. In exile they formed the Juncto, which with the recent elections has taken over the government. The things that the Juncto does during the coming year—the Bank of England, the Recoinage, &c.—are the beginnings of the new way of things that shall replace the old one that has died, or is dying. France lags, having more of lead and less of quicksilver in her constitution, and lacking a Juncto; but the same forces are at work there.

You need only look to Lyon for an example. When Lothar von Hacklheber journeyed to Lyon in April of 1692 and accepted, from M. Castan, half a million *livres tournoises* of French government obligations in exchange for silver deliverable at London, no one thought twice about it. It was a large transaction, to be sure, but altogether routine. If you had gone to him, or to any of the other German or Swiss bankers in Lyon, at that time, and said, "This is the last such loan that shall ever be made in Lyon, and it shall never be repaid," they'd have thought you a madman.

Yet all through 1692 Castan temporized, and promised to pay interest, and sought alternatives to paying it back. The bad harvest that autumn rendered payment quite out of the question, and the lines of *galériens* marching through Lyon en route to Marseille—mostly ordinary Parisians who had been caught looting bakeries—served to place the "sufferings" of Lothar in perspective. The immense military operation of last year consumed what money the Treasury had. The French victories (costly though they were) at Heidelberg, at sea, at Landen, and in Piedmont might have given Lothar some hope of seeing his money again. If so, that hope died in the winter just past, along with so many other things. The bankers of Lyon now look upon Lothar's April 1692 loan as the moment it all went wrong; the end of an epoch. My correspondents there tell me that real estate in that city is to be had for nothing now, because the Swiss and German bankers are all turning their backs on it, cutting their losses, packing their coffers, and moving out. One day France will have its equivalent of the Bank of England, and it will probably be in Paris; but not for a long time, and until then, her finances will be in perpetual confusion.

It is for all of these reasons that I have resolved to descend on Leipzig now. But in order for me to know how best to set my pieces on the board, as it were, vis-à-vis Lothar, I must have the very latest on the Esphahnians, and the machinations of Father Édouard de Gex. For I know that hardly a day passes without his pestering you for the latest news concerning Vrej and his movements about Hindoostan.

Here, we are still shopping for a conveyance. Boats in every country are as various as breeds of dogs. In Bohemia, in the forests that surround the headwaters of the Vltava, they fashion barges of oak, and float them down to be finished around Prague. These carry Silesian coal down to places like Magdeburg and Hamburg, where local boatmen buy them and fix them up for their own uses. So though they may have all looked the same as they were being wrought in Bohemia, where the waters of the Elbe began as raindrops dripping from pine-needles, by the time I inspect them in Hamburg, where the Elbe is a mile wide, each has become as unique as its owner. The notion of conveying a Duchess, her daughter, and her household three hundred miles up the Elbe is extraordinary to these boatmen, who as a rule do not venture more than one or two days' journey upriver; but some of the more adventurous spirits among them are warming to the idea, and I don't suppose it shall be long before we have come to terms with one of them, and set out. The spring thaws shall place an abundance of water under the flat bottom of our *Zille* (as these barge-boats are called), so that we shall not have to be so concerned with shoals; but by the same token, the vigorous flow of the river will make it impossible to sail upstream on any but the windiest of spring days, and so we shall progress only as fast as an ox-team on the river-bank can draw us. Figure ten miles a day, on average; from this and from your father's maps, you may put your mathematical acumen to use in guessing whither to post your reply. I guess Magdeburg; if you are slow, Wittenberg.

Eliza

Eliza to Pontchartrain
MARCH 1694

Monsieur,

A man of your erudition, a scholar as well as a nobleman, must know that the office of *contrôleur-général* comes with certain perquisites. If you have been slow to avail yourself of the same, it is not out of ignorance, but because your only thought is to be of service to the Most Christian King. I have long noted, but never mentioned this, for it was obvious that you were satisfied. But the latest letters from my friends in France are of a very grim cast, which has caused me to wonder whether you have, as you lay in bed in the dark hours of the night, regretted that you had not been more forward in looking after your own interests during those early years when France's prosperity was the envy of the world, and her credit as good as gold.

I would be remiss if I did not let you know of a certain opportunity. As you know, France has since ancient times owed money to any number of different creditors at any given time. Part of the job of the *contrôleur-général* is to see that these obligations are discharged by assigning them to sources of revenue; for example, if France owes such-and-such number of *livres* to Signore Fiorentino, the *contrôleur-général* might go to some French count and say, "This year, when you collect the taxes on your lands, send the proceeds to Signore Fiorentino, as we owe him a debt." A consequence of this is that not all French government debts are of equal value; for if the count, in the example above, was *honnête,* his lands bountiful, and the weather good, why, Signore Fiorentino would be repaid promptly and in full, while some other creditor, whose loan had been assigned to a less reliable source of revenue, might come up short-handed. It is this variability that makes the work of the *contrôleur-général* so endlessly absorbing. Not to mention *profitable;* for nothing in law or custom prevents the *contrôleur-général* himself from purchasing some loans that have gone bad, and then re-assigning them to more reliable sources of revenue, so that they are suddenly worth more. It is a perquisite of the office, and no one would give it a second thought if you were to avail yourself of it.

As it happens, for several years I have been purchasing underperforming loans from diverse petty nobles who did their parts to be of service to the King when the present war broke out. The total number of such transactions now numbers in the hundreds. The principals of all of these loans, summed, come to rather more than half a million *livres,* though I acquired them for less than a quarter of that amount. I will now sell them to you, Monsieur, for just what I paid for them, plus a soupçon of five percent. If, as I suspect, you lack the liquid assets necessary to close such a transaction, I will accept your word as a nobleman, and not think of being repaid until after you have had the leisure to plumb all of these obligations into adequate sources of revenue. Once you have accomplished that, you should be able to see that each of these loans is repaid in full, which means that you could in theory get back quadruple what you shall owe me.

No gratitude is expected, or desired; my only wish, as ever, is to be of service.

Eliza, duchesse d'Arcachon

Rossignol to Eliza
APRIL 1694

My lady,

I hope this finds you on a tidy and well-skippered *Zille* halfway up the Elbe. Please forgive me for the intemperate remarks contained in my previous letter. The situation in all places has become so bizarre, so suddenly, that I know not what to make of it. Half of London—the better half—is said to have been abandoned. Because there is no silver, Persons of Quality have no means of conveying rents from their lands in the country, to town; so they have no choice but to board up their town-houses and move to the country, where they can live on barter. It seems the worst possible moment for the Whigs to have taken power, and to have put in the Marquis of Ravenscar at the Exchequer; but perhaps it is the case that he, like you, perceives some opportunity where others see only confusion, and has chosen this moment to strike.

To business. You asked for the latest on the Esphahnians. I will tell you what I know.

You'll recall that after the severed head of your father-in-law turned up at his own birthday party on the evening of 14 October 1690, we heard little that was of any use on this channel for several years. Vrej Esphahnian had contrived to get a letter out from Egypt a few days before the duc d'Arcachon's demise, and several months later he posted a brief note from Mocha in which he directed his family not to make any effort to reply, as he could not predict where the currents of trade would next take him.

In the meantime I had not been idle. It was clear to me that the Esphahnians used some form of steganography in their letters, but I could not make out how they did it. The family was scattered among several hovels, entresols, and prisons around Paris. I hired thieves to rifle through their possessions, and at length found some letters that Vrej had sent to them from Spain and Barbary beginning in 1685. In the margins and interlinear spaces of these, I saw an inscription writ in letters of vermilion. It was plain enough that this was some sort of invisible ink, which had been made visible by some secret art known to the Esphahnians. By reading these, I was able to learn more of Vrej's story.

He had been sent to Spain early in 1685 to establish a family trading circuit there. But he had been taken by the Barbary Corsairs and enslaved. Yet his owner soon recognized that he had talents beyond pulling oars, and put him to work in a port city near Morocco, whence he was able to correspond with his family. From them, he learned of the disaster that had befallen the Paris Esphahnians after they had made the mistake of subletting their entresol to Jack Shaftoe. By this time they had been released from the Bastille, but one of them had died in prison, and their business was of course destroyed, so that in coming years many would drift in and out of debtors' prisons.

In 1688 Vrej's owner traded him to Algiers. There he became acquainted with another literate slave, a Jew of great intelligence, and over the course of several conversations with this Jew learned that Jack Shaftoe was still alive, as a galley-slave in the same city. During the winter of 1688–89, Vrej wrote to his family in Paris apprising them of this and proposing to find Jack and cut his throat, or arrange for it to be done, as revenge. Of course I do not have a copy of what was sent back in response; but it is easy enough to infer, from what Vrej wrote in his next letter, that older and wiser heads in Paris had prevailed. Jack Shaftoe was looked on as a sort of madman, a victim of possession, not responsible for his actions (though Vrej questions this, and suspects it is all an act), and no advantage to the family, temporal or spiritual, is seen in killing the poor man. Rather, it is suggested that Vrej seek some advantage in his dealings with the Jew.

As you will have anticipated, my lady, this Jew, this Armenian, and Jack, as well as several other galley-slaves, developed into the corps of pirates who have caused so much trouble since then.

All of these things were known to me, and to Father Édouard de Gex, by the end of the Year of Our Lord 1690. As you know, de Gex took the keenest imaginable interest in this. He began to ransack books of Alchemy for information about the vermilion ink: how it was concocted, and what vapor or infusion was required to make the hidden letters manifest on the page. With the connivance of his *cousine* the duchesse d'Oyonnax, he made the Esphahnians a great success among all the coffee-fanciers at Court, with the result that they have been able to move to Versailles and build that coffee-house on the Rue de l'Orangerie where you and I have spent so many stimulating hours. This had the effect that de Gex desired: All of the Esphahnians were gathered together in one house where they could be spied on with ease. When a letter came to them from some place such as Mocha, de Gex and I knew it first; and when a member of this family went out to buy something from a chymist, he was of necessity dealing with one of the Esoteric Brotherhood, well known to de Gex. And so by the middle of 1692 we had learned everything there was to know about the vermilion ink: how to compound it, and how to render it visible. Too, we knew of Vrej's movements about the Red Sea and the Persian Gulf. The one person who was wholly in the dark was Vrej himself. Because of his erratic movements, his family had not been able to send a letter to him since 1689, when they had been clinging to a wretched existence in Paris.

Finally in September of 1692 the pirates sailed to Surat, in Hindoostan, to get away from the Hell-hounds sent after them by Lothar von Hacklheber and various others they had injured. They were assaulted from an unexpected quarter by pirates of Malabar and their treasure was taken from them. Several, including Vrej, waded up on to the shores of Hindoostan where they dispersed. Vrej was press-ganged into the army of a regional king, a vassal of the Great Mogul whose *nom de guerre* is Dispenser of Mayhem. One might imagine that a man in such a position would be little better than a slave; however, it seems that, in the armies of the Mogul, Christian mercenaries enjoy a kind of elevated status—even when they are serving against their will! Or so I infer from the fact that Vrej was at last able to assemble the materials needed to concoct the invisible ink. And for the first time since his wanderings had begun, he was able to specify a return address. His letter reached France in November of 1692. De Gex and I steeped it in the chymical vapour that caused the scarlet letters to appear, and extracted the information I have just given you. Then I put my forgers to work making an exact duplicate of the letter, including the part written in invisible ink. This was delivered to the Café Esphahan and duly read by Vrej's kin. They immediately produced a letter in reply. Its outward contents were just the sort of mawkish drivel you would expect, but when de Gex and I exposed it to the vapour and read the hidden inscription, we found it to be rather more businesslike. In neat vermilion letters they told Vrej about the good fortune that the family had lately achieved.

I had been planning to have my forgers produce an exact copy of this, as we had done with the incoming letter; but de Gex had come under the spell of an idea, and formed a resolve to play a deeper game. He was extremely vexed that he had patiently bided his time for so many years only to learn that the Solomonic Gold had been lost to Malabar pirates, and had decided to grasp the nettle, as it were, and go to Hindoostan himself. To that end, he wished to cultivate Vrej as a source of intelligence, and, if possible, as an accomplice. But it was necessary to keep the matter a secret from other members of this pirate-band. The hidden channel of the vermilion ink was ideally suited to that purpose. And so the letter crafted by my forgers ended up being rather different from the original. It was written out on the cheapest paper we could gather up, with ink of miserable quality. The plaintext was much the same as in the original. But the invisible message was altogether different. In the letter that was actually posted back to Vrej, he is given the bad news that life has only gotten worse for the Esphahnians; two more of his brothers have perished in debtors' prisons, &c. However (according to this account, which de Gex concocted himself), the star of Jack Shaftoe has only soared higher; he is accounted a sort of picaresque hero now, and the story goes that he has pulled the wool over everyone's eyes, especially those of the pirates he travels with; for hidden in the treasure that was stolen is something of unimaginable value, known to Jack and to the Jew, but that they are concealing from their brethren.

The forged letter concludes by urging Vrej not to worry too much over the fate of his family in Paris, for, praise be to God, they have at last found an ally and a protector in one Father Édouard de Gex, a saintly man who knows of all the injustices perpetrated against the family, and who has taken a solemn vow to see to it that justice is done.

That forgery was sent off to Vrej in Hindoostan in December of 1692. The following April—about one year ago—Vrej's reply came in, and the scarlet letters might have been written in some unholy concoction of blood and fire, so infused were they with fury and lust for revenge. "The Lord has delivered him into my hands!" was what de Gex said upon reading it. I think he meant Jack Shaftoe, rather than Vrej. At any rate we produced a forged version whose invisible text was, of course, wholly different. In this version Vrej congratulates his family on their good fortune and asks to learn more of the glorious Café Esphahan, &c.

In this manner the correspondence has gone back and forth a few more times between Vrej and his brothers. Every word of it, of course, has passed through the mind and hand of de Gex, and been twisted one way or the other, so that Vrej and his brothers have developed utterly divergent pictures of what is going on.

Had you taken the trouble to ask me, you might have learned of all of these things prior to your departure for Germany. Since then, however, one more letter has come in from Vrej.

This letter was written in the court of the Great Mogul at Shahjahanabad where (one imagines) Vrej was reclining on silken pillows and being fed peeled grapes by bejewelled virgins, as he and what remained of his pirate-band had won a great battle against the Maratha rebels and thereby re-opened the high road from Surat to Delhi. Vrej relates the story in some detail. Word of it has already reached the courts of Europe via more than one channel and so I shall not say much about it here, on the assumption that you have heard or read other accounts. The general drift of Vrej's letter is that although he is being showered with rewards in Shahjahanabad, he cannot take any pleasure in them as long as he knows that his family are suffering in Paris; indeed, he would come home in the blink of an eye were it not for this saintly benefactor, Father Édouard de Gex, who was now looking after the family. Instead, Vrej proposes to tarry in Hindoostan so that he can get to the bottom of this story that I mentioned before— namely that there was something of extraordinary value secreted in the treasure of Bonanza. One would think that this had been irretrievably lost; but Vrej reports that some members of the pirate-band were taken as prisoners by the Malabar pirates. There exists the possibility that not all of them were slain instantly, tortured to death presently, or driven insane; i.e., that they are still alive in Malabar and know something about the lost treasure's whereabouts.

For his services to the Great Mogul, Jack Shaftoe has been made King of a region in southern Hindoostan for a term of three years, which, as bizarre as it sounds, is a customary way for that potentate to reward his generals. Soon Jack and the remnants of his band shall journey to his new kingdom for him to be enthroned. Vrej shall go with them, and promises to send his family news as soon as he has any to write down, and the means to post it.

That is all. Father Édouard, who was hoping for news more definite, is beside himself, and divides his time between the following three activities: one, uttering oaths that should never be heard from a priest. Two, seething, and trying to prevent himself from uttering any further oaths. Three, doing penance in various churches and chapels, to seek forgiveness for having let slip oaths. And so it is not an especially productive time for him; but between famine and lack of money it is no productive time for France either and so he does not stand out from the crowd.

Bonaventure Rossignol

Pretzsch, Saxony
APRIL 1694

PRINCESS WILHELMINA CAROLINE of Brandenburg-Ansbach had been sending letters to Eliza almost every week since the summer of 1689, which was when they had last seen each other. Caroline had been six years old then. Now she was almost eleven. The handwriting, and the contents of her letters, had changed accordingly. Yet as Eliza stood on the deck of her *Zille*—the slim, hundred-foot-long river-barge she had chartered in Hamburg—and scanned the green banks of the Elbe, she was looking for the young mother and the little girl she had bid farewell to in the Hague five years earlier. There was no helping it. To a child, nothing seemed more stupid in adults than their inability to come to grips with the fact that people grew. Unfathomably moronic seemed the aunt or grandpapa who exclaimed "You have grown!" at each reunion. Eliza knew this as well as anyone who has ever been a child. And yet she was ambushed by the two women on the quay. They had been waving to her as the *Zille*

drew near, and she had paid no more notice to them than to the cattle grazing in the undulating fields that rose up from the river's edge.

In her defense—if she needed any—she was exhausted from the length of the journey, and feeling especially woolly-headed today. And even if she'd been at her very sharpest, she might not have marked this quay because it was so humble. She had been on this river for a month, and had seen an uncountable number of wharves, piers, bridges, fords, and landings. Some, in cities, were vibrating entrepôts—little Amsterdams. Some, at the foot of barons' country estates, were Barock stone-piles and iron-snarls, meant to overawe the other Barons. Others were little more than flat places on the bank where farmers could bring their carts down to trade with barge-men. But the only reason this thing outside of Pretzsch rated a second look was that two women had risked their lives to come out and put their weight on it. A hundred years ago it might have supported a carriage and a team; two hundred, a house. Today, it was a slumping huddle of black piles slowly being transubstantiated into slime. Half the decking had been pilfered, and the other half was being used by shrubs and grass in lieu of soil. Those madly waving women showed bravery by putting themselves in its trust. The slenderer of the two showed a kind of reckless bravado by jumping up and down. They'd at least had the good sense to leave their wagon on terra firma—it was drawn up at the base of a mud track that meandered down the hill from a shaggy copse that might conceal a building. To either side of the wagon, a finger of stone was thrust into the air, as if to test the wind. Around these spread moraines of alienated blocks, bricks, and voussoirs, remnants of an arch that had been pulled down in some forgotten disturbance. In summer the loose stones would have been concealed by the leaves of the bushes and the sickly weed-trees that had insinuated roots among them, but winter had been even longer and deeper here than in France, and so most of these had not yet arrived at a firm decision as to whether they should put forth the effort of growing leaves, or simply stiffen up and die.

All of which made it no more or less decrepit than any other Elbe-side attractions that had passed in front of Eliza's uncaring eyes during the last month. It was not, however, the sort of place she would look for an Electress and a Princess.

Eleanor Erdmuthe Louisa, born a Princess, the daughter of the Duke of Saxe-Eisenach, had married the Margrave of Ansbach, John Frederick. When he had died, Eleanor and three-year-old Caroline had been turned out of the household and took up a poor wandering life among diverse minor courts of northern Europe. The center of gravitation round which they looped, and to which they frequently returned, was the court of the Elector and Electress of Brandenburg-Prussia, in Berlin. And a fine choice it was, for the Electress, Sophie Charlotte, had made of it a fair and fascinating place, replete with savants (e.g., Leibniz), writers, artists, musicians, &c. Sophie Charlotte and her redoubtable Mum, the Electress Sophie of Hanover, had taken Eleanor and Caroline under their wings, and been good to them.

But royalty was a family, which was to say that anyone fortunate enough to stay alive to the age when she became a sentient being would know in her bones that by having emerged from her mother's womb she had agreed to a pact, never to be broken or even questioned, whereby she'd receive all kinds of love and loyalty, but must repay every bit of it in kind. And whereas to a peasant family "loyalty" might mean slopping the hogs, to a royal it might mean *marrying* one, if that would help.

Brandenburg wished to form an alliance with Saxony, which lay immediately to its south, and thereby to worry it loose from the stern embrace of Austria. The alliance was to be sealed by the physical union of Johann Georg IV, the Elector of Saxony, with a suitable Princess from the House of Brandenburg. Eleanor was suitable, was available, and was there. And so she had married Johann Georg in Leipzig in 1692 and thereby become Electress of Saxony—so, equal in dignity to Sophie Charlotte, to Sophie, and to the six other Electors of the Holy Roman Empire. The newlyweds had moved to the Saxon electoral court at Dresden (which lay another sixty or so miles up the river from where Eliza was at this moment). Eliza had received a spate of Caroline-letters, and one Eleanor-letter, from there. But after a few months the Caroline-letters had begun to originate from this Pretzsch and the Eleanor-letters had stopped coming altogether. Even the maps of the father of Bonaventure Rossignol did not list any Pretzsch and so Eliza had had to ask Leibniz where it was. "A few hours' ride from Wittenberg," he had answered, and then declined to say anything more of it, which ought to have signified something to Eliza.

Caroline-letters tended to be full of talk about trees she had climbed, squirrels who had admitted her into their circle of trust, boys who had disgusted her, chess-games she had played via post against Leibniz, dreadful books she'd studied, wonderful books she'd read, the weather, logarithms, and timeless disputes among domestic animals. They told Eliza nothing about Johann Georg IV, about Dresden, or why they had moved to Pretzsch, or how Eleanor was doing. And so Eliza had assumed what would have been the case in France, namely that Pretzsch was some outlying château of the

Saxon court, as Marly was to Versailles, and that Eleanor, for whatever reason, favored it over life in the capital. And so ever since the
spires of Wittenberg had receded from view aft, Eliza had been scanning the hilltops above the river for some new Barock palace, with
terraced gardens leading down to a stone quay along the river, the
Electoral household drawn up in formation to greet her, perhaps a
consort playing music, the mother on the arm of her strapping husband the Elector, and the little girl. Her only concern had been that,
tired as she was, she might not be equal to the magnificence of it all.
Instead, this: above, a few leaning turrets and slumping eaves discernible through overgrown trees, a mud trough winding down to
the ruined dock where the two women were madly waving. It was so
at odds with Eliza's expectations that it made almost no impression
on her.

The day was saved by Adelaide, who could not talk yet, but who
had developed a keen interest in waving, and being waved to. The
apparition, in this empty countryside, of two women in bright
dresses, waving and waving and waving, could not have been better
calculated to draw her notice, and before long she was not only waving back but had to be chased down, snatched from the brink of a
watery demise, and physically restrained as she flung out both
chubby arms again and again toward the wavers. So it was that a pre-
verbal fourteen-month-old was able to perceive a simple truth that
had eluded Eliza: that they had reached the end of their journey and
were welcome among friends. Eliza gave word to the skipper. He
maneuvered the *Zille* alongside what remained of the quay. Eliza
pulled herself up out of the chair where she had been watching Germany go by, wiped sweat off her brow, and tried the experiment of
seeing whether the platform would support a third human.

Eleanor had broadened, sagged, lost teeth, shorn her hair, and
given up trying to conceal her old pox-scars beneath black patches,
as had been her practice in the Hague. She well knew how her looks
had declined, for she would not meet Eliza's eye, and kept turning
her face aside. What she did not understand was that the joy in her
face made up for all else; and moreover Eliza, who *felt* as run down as
Eleanor *looked*, was not of a mind to judge her unkindly. Eleanor
stood back half a pace, granting precedence to her daughter, who
was a glory. She was not exceptionally beautiful by the standards of
Versailles; however, she was more comely than nine out of ten
princesses. She had some spark about her, anyway, that would have
enabled her to outshine pretty people even if she'd been ugly, and
she had a self-possession that made her more watchable than any-

thing Eliza had laid eyes on since her weird audience with Isaac Newton. Eleanor hugged Eliza for a solid minute; in the same interval of
time, Caroline greeted everyone on the *Zille*, asked the skipper three
boat-questions, stuffed a bouquet of wildflowers into Adelaide's
hand, hitched the toddler up on her hip, told her to stop eating the
flowers, pranced across the cratered and shifting deck of the quay to
the shore, taught Adelaide how to say "river" in German, told her a
second time not to eat the flowers, pulled the flowers out of her
chubby fist, got into a violent row with her, patched it all up, and got
the little one giggling. She was now ready to go back to the house
and play chess with her Aunt Eliza; why the delay?

Pontchartrain to Eliza
APRIL 1694

My lady,

You have given me a strict command not to be grateful. I
know better than to disobey it. But you cannot command me
not to harbor *charitable* instincts. Of the benefit that I shall
reap from the transaction that you so cleverly devised, and
that your lawyers and mine have just consummated, I intend
to donate one quarter (after I have paid you your five percent) to charity. Alas, so many years have passed since I had
money to donate, that I have quite lost track of where the
deserving charities are to be found. Would you care to offer
any recommendations?

Ungratefully yours,

Ponchartrain

Eliza to Pontchartrain
MAY 1694

My ungrateful (but charitable) Count,

Your letter brought a smile to my lips. The prospect of discussing charities with you gives me one more reason to rush back to Versailles as soon as my business in Leipzig is finished. But do not forget that the government obligations I have sold to you are worthless until the *contrôleur-général* has assigned them to reliable sources of hard money revenue. As there is no money in France, or even in England, it must be got from other sources. Ships travel the sea bearing objects of tangible worth, and the laws of nations state that these may be taken as prizes during time of war. While the rest of France has been plunged into despair, Captain Jean Bart has presided over a golden age in Dunkerque, and often brings in prizes whose value is sufficient to cover the payments on those loans, supposing that the *contrôleur-général* wishes to manage it thus. As it may be some weeks before I can return to France, I recommend that you take up the matter directly with Captain Bart. If it bears fruit, why, then you and I may look forward to some delightful strolls in the King's gardens, during which we may plot how your generous donations may be put to work to better the world.

Eliza

The Dower-house of Pretzsch
APRIL AND MAY 1694

To suffer, as to doe,
Our strength is equal, nor the Law unjust
That so ordains.

—MILTON,
Paradise Lost

LIKE A GUINEA WORM, Eleanor's story had to be drawn out of her inch by inch. Its telling extended over a week, and was broken into a dozen installments, each of which was preceded by exhausting maneuvers and manipulations from Eliza and brought to a premature end by Eleanor's changing the subject or breaking down in tears. But the tiredness that Eliza had felt on the last day of the river-journey had developed into an influenza that kept her in bed for some days with aches and chills. So there was nothing else to pass the hours, and time favored Eliza.

The telling began when Eliza, sick, sore, woozy from mildew-smell and irritable because damp plaster kept falling from the ceiling onto her bed, asked: "A dower-house is where a dowager goes to live out her days after her husband has passed on; but yours still lives. So why are you in a dower-house?"

The answer—when all of the bits were spliced together and the preliminaries and digressions trimmed—was: The Elector Johann Georg IV belonged to a sort of fraternity whose members were to be found in every country in the world, and among every class of society: Men Who Had Been Hit on the Head as Boys. As MWHBHHB went, Johann Georg was a beauty. For some, the insult to the brain led to defects of the body, viz. wasting, unsightly curling of the fingers, twitches, spasms, drooling, &c. Johann Georg was not one of those; now in his late twenties, he could easily have found employment in Versailles as a gigolo for male or female clients—or both at the same time, as he was a great strapping stallion of a man, and who knew the limits of his body?

But *everyone* knew the limits of his mind. Eleanor might have known better than to marry him; but she had wanted to do her bit for the Brandenburgs, and to find a home for Caroline. He was rich and handsome; and though everyone knew he was a MWHBHHB, she had been assured, by many who knew him (Ministers of the Saxon court who in retrospect might not have been the most reliable sources) that he had not been hit all that hard. They pointed to his physical perfection as evidence of this. And (again, so easy to see in retrospect) they'd presented him to her, during their first few encounters, in settings ingeniously devised so that those aspects of his character attributable to his having been hit on the head as a boy had not been obvious. The wedding had been set for a certain date in Leipzig, a city easily reached from either capital (Berlin or Dresden) and large enough to accommodate two Electoral courts and a wedding party of noble men and women from all parts of Protestant Europe. Eleanor had gone there in the train of the Brandenburgs, and they had paid a call on her betrothed. The Elector of Saxony had received his bride-to-be in the company of a ravishing, expensively dressed young woman, and introduced her as Magdalen Sybil von Röohlitz.

Eleanor had heard the name before, always in a context of tawdry gossip. This woman had been Johann Georg's mistress for some years. Indeed they were said to be admirably matched, for though there was no evidence, visible or anecdotal, of her having been hit on the head as a girl, she might as well have been; despite lengthy and expensive efforts of her noble family to educate her, she could not read or write. And yet she was as perfect, as desirable a specimen of *female* beauty as Johann Georg was of *male.* The union made sense, in its way. There was a notable lack of brain power, but (a) the Doctors of Saxony were as one in saying that the imbecility of the Elector and of Fraülein von Röohlitz were not of the sort that is passed down to children, i.e., their offspring might be of sound mind, provided he were not hit on the head as a boy, and (b) the Countess's mother was said to be a clever one. *Too* clever; for she was in the pay of the Court of Austria, and doing all that she could to make Saxony into a fiefdom of that Realm. The Fräulein von Röohlitz had been Johann Georg's wife in all but name for some years and he'd given her a fortune, a Schloß, and a Court to go with it. Yet she was not of a rank to wed an Elector, or so insisted the old wise heads of the Saxon court, who were anti-Austria and pro-Brandenburg to a man. What Eleanor had seen and heard of these Saxons, from her distant and imperfect vantage-point in Berlin, had been only the faint noises off of a titanic struggle that had been carried out, over several years, in Dresden, between the pro-Brandenburg ministers of Saxony and the pro-Austria von Röohlitz faction. That Johann Georg had come to Brandenburg to woo her was evidence only that those ministers had, for a few months, got the upper hand. That her fiancé had now chosen to receive her, on the eve of their wedding, with his mistress draped all over him, and her draped in jewels that ought to have been gifts to Eleanor, proved that the struggle had lately swung the other way. Another prince, in such a circumstance, would have kept the mistress hidden away in her Schloß. The reality would have been no different but the presentation would have been comelier. But Johann Georg was a MWHBHHB and did not do things as other men. As Frederick, Elector of Brandenburg, looked on incredulously, and von Röohlitz watched in obvious delight, Johann Georg openly spurned Eleanor. And yet he had come to Leipzig with every apparent intention of going through with the wedding!

Frederick by now was acting in much the same rôle as Father of the Bride—though it was combined with that of one head of state negotiating an alliance with another, as well as that of a Doctor ministering to a village idiot. The meeting broke off. Most of those on the Brandenburg side of it were too nonplussed to be angry.

She married him. Eleanor Erdmuthe Louisa married Johann Georg IV, Elector of Saxony, albeit a few days later than planned, as everything had to be re-jiggered at the last minute. They moved to Dresden. The Elector promoted Magdalen Sybil von Röohlitz to the rank of Countess and kept her around. Libels began to circulate in the streets of Dresden in which it was argued that bigamy was no bad thing, having been practiced by any number of Biblical kings, and ought to be revived in Saxony. At about the same time, the Elector openly promised to marry the Countess von Röohlitz—*at the same time as he was still married to Eleanor.* The good Lutherans of Saxony pushed back against the idea of making bigamy the new law of the land, and even Johann Georg's impaired mind came to understand that he would never be able to marry two women at once.

Attempts to poison Eleanor's food commenced not long after. She might have been an easy victim in some other courts—a court, let us say, in which she had more enemies, and in which the enemies were not all mental defectives. But poisoning was a difficult and exacting business even for persons who had never been hit on the head, and the attempts of Johann Georg and Magdalen Sybil von Röohlitz were obvious, and were failures. Eleanor took as many clothes as she could pack in a hurry, and as many servants (three) as Johann Georg would allow her, and departed without taking another meal. This was how she and Caroline had landed at the dower-house of Pretzsch. Her sojourn here had hardened into a sort of exile, or imprisonment. As she had no money of her own, there was little practical difference. She and Caroline slept in the same room and barricaded the door at night in case Johann Georg should conceive some hare-brained plan to send assassins. Caroline, despite being an abnormally acute young lady when it came to squirrels and logarithms, had no idea that any of this was happening.

AT THE END OF TELLING THIS TALE, Eleanor looked better, albeit puffy around the eyes. She looked more like the dogged young Princess that Eliza had known at the Hague five years ago.

But any ground that she had gained by unburdening herself thus to Eliza, she gave back again in a few moments when, on the eighth day of Eliza's visit, she opened and read an ornate document that had been brought to the dower-house by a galloping courier. "Whatever is the matter?" Eliza asked. For she could not phant'sy what, to a woman in Eleanor's estate, could possibly be accounted Bad News; any conceivable change, it seemed, would be a step up.

"It is from the Elector," she announced.

"The Elector of—?"

"Saxony."

"Your husband?"

"Yes."

"What says it?"

"He has got word that I am entertaining a visitor, whose beauty and charm are renowned in all the courts of Christendom. He is pleased to learn that his Realm is graced by such a distinguished personage as the Duchess of Arcachon and of Qwghlm, and announces that he and the Countess shall arrive tomorrow to pay their respects to the Duchess, and to stay for a few days."

Eliza had summoned the strength to move to a chair by the sick-room's sole window. Cramped and dingy the dower-house of Pretzsch might be, but open fields surrounded it, with good climbing-trees. For some days Eliza had been too drained and listless even to read books; but she'd spent many hours in this chair, doing what she was doing now: watching Caroline and Adelaide play. The sheer number of hours that they could put into playing were a prodigy to Eliza, especially given that she felt a hundred years old. This had been her only form of contact with either of the girls since the day she'd arrived, for all had agreed it were best if Eliza were quarantined until she got better.

Eliza, draped in blankets like a statue for shipment, was rubbing the palms of her hands together. "Has the Elector ever had small-pox?" she asked.

"He does not bear scars of it, as far as I know. But as the marriage was never consummated, I have seen little of him. Why do you ask?"

"We have journeyed a great distance," Eliza said, "and called at more towns along the Elbe than I can remember. Given that, and given the sheer size of my entourage, there is always the possibility of someone's having picked up a disease en route. That is why travelers from abroad are frequently quarantined. Now, having heard so many lovely stories about the Elector of Saxony and the Countess von Röohlitz, I should be crestfallen if I missed the opportunity to make their acquaintances. But it would be most unfortunate if one of them were to fall ill of some malady that we brought up the Elbe. You will apprise them of this—?"

"I shall throw words in their general direction, to that effect," Eleanor said, "whether any shall stick I cannot say."

"By a long shot, however, the most sophisticated practice of the Turks is the institution of polygamy," Eliza said.

The Elector of Saxony, who really was a great penis of a man, all purple-red, and laced about with throbbing veins, and crowned with a tremendous curling black wig, sat up just a bit straighter. One eye, then the other, strayed in the direction of the Countess von Röohlitz. *She* was everything that Eliza could have anticipated from Eleanor's narration. Stuffed into a bag and smuggled a thousand miles to the southeast, she'd have sold, in a Constantinople slave-mart, for a whole stable of Arab race-horses. To ask her to make conversation, however, was a little bit like expecting a dog to cook his meat before eating it. Eliza had talked herself hoarse rather than shut up and listen to what these two would attempt to say to her. And like groundlings in a theatre, they were more than content simply to watch with open eyes, and, most of the time, open mouths.

"You don't say," said the Elector, after a while. "How do they . . . do it?"

Eliza let a beat or two pass in silence before letting go with a titter. She was not a great titterer by and large. This was a titter she had borrowed from a certain Duchess she had sat next to once at Versailles. She did not duplicate it very precisely, but here in the dower-house of Pretzsch it would serve. "Oh, monsieur," she went on, "your double entendre almost got by me."

"I beg your pardon—?"

"At first I supposed you meant, 'How did they institute the practice of polygamy?' but of course now I perceive you were really asking, 'How does the Sultan make love to two women, or more, at the same time?' I should be pleased to let you in on the secret, but I fear some of a more prudish disposition might object." And she kicked Eleanor in the shin under the table, and jerked her head toward the room's exit: which Eleanor had been pining for, as a prisoner regards a high window in the wall of his cell.

"I am exhausted," Eleanor announced.

"You look it," said the Countess, "or perhaps that is just age."

"Exhaustion or age—who can guess? I shall let it remain my little secret," Eleanor said equably. "I am sorry to leave the party so early, and when it appears that the conversation is about to take such a fascinating turn—"

"Or," said Eliza, catching the eye of Johann Georg, "to turn into something else."

"Pray, don't get up!" Eleanor said to her husband, who had shown not the slightest intention of doing so. "I'll to my bed, and shall see you all, I suppose, whenever you crawl out of yours. I do apologize once more for the miserable state of the accommodations." This last was aimed at her husband, who did not penetrate its meaning.

"Right," said Eliza, once the staircase, and the floorboards overhead, had let off creaking under the movements of Eleanor. She was in the salon now with the Elector of Saxony and his mistress, and she had their undivided attention. She brushed a bit of damp plaster out of her hair. "Where were we? Oh yes, the Chariot."

"Chariot?"

"I'm sorry, it is the name given to the technique that—in those countries that are enlightened enough to sanction the ancient Biblical practice of polygamy—is used by a Sultan when he is at a numerical disadvantage to his wives. I could try to describe it. A picture would be ever so much more effective, but I can't draw to save my life. Perhaps I should demonstrate it. Why, yes! That would be best. Would you be a dear, my good Elector, and flip yonder table upside down? I'll fetch an ottoman from the other room—"

"A what!?" barked Johann Georg, and his hand shifted to the hilt of his sword.

"As in a piece of furniture. We'll want something in lieu of reins—my dear Countess, if you'd care to unwind that silk sash from about your waist, 'twould serve."

"But the sash is holding up my—"

"—?"

"—ah, *j'ai compris*, madame."

"I knew you would, Fräulein."

"I HAD TO FUCK *SOMEONE*," Eliza mumbled through the hem of her blanket. "I suppose you'll think me a whore. But my son—I refer to the legitimate one—Lucien—died. Adelaide is a gem, but she was foolhardy enough to have been born female. My husband requires a legitimate boy."

"But—with *him*!?"

"You said yourself that his imbecility was not congenital."

"But how will you explain the *timing* of it!?"

"There is *nothing* that can't be explained away, if Étienne is willing to play along, and not ask difficult questions. And I think he is willing. None of it matters, probably."

"What do you mean by that?"

By way of an answer, Eliza—who was lying flat on her back in bed with a blanket over most of her face—thrust out a hand.

Eleanor screamed.

"Be quiet! They'll hear you," said Eliza.

"They—they have already left," said Eleanor from the uttermost corner of the room, whence she'd fled, quick as a sparrow.

"Oh. Then go ahead and scream all you like."

"When did the bumps appear?"

"I thought I felt one coming on yesterday. Had no idea they'd spread so rapidly." Eliza flipped the blanket down to expose her face. Earlier she'd counted twenty bumps, there, by feel, then lost interest. Eleanor gave her only the briefest glance before turning her face aside, and adopting a pose in the corner of the room like a schoolgirl who is being punished.

"So *this* is why you insisted Caroline and Adelaide be sent away to Leipzig!"

"You do a sick woman an injustice there. You yourself told me that the Elector could not take his eyes off Caroline. You mentioned it half a dozen times unbidden. She has only bloomed the more since he last raped her with his eyes. That alone was reason sufficient to get her out of the house."

"Does the Elector know?"

"Know that I have smallpox? Not yet."

"How could he have missed it?"

"First, most of these vesicles have broken out in the last few hours. Second, we did it in the dark. Third, many persons—including some who were not hit on the head as boys—are unclear as to the distinction between smallpox, and the great pox, or syphilis. Given the company he keeps, I cannot but think that Johann Georg has seen much of the latter!"

"What you have done is horrible!" Eleanor said, turning around, and, when she saw Eliza's face, thinking better of it.

"Oh, I've had worse."

"No! I mean, trying to get someone sick."

"You could have guessed yesterday that I had smallpox. You could have warned them off. You chose not to. So your outrage at this moment is very tiresome."

Eleanor could not frame any response to this.

"I don't know a single man at Versailles who has not killed someone, at least once in his life, directly or indirectly, by omission or commission. It is done commonly, and on the slightest pretexts. I might not have done what I did last night, had you not told me that the Elector desires Caroline. But knowing what I did of his lust for the girl, and his power over you, and knowing how it was likely to come out—well, I did what I did. Now, Eleanor, that is enough of talking about it. I really am spent. Last night took too much out of me at a time when I ought to have been conserving my strength. Now I'll pay the penalty. I wrote out instructions—in case of my death. It's under my pillow. I'm sleepy. Good-bye."

Jean Bart to Eliza
MAY 1694

My lady,

I take the liberty of sending you a first draft, only because the English Navy is massing in the Channel to lob more bombs on to French soil, a most tiresome practice of which they have lately become quite fond. They would prefer, of course, to destroy the many ships of our fleet (which all ought to be named *Eliza*, as we owe their existence to you). But these are *moving* targets, which their vessels are too slow to pursue, and their gunners too inept to hit, and so instead they have have taken to shooting at buildings. One is reminded of some old Baron who phant'sies himself a brave hunter, but is too shaky, senile, and blind to hit anything, and so stands in his garden blasting away at stuffed animals that his servants have propped up against the hedge.

But life, and this letter, are both too short to be wasted on the English and so I shall go straight to the point and pray you'll forgive my bald way of speaking.

My services are much in demand of late, as trade has stopped, owing to some confusion in the world of money. I do not understand it at all. You, I am certain, understand it perfectly. In between my perfect ignorance and your perfect knowledge stand the rest of humanity—innumerable persons of greater or less dignity, who *phant'sy* they understand it. Whatever the case may be, these persons know that your humble and obedient servant, Captain Jean Bart, is, at the present time, the only person making money in France (some small-minded pedants would assert that this is only by virtue of the fact that I steal things by force from their rightful owners; but this is a fine distinction that I shall leave to the Jesuits, so that one of them may one day come to me on my death-bed and inform me whether I'm bound for Heaven or Hell). Call it what you will, I bring money to France and deposit almost all of it into the King's coffers, in accordance with certain rules and procedures that have seen set down, or so I am told, to govern my *métier*, viz. Privateer. In consequence, I have been noticed by many persons, foreign and domestic, who are owed money by our government. They write me letters, sidle up to me at soirées, tug on my sleeve at the many levées and couchées to which I am invited; they loiter before my house, overhaul me on the high seas, pursue me down streets and garden-paths, send me wine, plant the most alluring whores in my very bed, mutter to me in the confessional, and threaten to kill me, all in the hopes that I shall, by some prestidigitation, channel the next treasure-ship to this or that port, so that it may fall into the hands of this or that local official who shall route the proceeds to this or that account.

You might recall that two years ago I took a large amount of silver from Lothar von Hacklheber, who waxed very wroth, and sent me the most impertinent letters, claiming that the money had been meant to cover some French government loan that had been made down in Lyon. I replied to his representative that Lyon was a long way from Dunkerque—I even offered to draw him a map—and I threw up my hands, knowing little and caring less of these Lyonnaise follies. In time, von Hacklheber stopped importuning me about this; but then after an all too brief respite he got after me again, claiming that the *contrôleur-général* had failed to make good on that Lyon loan. It seemed that he or his agents had inquired in every *pays* and arrived at the conclusion that the only way he would ever get his money back was through Dieppe; for in that port he had come to some sort of understanding with the local officials, such that, of the King's revenue that happened to come in there, some moiety would be diverted to the House of Hacklheber in repayment of the loan that it had extended to France.

Of course, I ignored him; though this did stick in my memory, for I recall that you had some sort of unpleasantness with Lothar von Hacklheber, though you would not part with any of the details; and in his communications, which were often of a most bizarre character, he made liberal use of your name.

A little bit more recently, I have begun to receive communications of a markedly similar nature from none other than the *contrôleur-général* himself, M. le comte de Pontchartrain, who is keen that I should get in the habit of bringing my prizes to the port of Le Havre. For it would seem that he has so arranged matters that any of the King's revenue passing through that port shall be channeled to some destination that is pleasing to him. He too has mentioned your name; for he knows of my passionate, wholly inappropriate and scandalous, and (so far) unrequited affection for you.

Now as a practical matter *nothing* of value has entered *either* Dieppe *or* Le Havre for some weeks, as both were attacked, bombed, and burnt by the British, in the manner I have already described. These disturbances have not hindered me from plying my trade, and so I have, during the same interval, garnered much treasure I would fain unload. Instead I have, perforce, kept it stored away in the holds of diverse ships—which, being *moving* targets, are perfectly safe from the British Navy. Why, in the hold of my own ship *Alcyon*, where I sit writing these words, are stored three-quarters of a million *livres tournoises* worth of silver and gold. I'll not unload such treasure in Dunkerque, for, as much as I love my hometown, its land connexions to France are too tenuous, and infested by highwaymen and Vagabonds. Dieppe or Le Havre, being closer to Paris, would be better—but which?

Far be it from me to spite the *contrôleur-général,* and so Le Havre is the obvious choice—yet just a few weeks ago you bestowed on me the honor of escorting you to Hamburg, so that you could pursue some errand among the Tatars, the Cossacks, or the Germans (as a sea-going man, I am unclear as to whatever fine distinctions might be observed, by geographers, among these landlocked tribes). Rumor has it that you are near Leipzig, the seat of Lothar von Hacklheber. It would seem, therefore, that my actions in respect of the gold and silver that is stored in my hold must have consequences for your venture. But I can't for the life of me make out what those consequences might be, and what is the best course for me to take.

To summarize, I am surrounded by persons who ask much of me but give me nothing that I desire. Far away are you, my lady, who have done more for me than anyone alive—and all simply because you are infatuated with me (don't bother denying it!). Yet you have never asked me for anything. And so, perversely, it is you, and no one else, whose bidding I would do in the matter. I hope that this finds you in good health in Crimea, Turkestan, Outer Mongolia, or wherever it is you have got to. Please know that I am awaiting some clarification from you as to whether I should call next at Dieppe, Le Havre, or some other port.

Your tumescent love slave,

(Capt.) Jean Bart

Leipzig
MAY 1694

And why then are we to despise Commerce as a Mechanism, and the Trading World as mean, when the Wealth of the World is deem'd to arise from Trade?

—DANIEL DEFOE,
A Plan of the English Commerce

PRINCESS WILHELMINA CAROLINE of Brandenburg-Ansbach wrinkled her nose, and flipped her braid back over her shoulder. "'Tumescent love slave'—is this some sort of French idiom? I can't make heads or tails of it."

"Noise! It is an idiocy that Captain Bart threw in at the end, for he knew that he had to wind up the letter, but could not make out *how*, and became desperate, and lost his wits. Thank God he is more even-tempered in battle! Pray don't dwell on that, my lady—"

"Why do you call me that? It's weird. Stop it!"

"You are a born Princess, and very likely to be a Queen some day. I am a made Duchess."

"But to me you are Aunt Eliza!"

"And to me you are my little squirrel. But the fact remains that you're doomed to be a Princess whether you like it or not, and you're going to have to marry someone."

"As happened to my mother," said Caroline, suddenly serious.

"Please do not forget that it happened twice. The second time around, she had to marry someone who was not suited for her. But the first time she was in a *good* marriage—to your father—and a perfectly wonderful Princess came of it."

Caroline blushed at this, and looked at the floor of the carriage. A whip-pop sounded from outside, and it lurched forward. They'd been stalled, for a time, outside the north gate of Leipzig. Caroline's eyes came up off the floor and gleamed in the light of the window. Eliza continued: "Why did your mother later end up in a bad marriage? Because things had gone against her—things she was powerless to do anything about, for the most part—and in the end she had very little choice in the matter. Now, why do you suppose I'm letting you read my personal correspondence from Captain Bart? To pass the time on the road to Leipzig? No, for if we only wished to make time pass, we could play cards. I show you these things because I am trying to teach you something."

"What, exactly?"

It was a good question, and brought Eliza up short. For a few moments there was no sound in the carriage except what came into it from without: the clopping of shod hooves, the crashing of rims on road, the oinking and grunting of the suspension. A shadow enveloped them, then fell away aft: They'd passed through the gate into Leipzig.

"*Pay attention*, that's all," Eliza said. "Notice things. Connect what you've noticed. Connect it into a picture. Think of how the picture might be changed; and act to change it. Some of your acts may turn out to have been foolish, but others will reward you in surprising ways; and in the meantime, simply by being active instead of passive, you have a kind of immunity that's hard to explain—"

"Uncle Gottfried says, 'Whatever acts cannot be destroyed.' "

"The Doctor means that in a fairly narrow and technical metaphysical sense," Eliza said, "but it's not the *worst* motto you could adopt."

And now for the tenth time in as many minutes Eliza reached up to scratch and probe at her face. In half a dozen places, small disks of black felt had been glued to it, covering crater-like excavations that smallpox had made in her flesh, but not had the good grace to fill back in before it had departed her body.

Most of what she knew about the progress of the disease, she knew second-hand, from Eleanor and the physician who had come to tend to her. Eliza herself had descended into a sort of twilight sleep. Her eyes had been open, and impressions had reached her mind, but the span of time she had spent in this trance—about a week—seemed both very long and very brief. Very brief because she remembered little of it—it was "when I had smallpox" to her now. Very long because, during it, she had heard every tick of the clock, and felt the budding of every pox-pustule, its growth as it peeled layers of skin asunder a slow steady agony that sparked whenever two pustules found each other and fused. In some places—particularly her lower back—those sparks had built to a wide-spread fire. Though Eliza had been too delirious to know it, these had been the moments when her life had hung in the balance, for if that fire had spread any further or burnt any brighter, her skin would have come off, and she'd not have survived it.

It was at such times that a physician would emerge to tell a room of hand-wringing loved ones that the case was very grave, and that the patient's life hung in the balance. Had it gone any further, the report would have changed to "not expected to survive," and everyone would have known, from this, that the disease had moved on to its sausage-grinder phase. In Eliza's case this had not happened. Fate had flipped a coin, and it had come up heads. The disease had nearly flayed her lower back and some parts of her arms and legs, and done damage internally, too. But it had spared her eyesight and left perhaps three dozen pocks on her face, of which most could be seen only in direct sun; of the ten or so that were obvious even by candlelight, some could be hid by a lock of hair or a high-collared dress, and the remainder got the black patch treatment. Eliza did not seriously intend to begin every day for the rest of her life by gluing these horrid objects to her skin, but today was special; she was venturing out of the dower-house of Pretzsch for the first time since she had arrived there six weeks earlier. She was going into Leipzig—which passed for a big city in these parts—and she was going to meet some people.

Of the six weeks at the dower-house, the first had been spent in (in retrospect) the prodrome of the illness, and culminated with the sending away of Caroline and Adelaide and the visit of the Elector and his mistress. After that it had been all pustules for two weeks. Eliza had not really come awake and begun to weave her impressions into coherent memories again until the twenty-fourth day; which happened to be the same day that the distant church-bells of Torgau and Wittenberg had begun to toll, announcing the deaths of the Elector of Saxony and his mistress. Eleanor was a widow for the second time. She was henceforth the Electress-Dowager of Saxony. Which meant she was living in the right house for once: The dower-house was where a dowager was supposed to live. The new Elector was Johann Georg's brother, August. August the Strong. He already had a hundred illegitimate children and was said to be hard at work on the second hundred, and his passion for engaging wild beasts in single combat would do nothing to improve Saxony's reputation at Versailles; but he had not been hit on the head, he bore no ill will toward Eleanor, and he didn't want to screw Caroline, so it looked like a win.

Eleanor had been called away to Dresden to attend her husband's funeral. And after Eliza's mattress and bedclothes had been immolated in a great bonfire down by the Elbe, and the scabs had fallen away to reveal her new face and body, Caroline and Adelaide had at last returned from Leipzig along with most of Eliza's retinue. So much for the fourth week; weeks five and six, then, had been time for Eliza to get her strength back. She had an idea that the pox had done to her entrails the same sort of things as it had done to her back, and so there had been problems for a while with eating, digestion, and elimination. Even if she'd bounced back like a rubber ball, there'd have been a delay while new garments were sewn for her, in smaller dimensions to fit her wasted frame, and with collars, sleeves, &c., to cover heavily cratered parts of her body. But the day before yesterday she'd noticed, all of a sudden, that she was bored. Yesterday had been devoted to the laying of plans. This morning she'd departed from the dower-house in a little train of borrowed and rented carriages. On the spur of the moment she'd decided to bring Caroline along with her (for Eleanor was busy organizing a Dowager-household), and little Adelaide, too (for she became obstreperous now if she did not have her Caroline to play with).

"WHAT IS THIS VENTURE of yours that Captain Bart speaks of in his letter?" Caroline asked her.

"Ay! That's difficult to explain!" Eliza said. "But I do not *have* to explain it, for you to get the point—which is that Captain Bart, ordinarily the most decisive, the most ruthless man on earth, cannot make up his mind whether to take his cargo to Dieppe or Le Havre, and feels obliged to send me a letter in Leipzig before acting. If I sat at home knitting and playing cards, he would feel no such compulsion, believe you me; but because I'm on the move, I am an unknown variable in the equation—"

"Which makes it more difficult for him to solve!" Caroline said. "Uncle Gottfried has been teaching me how to solve such problems using a thing he invented called matrices."

"Then you know more of it than I," said Eliza, not for the first time feeling a bit envious of this girl. "And you may show off your skills to your teacher now."

"Uncle Gottfried is here?"

The carriage had rolled to a stop. Eliza opened the door herself and allowed a footman to help her down. Caroline leapt out a moment later, landing bang on both feet, followed, after brief intervals, by her skirts and her braid.

They were in a square before a church from whose open doors organ-music was chanting. Not far away was the town square of Leipzig with its great dark Rathaus along one side, and narrow streets radiating from it, lined with trading-houses. Eliza was slowly turning round and round, taking the place in. But the look on her face was not of wonder but rather distracted, even a bit suspicious. "It is so small," she said.

"If you'd been living in Pretzsch it would seem ever so large!"

"Oh, but when we came here last—ten years ago, almost to the day—we'd been living in a shack in the mountains and it *did* seem large!"

"Who is this 'we?'"

"Never mind . . . but it is funny how one's mind works. I have built up a phant'sy of this as a great metropolis, whose trading-houses are immensely rich and powerful, but look at it . . . there are merchants in London, in Amsterdam, who could buy this whole town and slip it into a vest-pocket."

"Perhaps you should buy it then!" Caroline said, as a jest.

"Perhaps I already have." Eliza paused, blinked, and let out a breath, as if purging herself of all old memories and overblown phant'sies, then peered around sharply. "I have affairs to transact, and must leave you, for a few hours. Come!" She led Caroline through the doors of the church. It was empty just now. The organ-music was just someone practicing—someone not very accomplished, for he kept making mistakes, and each time he did, he came to a stop, and struggled to find the rhythm.

This place—the Nikolaikirche—lacked the dark, spooky look of so many churches. The vault was a semicircular barrel supported by fluted columns—but not of the Doric, Ionian, Corinthian, or any other known order of architecture. For the capitals were made to resemble sheaves of slender vertical palm leaves. The high vaults above, sluiced with clear white light rushing in through high windows, gathered themselves together and plunged down into these rich bundles of light green leaves, from which clusters of fruit peeked out. The altar rail described a broad half-circle with a gap in the center, like a pair of arms sweeping out to embrace the congregants. The font was a gilded goblet. Behind it, steps led up to an altar, above which a quicksilver Jesus hung from a plank. This part of the church—the Altarraum—was a sanctum of polished wine-colored and fleece-gray marble with many windows, giving a view of budding linden trees startled by pockets of breeze speeding invisibly through a blue heaven. The patterns in the marble suggested powerful turbulent motion—rapids, say, or lightning streaking through boiling clouds—arrested and silenced. Recalling the notion that if you knew the position and velocity of every particle in the universe at one moment of time, you'd know all—you'd be God. At the back of the church was a balcony claimed by a great organ of silver pipes in a white case in Roman style, lilies and palm leaves rampant. Hunched doggedly at the console was a man in a great periwig and a coat brocaded with hundreds of wee flowers. An elderly man in academician's robes loitered nearby, gazing down curiously at Eliza, Caroline, and other members of the entourage who were now straggling up the aisle; for Adelaide had been woken out of a nap by the stoppage of her coach, and had pursued her mother, and been pursued in turn by nurses, and by Eliza's guards, who were under orders not to let Adelaide out of their sight so long as they were on the hostile ground of Leipzig. The organist noticed all this, and raised his hands from the manuals, and the throaty singing of the organ-pipes seeped away, leaving in the still air of the church only the faint hiss of some leakage in the valves, and panting of a couple of pudgy schoolboys who'd been dragooned into pumping the bellows. Eliza applauded, and after a moment Caroline, recognizing the organist, followed suit.

"My lady. My lady," said Gottfried Wilhelm von Leibniz to Caroline and Eliza respectively; and then, to Adelaide: "My lady." Then, to Eliza: "I am sorry that your arrival in the Nikolaikirche, which ought to have been a moment of Grace and Beauty unalloyed, was dimmed by my maunderings."

"On the contrary, Doctor, the town is so quiet, your music brings life to it. Was that some new *Passacaglia* from Herr Buxtehude?"

"Just so, my lady. 'Twas brought hither in the pocket of a merchant of Lübeck, who means to have it printed and sold at the fair, a fortnight hence; I fetched one of the page-proofs and prevailed upon my old schoolmaster, Herr Schmidt—" the old man in the robes bowed "—to let me pick it out as I awaited your arrival."

Leibniz descended a stair to the floor of the church, and a lengthy round of bowing, curtseying, hand-smooching, and baby-adoration ensued. Leibniz's eyes lingered on Eliza's face, but not quite long enough to be offensive. It was to be expected that he'd be curious as to what the pox had done to her, and Eliza was content to have him look. He would return presently to such places as Hanover and Berlin, and propagate the news that the Duchess of Arcachon and of Qwghlm had come through it with only light disfigurement; that she could still see; and that her wits were intact.

"I was recalling my first visit to this town—and my first meeting with you—ten years ago, Doctor," Eliza said.

"As was I, my lady. But so many things are different now, of course. You mentioned that the town is quiet. Indeed. You will have speculated it is because the spring fair has not begun yet. That is what I supposed, when I arrived, some weeks ago. But since then I have learned that it is quiet for more reasons than meet the eye. Trade has all but stopped—"

"Owing to a mysterious, dire want of specie," Eliza said, "which is both cause and effect; for all who hear of it are transformed, as if by a magician's spell, into misers, and hoard whatever coin, plate, or bullion they have."

"You are familiar with the affliction, I perceive," Leibniz said drily. "So is our friend Dr. Waterhouse; for he tells me that the same plague has spread to London."

"Some would say it *originated* there," Eliza said.

"Others say Lyon," tried the Doctor, and watched Eliza's face a bit too sharply.

"Now you are fishing," said Eliza. Leibniz was pulled up short, but only for a moment; then he chuckled.

"Fishing for what? Is that another idiom?" Caroline demanded.

"He dangles bait before me, to see if I shall rise to it; for some trading-houses in this town have connexions of long standing to the *Dépôt* of Lyon, and if Lyon is bankrupt, why, it has consequences here. Do you have friends in Leipzig, Doctor, hungry for news?"

"I should not call them friends exactly; not any more."

"Well, I have enemies here. Enemies, and a boy who has not seen his mother in three years and seven months. I must make preparations to meet them. If you would be so good as to entertain the Princess for me, for a few hours—"

"No."

"What?"

"You are in error. Come with me." And Leibniz turned his back on Eliza, which was an arrestingly rude thing to do, and walked down the aisle and out of the Nikolaikirche into Leipzig. This left her no choice but to pursue him. Caroline pursued Eliza, and the rest of the train was drawn out behind them. Eliza turned back and with a significant look or two commanded the nurses to bundle Adelaide back into one of the carriages; she screamed at this, loud enough to draw looks from hookah-puffing Turkish merchants half a mile away.

"You are very rude. What is the meaning of this?"

"Life is short," said Leibniz, and looked Eliza up and down. It was a blunt allusion to smallpox. "I can stand in the aisle of the Nikolaikirche for two hours and try to get it across to you in words, and at the end of it you'll only say, 'I must see it with my own eyes.' Or I can take you on a five-minute walk and see the thing settled."

"Where are we going? Caroline—"

"Let her come along."

They walked across Leipzig's town square, which, the last time Eliza had seen it, had been a maze of leads and gaps among fragrant stacks of baled, barrelled, and trade-marked goods. Today it was all but empty, and sheets of dust skimmed across its paving-stones driven by spring gusts. Here and there, well-dressed men had clumped in twos and threes to smoke pipes and converse—not in the amused, aghast tones of merchants haggling over terms, but more as old men do on Sunday afternoons as they stroll out of church. As Eliza and Caroline followed the Doctor into the streets that issued from the square on the yonder side, they began to see business transacted, of a kind—but only at open-air coffee-houses, and nothing more weighty than a third cup of coffee, or a second slice of cake. The street was ventilated with broad vaulted arches, each of which, as Eliza knew, led into the court-yard of a trading-house. But half of them were closed, and in those that were open, Eliza spied, not throngs of hollering *commerçants* but unraveling knots of semi-idle men, smoking and sipping. For all that, though, the scene was never gloomy. It felt as though a holiday had been declared, not only for Christians, or Jews, or Mahometans, but for all at once. And this holiday was all the more enjoyable for being unwanted and unplanned. Leipzig was *calm*—as if the quicksilver that, as a rule, intoxicated these merchants were ebbing from their blood-streams. When they all came together in a place like Leipzig, a mad-ness came over them, and transformed them into a new kind of organism, as fish schooled. One such jumping, irritable, rapier-quick creature, if he were to appear in the town square of a medieval village, would be a useless, incomprehensible nuisance. But a thousand of them together amounted to something that worked, and that wrought prodigies that could never be imagined by villagers. That spell had been undone today, and the quiet of the village reigned.

A golden Mercury leapt from the keystone of an especially grand arch halfway up the street. The gates below it were closed. But they were not locked. The Doctor pushed one of them open, and extended an arm, inviting Eliza to precede him. She hesitated and looked both ways. This was a habit from Versailles, where merely to step over a threshold in the company of a person constituted a Move in the social chess-game, sure to be noted, talked of, and responded to; indeed people there might devote hours to engineering the details: seeing to it that certain persons were in positions to notice the event, and encoding messages in who preceded whom. *Here* it was faintly ridiculous, and she knew it; but the habit died hard. She looked, and acquired the knowledge that her entry into the House of the Golden Mercury was witnessed by half a dozen persons: an idler collapsed in a doorway, a Lutheran minister, a widow sweeping a stoop, a boy running a message, a Jew in a furry hat, and a very large bearded man with one sleeve empty and the opposite hand gripping a long staff.

This latter she recognized. From time to time, during the long barge-ride up the Elbe, she'd glimpsed such a figure striding along the riverbank, or betimes wading like a three-hundred-pound stork, darting at the water with a fish-spear. Here, he almost blended in. For Leipzig was the crossroads of the Venice-Lübeck and the Cologne-Kiev highways, and served as a catch-pot for all sorts of exotic ramblers, human oddities, and people who could not make up their minds which turn to take. She marked him only because she had seen him before. And in other circumstances she would have devoted the remainder of the week to puzzling over what he was doing here; but too much else was on her mind now, and this crowded Flail-arm out of her consciousness. She walked into the court of the House of the Golden Mercury as if she owned the place.

It was like a graveyard, save that instead of cenotaphs and headstones, it was cluttered with stacks and piles of goods: bales of cloth, barrels of oil, crates of china. She could not see far in any direction; but craning her neck she could see up five stories to the big cargo-doors let into the gables of the House. These were a-gape, swinging untended in the breeze. Within, the attics of the House of Hacklheber were empty. Their contents had all been let down into the courtyard, as if Lothar had decided to liquidate all. But there were no buyers.

Something plopped to the ground behind Eliza, and she heard Caroline give out a little gasp of surprise. Eliza spun on her heel and confronted a tiny savage—a pygmy with a tomahawk. He'd been stalking her through the courtyard, creeping along behind the piles of goods. He had sprung from the lid of a crate taller than his head to menace her in a narrow pass. But now he was having second thoughts, for he had trapped himself between Eliza and Caroline. He turned around to look at the latter. Gazing now at the back of his head Eliza saw a whorl of blond hair that needed washing, a precipitous cowlick that needed trimming, a small body, just stretching out through its sheath of baby fat, that needed a bath. He was dressed in a breech-clout and moccasins, and carrying a weapon made from a terra-cotta pot-sherd that some grownup had patiently lashed to a stick.

Caroline had got over being startled and was trying to pick between amusement and annoyance. "Boo!" she shouted. The little blond Indian spun around as if to run away, but remembered too late that his escape was blocked by Eliza. His eye met hers for a moment, and she recognized it as an eye that belonged to her. He dropped the tomahawk, the better to scramble over a netted pallet of sugar-loaves, and before she could call his name, he had vanished into a pretend Massachusetts.

Caroline laughed, until she met Eliza's eye, and took in her face; then she knew.

The court was surrounded by a covered gallery, where, when Eliza had last been here, men of the House of Hacklheber had sat at their *bancas* writing in their ledgers, and counting streams of outlandish coinage in and out of their massy strong-boxes. Eliza could see little of it now, save the tops of the arches; but a few moments later she heard a piping voice in German, making something known to "Papa," and a moment later, a rumble of a laugh, followed by some patient explanation.

Hearing that voice, Eliza by some instinct turned and gazed up at a three-storey balcony that projected out into the space above the court, all decked out with golden Mercurys and other Barock commerce-emblems. She had once seen Lothar up there, talking to the Doctor, and staring down at her and Jack; but the thing was deserted now, a still-life of dusty windowpanes, faded curtains, and moss-slicked stone.

The man had begun to declaim in a loping singsong. Eliza knew little German. She looked to Caroline, who explained, "He reads from a book of tales."

Eliza picked her way among the dusty goods, following the sound of that voice, until she stepped up onto the stone floor of the encircling gallery. This had been cleared of many of its *bancas*. Several paces away, a massive man squatted upon a black strong-box, all bound about with straps and hasps; but none of them was locked, which she looked on as suggesting it might be empty. The man had a great illustrated story-book open on one of his thighs. Perched on the other was the little blond Indian, who had leaned his head back on the man's bosom, and drawn up a corner of his breechclout to chew on it. His spindly legs straddled the man's leg. The moccasins pedaled slow air. He had got a falling look in his eyes, and the lids were unfolding. He glanced up at Eliza when she stepped into his field of view, but presently lost interest, and looked to his dreams. To him the appearance of the strange woman in the court of the house had been diverting, but only for a moment, and alarming, but only until "Papa" told him everything was going to be fine. "Papa," who was Lothar von Hacklheber, kept reading the story—not, Eliza, thought, out of any studied effort to ignore her, but because no parent who knows the rules of the game interrupts a story just when a child has tucked his wings and settled into the long glide to sleep. A pair of gold-rimmed half-glasses perched on Lothar's cratered nose, and when he reached the end of a page he would lick a finger, turn a page, and glance up at her with mild curiosity. The boy's lids drooped lower and lower, more and more of the breechclout made its way into his mouth to be sucked on—a sight that produced an ache in Eliza's breasts as they remembered what it was to let down milk. Presently Lothar shut the book, and glanced around for a place to set it—a gesture that brought Caroline running up to take it from his hand. Tightening a burly arm around the boy's chest, he leaned back, making of his body a sort of great pillowy couch, and somehow levitated to his feet. He turned his back on the visitors and padded on bare feet through a doorway, then laid the boy into a sort of makeshift Indian-hammock that had been strung diagonally across a disused office. After spreading some blankets over the child, he straightened up, emerged into the gallery, and pulled the door to behind him—leaving it cracked, as Eliza the mother well knew, so that he could hear if the boy cried.

"I had got the news that the Elector and his whore had died," said Lothar mildly, in French, "and wondered if a visit from the Reaper might not be in store for me as well."

Atop a bench on the edge of the court rested an array of weapons, dis-arranged, as if he and the boy had been at fencing-practice. Lothar scooped up a sheathed dagger, and in the same movement tossed it towards Eliza, who clapped it out of the air. "That *hashishin* stiletto that you have secreted in the sash of your dress is too small to dispatch one of my size with decent speed; pray use this instead." He was wearing a linen shirt that had not been changed in a while; now he ripped it open to expose his left nipple. "Right about there ought to do it. You may send the Princess of Brandenburg-Ansbach out first, if you would ward her tender eyes from so grisly a sight; or, if it's your purpose to raise her up to be another such as yourself, by all means let her watch and learn."

"Until this moment I had believed that the art of the masque had been developed to its highest in the Court of the Sun King," said Eliza in a quiet voice, so as not to wake the boy. "But now I see you know as much of it as anyone. What sort of mind invents a show like the one I have just witnessed?"

"What sort of mind," answered Lothar, "invades the tranquillity of a man's home and then denounces it as a show? This is the world, madame, it is not Versailles; we are not so devious, so recondite here."

Eliza tossed the dagger on to the floor. "You who kidnapped a baby, should not presume to deliver catechism to its mother."

"When an orphan, being raised by strangers, is brought to live with a family who loves it, does this even deserve the name of kidnapping? It seems rather like kidnapping's opposite. If you now announce that you are its mother, then I am disposed to believe you, for there is a marked resemblance; but this is the first time you have *admitted* it."

"You know perfectly well that to admit it then would have destroyed me."

Lothar turned to face his courtyard, and raised both hands. "Behold!"

"Behold what?"

"You speak of being destroyed as an abstraction, a thing you have read about, a phantom you fear as you lie in bed at night. Do not be satisfied with abstractions and phantoms, madame. Instead look upon destruction, for it is here. You have wrought it. You have destroyed me. But I have a boy who calls me Papa. If you had admitted to being his mother, and suffered destruction, what would your estate be to-day? And would it be better or worse than what you have?"

Eliza flushed at this: and not just her face but her whole body. It felt as though warm blood was washing into parts of her body that had been starved and pallid since the pox. She would have faltered, and perhaps even surrendered, if she'd not spent years steeling herself for this. Because the words of Lothar carried in them much that was true. But she had always known he would be formidable and that she'd have to bull ahead anyway. "You need not be destroyed," she said. "With a word, I can see to it that the loan is repaid, with interest."

"Stop, I pray you. Do you suppose my mind is as empty as this?"

He kicked the strong-box with the side of his foot and it boomed like a drum. "I know that you would never have come to Leipzig had you not so arranged matters that you could hold out to me the choice of destruction or salvation. It is all very ingenious, I am sure, the sort of thing I'd have found fascinating at your age; but I am not your age."

"Of course I am well aware that you have moved beyond money, to Alchemy—"

"Oh, you are? And I suppose you have some morsel to dangle above my mouth, where the Solomonic Gold is concerned?"

Having been anticipated thus made Eliza disinclined to say it, but she did: "I know who has it, and where; if that is your desire—"

"My desire was to conquer Death, which took my brothers young and unfairly," said Lothar von Hacklheber. "It is a common desire. Most come to terms with Death sooner or later. My failure to do so was an unintended consequence of a pact that my family had made with Enoch Root. In order for him to dwell among humankind he must don identities, and later, before his longevity draws notice, shed them. My father knew about Enoch—knew a little of what he was—and struck a deal with him: he would vouch for Enoch as a long-lost relative named Egon von Hacklheber, and suffer him to dwell among us under that name for a period of some decades, if, in exchange, 'Egon' would serve as a tutor to his three sons. Of the three, I was in some sense the quickest, for I came to know that Enoch was not like us. And I guessed that this was a matter of his having discovered some Alchemical receipt that conferred life eternal. A reasonable guess—but wrong. At any rate, it fired my interest in Alchemy until of late."

"And what came of late to damp that fire?"

"I adopted an orphan."

"Oh."

"It is trite, I know. To defeat Death, or to phant'sy that one has defeated it, by having a child. But I could not manage it before. For the same pox that slew my brothers left me unable to get a woman pregnant. I'll not speak of the motives that led to the taking of the boy from the orphanage where you kept him at Versailles. They were, as you have collected, quite beastly motives. I did not intend to love the boy. I did not even intend to keep him in my house. But as things came out, I did both—first kept him, then loved him—and as time went on, my mind turned to Alchemy, and to the lost Gold of Solomon, less and less frequently. I'd not thought of it for half a year until you reminded me of it just now."

"Then whatever other differences you and I may have, we are united in seeing it as foolishness."

"Oh, I don't think it is the least bit foolish," said Lothar, raising the pocked ridges where eyebrows had once sprouted, "all I said was that I no longer think of it. I'm ready to die. And whether I die rich or poor is of little account to me. But you are gravely mistaken if you believe that you can take Johann away from me. For that truly would be kidnapping; it would break his heart, and that would break yours."

"As to that, I am *not* mistaken. I *know* this, and have known it, ever since I learned, from the Doctor, that he was being raised as your son." Eliza looked up to solicit a confirmation from Leibniz. But it seemed that the Doctor had some minutes ago quietly taken Caroline aside, and led her off to some other corner of the courtyard so that Eliza and Lothar could talk privily.

"Son *and sole heir,*" Lothar corrected her, "though, thanks to your intrigues, I have nothing to will to him save debts."

"That could be changed."

"Then why do you not change it? What is it you want? Why are you here?"

"To see him. To hold him."

"Granted! Truly and happily granted. You may move in with me here, for all I care; you're welcome to do so. But you can't take him."

"You are in no position to dictate terms."

"Foolish girl! They're not my terms, and I am not dictating them! They are the terms of the world. You cannot admit to this world that you bore a child out of wedlock. You cannot even admit it to the boy—until he is older, perhaps, and able to fathom such things. You can take him back and give him to the Jesuits, who will raise him up to be a priest, who will fault his mother for having sinned. Or you can leave him in my care, and visit him whenever you will. In a year or two he'll be old enough to travel—he can visit you *incognito* in France, if that shall please you. He shall be a Baron and a banker, a gentleman, a Protestant, the cleverest scholar in Leipzig; but he shall never be yours."

"I know. I know all of these things—have known them for years."

Lothar's ravaged face was a difficult one to read, but he seemed exasperated now, or bewildered. "After all this," he said, "I did not expect you to be such a confused person."

"You did not? How unreasonable of you. You belabor me for being confused—yet *you* took the boy, not for love of him, but for hate of me, and out of lust for Alchemical gold—only to change your mind!"

Lothar shrugged. "Perhaps that is the real Alchemy."

"Would that such Alchemy could work its spell on me, and make me as content as you seem."

"I shall grant you this much," said Lothar. "The taking of the gold at Bonanza put me into a vengeful rage that kept me awake at night, and filled all of my days, for a long time, and drove me to hurt you as badly as I supposed you had hurt me. I wanted you to fathom my anger. You then went on to destroy me, cleverly and systematically, over a span of years. You used my own greed as a weapon against me. And if I seem content to you, why, in part it is because I have a son. But in part it is because of you, Eliza, your Barock fury, sustained for so long and expressed so Barockly. You showed, you expressed, what I once *felt;* and from that, I knew that I had struck home, that a spark had passed between us."

"Very well. Enough of this. Do you have, Lothar, a spare *banca* at which I could sit down for some minutes, and write a letter?"

Lothar spread his hands out, palms up, as if handing the place over to her. "Take your pick, madame."

SHE WOULDN'T HAVE NOTICED FLAIL-ARM if not for this gesture of Lothar's, so stealthily had the big amputee crept into the House. But as it happened, she turned on the balls of her feet to gaze into the court, and saw in the corner of her eye that a new thing had been added to the jumble-sale: a tall man with a beard, who had chosen this moment to step out from behind a crate. As before, he held a long walking-staff; but now something had been added to its end: the leaf-shaped warhead of a harpoon, its twin edges white where the whetstone had scoured them. This he hefted in his one hand, bringing it up above his shoulder, and he swung the shining adder's head about so that it pointed at the heart of Lothar.

Now Eliza—who only a couple of hours ago had been preaching to Caroline about the importance of noticing, and connecting—at last took her own advice. There was no telling how long it might have taken for her to recognize Flail-arm as Yevgeny the Raskolnik if he had not suddenly appeared gripping a harpoon, and making ready to kill Lothar; but these two *data* did the trick. She remembered now seeing this Yevgeny in the company of Jack in Amsterdam. Eliza had even borrowed his harpoon, and in a fit of pique hurled it at Jack. Yevgeny must have become, and might still be, a member of Jack's pirate-band. He must have peeled off from the group and come back to Christendom for some reason. He'd been keeping an eye on Eliza, and, in consequence, had found himself in Leipzig, before the gates of the house of the man who, as he supposed, was Jack's worst enemy. And now he was about three heartbeats away from doing what any red-blooded pirate would, when presented with such an opportunity.

This hefting and pointing of the harpoon was only the first move in some procedure that involved running some steps toward the prey. Yevgeny also extended his stump, which he had fortified with what appeared to be a cannonball on the end of a stick: a counter-weight to augment the force of the throw. Eliza began moving side-ways toward Lothar. She would interpose herself between harpoon and target, and Yevgeny would break off the attack. Yevgeny's blue eyes flicked towards her as she moved.

But a small person flitted out of the shades of the gallery. He had built up a running start and so was able to bound up and over the empty strong-box next to Lothar and thence to the top of the balus-ter that surrounded the courtyard. He already had an arrow nocked to his tiny bow, for as Yevgeny had stolen around the courtyard, get-ting into position to attack, Johann must have stalked him, and plot-ted intercepts, and looked for his opportunity. Eliza, seeing him flash across her vision, had already changed course, and flung out both arms toward the boy; but quick as a fingersnap he drew back his arrow and let it fly. Its blunted tip caught Yevgeny in the eye just as he was winding up to throw. The counterweight dropped like Thor's hammer. His body convulsed forward. The arm cracked like a knout. The harpoon was launched. It hurtled past Lothar's shoulder and crashed into the *banca* behind him. Lothar dropped onto his arse. Eliza, unable to stop herself, ran into Johann and hammered him off the railing; he tumbled into the dusty cobbles below and became one large abrasion. Yevgeny had ended up on his knees, staring forward. Eliza assaulted the baluster with her midsection and toppled over it, diving to the courtyard and catching her weight on her hands.

She, Johann, and Yevgeny now formed an equilateral triangle, maybe two yards on a side, in the court. Lothar, enthroned on his empty coffer, gazed down upon them in stupefaction. Yevgeny was no less dumbfounded. Johann was still winding up to bawl. Eliza, having just narrowly evaded death by smallpox, was the least taken aback, and the first to get up. She took a step toward Yevgeny. She didn't know Russian, and assumed he knew little French. But if he'd been a galley-slave in Algiers, he must know Sabir; so she scraped up a few leavings of that tongue that were to be found in rarely-visited corners of her brain, and said to him—quietly, so that only he could hear—"If your loyalty is to Jack, then know that *this* man is no longer your enemy. Instead go to Versailles and throw some harpoons at Father Édouard de Gex."

Yevgeny nodded once, clambered to his feet, and went up to the level of the gallery to extract the tool of his trade from the tool of

Lothar's. Because of the head's barbed flukes, this was not to be accomplished without half-destroying the *banca*; a task for which Yevgeny was superbly equipped in that he had the strength of ten men, and in lieu of one hand, a cannonball. A city-sacking's worth of splintering and shattering was packed into a brief span of time; then he popped up with the terrible head in his hand, and the shaft under one arm. He turned toward Lothar and favored him with a very civil nod and half-bow, then stalked out of the House of the Golden Mercury, glancing up once to get the sun's bearing.

"Who was *that*!?" asked Leibniz. He and Caroline had been oblivious to the harpoon-attack but had been drawn to the *banca*-demolition.

Eliza had Johann on her hip; he had got through all of the bawling and gone into child-shock.

"My dear Doctor," she answered, "if I explained every little thing to you, you'd grow bored with me, and stop writing me those charming letters."

"I simply wish to know, for practical reasons, whether you are being stalked by any more giant murderous harpooneers."

"He is the only one, as far as I know. His name is Yevgeny the Raskolnik."

"What's a Raskolnik?"

"As I said before, if I explain *everything*..."

"All right, all right, never mind."

> Our heart oft times wakes when we sleep, and God
> can speak to that, either by words, by proverbs, by
> signs, and similitudes, as well as if one was awake.
> —JOHN BUNYAN,
> *The Pilgrim's Progress*

She chose an ancient desk that had been dragged out into the court and left to die. Rain had fallen on it, and its planks had warped and split, and its drawers were stuck. But the sun shone on it, which felt good on her skin. From another *banca* she fetched a sheet of foolscap, and in a recess of this one she quarried out a glass inkwell whose cork was cemented in place by a rime of hardened ink. In the end the only way to get it open was to take that stiletto out of her waist-sash and scrape off the crust, then pry the cork loose. The ink had become sludge. She thinned it with saliva and gathered some of it up into a quill.

Leibniz and Caroline were sitting on crates, doing lessons: *"Tac-*

tics," said the Doctor, "are what the Duchess of Arcachon has been pursuing; Baron von Hacklheber has quite neglected *tactics* for *strategy*."

"Who won?" Caroline asked.

"Neither," said the Doctor, "for neither *pure* tactics nor *pure* strategy constitutes a wise course for a Prince, or a Princess. Perhaps the winner shall be Johann Jean-Jacques von Hacklheber."

"Let us hope so," said Caroline, "for he has been saddled with the most ungainly name I have ever heard."

Eliza to Jean Bart
MAY 1694

Captain Bart,

My dear friend Monsieur le comte de Pontchartrain, being the *contrôleur-général* of France, has, and shall have, numberless opportunities to channel the flow of the King's revenues in those ways that are most satisfactory to him, and so I feel I do him no great disfavor by suggesting that you sail your treasure-ship to the port of Dieppe, so that the King's loan to the House of Hacklheber may at last be repaid. France is helpless to defend her interests on foreign soil, so long as her credit, in foreign eyes, is bad; and repayment of even a single loan shall go far towards repairing the damage done in recent years. The German and Swiss bankers have already abandoned Lyon, but this need not prevent the payment from being sent through more modern channels, perhaps in Paris. It might help if you could suggest as much to the gentleman in Dieppe.

I thank you for having consulted me before taking action in this matter. Please know that one of the beneficiaries shall be your long-lost godson, who, as I write these words, is creeping up on me from behind with a bow and arrow, like a dirty little Cupid.

Eliza

"WHAT ARE YOU DOING, MADAME?"

"Finishing up a letter." She scattered sand across the page to blot it.

"To whom?"

"The most famous and daring pirate-captain in the world," Eliza said matter-of-factly. She let the sand slide off onto the ground, folded the letter up, and began ransacking the old desk's drawers for a bit of sealing-wax.

"Do you know him?"

Using a scrap of paper as a spatula, Eliza scraped some beads of sealing-wax out of a drawer-bottom. "Yes—and he knows you. He held you when you were baptized!"

Johann von Hacklheber quite naturally wanted to know more—which was how Eliza wanted it. He pursued her like an Indian tracker through the dusty rooms of the House of Hacklheber, pelting her not with arrows but with questions, as she scared up a melting-spoon, a candle, and fire. Presently she had a flame going under the blackened belly of the spoon. Into it she poured the crumbs of wax that she had looted from the desk: mostly scarlet, but a few black, and some the natural color of beeswax. Those on the bottom quickly succumbed to the heat. Those above stubbornly maintained their shapes. The similarity of these to smallpox-vesicles was very obvious to her. "When a thing such as wax, or gold, or silver, turns liquid from heat, we say that it has fused," Eliza said to her son, "and when such liquids run together and mix, we say they are con-fused."

"Papa says I am confused sometimes."

"As are we all," said Eliza. "For confusion is a kind of bewitchment—a moment when what we supposed we understood loses its form and runs together and becomes one with other things that, though they might have had different outward forms, shared the same inward nature." She gave the melting-spoon a little shake, and the beads of wax that had been floating on its top—which had become sacs of liquid wax, held together by surface tension—burst and collapsed into the pool of molten wax below, giving off a puff of sweet fragrance, vestiges of the flowers visited long ago by the bees that had made this stuff. It was sweeter by far than the telltale fragrance of smallpox, which she hoped never to smell again, though she caught a whiff of it from time to time as she moved about the town.

Before the black and red could mix together into mud, Eliza dumped the contents of the spoon onto her folded letter, and mashed her ring into it. The seal, when she pulled her ring away from it, was of scarlet marbled through with black and pale streaks—most attractive, she thought, and perhaps the beginning of a new trend at Court.

Lothar had summoned a rider who was willing to carry the message at least as far as Jena, where other messengers might be found to take it into the west. The rider waited just inside the gates with one horse that was saddled, and a second to spell it. Eliza handed him the letter and wished him Godspeed, and he mounted up without further ceremony and set to trotting down the street. When he reached the great square, he got his mount turned toward the west gate, and cantered out of sight. Along his wake were any number of curious onlookers, peering out the windows, and opening up the doors, of diverse factories and trading-houses. A man emerged from a door, pulling a big wig down over his stubbled scalp. He turned toward the House of the Golden Mercury and began to hustle toward it, eager to get some explanation from Lothar; and before he'd reached Lothar's gate, two others, not to be outdone, had fallen in stride with him. Eliza returned their courteous greetings as they went in the gate, curtseying to each in turn. But she did not follow them in. She stayed out in the street to watch the news spread and to hear the slow-building murmur of Leipzig coming alive.

BOOK 4

Bonanza

Southern Fringes of the Mogul Empire
LATE 1696

We say of some Nations, the People are lazy, but we should say only, they are poor; Poverty is the Fountain of all Manner of Idleness.

—DANIEL DEFOE,
A Plan of the English Commerce

A LAKE OF YELLOW DUST lapped at the foundations of some cobra-infested hills in the far west. Eastwards it ran to the horizon; if you went that way long enough, and survived the coastal marshes, you would reach the Bay of Bengal. To the north lay a country that was similar, except that it encompassed the richest diamond mines in the world; this was the King of Aurangzeb's favorite nephew, Lord of Righteous Carnage. To the south lay some hills and mountains that, except for the scattered citadels of the Marathas, were not really controlled by anyone just now. Beyond, at the very tip of Hindoostan, lay Malabar.

A pair of bamboo tripods supported the ends of a timber crosspiece that spanned a tiny puncture wound in the sheet of dust. The timber had been polished by a rope that slid over it all day long. On one end of that rope was a bucket, which dangled in the well-shaft. On the other end was a yoke thrown over the cartilaginous hump of a bullock. A gaunt man, armed with a bamboo cane, stood behind the animal. The bullock trudged away from the well. Here and there it would insolently pause and prod the dust with its snout for a minute or two, pretending that there was something edible there. The man would begin talking to it. At first his tone was conversational, then whining, then pleading, then irked, then enraged. Finally he would go to work with the cane and the bullock would stomp forward another few steps.

From time to time the bullock would reach the end of his rope, which signified that the bucket had emerged from the hole. The man with the bamboo cane would then shout at a couple of younger men who were dozing in the shade of the low dung rampart that surrounded the well's opening, giving it the general appearance of a giant rugged nipple. These men would bestir themselves, scale the rampart, get a grip on the bucket, swing it off to one side, and dump a few gallons of water onto the ground. The water would embark on a senseless quest for the nearest ocean. The bullock would turn round and come back.

These people were all People (as they name themselves in their language). The bucket-emptiers belonged to a separate subcaste from the bullock-spanker, but both could trace their lineage back for a hundred generations to the same ur-Person. And even if Sword of Divine Fire had not already known as much, it could have been guessed from following a given bucket-load of water downhill, and observing the scenery on either hand. For thousands of years' hourly bucket-emptyings had cut a meandering drainage channel into the dust. It careered and zigzagged for a mile, heading generally eastwards, until it petered out in a crazed salt-pan, which sported the locally renowned Large Hole in the Ground, and other improvements. In most places, a grown man could comfortably plant one foot on either side of the channel. In some parts one had to jump over it. In one stretch it spread out so wide that one needed a running start. Consequently the local children never wanted for sports and entertainment.

Each bank of the ditch was green from the water's edge to the point, about an arm's length away, where the desert took over again. Seen from the high ground at the well-mouth, it looked as if some Hindoo deity had dipped a quill in green ink and dragged it aimlessly across a blank parchment—which was not extremely far from what the People actually believed. Their king of the last two years and two hundred and forty-eight days scoffed at this creed, but since it had sustained them in adverse circumstances for a couple of thousand years, he had to admit it was no worse than any other religion.

The People furthermore believed that the same deity had divided the ditch's length (some two thousand paces in all) into five zones, and portioned them out to the five daughters of the ur-Person, and laid down certain rules as to what should be cultivated where. These five zones had inevitably been divided and subdivided as the five subcastes spawned from the loins of the five daughters had ramified into diverse clans, which had distinguished themselves from other clans by intermarrying with groups that were viewed as higher or lower, or, in some cases, destroyed themselves by not intermarrying *enough.* So each of those two thousand paces, on each side of the ditch, was now spoken for by *someone.*

Most of the someones were present and accounted for, dressed in brilliant fabrics, and squatting behind their tiny farms—therefore, packed shoulder-to-shoulder along the banks all the way from the well to the Large Hole in the Ground. Sword of Divine Fire had come to make his monthly inspection.

Sword of Divine Fire was mounted on a donkey. His aides, body-guards, and attendants were on foot, except for two *rowzinders* on horseback and one *zamindar* in a palanquin.

"Very well," said Sword of Divine Fire, "which is to say, it looks the same as last time, and the time before that."

His words were translated into Marathi by the man in the palan-quin, who then said, "Shall we have a look at the Large Hole in the Ground, then, and call it a day?"

"The Large Hole in the Ground can wait. First, we will inspect our potato," said Sword of Divine Fire.

This pronouncement, once it had been translated, touched off the most urgent conspirings and shushings among the aides, hangers-on, courtiers, camp-followers, and the *khud-kashtas* or head-men of the Ditch's various segments. Sword of Divine Fire gave his donkey a few smart heel-jabs and began steering for the Fourth Meander of the Third Part of the Ditch. His *zamindar* shortly caught up with him—the feet of his palanquin-bearers creating bursts of dust that flourished, paled, and dissolved in the still air.

"Your majesty's potato can hardly have changed much since the last visit. On the other hand, I am informed by the most highly placed sources that the Large Hole in the Ground is not only deeper—but wider, too!"

"We would view our potato," the king said doggedly. They were definitely getting close—the kids tear-assing around had the high noses and elongated skulls that set Fourth Meander folk apart from the less prestigious subcastes who cultivated the left bank of the Third Part. Only last week, one of them had been made an out-caste for Jumping the Ditch, i.e., having sex with one of the hillbilly girls on the Right Bank.

"Is one potato really so different from the next?" asked his *zamin-dar* philosophically.

"In general, no—but in our *jagir, there is no next!*"

"And yet—assuming that *some* potato materializes on your plate on the day specified, does the fate of a *specific* potato really amount to so much?"

"You are a tax collector, not a philosopher—mind your place."

"Excuse me, Your Royal Highness, but *we* were philosophizing when Aristotle's grandparents were banging rocks together."

"Where has it *gotten* you though?"

Ahead, Sword of Divine Fire could see the Flat Brown Rock, which—together with the Little Gray Rock, which stood about a hundred yards distant—accounted for most of the local topography. The Fourth Meander made a small excursion to go around it. The clan of the Flat Brown Rock Excursion were reputed to be the finest horticulturalists of the whole Ditch, and on cold nights were known to stay up sitting on their cabbages like hens warming their eggs. Normally, they would be turning round to smile proudly at their monarch. But today they squatted on the bank, hunched over with their backs turned to him, and refused to meet his gaze. Sword of Divine Fire could not fathom it until he noticed a gap forming in the line of persons. They were packed in nearly shoulder-to-shoulder, but still they were finding some way to shift sideways, creating an open space two yards across, which gradually expanded to three. In the center of that open space, a bony woman in a threadbare garment was hunched over a dead plant.

Sword of Divine Fire's reaction was succinct: "Fuck!" The woman cringed as if he'd hit her with a bullwhip. Then: "What has happened to our potato?"

"Sire, I launched an investigation as soon as I was informed. The *khud-kashta* of the Fourth Meander has been sternly brought to account. Furthermore, I have made discreet inquiries with Lord of Righteous Carnage, as well as with Shambhaji, to ascertain whether it might be possible to buy a replacement potato . . ."

"Come off it! Where's the money coming from? We can't even feed the bullock."

"If we put off purchasing a new rope . . ."

"The rope has been spliced so many times it's naught but splices. Besides! Jesus Christ! *Shambhaji!?* You asked *him*? I was sent down here to make *war* on Shambhaji."

"But you have not actually conducted an offensive operation against him in *years*."

"What, I'm besieging his citadel."

"You call it a Siege—others would describe it as a very long Picnic."

"In any event—Shambhaji is the *enemy*."

"In Hindoostan, all things are possible."

"Then where is my fucking potato!?"

Silence. Then the woman flung herself on the ground and began to beseech Sword of Divine Fire for mercy.

"Oh, splendid! Now she's probably going to go set fire to herself or something," the king muttered. Then he sighed. "What has your investigation turned up?"

"It may have been sabotage."

"Those Right Bankers, y'think?"

"Retribution for many Ditch-Jumpings."

"Well, I don't want to start a war," mused Sword of Divine Fire, "or my rutabaga will be next."

"I would not put anything beneath the Right Bank Vhadriyas, they are scarcely above apes."

"Tell 'em it's my fault."

"I beg your pardon, sire?"

"Karma. I looked crossways at a cow, or something . . . make some shit up. You're good at that, aren't you?"

"Truly you are the wisest ruler this kingdom has ever had . . ."

"Yeah, too bad my term's up in another four months."

Half an hour later, Sword of Divine Fire alighted from his donkey, and his *zamindar* emerged from his palanquin, and they stood together at the brink of the Large Hole in the Ground. All of the water that struggled out to the end of the Ditch emptied into this Hole. Members of the local Koli caste brought wagon-loads of black dirt hither from their dirt-mines in other parts of the *jagir* and dumped it into the hole. Then they pounded it with timbers, mixing it with the ditch-water, and drew off the liquor that floated on top and put it into a motley collection of pots and pans. These they boiled over fires made with wood brought down out of the hills by the people of the wood-splitter caste. When the pots had nearly boiled dry, they dumped their contents out into flat shallow earthenware trays and left them out under the sun. After a while, those trays filled up with a whitish powder—

"Who the hell is that man in the robe, and why is he eating my saltpeter?" demanded Sword of Divine Fire, visoring his eyes with one hand and gazing over towards the tray-farm.

Everyone looked over to see that, indeed, a figure in a long off-white robe—a cross between a Frankish monk's robe and an Arab *djellaba*—was nibbling at a handful of saltpeter-slush that he'd scooped up from one of the trays. His face was obscured by the hood of the robe, which he'd pulled over his head to shield himself from the sun.

A couple of *rowzinders* and three archers on foot—about half of Sword of Divine Fire's body-guards—bestirred themselves, and began trotting over that way, unlimbering weapons as they went. But the robed visitor turned out to have a sort of body-guard of his own:

two men on horseback who rode forth and took up positions on the flanks, and let it be known that they had muskets.

"Sire, this would appear to be a better-organized-than-usual assassination attempt," said the *zamindar*, stepping over to his palanquin and retrieving a musket of his own. "May I suggest you climb down into the Large Hole in the Ground?"

The king for his part pulled a pistol from his garment and checked the pan. "This fitteth not the profile of an assassination," he observed. "Perhaps they are wandering potato-merchants." He spurred his donkey forward, and rode past his body-guards, who had been stopped in their tracks by the appearance of those muskets.

As he drew closer to the robed man, he was surprised—but then again, not really—to observe a red beard. The visitor pulled his hood back to divulge a fountain of silver hair. He spat saltpeter on the ground and smacked his lips for a few moments, like a connoisseur of wine.

"I'm afraid it is contaminated with much that is not actually saltpeter," he said. "It would work for ballasting ships, but not for making gunpowder."

"Strange you should mention that, Enoch, as I may be needing some ballast soon."

"I know," said Enoch Root. "Unfortunately, many others in Christendom know it, too, Jack."

"That is most annoying, for I went to vast expense to bring in a scribe who knew how to employ cyphers."

"The cypher was broken."

"How is Eliza?"

"She is a Duchess in two countries."

"Does she know that I am a King in one?"

"She knows what I knew, before I left. Namely that there are tales of a Christian sorcerer who, some years ago, was traveling in a caravan to Delhi that was attacked by a Maratha army that came down out of the hills on elephants. The Marathas had the upper hand until nightfall, when they and their elephants alike were thrown into a panic by a cold fire that limned the warriors and the horses of the caravan without consuming them. This caravan reached Delhi without further incident, and Aurangzeb, the Great Mogul, according to his long-standing practice, elevated the victor to the rank of *omerah*, and rewarded him with a three-year *jagir*."

"And so you decided to come out and see who was putting your alchemical knowledge to such ill uses."

"I came for many reasons, Jack, but *that* was not one of them . . . I knew who the sorcerer was."

"Did you bring the thing I asked for?"

"We will speak of that later," Enoch said judiciously. "But I did bring two things you *should* have asked for, and forgot to."

"Hmm, let me think . . . I love riddles . . . a replacement penis, and a keg of decent beer?"

"I love riddles, too, Jack, but I hate guessing-games. Can we go somewhere that is not so, er . . ." And here Enoch Root turned his gaze one way, then the other, taking in most of the hundred-mile expanse between the hills and the coastal marshes. ". . . *exposed?*"

Jack laughed. "If it's privacy you want, you're in the wrong subcontinent."

"So you say—and yet there is more here than meets the eye, no?" said Enoch Root, staring Jack in the eye.

Jack rode back to his *zamindar* and said, "That gentleman over there is a buyer of saltpeter from Amsterdam."

"Is *that* the best you could come up with!?" answered Surendranath.

"'Twill serve, for now . . . I am going to take him on an inspection-tour of the dirt-mines. Dismiss the *khud-kashta*s with my compliments. Tell them not to give the potato-woman any grief. Meet me at the Royal Palace this evening, unless the roof has been blown off again, in which case, meet me by the tree."

"Sire, the dirt-mines are situated in a rowdy and treacherous *pargana*, quite infested with stranglers. Are you quite certain you do not want me to send the *rowzinders?*"

Jack sized up the two horsemen who had arrived with Enoch Root. "What do you make of them?"

"Mercenaries. Judging from their coloration, most likely Pathans."

"That was my guess, too, until I got closer. Methinks they are Christians with tans. They are barely even twenty years of age, but weathered like veterans, and they returned my gaze insolently."

"They handle their weapons like drilled musketeers," said the *zamindar.*

"They've made it all the way here, from Christendom . . ."

"But perhaps they are the last remnants of a whole Regiment."

"I believe I will be safe in their hands," Jack said.

"That's for me mum!" said the one.

"She's *me* mum, too, give 'im another!"

A large, bleeding fist filled most of Jack's visual field, getting rapidly bigger. Then lights flashed and a loud popping noise went off in the base of his skull.

"You can do be'er'n that, Jimmy!" said one, shoving the other aside. "Let me show you—now, how's about *that*! An' *that*! For our sainted mum!"

Suddenly they got six feet taller—either that, or Jack's head was resting on the ground. The one called Jimmy wound up for a kick.

"*That* is for mayakin' it neces'ry for us to travel all the way out to the butt o' the world to beat the bejesus out o' ye!"

Enoch hovered nervously in the background encouraging them to stop, or at least slow down—but they were having none of it.

"*That* is for bein' a friggin' shite-head!"

"Can you be more specific?" Jack said (he had found that a bit of levity sometimes worked wonders in these situations). But the words came out all a-mumble, for his lips stuck together whenever they got near each other—and they'd ballooned to the point where they were *always* near each other. But somehow the one named Jimmy understood, and went wide-eyed.

"Oh, you want *specificity*!? Danny, he's requested we wax *specific* at this time!"

Jack got up on all fours, then staggered to his feet. Being on the ground only tempted them to kick him, and that was worse, in the long run, than being punched.

"*That* is specifically for tayakin' up with another lady when the urth on Mum's grayave hadn't even been tamped down yet!"

"*That* is specifically for tradin' in yer French jools on a shite-load o' malarkey!"

Jack tumbled backwards into a stand of bamboo, and Jimmy and Danny—perhaps fearing cobras—did not come in after him. They stood where they were for a moment, getting their wind back. For the first time since Jimmy had tackled him out of the saddle a few minutes ago, it occurred to Jack that he was armed with a serviceable Janissary-sword, and knew a thing or two about how to use it; but cutting up his own flesh and blood wouldn't be right. Instead he eased it quietly from its scabbard and swung it into the base of a bamboo cane about as thick as his wrist, easily cutting it through. Then he staggered out of the thicket dragging it behind him.

"Powers o' Darkness!" Jack exclaimed, focusing his one eye that hadn't swollen shut on a point in the middle distance. "I do believe that elephant is fookin' that camel up the arse—or is it t'other way round?"

Jimmy and Danny turned around to look. Jack yanked on the bamboo, bringing it forward into his hands like a pike, and jammed the butt of it into Jimmy's left kidney, which caused Jimmy to topple backwards clawing at his lower spine with both hands. Danny turned round to see why Jimmy was screaming. Jack got the bamboo between his knees, sending him a-sprawl, and just as the young man's legs made a broad V in the air, Jack brought the cane down smartly. It was impossible to miss.

Stillness descended on the scene, save for the twittering of exotic birds and the groaning of the two lads.

"Enoch, if you could just keep an eye out for snakes, stranglers, and hordes whilst I give my boys a brief talking to."

"Glad to—but please do be brief."

"Now, Jimmy and Danny. Thank you for coming all the way out to Hindoostan to catch up with your dear father. You're probably afraid I'm going to be angry that you beat the shite out of me. But really it gives me no strong feelings one way or the other. I don't hold it against you that you turned out Irish, either. I wasn't there to make Englishmen of you, and so it's Irish you are, by default. That's all right; that can be remedied. But I must take exception to your say-ing—what was it? 'A shite-load o' malarkey.' You underestimate me, lads. Which you've plenty of reasons to do, I admit, since this is the first time you've ever laid eyes on me, and Mary Dolores's folk have been filling your heads with venom. I want you to understand that when I set forth on my trading voyage, twelve or thirteen years ago, I did it for you. And I'm still doin' it for you—I'm just not finished yet, is all. I've had diverse treasures to steal and Dukes to assassinate and pirates to escape from. But no voyage is finished until the ship drops anchor in London or Amsterdam—and you'll admit we're a hell of a long way from those places!"

Danny was the first to struggle to his feet. Still bent over at a right angle, he dug Jimmy's hand out of the brush and tried to heave him to his feet. "C'mon, now, Seamus, we've had our say—let's turn round an' head for Whitechapel now."

"Go if you must," Jack said, "but if you can bring yourselves to stay for a little while, I believe I can offer you transportation."

"Shahjahanabad is a basket of asps," Jack remarked the next day, as they were all riding through some wooded hills in the southeastern quarter of his domain. "Most of the Mogul's *omerahs* go there and become entangled with the intrigues and doings of other *omerahs*, not to mention diverse courtiers, concubines, eunuchs, Banyans of the *sodagar* and the *katari* class, Brahmins and Fakirs of diverse Hindoo sects, spies and intriguers from wild 'stans to the Northwest, the agents of the French, Dutch, and English East India Companies, and anyone else who just happens to be hanging around. Aurangzeb has a great palace there, which he stole from his pa and his brothers. So you see, lads, you're not the first men to violate the Fourth Commandment in Hindoostan—"

" 'Remember the Sabbath?' " quoth Jimmy, incredulous.

"Beg your pardon, I must've meant the Seventh."

" 'Thou shalt not commit adultery?' " said Jimmy and Danny in unison.

"I can see the Papists have left their mark on you lads—again, my fault."

"His Royal Highness meant to say the Fifth—honor thy father and mother," hollered Enoch Root—who, along with Surendranath, had been dropping farther and farther behind them, but who was still within earshot.

Danny made a sort of throat-clearing noise. "We came here to do that specifically—honor our mum, that is. It's just that in order to do it, we had to settle a score wi' Dad."

"Well, now that you've settled it," said Jack, pointing to various large swellings on his face, "shut up, because I'm trying to educate you. Before we embarked on *theologickal* disputations, I was talking about the Palace of the Great Mogul in Shahjahanabad, outside Delhi. It rises above the flood plain of a river, and on that plain, the Great Mogul stages mock-battles between armies of hundreds of elephants, and as many horse and camel. The expense, for elephant-feed alone, is damnable."

"Let's go! I ha' to see it!" exclaimed Jimmy, all starry-faced.

"Doahn't be such a shite-for-brayans!" said Danny. "Cahn't you perceive, he's tryin' to payant a picture of Oriental decadence?"

"I can perceive it as clearly as your ugly fayace! But I ha'n't rode all this friggin' way to beat up Dad an' then go hoahm! I'd not be above *seein'* a wee *sahmple* of Oriental decadence afore I leave— assoomin' that'd be all right wi' *ye*, Parson Brown."

"You'll see Oriental decadence and then some, if you'll only *shut up*—but you won't see it in *my* kingdom. Because the point I was leading up to is as follows. Among those *omerahs* is a fair sprinkling of Christian artillerymen—renegadoes and Vagabond soldiers from the armies of King Looie and the Holy Roman Emperor. Aurangzeb needs 'em, you see, because they've mastered the *al-jebr*, which is a sort of *mathematickal* sorcery that we had the good sense to steal from the Arabs. And by wielding this *al-jebr* they can predict where cannonballs will land, which is a useful thing to know in a battle. Consequently, Aurangzeb simply cannot make do without 'em."

"What has this t'do wi' *you*, Dad, who doahn't know *al-jebr* from *jabber*?" said Danny.

"In the clouded and furious imaginings of the Great Mogul, I am just another Frankish sorcerer. Which is to say that I could be reclining on a silken pillow in Shahjahanabad right now while some Hindoo lass played knick-knack on my *chakras*. But instead I am here!" And at this point Jack was secretly glad that his sons had been interrupting him the whole way, because the timing had worked out just as in some reasonably well-produced theatrical production: He spurred his donkey forward to the bare top of a hill and swept out a vast arc with his arm. "Look well and carefully upon these domains, my sons—for one day, they will *not* be yours!"

"Fook it in that case—we've already seen 'em," said Jimmy. "Which way to Shahjahanabad?"

"As you can see, my *jagir* resembles one of those large earthenware trays in which we make saltpeter. It has a flat hard bottom caked with salty mud, in which what little grows is immediately eaten. The sloped sides of the tray, then, are these ranges of hills that surround it on all sides—save in one place, down below us here, which—in this similitude—is the spout of the tray. It is a stretch of marshes, a sort of Reptile Paradise, that leads eventually to the Bay of Bengal."

"Beggin' your pardon, Dad, but your royal highness's *rayan* lasts another—what—four months?"

"One hundred sixteen days and counting."

"Then *whoy* should me 'n' Danny give a fook?"

"If you would shut up for ten consecutive minutes, I'd get to that," said Jack, and took advantage of his altitude to try to find Surendranath and Enoch Root—who seemed to think that the only purpose of going on journeys was to wander about and gawk at all and sundry. Not long after they'd all left the Royal Palace at Bhalupoor (Jack's summer capital, up in the hills), the Banyan and the alchemist had fallen into conversation. Not long after that, they'd evidently lost all interest in the incessant banter of the Shaftoes, and in the last few minutes they had dropped out of the caravan altogether. A retinue of spare palanquin-bearers, bodyguards, aides, and other *wallahs* had come along with them, and these were spreading out as the gap between Jack's and Enoch's group widened, trying to maintain some sort of contact; Jack could barely see the closest one, and could only hope that that fellow could see the next. The danger lay not in getting lost (for Surendranath knew the way better than Jack), and not in wild animals (according to Jimmy and Danny, Enoch could take care of himself), but in Thugs, Dacoits, and Maratha raiding-parties. Today's journey was taking them along the southern rim of the metaphorical Tray, and at no point were they more than a few miles away from some Maratha fort or outpost.

Jack realized with mild astonishment that Jimmy and Danny were actually listening to him.

"Oh, yes. Precisely *because* the Great Mogul hands out his king-ships on a strictly limited three-year term, every king must devote his energies, from the first day of his reign, to preparing for the day when he will be a king no more. Now here I could speak to you of details for twelve hours, and those of you who are fascinated by tales of Oriental decadence would hear much to marvel at. Instead I will summarize it as follows: There are two approaches to being a king. One, remain in Shahjahanabad and maneuver and strive against all the others in hopes that the Great Mogul will reward thee with another kingship at the end of the three years."

"I can guess two," said Danny. "Avoid Shahjahanabad as if 'twere a plague-town. Go dwell in your *jagir* and do all you can to suck it dry, so you can get out wi'a shite-loahd o' money . . ."

"Just like an English lord in Ireland," Jimmy added.

Jack heaved a great sigh; sniffled once; and wiped a tear from his eye. "My sons, you do me proud."

"That is the course you be steerin', then, Dad?"

"Not quite. Sucking this *jagir* dry is like getting blood from beef jerky. My illustrious predecessors have been sucking it dry for mil-lennia. Really it is one great sucking apparatus—there is a *zamindar* or chief tax collector, who does the sucking on behalf of whomever is king at the moment."

"That'd be the wog in the palankeen, then . . ."

"Surendranath is my *zamindar*. His agents hover over the markets in my two cities—Bhalupoor in the hills, where we stayed last night, and Dalicot on the coast, where we are going now. For those are the places where the produce of the earth or sea is exchanged for silver. And since I must pay my taxes to the Great Mogul in silver, that is the only place to collect it. The tax rate is fixed. Nothing ever changes. The *jagir* produces a certain meager income, and there is no way to increase it."

"So what've you been doin' all these years, Dad?" Jimmy de-manded.

"My first move was to lose some battles—or, at the very least, fail to win them—against the Marathas."

"Why? Y'know how t'make phosphorus. You could've scared those Marathas shitless and driven 'em into the sea."

"This was *tactical* losing, Danny boy. The other *omerahs*—I mean the intriguing types in Shahjahanabad—had heard tales of that phosphorus. It was in their nature to look on me as a dangerous rival. If I'd gone out and started winning battles, they'd've begun sending assassins my way. And I already have my hands full with French, Spanish, German, and Ottoman assassins."

"But by makin' yerself out to be a feckless Vagabond shite-for-brayans, you assured yourself of some security," said Jimmy.

"Moguls and Marathas alike want me to stay alive—for another one hundred and sixteen days, anyway. Otherwise I never would've lasted long enough for you boys to journey out and beat me up."

"But what then, Dad? Have you done *anything* here besides losin' battles and mulctin' wretches for pin-money?"

"Ssh! Listen!" Jack said.

They listened, and mostly heard their own stomachs growling, and a breeze in the trees. But after a few moments they were able to make out a distant *chop, chop, chop.*

"Woodcutters?" Danny guessed.

"Not just any wood, and not just any cutters," said Jack, spurring his donkey down off the hilltop and riding toward the sound. "Mark this tree over here—no, the big one on the right! That is teak."

"Tea?"

"*Teak. Teak.* It grows all over Hind."

"What's it good for?"

"*It grows all over Hind,* I said. Think about what that means."

"What's it mean? Just give it to us straight, Dad. We're no good at riddles," Jimmy said; at which Danny took offense.

"Speak for yourself, ninny-hammer. He's tryin' to tell us that nothin' succeeds in eatin' this type o' wood."

"Danny's got it," Jack said. "None of the diverse worms, ants, moths, beetles, and grubs that, sooner or later, eat *everything* here, can make any headway against teak-wood."

SEVERAL TALL TEAKS HAD BEEN felled in the clearing, but even so, Danny and Jimmy had to peer around for a quarter of an hour to realize what the place was. In Christendom there would have been a pit full of wood-shavings, and a couple of sawyers playing tug-of-war with a saw-frame the size of a bed-stead, slicing the logs into squarish beams, and looking forward to the end of the day when they could go home to a village some distance down the road. But here, a whole town had sprung up around these fallen trees. It had been a wild place before, and would be wild again in a year, but today, hundreds dwelt here. Most of them were gathering food, cooking, or tending children. Perhaps two score adult males were actually cutting wood, and the largest tool that any of them had was a sort of hand-adze. This trophy was being wielded by an impressive man of perhaps forty, who was being closely supervised—some would say nagged—by a pair of village elders who had an opinion to offer about every stroke of the blade.

The village's approach to cutting up these great teak-logs had much in common, overall, with how freemasons chipped rough blocks of stone one tiny chisel-blow at a time. At the other end of the village, some of them were scraping away at almost-finished timbers with potshards or fragments of chipped rock. Some of these timbers were square and straight, but others had been carved into very specific curves.

"That there would be a knee brace," Danny said, looking at a five-hundred-pound V of solid teak.

"Do not fail to marvel at how the grain of the wood follows the bend of the knee," Jack said.

"It's as if God formed the tree for this purpose!" said Jimmy, crossing himself.

"Aye, but then the Devil planted it in the middle of a million others."

"That might've been part of God's plan," Danny demurred, "as a trial and a test for the faithful."

"I think I have made it abundantly clear that I am no good at tests of that sort," Jack said, "but these *kolis* are another matter. They will wander the hills for weeks and look at every single tree. They'll send a child scampering up a promising teak to inspect the place where a bough branches off from the trunk, for that is where the grain-lines of the wood curve just so—and, too, it's where the wood is strongest and heaviest. When they've found the right tree, down it comes! And they move the whole village there until the wood has been shaped and the timbers delivered."

"I didn't think the Hindoos were seafarin' folk," Jimmy said, "other than wee fishin' boats and such."

"Most of these *kolis* will go to their graves, or to be precise, their funeral-pyres, without ever having laid eyes on salt water. They have been roaming the hills forever, going where they find work, supplying timbers for buildings, palanquins, and whatnot. When I became king they started coming here from all over Hindoostan."

"You must pay 'em *summat*. I thought you had no revenue."

"But this comes from a different purse. I am not paying these folk with tax money."

"Where is the friggin' money comin' from, then?" Jimmy demanded.

"More than one source. You'll learn in good time."

"He an' that Banyan must've made a shite-load of money when they brought that caravan home to Shahjahanabad," Danny observed.

"It wasn't just me and the Banyan, but the whole Cabal—or rather the half of it that had not fallen into the snares of Kottakkal, the *Malabar* pirate-queen."

"Hah! Now, *there* is your Oriental decadence!" Danny exclaimed to Jimmy, who was momentarily speechless.

"You have no idea," Jack muttered.

IT TOOK THEM ALMOST TWO hours to track down Enoch and Surendranath, who had wandered quite beyond the frontier of Jack's kingdom and into a sort of lawless zone between it and a Maratha stronghold. Through the center of that no-man's-land ran a small river in a large gulley—a steep-sided channel that the water had cut down through black earth every bit as slowly and patiently as the *kolis* whittling their beams.

"I should've predicted that we would find Enoch in the Black Vale of Vhanatiya," Jack said, when he finally caught sight of the alchemist down below.

"Who's that bloke in the turban?" Jimmy demanded, peering down over the lip of the gulley. Ten fathoms below them, in the bottom of the gorge, Enoch was standing in knee-deep water, conversing with a Hindoo who squatted in the shallows nearby.

"I have seen men like him once or twice before," Jack said. "He is a *Carnaya*, which I realize means nothing to you."

"Obviously he is a gold-miner," Danny said. The Carnaya was holding a round pan between his hands and swirling it around, causing a foamy surge of black river-sand to gyrate around its rim.

"If this were Christendom, where everything *is* obvious, he would be a gold-miner," Jack said. "But there is no gold, and naught is simple, in these parts."

"He must be panning for agates then," Jimmy said.

"An excellent guess. But there are no agates here." Jack cupped his hands around his mouth and hollered: "Enoch! It is a long ride to Dalicot, and we do not want to be caught in this country after dark!"

Enoch paid him only the slightest notice. Jimmy and Danny pounded down into the gulley, following their own avalanches into the river, which became cloudy—to the exasperation of the Carnaya.

Enoch wound up his conversation. There was much significant pointing, and Jack got the impression that directions were being given out. Jimmy and Danny peered at the Carnaya's pan, and at the heavy bags that he had filled with the results of his panning.

In time the whole caravan got re-assembled up above, and made ready for a forced march to Dalicot. "Be sure to check your pocket-compass," Enoch suggested before they set out.

"I know where we are," Jack said. But Enoch prevailed on him to check the compass anyway. Jack got it out and removed the cover: It was just a magnetized needle coated with wax and set afloat in a dish of water, and to get a reading, it was necessary to set it down on something solid and wait for a minute or two. Jack put it on a rock at the lip of the Black Vale of Vhanatiya, and waited for two minutes, then five. But the needle pointed in a direction that obviously was not north. And when Jack moved it to another rock, it pointed in a *different* direction that was not north.

"If you are trying to spook me, it has worked. Let's get the hell out of here," Jack said.

Their inspection of the Carnaya's equipment had left Danny and Jimmy baffled and suspicious respectively. " 'Twas nought more'n some dark matter, as dull and gross as anything I've ever seeyen," Danny reported.

"Certain gemstones look thus, before they have been cut and polished," Jack said.

"It was all sand and grit, nothing bigger'n a pin-head," Jimmy said. "But Jayzus! Those sacks were heavy."

Enoch was as close to being excited as Jack had ever seen him. "All right, Enoch—let's have it!" Jack demanded. "I'm king in these parts—stand and deliver!"

"You are not king *there*," Enoch said, nodding in the direction of the Black Vale, "nor in the place we will visit *tomorrow*."

Jimmy and Danny rolled their eyes in unison, and made guttural scoffing noises. They had been traveling in the company of Enoch the Red for half a year.

JACK WAS STANDING ON A beach, letting warm surf surge and foam around his sore feet, and watching a couple of Hindoo men working with a fragile-looking bow-drill, using it as a sort of lathe to shape a round peg of wood from the purple heartwood of some outlandish tree. "Peg-makers are a wholly different caste from plank-whittlers, and will on no account intermarry with them, though on certain days of the year they will share food," he remarked.

No one answered him; no one even heard.

Enoch, Jimmy, Danny, and Surendranath were standing on the beach a few yards away with their backs to him. On one side they were lit up by the reddish light of the sun, which (because they were so near the Equator) was making a meteoric descent behind the hills from which they had just descended. They were as motionless as figures in a stained-glass window, and in fact this was no mean similitude, since their heads were tilted back, their lips parted, their eyes clear and wide, much like Shepherds in the hills above Bethlehem or the Three Women in the empty tomb. Waves surged around their ankles and leapt up as high as their knees and they did not move.

They were beholding a vast Lady that lay on the beach. She was the color of teak. The light of the sun made her flesh glow like iron in a forge. She was far larger than the largest tree that had ever been, and so must have been pieced together from many individual bits of wood, such as this peg that the peg-maker was shaping next to Jack, or that plank that the plank-maker over there was assiduously sculpting out of a giant rough timber. Indeed, if they had come a year ago they might have seen her ribs jutting into the air, and courses of hull-planks still being cut to length, and it would have been evident that she had after all been pieced together. But in her current state it seemed as if she had just grown on the beach, and the way that the grain-lines of the teak followed her every curve did everything to enhance that illusion.

"Aye," Jack said, after he had allowed a proper silence to go by, "sometimes I think her curves are too perfect to've been shaped by man."

"They were not *shaped,* but only *discovered,* by man," said Enoch Root, and risked a single step towards her. Then he fell into silence again.

Jack busied himself inspecting various works higher up the beach. For the most part these were makers of planks and pegs. But in one place a shed of woven canes had been erected, and thatched with palm-fronds. Inside it, a woodcarver of higher caste was at work with his chisels and mallets; wood-chips covered the sandy floor and spilled out onto the beach. Jack went in there, bringing Surendranath as his interpreter.

"For Christ's sake! Look at her! Will you just look at her!? Look at her!" Then a pause while Jack drew breath and Surendranath translated this into Marathi, a couple of octaves lower, and the sculptor muttered something back.

"Yes, I see quite plainly that you were so good as to remove the elephant-trunk, and that the lady has a proper nose now, and for that you have my undying gratitude," Jack hollered sarcastically, "and as long as I am helping you with your self-esteem, sirrah, allow me to thank you for scraping off the blue paint. But! For! Christ's! Sake! Do you know, sirrah, how to count? You *do*!? Oh, excellent! Then will you be so good, sirrah, as to count the number of arms possessed by this Lady? I will patiently stand here while you take a full inventory—it may take a little while . . . oh, very good! That is the same reckoning that *I* have arrived at! Now, sirrah, if you will be so kind, how many arms do you observe on *my* body? Very good! Once again, we agree. How about Surendranath—how many arms has *he*? Ahh, the same figure has come up once again. And you, sirrah, when you carve your idols, you hold the hammer in *one*, and the chisel in *another*, hand—how many makes that? Remarkable! *Yet again* we have arrived at the same figure! Then will you please explain to me how come it is that This! Lady! is formed as you have formed her? *Why* the numerical *discrepancy*? Do I need to import a Doctor of *al-jebr* to explain this?"

Jack stormed out of the shed, followed closely by Surendranath, who was saying, "You *told* the poor fellow she was supposed to represent a *goddess*—what on earth were you *expecting*?"

"I was being *poetickal*."

Jimmy and Danny had long since clambered aboard, and were running from stem to stern and back again, hooting like schoolboys. Enoch had been walking about her, tracing short segments of arcs on the wet sand, and was now standing in violet light with the water up around his knees.

"My first thought was that she couldn't have been wrought by a Dutchman, on account of her marked dead-rise,* which will make her fast but will bar her from most Dutch harbors."

"There are no Dutch harbors around here, you'll notice," Jack observed.

"Her stem is strongly raked, more like a *jacht* than a typical East Indiaman. It looks as if two and maybe three exceptionally noble teaks were sacrificed to fashion that curve. There are no such trees in Europe any more, and so stems are pieced together, and rarely have such a rake. How did you find trees that were curved just so?"

"In this country, as you have seen, there is a whole sub-civilization of woodcutters who carry in their heads an inventory of every tree that grows between the Roof of the World in the north, and the Isle

---

* Meaning that seen in cross-section, her hull had a V shape instead of being flat-bottomed.

of Serendib in the south," Jack said. "We stole those trees from other *jagirs.* It took six months and was complicated."

"And yet her keel is no shorter, for all her stem-rake. So yet again, the builder seems to have valued speed above other desirables. Being so long and so rakish, she had to be narrow—quite a bit of volume has been sacrificed to that. And even more has been given up to riders and other reinforcements—you've put two ships' worth of teak into her. Expecting her to carry a lot of guns, are you?" Enoch asked.

"Assuming you've held up your end of the transaction."

"She should last thirty or forty years," Enoch said.

"Longer than most of us will," Jack answered, "present company excepted, that is—if the rumors about you are true."

"Anyone who looks at her will know she is hauling valuable cargo," said Enoch. "If ship-building is the art of compromise, then your builder has everywhere chosen speed and armament at the expense of volume. Such a ship can only pay for her upkeep if she is hauling items of small bulk and great value. She is pirate-bait."

"If there is anything we have learned in our wanderings, it is that *every* ship on the sea, even one as humble as *God's Wounds,* is pirate-bait," said Jack. "And so we have built a pirate-slayer. There is a reason why the Dutch make their merchantmen almost indistinguishable from their Ships of Force. Why should we go to the expense of fashioning a teak-built ship, only to lose her to some boca-neers six months after she is launched?"

Enoch nodded. Jack had become a bit furious.

"So let me hear your guess, Enoch. You said that she didn't look like a ship built by a Dutchman. Who was the shipwright, then?"

"A Dutchman, of course! For only they are so free in adopting outlandish notions—only they have the confidence. Everyone else only parrots them."

"You are both right and wrong," Jack said after a moment's pause, and then turned away and began slogging down the beach in the direction of a fire that had been kindled in the last few minutes, as the sun had finally disappeared and stars came out overhead. "Our shipwright is one Jan Vroom of Rotterdam. Van Hoek recruited him."

"His name is well-known. What on earth is he doing *here?*"

"It seems that in the days of Vroom's apprenticeship, shipwrights were held in high esteem by the V.O.C. and the Admiralty, and given a free hand. Each ship was built a little differently, according to the wisdom—or as some would say, the whim—of the shipwright. But recently the V.O.C. have become prideful, thinking that they know everything that will ever be known about how to build ships, and they have begun specifying sizes and measurements down to a quarter of an inch—they want every ship the same. And if a shipwright dares to show any artistry, why, then, some rival shipwright will be brought in to take measurements and write up a report, laying out how these rules and regulations have been violated, and causing no end of trouble. What it comes down to is that Jan Vroom did not feel appreciated. And when a worm-gnawed and weatherbeaten letter arrived in his hands, a couple of years ago, from an old acquaintance of his named Otto van Hoek, he dropped what he was doing and took passage on the next ship out of Rotterdam."

"Looks as if more followed," said Enoch, for they were now close enough that they could see a whole semicircle of muttering Dutchmen around the fire, lighting up their clay pipes with flaming twigs. In the middle were the red-headed captain, and a tall man with a blond-going-gray beard who was obviously Vroom. But four younger men were around them, listening and nodding.

"Before we interrupt these gentlemen, let us conspire in the darkness here," said Enoch.

"I'm listening."

"Along with these very Dutchmen, you imported some scribe, skilled—or so you were told—in the *cryptographickal* arts. You had this scribe write me an encyphered letter saying, 'Dear Enoch Root, I require forty-four large naval cannons, preferably of finest and most modern sort, please provide.' And several months later I decrypted and read this document in London—though not before some *spy* had intercepted it, and copied it out. At any rate, I read this document and I laughed. I hope you were laughing when you dictated it."

"A smile might have played round my lips."

"That is good, because it was an absurd request. And if you did not have the wit to recognize it as such, it would mean you had turned into some sort of addle-pated Oriental despot."

"Enoch. Do you, or do you not, have certain large metal items for me?"

"The items you refer to are not free for the taking. One does not acquire such goods without accepting certain obligations."

"You're saying you've found us an investor? That is acceptable. What are his terms?"

"You should rather say, *her* terms."

Jack levitated. Enoch clapped a hand on his shoulder and looked him in the eye. Enoch was facing toward the fire and the light glinted weirdly in the dilated pupils of his eyes: a pair of red moons in the night. "Jack, *it is not her.* She has done well for herself, it's true—but not so well that she can dispatch an arsenal halfway around the world, simply because a Vagabond writes her a letter."

"What woman *can?*"

"A woman you saw once, from a steeple in Hanover."

"Stab me!"

"And now you appreciate, I trust, how deep the matter is."

"But I should not have addressed the letter to Enoch Root, if I did not want it to become deep. What are her terms?"

The red moons were eclipsed for a little while. Enoch sighed. His breath on Jack's face was hot and warm like a Malabar breeze, and laced—or so Jack imagined—with queer mineral fragrances.

"*Investors* who dictate *terms* are common as the air, Jack," Enoch said. "This is a different matter altogether. You are not borrowing *capital* from an *investor* in exchange for specific *terms.* You are entering into a *relationship* with a *woman.* Certain things will simply be *expected* of you. I cannot even begin to guess *what.* If you and your partners fail to act as gentlemen *should,* you will incur the lady's displeasure. Is that specific enough? Is it clear?"

"It is neither."

"Good! Then this has been a successful conversation," Enoch said. "Now I must convey the same maddening ambiguity to your partners. That being accomplished, I must show due diligence, and—"

"What's that supposed to mean?"

"Certain items are conspicuously absent—such as masts and sails. Cordage. A crew. I cannot release the weapons until I have seen these. Also, her position on the beach is vulnerable."

"We will float her soon, and complete her on the water—as is traditional. If she had a few cannons on board she would be a difficult prize to take from land."

"Agreed. Have you made plans for her maiden voyage?"

"We were thinking perhaps of running saltpeter to Batavia, and then bringing spices back to one of the Great Mogul's ports—for Hindoostan consumes more spices than all Europe combined, and they have no lack of silver with which to pay for it."

"It is not a bad plan. But you may have a different plan tomorrow, Jack."

THE FOLLOWING AFTERNOON FOUND THEM in dangerous territory south of the Black Vale of Vhanatiya. The Carnaya miner had given Enoch deliberately misleading directions that would have led him directly into a Maratha trap. But Enoch had anticipated this, and tracked the miner through the hills like a hunter stalking wild game.

They passed for some hours through a high terrain overgrown with vicious scrub. All of the large trees seemed to have been cut down long ago and never grown back. Just when Jack was convinced that they were utterly lost in the most God-forsaken part of the world, he smelled camels, and they stumbled upon a caravan of Persians headed the same direction. This was a bit like running into a clan of kilted Scotsmen in the middle of the Sahara Desert.

The way became broad and trampled; Enoch no longer had to use his tracking skills. Finally even the scrub and thorn plants vanished. Like a few pebbles rattling down into a stoneware bowl, they descended into a rocky crater, maculated with schlock-heaps and filled with a perpetual miasma of wood-smoke.

"Even if your *taste* is abominable, I must grant you credit for *consistency*," Jack muttered. "How is it you always end up in the same sort of place?"

"By following the spoors of men such as the Carnaya," said Enoch, speaking in a hush, like a Papist who's just entered a basilica. "Now you see why I insisted that we come here alone—if we'd brought an escort of *rowzinders*, imagine how this place would have been upset."

"Isn't it *already*?" Jack asked. "What the hell are they up to? And why are those *Persians* here? And do my smoke-burnt eyes deceive me, or is that a contingent of Armenian long-range traders?"

Enoch said only: "Watch." So Jack followed Enoch and watched Enoch watch.

Now in the beginning Jack was certain that they had come to the place where all of Europe's teacups were manufactured, for there were clay-pits all over, and Hindoos squatted in them fashioning teacup-sized vessels. These were carried up to kilns to be fired. But if they were teacups, they were rough thick-walled ones without handles or decoration, and each came with a domed lid. And other peculiar operations were going on nearby: Canes of bamboo, and odds and ends of teak-wood, were being loaded into smoky furnaces to be turned into charcoal. Jack was certain that some of this teak was scrap left over from his ship-building project, and was peeved at first, then amused, to realize that his *kolis* had another operation going on the side.

Teak and bamboo were not the only vegetable matter being brought up to this stony vale. Wizened hill-people were staggering down under twig-bundles bigger than they were, and being paid in silver by important-looking characters. Jack did not recognize the twigs, but he gathered from the price paid for, and the reverence accorded, them that they were of some sort of plant sacred to the Hindoos.

All of these ingredients came together before a towering mud hearth, a sort of blazing termite-mound the size of a small church that rose from the center of the compound, looking twice as ancient as anything Jack had seen in Egypt. An old man with a priestly look about him squatted on his haunches next to a pyramid of rough teacups. He stirred his hand around in a sack of black sand just like what the Carnaya had panned out of the riverbank, and sifted it between his fingers into the crucible, seemingly feeling every single grain between his wrinkled fingertips, flicking away any that didn't feel right. Then he chose a few shards of charcoal and distributed them around atop the black sand, crumbling them into smaller bits as necessary, and finally plucked some leaves and blossoms from a giant spraying faggot of magic twigs and arranged these on the charcoal like a French chef placing a garnish atop a cassoulet. Then his hand went back into the sack of black sand and he repeated the procedure, layer upon layer, until the tiny vessel was full. Now the lid went on, and it was passed with great care to an assistant who sealed the lid in place with wet clay.

The finished crucibles, looking like slightly flattened balls of mud, were stacked like cannonballs near the great furnace. But they did not go in just now, because a firing was in progress: Jack could look in and see a heap of similar crucibles glowing in the heat like a bunch of ripe fruit.

"I'll be damned," said Enoch Root, "they are only red-, not yellow-hot. That means that the iron ore is not actually being melted. Instead the charcoal is being absorbed by the iron, though the iron is yet solid."

"Why doesn't the charcoal just burn?"

"No air can get into the sealed crucibles," Enoch snapped. "Instead it fuses with the iron to make steel."

"We've come all this way to watch a bunch of wogs make steel!?"

"Not just any steel." Enoch stroked his beard. "The diffusion must be very slow. Mark how carefully they tend the fire—they must keep it at a red heat for days. You have no idea how difficult that is—that boy with the poker must know as much of fire as Vroom knows of ships."

The alchemist continued gazing at the furnace until Jack feared they would remain in that very spot for as many days as the firing might take. But finally Enoch Root turned away from it. "There are secrets about the construction of that forge that have never been published in the *Theatrum Chemicum*," he said. "More than likely they are forgotten secrets, or else these people would have built more of them."

They moved on to a pile of crucibles that had been removed from the furnace and allowed to cool. A boy picked these up one at a time, tossing them from hand to hand because they were still too hot to hold, and dashed them against a flat stone to shatter the clay crucible. What remained among those smoking pot-shards was a hemisphere of spongy gray metal. "The egg!" exclaimed Enoch.

A smith picked up each egg with a pair of tongs, set it on an anvil, and struck it once with a hammer, then examined it carefully. Eggs that dented were tossed away on a discard-heap. Some were so hard that the hammer left no mark on them—these were put into a hod that was eventually carried across the compound to another pit where an entirely different sort of clay was being mixed up, according to some arcane recipe, by the stomping feet of Hindoo boys, while a village elder walked around the edge peering into it and occasionally tossing handfuls of mysterious powders into the mix. The eggs of metal were coated in thick jackets of this clay and then set aside to dry. The first clay had been red when wet and yellow when fired, but this stuff was grey, as if the clay itself were metalliferous.

Once the gray clay had dried around the eggs, these were carried to a different furnace to be heated—but only to a dull red heat. The difference become obvious to Jack only when the sun went down, and he could stand between the two furnaces and compare the glow of one with that of the other. Again, the firing continued for a long time. Again, the eggs that emerged were cooled slowly, over a period of days. Again they were subjected to the test on the anvil—but with different results. For something about this second firing caused the steel egg to become more resilient. Still, most of them were not soft enough to be forged after a single firing in the gray clay, and had to be put through it again and again. But out of every batch, a few responded in just the right way to the hammer, and these were set aside. But not for long, because Persians and Armenians bought them up almost before they had hit the ground.

Enoch went over and picked one of them up. "This is called *wootz*," he said. "It's a Persian word. Persians have been coming here for thousands of years to buy it."

"Why don't the Persians make their own? They seem to have the run of the place—they must know how it's done by now."

"They have been trying, and failing, to make *wootz* since before the time of Darius. They can make a similar product—your sons and I made a detour to one of their forges—but they cannot seem to manage *this*."

Enoch held the egg of *wootz* up so that fire-light grazed its surface and highlighted its terrain. Jack's first thought was that it looked just like the moon, for the color and shape were the same, and the rugged surface was pocked with diverse craters where, he supposed, bubbles had formed. On a closer look, these craters were few and far between. Most of the egg's surface was covered with a net-work of fine cross-hatched ridges, as if some coarsely woven screen—a mesh of wires—had been mixed into the stuff, and was trying to break free of the surface. And yet Jack had seen the crucibles prepared with his own eyes and knew that naught had gone into them save black sand, fragments of charcoal, and magic leaves. He pressed a fingertip against a prominent lattice of ridges; they were as hard as stone, sharp as a sword-edge.

"Those reticules grow inside the crucible, as plants do from seeds. And they are not only at the surface, but pervade the whole egg, and are all involved with one another—they hold the steel together and give it a strength nothing else can match."

"If this *wootz* is so extraordinary, why've I never heard of it?"

"Because Franks name it something else." Enoch glanced up, attracted by a distant ringing sound: a smith was smiting something. But it was not just some dull clod of iron. This was not a horseshoe or poker in the making. It rang with a noble piercing sound that put Jack in mind of Jeronimo wielding his rapier in the Khan el-Khalili.

The forge was about five minutes' walk away, and when they arrived they joined a whole crowd of Ottoman Turks and other travelers who had convened to watch this Hindoo sword-smith at work. He was using tongs to grip a scimitar-blade by its tang, and was turning it this way and that on an anvil, occasionally striking it a blow with a hammer. The metal was glowing a very dull red.

"It isn't hot enough to forge," Jack muttered. "It needs to be a bright cherry red at least."

"As soon as it is heated a bright cherry red, the lattice-work dissolves, like sugar in coffee, and the metal becomes brittle and worthless—as the Franks discovered during the Crusades, when we captured fragments of such weapons around Damascus and brought them back to Christendom and tried to find out their secrets in our own forges. Nothing whatsoever was learned, except the depth of our own ignorance—but ever since, we have called this stuff *Damascus* steel."

"Damascus steel comes from here!?" Jack said, jostling closer to the anvil.

"Yes—the reticules you saw in the egg of *wootz*, when patiently hammered out, at low temperature, produce the swirling, liquid patterns that we know as—"

"Watered steel!" Jack exclaimed. He was close enough, now, to see gorgeous ripples and vortices in the red-hot blade. Without thinking, he reached for the hilt of his Janissary-sword and began drawing it out for comparison. But Enoch's hand clapped down on his forearm to restrain him. In the same moment the forge was filled with a storm of whisking, scraping, ringing, and keening noises. Jack looked up into a dense glinting constellation of drawn blades: serpentine watered steel daggers, watered steel scimitars, watered steel *talwars*, Khyber swords, and the squat fist-knives known as *kitars*. Inlaid passages from the Koran gleamed gold on some blades, as did Hindoo goddesses on others.

Jack cleared his throat and let go of his sword.

"This gentleman with the hammer and the tongs is extremely well-thought-of among connoisseurs of edged weapons the world round," Enoch said. "They would be ever so unhappy if something happened to him."

"All right, all right, your point is well taken," Jack said, after they had, by dint of Enoch's diplomacy, extracted themselves from the forge with all of their body parts present and in good working order. "If we want valuable cargo for the ship's maiden voyage, there is no need to go to Batavia and load up with spices."

"Ingots of *wootz* will fetch an excellent price at any of the Persian Gulf or Red Sea ports," Enoch said learnedly. "You could trade them for silk or pearls, then sail for any European port—"

"Where we would all be tortured to death 'pon arrival. It is an excellent plan, Enoch."

"On the contrary, you might survive in London or Amsterdam."

"I had in mind going the opposite direction."

"It is true that in Manila or Macao you might find a market for *wootz*," Enoch said, after a moment's consideration. "But you would make out much better in the Mahometan countries."

"Let us strike out south and west towards the Malabar coast tomorrow."

"Will that not take us through Maratha territory?"

"No, they live in citadels up on mountain-tops. I know the way,

Enoch. We will pass through a couple of independent kingdoms that pay tribute to the Great Mogul. I have an understanding with them. From there we can pass into Malabar."

"Wasn't it Malabaris who stole your gold, and enslaved half of your companions?"

"That's one way to look at it."

"What is the other way?"

"Surendranath, Monsieur Arlanc, Vrej Esphahnian, and Moseh de la Cruz—our most cosmopolitan and sophisticated members— prefer to think of Malabar as a large, extremely queer, remote, hostile, and heavily armed *goldsmith's shop* in which we have made an involuntary *deposit*."

"We call such enterprises *banks* now."

"Forgive me, I haven't been in England for nigh on twenty years."

"Pray continue, Jack."

"They have our gold. We can never get it back. But it does them very little good, sitting there. Kottakkal, the Queen of the Malabar Pirates, can only *spend* so much of it fixing up her palace and refurbishing her ships. Beyond that, she must put that gold to work if she's to derive any benefit of having stolen it from us."

"Has she been putting it to work, then?"

"She owns twenty-five percent of our ship."

Enoch laughed—an uncommon event. He did more than his share of winking, smirking, chuckling, and deadpan commentary, but laughing out loud was a rare thing with him. "I am trying to imagine how I will explain to the Electress of Hanover, and heiress to the Throne of England, that she is now in partnership with Kottakkal, the Queen of the Malabar Pirates."

"Imagine how you're going to explain it to Kottakkal, please," Jack suggested, "because that will happen sooner."

Malabar
LATE 1696 AND EARLY 1697

THEY WERE TRAVELING NOW AS Hindoostani gentlemen: Enoch and
Jack each had a light two-wheeled carriage drawn by a pair of trotting bullocks. Each carriage could have accommodated two passengers, provided they were very close friends, but by the time Jack and
Enoch had packed themselves in with their diverse weapons, bundles, wine bottles, *et cetera*, there was only room for one. And that was
fine with Jimmy and Danny Shaftoe, who acted as if they'd never
seen anything quite this bizarre in all their travels, and could not
choose between being amused and disgusted. That was before they
discovered that their own horses could barely keep up with these
trotting bullocks over the course of a long night's march. Their
escort—eight musketeers and eight archers, siphoned off from the
endless Siege that Sword of Divine Fire had supposedly been prose-
cuting against the Marathas—had to jog the whole way.

By day the pace, combined with the sun, would have slain them
all in a few hours. So they woke up around sunset, lay about camp
for a few hours as the heat of the day seeped away into the earth and
sky, then got underway a couple of hours before midnight and hurried down roads and paths until dawn. Jack had made the trip several times, and had learned how to break it up into stages, each of
which ended in a mango- or coconut-grove near the walls of a town.
They would smooth out some ground and make camp as the sun
rose, and a few runners—adolescent boys of his *jagir*, well compensated for their exertions—would be dispatched to loiter outside the
town's gates until they were opened. These would go in and bargain
for victuals while the others slept in the shade of the trees. The
goods would then be delivered after sundown as the party readied
themselves for the next stage.

This was traveling of a wholly serious and businesslike nature,
and demanded certain adjustments of Jimmy and Danny, who in
their journey across Eurasia with Enoch Root had wantonly indulged

in side-trips and digressions. There was no time to do anything except cover ground, or make preparations to cover ground. There was no time even to talk.

Once they had escaped from Jack's blighted *jagir* the landscape was pleasant enough, but uniform and monotonous: ditched and irrigated fields alternating with groves of food-bearing trees, and occasional stretches of jungle covering hills, vales, and other areas that were not suited to agriculture. Sometimes they had to pass through such parts; the jungle seemed to rush out of the night to envelop them, and they moved forward with extreme care, expecting stranglers to abseil from overhead limbs, or large man-eating felines to explode from the brush. They had to ford several rivers, which in this part of the world meant wading through crocodiles. At one of these fords, Danny noticed a pair of largish reptilian nostrils closing in on a boy who was straggling behind the main group, and discharged his pistol in that general direction. It probably had no effect on the crocodile, but it scared the boy into catching up. At another ford, an immense crocodile carried away one of their donkeys.

The next day—or rather, the next evening—they woke up to find themselves in a black country of black men. It had been a long night's march and their bodies wanted to sleep but their minds did not. When they lay their heads down they could hear the earth thumping beneath them, like a gentle heartbeat, for this black earth was far richer in saltpeter than any in Jack's *jagir,* and the ground outside the walls of this town was pocked with holes where people labored with their thudding timbers all day long.

If the earth was full of thumps the air was just as full of strange cries, for every peasant working in the fields hollered "Popo!" every minute or so. Jack ended up sitting in the shade of a tree with Jimmy and Danny and Enoch, eating mangoes that literally fell into their laps, occasionally jumping up to sweep back plagues of ants, and watching these black Hindoos live their lives. A cool westerly breeze blew over them smelling of salt water, for they had almost crossed Hindoostan from east to west, and were nearing the Arabian Sea.

"Those field workers are Cherumans—a caste so low that they can pollute a Nayar from a distance of sixty-four feet," Jack explained, "whereupon the Nayar is obligated to kill them, and then purify himself with endless and pompous rites. So to save themselves from being killed, and the Nayars from being inconvenienced, they cry out *Popo!* all the time, to warn all comers that they are present."

"You're full o'shite as ever, Dad," said Jimmy with equal measures of contempt and affection.

A different cry sounded from around the road-bend: "Kukuya!

Kukuya!" As soon as they heard it, the Cherumans picked up their hoes and moved away from the road, depopulating a sixty-four-foot-wide strip to either side of it. Presently a small party of travelers came into view: a black-skinned woman, naked from the waist up except for her gold jewelry, riding a white horse, and a few servants on foot.

"If *that* be a Nayar, then let's go to where the Nayars live," Danny said.

"What the hell d'you suppose we've been doing for the last week?"

"There's more like her where we're going?"

"Yes—they run the place. They are a warrior caste. It's just like going to St. James's and gawking at the Persons of Quality: lovely ladies, and men with swords—who don't hesitate to use 'em."

After the sun had gone down, Jack sent his escort back to re-join the luxurious Siege. They lay about in that camp for the rest of the night dozing. At daybreak they were startled awake by a shouting match between a Cheruman, standing before a slab of rock sixty-four feet from the city limits, and a Banyan standing on the parapet of the wall. The Cheruman upended a sack of money onto the slab: cowrie-shells, Persian bitter almonds, and a few black coppers. Then he withdrew. A minute later the Banyan came out, deposited a bundle of goods, plucked off a few shells, almonds, and coppers, and went back into the town. The Cheruman returned and collected the bundle and whatever change the Banyan had left behind.

"Seems a wee bit *cumbersome*," Danny observed, watching incredulously.

"On the contrary, I deem it eminently practical," said Enoch Root. "If I belonged to a small warrior elite, my greatest fear would be a peasant uprising—ambushes along the roads, and so on. If I had the right to kill any peasant who came within a bow-shot of me . . ."

"You could relax an' enjoy the good life," Jimmy said.

After provisioning themselves in the town they turned south and followed the coast deeper into Malabar. From time to time they would pass a criminal who had been impaled on a javelin and left to die by the road-side, which only confirmed the impression that they were in a well-ordered place now, and had not taken any undue risks in sending their escort home. The heat of the sun in this far southern place was murderous, but the farther they went the closer the came to the Laccadive Sea with its cool onshore breezes, and in many stretches the road was lined with Palmyra palms whose enormous leaves cast volumes of shade on the way below.

They knew they were close to the court of Queen Kottakkal when frail racks began to line the road, all a-drape with those same palm leaves, which had been put there to dry and whiten. The Queen's scribes used them as paper. A lot of shouting could be heard up ahead.

"What're they hollerin' about?" Danny wondered.

"Maybe one of their ships just came back loaded to the gunwales with booty," Jack said, "or maybe a crocodile is loose in the town square."

The road opened up into the main street of a fair-sized port town consisting mostly of woven reed dwellings. There were occasional timber houses along the street, and these became more numerous and larger as they drew closer to the waterfront: the bank of a significant river that ran slowly and quietly through a deep-looking channel that broadened, a quarter of a mile downstream, to form an inlet of the Laccadive Sea. The town had doubtless stood here for æons but gave the impression of having just been set up in the midst of an ancient forest, as giant trees—teaks, mangoes, mahua, mahogany, coconut-palm, axle-wood, and one or two cathedral-sized banyan trees—stood between houses, and spread and merged overhead to create a second roof high above the palm frond thatchings that topped the buildings.

Young Nayar men were racing from house to house and tree-trunk to tree-trunk hollering at each other in extreme excitement. The travelers had only just come into view of the waterfront when a posse of Nayar boys burst out of a house and ran past them, completely ignoring them. Moments later those Nayars were pursued by a shower of arrows that came hissing down all around, some landing among the Shaftoes and lodging in the soft ground.

"Those black fookers are *shoowatin'* at us!" exclaimed Jimmy, yanking out his pistol and cocking the hammer.

"Not just *at* us, Jimmy boy," Jack said, in an ominously quiet voice.

All of the others turned to see Jack sprawled in his little two-wheeled carriage, both hands clutching his abdomen, where an arrow projected from his body at right angles. "It's a damned shame," he whispered. "Come all this way to die here and now . . ."

Jimmy was torn, like a man on the rack, between his desire to go and kill some black people, and the strictures of the Fifth Commandment. "Dad!" he cried, dismounting, and crossing over to the carriage in a couple of strides. He put his hand up to Jack's face as if to give him a tender caress—then clamped his father's jaw between thumb and fingers and wrenched his head this way and that, inspecting him. "You still bear the marks o' the beatin' we gayave ya—an' to think you'll carry 'em to yer grayave."

"To me they're like the sweet kisses I never had from the two of you—and never deserved—"

"Aw, Dad!" Jimmy cried, and planted one directly on Jack's lips. Fortunately from Jack's point of view it only lasted a few seconds—then Jimmy grunted, bit his father's lip, and spun away from him, clutching his ribs.

Danny was looking down on them coolly from the back of his horse, holding a bow whose string was still quivering. "When you're finished, tell me so I can go an' throw up. Then we've a score to set-tle with those Nayars, or what e'er the fook you call 'em."

Jimmy bent down stiffly and picked up the arrow that Danny had just loosed into his ribs. It had a blunt tip.

"Take two—you'll be needing 'em," Jack said, handing Jimmy the one that had bruised him in the stomach.

A couple of Nayars charged each other in the middle of the street nearby, and fell into a terrific duel with bamboo swords.

"I'm startin' to like the looks o' this town!" Jimmy said. "May we use firearms?"

"I do not think it would be considered sporting," Jack said, as Danny shot a blunt arrow into the chest of a strapping Nayar who was just emerging from a doorway. A dozen arrows swarmed from the windows of the same dwelling and knocked Danny out of the saddle.

"Ye basetards!" Jimmy bellowed, and charged the doorway before the snipers could nock a second flight of arrows.

"Run along and play, boys," Jack said—unnecessarily. He and Enoch slapped their bullocks' reins and went into motion. Soon the street debouched into a sort of waterfront plaza hacked out of the mangroves. Diverse small river-boats and coastal craft were tied up along the quay, reminding Jack, in a very imprecise way, of Thames-side. Turning their heads they could look downstream to the inlet that served as Queen Kottakkal's chief, and only, harbor. A dozen or so larger vessels rode at anchor there, and their appearance made Enoch chuckle. "Nowhere have I seen a more motley collection of pirate-vessels—not in Dunkirk, not even in Port Royal of Jamaica. Turkish galleots, Arab dhows, Flemish corvettes—is there anything they won't use?"

"To carry guns and to sail fast are the only requirements," Jack said. "The dhow, second from left, is the vessel she took from us."

And then both men naturally turned their heads to gaze south-wards across the river. The opposite bank was a stone bluff undercut by the current, so that it bulged out towards them slightly, then rose to a plateau some ten fathoms above their heads. This was not extraordinarily high, but it sufficed to command the river and the inlet with batteries of forty-eight pounders and mortars that could be seen, here and there, protruding from embrasures at the corners of Queen Kottakkal's palace wall. It was difficult to make out where the natural cliff left off and the built wall began, for both were concealed deep behind a mat of interwoven vines, some as thick as tree-trunks, that had grown outwards to a depth of yards. This hanging jungle was home to a whole nation of adventurous monkeys with prehensile tails. The vines that grew on the Queen's fortifications were of diverse species, but all of them seemed to be flowering. These were not roses or carnations but ripe dripping fleshy organs of sweet light, big as cabbages, grown in shapes that Euclid never dreamed off, organized in clusters, networks, and hierarchies. At the moment all were facing into the sun, so that the jungle-wall blazed with shocking color. It looked as if some fabulously wealthy pirate-nation had laid siege to the place and bombarded it with giant rubies, citrines, pearls, opals, lumps of coral, and agates, which had lodged in the cliff and been left there. It hummed and teemed with the energy of a million bees and a thousand hummingbirds that had been drawn to the place from all over the South Seas by the cataract of narcotic fragrance that came out of it. Compared to this, the mossy domes of the palace above and the blunt muzzles of its guns, were as dim as old paint.

Getting up there, if they had not been invited, would have been a short, fatal adventure. As it was, Jack and Enoch were conveyed across the river without losing any limbs to crocodiles, and ascended to the palace without running afoul of any trap-doors or poison-dart barrages. They followed a series of stairways—some external, winding up the stone cliff-face among the vines, and some internal, cut through the stone. Finally they emerged into a small courtyard surrounded by walls with many arrow-slits: a killing-ground for invaders. But a door was opened and so they entered into the palace.

Very little of Queen Kottakkal's palace was really indoors: It was a complex of gardens, terraces, temple-courts, and plazas divided one from the next by a sparse net-work of roofed galleries, with apartments situated here and there.

"Normally it is teeming with Nayars," Jack offered, "especially when so many pirate-ships are in the harbor. But they are all down in the town, enjoying the mock-battle."

He led Enoch on a short excursion down a gallery and across a garden to the very door of a large stone dwelling with diverse balconies and windows. But he drew up short when he noticed a sheathed sword leaning against the door-post. Jack shushed Enoch with a finger to his lips, and did not speak until they had put a hundred paces behind them.

"It was a good enough sword," Enoch said, "some sort of Persian *shamsir,* to judge from its extreme curvature and slender blade. But methinks you show it more respect than is warranted . . ."

"These Malabar women are as free with *men,* as Charles II himself was with *women,*" Jack explained. "In these parts, a man can never tell which children are *his.* Or to put it another way, every man knows his mother but hasn't the faintest idea who his *father* might be. Consequently, all property passes down the *female* line."

"Including the crown?"

"Including the crown. One peculiarity of this arrangement is that a man, going in to pay a call on a lady, never knows what *other* man he might discover in her bed. To prevent awkward situations, a gallant therefore leaves his weapon leaning against the door-post when he enters—as a sign to all who pass by that the lady's attentions are spoken for."

"So the Queen is passing some time with a Persian? Odd, that."

"The *weapon* is Persian. Dappa—our linguist—bought it in Mocha when we passed through there years ago. Of all of us, he is the only one who has made much headway in learning the Malabar language."

"He is putting it to good use!"

"He has *already* put it to good use by convincing the Queen that he and the others have a higher calling than to be slaves."

And with that Jack opened the door to another, much smaller apartment, and led Enoch through to a terrace at the back that looked out over the harbor. European-style tables and chairs had been brought out here. Two men were working over messes of palm-leaves covered with writing, figures, maps, and diagrams: Monsieur Arlanc and Moseh de la Cruz.

They were only mildly surprised to see Jack. Enoch Root required a bit of explanation—but once Jack adumbrated that the stranger had something to do with cannons, the others welcomed him. Moseh, Jack, and Monsieur Arlanc fell quickly into a detailed conversation about the ship. They were speaking Sabir, which was the only tongue they all shared. Enoch could not perfectly follow it. He drifted away to gaze out over the Laccadive Sea, and then turned his attention to some ink drawings that had been pegged to the wall.

"Is this art Japanese?" he inquired, breaking in abruptly.

"Yes—or at least, the fellow who made it is," Jack said. "We were just talking about him. Let's go and introduce you to Father Gabriel Goto of the Society of Jesus."

> I was driven out of my native country by a dreadful
> sound that was in mine ears, to wit, that unavoidable
> destruction did attend me, if I abode in that place
> where I was.
>
> —JOHN BUNYAN,
> *The Pilgrim's Progress*

Gabriel Goto had politely declined to work as a pirate and so
Queen Kottakkal had put him to work as a gardener. Some suspected
that he did not work very *hard*, for compared to most of the palace—
which was continually in danger of being overrun and conquered by
its vegetation—Gabriel Goto's plot was a desert. He'd been put in
charge of a courtyard in the landward corner of the palace grounds
that was perpetually shaded by tall trees and by an adjacent stone
watch-tower, yet sorely exposed to storm-winds, and poorly drained. It
had defeated many a gardener. Gabriel Goto settled the matter by
growing nothing there, except for moss, and the odd stand of bamboo. Most of the "garden" consisted of stones, raked gravel, and a
pond sporting a brace of bloated, mottled carp. Every so often the
Jesuit would drag a rake across the gravel or throw some food at the
fish, but most of the work involved in the upkeep was *mental* in nature,
and could not be accomplished unless his mind was clear. Clearing his
mind was an extraordinarily demanding project requiring him to sit
crosslegged on a wooden patio for hours at a time, dipping a brush
into ink and drawing pictures on palm leaves. At any rate, this corner
of the palace no longer bred mosquitoes and poisonous frogs as it had
formerly been infamous for doing, and so the Queen left him alone.

The results of Gabriel Goto's artistic labors were neatly stacked,
and in some cases baled, almost to the ceiling of the apartment
behind his patio. More recent work had been hung from lines to dry
in the breeze.

"It is the same landscapes over and over," Enoch Root observed,
browsing his way down a clothes-line of rugged and none-too-
cheerful-looking scenes: mostly hills and cliffs plunging into waters
speckled with outlandish square-sailed vessels.

"The work, as a whole, is called *One Hundred and Seven Views of the
Passage to Niigata*," said Moseh de la Cruz helpfully.

"This is my favorite: *Breakers on the Reef Before Katsumoto*," said
Monsieur Arlanc—delighted to have someone to speak full-dress
French to. "So much is suggested by so little—it is a humbling con-
trast with our *Barock* style."

"Bor-ing! Give me *Korean Pirate Attack in the Straits of Tsushima* any
day!" Jack put in.

"That is fine if you like vulgar sword-play, but I believe his finest work is in the Wrecks: *Chinese Junk Aground in Shifting Sands,* and *Skeleton of a Fishing-Boat Caught in Tree Branches* being two notable examples."

"Are *all* of his pictures about Hazards to Navigation?" asked Enoch Root.

"Have you ever seen a nautical picture that *wasn't?*" Jack demanded.

"Over here, you can see the *Massacre of Hara* triptych," said Moseh.

"Let's go find the samurai," Jack said. And they did, passing in a few steps through the wee house he'd fabricated out of sticks and paper—or, to be precise, palm leaves. His swords—a long two-hander and a shorter cutlass—rested one above the other in a little wooden stand. Jack went over and peered at the longer of the two. It had come from the collection of an Algerian corsair-captain, but according to Gabriel Goto it had unquestionably been forged in Japan at least a hundred years ago. And indeed the shape of its blade, the style of the handle, and the carving of the guard were unlike anything else Jack had ever seen, which argued in favor of its being from what by all accounts was the queerest country on the face of the earth. But the actual steel of the blade was (as Jack had noted, and remarked on, in Cairo years before) marked with the same swirling pattern shared by every other watered-steel blade, be it a Janissary-sword forged in Damascus, a *shamsir* from the forge of Tamerlane in Samarkand, or a *kitar* from the *wootz*-vale.

Having confirmed this memory to his own satisfaction, Jack straightened up and turned around and nearly butted heads with Enoch Root, who was just in the act of noticing the same thing. To his great satisfaction Jack saw amazement on the alchemist's face, followed by a few moments of what looked almost like fear, as he came aware of what it might mean.

"Let's hear what the artist has to say for himself," said Jack, and slid a translucent screen aside to reveal the flinty garden, and Gabriel Goto sitting with his back to them, holding a brush with an ink-drop poised on its sharp tip.

GABRIEL GOTO'S STORY
[AS NARRATED IN CLERICAL LATIN TO ENOCH ROOT]

"I have never seen Japan. I know it only from pictures my father drew, of which these are but miserable plagiarisms.

"From the others you have heard stories that are as complicated as a Barock church or Ottoman mosque. But the Japanese way is to be simple, like this garden, so I will tell my tale with as few brush-strokes as possible. Even so it will be too many.

"Those who have ruled Japan, be they monks, emperors, or shoguns, have always depended upon local knights, each of whom is responsible for looking after some particular piece of land—seeing to it that this land produces well and that the people who work it are orderly and content. Those knights are called Samurai, and as with the knights of Christendom, it is their responsibility to keep arms and to bear them in the service of their lord when called upon. My family have been Samurai for as long as we choose to remember. The lands for which we were responsible were of little account, being in a high cold stony place, and we were held in no special regard by others of our class.

"The story is related that an ancestor of ours had split his hold-ings between two sons, giving the paddies to his first-born and the rocks to the other. Each spawned his own branch of the family: one rich, dwelling in low-lands and distinguishing itself in wars, the other a clan of coarse mountain-dwellers, not known for their loyalty, but allowed to remain in existence because neither were they known for martial prowess.

"The tale of these two clans goes on for centuries, and is as fraught with complications as the history of Japan itself—someday when we are on a long sea-voyage perhaps I will relate more of it. What is important is that copper and then silver were discovered in the rocky up-lands. This was about two hundred years ago, at a time when the shogun turned his back on the affairs of the world and went into retirement, and Japan ceased being a unified country for a very long time—like Germany today. All power fled from Kyoto to the provinces, and each part of the country was controlled by a lord called a *daimyo*, something like a baron in Germany. These daimyos clashed and strove against each other ceaselessly, like stones on a pebble beach grinding each other. Ones who met with success built castles. Markets and cities formed round their walls. Markets require coins, and so each daimyo began to mint his own currency.

"What it amounts to is that this was a dangerous time to be a war-rior but an excellent time to be a miner. As my ancestors—being Buddhists—would have expressed it, the two clans were bound to opposite points of the Wheel, and the Wheel was turning. Those low-land warriors allied themselves with a daimyo who was not deserving of their trust, and lost two consecutive generations of males in battle. *My* ancestors—the uplanders—moved down from the mountains and into apartments in another daimyo's castle, not far from Osaka

Bay, near Sakai, which in those days was a free city devoted to foreign trade, like Venice or Genoa. This happened about a hundred and fifty years ago, which was the same time that the Portuguese began to come up from Macao in tall ships.

"The Portuguese brought Christianity and guns. My ancestors embraced both. To people living in Sakai in those days it must have seemed an intelligent choice. The harbor was crowded with European ships bristling with cannons and flying Christian banners from every spar. Also, the Jesuits liked to establish missions in poor areas, and despite the silver mines, our ancestral land was still poor. So when a mission was established there at the invitation of my great-great-grandfather, the miners and peasants embraced Christianity without hesitation. Here was a creed that preached to the poor and the meek, and they were both.

"At the same time my great-great-grandfather was learning the secrets of gunsmithing, and teaching this skill to the local artisans. Men whose fathers had hammered out hoes and shovels were now making firelocks worth a hundred times as much.

"Now the peasants who lived down below, working the paddies, began to make trouble for *their* Samurai, our cousins. Some of these peasants began to turn Christian, which our cousins abhorred; others were growing disrespectful of their lords, who seemed to have lost the mandate of heaven. In those days there was a thing called *katana-gari* which means sword-hunt, in which the Samurai would search the peasants' homes for armaments. They began to find not only swords but firearms.

"So naturally the cousins allied themselves with powerful men who sought to unify Japan. This tale extends across three generations and as many shoguns—the first two being Oda Nobunaga and Toyotomi Hideyoshi—and has more twists and turns than a game trail over the mountains. The long and the short of it is that they threw in their lot with Tokugawa Ieyasu, who, a hundred years ago, won the Battle of Sekigahara, in part by using foot-soldiers armed with guns. In that battle my cousins won glory, and they won even more in the storming and the destruction of Osaka Castle, which took place in the Year of Our Lord 1615. My father was eighteen years old at the time, and he was one of the defenders of that castle, and of the Toyotomi family which was extinguished on that day.

"The Wheel had turned again. The Tokugawa shogunate claimed a monopoly on the minting of coins—my family lost its chief source of revenue. Firearms were banned—another source of income vanished. Foreign trade was strictly controlled—Sakai became an island cut off from the rest of Japan. But worst of all, for my family, was that

Christianity had been outlawed. My father had not been the only Christian to have allied himself with the Toyotomi family, and Tokugawa Ieyasu believed that the Jesuits and the Toyotomis, allied together, were the only force that could defeat him. Both were extirpated.

"At the time of my father's birth there were a quarter of a million Christians in Japan and at the time of his death there were none. This did not occur all at once but gradually, beginning with the execution of a few Jesuit missionaries in the Year of Our Lord 1597 and culminating forty years later in a few great battles and massacres. My father perhaps did not really grasp what was happening until it was nearly finished. His brother had gone back to our ancestral land to look after the mines and practice Christianity in secret. My father remained in Sakai for a while trying to make a living in foreign trade. But first this fell under the strict control of the shogun, and from there it was gradually choked off. The Portuguese were banned altogether because they kept bringing over priests disguised as mariners. Sakai and Kyoto were closed to foreign trade altogether. Only Nagasaki was left open, and only to the Dutch, who—being heretics—did not care about saving Japanese souls from eternal fire, and only wanted our money.

"So my father had become a masterless Samurai, or *ronin*—one of a large host of Christian *ronin* brought into being by the policies I have described. He moved round to the opposite coast of Honshu—the coast that faces towards Korea and China—and worked as a smuggler. He smuggled silk, pepper, and other goods to Japan, and smuggled fugitive Christians out to Manila.

"Now, formerly my family had had no contacts with Manila whatsoever, because we were exporters of silver. If the commerce of Asia is like a fire, then silver is like the air blown into it to make it blaze up, and Manila is the bellows. For it is to Manila that the Spanish galleon sails every year, full of silver from the mines of New Spain. My family's mines could not compete against this, and so in generations past we had been more apt to trade with Macao, and other ports on the coast of China—a vast country that is eternally ravenous for silver.

"But in that time Japan refused to accept ships from Macao, even at Nagasaki, because Portuguese priests, who longed for martyrdom, used Macao as their point of departure. My father's contacts in Macao dried up, or moved to Manila. By that time he was no longer in the silver business anyway. So he began to trade between Manila and a certain smuggler's harbor in northern Honshu, near Niigata. His fame spread as far as Rome, and soon Jesuits began to arrive in

Manila from Goa in the west and Acapulco in the east, and to request him by name. He would take them up to Niigata, where they would be met by Japanese Christians who would take them up into the mountains to preach the Word of the Lord and serve holy communion in secret. But at the same time my father would bring aboard other Japanese Christians who had fled from this persecution. He would convey them down to Manila where there was, and is, a large community of such persons.

"So it went for a time. But in the Year of Our Lord 1635 the shogun decreed that thenceforward no Japanese could leave the Home Islands on pain of death, and that all Japanese currently abroad must return home within three years or face the same penalty. Two years after that, the Christian *ronin* staged a great rebellion on Kyushu and fought the forces of the shogun for half a year, but they were wiped out. Not much later the remaining Christians were obliterated at the Massacre of Hara. My father survived by virtue of several miraculous interventions by various Saints, which I will not enumerate since I know that you are a heretic who does not believe in such things, and made one last voyage to Manila where he took a young Japanese wife.

"I was born in Manila three years after Japan closed itself off from the world. When I was a boy I would beg my father to take me up on his boat so that I could see where we came from, but by then he was an old man and the boat was a worm-eaten wreck. He contented himself with painting pictures of the landmarks that he had used to navigate from Manila to his smuggler's cove on Honshu. My efforts here—*One Hundred and Seven Views of the Passage to Niigata*—are a miserable pastiche of the art that he made.

"My life has been uneventful by comparison. I grew up in Manila. The only people I ever saw were Japanese Catholics, and a few Spanish priests. Jesuit fathers taught me to read and write. Christian *ronin* taught me the martial arts. In time I took holy orders and was sent to Goa. I lived there for a few years, and developed some familiarity with the language of Malabar. Then I was dispatched to Rome, where I saw Saint Peter's and kissed the Holy Father's ring. I had hoped that the Pope would send me to Nippon to achieve martyrdom, but he said nothing to me. I was crushed, and in my self-indulgence I went through a time of doubting my faith. Finally I volunteered to travel to China to work as a missionary and perhaps be granted martyrdom there. I boarded a ship bound for Alexandria—but along the way we were captured by a galley of the Barbary corsairs. I killed a fairly large number of them, but then a member of my own ship's crew, seeking to curry favor with the Turks who were soon to be his masters, hit me from behind with a belaying-pin, and ended my struggle. The Turks took us back to Algiers and gave the one who had betrayed me slow death on the hook. Me they offered work on a corsair-galley, as a Janissary. I refused, and was made to pull an oar instead."

A paper door slid open, and from the darkness on the far side of it emerged a pair of ebony breasts and a tummy, followed in short order by their owner: Kottakkal, the Pirate Queen of Malabar. Behind her came Dappa, who was also naked from the waist up, but who had belted on his Persian scimitar. This accounted for the dim muttering sounds that had been audible through the paper wall for the last quarter of an hour: Dappa had been translating this story for the Queen.

She was a big woman, about as tall as an average European man, with broad hips that gave her exceptional stability when standing barefoot on the rolling deck of a pirate-ship, and were equally convenient to child-bearing—she had produced five daughters and two sons. She had a marvelous round belly covered in an expanse of smooth purplish-black skin. Jack always had the vague, dizzying sense that he was falling into it, and he suspected that other men felt the same. Her breasts showed the aftermath of many babies, but her face was quite beautiful: round and smooth except for a sword-scar under one cheekbone, with complicated lips that always had a knowing grin, or even a sneer, and eyelashes as black and thick as paintbrushes. Her head always seemed to be resting on a steel platter, or rather a whole stack of them, for whenever the Queen ventured out she wore—in addition to diverse gold bangles and rings—a stack of flat watered-steel collars that went over her head, and piled up into a sort of hard glittering neck-ruff.

Now the Queen spoke and Dappa translated her words into Sabir: "When we captured the gold-ship with Father Gabriel, Dappa, and Moseh—for *Jackshaftoe* and the others lacked the courage of those three, and had already lost their nerve, and jumped off into the water like panicked rats—"

Jack bowed low and muttered, "A pleasure to see you as always, Your Majesty." but the Queen ignored him and continued:

"At any rate, my men were about to put them to death, for they assumed that this would please me. But then Father Gabriel recognized us as Malabari, and spoke to me in a way that pleased me even more, and so I suffered them all to live."

"What did he say?" asked Enoch Root.

"He said, 'It is your prerogative to cut my head off, but then I cannot tell you the story of how the Vagabond named Quicksilver achieved his long-planned revenge against a Frankish Duke in Cairo, and stole this hoard of Mexican gold.' So I commanded him to tell me that tale before he was put to death. And this he did; but what he was *really* telling me was that he and his companions were worth more to me alive, as slaves, than as headless corpses bobbing in the Gulf of Cambaye."

"Your Majesty chose wisely," said Enoch Root.

"Often I have doubted it," said the Pirate Queen. "Dappa is a linguist, which (he informs me) means a man with an excellent tongue, and he has found more than one way of putting his tongue to work pleasing me. Gabriel Goto makes a good, if peculiar, garden. Moseh seemed like a useless mouth. Many times my advisors urged me to break the group up and sell them at a loss. Indeed I was on the brink of doing so several times in the early going, for there is an excellent slave-market in Goa and another in Malacca. But when Jackshaftoe secured his *jagir* from the Great Mogul, everything changed, and the construction of the ship began. Lately even my most skeptical captains have been vying with each other for the honor of supplying the ship's masts."

"I was wondering where you were going to obtain masts."

"Come with me, O Bringer of Armaments," said Queen Kottakkal, and whirled around and stalked out through Gabriel Goto's paper house. She moved so decisively that the wind of her passage peeled dry palm-leaves from stacks of finished artwork. The men hastened to catch up with her, creating a wind of their own, and gloomy drawings of Hazards to Navigation rose into the air and careered back and forth, spinning and sailing lazily on the heavy air. Among these Jack noticed some letters brushed in what he took to be the Japanese script—these were on rice-paper and had a weather-beaten and well-traveled look about them.

"What news from your brush-buddies in Nippon and Manila?"

Gabriel Goto's face did not betray any particular reaction, but he turned his head suddenly toward Jack. "Normally I do not look to you to voice any interest in the internal broils of Nippon and the exiled Christian *ronin* of Manila," he announced starkly.

"But now that I am a king of sorts I must broaden my interests—so indulge me."

"The shogun continues to hoard silver for internal use—which amounts to saying that he has been making the Dutch at Nagasaki accept gold coins for the goods that they unload from their ships. But recently the shogun devalued gold to the point that the Dutch are forced to take their compensation in the form of vast quantities of copper coins instead." He stopped and inspected Jack's face for signs of incomprehension or boredom. They were following the others across a courtyard where Hindoo statuary lurked in cascades of ripe flowers, and fountains fed melodious brooks.

"Don't be such a tease!"

"All such matters are now firmly controlled by a family called Mitsui—they have founded what you would call a banking house."

"I ween you've been in touch with your uncle's people—the miners."

"How did you know this?"

"Why, it's obvious that the devaluation of gold had great import for anyone running a copper mine in Nippon."

Gabriel Goto, seemingly shocked at having been found out, said nothing. They had entered into the Queen's apartments and were pursuing her down a gallery. She was deep in conversation with Enoch Root, but Jack got the impression that during the pauses, when Dappa was translating, Enoch was cocking an ear towards them.

Gabriel went on: "Since your inexplicable and new-found interest in Nipponese currency fluctuations is so marked, then, Jack, I shall warn you that it is all very complicated. The shogun has actually made several devaluations, trying to draw more metal from the ground and increase the supply of money, which in his view will bring about a corresponding increase in the amount of goods produced. Or so it seems from a miner's perspective—which, after all, is the only perspective *available* to me."

They were ascending a stone staircase, working against a current of cooler salt air. "Tell me of more complications," Jack said.

"You probably imagine my people still working the same land that we were bequeathed many centuries ago. But we lost that land as part of the evolutions I spoke of, and my surviving relatives fled generally northwards, to be closer to the smuggling ports, and farther from Edo. Edo has a million people now."

"It is impossible for a city to be that large."

"It is the largest city in Creation, and no place for Christians."

They had gained the top of the stairs now, and were crowding into a chamber that opened onto a balcony. From the rail of this balcony—the highest part of the palace—they could look down the vine- and flower-covered cliff below and out across the inlet where most of the Queen's pirate-fleet rode at anchor. The ships seemed to float in mid-air, such was the transparency of the water, and underneath them schools of bright fish maneuvered through coral formations.

"Behold!" said the Queen, sweeping out one bangle-covered arm. Actually she said something in Malabari, but obviously it meant "Behold" and Dappa did not bother with a translation.

A peculiar sort of cargo-handling operation was under way down below: two pairs of small boats, each pair lashed together abeam of each other with logs spanning the gap between them. One of these makeshift catamarans was following several lengths behind the other, and the distance between them was bridged by a colossal tree-trunk, spoke-shaved smooth, and painted barn-red.

Jack heard Dappa speaking in English to Enoch Root: "Normally I would not be so presumptuous as to proffer advice to you on any subject, least of all manners and protocol—but I urge you, sir, not to ask the Queen where she obtained that mast."

"I accept your counsel with gratitude," said Enoch Root.

It was obvious that the mast had just been brought in by one of the Queen's fleet: a frigate of European design. She was the largest ship in the harbor, but much smaller than the one being built on the beach in Dalicot, and so the mast dwarfed her—it was longer than the frigate's deck, and must have projected forward and aft before it had been unlashed and let down onto those boats.

The boat-crews were paddling toward the shore as gamely as they could, though half the men were laboring with bails; gouts of water flew from the boats in all directions and slapped the surface of the harbor, only to rush back in over the gunwales during the next swell. Jack wondered whether he was about to witness a disaster, until he heard men in the boats, and on the shore, laughing.

Then he turned his attention back to Gabriel Goto. "But if your family are reduced to Vagabonds, how comes it they know so much of currency devaluations—and how do they write you letters on fair-looking rice-paper?"

"The short answer is that they remain bound to the same ancient Wheel, which has not ceased to turn."

"The shogun wants metal to come from the ground—and in order to make it so, the House of Mitsui needs your cousins and nephews."

"That is not the only thing on the shogun's mind. In the far north, the Russians are on the move. Mostly it has been adventurers and fur-traders, ranging from outposts in Kamchatka, the Kurils, and the isles of the Aleuts. But there is a new Tsar in Russia named Peter, a man with a formidable reputation, who has even traveled to Holland to learn the art of shipbuilding—"

"I know all about this Peter," said Jack. "Jan Vroom worked by his side, and Peter wanted him to come to Russia and build ships there. But Vroom saw the prospect of more profit, and warmer climes, in the offer of van Hoek."

"In any event," said Gabriel Goto, "Peter's fame has reached the court of the shogun. Obviously Russia will one day threaten Nippon from the north. When that day arrives, Nippon will be defenseless against Peter's Dutch-style ships and *al-jebr*-trained gunners, unless we are well established in northern Honshu and on the vast island to the north—a wilderness full of blue-eyed savages, called Ezo, or Hokkaido."

"So your family may be doubly useful to the shogun. You can mine copper, and you have an interest in moving northwards."

Gabriel Goto said nothing, which Jack took to mean *yes.*

"Tell me—has the shogun's concern about this military threat led him to relax his ban on firearms?"

"He imports books of *rangaku,* which means 'Dutch learning,' so as to keep abreast of developments in fortifications and artillery. But the ban on guns will *never* be lifted," said Gabriel Goto firmly. "The sword is the symbol of nobility—it is what marks a man as a Samurai."

"How many Samurai are there in Japan?"

Gabriel Goto shrugged. "Their proportion to the entire population is somewhere between one in ten, and one in twenty."

"And there are a million souls in Edo *alone*?"

"That is what I am told."

"So, between fifty and a hundred thousand Samurai in that one city—each of whom must possess a sword?"

"Two—the long and the short. Many have more than one set, of course."

"Of course. And is watered steel as desirable there as it is everywhere else?"

"We may be isolated, but we are not ignorant."

"And where do the sword-smiths of Nippon get this kind of steel?"

Gabriel Goto inhaled sharply, as if Jack had strayed into the middle of his garden and left muddy foot-prints in the white gravel. "This is a great secret, the subject of legends," he said. "You know that most Japanese are Buddhists."

"Of course," said Jack, who hadn't known.

"Buddhism came from Hindoostan. And so did some of our other traditions that are very ancient—such as tea . . ."

"And steel," Jack said, "which for centuries has been imported, by the finest swordsmiths of Nippon, from India, in the form of small egg-shaped ingots with a distinctive cross-hatch pattern."

For once Gabriel Goto was openly dumbfounded. "How did you come to know this!?"

Down below, the narrow end of the giant mast had plowed into the beach. One pair of boats was being abandoned by drenched rowers. The other group was thrashing the water, trying to wheel the trunk around so it could be rolled up onto dry land. At a glance it seemed not to be moving at all. But move it did, as slowly as the minute-hand of a clock—as steadily as that mysterious Wheel that Gabriel Goto was always speaking of.

"You want to return to this homeland that you have never seen," Jack said. "It could hardly be more obvious."

Gabriel Goto closed his eyes and turned towards the Laccadive Sea. The onshore breeze blew his long hair back from his face and made his kimono billow like a colorful sail. "When I was a boy standing at my father's knee and watching him paint his pictures of the Passage to Niigata, he told me, over and over again, that Nippon was now a forbidden land to us, and that the places he was drawing were places I would never see. And that is just what I believed for most of my life. But let me tell you that when I stood in Saint Peter's, in Rome, waiting to kiss the Pope's ring, I looked up at the ceiling of that place, which was magnificently adorned by a painter named Michelangelo. Not in Latin, English, or Nipponese are there words to express its magnificence. And that is the very reason for its being there, for sometimes pictures say more than words. There is a place in that painting where the Heavenly Father reaches out with one finger toward Adam, whose hand is outstretched as I am doing here, and between the fingertips of the Father and the Son there is a gap. And something has leapt across that gap, something invisible, something that not even Michelangelo could portray, but anyway it has crossed from the Father into the Son, and the Son has been awakened by it, and been infused with awareness and purpose. At the moment that I stood there in Saint Peter's and saw all of these things, understanding suddenly came into my mind, bridging the gap of miles and years that separated me from my father, and I became aware for the first time. I understood that even though *with his words* he had forbidden me to return to Nippon, *in his pictures* he had told me that one day I *must* return—and in those same pictures he had given me the means."

"You believe that the *Hundred and Seven Views of the Passage to Niigata* are a sort of nautical chart, telling you how to return?"

"They are better than a chart," said Father Gabriel Goto of the Society of Jesus. "They are a living memory."

HALF THE TOWN WAS PULLED away from their mock-battle to heave the mast up onto the beach, and eventually three elephants were brought into play. Through the Queen's spyglass, which had evidently been pilfered from some Portuguese sea-captain's personal effects, Jack could see his sons—now half-naked, and covered with bruises—striving alongside Nayar youths to land this prize. Eventually it was paraded through the town, garlanded with flowers, bristling with incense-sticks, and then it was made the centerpiece of more merry-making, which continued into the night. In earlier years Jack would have been at the center of this, but as it was, he delegated the revelry to Jimmy and Danny, and spent most of the evening huddled with Enoch and the other members of the Cabal.

Everyone in the town slept late the next morning, save a few sentries and low-caste laborers. Jack reckoned it would be a simple matter to find his sons passed out under a palm-tree somewhere. But he could not find them. The tide was about to go out, and men on ships were calling his name. Jack returned to the top of the cliff, intending to wake up Monsieur Arlanc and ask him to search for Jimmy and Danny later. But on his way to the apartment where the Huguenot slept, Jack detected volcanic emanations from the Queen's chambers, and detoured thataway out of curiosity. As he approached her door he saw not just one but two sets of weapons leaned up against the door-posts: European muskets and cutlasses. Dim moanings, mutterings, and controversies emanating from the other side of that door told Jack that the boys had finally found what they had been looking for in the way of Oriental decadence, though Jack honestly could no longer tell it apart from the Occidental kind. In any event Jack left the boys there to pursue their own story while he sailed away to pursue his.

Two of Queen Kottakkal's ships sailed on that tide, and turned opposite ways when they cleared the harbor. The one on which Jack was a passenger planned to coast southwards until it rounded Cape Comorin at the tip of Hindoostan. Then it would turn north and sally through one of the gaps in Adam's Bridge—the chain of reefs and isles that stretched between the mainland and the Island of Serendib. From there it would be a short voyage to Dalicot, where the Cabal's ship was being built. Their eventual purpose was to raid shipping around the Dutch settlements of Tegnapatam and Negapatam, and the English ones at Tranquebar and Fort St. David, but they said they would be happy to deposit Jack on the shores of his *jagir*, which was not too far north of those places. Enoch Root, meanwhile, took passage on a northbound ship, intending to make a rendezvous in Surat with a Danish merchantman that was ballasted with cannons, and that wanted to unload them to make space for saltpeter and cloth.

THREE MONTHS LATER JACK WAS a King no longer: merely a Vagabond sailor infringing on the hospitality of the Malabar pirate-queen. He and van Hoek, Jan Vroom, Surendranath, Padraig Tallow, and various Dutchmen sailed into Queen Kottakkal's harbor aboard something that was close to being a ship. Her hull was painted and ballasted, her decks were in place, and a temporary foremast had been jury-rigged, giving her the ability to crawl through the water before a following wind. Her gunports were caulked shut. She was unarmed and helpless, but four of the Queen's pirate-ships had escorted, and occasionally towed, her around Cape Comorin. She had not been christened yet—it had been decided to save that ceremony for when the masts were stepped, the guns installed, and all members of the Cabal on hand.

The cannons had preceded them, and were stacked on logs just above the tide-line. Jack, ever disposed to view things from a wretch's standpoint, grasped right away that the movement of these objects from the hold of the Danish ship to their current position, concealed just within the first rank of palm trees, embodied a lavish expenditure of human toil—perhaps not so much as the Pyramids but still enough to give him pause.

For his part van Hoek, once he had sloshed ashore, stomped past the cannons without breaking stride, and did not even pause to light his pipe until he had encountered his three masts lying side-by-side in the middle of the town, out back of the Temple of Kali. He walked up and down the length of each one, stooping to inspect how they had been blocked up off the ground. He stood at their narrow ends and peered down them to check for undue curvature, and ambled up and down pounding on them with a pistol-butt and listening to the wood's reverberations with a hand cupped to his ear. He frowned at cracks, as if he could weld these imperfections shut with his furious gaze, and rested his hand contemplatively on places that had been scarred by the sawing friction of hawsers, collisions with spars, and impacts of pistol-balls. At first van Hoek seemed in the grip of something that approached panic, such was his anxiety that the masts would be found wanting. Gradually this eased into the quotidian fretting and continual state of low-level annoyance that Jack knew to be the perpetual lot of all competent sea-captains.

Then the Dutchman stopped for a while to gaze at the butt of the mainmast. Nowhere was it more obvious than from this standpoint that what they were really looking at, here, was a stupendous tree-trunk, most likely from a virgin forest in America. In other places its nature was somewhat concealed by the carpenters' work, and by bands of iron that had been hammered out in some enormous forge somewhere and, while still red-hot, slipped onto it like rings onto a finger so that as they cooled and shrank they would cut into the wood and become one with it. But here at the foot of the main-mast—which was almost as thick as van Hoek was tall—the tree's growth rings, and the boundary between heartwood and sapwood, were obvious even through diverse layers of tar, caulk, and paint. Van Hoek had gazed upon it twice as he circled round the mast, and seen nothing untoward, But on this third circuit he came in closer and began to hammer at the wood with the pistol-butt. Jack heard a solid *thunk, thunk* and then a sharp *whack;* a moment's silence; and then a cry from the Dutchman.

"What's amiss? Smash your finger?" Jack inquired. Meanwhile Jan Vroom came loping out of the trees, looking a bit peaked, asking in Dutch if van Hoek had discovered rot in the mast's heart.

Van Hoek was gazing incredulously at a flake of yellow metal embedded in the foot of the mainmast.

Now it was a longstanding tradition that whenever mariners stepped a mast they slipped a coin beneath it. Supposedly this was to placate sea-gods, or buy them passage to the afterlife when the ship went down to David Jones's Locker and took them with it. Normally such a coin became embedded in the bottom of the mast and could be viewed the next time it was pulled out. Masts that had been stepped several times had as many coins stuck to their bottoms. This particular mast had three of them, but they had been painted over, and so were visible only as blurred scabs. Van Hoek had just knocked a disk of paint clean off one of them with a blow of his pistol-butt. It was a French louis d'or. And that was how it came about that Jack Shaftoe, Otto van Hoek, Jan Vroom, and an ever-growing crowd of curious Nayar children found themselves staring into the face of King Louis XIV of France, stamped in fine gold, out behind the Temple of Kali in Malabar.

"Really the coiner was a flattering knave," Jack said. "In person he is not half so handsome as all that."

Van Hoek let go his pistol, yanked a dagger from his belt, and assaulted the mast. Jack guessed he was trying to get the point of the weapon beneath the coin and worry it loose; but the way he was flail-ing and jabbering he was unlikely to succeed. Anyway Vroom, who was two heads taller, grabbed van Hoek's arm on the backswing and stopped it. *"It is bad luck! Leave the coin be!"* Jack understood that much Dutch, anyway. He did not understand what van Hoek said in return—some sort of advanced calculus of luck, he gathered, in which the sacrilege of removing the coin was weighed against the ill omen of having a golden effigy of Leroy eternally planted in the heart of the ship.

Jack looked carefully left, right, and behind, in case cobras or crocodiles were creeping up on them, which in these parts was a routine precaution to take before fastening one's attention on any particular thing for more than a few moments. Then he stepped round this dangerous pair of struggling Dutchmen, drew out his own pistol, and struck one of the other coins. Paint fell away to reveal William of Orange on an English guinea. A blow to the last remaining coin produced King Carlos II on a Spanish doubloon.

"For God's sake, hasn't he died yet!?" Jack exclaimed. "Twenty years ago people were expecting him to drown in his own spit at the next moment."

Van Hoek calmed down and Vroom relaxed, but did not let go of his arms.

"As I read the signs, the Spanish made this mast in America for a treasure-galleon. English privateers then took it as a prize, or perhaps salvaged its wreck after some hurricanoe. Later those poor Englishmen ran afoul of the French Navy—courtesy of my old friend the duc d'Arcachon." Jack pointed with his pistol-barrel to each of the coins in turn as he made this all up. "That French ship later came east, escorting some merchant-vessels of the *Compagnie des Indes,* where God only knows what befell it. At any rate, the Wheel has now turned again—you may consult our new Pilot, Father Gabriel Goto, for more concerning the Wheel—and the mast is now ours. So let's put a fucking rupee underneath it and be on our way, shall we?"

"Still I do not like it," said van Hoek, and fired a broadside of spit at the golden Louis. He aimed high, but the tobacco-brown loogie rolled down over the coin like a cloud of battle-smoke darkening the face of the sun.

First they brought the cannons aboard, which was unspeakably tedious and toilsome, but gave them something to pass the time while Monsieur Arlanc, Vrej Esphahnian, and Moseh de la Cruz journeyed back and forth to and from the *wootz*-forge. Refining the terms of the deal was no less exacting than making watered steel from river-sand. Transporting gold north and *wootz*-eggs south across frequently hostile territory was no easier, and would have been impossible without pervasive bribery, and an escort of mounted Nayars; Jimmy and Danny came home with wild yarns of sword- and gun-play in jungle and mountain.

But the day came when the ship had been sufficiently ballasted, with cannons, cannonballs, *wootz*-eggs, and other heavy objects, that the masts could be stepped without risk of capsizing her. It was agreed that this would be as good a day as any to christen her. So Jack made ready a bottle of fizzing wine from the province of Champagne that he had acquired at staggering expense from a French factor in Surat. The Cabal assembled upon the shore of the river, where the three masts had been lashed together along with some lighter, more buoyant logs and made into a sort of raft. The river's current strove to push them out to sea, and this raft tugged at a line that had been tied around a tree-trunk a few yards upstream. A couple of juvenile crocodiles, no more than two yards long, had clambered up onto the mast-raft to warm themselves in the morning sun. Standing on the quay above said reptiles, Jack could gaze downstream to a flower-bedecked boat; a few hundred yards of mangrove-lined river; and finally out into the harbor where the mastless ship was riding at anchor with all of her cannons run out of her gunports in preparation to fire a salute.

The other members of the Cabal, dressed in the finest clothes they had, were already aboard the Queen's boat. Jack wasn't, because Queen Kottakkal had instructed him that "according to our traditions" he, Jack, was supposed to board last—after the Queen. And the Queen was still on the bank, talking to various Nayars who belonged to her court of pirate-captains and cavaliers. From time to time one of these Malabaris would glance interestedly at Jack. The Queen herself shot him an occasional glare. She had liked Jack's looks as much as he'd liked hers when he had made his first state visit to Malabar almost three years ago, and after a day or two of steamy flirtation Jack had leaned his Janissary-sword against the door-post of her apartments. He had been making the (in retrospect rash) assumption that the Queen would know why he was called Half-Cocked Jack, but that she would be familiar with certain Books of India—that Her Majesty would, in other words, know certain lore that would make Jack's shortcomings irrelevant.

As it had turned out—to make a long story (a story Jack wished every day he could forget) short—the tryst had gone more badly than Jack could ever have imagined. It turned out that Jack did not know the half of it where Books of India were concerned. That there existed certain advanced Books, unknown to, or at least unmentioned by, Eliza. That these Books enumerated diverse additional Sexes above and beyond the usual Male and Female, including a plethora of different categories of hermaphrodites. That each of these was not merely a Sex but a Caste unto itself, subject to diverse limits and regulations like any other caste. That, depending upon how certain ancient writings were translated into Malabari, Jack belonged to one or another of these hermaphroditic castes, and that consequently he ought to have gone about dressed in a certain type of clothing so that all and sundry would know what he was, and treat him well or poorly depending on whether they were of a lower or higher caste. That Queen Kottakkal was of a higher caste whose members were (to put it very mildly) not in the general habit of entertaining hermaphrodites in their bedchambers.

At any rate Anglo-Malabari relations had been set back centuries. Jack had barely escaped with his life. Moseh and other Cabal members who were the Queen's slaves had spent the better part of a year apologizing. Since then, Jack had had difficulty meeting the Queen's eye, and she had not spoken more than a few words to him—he had become a sort of out-caste, a sexual and social Cheruman.

Jack was reflecting upon these very topics, and watching a third, somewhat larger crocodile struggle up onto the mizzen-mast, when he realized with a bit of a shock that the Queen was speaking to him (albeit through Dappa), and in complete sentences, no less. She had boarded her boat now and was standing in the bow, facing upstream towards Jack. The rest of the Cabal, in their breeches, periwigs, robes, and kimonos, were seated behind her, listening with obvious curiosity.

"The gold is mine, Vagabond, not yours—dared you think otherwise?" said Dappa, translating for the Queen. Then, as an aside, he added, "She used a much more degrading term than 'Vagabond,' but . . ."

"You're trying to spare my feelings—I understand. Tell the Queen that she stole it from us fair and square, just as we did from the Viceroy, and I've never imagined else-wise. Dappa, do you think she is on the rag or something?"

The Queen responded, "Then why do you try to deceive me by sailing away over the horizon on a great ship in which I have invested so much of what is mine?"

"Dappa, have you not acquainted Her Majesty with the basic principles of the ship-owning business? Do I have to explain shares? Do I have to remind her that most of the ship's crew is to be hand-picked Malabaris? That both of her sons will be aboard? What is going on in her mind?"

"Very likely she is on the rag as you said," Dappa responded, "and in a bit of a Mood because her boys are leaving the nest."

The Queen said something. At the same moment she reached up with both hands and carefully removed one of the metal ornaments from her neck: a single watered-steel ring, like a dinner plate with a large hole in the center. She gripped it in one hand and curled it in towards her belly while turning sideways to Jack. Then suddenly her hand sprang outwards. The ring hissed through the air, narrowly missing Jack, and buried itself, shockingly deep, in the trunk of a tree.

"Stop talking to each other, and talk to me," she said. Another ring came off her neck, and every man within a hundred yards cringed. She flung this one at a closer target: the line mooring her boat to the quay. It sang through the rope as easily as flying through a shaft of sunlight and vanished into the water with a sizzle. The boat began to drift downstream. Jack caught movement in the corner of his eye and turned back to look at the masts: they too had gone into ponderous movement, and were adrift in the river now—Queen Kot-takkal's first throw had cut their line.

A third ring spun out and embedded itself in the mainmast next to a coil of rope with a throwing-lead tied to its end. "Mark that rope," said the Queen. "If you throw it to one of your friends on my boat, here, your masts are saved. If not, they drift out to sea, and all of you are my slaves to the end of your days."

"Are you certain you translated that aright?" Jack inquired.

"I translated it *perfectly*," said Dappa, gazing nervously at the departing masts.

"Have I gotten her general drift—that she wants me to swim through crocodile-infested waters to retrieve the masts?"

"The judicial machinery here is not well-developed," Dappa announced. "There is only one sort of trial: and that is Trial by Ordeal."

"I'm being put on *trial* here? For what offense?"

"For offenses you *might* commit in the future—which is to say that your honesty is being tried. Sometimes this might mean walking across fire. Other times, the defendant must swim through crocodiles. It is said to be an astonishing thing to watch—which may account for the custom's perpetuation. I can supply all manner of lurid detail later, after you have survived—"

"*If* I survive, you mean!"

"But for now, would you please *do something*!?"

As the Queen had begun flinging her lethal jewelry about, half a dozen Nayars had vaulted aboard the boat and trained loaded blunderbusses upon the other members of the Cabal. They could do nothing but sit tidily on their benches, like churchgoers, and watch Jack. Looking at them Jack was struck—and not for the first time, either—by the fact that, ever since Cairo, all of them had tended to look to Jack to take action. In other lives or other circumstances they might've been doers of deeds and leaders of men. But put 'em all together, pose 'em a problem, and they'd all turn their eyes Jack's way to see what he was going to do.

Which (come to think of it) had probably been noticed by Queen Kottakkal—so wise in the ways of men crowded together on armed Vessels, so backwards in her approach to judicial proceedings—and probably accounted for that it was Jack, and not van Hoek, or Moseh, who had been chosen to undergo the Trial by Ordeal.

The others followed his lead because of what he had done in Cairo. And Jack had done that deed because the Imp of the Perverse had somehow tracked him down in the Khan el-Khalili and convinced him that, rather than let the Duke live, and accept the perfectly reasonable deal that he was holding out, it would be better to slay him, and bring down consequences on himself and the others.

Everything that had happened since had been born in that moment. All of this Jack understood well enough. His only difficulty, just now, was that the said Imp had not followed him out as far as Malabar—or if it had, it had been waylaid by pirates and was now chained up in some dusty 'stan and being put to work (one could only suppose) getting rag-heads to do rash and imprudent things. At any rate the Imp was absent. And Jack—who at earlier times of his life would have dived without hesitation into the river—was strangely fixed to the spot, as if he were an old banyan-tree that had sunk a million roots into the earth. There were so many things to be said in favor of *not* attempting to swim through crocodiles that he simply could not move.

His comrades sat meekly in the Queen's boat, staring at him. Jack loved certain of those men as well as he'd ever loved anyone, not counting Eliza. But various experiences of war, mutilation, slavery, and Vagabonding had made him into a hard man. He knew perfectly well that any galley chosen at random from the Mediterranean would contain a complement of slaves every bit as deserving of freedom as van Hoek, Moseh, and the others, and that none of them would ever be free. So why swim through crocodile-infested waters for these?

His sons were on the boat. Jimmy and Danny were not even looking at him. They were affecting boredom, convinced he would fail them, as always.

Enoch was on the boat, too. One day, Enoch would escape from Malabar. It might take a hundred years, but Enoch would escape and return to Christendom and spread the tale of how Jack Shaftoe had lost his nerve in the end and consequently spent his last years as a hermaphrodite butt-slave in a heathen pagoda.

Jack noticed, as if from a distance, that he was sprinting down the river-bank.

The masts had a bit of a head start. Jack's path was eventually barred by mangroves, which formed a sort of living breakwater at the edge of the village. But there was a way through it, a path that people took over exposed roots and through brackish sumps, to get to the edge of the river where they would collect fish with nets or spears. Jack detoured through a cane house, snatching a couple of chickens as he ran across the yard. Too, a piece of bamboo caught his eye. It was rumored that you could wedge a crocodile's jaws open with such a thing and so he grabbed this and tucked it under his arm.

Then—moving as fast as a man could over wet slick tree-roots with one chicken-neck clenched in each fist—he picked his way out to the river-bank just in time to see the masts gliding by. They had reached a place where the river widened and slowed, and dropped silt on its bottom to form a submerged bar. Jack was praying that the masts would get hung up on this. But of course Queen Kottakkal's minions had put floats around the masts to make them ride high in the water and prevent it from happening.

The masts were ten yards away, moving at a fast walking pace. The intervening water was murky and still, broken only by nostrils and eyeballs, some of which were disconcertingly far apart. Jack estimated the number of animals at somewhere between eight and a dozen. They had observed him, and were beginning to cruise in his direction.

This was more or less how the Queen had planned it. In a few moments the masts would clear the bar and take to the harbor waters, which were much deeper and choppier. Jack could not swim in those waters; to stop those masts he had to make his move *here* in the shallows, and *here* was where all of the crocodiles lurked.

As an experiment Jack flung one of the chickens out. It did not fall nor fly, but wandered through the air for a while, then snagged a wing-tip in the water and plowed to a stop. Its head came up once to squawk. Then the surface was broken by an upper jaw about the size of a tavern bench. Jack only glimpsed it. The chicken vanished like a candle-flame thrust into water.

Like Frenchmen, crocodiles were what they were, and did what they did, and saw no point in making pretenses or apologies, and therefore possessed a sort of aplomb that Jack found admirable in a way. He wished only that God would send him some more mammalian enemies. Though, come to think of it, nothing was more evident than that Queen Kottakkal was a mammal—unless it was that she was his enemy, too. So perhaps it was a distinction without a difference.

The only plan Jack could conceive of was to throw the other

chicken in another direction and divert the crocodiles' attention long enough to make a dash for it. And this required shifting his burdens from hand to hand—the second chicken went to his right, the bamboo pole to his left. This was when he first became aware that the pole in question had a barbed metal head on one end. It was a fishing spear. A rope was trailing from the other end—Jack had been dragging it behind him, without knowing he was doing it, during his run through the swamp. Now he gave it a hard jerk. The knot at its far end (intended to keep the rope from slipping out of a fisherman's hand) bounced off a mangrove-root and came flying towards him. Jack dropped the spear and snatched the knot out of the air. Ten seconds later it was noosed round the neck of the second chicken. He now tossed the chicken into a momentarily crocodile-free zone about halfway between him and the masts. The crocodiles naturally converged on that place, their warty backs lifting the surface of the water without breaking through. Jack took advantage of this to jump down into the water, wade forward several steps (it came up to mid-thigh), and fling the spear in a high arc over the masts. It landed flat in the water on the far side of them. Or Jack guessed as much from the sounds made—he could not linger to watch its trajectory, because two crocodiles were already climbing over each other to reach him. Jack scampered back up onto mangroves and drew his sword before turning around.

The second chicken had long since been swallowed, without any tedious chewing, by a big croc. The rope was still attached—it ran up the crocodile's gullet, out of its mouth, and several yards across the water, over the mast-raft to the floating spear. As the masts moved downstream, the spear was dragged backwards across them, and inevitably the barbs in the spear-head snagged in some of the ropes binding the raft together. As to what happened inside of the crocodile's gut when the rope went taut and tried to pull the chicken out, Jack could only speculate—and as to what was going on in the mind of the *chicken* (which might be in some sense still alive), that was a matter for metaphysicians. The outward result was that the masts stopped moving and the crocodile became highly annoyed. Jack supposed that a very big and old crocodile must take a certain pride in his work, viz. swallowing and digesting whatever came along, and that an attempt to revoke a meal by yanking it out must be viewed, by such a Reptile, as a very serious affront. In any event it led to an amount of thrashing. And that led to a bit of good fortune Jack had not really looked for: All of the other crocodiles seemed to hear or feel this commotion and made it their business to get there as fast as they could—which was disturbingly fast.

Jack, anyway, was not slow to take advantage of this, the only opportunity he was likely to get. He waded halfway to the masts and faltered when he felt the river-bottom falling out from under his feet, and the current trying to sweep his legs. His boots and weapons would make swimming impossible. He kicked off a boot, and was about to abandon it when something prompted him to turn around. Nostrils were headed his way. He flung the boot towards them and it vanished as quickly as the chickens had. A few moments later, the second boot joined it. Now Jack pulled off the belt that supported his sword and scabbard. The belt he flung at the crocodile; it paused for one heartbeat to consume it. The sword he flung at the mast-raft; it had the good grace to stick there. The scabbard he made as if to throw at the crocodile. Watching him through bulging slit-pupil eyes, it opened its mouth to catch it; but Jack held on to this morsel, turned it vertical, and shoved it between the crocodile's jaws.

Now this turned out to be nothing more than a brief annoyance to the animal, and not the show-stopper Jack had been hoping for; but as Jack had demonstrated in diverse settings, sometimes it sufficed to be annoying. It took a few moments for this crocodile to shake the scabbard loose, and in that time Jack divested himself of his clothes. While another crocodile was swallowing those, naked Jack was swimming to the masts. While the two crocodiles were fighting over precedence, Jack was climbing onto the masts and retrieving his sword. A smaller crocodile came towards him with shocking speed, as if it were being towed on a rope behind a fleet ship, and made it halfway up onto the fore-mast on sheer momentum. Jack nearly took its head off and it fell into the water and became food for other crocodiles. Another stroke of the Janissary-blade severed the rope of the chicken and set the masts adrift again. The raft slowly began to move, and soon eased over the bar and into the harbor, spinning slowly in some vast unseen vortex.

The Queen's boat was waiting there, and with a couple of throws Jack was able to get the line over to his comrades, who proceeded to reel him and the masts in like a fish.

Jack sensed that he was already badly sunburnt; yet the equatorial sun was a soothing balm compared to the glare of Queen Kottakkal.

"I perceive the wisdom of your tradition, O Queen," Jack said as his mast-raft was brought alongside the royal barge, "for not one man in a thousand could survive the trial you set for me there. And as near as I can make out, one in a thousand is the normal proportion of honest men in any group . . ."

But here Jack's oration was rudely interrupted by screams from nearly every man on the boat. He turned around to see a giant croc-odile, twenty feet long if it was an inch. It was not so much *climbing onto* the masts as *thrusting them below* the surface of the water with its weight, and then gliding up over the submerged wood. This meant that it was advancing toward him. But then suddenly it was raining Shaftoes as Jimmy and Danny vaulted down between Jack and the reptile, each gripping a boat-paddle, and began waving these in the animal's face. It proceeded to chew its way up the wood as if the oars were breadsticks, and was well on its way to having Jimmy and Danny Shaftoe for lunch, and Jack for dessert, when the Nayars up on the boat opened fire with their blunderbusses.

A moment later the Malabar skies were split open by a long rip-pling train of explosions. Jack looked across the water to see the new ship obscured in a bank of gray smoke, and light jabbing out of it in all directions: The eager crew had misunderstood, and were firing a full salute to their approaching Queen and their ship's officers. Jack felt the masts bob upwards under his feet, and glanced over to see quite a bit of blood where the crocodile had been.

The guns of Queen Kottakkal's castle were firing a salute of their own now, and the Queen was ascending to the top of her barge to accept all of these honors. She had been overtaken by events, which happened to all monarchs; but like a good monarch she knew when to accept the strange verdicts handed down by Fortune and by croc-odiles.

JACK, IN A BORROWED Nayar loincloth, raised the Champagne-bottle over his head and drew a bead on the ship's bowsprit. "In the name of whatever passes for sacred in this hell-hole, I christen thee *Eli—*"

Halfway to its target, the bottle slapped into the suddenly out-thrust palm of Enoch Root.

"Don't name it after her," he said.

"Why not? That has *always* been my plan."

"Do you really think it will go unnoticed? The lady is in a delicate position . . . even the figurehead bears a dangerously close resem-blance to her."

"D'you really suppose it'll *matter*?"

"This ship is not destined to remain in Malabar forever. One day she will find her way back to some Christian port—and there are very few Christian ports *left* where Eliza is not, in some sense, embroiled."

"Well, what the hell should we name it, then? *Electress Sophie? Queen Kottakkal?*"

"Sometimes it is better to be indirect . . . then each and every one of those Ladies can *suppose* that the ship is *really* named after her."

"Not a bad idea, Enoch . . . but what does each of those three Ladies have in common?"

"Wisdom. Wisdom, and a kind of strength—a willingness to put her wisdom into effect."

"Say no more," Jack said, "I have seen the very Lady in plays." Then, turning his attention back to the ship: "I christen thee *Minerva.*" A moment later French wine was fizzing on his sunburnt flesh, and the cannons were firing all round. Dappa was translating all to Queen Kottakkal, who looked Jack in the eye and smiled.

BOOK 5

the Juncto

The Thames
FEBRUARY 1696

"A GREAT HEAP OF CORD-WOOD and kindling, saturated with oil, was found on the brink of the cliff at Dover," asserted Roger Comstock, Marquis of Ravenscar and Chancellor of the Exchequer, "ready to speed the news of his majesty's assassination across the Channel." Seated in the (more desirable) forward-facing bench of the boat, he held his head high, and gazed down the Thames as if combing the skies above the Nore for encrypted smoke-signals.

"It speaks well of the Jacobites that they have at last got their signals worked out," was all Daniel had to say. "They have used up half of France's wine and firewood celebrating *false* reports of William's demise."

Roger sighed. "You are as ever a fount of treasonous raillery. It is well that we meet on a water-taxi, where the only one who can overhear us, does not speak a word of English." This a playful dig at the Cockney manning the oar. If Daniel had made the same jest, he'd have been pitched overboard, and the waterman would have been acquitted, at the Old Bailey, on grounds of All Too Understandable Righteous Fury. Somehow Roger said it with the wink that was as good as a one-pound tip.

"When we parley in a coffee-house," Roger went on, "I flinch whenever you get that look on your face, and part your lips."

"Soon I shall follow that other Seditious Libeller, Gomer Bolstrood, across the sea, and your flinching days shall be at an end." Daniel, seated in the backward-facing seat, gazed wistfully toward Massachusetts.

"Yes, so you have been claiming, for the last ten years or so—"

"Closer seven. But to play fast and loose with *quantities numerical* is, of course, a perquisite—some would say, a necessity—of your office." Daniel rotated his head a few degrees to the left and nodded in the direction of Westminster Palace, still and for the next few seconds visible around the elbow of Lambeth. This was a reference to the Exchequer, an avalanche of ill-considered additions to the river-ward side of the same Palace. It was there that Daniel had gone to meet Roger, and thence that they'd departed on this boat a few minutes ago.

Roger turned around, following Daniel's gaze, but too late.

"I was looking at your Place of Business," Daniel said. "It seems to have disappeared behind all of those immense stacks of rotting timbers that have accumulated there in recent years, along the Lambeth river-bend, in consequence of that no one can buy anything because there is no money."

Roger blinked very slowly, once, which was a way of letting Daniel know that the jab had quite wounded him, but that the victim was in a forgiving mood.

"I should be ever so much obliged," Roger said, "if you would *attend* to the very important news I am projecting in the general direction of your bloody ears. Forty men—gentlemen and titled nobility of England, for the most part—gathered yesterday on Turnham Green to fall upon the King of England, on his way back from hunting, and murder him."

"Say, speaking of bloody ears—"

"Yes! He was among them."

People hated listening to Daniel and Roger converse, for they'd known each other much longer than was decent, proper, or good for them, and so were able to communicate in a stunted zargon of private allusions. *Bloody ears* was here a reference to Charles White, the Jacobite Tory who had made a habit of biting Whigs' ears off, and (or so 'twas rumored) later displaying them, in private, to like-minded friends, as trophies.

"In Calais, in Dunkirk," Roger continued, "you'll see ships crammed with French troops, waiting only for that signal-fire to blaze up before they set sail."

"I see that you are furious. I understand why. If I am *not*, it is only because this is all so bloody repetitive that I can scarcely believe I am hearing it! Did we not go through this already?"

"What an odd reaction."

"Is it? I could say the same about the bloody *money*. When are we to have money, Roger?"

"*Some*, Daniel, would say that the regrettable phænomena to which you allude were *consistent*, or *persistent*, or *constant* menaces to our liberties as Englishmen, and thus naturally to be confronted and subdued with manly vigor. For you to roll your eyes in this way, and deride them as merely *repetitious*—as if you were watching a *play*—is very strange."

"That is why I am getting ready to excuse myself, and go out to the lobby for air."

"The lobby is some labored metaphor, here, for Massachusetts Bay Colony?"

"Yes."

"What makes you suppose Massachusetts will seem any less repetitious? The news that I get from there is just one bloody Indian-raid, and Mather-tirade, after another."

"I shall be able to pursue work there, of an altogether novel character."

"Yes—so you keep telling the Fellows of the Royal Society—all two dozen of us."

"The correct figure is nearer *eight* dozen. But I take your meaning. We *have* dwindled. It is all because of Want of Novelty. I mean to fix that."

"Here is novelty for you: When you come in sight of the French naval base at Dunkirk—"

"That is the *second* time you have spoken to me as if I were about to go on a voyage to France. What is troubling your mind, to inspire such phant'sies?"

"Troubled mind or no, I am, am I not, the sole benefactor and Chairman of the Court of Directors of the Massachusetts Bay Colony Institute of Technologickal Arts?"

"Sir, I am not aware that the said Institute has even been Instituted yet. But if it *had*, you'd be the Prime Suspect."

"Is that a yes?"

"Yes."

"It follows that I am entitled to some say in how the sole employee goes about his work—do you not agree?"

"*Employees* get *paid*. They get paid *money*. Of which there *is* none."

"You are really the most exasperating chap. How have you spent the past fortnight?"

"You know perfectly well I've been up at Cambridge helping Isaac clean out his lodgings."

Roger affected astonishment. "I say, that wouldn't by any chance be Isaac Newton the savant—?—! Why ever is he leaving Cambridge?"

"Coming down here—*finally*—to run the Mint," Daniel allowed (this had been in the works for years; the Realm's political complications, and Isaac's mental disorders, had made it slow).

"They say he is the most brilliant fellow who ever lived."

"He would give that distinction to Solomon; but I am with you, sir."

"My goodness, do you suppose he'll be up to the task of stamping out a few bits of metal?"

"If he is not fettered by *Politicks*."

"Daniel, you offend me. What you have just said amounts to a suggestion that the Juncto is politically incompetent. May I remind you that Recoinage has been approved—by Commons as well as Lords? So we shall only have to put up with this rubbish for a little while longer." The Chancellor of the Exchequer reached into his shoe and pulled out a wad of Bank of England paper money he'd stuffed into it to keep his feet warm, and waggled it in the chilly air for emphasis. Then—disgusted by the sight of it—he chucked it over his shoulder into the Thames. Neither he nor the waterman looked back.

"That was a foolish and profligate waste," Daniel said. "We could've burned it to keep warm."

"Tally-sticks make more heat, guv'nor," volunteered the waterman, "and they are circulating at a discount of forty percent."

"Isaac will be sworn in at the Mint at the beginning of May," said Roger. "It is now February. How shall we occupy ourselves between now and then? Your intention is to carry forward that Comenius-Wilkins–Leibniz Pansophic Arithmetickal Engine–Logick Mill–Algebra of Ratiocination–Automatic Computation–Repository of all Knowledge project, is it not?"

"We need a better name for it," Daniel conceded, "but you know perfectly well the answer is yes."

"Then you really had ought to go have a chat with Leibniz first, or do you disagree?"

"Of course I don't disagree," said Daniel, "but even if money existed in this Realm, I should not *possess* any, and so I had not really considered it."

"I found some old *louis d'or*, pre-debasement, in a sock," Roger confided to him, "and should be pleased to advance them to you, while we wait for Isaac to stoke up the Mint."

"What on earth would I do with French coins?"

"Buy things with them," said Roger, "in France."

"We are at war with France!"

"It has been a very slow war of late—one battle of consequence in the last two years."

"Still—why should I go there?"

"It happens to be on the way to Germany, which is where Leibniz was, the last time anyone bothered to check."

"It would be more prudent to *avoid* France."

"But ever so much more convenient to go there direct—for that is where your *jacht* happens to be bound."

"I have a *jacht* now, too?"

"Behold!" proclaimed the Marquis of Ravenscar. Daniel was

obliged to swivel his head around and gaze downstream. They had, by this time, drifted past the Steelyard and were converging on the Old Swan Stairs, just above London Bridge. On the yonder side of the Bridge spread the Pool, which contained above a thousand ships.

"I haven't the faintest idea what it is you want me to behold," Daniel complained. "The Fishmongers?" For that was the closest thing along the azimuth that Roger was now forcibly indicating with bladelike thrusts of the hand.

"Oh, bloody hell," said Roger, "she is at Tower Wharf, you cannot see her from here, let us go and pay her a visit." And he alighted from the boat and stomped away up Old Swan Stairs without giving any money to, or even glancing back at, the waterman; who, however, seemed perfectly content. Roger must have an Understanding with him, as he seemed to with all London, a few Jacobites excepted.

FROM THE OLD SWAN, where they bated to warm themselves with pints, they could have walked half a mile along Thames Street and then applied themselves to the lengthy and complicated work of burrowing through the Tower's gates, bastions, causeways, and the micro-neighborhoods that had grown up around, and occluded, the same, as vegetation on infected heart-valves. But Roger was of a mind to see a thing on the river side, and so they walked only far enough to get round the end of the Bridge, then descended the terraced rectilinear cove of Lion Stairs, below the barnlike mass of the Church of St. Magnus Martyr, which Wren had rebuilt, but not got round to putting a tower or a steeple on yet. Another waterman consented to take them downriver from there. Swinging wide round the riotous congestion of Billingsgate and the broad Key before the Customs House, they pounced upon Tower Wharf. For the most part this presented itself to them as a quarter-mile-long wall jumping straight out of the river. But it was adorned here and there with cranes, guns, a wee crenellated castle, and other curios. Two stairs and one arched tunnel were cut into it, and the waterman kept guessing Roger would go to one of those; but the Marquis of Ravenscar kept exhorting him on, on to the downstream end, where two brigs and a ship had been made fast to the wharf. Daniel instinctively looked at the smaller and meaner vessels, until he recollected that he was in the company of Roger; then he had eyes only for what was high and gaudy. They were looking up at the bows of the three-master. Its figurehead was extraordinary. Not only because it was covered in many square yards of gold leaf—that was common enough—but because of its sculpture. It was a face carved into the front of a bulbous golden sphere that seemed to be hurtling forth with utmost impetuosity, drawing behind it a vast swirling wake of golden, silver, and copper flames. It was, Daniel realized, an anthropomorphic phant'sy of a Comet or a great fiery—

"Meteor!" Roger announced. "Or *Météore,* as her former owner, Monsieur le duc d'Arcachon, would have it." Then, to the waterman, "Take us up and down the length of her, and then, when Dr. Waterhouse has finished his inspection, we shall board her by yonder ladder. Daniel, I do hope you are in the mood for some ladder-climbing."

"I'd climb a *rope* to see this," Daniel returned.

"Mmm . . . any *sane* man, given a choice between scaling a rope, and going to France on a Duke's *jacht,* would choose the *latter* . . . so I shall take your remark as a commitment to be in Dunkirk in three days' time," said Roger.

EARLIER IN HIS LIFE DANIEL would have counted the guns of *Météore,* but as it was he had eyes mostly for the woodcarving and the decoration. The shipwrights had made it appear that *Météore* was draped and festooned from stem to stern with garlands of golden laurel. Victory spread her wings across the breadth of the sterncastle, and drew all those wreaths and festoons together in one hand like so many reins, while brandishing a sword in the other. Above the spreading wings was a row of windows. "Your cabin," Roger explained, "where refreshment awaits us."

They dined there on a roast quail prepared in *Météore*'s galley, "which had to be gutted and re-built," Roger said, "to remove the taint; for the late Duke had tastes abominable even to the French." The azure tablecloth was embroidered with gold fleurs-de-lis; Daniel suspected it might have been a flag once.

"Is this ship *yours* now, then, Roger?"

"Please do not be vulgar by speaking of *ownership,* Daniel; as everyone knows, she was taken as a prize from Cherbourg the *last* time the Frogs got ready to invade us, and became a trifle for the King to dispose of as he wished; he had thoughts of bestowing her upon his Queen, and so had her repaired—"

"What, the Queen?"

"The *ship.* But when smallpox took her from this world—the Queen, that is, not the ship—*Météore* became a useless bauble, scarcely worth the upkeep—"

"You got this ship *for free*!?"

"Damn all Puritans and their base obsession with how much it costs!" Roger bellowed, shaking a tiny drumstick at Daniel's brow as if it were the club of Hercules. "What *matters* is that the sentimental value of *Météore* to the de Lavardac family is very great. And who should be in Dunkirk just now but Eliza de Lavardac." Roger lost focus for some moments. "I hope it is not all true, what people say about her and the pox."

Daniel had seen the only woman he'd ever loved chewed up and vomited out by smallpox, and urgently desired a change of subject. "I begin to understand. The Whigs are seen as the party of the Bank, and of War. The Bank is said to be foundering and the War has ground to a halt."

"Mind you," put in Roger with one more admonitory shake of the drumstick, "the Bank shall succeed immensely, and we shall prevail over the French, all in good time; but it would help us if we could avoid losing the next election to Harley and Bolingbroke and his lot." Meaning the Tories.

"And so you would make some peace-offering to the French. Eliza is seen as a sort of bridge between France and England. You would please her and her husband by returning *Météore*. And you would like me to go along—?"

"Somewhat as you went to the Hague in the days before the Revolution," said Roger, "as the least likely imaginable diplomat."

"The more often I am sent on such missions the more likely I must seem," said Daniel, "but I shall go and deliver this boat to Eliza if that is what you want. From there it is on to Hanover."

"It is extraordinary you should mention Hanover," said Roger. "I have a message, too sensitive to commit to paper, that I should like you to deliver to our next Queen."

"Are you referring to Sophie of Hanover? You confuse me, for our next Queen is named Anne, and lives in England."

"Syphilitic like her sister and her dad," Roger mumbled, as if Princess Anne were only the most fleeting of distractions, "unlikely to have viable children—whereas Sophie was an unstoppable baby-maker in her day. Mark my words, if we can only suffer through to the end of these poxy, Popish Stuarts, we'll see Hanovers on the throne—and Hanovers are natural Whigs."

"How does that follow?"

"Hanovers are natural Whigs," Roger re-iterated. "Keep saying it to yourself, Daniel, an hundred times a day, until you believe it; and then say it to Sophie of Hanover as if you mean it."

"Well, do not look up, Roger, but I phant'sy that some natural Tories are spying on us from the Tower." Daniel cocked his head at a side-window of the cabin, which offered a prospect over the Wharf and the fortifications above and beyond it.

"*Really!?*"

"Oh yes indeed."

"The curtain-wall or—"

"Farther in, I should say. Do keep in mind that the Tower's a bit *crowded* with Tories today."

"I suppose it *would* be," said Roger. "Well done, Daniel! Perhaps you *do* have some future, after all, as a scheming political hack."

"You forget I used to make my living as one. Excuse me, Roger, but the gastro-colic reflex is having its way with me, and I must to the head."

"In truth or—"

"No, for I am stopped up in the bowels these three days; it is a diversionary ruse. Is there a prospective-glass to be found in this place?"

"Indeed, a lovely one, in that drawer—no, to the left—now down—and down again. There you have it."

"To perfect the illusion, I'll need something in lieu of a turd."

"Spotted Dick!" said Roger instantly, eyeing a brown log on a platter.

"I was thinking bangers," Daniel said, "but in English cuisine there are so many items of about the right size, shape, color and composition that it is easy to be overwhelmed by choices."

"In France, you'll find, there is greater variety in foods."

"So they keep saying." And Daniel, armed with a telescope in a hip-pocket and a length of Spotted Dick palmed in one hand, repaired to the head. In most ships this would have meant going all the way to the other end, and exposing his bum to London; but this being a ship of ducal luxury, there was, attached to this stateroom, a wee compartment, tacked on to the exterior of the hull proper, with a bench, with a hole, and three fathoms of open air between that and the water. Above the bench was a Barock window to admit light and vent fumes. Daniel made himself comfortable, cracked the window, and rested the prospective-glass on its sill, poking it out under the hem of the curtain.

Salt Tower, which anchored the southeastern corner of the fortifications that Henry III had, four hundred and some years ago, put up around what was now called the Inner Ward, looked to have been troweled together out of shivers and bits of other towers that had fallen down or been blown up. It was squarish in some places, roundish in others. Chimneys poked out here and there. In other parts were crenels or parapets. Diverse windows had been let into it whenever a whim to do so had taken the stonemasons. Or so it looked, at the end of half a millennium's improvements. Probably there was some inerrant logic behind the placement of every brick. Several kings named Edward had later surrounded all the Inner Ward stuff with a lower curtain-wall sporting its own museum of towers and bastions. It was over the guns and through the crenellations of the latter that Daniel now aimed his prospective-glass, and drew a focus on the flat top of Salt Tower above and beyond them. Salt was one of several of the old Inner Ward towers that were used as cells for prisoners of noble rank. It seemed to Daniel sometimes that half the people he knew had, at some point in their lives, been locked up in one or the other of these Towers—including Daniel himself. And so what might have seemed an incomprehensible Masonick salvage-yard to a common Newgate sort of prisoner, was as familiar to Daniel as a kitchen to a cook. He rapidly picked out, and drew focus on, two periwigged figures. They were standing on the very spot where, almost thirty years ago, Daniel had stood with the imprisoned Old-enburg and watched shipments of French gold come up the river under cover of night to buy England's foreign policy. Now all was reversed: These two men were peering down at *Météore*, which was on its way to France as part of an altogether different sort of Transaction. One of the men wore a wig of flaming red; this had to be Charles White, whose natural hair was the same color. His companion had a dark wig, a three-cornered hat, and a moustache, and was more difficult to make out. Both of them, presumably, had been rounded up following the betrayal, exposure, and failure of the assassination plot; but that only narrowed it down to a population of several thousand Tories who wanted King William dead badly enough to go and kill him. Conspicuous to Daniel was the dark-wigged man's curiosity about all that met his eye. To stare and point was rated bad manners, and not done by nobility, however these two chaps did nothing but. Charles White wanted chiefly to stare at *Météore*, and Daniel gave him something to notice by dropping three lengths of Spotted Dick down the hole. But his companion had eyes for London, and would not leave off staring, pointing, and tugging at White's sleeve to ask questions about this or that. He seemed particularly interested in the new developments of wharves and warehouses that had grown up along the banks of the river, spreading downstream towards Rotherhithe, in the last decades. Charles White was obliged to hold forth at some length, and to point out a few specifics. But once the dark-haired man had sated his curiosity, and gotten used to these novelties, he turned his attention towards older parts of London, and began to talk more and listen less. Charles White began to ask *him* questions. He began to relate anecdotes, with evocative hand-gestures and (Daniel supposed) expert wench-mimicry, planting limp wrists on his hip-bones, or cradling chin in curled fingers to deliver excellent punch-lines that evoked gusty laughter from both men—laughter with *recoil*, as both leaned back at the pelvis and exposed gleaming sweeps of teeth—like a pair of vipers rearing back to strike at each other. The dark man's teeth were recognizable even at this distance as having been made of the finest African elephant-ivory. Daniel, a free man, was intimidated by these prisoners, and stared at them raptly, like a hunter in a blind.

Dunkirk
MARCH 1696

IT WAS FAR FROM A warm day, especially with the wind coming in off the Channel; but the sky was perfectly cloudless, the waves of the sea had nothing to reflect except the saturated azure radiance of the sky, and in consequence this was one of those rare days when the ocean really was blue. That, and the glints of gold from wave-facets catching the direct light of the sun, seemed like a favorable omen for France.

Météore nearly had not been able to get in to the harbor at Dunkirk. It wasn't that she'd found a hostile reception. Midway across the Channel her crew had struck the Cross of St. George and run the fleur-de-lis up the mizzenmast, and the coastal batteries at Dunkirk had accepted this, or at least refrained from pulverizing them long enough for Daniel to explain himself, and send messages ashore. The difficulty had lain, rather, in finding room for one more ship in Dunkirk's harbor. (1) A modest invasion force had gathered there in the expectation that King William would be assassinated. This was nothing like the army that had massed near Cherbourg in '92, but it had been large enough that even now, a week after the plot had failed and the invasion had been cancelled, its remnants took up moorage-space. (2) Jean Bart, though he and his home town were as always well-fed, kept hearing reports from the interior of France that people were starving to death in large numbers; so he had sailed his fleet up north and fallen upon a hundred-ship convoy bringing Russian and Polish wheat out of the Baltic. He had defeated the Dutch naval squadron escorting it toward Amsterdam and diverted the entire convoy to Dunkirk. They were being unloaded as fast as cranes and stevedores could work, and the wheat was being taken in to famished France on endless wagon-trains that darkened the shore, and plugged the narrow ways of the town. (3) As bad as things were in France, they were worse to the north; reports had come in that during the winter just ending, one out of three Finns had died. And Scotland was not much better. Finland and Scotland were as far north as it was possible to go, and so those Finns and Scots who had been able to straggle out to the coasts and take ship had sailed south, and converged on harbors where food might be had. Many had ended up in Dunkirk.

No other ship would have been able to pass the Dunkirk breakwater, under such conditions; but when word made it up the chain of command that *Météore* had inexplicably returned, Captain Bart gave orders that room must be made for her; and so after some idling, *Météore* had been towed down a narrow lead among Baltic wheat-hulks, refugee-boats, invasion-transports, and ordinary Dunkirk fishing- and smuggling-craft to the anchorage of Bart's privateer fleet, and given a place of honor alongside Bart's flagship *Alcyon*. The first to come aboard had been a six-year-old boy armed with a wooden sword; the second, a noblewoman. She was gaunt, drawn, and black-patched compared to the last time Daniel had seen her, but he recognized her as the Duchess of Arcachon and (in England, and countries that recognized William) the Duchess of Qwghlm. And after he had talked to her for two hours, he was surprised by the awareness that she was still beautiful; just different.

And her internal fires had been banked. By the pox, he assumed at first. Then he guessed it was age—but she was not even thirty years old. On further consideration he decided it was because she had actually achieved things, and so needed not be as fierce as before. She was a Duchess twice over. She had made more fortunes than she'd lost. She had this six-year-old bastard, who seemed a fine lad, and gave every appearance of being one of those unusual children who survived to adulthood. She had a daughter of three, and a babe in arms, Louis de Lavardac, only a few weeks old—this implied she'd gone through at least as many miscarriages, stillbirths, and small-coffin funerals. Men sailed *jachts* across the sea and gave them to her, just to get her attention. And so perhaps her fires had been banked *by choice;* she'd had the sound judgment to know when to draw back, and let her investments and her children grow, and her plans come to fruition.

Daniel was invited to dine aboard *Alcyon* on the second day of his stay in Dunkirk—the day of the perfectly blue sky—and after he and Eliza and Jean Bart, the Marquis d'Ozoir, and a few other guests had sat round the table for some time, drinking coffee, talking, and letting the meal settle in their stomachs, Bart got up and took Jean-Jacques, or Johann as he was familiarly known, over to *Météore* to inspect her rigging. Daniel strolled round the decks with Eliza, drinking in the air and the sun, and watching Bart and his godson cavort about the decks, tops, and ratlines. For those two had forgotten about the ostensible purpose of the visit before they'd even come aboard the *jacht,* and it had turned into a sword-fighting tutorial. Bart was one of those who deemed it somehow dangerous to practice with anything other than a live, sharp, steel blade, and accordingly had armed Johann with a long knife. Bart drew a small-sword—a landlubber's weapon, as he was dressed for dinner, not privateering. He had drawn Johann into an exercise that appeared to consist mostly of knocking Johann down (not too roughly) whenever he committed the sin of being off balance.

"In London have people heard of Father Édouard de Gex, and what befell him?" Eliza wanted to know.

"I am too retiring, too peculiar to make the social rounds and hear all the latest," Daniel said, "and so maybe you are asking the wrong Englishman. He is a fierce Jesuit, close to the Marquise de Maintenon, and I have the vague notion that something bad happened to him—"

"You could say that," said Eliza. "He was strolling in the gardens of Versailles late in the summer. There is a place there called the Bosquet de l'Encelade—a pool and a fountain of several jets, depressed in the center of a great encircling bower, the whole surrounded by woods, and rather remote from the château. I used to read there. As de Gex was strolling along the circuit of the bower, he became aware—or so he told the story later—that someone else was there, padding along in the same direction, but lagging far enough behind as to remain hidden from view by the curvature of the bower. And so de Gex stepped through one of the portals that gives access to the lawn within—terraced rings of turf descending toward the pool. Cutting across the lawn, he turned around abruptly to look behind him, and saw what was recognizable as a human form. But it was difficult to make out through the lattice-work of the bower. 'Show yourself, whoever you are,' de Gex called, and after a brief hesitation his stalker emerged from one of those portals and was revealed as an immense one-armed man carrying a long staff—which proved, on second glance, to be a harpoon. Now, the fountain lay between them, and de Gex wanted to keep it that way, whereas this other chap wanted to get closer to de Gex, so that he could launch the weapon from shorter range and without having to pitch it through jets and spray. De Gex called for help, but in this secluded part of the garden, with the roar and hiss of the fountain, he could not know whether his cry had been heard. The harpooneer took to pursuing him. De Gex was uncertain whether to keep circling the fountain—which had the advantage that it kept his adversary in view—or to exit through the bower, flee into the grove, and go for help. In any event he did not have to dither over it for long, for as it turned out someone *had* heard his cry and come running to see what was the matter. De Gex took his eye off the harpooneer for a moment as his would-be rescuer emerged from the bower. When he looked back he saw the harpoon inbound; for his hunter, seeing that he was losing his chance, had made a desperate fling. De Gex tried to dodge it. Meanwhile it was diverted by a surging jet from a fountain. The details are unclear; suffice it to say that the fluked head of the weapon had to be excavated, by the King's surgeon, from deep in de Gex's upper thigh. It passed through the muscle on the outside of the limb and spared the great vessels and nerves that run along the inside; but the bone was damaged, an infection developed, and de Gex has, ever since, lingered at Death's door, in a sick-room at the chapter-house of the Jesuits in the town of Versailles."

"The attacker?"

"Bolted into the forest of the King's hunting-park and was tracked for some miles but never caught. Today I heard the news that de Gex has died. His cousin, Madame la duchesse d'Oyonnax, is looking after the arrangements—probably his body will be taken back to the family seat to be interred."

"It is an extraordinary tale," said Daniel. "As you have reasons for everything you do, I presume you had a reason for relating it to me?"

Eliza shrugged. "There was a feeling among some at Court that this was an assassin acting on orders from London, or some other Protestant capital. The plot to assassinate William on Turnham Green might have been tit-for-tat. I thought the Juncto might want to know as much."

"I shall pass it along, then, madame. The Juncto shall consider itself in your debt."

"I shall consider myself in yours, if you deliver the message."

"On the contrary, it will be my honor to be of service, madame."

"You might *also* be of service by escorting *him* home," said Eliza, nodding over toward Johann, "assuming he survives his fencing-lesson."

Johann had quickly tired of being knocked down by his godfather, and so the lesson had moved along to parts of the syllabus more fun and less practical: viz. hanging from ratlines with one hand whilst duelling the opponent with the other.

"I had supposed he *was* home," said Daniel.

"Home is Leipzig," said Eliza. "It is a long story—much longer than that of de Gex and the harpoon."

"I wonder if I might engage in some tit-for-tat by telling you a bit of news from my side of the water."

"Monsieur, I should be fascinated," exclaimed Eliza, suddenly coming alive. "How unlike you to volunteer something!"

Daniel blushed at this, but went on: "When I was at university I was terrorized by the Earl of Upnor—Louis Anglesey. Of course he has been dead since the Battle of Aughrim. But a few days ago I phant'sied I spied his ghost standing atop a bastion of the Tower of London. Then it came into my head that he must be Upnor's brother, Philip, Count Sheerness, who has not set foot in England for almost twenty years—he fled during the Popish Plot. England has forgotten him. But perhaps he has not forgotten England, and came back over at last to play some role in the complot to assassinate William."

"Then England certainly will not forget him again," Eliza said. "I wonder if he'll be suffered to leave the Tower alive."

"Were I a betting man, I'd bet yes. I'd bet he'll be back on this side of the Channel before summer. Oh, he'll be kept close for a while. Perhaps he'll even be tried. But no proof will be found that he was involved in the plot."

"What is your reason for telling me the story?"

"As it happens, I once was imprisoned in the same place. Some murderers were sent in to do away with me. But they were intercepted by a veteran sergeant of the King's Own Black Torrent Guards, one Bob Shaftoe, who I believe is known to you."

"Yes."

"He and I made a sort of compact. He would be of aid to me in doing away with my bête noire—the late Jeffreys—if I would assist him in recovering a certain young woman—"

"I know the story."

"Very well. Then you know she is a slave, once owned by the Earl of Upnor, but distributed to Count Sheerness as a part of Upnor's estate when Upnor was killed at Aughrim. I presume she has been on this side of the water, serving in Sheerness's household."

"Indeed. What is it you would have me do, Dr. Waterhouse?"

"The Black Torrent Guards have been in the Spanish Netherlands for some years, fighting the war, whensoever the Juncto could scrape together money for balls and powder. I thought perhaps you might know of some way of getting word to Sergeant Shaftoe that the owner of Abigail is in a tight spot just now, and unable to defend his *properties* on the Continent. Between that, and the lull in the fighting, there might be opportunity—"

"Other such opportunities have come his way in the past, but he has not been quick to take advantage of them," said Eliza, "because he has been looking after his nephews, and could not see a way to fulfill so many obligations at once. But his nephews must have reached the age of manhood by now. Perhaps he is ready."

"That must have vexed their uncle to no end," Daniel mused.

"Yes. But it must have made his life a good bit simpler, too," said Eliza. "So, consider the message delivered and your obligation discharged, Dr. Waterhouse."

"Thank you, your grace."

"You are most welcome."

"—"

"Is there anything else?"

"Nothing that I would dream of mentioning to any ordinary Duchess—or woman, for that matter. But as you have an interest in money, here is a curiosity for you."

Daniel reached into both hip-pockets at once. From each he drew a sheaf of printed bills, and held them out, rather like the two pans of a balance, so that Eliza could inspect them. The offerings on left and right were similar, but different. Clearly there had been a lot of work for engravers in London lately, for these documents had been pressed out by copper-plates of awesome complication: miles of line folded up into inches of space, like the windings of testicles. One depicted a goddess gripping a trident and sitting upon a great mound of coins. "Even by Barock standards, the most vulgar thing I've seen," Eliza pronounced it. BANK OF ENGLAND, it said; and below that was printed a florid and verbose assertion that it—which is to say, this piece of paper—was money. The bills on Daniel's opposite hand said LAND BANK and supported like claims—if anything, even more pompous.

"Whig," said Daniel, shaking the BANK OF ENGLAND bills, "and Tory," shaking the LAND BANK bills.

"You even have different money!?"

"The Bank of England was, as you must know, set up two years ago by the Juncto after it won the election. It is backed—these bills are backed—by the ability of the government to raise money from taxes, lotteries, annuities, and whatever other schemes the big brains of the Juncto can think up. Not to be outdone, the Tories set up their own Bank, backed by—"

"The land of England itself? How Tory-like."

"They are nothing if not consistent."

"Curious. Are these worth anything?"

"As always, you go to the heart of the matter. In the absence of any other money, these do circulate in London. The Marquis of Ravenscar, who gave these to me, asked that I present them to you, and try to—to—"

"To exchange them for specie?" Eliza laughed. "Cheeky fellow! So it is an experiment! A little foray into Natural Philosophy. He wishes you to gather some data on your Continental tour—to see if anyone outside of England heeds the promises stamped on these bills."

"Something like that. I am relieved that you take it in such good humor."

"Let me ask you this, Doctor: what is the exchange rate between Whig and Tory money?"

"Ah. At the moment, one of these—" he held up the Land Bank notes "—buys rather a lot of these." He indicated the Bank of England notes. "For many are of the view that the Bank of England has failed already, and the Land Bank is ascendant."

"Which amounts to saying that the Juncto will be cast down in the next election, and Harley will lead the Tories to victory."

"I dare not disagree—as much as I'd like it otherwise."

"Then I shall buy a few of these, in exchange for a Bill of Exchange, denominated in thalers, and payable at the House of the Golden Mercury in Leipzig," said Eliza, indicating the Land Bank notes, "but I shall exchange them immediately for a lot of these." She licked a finger and began to count off Bank of England notes.

"You place your trust in the Whigs? Roger shall be overjoyed."

"I place my trust in Newton," Eliza said.

"You refer to his new position at the Mint."

"I had more in mind the calculus."

"How so?"

"This is really a matter of derivatives, is it not?"

"Financial derivatives?"

"No, mathematical ones! For any quantity—say, position—there is a derivative, representing its rate of change. As I see it, England's stock of land represents a fixed quantity of wealth. But commerce I see as a derivative—it is the slope, the speed, the rate of change of the nation's wealth. When commerce stagnates, this rate of change is small, and money founded upon it is worthless. Hence the lopsided exchange rate you told me of. But when commerce thrives, all goes into rapid movement, the derivative jumps up, and money founded on it becomes of much greater value. Once Newton goes to work at the Mint, the supply of coin in England can only improve. Commerce, which has been frozen for lack of money, will surge, at least briefly. The exchange rate between these two currencies will swing the opposite way, long enough at least for me to take a profit."

"It is a way of looking at the thing I had not considered before," said Daniel, "and it sounds right to me. But if you ever have an opportunity to expound your theory to Isaac, I hope you'll use the word *fluxion* in place of *derivative*."

"What's a fluxion?"

"That," said Daniel, "is the problem in a nutshell."

An Abandoned Church in France
MARCH 1696

"I DO HOPE YOU'LL RECONSIDER, now, all of the unpleasant things you have had to say in the past about Satan." This was how Anne-Marie de Crépy, duchesse d'Oyonnax, greeted her cousin when his eyelids—which had been closed, three days ago, by a Jesuit father in Versailles—twitched open.

Father Édouard de Gex looked up at a black sky, framed in the aperture of his coffin. It was an uncommonly plush model, for a Jesuit. The brothers of his order had loaded him at first into a Spartan pine-plank box. But Madame la duchesse and her entourage had appeared just in time, and put a stop to it. "Imitation of Christ is all well and good during life, but my cousin is in Heaven now, and nothing prevents me from treating his earthly remains with decent respect; besides, I must accompany him all the way home, and I'd have the casket well sealed." And she had caused to be brought in to the sick-room a coffin so heavy it took four men to lift it: a coffin of oak, lined with lead, and cushioned better than most of the beds that courtiers slept on in Versailles. And so cunningly had it been wrought that even the pallbearers who carried it and its contents out to the street and set it on a flower-strewn gun-carriage would never have guessed that not only was it not sealed, but ventilation-slots ran all the way round the lip where the lid overhung the sides.

Oyonnax was now waving a phial of smelling-salts around under her cousin's nose. He tried to fend it off, but his arms were sluggish, and pinned to his sides by the overwhelming cushions. Finally he sat up, or tried to and failed and regretted it all in the same instant. The contraction of his abdominal muscles had ramifications as far down as the wounded thigh. The pain must have been desperate, for it brought him out of his stupor better than any smelling-salts. He managed to get an elbow under him, and Oyonnax reached in and rearranged cushions to prop him up. Then he was able to relax and look about himself. He could not have seen this from the satiny depths of the coffin, but: the gun-carriage, with him and the coffin on it, had been dragged up the aisle of a burnt-out church. The servants of Oyonnax had lifted the coffin up and set it crosswise on the altar— a granite plinth with all of its decorations burnt, weathered, gnawed, and looted away. The stone walls of the church stood mostly intact, though smoke had rendered them charcoal-black. The great beams of the roof had crashed to the floor as they'd burnt, and still lay there, like so many charred pews strewn around a floor that was knee-deep in shards of roof-tiles. Though from place to place, especially nearer the altar, wicker mats had been laid upon the burnt timbers so that well-dressed persons could sit upon them without soiling their fashions. Around the altar itself, the floor had been shoveled and swept clean, creating an open space where a pentagram had been daubed out in something that had dried to a thick brown crust. The altar, and de Gex, stood at the center of the pentagram.

"Holy Jesus, what I have I done—" said de Gex, and tried again to move; but the pain in his leg nearly killed him. He fell back and crossed himself.

Oyonnax laughed indulgently, and reached out to cradle her cousin's head in her hand. "I wondered how you would react."

"I had to escape from Versailles," said de Gex. "I was an imbecile before—it took me so long to understand the enormity of this conspiracy. Madame la duchesse d'Arcachon, of course, is at the center—but she is in league—always has been—with *L'Emmerdeur*. The Baron von Hacklheber was her enemy, but is now her friend. She operates with the Juncto hand-in-glove. Newton—the recoinage in England—all part of the same conspiracy! What could I do? D'Avaux displeased her, and was sent packing to Stockholm! Lucky he was not poisoned—or harpooned, as I was!"

"This sounds," said the Duchess, "like a little speech that you memorized, before you swallowed my sleeping-draught, so that you could recite it to St. Peter if you never woke up. I am not St. Peter, and this is the gateway to Hell, not Heaven. But if it pleases you to recite the speech anyway, pray continue."

"You must understand, *cousine*, that if there was nothing more to the conspiracy, I needn't have troubled you. For my Order is not without resources of its own; and when conjoined to the Office of the Holy Inquisition there is little in heaven or earth that could not be accomplished. But that was before I came to understand that she had seduced none other than Bonaventure Rossignol himself!"

"As much as I loathe her, I must admit this was a master-stroke. For who, other than *le Roi* himself, could be a more powerful ally for a subtle and conniving bitch like Madame la duchesse d'Arcachon?"

"Just so! I realized, then, that I was trapped like a fly in her web. For there is nothing that I do in this life that is not observed by hundreds of courtiers, all of whom gossip, and many of whom write letters. In consequence Rossignol must know everything I do, and must pass it on to Madame la duchesse d'Arcachon while they are fornicating! I then saw myself to be helpless, as long as I remained in this life—in this world. The failed assassination had given me—praise God and His mysterious ways—a convincing pretext for dying young. Hence the request I whispered into your ear—which must have struck you as very strange."

"Look about yourself, having been resurrected in this of all places, and tell me what is strange," said Oyonnax.

"Our Savior, having died on the cross, descended to the very pit of Hell before ascending once more into the light," de Gex remarked. "Still, I must know, *cousine*, if you invoked any of the Fallen ones—if my death and resurrection were effected by dæmonic necromancy or—"

"Dæmonic necromancy is so tedious, and fraught with unintended consequences," said Oyonnax, "when syrup of poppies does the job perfectly well. It is all a question of dosage—tricky to calculate, especially for one like you who was weakened."

"Why did you choose to bring me around *here* of all places, then?"

"It was ever my plan that if I were to miscalculate the dose, and if I opened the coffin to find you dead *in fact* as well as in *appearance*, then I should employ the arts of the necromancer to bring you back to life."

It took de Gex some moments to absorb this.

"But, *cousine*, I had always believed that you had only *affected* an interest in the Black Arts, when it was fashionable, years ago, when you were young and foolish. That you considered it all perfect nonsense."

"You have been *furious* at me, Édouard, for deeming it all nonsense! For to call Satan a figment of man's phant'sy is but one step from saying the same of God, is it not?"

"Indeed, *cousine,* I should rather you were a *sincere* Satanist than a *pretend* one; for the former recognizes God's majesty, and may be reformed, while the latter is an atheist, and doomed to the Lake of Fire."

"Then look about yourself, and draw your own conclusions."

"I see the relics and signs of the Black Mass, the candles still burning, the inverted cross. I conclude that there is hope for you. But I do not know yet whether there is hope for *me.*"

"What do you mean, Édouard?"

"You have been strangely reticent on the question of whether I was alive or dead when the lid came off the coffin; whether, that is, I am alive now because of smelling salts, or because you used necromancy on my corpse."

"Perhaps I shall tell you one day," said Oyonnax. She lifted a bundle of clothes off the floor and dropped it into his lap. "Change out of those Jesuit weeds and into these."

It was too much, in too short a time, for the opiated mind of de Gex. "I do not understand."

"Understand this: You ask too many favors of me. Perhaps I'm not as different as you phant'sy from Eliza. She is a businesswoman—she does nothing for free. *You,* cousin, have put me to an immense amount of trouble and expense. I have given you death, a splendid bespoke coffin, resurrection, safe transit out of Eliza's web, and now a new identity." She patted the bundle: it was a clerical robe, but light gray, not the black of the Jesuits. "You are now Edmund de Ath, a Belgian Jansenist."

"A *Jansenist!*?"

"What better disguise for a Jesuit than to become a Jesuit's nemesis? Put these on, shave your beard, and the transformation is complete. You can go on your quest to the East a new man. I'm sure the Jansenists in Goa, Macao, Manila, will be glad of your company!"

"The disguise should serve," said de Gex. "I thank you for it. For it and for all the rest."

"Have I not done much for you?"

"Obviously you have, *cousine,* but—"

"Then shave, put on your new garments, and let us be on our separate ways."

"I want only to know whether it was a chymist's receipt, or the Powers of Darkness, that brought me back to life!"

"Yes. You have already made that plain."

"And—?"

"And I thought I made it clear to you, Edmund de Ath, that I do not wish to answer your question at this time."

"But it is a simple thing for you to do! *And it makes all the difference.*"

Oyonnax smiled and shook her head. "You contradict yourself—how like a Jansenist! *Because* it makes such a difference, it can *never* be simple. Édouard, apply your Jesuitical logic for a moment. If I brought you to life with necromancy, it means you belong to the Legions of Hell now—*and* that I am a necromancer—which means I believe that both Satan and God are real—and therefore have hope of redemption, if only I agree to switch sides. Am I correct so far?"

"Indeed, *cousine,* you have reasoned as soundly as any man."

"On the other hand, if I did it all with drugs from the apothecary, then your soul belongs to God as it ever did. These trappings—" she indicated the pentagram, the candles "—are stage-props, nothing more—fetishes and relics of a ludicrous pseudo-religion that I hold in contempt, which I trotted out only to throw a fright into you—much as priests frighten peasants at church by prating about hell-fire. In which case I am a cynical atheist. Am I correct?"

"Yes, *cousine.*"

"And so *one* of us shall go to hell, the other to heaven. But we cannot both end up in the same place. I know which, you do not. I have the power to tell you, but I choose to withhold the knowledge. You may embark, whenever you feel ready, on your quest to recover the Solomonic Gold, but you'll do so not knowing the answer to your question."

De Gex shook his head, too a-mazed to feel the horror of his predicament. "They say necromancers hold in thrall those whom they have brought back to life," he said, "but I never thought it would work this way."

"To me a more apt similitude is the way a priest enslaves the minds of his parishioners," said Oyonnax. "But that is neither here nor there. I have lost count of the number of times some courtier has minced up to me and claimed he was enthralled by my beauty, wit, or perfume; of course it always turns out in the end that they are not enthralled at all. Still and all, I have often wondered what it would be like to have a thrall; and as you have so much hectored me, ever since we were children, about the prospects of my immortal soul, I can't think of anyone who more deserves it. Know that your empty coffin shall be interred with all due ceremony in the family mausoleum at Gex. Where Edmund de Ath shall lie one day, there's no telling; and where his soul shall end up is my secret."

Winter Quarters of the King's Own Black Torrent Guards Near Namur

MARCH 1696

"SERGEANT SHAFTOE REPORTING as ordered, sir," came a voice from the dark.

"I have got a letter addressed to you, Shaftoe," answered a different voice from the dark—a college-cultivated voice. "As a training exercise, I thought we might sally forth in search of some source of light, so that I could do something other than run my fingers over it."

"Captain Jenkins's company gathered some brush on their 'training exercise' this afternoon, and are burning it yonder."

"Ah, I phant'sied I smelled smoke. Where the devil did they find something to burn?"

"A wee sand-bar in the Meuse, three miles upstream. We've had our eye on it for several weeks. The French had not got to it yet, lacking swimmers. But Captain Jenkins's company has a man who can dog-paddle, when he has to. Today, he had to. He got over to this sand-bar with a line, and stripped it bare while the French watched shivering, and threw stones, from the opposite bank."

"That is the sort of initiative I look for in the Black Torrent Guards!" exclaimed Colonel Barnes. " 'Twill serve them well in the years to come!"

The conversation to this point had been transacted through a wall of mildewy canvas, for Colonel Barnes was on the inside, and Sergeant Shaftoe the outside, of a tent. The sentences of Barnes were punctuated by thumping and clanking as he got sword, boot, peg-leg, and topcoat on. The tent was a ghostly cloud under starlight. It bulged at one end as Barnes pushed his way out through the flaps; then he became perfectly invisible. "Where are you?"

"Here."

"Can't see a bloody thing," Barnes exclaimed, "it is an excellent training exercise."

"You could be living in a house, with candles," said Bob Shaftoe, not for the first time.

Indeed, Barnes had passed most of the winter in a house up the road from this, the winter camp of his regiment; but some piece of news from England, recently received and digested, had prompted him to vacate, to take up lodgings in a tent among his men, and to begin referring to everything they did as a training exercise. The change had been much noted but little understood. They'd not taken part in anything like a military engagement since half a year ago, when they had participated in King William's successful siege of Namur. Since, they'd done naught but live on the land, like field-mice. And since the trees and brush had all long since been cut down and burnt, and the farms trampled to unproductive mud-flats, and the animals hunted and eaten, living on this land required some ingenuity.

The brush-fire was, as both men knew, on the opposite side of a swell in the earth, where Captain Jenkins's company had made its camp. To get there, they had to walk through the camp of Captain Fletcher's company, which in daylight would have taken all of thirty seconds. With a lanthorn it might have taken a minute or two. But the Black Torrent Guards' last candle had vanished several days previously, and in the most ignominious way possible, viz. nicked from Colonel Barnes's coat-pocket by rats when he ventured out to use the latrine, and carried away to be eaten. And so the passage through Captain Fletcher's company's camp was, as both men knew, to be an infinitely gradual shuffling and sliding through a three-dimensional labyrinth of tent-ropes and clotheslines. It seemed an opportune time to speak of difficult matters—for there was no way, in darkness, to look someone in the eye.

"Err . . . it is my duty to inform you," said Bob, "that private soldiers James and Daniel Shaftoe are absent without leave."

"Since how long?" asked Barnes, sounding interested, but not surprised.

"That might be debated. Three days ago, they claimed they had come upon the spoor and tracks of a feral pig, and requested leave to hunt it down. They vanished over the horizon, in the direction of Germany, not long after permission was granted."

"Very good—an excellent training exercise."

"When they did not return after one, then two days, yet their sergeant was disinclined to think the worst of them—"

"The expectation of bacon for breakfast had impaired his judgment. As my own mouth is almost too full of saliva for me to speak, I must say that I understand."

"Now still Jimmy and Danny are not back. I must assume that they have deserted."

"They trained only too well, and learned the lesson too soon," Barnes reflected. "Now their lives shall be forfeit, if they are caught."

"Oh, they shan't be *caught*," Bob assured him. "You forget that before I taught them to be English soldiers, Teague Partry taught them to be rapparees."

"Do you want leave to hunt them down? It would be an excellent—"

"No, sir," said Bob, "and would you please explain your incessant jesting about everything we do being a training exercise?"

"I have a soft spot in my heart for the men of my regiment—*most* of them, anyway," said Barnes, "and would see as many of them as possible survive what is to come."

"What, then, *is* to come?" Bob asked, "and how does brush-gathering and pig-chasing make us more fit for it?"

"This war is over, Bob. Ssh! Don't tell the men. But you may be assured there'll be no fighting in the year to come. We shall occupy this ground, as a bargaining-chit for diplomats to shove to and fro on a polished tabletop somewhere. But there'll be no more fighting."

"That is what is always *claimed*," said Bob, "until a new front is opened, and a campaign launched."

"True enough—in your boyhood," said Barnes. "But you must adjust your thinking now, and take into account that the money is all gone. England has ninety thousand men under arms. She can *afford* perhaps *nine* thousand; and she is *willing to pay for* many fewer than that—especially if the Tories throw down the Juncto, as seems likely."

"The Black Torrent Guards are an elite regiment—"

"You really *must* fucking listen to me, Shaftoe . . ."

Barnes's voice was getting fainter and falling away aft.

"I am listening sir," said Bob, "but mind you don't stand still and declaim for too long in one place, lest mud swallow up your peg."

"Shut up, Shaftoe!" said Barnes; but renewed sucking and squelching noises told that he had heard Bob's counsel too late. There was a long grunt of effort terminated by a succulent pop as he drew his prosthesis out of the mire.

"Yes, sir."

"It is *all* going away, man! Every bit of it. An elite regiment, you say? Then some draughty chamber in the Tower of London may be set aside, and a sign nailed to the door reading 'King's Own Black Torrent Guards,' and if I am very fortunate, and if my lord Marlborough intercedes, and fights hard for us, I may be allowed to go behind that door from time to time and push a quill about. On

frightfully important occasions of state, I may be prevailed upon to
rake together a skeleton Company and dress them up in uniforms so
that they may parade before a visiting Embassy, or some such. But I
say to you, Bob, that a year from now everyone in this regiment, with
a very few lucky exceptions, shall be a Vagabond. If Jimmy and
Danny have deserted, and taken to the road, it is only because they
have had the wit to anticipate this."

"Mmph. I have oft wondered over the amount of time you spent
in yonder house, over the winter, reading letters from London."

"I know you have from the queer looks you sent my way."

"Since the Year of Our Lord 1689," said Bob, "I have spent all of
about three weeks in England. As I cannot read, all that I know of
the place now consists of rumors. Your predictions seem unlikely to
me—if you are correct, it means England has gone mad. But I do not
have knowledge of my own to set against yours, in a debate; and in
any case I do not have the standing to over-rule you, sir, if you have
made up your mind to turn your Regiment's winter quarters into a
training-ground for Vagabonds."

"It is more than that, Shaftoe. For their own sakes, I would that
these men would survive the coming lean years. And for England's
sake I would conserve this Regiment. Even if we be disbanded for
some years, yet the day shall come when we are mustered again, and
on that day I'd fain re-constitute the King's Own Black Torrent
Guards from *this* lot, and not, as is customary, from some random
collection of criminals, shake-rags, and Irishmen."

"You want them to stay alive—if possible *honestly*," Bob translated,
"and you want me to know where they are to be found, so that we
can call them up again, if there is a need, and if there be money to
pay them."

"That is correct," said Barnes. "Of course, we can't tell them any
of this!"

"Of course not, sir," said Bob. "They'll have to work it out for
themselves."

"As did Jimmy and Danny. Now! It is time to read your letter.
Fetch me a burning bush and I shall play Jehovah to your Moses."

Bizarre witticisms such as this were the price Bob Shaftoe had to
pay for having a colonel who'd trained as a churchman. He trudged
over to the feeble campfire that Captain Jenkins's company had made
in the midst of their encampment, requisitioned one uprooted shrub
from their brush-pile, and shoved it into the coals until it began to
burn. Then he hastened back to Barnes and held it up like a candelabra, from time to time waving it about to make it blaze up. Smoldering leaves snowed down upon the page and on the epaulets and the

three-cornered hat of Barnes, and he shrugged or blew them off as he read.

"It is from your lovely Duchess," said Barnes.

"I had guessed as much."

Barnes read for a bit and blinked and sighed.

"Am I allowed to know that it says, sir?"

"It concerns your woman."

"Abigail?"

"She is in a house not thirty miles from here . . . a house that is for the time being unguarded, as the proprietor has been locked up in the Tower of London. How fortuitous, Sergeant!"

"What is fortuitous, sir?"

"Don't play the fool. Just at the moment when you must lay plans for a new life as an unemployed civilian, your two chief sources of distraction and gratuitous complications—Jimmy and Danny—have absented themselves, and you are presented with an opportunity to take a wife!"

"*Take* is an apt word in this case, sir, as she is the legal property of Count Sheerness."

"Why should that trouble us? If Jimmy and Danny can run off in quest of a feral pig, cannot we steal you a wife?"

"What d'you mean *we*, sir?"

"I am altogether decided on it!" Barnes proclaimed, and thrust the corner of the page into the bush, setting it ablaze. "To establish you in a stable and happy domestic arrangement is to be a linch-pin of my strategy for keeping the Black Torrent Guards together! Besides which, it shall be an excellent training exercise."

The Track to Pretzsch
APRIL 1696

God has chosen the world that is the most perfect, that is to say, the one that is at the same time the simplest in hypotheses and the richest in phenomena.

—LEIBNIZ

"It is the very last fate I should ever have imagined, that two unmarried and childless wretches should end up running a service to deliver children from city to city," said Daniel.

As the carriage had thumped and veered out of Leipzig up the high road toward Wittenberg, and (later) the very, very low road to Pretzsch, he had settled like a great heap of sand, grabbing pillows and stuffing them under the boniest parts of his frame, and bracing his feet against the base of the bench that supported his companion, Gottfried Wilhelm Leibniz.

If Daniel was a heap of sand, Leibniz—far more hardened than Daniel to long-range coach travel—was an obelisk. He sat perfectly upright, as if ready to dip quill in ink-pot and begin penning a treatise. He raised his eyebrows and looked curiously at Daniel, who was now only a few degrees shy of supine, with a knee practically wedged in Leibniz's groin.

Daniel had assumed his ears had deceived him when the Duchess of Arcachon and of Qwghlm had asked him to deliver Johann to Leipzig. But he had done it—only to discover Leibniz was there, rather than in Hanover, where Daniel had expected him. News had reached Hanover and Berlin that Eleanor, the Electress-Dowager, had fallen gravely ill in the Dower-house of Pretzsch. It seemed likely she would not survive; and if she perished, someone would be required to transport a grieving Princess Caroline to her new foster-home at the Electoral court at Berlin. And who had been chosen for this duty? Leibniz.

Leibniz considered it for a few moments, then said: "Say! How is the youngest son of the Duke of Parma faring these days? Has he recovered from that nasty rash?"

"You have quite lost me, sir. I do not even know the *name* of the Duke of Parma, much less the medical condition of his youngest son."

"That was already obvious," said Leibniz, "for he *has* no sons—two daughters only."

"I am beginning to feel like the Dim Interlocutor in a Socratic dialogue. What is your point?"

"If you asked the Duke of Parma about Leibniz, he might recognize the name vaguely, but he would know nothing of Natural Philosophy, and of course it is absurd to think he would entrust a daughter to me, or you, on a journey. Almost all the nobility are like the Duke of Parma. They don't know, or care about, us, and we know little of them."

"You are saying that I have fallen victim to observational bias?"

"Yes. The only nobility who suffer the likes of you, or of me, to come within a mile of them, are those exceedingly peculiar few who

(God help them!) have taken an interest in Natural Philosophy. They used to be more numerous, but now I can count them on the fingers of a hand: Eliza, Sophie, and Sophie Charlotte. Those are the only ones we get to talk to. They are desirous of exposing their young ones to Natural Philosophy. Given a choice between the likes of you or me, Daniel, *versus* some available—which is to say idle—retainer, uncle, stooge, or priest who would be inclined to ignore, molest, corrupt, or convert the child en route, such a woman will unfailingly choose the Natural Philosopher; for the worst *we* will do is bore them."

"I believe I did just that with little Johann," said Daniel. "He would respond better, I do believe, to a curriculum centered wholly on Weaponry and its uses. In the absence of weapons, he prefers unarmed combat. I do believe I learned more wrestling-holds from *him* than he Philosophy from *me*."

"That should serve you well when you get to Massachusetts," said Leibniz gravely, "for the Indians are said to be brave wrestlers all."

"After he has fenced with Jean Bart on the deck of a warship, to be shut up in a carriage with the likes of me for several days was a miserable fate."

"Pfui! A slow and excruciating death by lockjaw is the *miserable fate* of those who play too much with edged weapons," said Leibniz. "Eliza knows this. You served her well, even if Johann is too young to appreciate it! Tell me, did he really show *no* curiosity at all?"

"The foolish boy gave me an opening, by discoursing too much of mortars and cannons," Daniel admitted. "We got into parabolas. I halted the carriage in a field between Münster and Osnabrück and we scattered some peasants by conducting a systematic trial, first with archery, later moving on to firearms."

"You see? He'll never forget that! Every time Johann sees a Projectile Weapon—which in this benighted world means every five minutes—he'll know that they are useless without mathematicks."

"How far are we from this Pretzsch?"

"You are deceived by the understated style of the place," said Leibniz. "Behold, we are *in* Pretzsch, and have been for some minutes." He slid his window open, laid a hand atop his wig to prevent its ending up under a wheel-rim, and thrust his head out. "The Dowerhouse is dead ahead."

"What will you discourse of with the orphan," Daniel asked, "assuming she does not share Johann's curiosity about weapons?"

"Whatever she likes," Leibniz said. "She is after all a Princess, and almost certain to be a Queen one day." He regarded Daniel skeptically.

"All right," said Daniel, moving. "I'll sit up straight."

THE TRAIN WAS THREE CARRIAGES, a baggage-wain, and several mounted dragoons. The latter had been sent down from Berlin, which was to say they were Brandenburgish/Prussian. Leibniz had met up with these Berliners in Leipzig. This had occurred only an hour after Daniel—who'd only just dropped off Johann, and cashed his Bill of Exchange, at the House of the Golden Mercury—had tracked down Leibniz. The union of these three separate parties was under the command of a Brandenburger noble who was also a captain of dragoons. He was adamant that they must press on across the Elbe and get into Brandenburg territory before nightfall, lest some Saxons give in to the temptation to make things complicated. Daniel found this a little ridiculous, but Leibniz saw wisdom in it. For Caroline might be an impoverished orphan living out in the middle of nowhere, but she was still a Princess, and to have a Princess in one's custody, voluntary or in-, was to have power. And though Augustus the Strong, Elector of Saxony, was a much better man than his late brother, yet there was no end to his crafty scheming; who knew if he might snatch Caroline up on a pretext and marry her off to some Tsarevich. So the collection of Caroline and her one item of baggage from the Dower-house of Pretzsch was carried through with a brusqueness normally reserved for kidnappings and elopements. This didn't make it easier for the orphan Princess, but nothing could have done so, and a lingering farewell might have made it harder. By her choice she shared Leibniz's coffee-brown, flower-painted carriage with him and Daniel. Tears and smiles passed alternately across her face like squalls and sunbeams on a gusty March day. She was thirteen.

The train crossed the Elbe on a nearby ferry and pounded down the road for some hours until they reached Brandenburg, then stopped for the night at an inn on the Meißen-Berlin road. The next day they got a late start. Some fifty miles separated them from the Palace of Charlottenburg and the hospitality of its namesake, the Electress Sophie Charlotte. "Pray consider me at your disposal, your highness," said Leibniz. "The road is long, and I shall deem it a high honor to be of whatever assistance I may in making it seem shorter. We may pursue your mathematicks-lessons, which have been neglected during the illness of your late mother. We may discourse of theology, which is something you should tend to; for in the Court of Brandenburg-Prussia you'll encounter not only Lutherans but Calvinists, Jesuits, Jansenists, even Orthodox, and you'll need to keep your wits about you lest some silver-tongued zealot lead you astray. I have a blockflöte, and could attempt to give you a music-lesson. Or—"

"I would hear more of the work that Dr. Waterhouse purposes to undertake in Mas-sa-chu-setts," said the Princess carefully. She had got wind of this from remarks overheard yesterday.

"A fitting topic, but in the end a very broad one," said Leibniz. "Dr. Waterhouse?"

"The Massachusetts Bay Colony Institute of Technologickal Arts," began Daniel, "has been founded, and will sooner or later be endowed, by the Marquis of Ravenscar, who looks after his majesty's money, and who is a great Whig. That means he belongs to a faction whose bank and whose money are founded on Commerce. They are ever opposed to the Tories, whose bank and money are founded on Land."

"Land seems much the better choice, being fixed and stable."

"Stability is not always a good thing. Think of lead and quicksilver. Lead makes good ballast, rooves, and pipes, but is sluggish, while quicksilver has marvelous properties of speed, flexibility, fluidity . . ."

"Are you an Alchemist?" Caroline demanded.

Daniel colored. "No, your highness. But I will go so far as to say that Alchemists think in metaphors that are sometimes instructive." He shared a private look with Leibniz, and smiled. "Or perhaps we are all born with such habits of thought ingrained in our minds, and the Alchemists have simply fallen into the trap of making too much of them."

"Mr. Locke would disagree," said Caroline. "He says we start out a *tabula rasa* . . ."

"It might surprise you to learn that I know Mr. Locke well," Daniel said, "and that he and I have argued about it."

"What has he been up to lately?" Leibniz asked, unable to hold himself back. "I've been working on a reply to his *Essay Concerning Human Understanding* . . ."

"Mr. Locke has spent much time in London of late, debating Recoinage; for while Newton would devalue the pound sterling, Locke is a staunch believer that the standard laid down by Sir Thomas Gresham must never be tampered with."

"Why do England's greatest savants spend so much time arguing about coins?" Caroline asked.

Daniel considered it. "In the old world, the Tory world, when coin was nothing more than an expedient for moving rents from the country to London, they would never have paid it so much notice. But Antwerp suggested, and Amsterdam confirmed, and London has now proved, that there is in Commerce at least as much wealth as in Land; and still no one knows what to make of it. But money makes it all work somehow, or, when it is managed wrong, makes it collapse. And so coins are as worthy of the attention of savants as cells, conic sections, and comets."

Leibniz cleared his throat. "The way to Berlin is long," he said, "but not *that* long."

Daniel said, "The Doctor complains of our digression. I was speaking of the new Institute in Boston."

"Yes. What is to be the nature of its work?"

Here Daniel was stumped; which was odd, and embarrassing. He did not quite know where to begin. But the Doctor, who knew Caroline much better, said, "If I may," and gratefully Daniel gave the floor to him.

Leibniz said, "Persons such as your highness, who woolgather, and ponder things, are apt to be drawn into certain labyrinths of the mind—riddles about the nature of things, which one may puzzle over for a lifetime. Perhaps you have already visited them. One is the question of free will versus predestation. The other is the composition of the continuum."

"The *what* of the *what*?"

"Simply that if you begin with observable things around you, such as yonder church-tower, and begin dividing them into their component parts, viz. bricks and mortar, and the parts into parts, where does it lead you in the end?"

"To atoms?"

"Some think so," said Leibniz, agreeably enough. "At any rate, it happens that even the *Principia Mathematica* of Mr. Newton does not even attempt to settle such questions. He avoids these two labyrinths altogether—a wise choice! For in no way does he address the topic of free will versus predestation, other than to make it plain that he believes in the former. And he does not touch on atoms. Indeed, he is reluctant even to divulge his work on infinitesimal mathematics! But do not be misled into believing that he does not have an interest in such things. He does, and toils night and day on them. As do I, and as will Dr. Waterhouse in Massachusetts."

"Do you toil on these two problems *separately* or—"

"A most important question, and one I should have anticipated," said Leibniz, clapping his hands. "I should have mentioned that both Newton and I share a suspicion that these two problems are connected. That they are not two separate labyrinths, but a single large one with two entrances! You can enter either way; but by solving one, you solve the other."

"So, let me see if I am understanding you, Doctor. You believe that if you understood the composition of the continuum—which is to say, atoms and whatnot—"

Leibniz shrugged. "Or monads. But pray continue."

"If you understood that, it would somehow settle the question of free will versus predestination."

"In a word: yes," said the Doctor.

"Atoms I understand better," began Caroline.

"No, you only phant'sy you do," said Leibniz.

"What's to understand? They are wee hard bits of stuff, jostling one another . . ."

"How big is an atom?"

"Infinitely small."

"Then how can they touch each other?"

"I don't know."

"Supposing they do, by some miracle, come in contact, what happens then?"

"They bounce off each other."

"Like billiard balls?"

"Precisely."

"But, your highness, have you any idea just how complicated a billiard ball must be, to bounce? It is a fallacy to think that that most primitive of entities, the atom, can partake of any of the myriad qualities of a polished spherical lump of an elephant's tusk."

"Very well, then, but, too, sometimes they stick together, and form aggregates, more or less porous . . ."

"How does the sticking-together work? Even billiard balls can't do that!"

"I haven't the faintest idea, Doctor."

"Nor does *anyone,* so do not feel bad about it. Not even Newton has figured out how atoms work, for all his toil."

"Does Mr. Newton work on atoms too, then?" asked Caroline. It was directed at Daniel.

"All the time," said Daniel, "but this work is called by the name Alchemy. For a long time I could not fathom his interest in it; but finally I came to understand that when he did Alchemy he was trying to solve this riddle of the two labyrinths."

"But when you go to Massachusetts you'll do no Alchemy at your Institute, will you, Dr. Waterhouse?"

"No, your highness, for I am more persuaded by *monads* than *atoms.*" He glanced at Leibniz.

"Eeyuh, that's what I was afraid of!" said Caroline, "for I do not understand those one bit."

"I believe we have established," said Leibniz in a gentle voice, "that you do not understand *atoms* one bit—whatever illusions you may have nourished to the contrary. I hope to disburden your highness of the idea that, in looking for the fundamental particle of the universe, atoms are a simple and natural choice, monads not."

"What's the difference between a monad and an atom?"

"Let us first speak of how they are the same, for they have much in common. Monads and atoms both are infinitely small, yet everything is made out of them; and in considering how such a paradox is possible, we must look to the interactions among them: in the case of atoms, collisions and sticking-together, in the case of monads, interactions of an altogether different nature, which I shall come to presently. But either way, we're obliged to explain the things we see—like the church-tower—solely in terms of those interactions."

"Solely, Doctor?"

"Solely, your highness. For if God made the world according to understandable, consistent laws—and if nothing else, Newton has proved that—then it must be consistent through and through, top to bottom. If it is made of atoms, *then it is made of atoms,* and must be explained in terms of atoms; when we get into a difficulty, we cannot suddenly wave our hands and say, 'At this point there is a miracle,' or 'Here I invoke a wholly new thing called Force which has nothing to do with atoms.' And this is why neither Dr. Waterhouse nor I loves the Atomic theory, for we cannot make out how such phænomena as light and gravity and magnetism can possibly be explained by the whacking and sticking of hard bits of stuff."

"Does this mean that you *can* explain them in terms of monads, Doctor?"

"Not yet. Not in the sense of being able to write out an equation that predicts the refraction of light, or the pointing of a compass-needle, in terms of interactions among monads. But I do believe that this type of theory is more fundamentally coherent than the Atomic sort."

"Madame la duchesse d'Arcachon has told me that monads are akin to little souls."

Leibniz paused. "*Soul* is a word frequently mentioned in connexion with monadology. It is a word of diverse meanings, most of them ancient, and much chewed over by theologians. In the mouths of preachers it has come in for more abuse than any other word I can think of. And so perhaps it is not the wisest choice of term in the new discipline of monadology. But we are stuck with it."

"Are they like human souls?"

"Not at all. Allow me, your highness, to attempt to explain how this troublesome word *soul* became entangled in this discourse. When a philosopher braves the labyrinth, and sets about dividing and subdividing the universe into smaller and smaller units, he knows that at *some* point he must stop, and say, 'Henceforth I'll subdivide no further, for I have at last arrived at the smallest, elemental, indivisible unit: the fundamental building-block of all Creation.' And then he can no longer dodge and evade, but must finally stick his neck out, as it were, and make an assertion as to what that building-block is like: what its qualities are, and how it interacts with all the others. Now, nothing is more obvious to me than that the interactions among these building-blocks are stupefyingly numerous, complicated, fluid, and subtle; just look about yourself for irrefutable proof, and try to think what can explain spiders, moons, and eyeballs. In such a vast web of dependencies, what laws are to govern the manner in which one particular monad responds to all of the other monads in the universe? And I do mean *all;* for the monads that make up you and me, your highness, feel the gravity of the Sun, of Jupiter, of Titan, and of the distant stars, which means that they are sensitive of, and responsive to, each and every one of the myriad monads that make up those immense bodies. How can they keep track of it all, and decide what to do? I submit that any theory based on the assumption that Titan spews out atoms that hurtle across space and whack into my atoms is very dubious. What is clear is that my monads, in some sense, *perceive* Titan, Jupiter, the Sun, Dr. Waterhouse, the horses drawing us to Berlin, yonder stable, and everything else."

"What do you mean, 'perceive'? Do monads have eyes?"

"It must be quite a bit simpler. It is a logical necessity. A monad in my fingernail feels the gravity of Titan, does it not?"

"I believe that is what the law of Universal Gravitation dictates."

"I deem that to be *perception*. Monads perceive. But monads *act* as well. If we could transport ourselves much closer to Saturn, and get into the sphere of influence of its moon Titan, my fingernail, along with the rest of me, would fall into it—which is a sort of collective action that my monads take in response to their perception of Titan. So, your highness: What do we know of monads thus far?"

"Infinitely small."

"One mark."

"All the universe explainable in terms of their interactions."

"Two marks."

"They perceive all the other monads in the universe."

"Three. And—?"

"And they act."

"They act, based on what?"

"Based on what they perceive, Dr. Leibniz."

"Four marks! A perfect score. Now, what must be true about monads, to make all of these things possible?"

"Somehow all of these perceptions are flooding into the monad, and then it sort of decides what action to take."

"That follows unavoidably from all that has gone before, doesn't it? And so, summing up, it would appear that monads perceive, think, and act. And this is where the idea comes from, that a monad is a little soul. For perception, cogitation, and action are soul-like, as opposed to billiard-ball-like, attributes. Does this mean that monads have souls in the same way that you and I do? I doubt it."

"Then what sorts of souls *do* they have, Doctor?"

"Well, let us answer that by taking an inventory of what we know they do. They perceive all the other monads, then think, so that they may act. The thinking is an internal process of each monad—it is not supplied from an outside brain. So the monad must have its own brain. By this I do not mean a great spongy mass of tissue, like your highness's brain, but rather some faculty that can alter its internal state depending on the state of the rest of the universe—which the monad has somehow perceived, and stored internally."

"But would not the state of the universe fill an infinite number of books!? How can each monad store so much knowledge?"

"It does because it has to," said the Doctor. "Don't think of books. Think of a mirrored ball, which holds a complete image of the universe, yet is very simple. The 'brain' of the monad, then, is a mechanism whereby some rule of action is carried out, based upon the stored state of the rest of the universe. Very crudely, you might think of it as like one of those books that gamblers are forever poring over: let us say, 'Monsieur Belfort's Infallible System for Winning at Basset.' The book, when all the verbiage is stripped away, consists essentially of a rule—a complicated one—that dictates how a player should act, given a particular arrangement of cards and wagers on the basset-table. A player who goes by such a book is not really thinking, in the higher sense; rather, she perceives the state of the game—the cards and the wagers—and stores that information in her mind, and then applies Monsieur Belfort's rule to that information. The result of applying the rule is an action—the placing of a wager, say—that alters the state of the game. Meanwhile the other players around the table are doing likewise—though some may have read different books and may apply different rules. The game is, *au fond*, not really that complicated, and neither is Monsieur Belfort's Infallible System; yet when these simple rules are set to working around a basset-table, the results are vastly more complex and unpredictable than one would ever expect. From which I venture to say that monads and their internal rules need not be all that complicated in order to produce the stupendous variety, and the diverse mysteries and wonders of Creation, that we see all about us."

"Is Dr. Waterhouse going to study monads in Massachusetts, then?" Caroline asked.

"Allow me to frame an analogy, once more, to Alchemy," Daniel said. "Newton wishes to know more of atoms, for it is through atoms that he'd explain Gravity, Free Will, and everything else. If you visited his laboratory, and watched him at his labours, would you see atoms?"

"I think not! They are too small," Caroline laughed.

"Just so. You instead would see him melting things in crucibles or dissolving them in acids. What do such activities have to do with atoms? The answer is that Newton, unable to see atoms with even the finest microscope, has said, 'If my notion of atoms is correct, then such-and-such ought to happen when I drop a pinch of this into a beaker of that.' He gives it a go and sees neither success nor failure but some other thing he did not anticipate; then he goes off and broods over it, and re-jiggers his notions of atoms, and devises a new *experimentum crucis,* and re-iterates. Likewise, if your highness were to visit Massachusetts and see me at work in my Institute, you'd not see any monads lying about on counter-tops. Rather you would see me toiling over machines that are to *thinking* what beakers, retorts, *et cetera,* are to atoms: Machines that, like monads, apply simple rules to information that is supplied to them from without."

"How will you know that these machines are working as they ought to? A clock may be compared to the wheeling of the heavens to judge whether it is working aright. But what is the action that your machine will take, after it has applied the rule, and made up its mind? And how will you know whether it is correct?"

"That is easier than you might suppose. For as Dr. Leibniz has pointed out, the rules need not be complicated. The Doctor has written out a system for conducting logical operations through manipulation of symbols, according to certain rules; think of it as being to propositions what algebra is to numbers."

"He has already taught me some of that," said Caroline, "but I never phant'sied it had anything to do with monads and so forth."

"That system of logic may be imbued into a machine without too much difficulty," said Daniel. "And a quarter of a century ago, Dr. Leibniz, building upon the work of Pascal, built a machine that could add, subtract, divide, and multiply. I mean simply to carry the work forward. That is all."

"How long will it take?"

"Years and years," said Daniel. "Longer, if I were to try to do it amid the distractions of London. So, as soon as I have delivered you to Berlin, I shall begin heading west, and not stop for long until I have reached Massachusetts. How long shall it take? Suffice it to say that by the time I have anything to show for my labors, you'll be full-grown, and a Queen of some Realm or other. But perhaps in an idle moment you may recall the day you went to Berlin in a coach with two strange Doctors. It may even occur to you to ask yourself what became of the one who went off to America to build the Logic Mill."

"Dr. Waterhouse, I am certain you shall come to mind more frequently than that!"

"Difficult to say—your highness shall have many distractions. But I hope I am not being too forward in saying that I should be honored to receive a letter from your highness at any time, if you should wish to inquire about the state of the Logic Mill. Or, for that matter, if I may be of service to your highness in any other way whatsoever!"

"I promise you, Dr. Waterhouse, that if any such occasion arises, I shall send you a letter."

As best he could in a moving carriage, Daniel—who had sat up admirably straight all through the interview—bowed. "And I promise your highness that I shall respond—cheerfully and without a moment's hesitation."

A House Overlooking the Meuse Valley
APRIL 1696

BEFORE THE MANOR-HOUSE'S GATES, two equestrians parleyed: a stout, peg-legged Englishman in a coat that had been drab, before it had got so dirty, and a French cavalier. They were ignored by two hundred gaunt, shaggy men with shovels and picks, who were turning the house's formal garden into a system of earthen fortifications with interlocking fields of fire.

The Englishman spoke French in theory, but perhaps not so well in practice. "Where are we?" he wanted to know, "I can't make out if this is France, the Spanish Netherlands, or the Duchy of bloody Luxembourg."

"*Your men* appear to believe it is part *d'Angleterre!*" said the cavalier reproachfully.

"Perhaps they are confused because an Englishman is said to reside here," said the other. He gave the Frenchman an anxious look. "This *is*—is it not—the winter quarters of Count Sheerness?"

"Monsieur le comte de Sheerness has chosen to establish a household here. During intervals between campaigns, he withdraws to this place to recover his health, to read, hunt, play the harpsichord—"

"And dally with his mistress?"

"Men of France have been known to enjoy the company of women; we do not consider it a remarkable thing. Otherwise I should have appended it to the list."

"But what I'm getting at is: There *is* a feminine presence here? Maids and whatnot?"

"There *was*, when I went out this morning to ride. Whether there is any more, I can only speculate, Monsieur Barnes, as the place has been invested, and I cannot get into it!"

"Pity, that. Say, monsieur, do tell me, is this French soil or not?"

"Like a banner in the wind, the border is ever-shifting. The soil we stand upon is not presently claimed by *La France,* unless *le Roi* has issued some new proclamation of which I have not been made aware yet."

"Ah, that's good—these chaps have not invaded France, then— now, *that* would be embarrassing."

"Monsieur. There are *some* commanders in *some* armies who would find it embarrassing that two entire companies of their Regiment had deserted and wandered thirty miles from their assigned quarters and laid siege to the country house of a nobleman!"

"I believe it is now *you and I* who are laying siege to *them,*" observed Barnes, "as *they* are on the inside, and we on the *out!*"

The cavalier did not take the jest very well. "In wartime there are always deserters and foraging-parties. For this reason Monsieur le comte de Sheerness left orders, when he went to Londres, that musketeers were to be billeted in the stables, and the perimeters of the estate were to be patrolled night and day. In recent days these sentries have reported seeing more strange men than usual about the place, which I attributed to the spring thaw; I assumed, as *anyone* would, that they were *French* soldiers who had deserted from some regiment on the Namur front that had disintegrated from pestilence or want of food. Indeed, when I went out riding this morning, I had it in mind that when I returned to the house I ought to send word to a company of cavalry that is billeted some miles to the north, and ask that they ride down to round up a few of these deserters and hang them. *Never* did it enter my mind that they might be *Englishmen* until I was out for a gallop in a pasture down the road, and came upon a whole nest of them, and heard them talking in their jabber. I rode back to the house to find that, in my absence, upwards of a hundred men had emerged suddenly from the wooded ravines that lead down to the Meuse, and taken the estate in a *coup de main!* As I looked on in astonishment, the number doubled! I was going to ride north to summon help, but—"

"The roads had been blocked," said Barnes. "And then haply I came along. Thank God! For there is still time to prevent this from developing into some sort of an incident."

The cavalier's eyebrows leapt up so high as to almost disappear beneath the verge of his periwig. "Monsieur! It is already an incident! Under no circumstances do the rules of war allow such a thing as this!"

"I agree fully, and you have my abject apologies as an English gentleman, monsieur. But only listen and consider what Count Sheerness himself would do, were he here. The Count is an Englishman, living in France, and commanding a regiment that, I need hardly tell you, fights nobly and loyally on the French side. Yet in the halls of Versailles, courtiers, who are not here to witness his gallantry on the field of battle, must be whispering, 'Can we trust this Anglo-Saxon not to betray us?' Ludicrous, I know, and unfair," Barnes continued, holding up a hand to calm the cavalier, who looked as if he were about to lash the impertinent Barnes with his riding-crop, "but in these muddled times, an unfortunate fact of human nature. Now yonder band—"

"I should name them a *battalion,* not a band!"

"—of English deserters—"

"Strangely well-disciplined ones, monsieur—"

"Wandering lost, far behind enemy lines—"

"Is it wandering? Are they lost?"

"Have made camp, by a perverse accident, on the grounds of the quarters of Monsieur le comte de Sheerness. It means *nothing,* as you and I can plainly see; but there are those at Versailles who are bound to read *something* into it! Count Sheerness is detained in the Tower of London, is he not?"

"Obviously you know perfectly well that he is."

"Some will allege, perhaps, that he is not so much *detained* as a *willing guest,* coöperating with King William, and with the King's Own Black Torrent Guards, which happen to be headquartered in the Tower."

The cavalier was now so incensed that all he could do, short of murdering Barnes on the spot, was to wheel his mount, gallop some yards down the road, wheel it again, and gallop back. By the time he had returned from this excursion, he had parted his lips to deliver some choice remark to Barnes; but Barnes, who had nudged his saber a few inches out of its scabbard, now drew it out altogether, and pointed it through the iron-work of the gate. This drew the cavalier's attention, first to the saber itself, and then to half a dozen men standing attentively just inside the gate with loaded muskets cradled in their arms.

"These," Barnes announced, "*are* the King's Own Black Torrent Guards. I recommend we get them out of here as quickly as possible, before there is serious trouble."

"As I suspected," said the cavalier, "it is a kind of blackmail. What is it you want?"

"I want you to take this opportunity to be silent, monsieur, and to bide here for a time, so that I may go within and parley with their leaders, and convince them that it is in their best interests to depart immediately and without pillaging."

The cavalier, after another look at the musketeers, and at another such formation that had appeared on the road nearby, accepted those terms with a nod. Barnes nudged his nag to the gate, which was opened for him. He dismounted and crunched down the gravel path into the château.

Five minutes later, he was back. "Monsieur, they will leave," he announced. Which had been obvious anyway, for as soon as he had entered the house the men had ceased digging, and begun to gather their things, and to form up in the garden by platoons.

"There is a complication," Barnes added.

The cavalier rolled his eyes, sighed, and spat. "What is the complication, monsieur?"

"One of my men came across something in the house that, I regret to inform you, is not the rightful property of Count Sheerness. We are taking the item in question with us."

"So, monsieur, it is as I knew all along. You are thieves. What is this prize, I wonder? The plate? No—the Titian! I suspected you had an eye for art, monsieur. It's the Titian, isn't it?"

"On the contrary, monsieur. It is a woman. An Englishwoman."

"Oh no, the Englishwoman stays here!"

"No, monsieur. She goes. She goes with her husband."

"Her husband!?"

IT HAD BEEN UPWARDS OF thirty years since Bob Shaftoe had shinnied up a drainpipe to break into the home of a rich man. But the women of the household had, like birds, flown upwards by instinct, and availed themselves of every stair that presented itself to them, until they nested in an attic. An eyebrow window protruded from the roof, and worried faces flashed in it. Bob, rather than see doors smashed down and the house torn apart, ascended to that roof, belly-crawled up the roof-tiles, kicked out the window, somersaulted to the floor, and parried a rush and a thrust from some kitchen-wench who had thought to snatch up a butcher-knife before abandoning her post. He got this one by the wrist, spun her around into a hammerlock, pried the knife from her grip, and held her as a shield before him, in case any of the four other women in this attic had like intentions. She smelled of carrots and thyme. She shouted something in French that he was sure meant, "Run away!" but not a one of them moved. The booming on the attic-door proved they had no route of escape that way.

They looked at him. Their faces were turned to the light pouring in through the wrecked window. One was a crone, two were matrons, too old and stout to be Abigail. One was the right age, and shape, and coloration. His heart jumped and stumbled. It wasn't her. "Damn it!" he said, "do not be afraid, you'll not be touched. I seek Miss Abigail Frome."

Four pairs of eyes shifted slightly from Bob's face to that of the woman he was holding.

Then her entire weight was pressing him back, and he had to let go her wrist to catch her. In his life he had learned a few things about unarmed combat, including a trick or two for escaping from a hammerlock. This, though, was a new one: faint dead away into your captor's arms.

SHE CAME AROUND THREE MINUTES later, diagonal on a bed one storey below. Bob bobbed in and out of her field of view. He'd draw near to count her freckles, then would remember that a life of military serv-ice had made him a frightful thing to look upon, and so, to spare Abi-gail's tender eyes, he would withdraw, and make a circuit of the room's windows, inspecting the trench-work of the soldiers below. Some of them were doing it a little bit wrong. He mastered the urge to fling up a sash and bawl at them. He flicked his eyes up to scour the horizon for vengeful French Horse-regiments. When Abigail reached up to rub her nose, he kept an eye on her, in case she had secreted on her person any more cutlery. But he need not have both-ered. This was not a tempestuous assassin he was looking at. She was a schoolgirl from a small town in Somerset, of a sweet and level dis-position, but inclined to be a bit daft about practical matters, which was how Bob had met her in the first place, and how he had lost his heart to her. To rush at him with a knife, as she had just done, was not typical of her character, but it was a fair sample of the less than prac-tical side of her nature, which Bob, who had nothing but practical in *his* makeup, needed and wanted. He had seen this, eleven years ago, in the time it had taken his heart to skip three beats. And in a sort of miracle—the only miracle that Bob had ever been party to—this girl had seen in *him* what *she* wanted. *Wanted,* both in the sense that meant *was lacking,* and the sense that meant *desired.*

Beds of the time had a lot of pillows, as it was the practice to sleep half-sitting up. Abigail had been flung down flat by Bob, but now pushed herself up against the pillows so that she could eye him pacing about the room.

"Bloody hell!" were his first tender words to her. "There is no time! I know you remember me, or you would not have fainted."

She was still pale, and not inclined to move more than she had to, but a smile came on her face, giving her the placid look of a Virgin Mary in a painting. "Even if I had it in me to forget you, my lords Upnor and Sheerness would have made it impossible. It was strange how oft they felt moved to relate the story of how you stood on the bridge and challenged Upnor on my behalf."

"Oh, that was ignominious."

"True, they told the tale to make fun of you; but to me 'twas a love-story I never tired of hearing."

"Still, ignominious. As was my *second* meeting with Upnor, which you might not have heard about. Thank god Teague happened along with his stick! But we have no time for this. Oh, bloody hell, here he comes!"

"Who!?" cried Abigail.

"Didn't mean to alarm you, Miss. It is not Monsieur le comte. It's Colonel Barnes. He approaches. Do you mark his peg-leg beating time on the stairs? We must get out of this place."

Bob moved toward the door of the bedchamber. Abigail watched with a wrinkled brow, not knowing whether it was Bob's intention to flee; to barricade it; or to welcome the Colonel. But instead some detail of it caught Bob's notice. He reached out and touched—caressed—the upper hinge: two straps of forged iron, one fixed to the door, the other to the post, joined by a short rod of iron about as thick as his little finger. "Quickly then: a few moments in Taunton market-square, eleven years ago, helping you with that silly banner, when the wind had gusted, and blown it down—you remember? Those moments are to my life what this hinge-pin is in the case of the door; which is to say that all pivoted, and pivots, about it; it is what I am about, as it were, and at the same time, it holds all together. Take it away—" And here Bob, not trusting his tongue, on an impulse drew a knife from his belt, shoved it under the mushroom-shaped head of the pin, and popped it loose. Lifting the door up with one hand, he jerked the pin up and out with the other; then he let go. The pin clanged to the floor. The door fell askew and cracked, and would not move properly any more, but hung sadly askew and wobbled.

"We've another moment now, unfortunately no longer than the first. What's it to be, Abigail?"

"What do you mean exactly?"

Barnes stepped carefully into the room, eyeing the broken door. He gave Bob a Significant Look; then, remembering his manners, turned smartly toward Abigail and bowed. "Miss Frome! Sergeant Shaftoe has extolled your beauty so many times I have grown bored of him; seeing you in the flesh, I understand, and repent, and shall never again yawn and drum my fingers on the table, when the topic arises, but join in chorus with Sergant Bob."

"Thank—" Abigail began, but Barnes had already moved on.

"Have you asked her yet?"

"No, he hasn't," Abigail said, for Bob was dumbstruck.

"Drop," said Barnes, "ask."

Bob smashed down on to his knees. "Will—"

"Yes."

"Abigail Frome will you take—" began Barnes.

"I do."

"Robert Shaf—"

"I do."

"—nounce you man and wife. You may kiss the bride—*later*. Let's get the bloody hell out of here!" said Colonel Barnes, and fled the room; for he phant'sied he'd spied something through the window.

"Fetch me that hinge-pin, husband," Abigail said, "in lieu of a ring."

SEVERAL PLATOONS OF MUSKETEERS were already formed up anyway in the forecourt of the house, and so it did not impose any significant further delay for them to line up on both sides of the path and form an arch of bayonets for Mr. and Mrs. Shaftoe to run through. It was too early for spring flowers, but some private had the presence of mind to hack a branch from a budding cherry-tree and slap it into Abigail's arms. A white horse was pillaged from the stables and bestowed on the newlyweds as a wedding-present. Members of the household staff looked on through windows, and cooed and waved tea-towels. The French musketeers who were supposed to be guarding the place, and who had been disarmed, and herded into a dry fountain, wept for joy and blew their noses. Even the cavalier who had been giving Barnes such a hard time could only look the other way, shake his head, and blink. He was indignant to have been made the small-minded villain in this story, and wished he could have spoken more to Barnes, and let him know that, if he had only been made aware of the nature of the errand, he might have served Venus instead of Mars.

Barnes and the Shaftoes, distributed between two horses, inspected the troops a last time.

"You have done well by your Sergeant to-day," Barnes announced, "and repaid a small portion of that debt you owe him for having kept you alive through so many battles. Now, back to training! Today's exercise is called 'melt away into the countryside.' It has already commenced, and you are already doing a miserable job of it, being bunched together in plain view!"

Private soldiers began to break ranks and vault walls. A senior sergeant approached Barnes, and lodged a protest: "There's no countryside to melt into, sir! We've got one foot in bloody France, all the trees are cut down, we are thirty miles behind enemy lines—"

"That is what makes it such a superlative training exercise! If we were in bloody Sherwood Forest, it'd be easy, wouldn't it? Here is a suggestion: As long as you keep your gob shut, they'll assume you are starveling deserters from the French Army! Now, get you all gone. I shall see you all back at quarters in a few days. I must convey Mr. and Mrs. Shaftoe to the sea-coast, that they may go to London and set up housekeeping. You shall all be welcome at their house!"

Abigail here for the first time looked a little less than radiant. But the joy came back into her face again as those Black Torrent Guards who had not yet melted away into the countryside broke into cheers. Bob got the white horse moving, and trotted round the circuit of the gardens, accepting in turn the cheers of various small mobs of soldiers, of the French maids in the windows, and the musketeers in the fountain; and then it was through the gate and out on to the road. Following Barnes—who was halfway to the western horizon already—they took off hell-for-leather. Abigail, straddling the horse's croup, pressed her cheek into the hollow between Bob's shoulder-blades, wrapped her arms about his waist, and clasped her hands together. Bob, feeling a hard thing jammed into his belly, looked down to see Abigail's fingers interlocked about the hinge-pin.

Herrenhausen Palace, Hanover

AUGUST 1697

"FRANCE WILL SHED all of the lands she has conquered since 1678—except for Strasbourg, which Louis seems to have conceived a great liking for—on the condition they remain Catholic," said the fifty-one-year-old savant. He ticked another item off a list that he had spread out on a Dresden china dinner-plate blazoned with the arms of the Guelphs.

Then he glanced up, expecting to see the hem of the sixty-seven-year-old queen's ball gown hovering just above the tabletop. Instead, the garment—miles of gathered silk, made dangerous by an underlying framework of bone and steel—whacked him in the face, and stripped off his spectacles, as the Electress of Hanover made a smart about-face.

"It took me a week to grind these lenses." Gottfried Wilhelm Leibniz leaned sideways to rake his spectacles up off the floor. He had to keep his head upright to prevent his biggest and best wig from sliding off his bald, sweaty scalp. This gave him a crick in the neck, however enabled him to get a charming view of muscular white calves pumping in and out as his patroness stormed down the mid-line of the banquet-table.

"This is *news*," she complained, "I could get it from *any* of my Privy Councillors. From *you* I expect better: gossip, or philosophy."

Leibniz got to his feet, and took part of his chair with him; his vacant scabbard had got locked up in a bit of Barock wood-carving. The sound of a blade whipping through the air made him cringe and duck. "Almost got it!" Sophie exclaimed, fascinatedly.

"Gossip . . . I am trying to think of some gossip. Er, your daughter's palace in Berlin continues to shape up splendidly. The courtiers there are all in an uproar."

"The same uproar as *last* week, or a *different* one?"

"With every day that passes, with every new statue and fresco that is added to the Charlottenburg, it becomes more and more difficult to deny the awkward—the embarrassing—the monstrous fact that Frederick, the Elector of Brandenburg and probable future King of Prussia, is in love with your daughter."

"Why should that be the cause of an uproar?"

"Because they are *married* to each other. It is viewed as bestial—perverse."

"Really it is because of what the courtiers all believe about me."

"That you *planted* Sophie Charlotte there to control Frederick?"

"Mmmm."

"Well, *did* you?"

"If I *did*, it obviously *worked*, and that is what the courtiers cannot abide," Sophie answered vaguely. She now whirled again, her formidable Hem shredding a few centerpiece snapdragons, and ran down the table with silk ribbons trailing behind her like battle-streamers. She made another vicious cut with the sword. Candle-tops scattered and came to rest in splashes of their own wax, spinning out threads of smoke. "I could finish this in an instant if this *verdammt* burning bush were not in my way," she said meditatively, pointing the sword at a candelabra that had been hammered together out of several hundred pounds of Harz silver by artisans with a lot of time on their hands.

A few servants, who had to this point kept as far as they could from the Electress, peeled their backs off the wall of the dining-hall and scuttled inwards toward the offending fixture, knees flexed and hands raised. Sophie ignored them and tilted the rapier this way and that, letting the light of the surviving candles trickle up and down the blade. "No wonder you could not wrest it out of its scabbard," she said, "it was rusted in place, wasn't it?"

". . ."

"What if I had to call upon you to defend my realms, Doctor?"

"Swordsmen are gettable. I could fashion a hell of a siege-engine, or make myself useful in some other wise."

"Make yourself useful now! I do not need to hear gossip from Berlin. My daughter sends me more than I need, and little Princess Caroline has been posting me the most excellent letters—your doing?"

"I have taken some interest in her education since the untimely death of her mother. Sophie Charlotte has become the next best thing, however, and I sense I am needed less and less."

"*Ach*, now I can move, but I cannot *see*," complained Sophie, squinting up towards a fresco shrouded by poor light and ancient congealed smoke. "I can't tell the painted-on *Furies* from the living *bat*."

"I believe those would be harpies, your majesty."

"I will show you what a harpy is, if you do not begin doing your job!"

"Right . . . well, Louis XIV has a mickle abscess on his neck. That's not very good, is it? Right, then . . . the French will now recognize William as King of England, and all of the titles he has bestowed. So, to mention a few examples, John Churchill is now Earl of Marlborough, the Duchess d'Arcachon is now also the Duchess of Qwghlm."

"Arcachon-Qwghlm . . . yes . . . *we have heard of her,*" Sophie announced, making a momentous decision.

"She'll be overjoyed, your Electoral Highness, that you recognize her existence. For she respects no monarch in this world more than your Electoral Highness."

"What about her own liege-lords, Louis and William? Does she not respect *them?*" inquired her Electoral Highness.

"Er . . . *protocol,* I'm sure, forbids the Duchess from preferring one over the other . . . besides which, both of them are, sorry to say, *men.*"

"I see what you mean. Does this double Duchess have a Christian name?"

"Eliza."

"Children? Other than—unless I'm mistaken—that energetic little bastard who is always following my banker around."

"Two surviving children thus far: Adelaide, four, and Louis, going on two; the latter is the personal unification of the Houses of Arcachon and of Qwghlm, and, if he survives his father, will become lord of a hyphenated Duchy, like Orange-Nassau or Brandenburg-Prussia."

"Arcachon-Qwghlm doesn't have quite the same ring to it, I'm afraid. What are her pastimes?"

"Natural Philosophy, amazingly complex financial machinations, and the abolition of slavery."

"*White,* or *all* of it?"

"I believe she means to begin with white, and then leverage legal precedents thus obtained to extend it to all."

"Scarcely matters to us," muttered Sophie, "we have no black-amoors hereabouts, and no fleet with which to go and get them. But it seems a bit, I don't know, quixotic."

Leibniz said nothing.

"Quixotic is fine!" Sophie allowed, "we enjoy a dash of quixotic, as long as it is not boring. She is never boring about it, is she?"

"If you take her aside and really press her on it, she can go on at some length about the evils of slavery," Leibniz conceded, "but otherwise she is the very soul of discretion, and never heard to utter more than a few words on the topic in polite company."

"Where is she?"

"She spends most of her time in London lately, looking after an unfathomably lengthy and tedious Judicial Proceeding involving one Abigail Frome, a white slave, but maintains residences in St.-Malo, Versailles, Leipzig, Paris, and of course the Castle on Outer Qwghlm."

"We would meet her. We are grateful that she took Princess Caroline under her wing when the poor child was forgotten and alone. We share her passion for Natural Philosophy. We may require someone of her talents to assist us in the management of our ship *Minerva* and to ensure that the profits are not illicitly diverted to the coffers of our partner, Kottakkal, the Pirate-Queen of Malabar."

"I am afraid you quite lost me there, your Electoral Highness!"

"*Do* try harder to keep up, Doctor Leibniz, I hired you because people said you were *clever*."

"It shan't happen again, your Electoral Highness . . . er . . . you were on to something about a ship?"

"Never mind the ship! The most important thing is that this Eliza shall bring us the most excellent gossip from London; gossip that it is our duty to hear, as we or our heirs are likely one day to be crowned monarchs of England. And so if Eliza comes to this part of the world to pay a call on her bastard . . ."

"I'll see to it that she puts in an appearance here, your Electoral Highness."

"Done! What is next on the list?"

"Whitehall Palace burnt down."

"The whole thing? I was led to believe it was quite . . . rambling."

"According to the few people remaining in London who will still write to me, it is all smoking ruins."

"Ve must speak Englisch ven ve speak of Englant!" the Electress decreed. "I never get to practice othervise."

"Right. In English, then: As soon as the war ended, the Whigs were cast out—"

"The Yuncto?"

"Very good, your majesty, you have it right, the Yuncto is cast into the outer darkness, the Tories are ascendant."

"How fortunate for William," Sophie said drily. "Just when he needs a new palace built, the king-loving party gets its hands on the treasury."

"Which happens to be completely empty at the moment, but that problem is being worked on by clever fellows, fear not."

"Now the conversation really is about to become very boring indeed," Sophie reflected, "as we are on to revenue and taxes. The bat will go to sleep up there, snuggled up next to a naiad or a dryad, and not come awake until the middle of dinner."

"Everything said of the Tsar would suggest he'll not be troubled by a *bat*. You could have *wolves* and *bears* in here and he would not look twice."

"I am not trying to make Peter feel *at home*," Sophie said frostily, "but to show him that, somewhere between Berlin and here, he at last crossed the frontier of *civilization*. And one lovely thing about civilization is *philosophers* capable of making interesting conversation."

"Right. So we are finished with gossip, then, and—"

"—and on to the latest developments in philosophy—Natural, or Unnatural, as you prefer. Stand and deliver, Doctor Leibniz! Whatever's the matter? *Bat* got your tongue?"

"The English savants are all busy toiling at practical matters—Mints, Banks, Cathedrals, Annuities. The French are all under the shadow, if not the actual boot, of the Inquisition. Nothing of interest has been heard out of Spain since they kicked out the Jews and the Moors two hundred years ago. So when you inquire after Philosophy, Majesty, you inquire—and I do not wish to seem self-important when I say this—after *me*."

"Am I not allowed to inquire after *my* friend in *my* house?"

"Of course, I just . . . well . . . never mind. I have been corresponding with those Bernoulli brothers rather a lot. Nothing important. You know I have always been fascinated with symbols and characters. The calculus has brought us new ideas for which we want new symbols. For differentiation, I like a small letter *d*, and for integration, a sort of elongated *S*. That's how the Bernoullis have been doing it, and it suits them well. But there is another Swiss mathematician, a fellow who was once viewed as quite a promising young savant-in-the-making, by the name of Nicolas Fatio de Duillier."

"That one who saved William of Orange from a kidnap-plot?" asked Sophie, planting the tip of Leibniz's rapier in the tabletop and flexing it absent-mindedly.

"The same. He and the Bernoullis have been corresponding."

"But you said, very meaningfully, that this fellow was *once* viewed as promising."

"His work the last few years has been laughable. He is not right in his head, or so it would seem."

"I thought it was *Newton* who had gone out of his mind."

"I am coming to Newton. He—Fatio, that is—and the Bernoullis have, 'twould seem, been carrying on one of these slow-smoldering disputes. They send him a letter using the little *d* and the stretched-out *S*, and, tit-for-tat, he sends them one back using a little dot for differentiation and some sort of abominable "Q"-notation for integration. This is how Newton writes calculus. It is a sort of shin-kicking contest that has been going on for years. Well, a few months ago it *blew up*. Fatio published an article saying some very uncomplimentary things about your humble and obedient servant right here, and attributing the calculus to Newton. Then the Bernoullis cooked up a mathematicks problem and began sending it round to the Continental mathematicians to see if any of them could solve it. None of them could—"

"Not even *you!*?"

"Of course I could solve it, it was just a calculus problem and it had only one purpose, which was to separate the men—which is to say, those who understood the calculus—from the boys. They then sent the damned thing to Newton, who worked it out in a few hours."

"Oh! So he is *not* out of his mind!"

"For all I know, Majesty, he may be *entirely* out of his mind—the point is, he is still without rival, when it comes to mathematicks. And now, thanks to those mischievous Bernoullis, he believes that I and all the other Continental mathematicians do conspire against him."

"I thought you were going to talk philosophy now, not gossip."

Leibniz inhaled to say something, stopped, and sighed it all out. Then he did it again. Then a third time. Fortuitously, the bat chose this moment to come out of hiding. Sophie was not slow to jerk the rapier free from the tabletop and return to the hunt. After a bit of random flitting here and there—for the bat seemed to phant'sy that the keening tip of the rapier was some sort of blindingly fast insect—it settled into a hunting pattern, swinging around the long perimeter of the dining room, but judiciously avoiding the corners, plotting therefore a roughly elliptical orbit. The table was planted across one end of the room and so the bat flew across it twice on each revolution. Sophie's strategy, then, was to plant herself on the table just where she predicted the bat would over-fly it as it came in from its long patrol of the room. Missing it there, she could then rush down to the other end to take another hack at it when it rebounded from the near wall and passed over again, outward-bound.

"Your majesty's situation vis-à-vis the bat is very like that of a terrestrial astronomer when the earth's orbit—a segment of which is here represented by the table—is intersected by that of a comet, crossing over twice, once inbound towards Sol, and once outbound." Leibniz nodded significantly at the dazzling blaze of the candelabra, which had been set down on the floor between the table and the wall.

"Less sarcasm, more philosophy."

"As you know, the library is being moved here—"

"I just thought, what's the use of having a library if I must journey to Wolfenbüttel to use it? My husband never cared much for books, but now that he spends all his time in bed—"

"I do not criticize, Majesty. On the contrary, it has been good to withdraw from day-to-day management of the collection, and turn my attention to the library's true purpose."

"Now you really have got me confused."

"The mind cannot work with things *themselves*. I see the bat over yonder, my mind is aware of it, but my mind does not manipulate the bat *directly*. Instead my mind is (I suppose) working with a symbolic representation of the bat that exists inside my head. I can do things to that symbol—such as imagining the bat dead—without affecting the real bat itself."

"All right, so thinking is manipulation of symbols in the head, I have heard this from you before."

"A library is a sort of catalog or warehouse of all that men think about—so by cataloging a library I can make a more or less orderly and comprehensive list of all the symbols that sapient beings carry around in their heads. But rather than trying to dissect brains and ransack the actual gray matter for those symbols—rather than use the same sorts of symbolic representations that the brain manipulates—I simply assign a prime number to each. Numbers have the advantage that they may be manipulated and processed with the aid of machines—"

"Oh, it's *that* project again. Why don't you stick to monads? Monads are a perfectly lovely subject and you don't need machines to process them."

"I *am* sticking to monads, Majesty, I work on the monadology every day. But I am also working on this other thing—"

"You used to call it something else, didn't you? This is the 'I need an infinite amount of money' project," said Sophie distractedly, and made a rush down the table.

Leibniz ambled out into the center of the room, where it was a geometric impossibility for the tip of the blade to reach him. "The only sense in which it requires an infinite amount of money," he said with great dignity, "is that it requires *some* money every year, and I hope it shall go on *forever*. Now, I tried to fix up your silver mines— that didn't work because of *sabotage*, and because we had to compete against Indian slave labor in Mexico. I am sorry it failed. So then I went to Italy and set everything up so that you might, Parliament willing, become the next Queen of England. According to the Tories who are running the Land Bank, the value of that country is 600 million *livres tournoises*. They are selling grain and importing gold at a terrific clip. There is money there, in other words—not an infinite amount, but enough to pay for a few arithmetickal engines."

"Not only does Parliament have to vote on it, but also lots of people have to die in the right order, before I can be Queen of England. First

William, and then Princess Anne (who would be Queen Anne by that point) and then that little Duke of Gloucester, and any other children she might have in the meantime. I am sixty-seven years old. You need to seek support elsewhere—eeeYAHH! There you are! Invade my dining room, will you! Doctor Leibniz, how do you like my cooking?"

The sword was no longer moving. Leibniz ventured closer, keeping his eyes fixed on Sophie's powdered face, then traced a line from her soft, plump white shoulder, down the sleeve of her dress, across a rubble of jewelry encrusting her wrist and fingers, down the rusty rapier-blade, to a Dresden china plate where a deceased bat lay, wings arranged artfully as if it had been put there as a garnish by a French chef. "The comet has come to earth!" she proclaimed.

"Oh, how very poetickal you are, Mummy!" exclaimed a voice from behind Leibniz.

Leibniz turned around to face the door and discovered a large bloke, nearing forty, but with the face and manner of a somewhat younger man. George Louis, or Georg Ludwig as he was called in the vernacular, seemed to have only just realized that his mother was standing on a table. He blinked slowly a few times, froglike.

"The comet is approaching, er, the tree," he said uncomfortably.

"The *tree*!? Comets don't approach trees!"

"He has been ensnared, as it were, by the net cast by the falcon."

"Falcons don't cast nets," Leibniz blurted, unable to stop himself. The look he got in return from George Louis made him wish that he hadn't handed his only means of self-defense to Sophie.

"What does it matter, since it's all nonsense to begin with!? Once you've made up your mind to speak in ridiculous figures, instead of saying things straight out, why bother with making it all *consistent*?"

"George, my firstborn, my pride, my love. What are you trying to say to us?" Sophie asked indulgently.

"That the Tsar is approaching the Herrenhausen!"

"So the Tsar is the comet?"

"Of course!"

"We were using 'comet' to mean this bat."

The corners of George's mouth now drew back and downwards so far that his lips ceased to exist and the slit between them took on the appearance of a garrotte. He threw a dark look at Leibniz, blaming him for *something*.

"Who is the falcon, your royal highness?" Leibniz asked him.

"Your fawning disciple—*and my little sister*—Sophie Charlotte, Electress of Brandenburg, Dr. Leibniz."

"Splendid! So the metaphor of the net was to say that she had *ensnared* Peter by her charm and wiles."

"He passed through Berlin like a cannonball—didn't even slow down—she had to hunt him down like a fox at Koppenbrügge—"

"Do you mean, Sophie Charlotte was like a fox, in that she was so clever to hunt down the cannonball? Or that the Tsar was foxlike in his evasions?" Sophie asked patiently.

"I mean they are coming right now."

"Go to your father's bedchamber. Send the *embalmers* away," Sophie commanded, meaning the physicians. "Get your father to understand that someone very tall, and frightfully important, may swim into his vision, and that he should try to mumble a pleasantry or two if he is feeling up to it."

"Yes, Mummy," said the obedient son. With a parting bow for his mother, and a momentary eye-narrowing at Leibniz, George Louis took his leave.

It felt now as if Sophie and the Doctor ought to say something concerning George Louis, but Sophie very deliberately *didn't* and Leibniz easily decided to follow her lead. There was a brief upwelling of chaos and hilarity as Sophie was brought down to floor level again (she threatened to jump, and probably could have), but word had reached them that the Tsar of All the Russias had entered the building, preceded by Sophie Charlotte, who was essentially dragging him in by the ear. If this had been an official state visit they'd have had plenty of time to get ready. As matters stood, Peter was traveling *incognito* and so they were going to behave more or less as if he were a country cousin who had decided to drop by for dinner.

Clanking noises and guttural accents approached, and the avian trilling of Sophie Charlotte's laughter! A couple of ladies-in-waiting darted in on Sophie to tuck in loose hair-strands and yank down on her bodice; she counted to ten and slapped them away. Behind her one servant, moving in a posture of awful dignity, bore the bat-plate out of the room while another replaced it with a clean one. Still others made frenetic repairs to the candelabra and the centerpiece. "Doctor! Your sword!" Sophie exclaimed. She snatched the moist weapon up off the table and, in an absent-minded way, made for Leibniz as if to impale him. Leibniz side-stepped politely, took the weapon by its hilt, and then embarked upon the project of trying to get it back into its scabbard. The tip had to be introduced into an opening that was too small for Leibniz to even *see*, inasmuch as he had pocketed his spectacles, and he was loath to touch the bat-smeared metal with the fingers of his other hand. So when the Tsar's advance-guard rounded the corner into the room, he was still standing directly before the entrance holding it up in a posture that was ambiguous. The guards, who were not paid to be meditative, could not really discern, at a moment's glance, whether he was yanking the blade out, or shoving it in.

Three swords screamed out of their scabbards as one, and Leibniz glanced up to discover the blades—quite a bit shinier than his—triangulated on the base of his neck. In the same instant—possibly because he had gone slack with terror—the tip of his blade happened to blunder into his scabbard, and down it slid, until rust-blockages froze it about halfway in. Leibniz's arms had dropped to his sides like damp hawsers. The heavy guard of his rapier reciprocated back and forth on its springy blade going *wuv, wuv, wuv.* Twenty-five-year-old Peter Romanov entered the room on the arm of twenty-nine-year-old Sophie Charlotte. Or Leibniz (who was standing motionless, with his chin high in the air to keep it from being shaved) assumed this fellow must be the Tsar, from the fact that he was the tallest human being that Leibniz had set eyes on in his whole life. For all his immensity, he had a gracefully drawn-out frame, and his face—clean-shaven except for a dark moustache—still had a boyish softness about it. When he tore his dark, quasi-Mongol eyes away from Sophie Charlotte (not easy in that she was very likely the most lovely and interesting female he had ever seen) and got a load of the tableau in the dining room, he came to a stop. His left eye twitched shut as if he were winking, then struggled open, then did it again. Then the whole left side of his face contorted as if an invisible hand had gripped his cheek and twisted it. He pulled free of Sophie Charlotte's arm and clapped both hands over his face for a few moments, possibly from embarrassment and possibly to hide this twitching. Then both hands lunged out as he strode forward. He was so shockingly colossal that it seemed as if he were diving forward, launching himself towards his three guards like an immense bat. But he remained on his feet. He grabbed the two guards on the flanks by the scruffs of their necks and drew them together so that they collided with the one in the middle; and holding them all together in a bear-hug he screamed at them for a while in what Leibniz took to be the tongue of Muscovy. Leibniz stepped backwards until he was behind and beside Sophie, then got both hands together on his sword-pommel and rammed it all the way home in a series of sharp yanking gestures. By that time, Peter had switched over to whorehouse German. "I would borrow three large wheels!"

"What for?" Sophie Charlotte inquired, as if she and everyone else in the room did not already know.

"Merely breaking all of the bones in their bodies does not cause sufficient pain to punish them for this crime. But if they are first tied to a wheel, which is continually rotated, the shifting of their weight causes the broken bone-ends to jar and grind against each other—"

"We have this form of punishment, too," Sophie Charlotte said. "But," she added diplomatically, "we have not actually employed it recently, and our punishment-wheels are in storage. Mother, may I introduce Mr. Romanov. Mr. Romanov is from Muscovy and is traveling to Holland to visit the ship-yards. He is very very very interested in ships."

"Pleased to make your acquaintance, Mr. Romanov," said Sophie, allowing the giant Tsar to spring forward and kiss her hand. "Did my daughter show you my gardens and greenhouses as you drove in?"

"She told me of them. You walk in them."

"I *do* walk in them, Mr. Romanov, for hours and hours every day—it is how I preserve my health—and I am terribly afraid that if these three wonderful gentlemen were to be mounted on wheels and broken and rotated for days and days screaming with the torments of the damned as they slowly died, that it would quite spoil my recreations."

Peter looked somewhat baffled. "I am merely trying to—"

"I *know* what you are trying to do, Mr. Romanov, and it is so very dear of you."

"He is worried about Raskolniki," Sophie Charlotte said helpfully.

"As very well he *should* be!" Sophie returned without hesitation.

"They believe that I am the Antichrist," Peter said sheepishly.

"I can assure you that Doctor Leibniz is in no way offended to have been mistaken for a Raskolniki, are you, Doctor?"

"In a strange way I am almost honored, your majesty."

"There, you see?"

But Peter, upon hearing Leibniz's name, had turned questioningly to Sophie Charlotte and said something no one could quite make out—except Sophie Charlotte. She got a look of joyous surprise on her face, causing every male heart in the room to stop beating for ten seconds. "Why, yes, Mr. Romanov, it *is* the same fellow! Your memory is quite excellent!" Then, for the benefit of everyone else, she continued, "This is indeed the same Dr. Leibniz who gave me the tooth."

A ripple of mis-translation and conjecture spread outwards through the carnival of Prussians, Muscovites, Tatars, Cossacks, dwarves, Dutchmen, Orthodox priests, *et cetera*, who had piled up behind them. Sophie Charlotte clapped her hands. "Bring out the tooth of the Leviathan! Or whatever it was."

"Some sort of giant elephant, I rather think, but with plenty of hair on it," Leibniz put in.

"I have seen such beasts frozen in the ice," said Peter Romanov. "They are bigger than elephants."

George Louis had returned from his errand and had been skirting the back of the crowd trying to find a way in without getting into a shoving-match with any Cossacks. The crowd parted to admit one of Sophie Charlotte's footmen, who glided in carrying a tray with a velvet pillow on it, and on the pillow, a rock still nestled in torn-up wrapping paper. George Louis followed the lead and took up an appropriate position next to his mother, and got an expression on his face that said, *I am ready to be introduced and to have a jolly good time playing along with this incognito business,* but everyone else—especially Peter—was gazing at the rock instead. It was pinkish-brown, and about the size of a melon, but sort of Gibraltar-shaped, with a flat, angled grinding-surface on the top and a system of rootlike legs below. There was a lot of rude behavior going on in the outer fringes of Peter's retinue, as diverse furry muscular steppe-dwellers jostled for position. They seemed to have convinced themselves that "Tooth of the Leviathan" was a flowery monicker for some very large diamond. Men who were eager to lay eyes on the treasure collided with others who already had, and were recoiling in dismay. Meanwhile Leibniz had been nudged up to the front by Sophie, who did not believe in breaking her minions on the wheel, but was not above delivering swift jabs to the arse and kidney with her bejewelled knuckles. Leibniz bellied up to the tooth and caught the edge of the underlying tray, which was almost too heavy for the servant to hold up. Sophie Charlotte's heavenly face was beaming at him. Next to it was the Tsar's watch-chain. Leibniz began to tilt his head back, and did not stop until he was gazing at the undersurface of Peter's chin. His wig slipped and Sophie cuffed him in the back of the head to set it aright, and said: "The Doctor is hard at work on a wonderful project in Natural Philosophy, which my son does not understand, but which should produce miraculous results, provided some wise monarch can only supply him with an infinite amount of money."

At this Leibniz naturally winced, and George Louis chuckled. But Tsar Peter thought about it very gravely, as if an infinite amount of money was a routine sum for him to bandy about in his budget-meetings.*

"Could it make ships better?"

"Ships and many other things, Mr. Romanov."

That did it; Peter hurled a frightfully significant glare at some advisor, who cringed back half a step and then fastened a raptor-like gaze upon Leibniz's face. The Tsar, having settled that much, brushed past the Doctor on his way to greet George Louis.

---

* Maybe it was a translation problem; the German word for infinite is *unendlich,* or, roughly, unendly, without an end, and perhaps it came through to the Tsar as "a certain amount every year."

BOOK 4

Bonanza

Japan
MAY 1700

Dappa exchanged Malabar-words with three black sailors who had just hauled in the sounding-lead, then turned toward the poop deck and gave van Hoek a certain look. The captain stretched out a mangled hand towards the bow, then let it fall. A pair of Filipino sailors swung mauls, dislodging a pair of chocks, and the head of the ship pitched upward slightly as it was relieved of the weight of the anchors. Their chains rumbled through hawse-holes for a moment, making a sound like Leviathan clearing its throat. Then chains gave way to soft cables of manila that slithered and hissed across the deck for quite a few moments, gathering force, until everyone abovedecks began to doubt if the Malabari sailors with the sounding-lead had really gotten it right. But then the life seemed to go out of those cables. They coasted to a stop, and the Filipinos went to work recovering the slack. The sails had all been struck, but the wind that they had ridden in from the Sea of Japan found purchase on *Minerva's* hull and nudged her forward into the long shadow of a snow-topped mountain, creating the curious impression that the sun was setting in the east.

Jack, Vrej Esphahnian, and Padraig Tallow were up around the foremast, stowing the few paltry sails that van Hoek had used to bring *Minerva* into this cove. Jack and Vrej were up in the ratlines while Padraig, who had lost his left leg during a corsair-attack around Hainan Island, was stomping around on a hand-carved peg-leg of jacaranda wood, humming to himself and pulling on ropes as necessary. These men were all shareholders in the enterprise, and normally did not do sailors' work. But today most of the ship's complement was down on the gundeck. The ship had developed a ponderous side-to-side roll that was obvious to Jack, high up in the ratlines. This told him, without looking, that all of the cannons had been run out as far as they could go, and were protruding from their gunports, giving *Minerva* the appearance of a hedgehog. The

679

Japanese lurking in the forests that lined this cove would not have to consult their books of *rangaku,* Dutch Learning, to understand the message.

Gabriel Goto was standing at the bow in a bright kimono. Gazing down on him from above, Jack saw his shoulders soften and his head bow. The *ronin* had shaved, cut, greased, and knotted his grizzled hair into a configuration so peculiar that it would have gotten him burnt at the stake, or at best beaten to a pulp, in most jurisdictions; but here it was apparently as *de rigueur* as wigs at Versailles. Gabriel Goto did not have to worry about looking strange in Western eyes ever again, once he set foot on yonder shore. Because either the whole Transaction was a trap, and he would be crucified on the spot (the customary greeting for Portuguese missionaries), or else it was on the up-and-up, and he would become a Japanese in good standing once again—a Samurai looking after some scrap of mining country in the north, and keeping his religious opinions—if he still had any—to himself.

"His journey is over," Enoch Root observed, when Jack descended to the upperdeck. "Yours is about halfway along, I should say."

"Would that it were," Jack said. "Van Hoek tells me that we have another forty degrees to travel eastwards, before we reach the Antipode of London. After all these years I am not even close to halfway."

"That is only one way to measure it," Enoch said. He had been crouched on the deck, arranging some mysterious instruments and substances in a black chest. Now he stood up and nodded at some particular feature that his eyes had marked on the shore. "You might instead say that no place is less accessible from London, than this."

"Or that no place is harder to reach from here than London," Jack said. "I take your point."

They stood and looked at Japan for a while. Jack had not been sure what to expect. Nothing would have surprised him: castles floating in air, two-headed swordsmen, demons enthroned on tops of volcanoes. They'd finally reached one of those places that were not shown on the Doctor's maps in Hanover, save as vague sketchings of shorelines with nothing in back of them. If phantasms existed anywhere on the globe, they'd be here. But Jack saw none. Now that they had been here long enough to begin picking out details, Jack could perceive buildings here and there. They had an Oriental look about them, to be sure. But *Minerva* had been trading in East Asia for two years, as slow progress was being made towards today's Transaction, and they had seen Chinese roofs in many places: Manila, Macao, Shanghai, even Batavia. These Japanese buildings seemed much the same. Smoke came from their chimneys as it did in every other place where weather was cold. Hilltops had watch-towers on them, coastlines had piers, fishing-boats and fishnets were drawn up on beaches just as they had been at the foot of Sanlúcar de Barrameda. A few Japanese crones were out on a rock with baskets, gathering seaweed, but Jack had seen Japanese Christians doing the same thing near Manila. There were no demons and no phantasms.

"In truth? I feel as if I've already been round the world," Jack said. "The only thing separating me from London is Mexico, which I have seen on maps, and know to be but a narrow isthmus."

"Don't forget the Pacific and Atlantic Oceans," Enoch said. He began closing up several latches and locks of the little chest.

" 'Tis naught but water, and we have a ship," Jack scoffed. Every Filipino within earshot crossed himself, taking Jack's words as a more or less direct request for God to strike Jack, and anyone near him, dead. "In truth, I was considering this very subject the night before we departed Queena-Kootah, when we were all convened, there, at the new Bomb and Grapnel, at the foot of Eliza Peak, enjoying the balmy breezes and drinking toasts to Jeronimo, Yevgeny, Nasr al-Ghuráb, Nyazi, and others who could not be with us."

"Oh? You did not seem to be in any condition to consider *anything*."

"You forget I am no stranger to mental impairments, and have learned to get by with them," Jack said. "At any rate. My ruminations—"

"*Rum*-inations?"

"*Roominations* ran along these general lines: You gave me advice not to name this ship after Eliza, for one day the Vessel might arrive in the same city as the Lady and give rise to whisperings and inferences that he might find embarrassing or even dangerous. Fine. So when we first dropped anchor before Queena-Kootah, a couple of years ago, and Surendranath ventured ashore to trade with the Moorish natives, and learnt that they stood in need of a new Sultan—I say, when we became aware that the place was essentially being *given* to us—I looked at that beautiful snow-capped mountain and named it Eliza. Because it was warm, fertile, and beautiful below, while being a bit frosty and inaccessible at the top—yet possessing a *volcanick* profile foretelling explosions—"

"Yes, you have explained the similitude in great detail on several occasions."

"Righto. But I reckoned it was safe to use Eliza's name *there*, as it was so far away from the cities of Christendom. But later—after we had installed Mr. Foot as Sultan, and Surendranath as Grand Wazir, and they had built the Bomb and Grapnel anew—European ships began to drop anchor there, and old sea-captains began coming ashore, and some of them *knew* Mr. Foot from of old. They resumed conversations that had been interrupted by tavern-fights thirty years earlier at the first Bomb in Dunkirk. And I began to understand that even Queena-Kootah is not so terribly far from London. Standing on a ship in Japan, I am closer to London than ever I was standing on the banks of the Thames as a mud-lark boy."

"We must needs see to certain matters before you go for a stroll down the Strand," said Dappa, who was perched above them on the fo'c'sle-deck like a raven. "Such as whether we will be suffered to leave Japan alive. You have no idea how illegal this is."

"In truth I have a fairly good idea," Jack demurred.

But there was no stopping Dappa. "If this were Nagasaki, boats would have come out already to remove our rudder and take it ashore—armed Samurai would be searching every cranny of the ship for stowaway Jesuits."

"If this were Nagasaki we would not even be able to enter or leave the harbor without a Japanese pilot to help us over the rocks, and even then we would have to drop anchor several times and wait for tides—so we'd be helpless," Jack said. "As it is, we can be on our way at a moment's notice, provided we don't mind cutting our anchor-cables."

"When night falls we shall be desperately vulnerable to boarders," Dappa returned.

"We are in high latitudes for once—it is near the middle of the year (though you'd never guess it from the temperature)—and the day is long," Jack said, stepping around to a new position where he could get a clear view of the sun rising over the mountains of Japan. The water of the harbor was glancing light into his eyes so that it looked like a sheet of hammered copper. A longboat was clearly silhouetted on it, headed their way. "Damme, these Japanese are punctual—it is not like Manila."

"Chinese smugglers they accept grudgingly. It pleases them not to have a Christian ship drop anchor here. They want rid of us."

Van Hoek came by and said, "I had Father Gabriel write, in his last communication, that the transfer of metal would continue until the sun was four fingers above the western horizon—not a moment longer."

Every man on the ship who was not manning a cannon gravitated to the rail to watch the Japanese boat approach. As it drew closer, and the sun came clear of the rugged horizon, they were able to see a dozen or so commoners in drab clothing pulling on the oars, and, in the middle of the boat, three men wearing the same hair-do as Gabriel Goto, each armed with a pair of swords, and dressed in kimonos. Packed in around them were half a dozen archers in outlandish helmets and metal-strip armor. The boat was moving almost directly up-wind and so had not bothered raising her one sail, but from the mast she was flying a large banner of blue silk blazoned with a white insignia, a roundish shape that like the art of the Mahometans did not seem to be a literal depiction of anything in particular, but might have been thrown together by a man who had seen a flower once.

A fresh breeze was rising up out of the Sea of Japan as the day got under way, and no one needed to consult a globe to guess that this air had originated over Siberia. It was the first time Jack had felt cold since he had left Amsterdam—a memory that caused him to rub absent-mindedly at the old harpoon-scar on his arm, which at the moment was all covered with goose-pimples. The crew of Filipinos, Malabaris, and Malays had never felt anything like this, and muttered to one another in astonishment. "Make sure they understand that this is only a taste of what will come when we are crossing the Pacific, or rounding Cape Horn," van Hoek said to Dappa. "If any of them desires to jump ship, Manila will be his last opportunity."

"*I* am giving thought to it *myself,*" Dappa said, rubbing and spanking himself. His eyes crossed for a moment as he gazed in alarm at steam rising from his own mouth. "I could be a publican at the new Bomb and Grapnel . . . and never feel cold, except when I had snow brought down from Eliza Peak, and scooped a handful of it into a rum-drink. Brrr! How can those men stand it?" He nodded across fifty yards of chop to the Japanese boat. The Samurais were kneeling there stolidly, facing into the wind, which made their garments billow and snap.

"Later they will go boil themselves in vats," Enoch said learnedly.

"When I saw Goto-san's get-up," Jack said, "I supposed that he'd had it pieced together of scraps collected from *Popish Churches* and *whorehouses,* such are the colors. Yet compared to what those sourpusses in the boat are wearing, Father Gabriel's togs look like funeral-weeds."

"They put French Cavaliers to shame," Enoch agreed.

In a few minutes the Japanese boat advanced into the lee of *Minerva* and drew up alongside her. Lines were thrown back and forth, and a pilot's ladder unrolled from the upperdeck. The protocol of what followed had been worked out in such detail that van Hoek had to consult a written list: First, the Cabal gathered near the mainmast and said farewell to Gabriel Goto. Jack, for his part, had never felt especially friendly toward the man, but now he remembered the *ronin* doing battle against the foe at the needle's eye in Khan el-Khalili, and his nose ran and tears came to his eyes. Gabriel Goto was recalling the same thing, for he bowed low to Jack and said in Sabir: "I have been a *ronin* all my life, Jack, which means a Samurai without a master—except for that one day in Cairo when I swore allegiance to you, and for a brief time knew what it was to have a Lord and to fight as part of an Army. Now I go to a place where I will have a new Lord and serve in a different Army. But in my heart I will always owe my first allegiance to you." And then he removed the two swords, the *katana* and the *wakizashi*, from the belt of his garment, and presented them to Jack.

Dappa, van Hoek, Monsieur Arlanc, Padraig, and Vrej Esphahnian each stepped forward to exchange bows with the Samurai. Moseh, Surendranath, and the Shaftoe boys had remained behind in Manila and had already said their good-byes on the banks of the Pasig. Finally Gabriel Goto strode over to the top of the ladder and threw one leg over the gunwale and began to descend, rung by rung, vanishing below the teak horizon. For a moment only his head was visible, his face clenched like a fist, a few stray strands of hair whipping around in the wind. Then it was only his top-knot. Then he was gone.

Jack sighed. "We are a Cabal no longer," he said. "What began on the roof of the *banyolar* in Algiers has dissolved in this Japanese smugglers'-cove."

"We are all business partners now, and not brothers-in-arms," said Dappa.

"There is no difference to *me*," said Vrej Esphahnian, moderately annoyed. "Why should the bonds holding a business partnership together be inferior to those joining brothers-in-arms? For me the venture does not end here—it only begins."

Jack laughed. "A great adventure to other men is a routine thing for an Armenian, it seems."

A different top-knot appeared at the gunwale, and a different Samurai came aboard and exchanged bows with van Hoek. It was obvious from the way he looked around that he had never seen a ship of any size before, to say nothing of sailors with red hair, blue eyes, or black skin. But he kept his composure and carried on with the next phase of the protocol: van Hoek presented him with a single egg of *wootz*, which had been cleverly boxed and wrapped, with great ceremony, by an ancient Japanese lady in Manila. The Samurai made as great a ceremony of unwrapping it, then handed it off to one of his archers, who had to scamper up the ladder to get it.

Van Hoek gave the visitor a tour of *Minerva*'s hold, where many more eggs of *wootz,* and diverse other goods besides, were waiting for inspection. Meanwhile Enoch Root caused his black chest to be lowered into the boat. Then he descended the ladder. In a few minutes he was followed by the Samurai, who'd finished his inspection belowdecks. The Japanese boat cast off its lines, raised a sail, and quickly made its way into a pier, where it was tied up next to a much larger vessel, a sort of cargo-barge that looked as if it might be used for ferrying goods between shore and ship. Under the watchful spy-glasses of various men on *Minerva,* everyone disembarked onto the pier. Enoch was escorted to a sort of warehouse on the shore.

Half an hour later the alchemist came out by himself and boarded the boat. Immediately it shoved off and began rowing towards *Minerva.* At the same time a few score boat-men swarmed over the barge and cast off its mooring-lines, and began laboring with oars and push-poles to move it away from shore.

Enoch Root ascended the pilot's ladder like a young man, though when his face appeared above the rail he had a grave look about him. To van Hoek he said, "I performed every test I know of. More tests than the assayers in New Spain will likely do. I submit to you that the stuff is as pure as any from the mines of Europe." To Jack the only thing he said was, "It is a very strange country."

"How strange?" Jack asked.

Enoch shook his head and answered "Enough to make me understand how strange Christendom is." Then he retired to his cabin.

Minerva's sailors pulled his belongings up on ropes: first his chest of alchemical whatnot, and second a box, still partly covered in gaudy wrapping paper. Dappa caught this as it was hoisted over the rail and set it down on a table that they'd brought up from van Hoek's wardroom. Nestled in crumpled paper inside the box was an egg of fired clay: a flask, stoppered at one end by a wooden bung. Wax had been dribbled over this to seal it, but Enoch Root had already violated the seal so that he could perform his tests. Dappa thrust his hands down into the nest of paper and cupped the egg in his hands and raised it up into cold blue sunlight. Van Hoek drew out his dagger and used its tip to worry the bung loose. When this had been removed, Dappa tipped the flask. Fluid sloshed inside with momentum so potent that it nearly pulled him off his feet. A bead of liquid silver leapt out into the sun and built speed until it struck the tabletop with the impact of a hammer. Then it exploded in a myriad gleaming balls that glided across the table and cascaded over its edge like a waterfall and spattered heavily on *Minerva*'s deck. The quicksilver probed downhill, seeking gaps between planks, spattering down into the gundeck and making an argent rain among the men who stood tense by their guns. A murmur and then a thrill ran through the ship. It was to every man aboard as if *Minerva* had received a second christening, with quicksilver instead of Champagne, and that she was now re-consecrated to a new mission and purpose.

It was high noon before the barge was alongside *Minerva* and the transfer of cargo could begin. This was an awkward way to do it, but the Japanese officials would on no account suffer *Minerva* to approach shore. With larger cargo it would have been well nigh impossible. But *Minerva* was laden with *wootz*, silk, and pepper, and the barge carried nothing but flasks of quicksilver, and bales of straw for packing it. Any of these items could be passed or thrown from hand to hand, and once they had got it organized the transfer went on at a terrific pace— a hundred men, sweating and breathing hard, could transfer tons of cargo in a minute. Steel, spice, and silk streamed out of *Minerva*'s holds and were replaced by quicksilver. The outgoing and incoming flows grazed each other at one place on the upperdeck, where Monsieur Arlanc and Vrej Esphahnian sat at the table facing each other, each armed with a stockpile of quills, one tallying the quicksilver and the other tallying other goods. Every so often they would call out figures to each other, just making sure that the flows were balanced, so that *Minerva* would not rise too high or sink too low in the water.

Enoch Root emerged, rubbing sleep from his eyes, when the transfer was perhaps two-thirds complete. He flicked his eyes at Jack, and then van Hoek, and then returned to his cabin.

Twenty seconds later Jack and van Hoek were in there with him.

"I was trying to sleep but that lanthorn kept me awake," Enoch said, nodding at an oil lamp that was suspended from the ceiling of his cabin on a chain. It was swinging back and forth dramatically even though the ship was only rocking slightly from side to side.

"Why don't you take it down?" Jack asked.

"Because I think it is trying to tell me something," Enoch said. He then turned his gaze on van Hoek. "You told me, once, that every harbor, depending on its size, has a characteristic wave. You said that even if you were lying in your cabin with the curtains drawn you could tell the difference between Batavia and Cavite simply by the period of the waves."

"It's true," van Hoek said. "Any captain can tell you stories of ships that were proven seaworthy, but that were cast away entering an unfamiliar harbor, because the period of that harbor's waves happened to match the natural frequency of the ship's hull."

"Every ship, depending on how it is ballasted and laden, rocks in a particular rhythm—just as this lantern swings at a fixed rate," said Enoch, explaining it for Jack. "If waves strike that ship in the same rhythm, then she soon begins moving so violently that she overturns and is cast away."

"Just as a lute-string that is plucked makes its partner, which is tuned to the same note, vibrate in natural sympathy," said van Hoek. "Go on, Enoch."

"When we sailed into this harbor early this morning, my lanthorn suddenly began to swing so violently that it was bashing against the ceiling and spilling oil about the cabin," Enoch said. "And so I took it down and adjusted the chain to a different length, as you see it now." Enoch now lifted the lanthorn's chain from its hook in the ceiling-beam, and began to feel his way along, link by link, until he came to one that was worn smooth. "This is how it was when we entered the harbor," he said, and then re-hung the lanthorn so that it dangled a few inches lower than before. He pulled it away to the side and then let it go, and it began swinging back and forth in the center of the cabin. "So it follows that the frequency we observe now—swing, swing, swing—is tuned to the natural period of this harbor's waves."

"With all due respect to you and your friends of the Royal Society," van Hoek said, "can this demonstration not wait until we are out in the middle of the Sea of Japan?"

"It cannot," Enoch said calmly, "because we will never reach the Sea of Japan. This is a death-trap."

Van Hoek was about to spring to his feet, but Enoch restrained him with a hand on the shoulder, and glanced out his cabin window lest they be observed by some Japanese. "Hold," he said, "it is a subtle trap and subtle we must be to escape it. Jack, on my bed there is a flask."

Jack, who was too tall to stand upright in the cabin, crab-walked sideways a step or two, and found one of the quicksilver-flasks nestled among Enoch's bed-clothes.

"Hold it out at arm's length," Enoch said.

Jack did so, though it took the strength of both arms. The quicksilver inside the flask swirled about as he moved it, but then it settled. His hands became still. Then the liquid metal began sloshing back and forth, forcing his hands to move left, right, left, right, no matter how hard he tried to hold it still.

"Mark the lantern," said Enoch. Attention shifted from the sloshing flask to the swinging light.

Van Hoek saw it first. "They move at the same period."

"Which is the same as what?" Enoch asked, like a schoolmaster leading his pupils forward onto new ground.

"The natural rhythm of the waves at the entrance to this harbor," Jack said.

"I have tried three flasks in this way, and all of them slosh at the same frequency," Enoch said. "I submit to you that they have been tuned, as carefully as the pipes in a cathedral-organ. When this ship is fully loaded, and we try to sail out the harbor's mouth—"

"We will hit those waves . . . ten tons of quicksilver will began to heave back and forth . . . we will be torn apart," van Hoek said.

"It is a simple matter to remedy," Enoch said. "All we need is to go down and open the flasks and fill each one up so that they cannot slosh. But we must not let the Japanese know that we have figured out their plan, or else they will swarm on us. The warehouse on shore has an oily smell. I believe that there are many archers concealed in the woods, waiting with fire-arrows."

THEY FINISHED THE TRANSFER OF goods with plenty of daylight left. The Samurai in charge of the barge bid them farewell with a perfunctory bow and then turned his attention to getting his hoard of exotic goods in to shore. Van Hoek ordered preparations made for sailing, but they were of a highly elaborate nature, and took much longer than they might have. Belowdecks he had pulled one man off of each gun crew and put as many as he could muster to work unstoppering the quicksilver-flasks and decanting the mercury from one to the next, until each one was brim-full. Aboard ship there was never a shortage of pitch and black stuff used for caulking seams, and so each one of the flasks was sealed shut in that way. Half an hour before sunset van Hoek ordered the anchors weighed, a procedure that lasted until twilight had fallen over the harbor.

From that point onwards it was mad, black toil for many hours. There was a full moon (they'd planned it that way long in advance, so that they'd have better light during the tricky parts of the journey) and it shone very bright in the cold sky. As they traversed the harbor entrance, all of the ship's officers gathered in Enoch's cabin to watch the one quicksilver flask that had not been changed; it seemed to come alive at a certain point, when the rhythmic waves struck the hull, and thrashed around as if some djinn were trapped inside trying to fight its way out.

This was the point when the Japanese must have realized that their trap had been foiled, and out they came in longboats that were all ablaze with many points of fire from burning arrows. But van Hoek was ready. Abovedecks, the riggers had quietly readied all the courses of sail that *Minerva* had to offer, and they spread it all before the wind as soon as they heard the war-drums booming from the shore. Belowdecks, every cannon had been loaded with grape-shot. The Japanese boats could not hope to match *Minerva*'s speed once she got under way, and the few that came close were driven back by her cannons. All of about half a dozen burning arrows lodged in her teak-wood and were quickly snuffed out by officers with buckets of sand and water. They were able to get well clear of the shore, and of their pursuers, by the moon's light.

When the sun rose over Japan the next morning, a soldier's wind came up out of the west—which meant it blew perpendicular to their southerly heading, and was therefore so easy to manage that even soldiers could have trimmed the sails. Nevertheless van Hoek kept her speed low at first, because he was concerned that the flasks would shift about in their straw packing as they entered into heavier seas. As *Minerva* worked through various types of waves, van Hoek prowled around her decks sensing the movements of the cargo like a clairvoyant, and frequently communing with the spirit of Jan Vroom (who had died of malaria a year ago). His verdict, of course, was that they'd done a miserable job of packing the flasks, and that it would all have to be re-done when they got to Manila, but that, given the hazards of pirates and typhoons, they had no choice but to raise more sail anyway. So that is what they did.

They added one or two more knots to their speed thereby, and after three days, ran the Straits of Tsushima: a procedure that might have been devised by some fiendish engineer specifically to drive van Hoek mad with anxiety, as it involved running down a complex and current-ridden, yet poorly charted chute hemmed in on one side by pirate-islands of Korea and on the other by a country (Japan) where it was death for a foreigner to set foot. The paintings of Gabriel Goto's father were of very little use because that *ronin* had been piloting a boat of much shallower draft than *Minerva* and invariably chose to hug shorelines and squirt through gaps between islands where *Minerva* could not go.

At any rate they made it through, and putting the mountains of Japan on their larboard quarter they ventured into the East China Sea. Immediately the lookout identified sails to larboard: a ship emerging through a spacious gap between certain outlying Japanese islands, and coming about into a course roughly parallel with their own. This was curious, because the charts showed nothing but Japanese land in the direction from which the ship had come—beyond that, it was the Pacific Ocean for one hundred degrees, and then vague sketches of a supposed American coastline. And yet this ship was unmistakably European. More to the point, as van Hoek announced after peering at it for a while through his spyglass, it was Dutch. And that settled the mystery. This was one of those Dutch vessels that was allowed to sail into the harbor of Nagasaki and anchor before Deshima—a walled and guarded island-compound near that city, where a handful of Europeans were suffered to dwell for brief periods as they traded with the representatives of the Shogun.

Now van Hoek ordered that the Dutch flag be run up on the mizzenmast, and had them fire a salute from the ship's cannons. The Dutch ship responded in kind, and so after exchanging various signals with flags and mirrors, the two vessels fell in alongside each other, and gradually drew close enough that words could be hollered back and forth through speaking-trumpets. Every man on board who knew how to write was busy writing letters for himself, or on behalf of those who couldn't, because it was obvious that this Dutch ship was headed for Batavia, and thence west-bound. Within a few months she would be dropping anchor in Rotterdam.

This was when they lost their Alchemist.

When it came clear that they were about to lose their Adult Supervision, Jack felt panic under his feet like a swell pressing up on the ship's hull. But he did not suppose that it would instill confidence, among the crew, for him to break down and blubber. So he acted as if this had been expected all along. Indeed, in a way it had. Enoch Root had shown inhuman patience during the last couple of years, as the transaction of the quicksilver had been slowly teased together, and there had been plenty of interesting diversions for him in the Chinese and Japanese *barangays* of Manila, the countless strange islands of the Philippines, and in helping to establish Mr. Foot as the White Sultan of Queena-Kootah. But it was long since time for him to move on.

He had taken up an interest in the vast territories limned on Dutch charts to the South and East of the Philippines: New Guinea; the supposed Australasian Continent; Van Diemen's Land; and a chain of islands sprawling off into the uncharted heart of the South Pacific, called the Islands of Solomon.

Enoch stood on the upperdeck, waiting for his chests and bags to be lowered into the longboat. As he often did in idle moments, he reached into the pocket of his traveling-cloak and took out a contraption that looked a bit like a spool. But a poorly made one, for the ends of the spool were bulky, and the slot in between them, where the cord was wound, was narrow. He unwound a couple of inches of cord and slipped his finger through a loop that had been tied in its end. Then he allowed the spool to fall from his hand. It dropped slowly at first, as the spool's inertia resisted its tendency to unwind, but then it picked up speed and plunged smoothly toward the deck. Just shy of hitting the planks it stopped abruptly, having unwound its meager supply of cord. At the same moment Enoch gave a little twitch of the hand, and the spool reversed its direction and began to climb up the string.

Jack glanced across several fathoms of open water toward the Dutch ship. A dozen or so sailors were watching this miracle with their mouths open.

"They cannot see the string at this distance," Jack commented, "and suppose you are doing some sort of *magick.*"

"Any sufficiently advanced technology is indistinguishable from a yo-yo," Enoch said.

"That could not hurt a sparrow," Jack said. "I prefer the original type with the rotating knives."

"All well and good for striking prey off tree-limbs in the Philippine jungle," Enoch said, "but it gets uncomfortable, carrying such weapons about in one's pocket."

"Where art thou and thy yo-yos bound?"

"It is rumored that the purple savages of Arnhem Land also make throwing-weapons that return to the thrower," Enoch said, "but without a string, or any other such physickal connexion."

"Impossible!"

"As I said—'Any sufficiently advanced tech—'"

"I heard you the first time. So it's off to Arnhem Land. And then?"

Enoch paused to check the progress of the boat-loading, and seeing that he still had a minute or two, related the following: "You know that our entire Enterprise hinges on our being able to corrupt certain Spanish officials and sea-captains, which is not inherently difficult. But we have had to spend countless hours wining and dining them, and listening to their interminable yarns and sea-fables. Most of these are tedious and unremarkable. But I heard one that interested me. It was told me by one Alfonso, who was first mate aboard a galleon that left Manila for Acapulco some years ago. As usual they attempted to sail north to a higher latitude where they could get in front of the trade wind to California. Instead they were met by a tempest that drove them to the south for many days. The next time they were able to make solar observations, they discovered that they had actually crossed the Line and were several degrees south. Now the storm had washed away all of the earth that they had packed around their hearth in the galley, making it impossible for them to light a cook-fire without setting the whole galleon ablaze. So they dropped anchor near an island (for they'd come in sight of a whole chain of 'em, populated by people who looked like Africans) and gathered sand and fresh water. The water they used to replenish their drinking-jars. The sand they packed around their hearth. Then they continued their journey. When they arrived at Acapulco, the better part of a year later, they discovered nuggets of gold under the hearth—evidently that sand was auriferous and the heat of the fire had melted the gold and separated it from the sand. Needless to say, the Viceroy in Mexico City—"

"The same?"

Enoch nodded. "The very same from whom you stole the gold before Bonanza. He was informed of this prodigy, and did not delay in sending out a squadron, under an admiral named de Obregon, to sail along that line of latitude until they found those islands."

"Would those be the Solomon Islands?"

"As you know, Jack, it has long been supposed that Solomon—the builder of the Temple in Jerusalem, the first Alchemist, and the subject of Isaac Newton's obsessions for lo these many years, departed from the Land of Israel before he died, and journeyed far to the east, and founded a kingdom among certain islands. It is a part of this legend that this kingdom was fabulously wealthy."

"Funny how no one ever makes up legends concerning wretchedly poor kingdoms—"

"It matters not whether this legend is *true,* only that some people *believe* it," Enoch said patiently. He had begun to do tricks with the yo-yo now, making it fly around his hand like a comet whipping around the sun.

"Such as this Newton fellow? The one who reckoned the orbits of the planets?"

"Newton is convinced that Solomon's temple was a geometrickal model of the solar system—the fire on the central altar representing the sun, *et cetera.*"

"So he would fain know about it, if the Islands of Solomon were discovered . . ."

"Indeed."

". . . and no doubt he has already perused the chronicles of that expedition that was sent out by our friend in Bonanza."

Enoch shook his head. "There are no such chronicles."

"The expedition was shipwrecked?"

"Shipwrecked, killed by disease . . . the vectors of disaster were so plentiful that the accounts cannot be reconciled. Only one ship made it to Manila, half of her crew dead and the rest dying of some previously unheard-of pestilence. The only one who survived was one Elizabeth de Obregon, the wife of the Admiral who had commanded the squadron."

"And what does she have to say for herself?"

"She has said nothing. In a society where women cannot own property, Jack, secrets are to them what gold and silver are to men."

"Why did the Viceroy not then send out another squadron?"

"Perhaps he did."

"You have grown coy, Enoch, and time grows short."

"It is not that I am coy, but that you are lazy in your thinking. If such expeditions had been sent out, and found nothing, what would the results be?"

"Nothing."

"If an expedition had succeeded, what result then?"

"Some chronicle, kept secret in a Spanish vault in Mexico or Seville, and a great deal of gold . . ." Here Jack faltered.

"What did you expect to find in the hold of the Viceroy's brig?"

"Silver."

"What found you instead?"

"Gold."

"But the mines of Mexico produce only silver."

"It is true . . . we never solved the mystery of the origin of that gold."

"Do you have any idea, Jack, how many alchemists are numbered among the ruling classes of Christendom?"

"I've heard rumors."

"If a rumor got out among those people—kings, dukes, and princes—that the Island of Solomon had been discovered, and gold taken from there—not just any gold, mind you, but gold that came from the furnaces of King Solomon himself, and was very close to being the pure stuff of the Philosopher's Stone and the Philosophick Mercury—I should think that it would excite a certain amount of interest. Wouldn't you say?"

"If rumor got out, why, yes—"

"It always gets out," Enoch explained flatly. "Does this help to explain why so many great men are so very angry with you?"

"I never thought it wanted explanation. But now that you mention it . . ."

"Good. And I hope it also explains why I must go and see these Solomon Islands myself. If the legends are true, then Newton will want to know all about it. Even if they are nothing more than legends, those islands might be a good place for a man to go, if he wanted to get away from the world for a few years, or a few centuries . . . in any event, that is where I am bound."

The yo-yo came up sharply into Enoch's palm and stopped.

THE SEA-VOYAGE FROM JAPAN to Manila had in common with all other sea-voyages that it was all about latitudes. Van Hoek, Dappa, and several others aboard knew how to find their latitude by observing the sun's position in the sky. The sun came out at least once a day and so they always had a good idea of which parallel they were at. But there was no way to reckon longitude. Accordingly, van Hoek's charts and records of Hazards to Navigation tended to be organized by latitude. Along certain parallels they had nothing to worry about, because in this part of the world (according to the documents) no reefs or islands existed there. But along certain other parallels, hazards had been discovered, and so whenever *Minerva* was found to be in such latitudes the mood of the ship changed, sail was reduced, lookouts added, soundings taken. They might have been a hundred miles due east or due west of the Hazard in question; not having any idea of their longitude, there was simply no telling. Since the voyage from Japan to Manila was a north-to-south one, their degree of latitude, and their degree of anxiety, were changing every moment.

Other than reefs and islands, the chief hazards were typhoons, and the kingdom of Corsairs who had wrested Formosa from the Dutch some years previously, and through whose waters they had to sail in order to reach Luzon. On this voyage both of those hazards struck on the same day: Corsairs sighted them and fell into an intercept course, but before they could close with *Minerva,* the weather began to alter in ways that suggested an approaching typhoon. The Corsairs broke off the pursuit and turned their energies to survival. By this point *Minerva* had ridden out several such storms, and her officers and crew knew how it was done; van Hoek could make educated guesses as to how the direction of the wind would change over the course of the next two days, and how its strength would vary according to their distance from its center. By setting some storm-sails and managing the tiller personally, he was able to arrange it so that they were not driven against the isle of Formosa. Instead the typhoon flung them out to the south and east, into the Philippine Sea, which was deep water with no obstructions. Later, when the weather cleared and they could shoot the sun again, they sought out a particular latitude ($19°\ 45'$ N) and followed that parallel west for two hundred miles until they had passed through the Balintang Channel, which separated some groups of small islands north of

Luzon. Turning to the south then, they made way with great care until the hills and headlands of Ilocos—the northwestern corner of Luzon—came into view.

At that moment the character of the voyage changed. Three hundred miles separated them from the point of Mariveles at the entrance to Manila Bay, and it would all be coastal sailing, which meant contending with weak and fickle winds, and taking frequent soundings, and dropping anchor at night lest they run aground on some unseeable hazard in the dark. Some days they made no progress whatever, owing to contrary winds—by day, they traded with locals for fresh fruit and meat brought out in long dual-outrigger boats, and by night they patrolled *Minerva*'s decks with loaded blunderbusses, waiting for those same locals to steal out in the same boats and creep over the gunwales with knives in their teeth.

At any rate, ten days of this sort of travel brought them, late one afternoon, to the point of Mariveles, where several rocks projected from the surf like daggers. The garrison on the nearby island of Corregidor caught sight of *Minerva* around sunset and lit some fires to prevent her from running aground. By triangulating against these they were able to bring the ship gingerly around the south side of the island and drop anchor in the bay there. The next morning the Spanish ensign in command of the garrison came out on a longboat for an hour's visit; they knew him thoroughly, as *Minerva* had passed this way a dozen or so times on her triangular voyages among Manila, Macao, and Queena-Kootah. He gave them the latest jokes and gossip from Manila and they gave him some packets of spices and a few trinkets they'd picked up in Japan.

They weighed anchor and sailed across Manila Bay. The Spanish castle on the point of Cavite came into view first, and later they could make out, beyond it, the bell-towers and fortifications of Manila, and a thicket of masts and spars, shot through with furling silk banners, around the outlet of the Pasig River. It was the expectation of most aboard that they would make direct for there. But as they weathered the point of Cavite and entered into calmer water in the lee of the castle, van Hoek ordered most of the sails taken in. A *banca*—a sort of longboat hewn from the trunk of a single colossal tree—came toward them, and as it drew closer, Jack was able to recognize Moseh and Surendranath, who had stayed behind to settle some business affairs, and Jimmy and Danny, who had been acting as their bodyguards. One by one these men clambered up the pilot's ladder and joined their brethren on the upperdeck. Moseh and Surendranath went back into van Hoek's wardroom to confer with the captain and the other chief men of the enterprise. Jack could have participated in this meeting but declined to because he could tell from the look on Moseh's face that it had all gone more or less well, and that their next voyage would be eastbound.

This was the innermost harbor of Manila Bay: a hammock-shaped anchorage slung between two points of land several miles apart, each of which had been built up into a fortress by the Spaniards, or rather by their Tagalian minions, during the century and a half that they had held sway over these islands. The closer of the two forts, just off their starboard, was Cavite: a conventional square, four-bastioned castle thrust out into the water on a slender neck of land, so that the bay served as its moat. A ditch had been dug across that neck so that the landward approach could be controlled by a drawbridge. This ditch was situated at some distance from the castle proper, and the intervening space had been covered with buildings: a crowd of cane houses with more substantial wood-frame dwellings rising out of it from place to place, and three stone churches that had been erected, or were being erected, by various Popish religious orders.

The opposite end of the harbor was the city of Manila proper. The Spaniards had taken a small peninsula framed on one side by the Bay and on two others by rivers: the Pasig, and a welter of pissant tributaries that joined the Pasig just short of where it emptied into the Bay. They had enclosed this peninsula in a modern sort of slope-sided wall, a couple of miles in circuit, and erected noble bulwarks and demilunes at its corners, rendering it impregnable to land assault by Dutch, Chinese, or native legions. The outlet of the Pasig was dominated by a considerable fortress whose guns commanded the river, the Bay, and certain troublesome ethnic *barangays* across the river.

From this point of view—or any point of view, for that matter—it did not look like a fabled citadel of inconceivable wealth. If the Spaniards had built Manila anywhere else, her church-spires and watch-towers would have reached into the clouds. As it was, even the noblest buildings hugged the ground and had a stoop-shouldered look about them, because they had learned the hard way that anything more than two storeys high, and built of stone, would be brought down by an earthquake while the mortar was scarcely dry. So as Jack stood there on *Minerva*'s deck he perceived Manila as something very dark, low, and heavy, and overlaid with smoke and humidity, softened only a little by the high coconut palms that lined her shore.

This was just the sort of weather that culminated in a bracing thunder-shower—a fact *Minerva*'s crew knew well, for Manila had been their home port for most of the three years since the ship had made her maiden voyage out of Malabar, and at any rate half the crew had grown up along the shores of this bay. They also knew that this bay offered no protection from north winds, and that a big ship like *Minerva* would be cast away if she were caught between Cavite and Manila when the wind shifted round that way; she would run a-ground in the shallows and fall prey to Tagalians who would come out in their tree-trunk boats and Chinese *sangleys* who would come out in their sampans to salvage her. So instead of being boisterous, as one might reasonably expect of sailors who'd just made a perilous and improbable voyage to Japan and back, they were solemn as monks on Sunday, and angrily shushed anyone who raised his voice. Malabaris had suspended themselves in the ratlines like spiders in webs and were hanging there motionless with eyes half closed and mouths half open, waiting for meaningful stirrings in the air.

The sky and air were all white, and of a uniform brightness, so that it was impossible to get even a general notion of where the sun might be. According to the hour-glasses they used to keep track of watches, it must be an hour or so before sunset. The whole bay was as still and hushed as *Minerva*'s upperdeck; the only noise, therefore, came from the vast shipyard that spread along the shore below the sullen arsenal of Cavite. There five hundred Filipino slaves were at work under the whips and guns of helmeted Spaniards, constructing the largest ship Jack had ever seen. Which, considering the places he had been, meant that it was very likely the largest ship the world had seen since Noah's Ark had run a-ground on a mountain-top and been broken up for firewood.

Piled on the shore in pyramids were the stripped boles of giant trees that these Filipinos, or others in the same predicament, had cut down in the bat-infested jungles that crowded in along the shores of Laguna de Bay (a great lake just inland of Manila) and floated in rafts down the Pasig. Some of the workers were cutting these into beams and planks. But the great ship was close to being finished and so the demand for huge timbers was not what it had been months ago when the keel and frames had stood out like stiff fingers against the sky. Most of the laborers were concerned with finer matters now: making cables (indeed, Manila made the finest cordage in the world), caulking joints between hull-planks, and doing finish carpentry on the cabins where the most ambitious merchants of the South Seas would dwell for most of the next year, or drown within weeks, depending on how it went.

"Dad, either my eyes play tricks, or else you've finally traded in that Mahometan spadroon for *proper* armaments," said Daniel Shaftoe, eyeing the *katana* and *wakizashi* of Gabriel Goto, thrust into Jack's belt.

"I've been trying to grow accustomed to 'em," Jack allowed, "but it's all for naught. One-handed is how I learned to fight, and it's all I'll ever know. I wear these to honor Goto-san, but when next I venture into some place where I might need to do some *defensing*, it's the Janissary-sword I'll be wearing."

"Aw, it ain't that hard, Dad," said Jimmy, coming up to shoulder past his brother. "By the time we reach Acapulco we'll have you swingin' that *katana* like a Samurai." Jimmy patted the hilt of a Japanese sword, and now Jack noticed that Danny was armed in the same manner.

"Been broadening your horizons?"

"Manila is better than the *'varsity*," Danny proclaimed, "as long as you remain a step ahead o' that pesky *Spanish Inquisition* . . ."

"From the fact that Moseh is still alive, and has all his fingernails, I'm guessing you succeeded there."

"We fulfilled our obligations," Jimmy said hotly. "We took lodgings on the edge of the *barangay* of the Japanese Christians—"

"—an orderly place—" Danny offered

"Perhaps a bit *too* orderly," Jimmy said. "But we were hard up against the wicker walls of the *sangley* neighborhood, which is a perpetual riot, and so whenever the Inquisitors came after us we withdrew into that place for a while, and kept a sharp eye on one another's backs until such time as Moseh could settle the matter."

"I did not appreciate that Moseh had any such influence with the Sons of Torquemada," Jack said.

"Moseh has let it be known, to a few of the Spaniards, what we are planning," said Danny. "Suddenly those Spaniards are our friends."

"They call off the Inquisitor's dogs whenever Moseh lets out a squawk," Jimmy said airily.

"I wonder what their friendship will cost us," Jack said.

"They'd be more expensive as enemies, Dad," Danny said, and in his voice was a confidence that Jack had not felt about anything in about twenty years.

The teak deck was changing color from a weathered iron-gray to a warmer hue, almost as if a fire had been kindled belowdecks and was trying to burn its way through. Jack looked away toward the exit of the bay, and saw the cause: The sun, now a hand's breath above the horizon, had bored a hole through the miasma of vapor over the bay. Wisps and banks that still lurked in pockets of shade and stagnant coves round the foundations of the arsenal were fleeing from its sudden heat like smoke driven before a gust. For all that, the air was still. But a faint rumble prompted Jack to turn around and look east. Manila stood out in the clear now, her walls and bastions glowing in the sunlight as if they had been hewn out of amber and lit from behind by fire. The mountains behind the city were visible, which was a rare event. By comparison with them, the highest works of the Spaniards were low and flat as paving-stones. But those mountains in turn were humbled by phantasmic interlocking cloud-formations that were incarnating themselves in the limitless skies above, somewhat as if the personages and beasts of the Constellations had become fed up with being depicted in scatterings of faint stars, and had decided to come down out of the cosmos and clothe themselves in the stuff of typhoons. But they seemed to be having a dispute as to which would claim the most gorgeous and brilliant vapors, and the argument showed every sign of becoming a violent one. No lightning had struck the ground yet, and the cataracts of rain shed by some clouds were swallowed by others before they descended to the plane of the mountain-tops.

Jack altered his focus to the yards of *Minerva,* which compared to all of this were like broom-straws tangled together in a gutter. The men of the current watch were quietly making ready to be hit. Below, the head men of what had formerly been the Cabal had emerged from van Hoek's cabin and were moving forward. Some of them, such as Dappa and Monsieur Arlanc, had gone to the trouble of changing into gentlemanly clothes: breeches, hose, and leather shoes had been broken out of foot-lockers. Vrej Esphahnian and van Hoek were wearing actual periwigs and tri-cornered hats.

Van Hoek stopped just in front of the mainmast, at the edge of the quarterdeck, which loomed above the broadest part of the upperdeck like a balcony over a plaza. Most of the ship's complement had gathered there, and those who couldn't find room, or who were too short to see over their fellows' heads, had ascended to the forecastledeck whence they could look aft and meet van Hoek's eye from the same level. The sailors had grouped themselves according to color so that they could hear translations: the largest two groups were the Malabaris and the Filipinos, but there were Malays, Chinese, several Africans from Mozambique by way of Goa, and a few Gujaratis. Several of the ship's officers were Dutchmen who had come out with Jan Vroom. To look after the cannons they had rounded up a French, a Bavarian, and a Venetian artilleryman from the rabble of mercenaries that hung around Shahjahanabad. Finally there were the surviving members of the Cabal: van Hoek, Dappa, Monsieur Arlanc, Padraig Tallow, Jack Shaftoe, Moseh de la Cruz,

Vrej Esphahnian, and Surendranath. When Jimmy and Danny
Shaftoe were added, the number came to a hundred and five. Of
these, some twenty were active in the rigging, readying the ship for
weather.

Jack ascended the stairs to the quarterdeck and took up a position behind van Hoek, among the other share-holders. As he turned
round to look out over the upperdeck—facing in the general direction of Manila—one of those constellation-gods in the sky above the
city, furious because he had ended up in possession of nothing more
than a few shredded rags of dim gray-indigo stuff, flung a thunderbolt horizontally into the mid-section of a rival, who was dressed in
incandescent coral and green satin. The distance between them
must have been twenty miles. It seemed as if a sudden crack had
spanned a quarter of Heaven's vault, allowing infinitely more brilliant light to shine through it, for an instant, from some extremely
well-illuminated realm beyond the known universe. It was just as well
that the crew were facing the other way—though some of them
noticed startled expressions on the faces of the worthies on the quarterdeck, and swiveled their heads to see what was the matter. They
saw nothing except a blade of rain sinking into the black jungle
beyond Manila.

"It must have been Yevgeny, throwing a cœlestial Harpoon, to
remind van Hoek that brevity is a virtue," Jack said, and those who
had known Yevgeny chuckled nervously.

"We have lived through another voyage," van Hoek announced,
"and if this were a Christian ship I would take my hat off and say a
prayer of thanksgiving. But as it is a ship of no one particular faith, I
shall keep my hat on until I can say my prayers alone later. Go you all
to your temples, pagodas, shrines, and churches in Manila this night
and do likewise."

There was a general muttering of assent as this was translated.
Minerva had no fewer than three cooks, and three completely differ-
ent sets of pots. The only group who did not have their own were the
Christians, who, when it came to food, would balk at nothing.

"Never again will this group of men be all together in one place,"
said van Hoek. "Enoch Root has already bid us farewell. Within a
fortnight Surendranath and some of you Malabaris will set sail for
Queena-Kootah on the brig *Kottakkal* so that the rightful share of
our profits may be conveyed to the Queen of the same name. In time
Padraig will join them. He, Surendranath, and Mr. Foot will pursue
happiness in the South Seas while the rest of us journey onwards.
You sailors will disperse into Manila tonight. Some of you will return

to this ship in one month's time to prepare on our great voyage. Others will think better of it."

Van Hoek now yanked out his cutlass and aimed it at the titanic ship that was being finished before the arsenal of Cavite. "Behold!" he proclaimed. All heads turned toward the mountainous galleon, but only for a moment; then attention turned to the weather. A wind had finally been summoned up, and it came from the east but showed signs of swinging round to the north. But the watch had a sail ready on the maintop, and they raised it now and let the wind bite into it, and trimmed it so as to bring *Minerva* about and convey her toward deeper waters in the center of the bay.

"A great ship for a great voyage," van Hoek said, referring to the Spanish behemoth. "That is the Manila Galleon, and soon it will be laden with all the silks of China and spices of India and it will sail out of this bay and commence a voyage of seven months, crossing half of the terraqueous globe. When the Philippines fall away to aft her anchors will be brought up and stowed in the nethermost part of her hold, because for more than half a year they'll not see a speck of dry land, and anchors will be as much use to her as bilge-pumps on an ox-cart. Northward she'll sail, as far north as Japan, until she reaches a certain latitude—known only to the Spaniards—where trade winds blow due east, and where there are no isles or reefs to catch them unawares in mid-ocean. Then they'll run before the wind and pray for rain, lest they die of thirst and wash up on the shores of California, a ghost-ship crowded with parched skeletons. Sometimes those trade-winds will falter, and they'll drift aimlessly for a day, then two days, then a week, until a typhoon comes up from the south, or Arctic blasts come down out of the polar regions and freeze them with a chill compared to which what made us shiver and chafe so in Japan is as balmy as a maiden's breath against your cheek. They will run out of food, and wealthy Epicureans, after they've eaten their own shoes and the leathern covers of their Bibles, will kneel in their cabins and send up delirious prayers for God to send them just one of the moldy crusts that earlier in the voyage they threw away. Gums will shrivel away from teeth, which will fall out until they must be swept off the deck like so many hailstones."

This similitude was apparently improvised by van Hoek, for a barrage of pea-sized hail had just sprayed out of a low swirling cloud and speckled the deck. All hands looked at the hail and dutifully imagined teeth. A gust came across the water, decapitating a thousand whitecaps and flinging their spray sideways through the air; it caught them upside their heads, and in the same instant the sail popped like a musket-shot and the whole structure of the ship heaved and groaned from the impact. A rope burst and began thrashing about on the deck like a living thing as the tension bled out of it and its lays came undone. But then this momentary squall subsided and they found themselves working into a blustery north wind, across the darkling bay. The sun had plunged meteorically into the South China Sea, and its light was now overmatched by the lightning over Manila, which had merged into a continuous blue radiance that a person could almost read by.

"One day, long after they've given up hope, one of these wretches—one of the few who can still stand—will be up on deck, throwing corpses over the rail, when he'll see something afloat in the water below: a scrap of seaweed, no bigger than my finger. Not a thing you or I would take any note of—but to them, as miraculous as a visitation by an angel! There'll be a lot of praying and hymn-singing on that day. But it will all end in cruel disappointment, for no more seaweed will be observed that day, or the next, or the next. Another week they'll sail—nothing! Nothing to do but run before the wind, and try with all their might to resist the temptation to cannibalize the bodies of the dead. By that point the most saintly Dominican brothers aboard will forget their prayers, and curse their own mothers for having borne them. And then another week of the same! But finally the seaweed will appear—not just a single bit of it, but two, then three. This will signify that they are off the coast of California, which is an island belted all around with such weeds."

Jack noticed at about this time, that the blue-green light had grown much brighter, and had become steady and silent as if some eldritch Neptunian sun had risen out of the water, casting light but no warmth. Fighting a powerful instinctive reluctance, he forced himself to look up into the spars and rigging of the mainmast. Every bit of it—every splinter of wood and fiber of cordage—was aglow with crackling radiance, as if it had been dipped in phosphorus. It was a sight worthy of a good long look, but Jack made himself look down at the crowd on the quarterdeck instead. He saw a pool of upturned faces, teeth and eyes a-gleam, a well of souls gazing up in wonder.

"First 'twas Yevgeny—now Enoch Root is putting in his tuppence worth," he joked, but if anyone did so much as chuckle, the sound was swallowed up in the susurration of waves against the hull. Van Hoek turned and glanced at Jack for a moment, then squared off again to continue his terrible Narration. The weird Fire of Saint Elmo had crawled down the mast to dance round the fringes of his tri-cornered hat, and even the curls of his goat-hair wig had become infected by sparks that buzzed and rustled as if alive. The individual hairs of that long-dead goat were now re-animated as if by some *voudoun* chaunt, and began trying to get away from each other, which entailed straightening and spreading out-wards. The quivering tip of each hair was defended by a nasty corona.

Van Hoek paid it no mind; if he was even aware of it, he evidently saw it as a way to add emphasis to his words. "Yet their ordeal is not finished, but only takes a different form; now they must endure the torment of Tantalus, for that land of milk and honey is the domain of savages, and no victuals are to be found on her shores—only sudden and violent death. Now they must sail for many long days down that coast, moving ever southeastward, making occasional desperate forays on to the land to scavenge fresh water or game. Finally one day they spy a Spanish watch-tower glowering down upon 'em from a stony mountain-top above the sea. Signals are exchanged, letting those on the ship know that riders have been sent out, galloping down the King's Highway to the City of Mexico to spread the news that this year's Manila Galleon has not been cast away or sunk in a storm but, *mirabile dictu,* has survived. Several days more and then a Spanish town comes into view. Boats come out bearing the first fruit and vegetables that these travelers will have eaten in half a year. But, too, they bring tidings that both French and English pirates have rounded Cape Horn and are prowling the coast—many dangerous miles still separate them from their destination of Acapulco . . ."

The Saint Elmo's Fire was dying down now, and the miraculous pocket of calm in which they had drifted for the last several minutes was giving way to something a bit more like a thunderstorm. A big roller got under the hull, and the faces on the upperdeck undulated like a field of grain as every man sought his balance.

"As I said, we will be departing a few weeks after the Galleon, and we require sailors . . ." van Hoek began.

"Er, excuse me there, Cap'n," Jack said, "your description of the voyage's terrors was most affecting, and I'm sure every man jack has shited his breeches now . . . but you have forgotten to include any *countervailing* material. Having aroused the *fear,* you must now stimulate the *avarice,* of these sailors or else they will jump overboard and *swim* to shore right now, and will *never* enlist again."

Van Hoek now got a contemptuous look which Jack was only able to see with the help of a convenient triple lightning bolt. "You sorely underestimate their intelligence, sir. It is not necessary to come out and state *everything* so directly. A well-formed Narration says as much by what is left *out* of it as by what is put *in*."

"Then perhaps you should have left more *out.* I have some experience in matters *theatrickal,* sir," Jack said, "which is applicable here insofar as this quarterdeck resembles nothing so much as a stage, and *those,* to my eye—notwithstanding your very generous estimate of their intelligence—look like nothing so much as groundlings, knee-deep in hazelnut shells and gin-bottles, waiting—*begging*—to be hit over their heads with some direct and unambiguous *message.*"

A lightning-bomb detonated over Manila.

"There is your message," van Hoek said pointing toward the city, "and your groundlings will go into it tonight, and dwell in that Message for the next two months. You have dwelt there, too, Jack—did the Message not reach your ears?"

"I may have heard faint whisperings—could you *amplify* it?"

"Of all the enterprises to which a man can devote his energies," van Hoek began grudgingly, raising his voice, "long-distance trade is the most profitable. It is what every Jew, Puritan, Dutchman, Huguenot, Armenian, and Banyan aspires to—it is what built the Navies and palaces of Europe, the Court of the Great Mogul in Shahjahanabad, and many other prodigies besides. And yet in the world of trade, it is common knowledge that no circuit—not the slave trade of the Caribbean, not the spice trade of the Indies—exceeds the Manila-to-Acapulco run in sheer profit. The wealthiest Banyans in Surat and bankers in Genoa lay their perfumed heads on silken pillows at night, and dream of sending a few bales of cargo across the Pacific on the Manila Galleon. Even with all the dangers, and the swingeing duty that must be shelled out to the Viceroy, the profits never fall below four hundred percent. *That* city is founded upon such dreams, Jack. We are all going to go there now."

Van Hoek finally shut up at this point, and in the silence that followed he realized that, down below him on the upperdeck, his rant was being dutifully translated into diverse heathen tongues. The translators took more or less time to relate it, depending on the wordiness of their several languages and how much they edited out or how freely they embellished. But when the last of them finally wound up his oration, a light pattering started up. Jack flinched, thinking it was more hail. But then it grew into a heavy, stomping roar, and he recognized it as applause. Dappa thrust both index fingers into his mouth and emitted a piercing noise. Van Hoek seemed startled at first; then understanding dawned, and he turned to Jack, removed his hat, and bowed.

BOOK 5

the **Juncto**

Berlin

JANUARY 1700

At bottom, all our experience assures us of only two things, namely, that there is a connection among our appearances, which provides us the means to predict future appearances with success, and that this connection must have a constant cause.

— LEIBNIZ

G. W. Leibniz, President
Berlin Academy
Berlin, Prussia
To Mr. Daniel Waterhouse, Chancellor
Massachusetts Bay Institute of Technologickal Arts
Newtowne, Massachusetts Bay Colony
Dear Daniel,

The appearance of your letter on the doorstop of my Academy brought unlooked-for cheer to an otherwise frosty Berlin day, which developed into pleasure when I read that your Institute now has a roof over its head, and joy when you expressed your continued desire to collaborate with me. I confess that when two years passed without word from you, I thought you had been killed by Indians or hanged for a witch!

Much has happened since we last exchanged letters. You have probably noticed that I have a new address (Berlin) and what is more, it is in a new kingdom (Prussia). The monarch you knew by the name Elector Frederick III of Brandenburg is now called King Frederick I of Prussia. He is the same chap, still joyfully married to the same Sophie Charlotte, living in and ruling from the same palace that he built for her in Berlin, but he has (through machinations that would only disfigure this letter) persuaded the Holy Roman Emperor in

Vienna (still Leopold I, in case you have not been keeping up) to suffer him to use the title of King. His family (the Hohenzollerns) have been the Dukes of Prussia as well as Electors of Brandenburg for so many generations that it made sense to merge the two countries. The result is called Prussia but still ruled out of Brandenburg.

Sophie is as vigorous and crafty as always. She and her daughter have deemed it unwise to give the appearance of being too close, as this would give the idea, to friends and foes alike, that Sophie was now controlling an immense German state stretching from Königsberg in the east almost all the way west to the Rhine. For various reasons she prefers to seem instead like a contented elderly widow; so she lets her son George Louis think that he rules Hanover, and she travels to Berlin only occasionally, to pinch the cheeks of her grandchildren and put on a great show of harmlessness.

I shuttle back and forth between Hanover and Berlin all the time, to the point where the more bloody-minded Berlin courtiers were beginning to whisper that I must be acting as a secret conduit for Sophie's influence. The problem being that I could not point to any official reason why I should be in Berlin so frequently. The real reasons (to have interesting conversations with Sophie Charlotte and her brilliant circle of friends, and to tutor Princess Caroline) are scoffed at by that sort of person.

Hence the Berlin Academy, of which I am the first president. It seems like the sort of institution that a King ought to found (the fashion having been established, of course, by your Charles II with his Royal Society) and so doing it makes Frederick's new title seem that much more richly deserved. And being its president gives me an excuse to be in Berlin whenever I wish.

And it is well that I have *something* to belong to other than the Royal Society! By now you have probably received copies of the dreadful publications of last year: volume three of Wallis's work, in which my twenty-five-year-old correspondence with Newton is exposed to the whole world, and made to seem like something other than what it really was, and Fatio's *Lineae Brevissimi Descensus,* which is yet another bitter assault on me. A school of thought seems to be developing, according to which I had no inkling of the calculus until I stole the whole thing from Newton around 1677. Apparently my years of toil in Paris under the tutelage of Huygens count for nothing!

I had best not begin to rant and rave about this. Let me instead turn to some of your questions.

Yes, I still correspond with Eliza. How could I not? But, as many people do when they have children, she settled, at some point, into a more steady kind of life, and since has not written to me as frequently. When the peace treaty was signed between France and the allies three years ago, her title as Duchess of Qwghlm was recognized by the French court, and she began to travel frequently to England—though almost never with her husband. She keeps a town-house near St. James's and has even journeyed to Qwghlm occasionally to renew her ties to the place of her birth. Once or twice a year she journeys to my part of the world to spend time with her bastard son and to pay a call on Sophie. Her husband, with his long-standing connexions to the Navy, is more fond of Qwghlm than she is, and seems to phant'sy that the massive Castle there has the makings of a country house—though it is difficult to think of a more outlandish and wretched setting for one! And so he is there several months this last year over-seeing a project to rebuild one part of that ruin, and make it over into a villa and a proper seat for the nascent Duchy of Arcachon-Qwghlm. Some in London grumble that he is get-ting ready to turn Qwghlm into a French naval base, à la Dunkerque. But I cannot imagine Eliza allowing any such thing to happen.

As a way of making a name for herself in London society she supports a charity for Vagabond-soldiers, which has been a pet cause of hers for some years. After the peace treaty was signed and the Tories came into power, the size of England's army was drastically reduced, many regiments disbanded, and out-of-work soldiers have been roaming around the country making trouble ever since. Eliza's obvious concern for them is an implicit criticism of Tory policies, which should put her in a good position if the Juncto ever returns to power.

Concerning her opposition to Slavery, she is not as outspo-ken, even though her feelings run deeper. She knows that to make a pest of herself on this topic would cause her to be ejected from society altogether, and to lose any hope of effect-ing change. Those in the legal profession are well aware of the work she has done in the last few years to secure freedom for some of the Taunton maids who were enslaved by Jeffreys after Monmouth's Rebellion.

It is well that she maintains good relations with the Whigs.

As you must know if you get any letters from London at all, they are close to Princess Anne, who will probably reign over England sooner or later. And they are the party of active foreign policy—or, setting aside euphemisms, of war. That wretch, King Carlos II (the Sufferer) of Spain, who has been on his death-bed for something like thirty-five years now, cannot possibly live much longer—no, really!—and when he dies there will certainly be another great war. For make no mistake. Louis XIV covets Spain, with her Empire and her mines and her mints. It must be admitted that the duc d'Anjou has as good a claim to the throne as anyone else. Never mind that he happens to be the loyal and obedient grandson of Louis XIV!

If you do not get a lot of mail, you might be saying, wait! I thought the matter had been settled by treaty, and that the Electoral Prince of Bavaria was going to be King of Spain. But he has died, suddenly and strangely. The Empire has nominated its own candidate: Archduke Charles, the younger son of the Holy Roman Emperor. There is public talk of negotiations and partition-treaties, but private preparation for war. And as the stakes of that war will be Spain, the beating heart that circulates silver and gold through the world's markets, we may expect that it will be harder-fought even than the last one.

But on to more interesting matters.

You say you would collaborate with me. I will try to dissuade you by mentioning two facts. First, it is now clear that you will be ostracized from the Royal Society if you associate your name with mine. Second, we will be working for a chap who has his minions broken on the wheel if they incur his displeasure. No, I am not talking about my new King of Prussia, but about a taller monarch who lives farther to the east and owns about half of the planet.

If I have not scared you away yet, then consider the nature of the work. The thing I want to make embodies very little that is beautiful or elegant mathematically. It will consist of two components: a mechanical system for performing arithmetickal and logical operations upon numbers, and a vast compendium of *data* that will inform the operations of that machine. Much work remains to be carried out on both of these fronts. The former promises more satisfaction, in that it is a practical pursuit, akin to Hooke's watch-making, and one may see the machine take shape on the workbench, and point to this gear or that shaft with a measure of pride. But I fear it is not what really demands our attention now. Think of how the art of watch-making has advanced during our lifetimes alone, beginning with Huygens's pendulums, &c., and extrapolate this into the future, and you will readily agree that arith-metickal engines will only get better with time. On the other hand—with due respect for the work that you and Wilkins did on the Philosophical Language—we have only just embarked upon the amassing of the *data* and the writing-out of the logi-cal rules that will govern the machine's workings.

You are the protégé of Wilkins and the only man still living who worked on that project; on his deathbed he passed his mantle on to you. It follows that you are the man best suited to assemble and organize the *data* that our machine shall require, and to place it in a form that may be read and understood by a machine. This is a matter of assigning prime numbers to the symbols and then encoding them in some medium, probably as binary digits. The medium needs to be something enduring, for it may be many generations before machines can be con-structed that are capable of doing the work. Best would be thin sheets of gold.

For my part, I confess I have a thousand distractions, which conspire to make me a poor collaborator indeed. Any work that demands a vast amount of un-interrupted time is impossi-ble for me—which is why I have suggested that you, alone in your quiet Massachusetts cabin, are better qualified to draw up the immense symbol-tables.

Setting aside political entanglements, calculus-controversies, and the three Ladies (Sophie, Sophie Charlotte, and Princess Caroline) who never stop asking me to explain things to them, my chief project, at the moment, is the monadology.

At any rate, what it comes down to is that my life for the next several years will consist of flying back and forth between Hanover and Berlin (with perhaps the occasional excursion to St. Petersburg!) trying to work out a beautiful set of logical rules. That matches well with the other part of the arith-metickal engine project, namely, writing down the set of rules that will govern how it processes symbols. As a matter of fact I should like to think that these two sets of rules—the one gov-erning monads, the other governing the mechanical mind—will turn out to be one and the same. So I propose to take on this part of the undertaking myself, as it is so similar to what I am doing anyway.

That is my proposal for how we might collaborate, Daniel, and I hope it pleases you. The Tsar is fearsome it's true, but he is far away from you, and extremely distracted putting down the Raskolniki and the Streltsy and making war on the Swedes. I do not think you need to fear him. Hard as it might be to believe, there is no monarch in the world more committed to advancing what you call the Technologickal Arts. I believe that if I were to ask him for a ton of gold, explaining that we wanted to use it to store *data,* he would hand it over in a moment. But first you and I need to come up with some *data* so that those plates will not remain as blank as Mr. Locke's *tabula rasa.*

Yours affectionately,

Leibniz

BOOK 4

Bonanza

The Pacific Ocean
LATE 1700 AND EARLY 1701

Such are the Diseases and Terrors of the long
Calms, where the Sea stagnates and corrupts for
Want of Motion; and by the Strength of the Scorching Sun stinks and poisons the distrest Mariners,
who are rendered unactive, and disabled by
Scurvies, raging and mad with Calentures and
Fevers, and drop into Death in such a Manner, that
at last the Living are lost, for Want of the Dead, that
is, for want of Hands to work the Ship.

— DANIEL DEFOE,
A Plan of the English Commerce

MINERVA DROPPED ANCHOR below the burning mountain of Griga in
the Marian Islands on the fifth of September. The next day the
Shaftoe boys and a squad of Filipino sailors went ashore and
ascended to the rim of a secondary cinder-cone on the western slope
of the mountain proper. They established a watch-post there, within
sight of *Minerva*. For two days they flew a single flag, which meant *We
are here, and still alive.* The next day it was two flags, which meant *We
have seen sails coming out of the west,* and the day after that it was three,
meaning *It is the Manila Galleon.*

Van Hoek had the crew make preparations for departure. The
next morning the Shaftoe boys struck their camp and came down,
still coughing and rubbing their eyes from the fumes that hissed out
of that cinder-cone day and night, and after splashing around glee-
fully in the cove for a few minutes, washing off dust and sweat, they
came out to *Minerva* in the longboat and announced that the
Galleon had commenced her long northward run at dawn.

For two days they wove a course among the Marian Islands—a
chain that ran from about thirteen degrees at its southern end, to
about twenty degrees at the north. Some of the islands were steep-

715

sided volcanoes with deep water all around, but most were so flat that they did not rise more than a yard or two above the level of the ocean, be they never so large. These were belted all round with dangerous shallows, and yet they were easy to overlook in darkness or weather. So for a few days their energies were devoted to simply not disembowelling themselves on coral-reefs, and they did not see the Manila Galleon at all.

Some of the islands were populated by stocky natives who came and went in outrigger canoes, and one or two even had Jesuit missions on them, built of mud, like wasps' nests. The sheer desolation of the place explained why they'd chosen it as a rendezvous point. If *Minerva* had set out from Cavite on the same tide as the Galleon, it would have been obvious to everyone in the Philippines that some conspiracy had been forged. Almost as bad, it would have added several weeks to the length of *Minerva*'s voyage. The Manila Galleon was such a wallowing pig of a ship, and had been so gravely overloaded by Manila's officialdom, that only a storm could move it. The exit from Manila Bay, which took most ships but a single day, had taken the Manila Galleon a week. Then, rather than taking to the open sea, she had turned south and then east, and picked her way down the tortuous passages between Luzon and the islands to the south, anchoring frequently, and occasionally pausing to say a mass over the wrack of some predecessor; for the passage was marked out, not with buoys, but with the remains of Manila Galleons from one, ten, fifty, or a hundred years past. Finally the Galleon had reached a sheltered anchorage off a small island called Ticao. She had dropped anchor there and spent three weeks gazing out over twenty miles of water at the gap between the southern extremity of Luzon, and the northern cape of Samar, which was called the San Bernardino Strait. Beyond it the Pacific stretched all the way to Acapulco. Yet Luzon might as well have been Scylla and Samar Charybdis, because (as the Spaniards had learnt the hard way) any ship that tried to sally through that gap when the tides and the winds were not just so would be cast away. Twice she had raised anchor and set sail for the Strait only to turn back when the wind shifted slightly.

Boats had come out to the Galleon at all hours to replenish her stocks of drinking water, fruit, bread, and livestock, which were being drawn down at an appalling rate by the merchants and men of the cloth who were packed into her cabins. Indeed this had been the whole point of taking the route through the San Bernardino Strait, for by going that way they had been able to get two hundred and fifty miles closer to the Marianas without passing out of sight of the Philippines.

When finally she had broken out on the tenth of August—a month and a half after departing Manila—she had done so fully provisioned. Almost as important, the officials, priests, and soldiers who had stood by at the foot of Bulusan Volcano to witness and salute the great ship's departure had seen her venture forth into the Pacific *alone.*

Minerva had sailed out of Manila Bay two weeks after the Galleon and had gone for a leisurely cruise round the northern tip of Luzon, then had looped back to the south and taken shelter in Lagonoy Gulf, which emptied into the Pacific some sixty miles to the north of the San Bernardino Strait. There, by trading with natives and making occasional hunting and gathering forays, they had been able to keep their own stocks replenished while they had waited for the Galleon to escape from the Philippine Islands. Padraig Tallow had been among the crowd at the foot of Bulusan watching that event, and he'd thrown his peg-leg over the saddle of a horse and ridden northward until he had come to a high place above the Gulf of Lagonoy whence he could signal *Minerva* by building a smokey fire. *Minerva* had fired the Irishman a twenty-gun salute and hoisted her sails. Padraig Tallow's doings after that were unknown to them. If he'd stayed in character, he'd have stood where he was until the tip of *Minerva*'s mainmast had sunk below the eastern horizon, weeping and singing incomprehensible chanties. If things had gone according to plan, he'd then ridden his horse through the *bundok*, following the tracks from one steamy mission-town to the next, until he'd reached Manila, and he and Surendranath, and the one son of Queen Kottakkal who'd survived the last years' voyaging, and several other Malabaris were now making their way down the long coast of Palawan to join Mr. Foot in Queena-Kootah.

For her part *Minerva* had sailed almost due east for fifteen hundred miles to the Marianas, passing the Manila Galleon somewhere along the way.

Now they sailed north out of those islands without ever catching sight of her. This was just as well for all involved in the conspiracy—including all of the Galleon's officers. The bored Jesuits and soldiers scattered among those islands would see the Galleon, and would see *Minerva*, but would never see them *together.*

Weather made it impossible to observe the sun or look for the Galleon's sails for two days after they put the Marianas behind them. Then the sun came out, and they traversed the Tropic of Cancer and sighted the Galleon's topsails, far to the east, at almost the same moment. It was the fifteenth of September. Even before the northernmost of the burning islands of the Marianas had sunk below the southern horizon, they had gone off soundings, which meant that their sounding-lead, even when it was fully paid out, dangled miles above the floor of an ocean whose depth was literally unfathomable. After several days had gone by without sighting land they had brought *Minerva*'s anchors up on deck and stowed them deep in the hold.

They traversed the thirtieth parallel, which meant that they had reached the latitude of southern Japan. Still they continued north. They could not keep the Galleon in sight all the time, of course. But it was not necessary to follow in her wake. They had only two requirements. One was to discover the magic latitude, known only to the Spanish, that would take them safely to California. The other was to arrive in Acapulco at about the same time as the Galleon, so that certain officers aboard that ship could smooth the way for them. With her narrow hull *Minerva* could not carry as many provisions as the Galleon, but she could sail faster, and so the general plan was to speed across the Pacific and then tarry off California for a few weeks, surviving on the fresh water and game of that country, while keeping a lookout for the Galleon.

But they could not bolt east until they were sure of the right latitude, and so every day they posted lookouts at the top of *Minerva*'s foremast and had them scan the horizon for the sails of the Manila Galleon. Having sighted her, they would plot a converging course, and creep closer until they could see how her sails had been trimmed. The winds almost always came from the southeastern quarter of the compass rose, and every time they caught sight of the Galleon she seemed to be going free, which was a way of saying that the wind was coming in from behind her and from one side—in this case, the starboard. In other words the Galleon's captain was still bending all his efforts to gain latitude, and seemed not to know or care that he had five thousand miles to cover eastwards; or that every degree he went north was a degree he'd later have to go south (Manila and Acapulco lying at nearly the same latitude).

They spent a few days becalmed at thirty-two degrees, then advanced due north to thirty-six degrees, then encountered weather. At the beginning this came out of the east, which made van Hoek extremely nervous that they would be cast away on the shores of Japan (they were at the latitude of Edo, which Gabriel Goto had claimed was the largest city in the world, and so it wasn't as if the wreck of their ship would go unnoticed). But then the wind shifted around to the northwest and they were forced to put up a storm-sail and scud before it. The weather was not nearly as threatening as the waves, which were mountainous.

It happened sometimes that when a wind shifted violently, or a ship was miserably handled, or both, the wind would blow in over the head and strike a ship's sails directly in the face, plastering the canvas back over the rigging, and frequently slamming crew-members off of their perches. The ship would be flung into disarray. She'd go dead in the water, making her rudder quite useless, and would drift and spin like a stunned fish until she was brought in hand again. This was called being taken a-back, and it could happen to persons as well as ships. Jack had never seen van Hoek taken a-back until the Dutchman emerged from belowdecks at one point to see one of those waves rolling toward them. Its crest of foam alone was large enough to swallow *Minerva*.

The only way to survive seas like these was to manage rudder and a few scraps of canvas in such a way that the waves never struck the ship broadside. That was the only thing the men on *Minerva* thought about for the next forty-eight hours. Sometimes they stood poised on watery mountain-tops and enjoyed the view; seconds later they'd be in a trough with seemingly vertical walls of water blocking their vision fore and aft.

After Jack had been awake for some thirty consecutive hours, he began to see things that weren't there. For the most part this was preferable to seeing the things that *were*. But strangely enough—with so many natural dangers all around—the one fear that obsessed him was that they would collide with the Manila Galleon. Early in the storm he had seen a great wave coming in the corner of his eye, and phant'sied somehow that it was the Galleon riding a storm-crest; the dark bulk of the wave he took to be her hull of Philippine mahogany, the foamy crest he imagined was her sails. Of course in such a storm she wouldn't have canvas up at all, but in this momentary dream she was a ghost-ship, already dead, and riding the storm with every inch of canvas stretched out before the wind. Of course it was really nothing more than just another damned great wave and so he forgot this apparition in the next instant.

Every wave that came their way was a fresh challenge to their existence, as formidable as anything the Duc d'Arcachon or Queen Kottakkal had flung at them, and had to be met and survived with fresh energy and ingenuity. But they kept coming. And late in the storm, when Jack and everyone else on the ship had entirely lost their minds, and were surviving only because they were in the habit of surviving, the phant'sy of the ghost-Galleon came back and haunted him for long hours. Every wave that came towards them he saw as the underside of the Galleon's hull, the barnacled keel coming down on them like the blade of an axe.

He woke up lying on the deck, in the same position where he had collapsed hours before, at the end of the storm. Bright light was in his eyes but he was shivering, because it was damnably cold.

"Thirty-seven degrees . . . twelve minutes," croaked van Hoek, working nearby with a back-staff, "assuming . . . that I have the day right." He paused frequently to heave great laboring sighs, as if the effort of forcing words out was almost too much for him.

Jack—who'd been lying on his stomach—rolled onto his back. His arms had been pressed underneath him the whole time he'd been asleep, and were completely numb and dead now, like sopping rags a-dangle from his shoulders. "And what d'you suppose the day is?"

"If that storm lasted a mere two days, I am ashamed at selling myself so cheaply. For a two-day storm should not leave a sea-captain half dead."

"You are half dead? I am at least three-quarters dead."

"Further evidence that it was more than two days. On the other hand, we could not have survived four days of that."

"I am not some Jesuit, bent on arguing. If you call it three days, I will agree."

"Then we agree that this is October the first."

"Any sign of the Galleon?"

Van Hoek squinted up. "No one has the strength to go above and look. I doubt she survived. So big, and so overloaded . . . now I understand why they build a new one every year. Even if she survived, she'd be worn out."

"What do we do in that case?"

"North," said van Hoek. "They say that if we turn east too soon, we will make it most of the way across the Pacific, only to be becalmed, almost within sight of America, where we'll starve to death."

This conversation happened at dawn. It was midday before *Minerva*'s topmasts could be raised again, and midafternoon before she was under way, sailing north by northeast. Every man was busy repairing the ship, and those who had no skills at carpentry or rope-work were sent down to the bilge to collect quicksilver that had trickled down there from broken flasks.

Two days later they grazed the fortieth parallel, which put them at the same latitude as the northern extremes of Japan. Van Hoek finally consented to sail towards America. His intention was to hew closely to forty degrees, which (according to a bit of lore he had pried out of a drunken Spanish sea-captain in Manila) would lead eventually to Cape Mendocino. But this went the way of all intentions a day later when he discovered that some combination of winds, currents, and wandering compass-needle had driven them down almost to thirty nine degrees. He laughed at this, and that evening when they gathered in the dining cabin to saw at planks of dried beef and flick maggots out of their beans, he explained why: "Legend would have it that the Spaniards have found out some secret way across the Pacific Ocean. It is a good legend because it prevents Dutchmen, Englishmen, and other prudent Protestants from attempting the voyage. But now I know the truth, which is that they *wander* across, driven north and south willy-nilly, placing their lives and estates in the hands of innumerable saints. So let us drink to any saints who may be listening!"

Thus they wandered for most of October. It turned out that the storm had done irreparable injury to the foremast, rendering it more trouble than it was worth, and so they lost a knot or two. Sometimes the wind would grow frigid and bear down out of the north, pushing them toward the latitude of thirty-five degrees, which was the lowest that van Hoek would tolerate. Then they would have to work painstakingly into the wind. The cold spray blew into the faces of the Filipino and Malay sailors like chips of flint. Van Hoek's insistence on remaining far to the north led them to grumble. Jack did not think they were going to mutiny, but he could easily imagine circumstances in which they *would*. The difference in climate between thirty-five and forty degrees was considerable, and winter was making no secret of its intentions.

They had no idea where they were. Indeed, the very notion of being somewhere lost its hold on their minds after they had gone for a month without seeing any land; if some Fellow of the Royal Society had been a-board with a newfangled instrument for measuring longitude, the figures would have meant nothing to them. Van Hoek made estimates based on their speed, and at one point announced that they had probably crossed over the meridian dividing the East from the West Hemisphere. But under close interrogation from Moseh, he admitted that it might have happened last week or that it might happen a week in the future.

Jack saw no difference between East water and West water. They were in a part of the world that, on the Doctor's maps, either had not appeared at all (it being considered sinful wastefulness to leave such a large expanse of fine vellum blank) or else had been covered up by some vast Barock cartouche with words printed on it in five-hundred-mile-high letters, surrounded by bare-breasted mermaids blasting away on conch-shells. *Minerva* had crawled underneath the legends, compass-roses, analemmas, and cartouches that were superimposed on all the world's maps and globes, and vanished from all charts, ceased to exist. Jack had a phant'sy of some young Princess in a drawing-room staring at a map, and seeing a bit of movement under the eastern edge of some bit of engraver's *trompe l'oeil,* a scrap of faux-weather-beaten scrollwork where the cartographer had writ his name. She would suppose it to be a wandering silverfish at first— then, peering at it through a magnifying lens, would resolve the outlines of a certain ship filled with mercury . . .

Anyway, he was not the only man aboard seeing strange visions, for one day early in November, the lookout let out a wail of mingled fear and confusion. It was not a cheering kind of sound, coming from a lookout, and so it got the attention of every man on board.

"He says that there is a ship in the distance—but not a ship of this world," Dappa said.

"What the hell does that mean?" van Hoek demanded.

"She sails upside-down. She leaps from place to place and her form shifts, as if she were a droplet of quicksilver trapped between sea and sky."

Jack found this marvelously poetickal, but van Hoek was all ready with a tedious explanation: "Tell him he is only seeing a mirage. It might be another ship that lies over the horizon, or it might be a reflection of our own vessel. But there is probably not another ship within two thousand miles of us, and so it is most likely the latter."

But every man who was not busy with something else ascended the ratlines and got in position to view this entertainment. Jack got up sooner and higher than most. As a shareholder, he slept in a cabin instead of belowdecks, and as an Englishman he kept his windows open unless there was a positive hurricane blowing, and he had escaped the never-ending round of catarrhs, influenzas, rheumatic malfunctions, and fœbrile disorders that eddied through the crew. At any rate he had more energy and better lungs than they did and so he climbed all the way to the topmast trestletrees: high enough that he could take in *Minerva*'s whole length at a glance. At first the mirage was not visible, but van Hoek said that this was the common way of mirages and to be patient. So while he was being patient in the topmast trestletrees, Jack looked down at the crew, struggling up the ratlines and coughing, spitting, and scratching themselves just like the audience in a theatre, waiting for the show to begin. This was not such a bad similitude either. From the point of view of a drawing-room Princess, *Minerva* had vanished underneath a florid mermaid-cartouche. But from *Minerva*'s point of view, it was the world that had disappeared—somewhat as players do when the story pauses between acts. With their wigs, costumes, swords, and stage-props they exeunt; nothing happens for a while; the audience shifts, mutters, farts, cracks hazel-nuts, hawks up phlegm; and if it is a better class of theatre, there begins a little play-within-the-play, an *entr'acte*.

"*Mira!*" someone shouted, and Jack looked up to see it.

The phantom-ship appeared to be no more than a cannon-shot away from them. At times it appeared quite normal and solid. Then it would split into two symmetrical images, one right-side-up and one upside-down, or it would warp and flit about, like a drop trapped between panes of glass and being moved hither and thither by the pressure of a finger.

But when it was solid and stable for a moment, it was obviously not *Minerva* but some other ship. It had men on it, and they had trimmed her sails to run before the wind, just as *Minerva* was doing. Several of them had climbed into her rigging to gawk and point at something.

"Does she have any cannon run out?" van Hoek inquired.

"It would be a strange part of the world to go a-pirating," said Dappa.

"Hmph!"

"She is running up a flag," said Moseh de la Cruz. "She must see us, as we see her!"

Red silk bloomed in the mirage, a sudden billowing of flame. In the middle of it a gold cross and some other heraldic designs. Every man sighed at once.

"It is the Manila Galleon!" Jack announced.

At this news van Hoek finally bestirred himself. He climbed to the maintop and began trying to fix his spyglass on the mirage, which was like trying to spear a flea with a jack-knife. There was a certain amount of cursing in Dutch. Jack had spent enough time with van Hoek to know why: For all her bulk and shoddy construction, the Manila Galleon had not only survived; she had come through the storm in better condition than *Minerva*, or at least without losing any of her masts.

After that it hailed for two straight days. One of the older sailors remarked that hail never occurred far from land. The wind came about into their teeth, and as they'd been pushed by inscrutable currents dangerously close to thirty-five degrees, they had no choice but to sail northwest for a day. When the weather cleared and the trade-wind returned, and they were able to steer towards California again, someone sighted a school of tunny fish. All agreed that tunny never ventured far from land—all except for van Hoek, who only rolled his eyes.

The day after that they once again caught sight of the Manila

Galleon in a mirage. This time—though the image was fleeting and warped—they saw a jab of flame, which probably meant that the Galleon had fired a cannon in an effort to signal them. All hands shushed each other, but if any sound reached *Minerva* it was drowned out by the shushing. Accordingly van Hoek refused to fire an answering signal; the Galleon, he said, might be a hundred miles away, and there was no point in wasting gunpowder.

That evening one far-sighted man insisted he saw a column of smoke to the southeast, which he took to be an infallible sign of land. Van Hoek said it was probably a waterspout. Still, several men loitered at that quarter of the ship, looking at it while the sun went down. Sunsets at this latitude, in November, were long and gradual, so they had plenty of time to look at this apparition, whatever it was, as the horizontal red light of dusk reflected from it.

Eventually the sun went down, of course, though some clouds high in the eastern sky continued to reflect back a faint glow for a while afterwards.

But there was one spot that refused to stop glowing, as if a spark of sun had flown off and gotten lodged there. It lay over the horizon, along the same bearing as the column of smoke or waterspout seen earlier. Van Hoek now revised his explanation: it was most likely an uncharted volcanic island in the middle of the Pacific. As such it might be naught more than a hot rock. On the other hand it might have streams of fresh water, and birds that could be shot and eaten. Every mouth on the ship was, in an instant, flooded with saliva. So he ordered a change in course, and had more canvas raised, since tomorrow weather might close in and make it difficult to see the volcano and easy to run aground on it.

At first he estimated the distance to the volcano at a hundred miles or more. But the light (which at first they'd seen only by its reflection on a cloud layer above) popped up over the horizon almost immediately, and van Hoek halved the estimate. Then, when flickerings in that light became clearly visible, he halved it again. Finally he declared that this was no volcano but something entirely different, and then everyone understood that, whatever it was, they were no more than a few miles away from it. Van Hoek ordered a prudent reduction in speed. Every man was abovedecks now, bumping into things because dazzled by the light.

They were close enough to see that it was an enormous fire that had by some miracle been kindled on the very surface of the ocean. Crackles and roars came out of it, and it billowed and stretched easily, sometimes drawing itself up and surging hundreds of yards straight up into the air, other times growing squat and spreading out over the hissing surface of the calm sea. At times black shapes became visible in its heart: suggestions of massive ribs, and a broken mast clothed in fire. Sparks of green, red, and blue flame appeared here and there as exotic Oriental pigments and minerals were reached by the flames.

At some point they could no longer deny that they were hearing screams. *"Socorro! Socorro!"* The Spanish word for *help* had a sorrowful rather than an urgent sound. There was sentiment for going in closer, but "We wait for the magazine" was all van Hoek would say. Jack saw a red-hot cannon finally break through the charcoal beams that were supporting it. It dropped clumsily into the bilge and ejaculated a vast cloud of steam that blurred and dimmed the fire-light. One man with a very loud voice was crying *"Socorro! Socorro!"* But then he changed over into some Latin prayer.

He was halfway through it when all of the gunpowder on the Manila Galleon exploded at once. Flaming planks streaked away in every direction, blazing with the white heat of a forge as air shrieked over them, rapidly burning away to black cinders that plopped and sizzled in the water all around. Some landed on the ship and burnt little holes through her sails or started small fires on her deck, but van Hoek had long since ordered men to stand by with buckets, and so all flames were smartly doused.

It was near dawn before they could mount any serious attempt to look for survivors. The longboat had been taken apart and stowed, and in the darkness it took hours to get its pieces out, put it together, and launch it. Though no one came out and said as much, it was understood (as how could it not be) that everyone aboard *Minerva* was starving to death *to begin with* and that matters would only get worse with each survivor that was plucked out of the water.

At dawn they set out in the longboat and began rowing toward what had been the Galleon. She had burnt to the waterline, and now was just a shoe, a sole afloat in the Pacific, likely to fill up and sink as soon as the seas rose. Curls of cinnamon-bark dotted the surface of the water, each one looking like a small burnt ship itself. Around the hulk spread a morass of Chinese silk, ruined by fire and sea-water but still more gaily colored than anything their eyes had seen since their final whorehouse-visits in Manila four months earlier. The silk caught on the longboat's oars and came out of the water with each stroke, giving them gorgeous glimpses of tropical birds and flowers before sliding off and sinking into the gray Pacific. A map floated on the surface, a square of white parchment no longer parched. Its ink was dissolving, images of land, parallels, and meridians fading away until it became a featureless white square. Jack fished it up with a boat-hook and held it above his head. "What a stroke of luck!" he exclaimed, "I do believe this map shows our exact location!" But no one laughed.

"MY NAME," SAID THE SURVIVOR, speaking in French, "is Edmund de Ath. I thank you for inviting me to share your mess."

It was three days since Jack had pulled him out of the drink and slung him over one of the longboat's benches; this was the first time de Ath had emerged from his berth since then. His voice was still hoarse from inhaling smoke and swallowing salt-water. He had joined Jack, Moseh, Vrej, Dappa, Monsieur Arlanc, and van Hoek in the dining cabin, which was the largest and aft-most cabin on the quarterdeck; its back wall was a subtly curved sweep of windows twenty feet wide, affording a splendid view of the sun setting into the Western Pacific. The visitor was drawn inevitably to those windows, and stood there for a few moments with the ruddy light emphasizing the pits and hollows of his face. If he put on two or three stone— which he was likely to do when they reached New Spain—he'd be handsome. As it was, his skull stood a bit too close to the surface. But then the same was true of every man aboard this ship.

"Everything is idiotically plain and stark here, and that goes for the view as well," Jack said. "A line between water and sky, and an orange ball poised above it."

"It is Japanese in its simplicity," said Edmund de Ath gravely, "and yet if you only look deeper, Barock complexity and ornament are to be found—observe the tufts of cloud scudding in below the Orb, the delicate curtseying of the waves as they meet—" and then he was off in high-flown French that Jack could not really follow; which prompted Monsieur Arlanc to say "I gather from your *accent* that you are Belgian." Edmund de Ath (1) took this as an insult of moderate severity but (2) was too serene and poised to be troubled by it unduly. With Christian forbearance he responded with something like, "And I gather from the company you keep, monsieur, that you are one of those whose conscience led him to forsake the complexity and contradictions of the Roman church for the simplicity of a rebel creed." That this Belgian friar refrained from using the word *heretic* was noted silently by every man in the cabin. Again he and Arlanc went off into deep French. But van Hoek was clearing his throat a lot and so Jack finally broke in: "The maggots, weevils, mealworms, and mold in those serving-dishes aren't going to keep fresh all night!"

The only food remaining on the ship was beef jerky, some dried fish, beans, and biscuit. These were steadily being converted into cockroaches, worms, maggots, and weevils. They had long since stopped observing any difference between food that had and that had not undergone the conversion, and ate both in the same mouthful.

"According to my faith, I am not allowed to eat any *flesh* on Friday," said Edmund de Ath, "and so someone else may have my portion of *beans*." He was gazing bemusedly at a raft of maggots that had floated to the surface of his bowl. Van Hoek's face grew red when he understood that their new passenger was making jests about the food, but before the Dutchman would leap up and get his hands around the throat of the Belgian, Edmund de Ath raised his eyes to the red horizon, delved blindly with his spoon, and brought a stew of beans and bugs to his mouth. "It is better fare than I have had in a month," he announced. "My compliments, Captain van Hoek, on your *logistical* acumen. Rather than trusting to some *saint* as the Spanish captains do, you have used the brain God gave you, and provisioned the ship *responsibly*."

The diplomacy of de Ath only seemed to make van Hoek more suspicious. "What sort of Papist are you, to make light of your own faith?"

"Make light of it? Never, sir. I am a Jansenist. I seek reconciliation with certain Protestants, finding their faith nearer truth than the sophistry of the Jesuits. But I would not bore you with tedious *theologickal* discourse—"

"How about Jews?" asked Moseh gravely. "We could use an extra Jew on this ship, if you could stretch your principles *that* far."

"I will not stretch my principles, but I will stretch my *mind*," said Edmund de Ath, refusing to be baited. "Tell me, what do the *rebbes* say concerning the eating of larvae? Kosher, or *trayf*?"

"I have been thinking of writing a scholarly treatise on that very subject," said Moseh, "but I need access to certain rabbinical writings that are not available in Captain van Hoek's library of nautical lore and picaresque novels."

Everyone laughed—even Monsieur Arlanc, who was hard at work grinding a fragment of boiled jerky against the tabletop with the butt of his dagger. His last remaining tooth had fallen out a week ago and so he had to chew his food manually.

They had spent so many years together that they had nothing to say to one another, and so this new fellow—whether they liked him or not—held their attention fast, no matter what he did or said. Even when he was answering Vrej Esphahnian's questions about Jansenist views towards the Armenian Orthodox Church, they could not look at anything else.

After dinner, hot sugar-water was brought out. Dappa finally broached the subject they all wanted to hear about. "Monsieur de Ath, you seemed to take a dim view of the Manila Galleon's management. Without intending disrespect for the recently departed, I would like to know how the disaster came about."

Edmund de Ath brooded for a while. The sun had set and candles had been lit; his face stood out pale, floating in the darkness above the table. "That ship was as *Spanish* as this one is *Dutch*," he said. "The overall situation was more desperate, as the ship was slowly disintegrating and the passengers were unruly. But the atmosphere was gay and cheerful, as everyone aboard had given themselves over to the verdict of Fortune. The chief distinction between that ship and this is that *this* is a single unitary Enterprise whereas the Manila Galleon belonged to the King of Spain and was a sort of floating bazaar—a commercial Ark supporting diverse business interests, many of which were naturally at odds. Just as Noah must have had his hands full keeping the tigers away from the goats, so the Captain of the Galleon was forever trying to adjudicate among the warring and intriguing *commerçants* packed into her cabins.

"You'll recollect that a few days ago we had two days of hailstorms. Several of the merchants who'd bought passage on the Galleon had brought aboard servants from balmy climes where cold air and hailstones are unheard of. These wretches were so unnerved by the hail that they fled belowdecks and secreted themselves deep in the hold and would not be fetched out for anything. In time the weather cleared, and they emerged to be soundly beaten by their masters. But about the same time, smoke was observed seeping out from one of the hatches. It appears likely that one of those servants had brought a candle below with him when he had gone down fleeing the hailstorm. Perhaps they had even kindled a cook-fire. The truth will never be known. In any event, it was now obvious that a slow smoldering fire had been started somewhere down amid the countless bales of cargo that the merchants had stuffed into the hold."

Van Hoek rose and excused himself, for from the point of view of ship's captain the story was finished. There was no point in hearing the details. The others remained and listened.

"Now, many ponderous sermons could be written about the rich pageant of greed and folly that played out over the next days. The correct action would have been to man the pumps and drench everything in the hold with sea-water. But this would have ruined all of the silks, and caused incalculable losses, not only for the merchants but for the ship's officers, and various of the King's officials in Manila and Acapulco who had bales of their own in the hold. So the captain delayed, and the fire smoldered on. Men were sent below with buckets of water to find and douse the fire. Some returned saying that the smoke was too thick—others never came back at all. Some argued that the hatches should be opened and bales brought out onto the deck, but others who had more knowledge of fires said that this would allow an in-rush of air that would cause the fire to billow up and consume the Galleon in a moment.

"We sighted your ship in a mirage, and fired a signal-cannon hoping you would come to our aid. There was disagreement even concerning this, for some supposed you were Dutch pirates. But the captain told us that you were a *merchant*-ship loaded with quicksilver, and confessed he had made an agreement with you in secret, that he would guide you across the Pacific and grease the path for you in Acapulco in return for a share of your profits."

"Was everyone shocked and dismayed?"

"No one batted an eye. The signal cannon was fired forthwith. No answer came back to our ears: only the silence of the Pacific. At this, madness descended on the Galleon like a Plague. There was an insurrection—not merely a mutiny but a three-sided civil war. Again, someday it will make for a great allegory-tale that preachers may recite from pulpits, but the way it came out was that those who wanted to unload the cargo-hold prevailed. Hatches were opened— smoke came out, which you must have seen on the horizon—a few bales were hoisted out—and then, just as some had predicted, flames erupted from below. I saw the very air burning. A boiling flame-front came towards me, trapping me against the rail, and I toppled overboard rather than be roasted alive. I climbed onto one of the bales that had been thrown overboard. The ship crept downwind, slowly getting farther away from me, and I watched the final catastrophe from a safe distance."

Edmund de Ath bowed his head slightly, so that arcs of reflected candle-light gleamed in the tear-filled channels beneath his eyes. "May Almighty God have mercy on the hundred and seventy-four men and the one woman who perished."

"You may scratch the one woman off that list, at least for the time being," Jack said. "We plucked her out of the water fifteen minutes after you."

There was a long pause, and then Edmund de Ath said: "Elizabeth de Obregon survived?"

"If you call this surviving," Jack answered.

"He *swallowed*!" said Monsieur Arlanc the next day, having cornered Jack up at the head. "I saw his Adam's apple move."

"Of course he swallowed—he was eating dinner."

"Dinner was finished!"

"All right, he was drinking sugar-water then."

"It was not that sort of a swallow," said Monsieur Arlanc. "I mean he was perturbed. Something is not right."

"Now Monsieur Arlanc, consider it: What could de Ath possibly find troubling about the poor lady's survival? She's half out of her mind anyway."

"People who are half out of their minds sometimes forget discretion, and say things they would normally keep secret."

"All right, then, perhaps he and the lady were having a scandalous *affair de coeur*—that would explain why he's been sitting at her bedside ever since."

Jack was sitting in a hole, his buttocks dangling over the Pacific, and Monsieur Arlanc was standing next to him; together they gazed down the length of the ship for a few moments. The several divisions and subdivisions of the current watch were distributed among the masts and sail-courses, running through a drill that every man knew in his sleep, trimming the sails for new weather that was bearing down on them out of the northwest. Their limbs were swollen from beri-beri and many of them moved in spasmodickal twitches as their feet and hands responded balkily to commands from the mind. On the upperdeck, in the middle of the ship, a dozen Malabaris were standing around a corpse stitched up in a sheet, joining in some sort of heathenish mourning-chant prepatory to flinging it overboard. A scrap of cordage had been lashed around its ankles and made fast to an empty drinking water jar packed with pot-shards and ballast-sand, so that the body would be pulled smartly down to David Jones's Locker before the sharks who swarmed in the ship's wake could make sport with it.

"We gained two mouths from the Galleon, and fretted about going hungry on that account," Jack mused. "Since then three have died."

"There must be some reason for you to sit there and tell me things of which I am already aware," said Monsieur Arlanc, mumbling pensively through swollen gums, "but I cannot fathom it."

"If strong sailors are dropping dead, what chance has Elizabeth de Obregon?"

Monsieur Arlanc spat blood over the rail. "More chance than I have. She has endured a voyage that would slay any man on this ship."

"Are you trying to tell me that there is a worse voyage in all the world than *this* one?"

"She is the sole survivor of the squadron that was sent out from Acapulco years ago, to find the Islands of Solomon."

Now Jack was glad in a way that he was sitting on the head, for it was a pose well-suited to profound silent contemplation. "Stab me!" he said finally. "Enoch told me of that expedition, and that the only survivor was a woman, but I had not drawn the connexion."

"She has seen wonders and terrors known only to the *Spaniards*."

"In any event she is very sick just now," Jack said, "and so it is no wonder that Edmund de Ath sits at the lady's bedside—we'd expect no less of a priest."

"And nothing more of a *blackguard*."

Jack sighed. The corpse went over-board. Several Filipino idlers—which meant tradesmen not attached to any particular watch—were arguing about ducks. A flight of ducks had been sighted in the distance this morning and several were of the opinion that ducks were never seen more than a few miles from land.

"It is in the nature of men cooped up together aboard ship that they fall to infighting at some point," Jack finally said.

Monsieur Arlanc grinned, which was an unspeakably nasty sight: his gums had peeled back from his mandibles to show blackening bone. "It is some sort of poetic justice. You turn my faith against me by arguing that I am predestined to distrust Edmund de Ath."

MONSIEUR ARLANC DIED a week later. They held on to his corpse for as long as they could, because a fragment of kelp was sighted in the water almost at the moment of his death, and they hoped that they could make landfall and bury him in the earth of California. But his body had been well decayed even while he'd been still alive. Dying scarcely improved matters, and forced them to make another burial at sea. It was just as well that they did. For even though kelp-weeds continued to bob in the waves around Minerva's hull, it was not for another ten days after they threw the Huguenot's corpse overboard that they positively sighted land. They were just below thirty-nine degrees of latitude, which meant they'd missed Cape Mendocino; according to the vague charts that van Hoek had collected in Manila, and a few half-baked recollections of Edmund de Ath, the land they were looking at was probably Punto Arena.

Now the so-called idlers, who really had been idle for most of the last several weeks, worked night and day re-making *Minerva* for a coastal voyage. The anchors were brought up out of the hold and hung on the ship's bow. Likewise cannons were hoisted up from storage and settled on their carriages. The longboat was re-assembled and put on the upperdeck, an obstruction to the men of the watch but a welcome one. While these things were being done *Minerva* could not come too near the coast, and so they put the distant mountains of California to larboard and coasted southwards for two days, sieving kelp up out of the water and trying to find some way to make it palatable. There were clear signs of an approaching storm, but as luck had it, they were just drawing abreast of the entrance to the great bay of California. As the wind began to blow hard off the Pacific they scudded between two mighty promontories that were lit up by golden sunlight gliding in beneath the storm-clouds. Changing course to the south, they were then able to navigate between a few steep rocky islands and get through a sort of bottle-neck. Beyond it the bay widened considerably. It was lined with salt-pans reminiscent of those at Cadiz, though of course no one was exploiting these. They dropped anchor in the deepest water they could find and readied the ship to wait out the storm.

WHEN THE WEATHER lifted three days later they found that they had dragged their anchor for a short distance. But not far enough to put them in danger, for the bay behind the Golden Gate was vast. Its southern lobe extended south as far as the eye could see, bounded on both sides by swelling hills, just turning from green to brown. The crew of *Minerva* now embarked on a strange program of eating California, beginning with the seaweed that floated off-shore, working their way through the mussel-beds and crab-flats of the intertidal zone, chewing tunnels into the scrub that clung to the beach-edge and perpetrating massacres of animals and birds. Foraging-parties would go out one after the next in the longboat, and half of them would stand guard with muskets and cutlasses while the others ransacked the place for food. Certain parts of the shoreline were defended by Indians who were not very happy to see them, and it took a bit of experimentation to learn where these were. The most dangerous part was the first five minutes after the longboat had been pulled up on the beach, when the men felt earth beneath their feet for the first time in four months, and stood there dumbfounded for several minutes, their ears amazed by the twittering of birds, the buzzing of insects, the rustle of leaves. Said Edmund de Ath: "It is like being a newborn babe, who has known nothing but the womb, suddenly brought forth into an unimagined world."

Elizabeth de Obregon emerged from her cabin for the first time since Jack had carried her in there, all wet and cold from the Pacific, on the night the Galleon burned. Edmund de Ath took her for a feeble promenade around the poop deck. Jack, lying on his bed directly beneath them, overheard a snatch of their conversation: "*Mira,* the bay seems to go on forever, no wonder they believed California was an island."

"It was your husband who proved them wrong, was it not, my lady?"

"You are too flattering, even for a Jesuit, Father Edmund."

"Pardon me, my lady, but I am a Jansenist."

"Yes, I meant to say Jansenist—my mind is still addled, and I cannot tell waking from dreaming sometimes."

"That promontory to the south of the Gate would be a brave place to build a city," said Edmund de Ath. "A battery there could control the narrows, and make this entire Bay into a Spanish lake, dotted with missions to convert all of these Indians."

"America is vast, and there are many nice places to build cities," said Elizabeth de Obregon dismissively.

"I know, but just *look* at this place! It's as if God put it here to be built on!"

They tottered onwards and Jack heard no more. Which was just as well—he'd heard enough. It was a type of clever, courtly conversation the likes of which he had not been forced to listen to since he'd left Christendom behind, and it filled him with the same old desire to run abovedecks and throw those people overboard.

As Elizabeth de Obregon ate of the fruits and greens of California and recovered her strength, she began to emerge from her cabin more frequently and even to join them in the officers' mess from time to time.

After Jack had related certain things to his partners, and after they'd allowed a day or two to pass, Moseh turned to Elizabeth one evening as they were dining, and remarked, "The situation of this Bay seems so fair that it will probably attract simpletons from all over the world . . . doubtless the *Russians* will throw up a fort on that promontory any year now."

Elizabeth looked politely amused at the reaction of Edmund de Ath, who turned red and began to chew his food very slowly. She turned to Moseh and said, "Pray tell, why wouldn't *sophisticated* men build here?"

"Ah, my lady, I would not bore you with the tedious speculations of the Cabbalists . . ."

"On the contrary, my family tree is full of *conversos,* and I love to steep myself in the wisdom of the rabbis."

"My lady, we are near the latitude of forty degrees. The golden rays of the sun, and silver rays of the moon, strike the surface of the globe at a *glancing* angle here, rather than shining down *vertically* onto the ground. Now it has been understood by *Cabbalistickal* sorcerers, ever since the days of the First Temple, that the diverse *metals* that grow in the earth, are created by certain *rays* that emanate from the various heavenly bodies, penetrate the Earth, and there combine with the Elements of Earth and Water to create gold, silver, copper, mercury, *et cetera,* depending on which Planet emanated the Ray. *Videlicet,* the rays of the Sun create Gold, those of the Moon Silver, *et cetera, et cetera.* And it follows naturally that Gold and Silver will be found most abundantly in sunny places near the Equator."

"The Alchemists of Christendom have either *borrowed* this insight from your Cabbalists, or discovered it on their own," said Elizabeth.

"As you know, Lady, the great metropolises of *al-Andalus,* Cordoba and Toledo, were crucibles in which the most learned men of Christendom, of *dar al-Islam,* and of the Diaspora commingled their knowledge . . ."

"I thought the function of a crucible was to *purify* and not to *intermix,*" said Edmund de Ath, and then put on an angelic face.

"To fall into discussion of alchemichal arcana would be to do the lady a disservice," said Moseh. "She informs me that the sages of the King of Spain are well-acquainted with the nature and properties of the astrologickal emanations. Yet any half-wit who glances at a map could have inferred that that the *Rey* knows all about the *rays,* for it has ever been the wise policy of the Spanish Empire to follow the Line, and establish colonies in the auriferous belt where Sun and Moon beat straight down on the earth. Leave *California* and *Alyeska* to the wretched Russians, for gold will *never* be discovered in *those* places!"

"I confess I am somewhat taken a-back," said Edmund de Ath, "as I never dreamed until now that I was sharing a ship with a *Cabbalistic* sorcerer."

"Don't hang your head so, monsieur. The North Pacific is not generally considered a Jewish neighborhood . . ."

"What possessed you to venture out this way, sir?" asked Elizabeth de Obregon. The sight of land, and fresh food, had brought her back to life, and now this fencing-match between the Jansenist and the Jew was taking years off her age.

"My lady, you do me a favor to pretend interest in my obscure researches," said Moseh. "I'll return the kindness by being as brief as possible: there is an occult legend to the effect that King Solomon, after building the Temple on Mount Zion—"

"—journeyed far to the East and built a Kingdom on some island there," said Elizabeth de Obregon.

"Indeed. A kingdom of vast wealth to be sure, but—more importantly—an Olympian center for alchemical scholarship and Cabbalistic research. There the secrets of the Philosopher's Stone and the Philosophic Mercury were first brought to light—in fact, all the lucubrations of our modern-day Alchemists and Cabbalists are but a feeble attempt to pick over the scraps left behind by Solomon and his court magicians. After I had journeyed to the frontiers of learning during my youth, I reached the conclusion that I could only learn more by seeking out the Solomon Islands and going over them inch by inch."

Now it was Elizabeth's turn to become pink in the face. "Many have died trying to discover those islands, rabbi. If your tale is true, you are fortunate to be alive."

"No more fortunate than *you*, my lady."

Now Elizabeth de Obregon locked her gaze upon Moseh, and mystickal Rays passed back and forth between them for a while, until Edmund de Ath could not endure it any longer. He said, "Can you share your findings with us, sir, or must the results be locked up in some encyphered Torah somewhere?"

"The *results* are still *resulting*, sir, there is no definite report to be made."

"But you've left the Solomon Islands!"

"*I* have. That much is obvious. But did you really think I could have journeyed there *alone*? Of all those who went, monsieur, I am the *least*. A mere errand-boy, sent this way to fetch a few necessaries. The rest are still there, hard at work."

PLAYING WITH THE MINDS of Edmund de Ath and Elizabeth de Obregon made for excellent sport, and if done right, might even keep Jack, Moseh, and company alive when they reached Acapulco. But it was a sport Jack could only *watch*, since neither of those two would seriously entertain the idea of having a conversation with him. To Jack, the lady showed faint, perfunctory gratitude, and to all others she showed a sort of amused tolerance—all except Edmund de Ath, who was the only one she treated as an equal. This galled Jack far more than it should have. It was years since he'd been a king in Hindoostan and he should have been used to his reduced status. But being around this Spanish gentlewoman made him want to go back to Shahjahanabad and enlist in the service of the Great Mogul once more. And he was on his own ship!

"The only cure for it is to become a merchant prince," said Vrej Esphahnian, as they were sailing out of the Golden Gate on a cold, clear morning. "And that is what we are working toward. Learn from the Armenians, Jack. We do not care for titles and we do not have armies nor castles. Noble folk can sneer at us all they like—when their kingdoms have fallen into dust, we will buy their silks and jewels with a handful of beans."

"That is well, unless pirates or princes take what you have so tediously acquired," Jack said.

"No, you don't understand. Does a farmer measure his wealth in pails of milk? No, for pails spill, and milk spoils in a day. A farmer measures his wealth in *cows*. If he has cows, milk comes forth almost without effort."

"What is the cow, in this similitude?" asked Moseh, who had come over to listen.

"The cow is the web, or net-work of connexions, that Armenians have spun all the world round."

"It has never ceased to astonish me how you find Armenians everywhere we go," Jack admitted.

"In every place where we have tarried for more than a few days: Algiers, Cairo, Mocha, Bandar-Abbas, Surat, Shahjahanabad, Batavia, Macao, Manila—I have been able to invest some small fraction of my profits in the diverse enterprises of other Armenians," Vrej said. "In some cases the amounts were trivial. But it does not matter—those men know me now, they are knots in my net-work, and when I return to Paris, even if we lose *Minerva* and everything aboard her, I'll be a wealthy man—not in *milk* but in *cows*."

"Avast there, Vrej," Jack said, "I am not a superstitious man, but I do not love to hear this talk of losing *Minerva*."

Vrej shrugged. "Sometimes a man must accept a great loss."

An awkward stillness for a few moments, made more excruciatingly obvious by the shouting of the riggers as they trimmed the sails for a new course. *Minerva* was leaving the Golden Gate behind, and coming about into a new southeasterly course along the coast. She'd follow this general heading for some two thousand miles to Acapulco.

Finally Moseh said, "Well, I *am* a superstitious man, or at least a *religious* one, and I have been pondering this: When is my trading-voyage finished?"

"When you drop anchor in London or Amsterdam and come ashore with Bills of Exchange, or imported goods," Jack said.

"I cannot eat those."

"Very well, change them into silver and buy bread with it."

"So I have bread then. But did I need to sail around the world for bread?"

"Bread you can get anywhere," Jack admitted, then glanced at the open Pacific to starboard. "Save *there*. Why sail round the world, then? For entertainment, I suppose. We do what we have to do, Moseh, and are not frequently given diverse *choices*. What are you getting at?"

"I believe my journey ended when we crossed the Sea of Reeds and escaped from bondage in Egypt," Moseh said. "Nothing since then has brought me satisfaction."

"Again, though, you've had no choices available."

"Every day," Moseh said, "every day I've had choices, but I've been blind to them."

"You are being too Cabbalistickal for me," Jack said. "I am an Englishman and will go to England. You see? Very simple and plain. Now I will ask you a question that should have a simple answer: When we get to Acapulco, will you be in the Wet or the Dry Group?"

"Dry," said Moseh, "dry forever."

"Very well," said Vrej after another of those awkward silences, "as we've lost poor Arlanc, it follows that I shall have to be Wet. And that sits well with me, for I am eager to see Lima, the Rio de la Plata, and Brazil, and after all we've endured, Cape Horn holds no terror for me."

Dappa happened along. "For a man without a country, the ship is the only choice. Brazil and the Caribbean are awash in African slaves and I cannot learn or tell their stories unless I voyage there and talk to them."

"Then since van Hoek obviously goes with the ship, I'm obligated to be Dry," Jack said, "and my boys will go with me."

They all stood silently for a few moments, caught between a raw Pacific wind and the coast of California. Then every one of them seemed to understand how many preparations lay ahead of him, and each went his own way.

"THE BEST TIME TO NEGOTIATE is before negotiations have begun," said Moseh, as he and Jack watched the longboat crawl towards the shore of the port of Navidad. The Alcalde of Chiamela, several priests, and a few men in the full Conquistador get-up stood there waiting for it. "Or anyway that is what I learned from Surendranath, and I hope it has worked in this case."

Jack noticed that, as Moseh was saying this, he was fingering the scrap of Indian bead-work he had inherited from his Manhattoe ancestors. It was something that Moseh did, in an absent-minded way, whenever he was afraid of getting a raw deal. Jack decided not to mention it.

After two weeks of working their way down the coast of California they had crossed the Tropic of Cancer and weathered the bald promontory of Cabo San Lucas on New Year's Day of 1701. Then they had set their course due southeast so as to traverse the mouth of the Gulf of California, a journey that had ended up taking several days because the Virazon, or northwest wind down the coast, had failed. Eventually they had come in sight of the trio of islands called the Three Marys, which lay off the bony elbow of New Spain, Cabo Corrientes—the Cape of Currents. Two rather tense days had followed. Those two Capes (San Lucas and Corrientes) formed the gate-posts of the long narrow body of water that ran between lower California and New Spain, which was called a Strait by those who still believed California was an island and a Gulf by those who didn't. Whether it was a Strait or a Gulf, the Three Marys had a commanding position near its entrance. Yet they were far enough north to be out of reach of the Spanish authorities in Acapulco. Consequently they were a popular place for English and French pirates to spend winters. And to this human danger were added certain natural ones: the Three Marias were nearly joined to Cabo Corrientes by vast shallows. Even if they'd been able to salvage the latest Spanish charts from the Manila Galleon—which they hadn't—these would have been nearly useless, because the powerful currents passing between the two Capes in and out of the Strait or Gulf shifted the sands from one tide to the next. The only persons in the world who would have the cunning to pilot a ship in that area would be the aforementioned pirates—if there were any. If there were, and they were English, they might or might not be the natural allies of *Minerva*. If French they would certainly be enemies.

But a nerve-wracking circuit of Maria Madre, Maria Magdalena, and Maria Cleofas had not turned up anything beyond a few decaying bivouacs, some abandoned and some manned by skeleton crews of dumbfounded wretches who fired guns in the air in weak bids to beckon them closer. "This year's crop of pirates—if any made it around Cape Horn—must be wintering in the Galápagos," van Hoek had said one night at mess, as they supped on the meat of some tortoises that had been captured from the longboat.

"The only pirates are *we*," Dappa had remarked. This had not sat very well with van Hoek, but it had made something of an impression on Elizabeth de Obregon and Edmund de Ath. They had excused themselves early, withdrawn to the taffrail, and had yet another in their seemingly un-ending series of obscure conferences. "They'll be re-writing their damned letters all night long," Jack had predicted.

More conferences, and more re-writing, had followed the next day, as they'd dropped anchor off Maria Madre (the largest of the islands) and used the longboat to ferry Heavy Objects back and forth between *Minerva* and shore. Elizabeth and Edmund were confined to their cabins the whole time, and the longboat's load was covered with sailcloth whenever it was within view of their windows. The cargo hold was off limits to them. There was no way for them to know what had been done. The obvious interpretation was that part of the quicksilver had been taken ashore and buried, and stones brought out from the island to ballast the ship. But it might just as well have been a mountebank's shell-game: quicksilver-flasks going in to shore and then coming right back out again to be put back in their places in the hold.

The same performance had been repeated two days later on the Cape of Currents itself. Only then had van Hoek given the order they'd all been waiting for: to put that Cape behind them and run before the Virazon, coasting southeast into the country of New Galicia, the northernmost part of the coast that was really settled. The mountains and volcanoes of that country looked empty and barren, but after the sun went down they saw a signal-fire blazing on a high remote summit and knew from this that they had been sighted by the sentinel who was posted there. It meant that a rider was now galloping post-haste towards the City of Mexico, a journey of five hundred miles across terrible mountains, to deliver the news that a great ship had come out of the West. According to Elizabeth de Obregon, the people of Mexico (who were almost all monks and nuns, as the Church owned all of the land in the city) would begin to pray around the clock as soon as they heard that news, and would not stop until letters arrived from other watchers, farther down the coast, confirming that it was indeed the Manila Galleon.

Of course in this case it *wasn't,* and so the letters would say something else. As the only two survivors of the disaster, Elizabeth and Edmund would perforce be the authors of those letters. Van Hoek would make a report, too, as a courtesy to the Viceroy. Much hinged upon how exactly those letters were worded, and on how *Minerva*'s involvement was explained. The two survivors had spent much of the journey from the Golden Gate to Cabo San Lucas writing and rewriting them, and had continued to make revisions until a few minutes before the documents had been placed on the longboat and despatched toward the shore. *Minerva* had cruised past the port of Chiamela, which was large and well-sheltered by islands but too shallow for large ships, and continued a few hours down the coast to the deep-water port of Navidad. By then it must have been obvious to the Alcalde of Chiamela, who was pursuing them on horseback the whole way, that this was no Manila Galleon, and that something had gone wrong. But not until *Minerva's* longboat pulled to within shouting distance of Navidad did anyone who'd not been on the voyage learn of what had happened in the middle of the Pacific. There was a suitable eruption of wailing, cursing, praying, and (eventually) bell-clanging when this bit of intelligence finally sparked across the gap. Moseh winced empathetically and turned his attentions back to Jack.

"Though they were our captives in all but name, Ed and Elsie" (here he used Jack's names for the two passengers) "might have said to us: 'You men of *Minerva* are starving, your ship needs repairs, your cargo is valueless save at the mine-heads of New Spain and Peru. Only at the great ports of the King of Spain, such as Acapulco, Panama, and Lima, have you any hope of trading your quicksilver for what you so desperately need. If you are barred from those ports, you shall be exiled to a few wretched pirate-islands, for in your current plight you've scant hope of weathering Cape Horn. A few words on parchment, signed and sealed by us, determine whether you'll be welcomed as heroes or hunted down as scurvy pirates.' "

"They *might* have said that," Jack agreed. "But they didn't."

"They didn't. If they had, it would have meant we were negotiating, which was best avoided. So before the subject was even broached I went into my Cabbalist act and gave Ed and Elsie to believe that I was naught more than an errand-boy for a legion of wizards and alchemists in the Islands of Solomon. That, and the caches of quicksilver that we might or might not have buried on Maria Madre and Cabo Corrientes, put us in a stronger position than we really deserve."

"Dappa has read their letters," Jack remarked. "He admits that their Latin is high-flown and abstruse, and that he may be overlooking much that is nuanced. But he seems to think that the survivors' accounts depict us in a favorable light."

"At the very least we should avoid summary execution," Moseh allowed.

"There you go again—always the optimist."

The port of Navidad despatched a boat of its own to bring out some provisions. The only cure for scurvy was to go ashore, but since they had arrived at the Golden Gate and begun to eat the fruits of the earth again, teeth had stopped falling out and gums had pinkened. Whatever was on this boat should tide them over to Acapulco. As it turned out, the boat carried not just food, but also tidings from Madrid: King Carlos II, "The Sufferer," had finally died.

Of course hardly anyone on *Minerva* cared, and in any case it was not much of a surprise, as all of Christendom had been waiting for it to happen for three decades. But as they were in the Spanish Empire now, they tried to look solemn. Edmund de Ath crossed himself. Elizabeth de Obregon covered her face and went into her cabin without saying a word. Jack naïvely supposed she was praying the rosary for her dead monarch. But when he next went to his own cabin for a cat-nap he could hear the *scribble, scribble* of her quill, inscribing yet more letters.

They sailed for another week along a coast lined with cacao and vanilla plantations, and on the 28th of January came in sight of the first city they'd seen since leaving Manila in July. It was a shoal of mean little shacks that looked in danger of being shrugged into the water by the green mountains rising up behind. They could have sailed right past it, mistaking it for a wretched fishing-village, if not for the fact that a large castle stood in the middle.

The steepness of those mountains suggested a deep-water harbor. This was confirmed by a few large ships that had come in so close to shore that they were tied up to trees! But the passage in to that harbor was winding; the *barque de négoce* that came out to meet them had to put her three lateen sails through any number of difficult evolutions just to get out into blue water. This barque sported two six-pounders on either side of her high stern as well as a dozen or so swivel-guns distributed around her gunwales. In other words, compared to a Dutch East Indiaman like *Minerva* she was essentially unarmed. But the gaudy encrustations wrapped around her stern, and the fabulously complex heraldry on her ensign, told them that this barque had been sent out by someone important: according to Elizabeth de Obregon, the castellan, who was the highest authority in Acapulco. The two survivors of the Galleon were welcomed aboard this barque. *Minerva* was told not to enter the harbor, but to proceed several miles down the coast to a place called Port Marques.

Van Hoek had heard of it; Port Marques was the semi-official smugglers' port, frequented by ships that came up from Peru with pigs of silver and other contraband that it would be unseemly to unload directly beneath the windows of the Castle of Acapulco. So they passed Acapulco by, with no sense of regret, as every building there was either a mud hovel or a monastery, and a few hours later dropped anchor before Port Marques. This was even more ragged and humble, being little more than a camp inhabited by Vagabonds, blacks, mulattoes, and mestizos.

Moseh went ashore on the first boat-load, fell on his face in the sand, and kissed it. "I will never set foot on a ship again as God is my witness!" he hollered.

"If you are talking to God, why are you speaking Sabir?" shouted Jack, who was watching from the poop deck of *Minerva.*

"God is far away," Moseh explained, "and I must rely on men to keep me honest."

LATER DAPPA WENT ASHORE and talked to some of the black men camped on the beach. There was a group of half a dozen who had come from the same African river as he, and spoke a similar language. Each of them had been captured by other Africans and sold down the river to Bonny, where he had been branded with the trademark of the Royal Africa Company and eventually loaded on an English ship that had taken him to Jamaica.

Each of them had come, in other words, from a part of Africa notorious for breeding lazy and rebellious slaves, and each had acquired some additional defect en route: infected eyes, gray hair, excessive gauntness, mysterous swellings, or contagious-looking skin diseases. Therefore none of the planters had wanted to buy them, or even take them for free. Obviously the captain of the slave-ship had no intention of taking such refuse slaves back to Africa and so they were simply abandoned on the dock of Kingston, where it was hoped and expected they'd die. And indeed there was no better place for it, as Kingston was perhaps the filthiest city on the planet. Most of the refuse slaves obligingly died. But each of the ones in this little band had separately made his way inland, and entered into a sort of Vagabond life, joining together in bands with escaped slaves and native Jamaicans and roving about the island stealing chickens and trying to stay one step ahead of the posses sent out after them by plantation-owners.

This particular group had drifted to an unsettled stretch of coast towards the western tip of Jamaica, where fishing was rumored to be good. About a year later they had encountered a brig full of English adventurers sailing out of the west, i.e., from the general direction of New Spain. These Englishmen—who, to judge from their description, were likely nothing more than incompetent or luckless bocaneers—had lately been reckless enough to find a route through a barrier reef that had hitherto barred access to a certain part of the Mosquito Coast, seven hundred miles due west of Jamaica. Now they were making a foray to Kingston to collect gun-powder, musket-balls, swine, and other necessaries, so that they could go back and establish a settlement.

Here the narrator—an African by the name of Amboe, with a bald head and grizzled beard—jumped over what must have been a somewhat involved negotiation, and said simply that he and a dozen of his band had decided to leave Jamaica and throw in their lot with these boca-neers, and had helped establish a rudimentary village at a place called Haulover Creek near the mouth of the river Belice. But it was a pestilential place, and the Englishmen got drunker and nastier every day, and so those who'd survived the initial rounds of diseases and hurricanes had pulled up stakes and moved inland, passing through a land of jungle-covered Pyramids (lengthy, implausible yarns deleted here), and straying across the Isthmus of Tehuantepec (or so Jack—who'd been studying maps—inferred), to the Pacific Coast, and then wandering up this way.

Acapulco, Amboe explained, was far too hot, cramped, and famished to support many Spaniards and so for most of the year its hovels were occupied by the wretched soldiers of the garrison, a few missionaries who did not care whether they lived or died, and people like these: Indians, refuse-slaves, and the like. Only when the Manila Galleon or the Lima treasure-fleet was expected did white men swarm down out of the mountains and kick out the squatters and turn Acapulco into a semblance of a real city. This had just happened a week ago, which explained why so many rabble were camped on the beach at Port Marques; but word had already gotten around that the ship was not the Manila Galleon, and disappointed merchants were already streaming out of town in droves, leaving behind empty buildings that the beach-people would soon move back into.

Naturally all of *Minerva*'s crew wanted to come ashore, but van Hoek only let them do so one watch at a time, and he insisted that men stand by the longboat with muskets. He was worried, in other words, that the Spaniards would try to seize the ship on some pretext, and that she would have to fight her way out onto the main and make for Galápagos or some other pirate-haven. Jack for his part was inclined to believe that the Spaniards would see things their way. If *Minerva* came under attack she would either flee or be sunk, and in either event the quicksilver in her holds would never arrive at the mine-heads of New Spain. And if she were not received hospitably and dealt with fairly, she could sail down the coast to Lima and the quicksilver would end up at Potosí, the greatest mine in the world.

In any event there was a pause while the accounts of Edmund de Ath and Elizabeth de Obregon were sent by express to Mexico City, and (presumably) pondered by important people, and orders sent back by express. This ended up taking sixteen days. Van Hoek never once came ashore, but remained aboard his ship, doing sums in his cabin or pacing the poop deck with a spyglass, scanning the horizon for armadas. Vrej Esphahnian ventured into Acapulco to procure the wood and other items needed to repair *Minerva*'s foremast. He ended up being absent for two nights and a day, and van Hoek was getting ready to send out a rescue party when a barge emerged from Acapulco Harbor's broad southeastern entrance and came their way, laden with what they wanted. Vrej was posed insouciantly on a new foremast, and explained the delay by informing them that Acapulco was that rarest of places, an important trade-port without a single Armenian, and so he had been forced to deal with slower minds.

Minerva's idlers were now idle no more, as the new foremast had to be stepped and rigged. That procedure might have been interesting to Jack if it had been done in mid-ocean where there was nothing else to look at, but as it was, being on land had reminded him of how much he hated being aboard ship. He spent those days ashore, making friends with diverse Vagabonds and ne'er-do-wells, learning which of them were idiots and which merely independent-minded. Amboe and his band were obviously of the latter type, but most of these beach-people did not have such informative Narrations to tell, and Jack could sound them out only through carousing with them over a period of weeks. Jack had long since lost interest in carousing *per se,* but he recalled how it was done, and could still put on a performance of carousing that looked sincere but was in fact wholly affected, shrewd, and calculating. He was helped in this by his two sons, who really meant it.

Gentlefolk liked to claim that horsemanship was a noble art. If that were true, then half of the renegadoes on the beach at Port Marques were bastard sons of Dukes and Princes. New Spain bred horses the way London bred fleas, and many of these mulattoes and mestizoes could ride like cavaliers, even bareback. Jack of course was the last man on earth who'd ever believe that riding well was a sign of superior breeding. But he did know that riding badly was its own punishment, and that spirited horses could smell fools and poseurs from a mile away. Some of the Port Marques crowd would entertain themselves by roping wild beach-mustangs and riding them up and down the sand, forcing them against their will to gallop into breaking waves. From a musket-shot away Jack could see the white teeth of those riders as they laughed, and later on, as they gathered around driftwood-fires to eat the food of the country (maize flat-bread wrapped around meager helpings of beans and spicy stews), he would seek those men out and try to learn something of them, and he would ply them with rum to see if they had a weakness for liquor. Of all of these, the best man, in Jack's opinion, was an African named Tomba, a member of Amboe's band. Tomba was not a refuse slave; he had escaped from a sugar plantation in Jamaica. The scars on his back confirmed part of his story, which was that he'd fled to avoid being beaten to death by an overseer. The time he'd spent on the plantation, and at the English settlement on Haulover Creek, had given Tomba some knowledge of English, and he spent several long evenings sitting by the fire with Jimmy and Danny Shaftoe talking about what sons of bitches Englishmen were in general.

Almost three weeks after *Minerva* had dropped anchor at Port Marques, Edmund de Ath came out alone one morning from Acapulco, bearing sealed letters from the Viceroy. One was addressed to van Hoek and another to the Viceroy's counterpart in Lima. Van Hoek opened his in *Minerva*'s dining cabin, in the presence of de Ath, Dappa, Jack, and Vrej.

Moseh's vow compelled him to remain ashore. Later Jack rowed in on a skiff and found the Jew eating a taco.

"These Vagabond-boots are longing to Stray," Jack said. "I reckon that tomorrow we will round up a posse of these *vaqueros* and *desperadoes* and begin to assemble a mule-train."

Moseh finished chewing a bite of his taco and swallowed carefully. "The news is good, then."

"We are all vile hereticks and profiteers, says the Viceroy, and ought to be whipped all the way to Boston . . . but Edmund de Ath has put in a good word for us."

"Is that Ed's version or . . ."

"It's right there in black and white in the middle of the Viceroy's letter, or so literate men assure me."

"Very well," said Moseh, dubiously. "I do not like being beholden to that Jansenist, but—"

"We are beholden to him anyway," said Jack. "Do you recollect the fellow we had dealings with in Sanlúcar de Barrameda?"

"That *cargador metedoro*? It's been a while."

"You don't have to remember him *personally*, but only the class he belonged to."

"Spanish Catholics who front for Protestant merchants . . ."

". . . because hereticks are barred from doing business in Spain. You've got it."

"The Viceroy wants our quicksilver," Moseh said, "but as long as the Inquisition is active in Mexico City, he cannot allow Protestants and a Jew to roam about transacting business in his country. And so he insists that we nominate a Papist to act as our *cargador metedoro*."

"Just so," Jack said.

"And—don't tell me—Edmund de Ath is our man. I am uneasy."

"You are always uneasy, and more often than not, for the best of reasons," Jack said, "but for God's sake look about you and consider our situation. We must have a Catholic and that is all there is to it. There are many to choose from, but as a Belgian Jansenist, Ed is the least Catholic Catholic we are likely to find, and at least we know something about him."

"Do we? The only person who can testify as to his character is Elizabeth de Obregon, and she's been under his spell ever since she came to."

Jack sighed. "Do I need to tell you that you've been out-voted?"

Moseh flinched. "I never should have given any of you voting privileges . . . that was never part of the Plan."

"We're not putting him in control of the ship," Jack said, "just allowing him to act as our front here and in Lima. He'll sail down that-a-way aboard *Minerva* and sell whatever quicksilver we do not off-load here. At that point, his role in the enterprise is finished. *Minerva* leaves him on the dock in Lima, rounds Cape Horn, and makes rendezvous with us in Vera Cruz or Havana a year or two later. Edmund de Ath can stay in Peru and try to convert the Incas to Œcumenicism, or he can come back to Mexico . . . it matters not to us."

"It matters not to *me,* for my voyaging days have ended," said Moseh. "If Edmund de Ath tries to do any mischief I'll put on my poncho and *sombrero* and ride north with saddlebags full of silver."

"Very well," Jack said, "but first you had better learn how to ride. It is more difficult than pulling on an oar."

Charlottenburg Palace, Berlin
JULY 1701

"Your highness, when I was a boy—rather younger than you are now, hard as that might be to imagine—I was locked out of a library for a time, and I did not care for it at all," said the bald man leading the young woman down the gallery. "I pray you understand how it has pained me to have locked *you* out of *yours* for the last week—"

"It's not really mine, is it? The library is the property of Uncle Freddy and Aunt Figgy!"

"But you have made it yours by spending so much time there."

"While it was closed, you've brought me every book I asked for without delay, Doctor. So whyever should I mind?"

"It's true, Highness, my desire to apologize to you is wholly irrational, Q.E.D."

"Is it just one of those Barock apologies that courtiers put at the beginnings of letters?"

"I should hope not. An apology may be *heartfelt* without being *rational*."

"Whereas a courtier's apology is the opposite," said the Princess, "in that it is *insincere* but *calculated*."

"It is well said—but said too loudly," answered the proud Doctor. "Your voice carries for a mile down these echoing galleries; and a courtier who has just snatched an indiscretion out of the air will prance about to all the salons like a puppy who has just stolen a drumstick."

"Then let's in *here*, where my voice will be muffled by books, and where courtiers never venture," answered Caroline, and paused before the doors to the library, waiting for Leibniz to open them for her.

"Now you will see your birthday present, and I hope you like it," said the Doctor, drawing a key on a blue silk ribbon from his pocket. The key was a rod of steel having a fabulously ornate handle at one end, and at the other, a sort of three-dimensional maze carved into a steel cube. He inserted this into a square hole in the door-lock, wiggled it to and fro to make it one with the mechanism concealed inside, then turned it. Before opening the doors, he removed the key from the lock and hung it on its blue ribbon around the Princess's neck. "Since you cannot carry your present with you, I hope you'll carry this key as a token. May you never be locked out again."

"Thank you, Doctor. When I am Queen of some country or other, I shall build you a library greater than that of Alexandria, and give you a golden key to it."

"I fear that I shall be too old and blind to make good use of the *library*—but I shall accept the *key* with gratitude, and carry it to my grave."

"That would be irresponsible of you—then no one else would be able to get into the Library!" Caroline answered, with a roll of the eyes, and a sharp sigh of exasperation. "Open the doors, Doctor, I want to see it!"

Leibniz unlatched the double doors, turned around, and backed through them so that he could watch her face. He saw light reflected in her blue eyes: light from high windows all around the room, and from sparking fire-works set in buckets of sand to make it look like one great birthday-cake.

The library had been built two stories high, with a catwalk all around, halfway up, to afford access to the higher shelves, and its walls and the frescoed vault overhead had been generously arched with windows so that "Aunt Figgy" (short for Figuelotte, as Queen Sophie Charlotte was known to her family) and her bookish friends could read into the evening without need of candles. The high windows had been cracked open to let the room breathe in warm summer air and to exhale the smoke from the fizzing sparklers. The frescoes depicted the same assortment of Classical scenes that covered the ceiling of every rich person in Christendom nowadays, though the gods and goddesses had been provided with blond hair and blue eyes so that Jupiter might as well have been Wotan. *Trompe l'oeil* made it look as if the library had no ceiling but was open to the blue skies, and the gods were all springing out of frothy clouds. The writhing columns of smoke from the fireworks spread out against the plaster-work and swirled about to make the illusion that much better.

A cheer and a little song followed, from the dozen or so people who had come to wish Caroline *Glück* on her *Geburtstag*. It was a small party, for a Princess, and it was an older crowd. Sophie was the eldest of all at seventy-one—she had come out from Hanover, crammed into a carriage with Leibniz and her grandchildren: George August (who was a few months younger than Caroline) and Sophie Dorothea (four years younger yet). Sophie Charlotte (Figuelotte), Queen of Prussia and the mistress and namesake of the palace, was here with her son Frederick William, a legendary brat of thirteen. Filling out the guest list was the motliest collection of metaphysicians, mathematicians, radical theologians, writers, musicians, and poets ever brought together for a princess's eighteenth birthday.

The Queen of Prussia liked to stage operas, when she wasn't inciting riotous dinner-table debates among her friends, and the only sense in which she was ever a tyrant was in ordering some poor physicist to don a mad-cap and warble a role for which he was untrained and ill-suited. Princess Caroline had been dragooned, from time to time, to sing a Nymph or Angel part. Nothing, except perhaps for fighting side-by-side in a war, forged bonds among disparate persons so well as performing together on stage, and so Caroline had become a great friend of these grownups, her fellow-sufferers on the boards of the Charlottenburg.

With wine-glasses and sparklers in hand they had gathered round a pedestal that had been built of polished cherry-wood in the center of the library. Surmounting this, and spreading out above the heads of the revelers, was a large spherical object—

"A cage!" Caroline exclaimed.

Dismay flowed over Leibniz's face. But very soon that emotion gave way to a sort of distracted, intrigued look, as his curiosity had been somehow provoked. He bobbed his head in a way that might have been a nod, or a bow. *"C'est juste,"* he said. "Geometers have, with their parallels and meridians, *ruled* the globe that, being unmarked, save by irregular coastlines and river-courses, seemed wild to eyes that only in *order* could see *beauty*. But one who loves Nature for her *variety* might see the geometers' devices as a disfigurement—no bird is as beautiful when seen through the bars of a cage, as it is in the wild. But I pray, Highness, that you will construe this rather as an inventory of the known. It is a map of the world, not as flattened out by cartographers, but as it *is*."

The globe had been set at an angle, as the earth was tilted with respect to the ecliptic. An unexplored portion of the South Pacific bore on the pedestal. Not far away from it, the south pole presented itself just at the level of Caroline's head. This globe was indeed fashioned like a spherical bird-cage, with curving brass bars following the lines of longitude and latitude. Most of it (the oceans) was openwork. But the continents were curved plates of brass riveted to those bars. They were mounted to the *inside* of the cage, rather than the outside, so that the bars passed in front of them—at least, for the celebrants who were standing around it. An irregular, wholly facti-tious continent had been placed around the south pole, represent-ing the hypothetical land of Antarctica, and this had a round hatchway cut into it, and steps leading up to it from the floor.

Dr. Krupa (a Bohemian mathematician who had become a sort of permanent houseguest here) said, "Highness, some have proposed that at the world's poles are openings where one may descend into the earth's interior. Here is your opportunity personally to put that hypothesis to the test."

The Princess appeared to have forgotten that anyone else was in the room, and had not even said hello to Aunt Figgy or to Aunt Sophie. She stood for a moment at the base of the steps, the O of her mouth an echo of the big hole that was about to swallow her up. Even Frederick William shut up for a moment, sensing a *frisson* run-ning through the assembled grownups, but not having the first idea why. That Princess Caroline of Ansbach had once been a little pen-niless orphan had been long forgot by most. But something about her pose there, below that hole in the Antarctic, unaware of all the people standing about, called to mind the orphan who had showed up on Sophie Charlotte's doorstep five years ago, escorted by two Natural Philosophers and a brace of Prussian dragoons.

Then she got a smile on her face and climbed up through the hole. The grownups resumed breathing and applauded—giving Frederick William the diversion he needed to loop round behind the crowd and slam George August over the head with a book. Leib-niz, who had not spent much time around children, watched this dumbfounded. Then he noticed Sophie regarding him with amuse-ment. "It begins," she said, "already the boys are vying for Caroline's attention."

"Is *that* what they're doing?" Leibniz asked incredulously as George August,* who was five years older than, and twice the size of, his assailant, body-slammed Frederick William† against a smaller and more traditional sort of globe that had been shoved into a corner to make way for the new one. The papier-mâché sphere crumpled inward and Frederick William ended up wearing it on his head, mak-ing him look like some antipodean creature with a monstrously over-sized brain.

These antics had gone unnoticed, or been deliberately ignored, by Monsieur Molyneux, a Huguenot writer who had been haunting

---

* The future King of England.
† The future King of Prussia

Berlin since his family had been wiped out in Savoy. "Why indeed should we *not* view the world as a cage in which our spirit has been imprisoned?" he reflected.

"Because God is not a prison-warden," Leibniz answered sharply, but stopped when an elbow even sharper (Sophie's) caught him in the ribs.

Princess Caroline had taken her seat: a swivel-stool mounted in the middle of the globe. Planting one of her party-shoes at the junction of the Twentieth West Meridian and the Fortieth South Parallel, so that the toe seemed to breach out of the South Atlantic like an immense white whale, she gave a little kick that sent her spinning around. "I'm rotating!" she reported, "the world is revolving around me!"

"Solipsistic, that," somone remarked drily.

"It is more than that," Leibniz said, "it is a profound question of Natural Philosophy. How indeed can we tell whether we do stand still in a rotating universe, or spin in a fixed cosmos?"

"*Eeehuhh*, I'm dizzy!" Caroline said, explaining why she had planted her feet, and stopped.

"There's your answer," Dr. Krupa said.

"Not at all. You assume that dizziness is a symptom—internally produced—of our spinning. But why might it not just as well be an effect exerted upon us from a distance, by a revolving universe?"

"No one should be forced to listen to metaphysics at her eighteenth birthday-party," Sophie decreed.

"It's dark in here," Caroline said, "I can't see the maps."

Wladyslaw—a Polish tenor who sang the lead in just about every one of Sophie Charlotte's operas—lit a fresh sparkler and handed it through the central Pacific Ocean to Caroline. Leibniz's view of the girl happened to be blocked by Brazil, but he saw the inside of the sphere light up as the sparkler was drawn into the middle; the freshly buffed brass seemed to ignite as it sieved the light from the air and spilled it out in every direction. For a moment it seemed as if the globe-cage was filled with flame, and Leibniz's heart ached and pounded with fear that Caroline's dress had caught fire; but then he heard her delighted voice, and decided that the fear he felt was of something else, of some larger and longer calamity than the fate of one orphan Princess.

"I can see now all the rivers set in turquoise, and all the lakes, too, and forests of green tortoise-shell! The cities are jewels, which the light shines through."

"It is how the world would look if it were transparent and you could sit in the middle looking outward," said Father von Mixnitz, a Jesuit from Vienna who had somehow arranged to get himself invited.

"I am aware of that," said Caroline, annoyed. A long, irritable silence followed. Caroline was quickest to forgive and forget. "I see two ships in the Pacific, and one is full of quicksilver, and the other is full of fire."

"I do not recall putting those in the drawings," Leibniz joked, trying to obey Sophie's command to lighten things up a bit. "I shall have to have a word with the workmen about that!"

"Consider this, your royal highness," continued Father von Mixnitz, "you may spin yourself all the way round, three hundred and twenty degrees—"

"Three hundred and *sixty*!"

"Yes, highness, that is what I meant to say—three hundred and *sixty* degrees—and never shall you pass out of sight of the Spanish Empire. Is it not remarkable, how vast, how wealthy, are the dominions of Spain?"

"Aunt Sophie says it may be the dominions of France soon," Caroline demurred.

"Indeed, the French pretender does sit on the throne in Madrid at the moment . . ."

"Aunt Sophie says it's the woman behind that throne who matters."

"Indeed," the Jesuit said, twitching his eyes toward Sophie, "many argue that the duc d'Anjou, or King Philip V of Spain as he styles himself, is a mere pawn of the princesse des Ursins, who is herself a notorious soulmate of Madame de Maintenon—but this is beside the point, as Anjou cannot possibly endure long on the Spanish throne, when he is opposed by women far more cunning, more powerful, and more beautiful."

"Aunt Sophie says she does not care for flatterers," said the voice from the center of the brass world.

Sophie, who had been about to squash the priest like a bug, now did something rare for her: She hesitated, torn between annoyance with the Jesuit and delight in Caroline.

"It is no flattery, highness, to say that Sophie, in league with King William, or Queen Anne as the case may one day be, is a stronger hand than Maintenon and des Ursins. All the more so if the *rightful* heir to the Spanish throne—Archduke Charles—were wed to a Princess in the mold of Sophie and Sophie Charlotte."

"But Archduke Charles is Catholic while Aunt Sophie and Aunt Figgy are Protestants—as am I," said Caroline, absent-mindedly kicking at meridians to twist herself left, right, left, right, peering first to one side, then the other, of the Isthmus of Panama.

"It is hardly unheard-of for Persons of Quality to change their religion," the Jesuit said. "Especially if they are intellectually active, and are presented with compelling arguments. As I am taking up residence here in Berlin, I shall look forward to exchanging views with your royal highness on such matters in coming years, as you grow in wisdom and maturity."

"We needn't wait," Caroline said helpfully. "I can explain it to you now. Dr. Leibniz has taught me all about religion."

"Oh, has he now?" Father von Mixnitz asked uneasily.

"Yes, he has. Now tell me, Father, are you one of those Catholics who still refuses to believe that the Earth goes round the Sun?"

Father von Mixnitz swallowed his tongue and then hacked it back up. "Highness, I believe in what Dr. Leibniz was saying just a minute ago, namely, that it is all *relative*."

"That's not *exactly* what I said," Leibniz protested.

"Do you believe in the transubstantiation of the bread and the wine, Father?" Caroline asked.

"How could I be a Catholic if I did not, Highness?"

"This is not how we do birthday parties in Poland," commented Wladyslaw, ladling himself another cup of wine.

"Hush! I am enjoying it greatly," Sophie returned.

"What if you ate it and then you got sick and threw up? When it came out, would it be Jesus's flesh and blood? Or would it detransubstantiate on the way out, and become bread and wine again?"

"Such solemn questions do not comport with the frothy imaginings of an eighteen-year-old girl," said Father von Mixnitz, who had gone all red in the face and was biting the words off one at a time, as if his tongue were a trip-hammer in a mill.

"Here's to frothy imaginings!" said Queen Sophie Charlotte, raising her glass with a beautiful smile; but her eyes were like those of a falcon tracking a mink as she watched Father von Mixnitz take his leave and stalk out of the room.

"What else do you see in the empty places, besides the ships of quicksilver and of fire?" asked Dr. Krupa.

"I see the very first ship sailing into the Tsar's new city of St. Petersburg. It is a *Dutch* ship, I phant'sy. And in the Atlantic and the Caribbean, ships of the Dutch and of the English sailing to war against the French and the Spanish . . ." but suddenly her sparkler fizzled out. A groan of sympathy ran through her audience. "Now I can see *nothing*!" she complained.

"The future is a mystery," Sophie said.

Sophie Charlotte's smile had been forced and fragile the last few minutes. "At least she got to use the thing as it was intended for a few minutes," she said to Leibniz.

"What do you mean, Majesty?"

"I mean, *innocently,* as a wonder to marvel at—and *not* as a Visual Aid for choosing her husband."

"She can learn all she needs to know of husband-choosing from you, Majesty," Leibniz answered. Those words led to a brief sweet moment between the savant and Sophie Charlotte—which was cut short by Frederick William, who came running in to shield himself behind his mother's skirts. George August had ascended to one of the library catwalks with a big fire-stick he had plucked from a sand-bucket. Copying his pose directly from the fresco above, he drew back and aimed it at his cousin just like Jupiter readying a thunderbolt.

Leibniz excused himself so that Sophie Charlotte could scold her son. As he passed beneath the globe he saw Princess Caroline's shoes flashing out first to one side, then the other, as she reciprocated to and fro, first towards George August, then towards Frederick William. She was singing a little nursery rhyme she had picked up from her English tutor: "Eeny, meeny, miney, moe . . . catch a suitor by the toe . . . to England or Prussia shall I go . . . to be made high or be laid low . . . eeny, meeny, miney, moe."

BOOK 4

Bonanza

Mexico City, New Spain

SUKKOTH 1701

That Golden Sceptre which thou didst reject
Is now an Iron Rod to bruise and breake
Thy disobedience.

—MILTON,
Paradise Lost

"*CARAMBA!*" EXCLAIMED DIEGO DE FONSECA, "a *cucaracha* has fallen onto the *tortillas* of my wife!"

Moseh had seen it before de Fonseca had, and had jumped to his feet even before the initial *Caramba!* had echoed off the far wall of the prison's courtyard. As he reached over the table, the beads of his colossal rosary—walnut-shells strung on a cowhide thong—whacked the rim of a honey-filled serving-crock. His arm shot free of its sleeve, revealing a ladder of welts and scars, some fresher than others. His shoulder-joint rumbled and popped like a barrel rolling over cobblestones. Most of the men at the table felt twinges of sympathetic pain in their own shoulders, and inhaled sharply. Moseh's ingratiating smile hardened into a scary grimace, but he got a grip on Señora de Fonseca's tortilla-plate and pulled it clear. "Allow me to fetch some fresh ones . . ."

Diego de Fonseca glanced sidelong at his wife, who had tilted her head back, reducing her chin count to a mere three, and was glaring at the net-work of vines above the table, which was vibrant with six-legged life. The Director, who was not a thin specimen either, leaned slightly towards Moseh and said, "That is most Christian of you . . . but we prefer our *tortillas* made with rich lard, and in fact have never seen them made with olive oil before—"

"I could send out an Indian, Señor Director—"

"Don't bother, we are satiated. Besides—"

"I was just about to say it!" Jack put in. "Besides, you and the Señora get to go *home* tonight!"

Diego de Fonseca adjusted the set of his jaw slightly, and favored Jack with the same look his wife had aimed at the cockroach moments earlier. Fortunately, Señora de Fonseca's attention had been drifting: "Over *there,* you pay such attention to *cleanliness,*" she observed, casting a look down an adjacent gallery, where several prisoners were sweeping the paving-stones with bundles of willow-branches. "Yet you lay out your feast with nothing to protect you from the sky, save this miserable thatching of infested vines."

"I gather from your tone that you are *bemused* by our *ineptitude* where a señora less imbued with Christian charity would be *angry* at our *rudeness,*" Moseh said.

"Quite! Why, those fellows with the willow-branches are not so much *sweeping* the pavement as *spanking* it!"

"Those are from that batch of Jewish monks we arrested at the Dominican monastery three years ago," said Diego.

From any other Inquisition prison warden, this might have sounded judgmental—even condemnatory. But Diego de Fonseca presided over what was widely held to be the mellowest and most easy-going Inquisition prison in the whole Spanish Empire, and he said it in mild conversational tones. Then he popped a honey-dipped pastry into his mouth.

"That explains it!" said Moseh. "Those Dominicans are so rich, each monk hires half a dozen Indians as housekeepers, and consequently they know nothing of the *domestick* arts." He cupped his hands around his mouth. "Say, Brother Christopher! Brother Peter! Brother Diaz! There are *ladies* present! Try to move some dirt as long as you are sweeping the courtyard, will you?"

The three monks straightened up and glared at Moseh, then bent their backs again and began scraping dust across the stones. Clouds of volcanic ash built up and rose around their knees.

"As for this wretched covering, I can only beg you pardon, señora," continued Moseh. "We like to lie out in this place and recuperate after a question-and-answer session with the Inquisitor, and so we have been training the vines to grow thus, to shade us from the mid-afternoon sun."

"Then you need to give them manure, for I can clearly see stars coming out through the gaps."

To which the obvious response was *Manure!? We get no shortage of that from the priests, and give all of it back to the Inquisitor,* but before Jack could say it, Moseh silenced him with a look, and said: "Insofar as the vines cover us, we thank Lord Jesus, and insofar as they don't, we are reminded that in the end we are all dependent on the protection of God in Heaven."

The feast had been brought in by the prisoners' families and laid out on a long deal table at the edge of the prison courtyard, under a makeshift awning of bougainvilleas. It was a lot of harvest-time food: particularly squashes, baked with Caribbean sugar, cinnamon from Manila, and an infinity of beans. Jack had taken a liking to mushy food since losing most of his teeth crossing the Pacific. Up in Guanajuato he'd hired an Indian to make him a new set out of gold and carven boar's tusks, but this accessory had been mislaid, somewhere along the line, after he and Moseh had fallen into the hands of the Inquisition. He guessed that some *familiar* or *alguacil* was chewing his pork with Jack's teeth at this very moment, probably just over the wall in the dormitories of the *Consejo de la Suprema y General Inquisición.*

"Consider your apologies accepted, and your flattery disregarded," said Señora de Fonseca. "But a lady who attends a social function in a prison, organized by men—hereticks and infidels at that!—does not expect that the niceties will be observed. That is why every man seeks a wife, no?"

There followed a long silence, which quickly became embarrassing to those hereticks and infidels, and then stretched out to a point where it seemed likely to become fatal. Finally Jack kicked Salamón Ruiz under the table. Salamón had been rocking back and forth on his bench and muttering something. When Jack's boot impacted on his shin he opened his eyes and shouted, "Oy!"

Then, amid sharp inhalations from all around the table, stretched it out thus: *"Oigo misa!"*

"You are going to Mass!?" said Diego de Fonseca, perplexed.

"Misa de matrimonio," said Salamón, and then finally remembered to unclasp his hands and grope for the hand of his supposed *novia,* this evening's nominal guest of honor, Isabel Machado, who was seated on his right. He had never seen the girl before, and for a moment Jack was afraid he was going to grab the wrong woman's hand. "In my *head,* you know, I was going to Mass on my wedding day."

"Well, keep your hands out of your lap when you're doing it please!" Jack returned. The comment was not well received by the warden's wife, but Moseh plastered it over by rising to his feet and hoisting his chocolate-cup into the air: "To Isabel and Sanchez,* whose betrothal we celebrate tonight, may the Inquisitor be merciful to Sanchez, may the *auto da fé* be of the non-violent sort, and may their marriage be long and prosperous."

That toast led to others, which continued in chocolatey volleys

---

* Salamón went by the name Sanchez.

until the Cathedral bells rang vespers. Then the dinner broke up as the prisoners and their guests got to their feet and began to walk in a long uneven procession around the perimeter of the courtyard.

"To walk around thus after eating is a custom up north," Jack heard Moseh explaining to Señora de Fonseca.

"In Nuevo Leon? But that place was settled by Jews!"

"No, thank God, I meant the new mining country: Guanajuato, Zacatecas . . ."

She shuddered. "Brr, it is a land of Vagabonds and Desperadoes . . ."

"But pure-blooded Christians all. And after a big meal they always march around the town square seven times."

"Why seven?"

"Five times for the Five Wounds of Christ," Jack blurted out, "and three for the three persons of the Trinity."

"But five and three make *eight*!" observed Señor de Fonseca, now becoming interested.

Moseh now literally stepped in between Jack and the Fonsecas and continued, "All right, I did not wish to bore you with all of the details, but really the tradition is this: *formerly* they would go eight times around, turning always to the right. Then they would reverse direction and march around four times, one for each of the four gospels, turning to the left. Then reverse again and three additional times to the right, one for each of the crosses on Calvary. But then some Jesuit came along and pointed out that five and three, take away four, add three, make seven all together, and so why not simply go around seven times and leave it at that? Of course he was not taken seriously until they got a new priest up there, who had gout in one foot, and did not like so much walking. A letter was sent to the Vatican. Twenty years later the answer came back that the Jesuit's arithmetick had been examined, and determined to be sound. By that time the gouty priest had died of a fever. But his replacement was in no position to argue sums with the Pope, and so the tradition was established anyway."

Visibly exhausted, Moseh now lapsed into silence, as did the Fonsecas, who had been driven into a profound stupor. Not until several orbits of the courtyard had been tallied up did anyone speak again.

"Damn all this dust!" said Diego de Fonseca, waving a flabby hand before his face. The monks who had been sweeping earlier were now shaking their branches in the air, releasing clouds of Popocatepetl ash.

"I heard unfamiliar screaming today," Jack remarked. "Sounded as if someone was being given the *strappado,* but I didn't recognize his voice."

"It is a *Belgian* priest, supposedly with *heretickal* leanings—they brought him up from Acapulco," said the warden. "I believe he is a material witness in *your* case."

FATHER EDMUND DE ATH was sitting in his cell staring with a kind of dull curiosity at his own arms, which were laid out on the table in front of him like lamb shanks in a butcher's shop. They were still attached to his shoulders, but they were bloated and bluish, except around the wrists where ropes had sawn nearly to the bone. The only part of him that moved was his eyeballs, which swiveled toward the door as Jack and Moseh entered.

"You know, there was a monk in Spain who was thrown into the common jail for some petty crime, fifty or a hundred years ago," said de Ath. He was speaking in a quiet voice. Jack and Moseh knew why: the *strappado* ripped all of the muscles around the ribs and spine, giving the victim every incentive to breathe shallowly for the next couple of weeks. Jack and Moseh came round to either side and bent close so that de Ath could get by with a mere whisper. "After a few days in the squalor of that jail, he called the jailer over and uttered certain heretickal oaths. Of course the jailer denounced him to the Inquisition without delay. Before the next sundown, this monk had been moved to the Prison of the Inquisition, where he had his own cell, clean and well-ventilated, with a chair and—ahh—a table."

"A table's a good thing to have," Jack allowed, "when your arms have been pulled out of their sockets, and have nothing to support their weight save a few strands of gristle."

"You are not really a heretick, are you, Father?" asked Moseh.

"Of course not."

"So it follows that you believe in turning the other cheek, that the meek shall inherit the earth, *et cetera?*"

"*¿Como no?* As the Spaniards say."

"Good—we shall hold you to it," said Jack, raising one foot and planting it in the middle of de Ath's chest. He grabbed one of the priest's hands and Moseh the other. A violent shove sent the victim toppling backwards in his chair. Just as he was about to bash his head on the stone floor, Jack and Moseh jerked as hard as they could on de Ath's arms, yanking him back up like Enoch Root's yo-yo. A loud pop sounded from deep in each shoulder. The scream of Edmund de Ath, like the blowing of the legendary horn of Roland, could presumably be heard several mountain ranges away. Of course it emptied his lungs, which forced him to draw a deep breath, which was so painful that he had to scream some more. But after a while this Oscillatory Phenomenon damped out and de Ath was left in the same position as before, viz. sitting bolt upright with his arms on the table. But now he was cautiously clenching and unclenching his fists, and in the light of the candles that Jack and Moseh had brought in, it seemed his flesh was becoming a pinker shade of gray.

"Pardon me while I try to come up with theologickal analogies for what you just did to me," he said.

"You could do that until the *vacas* came back to the *hacienda,* I'm sure," said Moseh.

"Now that we are all devout Catholics we'll have plenty of opportunities to listen to homilies," Jack said. "For now, only tell us what you know of the proceedings against us."

Edmund de Ath said nothing for a long time. In Mexico, time was as plentiful as silver.

"The warden says you are a witness," Moseh said, "but they would not torture you unless you were also a suspect."

"That much is obvious," agreed de Ath, "but as you know perfectly well, the Inquisition never tells a prisoner what the charges are against him, or who denounced him. They throw him in prison and tell him to confess, and leave him guessing what he's supposed to confess *to.*"

" 'Tisn't hard for *me* to guess," Jack said. "I'm an Englishman missing the end of his dick, which means the only question is: Jew, or Protestant?"

"I hope you've been wise enough to tell them you're a Jew who was never baptized."

"That I have. Which—assuming they *believe* me—marks me as an *infidel.* And as this Church of yours thinks it is its mission to *preach* to infidels rather than *burn* 'em, I'm likely to escape with nothing worse than having to listen to a whole lot o' preaching."

"Your sons?"

"When the *alguaciles* came for me and Moseh, they were on a trip to Cabo Corrientes to dig up some of that buried quicksilver. No doubt they are drinking *mezcal* in some mining-town saloon about now."

"And you, Moseh?"

"They can see perfectly well I'm half Indian, so they've pegged me as a *mestizo* spawned by one of those crypto-Jews who went up to Nuevo Leon a hundred years ago."

"But that lot was exterminated in the *autos da fé* of 1673."

"Ridding a country of Jews is easier than purging every last phant'sy and suspicion from an Inquisitor's mind," Moseh returned. "He supposes every Indian between San Miguel de Allende and New York has a Torah concealed in his breech-clout."

"He wants to find that you are a heretick," said Edmund de Ath.

"And hereticks burn," Moseh added.

"Only if they are *unrepentant*," said Edmund de Ath, and his eyes followed the lines of Moseh's tunic until they found the rosary. "So you have made the decision to pass as a Christian, and avoid the stake. As soon as you are set free you'll go far away and become a Jew again. That is exactly what the Inquisitor *suspects*."

"Go on."

"He has been asking me questions about you. He would like for me to testify that you are a sham Christian and an unrepentant Jew. That is all he needs to burn you over a crackling mesquite fire . . . your only choice then would be to accept Christ as they were tying you to the stake . . ."

"In which event they'd charitably strangle me as the flames were rising—or, I could live for a few minutes longer as a devout Jew."

"Albeit an uncomfortable one," Jack concluded.

"Jack, he would also like for me to testify that you and Moseh prayed together in Hebrew, and observed Yom Kippur aboard *Minerva*."

"Go ahead, it just confirms I'm an infidel."

"But now that you are pretending to be a Catholic you've burned that excuse—any lapses make you a heretick."

Jack now became mildly irked. "What is your point? That you could, with a few words, send me and Moseh to the stake? We already knew that."

"There must be something more," Moseh said. "A *witness* they would not torture. Edmund has been accused of *something* by *someone*."

"Under normal circumstances there would be no guessing who my accuser was," said de Ath, "since the Inquisition keeps such matters a secret. But here in New Spain, no one knows me except for those who disembarked from *Minerva* in Acapulco. Obviously you two did not denounce me to the Inquisition." De Ath said this deliberately, and looked Jack and then Moseh in the eye, examining each for signs of a guilty conscience. Jack had been subjected to this treatment countless times in his life, first by Puritans in English Vagabond-camps and subsequently by diverse Papists eager to hear him confess all his colorful sins. He met the gaze of de Ath directly, and Moseh looked back at the Belgian with a sorrowful look that showed no trace of guilt or nervousness. "Very well," said de Ath, with a faint, apologetic smile. "That leaves only—"

"Elizabeth de Obregon!" Moseh exclaimed, if a whisper could be an exclamation.

"But she was your *disciple*," Jack said.

"*Judas* was a disciple, too," de Ath said quietly. "Disciples can be dangerous—especially when they are not right in the head to begin with. When Elizabeth returned to awareness in that cabin on *Minerva,* mine was the first face she saw. I believe now that my face must somehow haunt her nightmares, and that she seeks to exorcise it in flames."

"But we thought—"

"You *imagined* I was exerting some sinister influence on a susceptible mind—I know you did," said de Ath. "In fact, I was ministering to one who was not right in mind or body. Ever since that disastrous expedition to the Islands of Solomon she had been a little daft—confined to a nunnery in Manila. Finally her family in Spain arranged for her to come home, which is how she ended up on the Manila Galleon. To outward appearances she was entirely sane. But the fire on the Galleon burned away what was left of her good sense. By treating her with tincture of *opium,* and staying by her side at all times, I was able to keep her madness in hand as long as we remained aboard *Minerva.* But when I became the *cargador* for your enterprise, my responsibilities took me down to Lima. Elizabeth came here to Mexico City. I am afraid she has fallen under the influence of certain Phanatiqual *Jesuits* and *Dominicans.* Churchmen of that stripe loathe such as me, because I keep a civil tongue in my head when talking to Protestants. I fear that they have preyed upon Elizabeth's mind and that in her madness she has said things about me that have made their way to the stupendous and omniscient annals of the *Consejo de la Suprema y General Inquisición.* The Inquisitor wants to make me, and by extension every other Jansenist, out to be a heretic. Along the way he would like for me to utter words that would send both of you to the stake."

Jack sighed. "Now I'm *glad* we did not invite you to the feast—you are so depressing to talk to."

Edmund de Ath attempted to shrug, but this hurt a lot, and all the muscles on his skull stood out for a few moments, making him look like a woodcut in an anatomy book that Jack had once seen flying through the air in Leipzig. When he could speak again he said, "It is just as well—my faith would not allow me to participate in your *Sukkoth* even though you cleverly disguised it as a betrothal-feast."

Moseh laced his fingers together and stretched his arms, which was a noisy procedure. "I am going to bed," he said. "If they are looking for reasons to burn you, Edmund, and if you are not giving them any, it follows that Jack and I will soon be dangling from the ceiling of the torture-chamber while clerks stand below us with dipped quills. We'll need our rest."

"If any one of us breaks, all three of us burn," said de Ath. "If all three of us can stand our ground, then I believe they will let us go."

"Sooner or later one of us will break," Jack said wearily. "This Inquisition is as patient as Death. Nothing can stop it."

"Nothing," said de Ath, "except for the Enlightenment."

"And what is that?" Moseh asked.

"It sounds like one of those daft Catholicisms: The Annunciation, the Epiphany, and now the Enlightenment," Jack said.

"It is nothing of the sort. If my arms worked, I'd read you some of those letters," said de Ath, turning his head a fraction of a degree towards some scrawled pages on the end of this table, weighed down by a Bible. "They are from brothers of mine in Europe. They tell a story—albeit in a fragmentary and patchwork way—of a sea-change that is spreading across Christendom, in large part because of men like Leibniz, Newton, and Descartes. It is a change in the way men think, and it is the doom of the Inquisition."

"Very good! Well, then, all we must needs do is hold out against the *strappado,* the *bastinado,* the water-torture, and the thongs for another two hundred years or so, which ought to be plenty of time for this new way of thinking to penetrate Mexico City," said Jack.

"Mexico City is run out of Madrid, and the Enlightenment has already stormed Madrid and taken it," de Ath said. "The new King of Spain is a Bourbon, the grand-son of King Louis XIV of France."

"Feh!" said Moseh.

"Eeew, *him* again!" said Jack. "Don't tell me I'm to peg my hopes of freedom on *Leroy*!"

"Many Englishmen share your feelings, which is why a war has been started to settle the issue, but for now Philip wears the crown," said Edmund de Ath. "Not long after his coronation he was invited to the Inquisition's *auto da fé* in Madrid, and sent his regrets."

"The King of Spain failed to turn up for an *auto da fé*!?" Moseh exclaimed.

"It has shaken the Holy Office to its bones. The Inquisitor of Mexico will probe us once or twice more, but beyond that he'll not press his luck. Scoff all you like at the Enlightenment. It is already here, in this very cell, and we shall owe our survival to it."

THE PRISON OF THE INQUISITION lay not far from the Mint where, in theory, every ounce of silver that came up out of the mines of Mexico was turned into pieces of eight. In practice, of course, somewhere between half and a quarter of Mexico's treasure was smuggled out of the country before the King could take his fifth, but still the amount that came down into Mexico City sufficed to mint sixteen thousand pieces of eight every day. This was a large enough number to mean almost nothing to Jack. *A couple of thousand an hour* began to make sense to him. The booming and grinding of heavy silver-carts on the cobblestones beyond the prison walls gave a feeling of the sheer mass of metal involved.

One afternoon he was taking the air in the prison courtyard, letting the sun shine on some fresh thong-wounds that twined around his body like purple vines. It was a still and sultry day. Mexico City spread for no more than a mile in each direction and so Jack was able to hear something from every quarter: rugs being flapped out of windows; iron wheel-rims on stone pavers; whip-cracks; disputes at the Market; protesting mules, chickens, and swine; aimless chantings of diverse religious orders—the same noises as any city in Christendom, in other words, though the thin bony air of this high valley seemed to make sounds carry farther, and to favor harsh sounds over soft ones. Too, there were certain sounds unique to this country. The chief food was maize and the chief drink was chocolate, and both had to be ground between stones as the first step in their preparation, so any group of human beings in New Spain that was not positively starving to death was attended by a dim gnawing sound.

Jack had tied a strip of cloth over his eyes so that he could lie in the sun comfortably, and had unrolled a straw mat on the stones of the courtyard to even out the bumps somewhat, but except for a few negligible layers of skin, hair, and straw, his skull was in direct contact with the stones. Even if he stopped up his ears with his fingers, blocking out the noises of living things, certain vibrations of a mineral nature were still conducted into his head through that route, and even when no carts happened to be passing by, Jack fancied he could sense the omnipresent grumble of those grinding-stones, thousands of granite molars chewing the maize and cacao of this country. Which might be mistaken as the deepest ground-note, the continuo-line of this neverending Mass that was Mexico City. Except that there was another note even more pervasive. Jack did not hear it for a while, or if he did he could not disentangle it from the city's other noises. But after he had been lying there for some time he went half to sleep and had some strange vision that, if he'd been a Papist, probably would have been accounted a miracle and got him nominated a Saint. The vision was that his body was a body of light, rising up and growing as it rose, as bubbles do when they come up out of a black depth, but that it was bound with thongs of darkness, somewhat as the light of a lanthorn appears to be gibbeted by the straps of iron that clasp it all round. At any rate, something about this sun-intoxicated state of mind, and the general drugged stupor that followed a torture-session, caused the brocade of sounds to unravel itself and come apart into its several threads, yarns, warps, and woofs. And in this way Jack became aware of the sound of the Mint.

Years before, he had seen a coiner at work making thalers in the Ore Range, and so he knew that underneath all of the ceremonies and offices, this Mint must be nothing more than a few men with hammers pounding out the coins one at a time. To make sixteen thousand pieces of eight per diem, they had to have several coiners working at once, each with his own hammer and die. Each hammer-blow was another eight bits given the sacred imprint of the King of Spain and sent out into the world. Sometimes several coiners would bring their hammers down in quick succession and Jack would hear a cluttered barrage of rings, other times there would be anomalous pauses during which Jack phant'sied the whole Spanish Empire was holding its breath, fearing that the silver had run out. But for the most part the coiners worked in a shared rhythm, each taking his turn, and the rings of the hammers came steadily, about as frequently as the beats of Jack's heart. He put his hand to his breast to prove it. Sometimes his heart would beat in perfect synchronization with the coiners' hammers for several beats in a row, and Jack wondered whether this was more true among persons who had been born and raised in this city.

Like a heartbeat, the sound of pieces of eight being born was not normally audible, but if you sat very still you could sense it, pervading the streets of Mexico City as the blood did the body; and Jack already knew that in certain remote places like London, Amsterdam, and Shahjahanabad, you could detect its pulse, just as you could count a man's at a certain place on the wrist, far away from the beating heart.

Jack had never had much use for Spaniards, having always tended to view them as Englishmen gone spectacularly wrong, grapes that had turned to vinegar, a reasonably promising folk who'd been made utterly deranged by being trapped between *la France* and *dar al-Islam*. But lying there in the fist of the Inquisition listening to the grinding of the tortilla-stones and the ringing of the coiners, Jack was forced to admit that they were as vast and queer in their own way as the Egyptians.

Jack would never have accused himself of being a wise man, but he prided himself on cunning. Wisdom or cunning or both told him that he'd best ignore de Ath's ravings about the Enlightenment and keep his attention fixed on nearer and more practical matters. The crypto-Jews who occupied the cells of this prison were an odd lot, but they knew quite a lot about the workings of the Mexican Inquisition—as how could they *not*. It was the rule in most Inquisition prisons to keep every prisoner in solitary confinement, for years at a time if need be, in the hope that he or she would finally break down and confess to some heresy that the Inquisitor had not even suspected, or even dreamed of—supposedly whole new categories of Sin had been discovered, or invented, in this way. But the only rule that Diego de Fonseca enforced in *his* prison was that the inmates were not supposed to leave, and he'd even bend *that* rule for a few hours or a night, if you promised to come back.

Consequently Jack, while lying in the sun of the courtyard recovering from various torture-sessions, had already had plenty of opportunities to listen to his fellow-inmates holding forth on the dark glories of the Inquisition. At the drop of a hat they'd tell the tale of the *auto da fé* of 1673 or of 1695, how many were burnt and how many merely humiliated. Even allowing for routine exaggeration, there was no avoiding the conclusion that an *auto da fé* was a colossal event, something that happened only once or twice in an average person's lifetime, and a spectacle that *peons* would travel for days just to witness.

None of which was exactly comforting—until it was learned, a week or two after the arrival of Edmund de Ath, that the Inquisitor had scheduled an *auto da fé* for two months hence, which put it shortly before Christmas. Obviously such an enormous pageant could not be re-scheduled once a date had been set, and so if the three *Minerva* prisoners could only hold out until mid-December they would probably be punished and set free. But in the meantime the Inquisitor had every incentive to break them.

A single gifted torturer acting free of bureaucratic restrictions probably could have gotten Jack, Moseh, and Edmund to say anything he wanted them to in a few minutes' work. But Inquisition torture was ponderous and rule-bound. A large staff of doctors, clerks, bailiffs, advocates, and Inquisitors had to be present, and by the looks of things it was no easy task finding openings on so many important men's schedules. Torture-sessions would be arranged a week in advance and then cancelled at the last minute because some important participant had come down with a fever or even died.

In spite of these difficulties, during the month of November, men rammed a length of gauze down Jack's throat into his stomach and then poured water down it until his abdomen swelled up, and it felt as if gunpowder were burning inside of him, filling his guts with smoke and fire. Edmund de Ath was tied to a table and thongs tightened round various parts of his body until the skin burst under the pressure.

But Moseh went into the torture-chamber and came out half an hour later looking rather all right—fine, in fact—so unruffled, really, that it made Jack want to share some pain with him, when he sauntered over and joined Jack and Edmund de Ath under the patchy shade of the vines. "I confessed," he announced.

"To being a heretick!?"

"To having money," Moseh said.

"I didn't know that you'd been *accused* of that."

"But when you are in the hands of the Holy Office you *never* know. You just have to figure it out, through silent meditation, and give them the confession that they *want*. I've been ever so slow. But finally it came to me the other day—"

"Through silent meditation?"

"No, I'm afraid it was a bit more mundane. Diego de Fonseca came to my cell and asked me for a loan."

"Hmmm—I knew he was meagerly compensated, but that he is begging from his own prisoners comes as news to me," said Edmund de Ath.

"The *alguaciles* brought you straight to this prison from Acapulco—you never had to *buy* anything in Mexico City," Jack said. "*We* came here once or twice selling quicksilver to the owners of mines. Food is cheap enough, which explains why there are so many Vagabonds in the suburbs. But the scarcity of all other goods, and the over-supply of silver, make this an expensive place to be respectable."

Moseh nodded. "I talked to many old Jews in New Amsterdam and Curaçao who told me that in the old days the Inquisition supported itself by confiscating goods from Jews. But here in Mexico they did their job so well that they've run out of Jews—they've been reduced to stealing the occasional burro from some mestizo who took the Lord's name in vain. So finally I had what you might call a little Enlightenment of my own, and I understood what the Inquisitor really wanted. I confessed to nothing except having a lot of silver, and offered to make due penance for this crime on the morning of the *auto da fé*. With that my ordeal—*our* ordeal—was over and done with."

Mexico City

DECEMBER 1701

NOT SHOWING UP FOR AN *auto da fé* was regarded as a Bad Idea everywhere in the Spanish Empire, and especially in Mexico City. Every
scrap of land in the town was owned by the Church, and the Holy Sur-
veyors of Rome had (or so Jack phant'sied) come out here and
planted Trinitarian transits on the land that had been miraculously
reclaimed from Lake Texcoco and hung holy plumb-bobs made of
saints' skulls and stretched cords of spun angels' hair, driven cruci-
fixes into the ground at strategickal Vertices, and platted the land
into quadrilaterals, each one butted snugly against the next; angels
might slip through the interstices, but never Indians nor Vagabonds.
These parcels had been entrusted to various religious Orders, viz.
Carmelites, Jesuits, Dominicans, Augustinians, Benedictines, *et cetera*,
each of which had lost no time in erecting a high stone wall around
its property-line to shield it from the intrigues and supposed heresies
of the neighboring Orders. This accomplished, they had got to work
filling in the middle with churches, chapels, and dormitories. The
buildings sank into the soft ground almost as quickly as they were
built, which made the place seem much beyond its true age of about
a hundred and eighty years. At any rate there was no place to live in
Mexico City that was not controlled by one Order or another, and
consequently no way not to show up for an *auto da fé* without its being
noticed by someone who'd be apt to take it the wrong way.

In spite of—or on second thought, maybe *because* of—their tendency to live cloistered behind high walls, the men and women of
these diverse Orders loved nothing better than to dress up in peculiar clothing and parade through the streets of the city, bearing religious effigies or fragments of saints' anatomies. When Jack had been
abroad in this city as a free man, these never-ending processions had
been an absolute menace, and an impediment to commerce. Sometimes one procession would collide with another at a street-corner
and monks would come to blows over which Order had precedence.

An *auto da fé* was one of the few occasions significant enough to get every single nun from the city's twenty-two convents and every friar from its twenty-nine monasteries all processing at one time, in more or less the same direction. So all of them were present.

Of course Vagabonds always found a way to exist. Around here they seemed to dwell outside the walls, which was where important people liked them to stay. Not ten years earlier, they had gathered in the *zócalo* in sufficient numbers to burn the Viceroy's palace down. Since that event, Count Montezuma had tended to get a little jumpy whenever rabble gathered near his dwelling in large numbers; his rebuilt palace had high walls with plenty of loop-holes for broadcasting grapeshot into any inconvenient crowds. The Vagabonds, *criollos,* the mountain-dwelling Indian *peons,* the *desperadoes* from the mining-country up north, these were only permitted to gather in the City on certain occasions, and an *auto da fé* was one of them. Of course they had no formal place in the procession of processions that wound its way through the streets to the *zócalo,* but cheerfully insinuated themselves among and between the nuns and monks, the three- or four-hundred-strong staff of the Cathedral, the *asesors, fiscals, alquaciles,* and *familiares* of the Holy Office of the Inquisition, and diverse priests, friars, nuns, *oidors,* and *fiscals* who happened to be passing through en route to or from Manila or Lima. Despite the now well-known fact that the new French King of Spain had snubbed the *auto da fé* of Madrid, all of the King's representatives in Mexico City turned out: the Viceroy and all his household and courtiers, the various ranks and hierarchies of civil servants, the officers of foot and of horse in their ostrich plumes and polished helmets, and as many of the garrison's soldiers as could be spared from guarding the five gates and innumerable walls of this City.

Jack and Moseh had made it their business to know about the men who ran the Mint, and so as they and the other prisoners were marched out into the *zócalo* and made to stand in ranks before the grandstands that had been erected there, Jack was able to pick them out easily. The *Apartador,* the head of the Mint, was a Spanish count who had bought the office from the previous King for a hundred thousand pieces of eight, which was a bargain. He was there with his wife and daughter, all wearing the finest clothing Jack had seen since his last trip to Shahjahanabad (Jack, as a king, had been obliged to show up for the annual ceremony at which the Great Mogul sat cross-legged on one pan of an enormous scale, and silver and gold were heaped up on the opposite pan by his diverse *omerahs,* king, courtiers, and foreign emissaries until the jewel-covered crossbar finally went into motion and became level, leaving the Mogul suspended on his pan, balanced by his annual revenue, and modestly accepting the applause and gun-salutes of his subjects; on that occasion, Jack had done his part by heaving a big sack of coins onto the pan—taxes collected by Surendranath in the few wretched bazaars of Jack's domain—at least half of which had been pieces of eight minted decades earlier under the direction of some predecessor of this Count who was now peering down at Jack from the highest bench of the grandstand). Arrayed below him and his family were those Treasurers not currently on duty (Moseh had estimated these earned fifty to sixty thousand pieces of eight annually), the Assayers and Founders (some fifteen thousand annually), and farther down, in humble but still very good clothing, a plethora of Cutters, Clerks, Under-clerks, *Alcaldes,* and various ranks of Guards; close to the very bottom, numerous Foremen and *Brazajereros* who stoked the fires, and finally the brawny young *criollo* men who actually struck metal with metal and turned disks of silver into pieces of eight: the Coiners.

Seated near all of the Mint people were the three merchants who supplied them with most of their business. Technically any miner who came into the city with silver could have it minted, but in practice most miners sold their pigs to these few merchants who had made it their business to act as middle-men, and make sure that the Minters were duly wined, dined, coddled, and bribed at all times. They were not easy to pick out in the midst of their enormous and well-dressed families, but finally Jack caught sight of one of them looking right back at him through a spyglass. The fellow recognized Jack in the same instant, took the glass away from his eye, and made a remark to a younger man seated next to him. For to the churchmen of Mexico City, Jack and Moseh and Edmund de Ath might be foreign hereticks, but to anyone connected to the Mint they were the men who had the quicksilver, and who could modulate the flow of pieces of eight by putting more or less of it on the market.

They did not look the part of quicksilver magnates today. All three of them were wearing dunce-caps, and large sack-like yellow over-garments with giant red Xs on them, called *sanbenitos.* If these had been decorated with pictures of angels, devils, and flames, it would have signified that their wearers were to be burnt at the stake outside the city gates at the end of the day. The red X, on the other hand, meant only that the wearer was a Blasphemer in Recovery who would have to wear this garment whenever he ventured out of doors for the next several years. Jack had never been the sort to care about clothing, but he knew that the decorations he wore today were of high import not only to himself but to everyone connected with the Mint—which meant everyone in Mexico City, except for the hapless

Inquisition, which was run out of Rome and had no way to dip its fingers into the running river of silver except by arresting and shaking down the likes of Jack and Moseh. At any rate, the fact that he and his comrades were wearing red Xs was probably influencing a market somewhere even at this very moment. And given that all news eventually reached Amsterdam, Jack now devoted half an hour or so to a little phant'sy about a blue-eyed woman sitting in a coffee-house along the Damplatz, hearing this bit of news, and connecting it to a certain Vagabond she had run around with when she was young.

He knew that his sons must be somewhere inside the city, or else his *sanbenito* would be decorated with pictures of flames. It took a full hour for his eyes to find them, which was not so terribly long since the *auto da fé* was an all-day event. The stands filled one end of the *zócalo* (they had been a-building for two months) and everyone in them was gleaming and glorious to some degree, whether it was the Archbishop who reigned over the ceremony from the highest and most central altar, or the coiners' wives in their best dresses. But there was an undeniable tendency for the costumes to become more drab as they got farther from the Archbishop, so the transition to the common folk standing on the pavement in their undyed homespun stuff was almost seamless. Beyond that point they only got plainer and browner as they spread around the edges of the *zócalo,* to the point where they almost faded away into the rough-hewn stone walls. In such a place Jack finally saw three men, two brown and one black, holding the reins of some burros. Their faces were shaded under the vast brims of their *sombreros.* But Jack could have recognized them from the burros alone. Those animals were still crusted with the yellow dust of the high country and the sweat of traveling through it, and each of them had smallish saddlebags sewn of the heaviest ox-hide and scored in countless places from brushes with cactus-thorns. Those were the saddlebags used to bring silver down to the mints. This morning they were hanging limp on the burros' flanks. Their contents had been transferred to the vaults of the Inquisition, where they rested safe among piles of documents listing every heresy that had ever been committed or imagined in the New World.

The ceremony was all in Latin. Sunstroke probably would have slain them all if it hadn't been December. About four hours into it, Jack noticed that Moseh was humming to himself, which was the one thing Jack would never have expected. He was tempted to bend his head close to Moseh's, but given that he was wearing a dunce-cap three feet high, the movement would have been about as subtle as dancing a tarantella on the Lord's Table. So he stood straight, along with everyone else in Mexico. To his other side Edmund de Ath was muttering some Latin phrases of his own, but rather than closing his eyes and bowing his head, he seemed to be staring straight forward into a phalanx of wealthy nuns seated below and to the left hand of the Archbishop. Jack had nothing but time, and so he looked at each nun in turn until finally he recognized Elizabeth de Obregon staring right back at him.

The *auto da fé* continued there until shortly after sundown and then devolved: the nuns and monks marched away in color-coded processions and the poor people staged a bread-riot. Which seemed like an interesting story, but Jack wanted no part of it. He and Moseh and Edmund de Ath made rendezvous with Jimmy and Danny and Tomba, and out of the city they went.

When finally it was safe to talk out loud, Jack said to Moseh, "Never was a Jew so happy during an *auto da fé*—have you been chewing those *Peruvian* leaves that the Spaniards are so fond of?"

"No, I was watching the sun swing low over the mountains and pondering matters *astrologickal*. First: This is the shortest day of the year in the *Northern* Hemisphere and the longest in the *Southern*, which is good for us at both ends. *Here* it made the ceremonies an hour or two shorter than they might have been, and much cooler. Down *Tierra del Fuego* way, the weather's as balmy as it ever gets, and the days exceptionally long. If van Hoek knows what he's doing— which I think he does—he'll be venturing into the Straits of Magellan about now. Which brings me to my Second observation, namely: a new year is about to begin. It is the second year of the Eighteenth Century, and van Hoek will celebrate it (God Willing) by rounding Cape Horn, and I will celebrate it by trading this cursed *sanbenito* for a *poncho* and this dunce-cap for a *sombrero* and riding north, beyond the reach of the Inquisition. It is the Century of the Enlightenment—I can feel it!"

"You *have* been chewing leaves from Peru," Jack concluded.

That night they lodged at an inn where they had to suspend their boots and stirrups from the ceiling in order to prevent them from being carried away and eaten by rats. They paid an outrageous price and departed before dawn, and after getting clear of certain fœtid suburbs where Vagabonds dwelt, they began the first leg of their journey north: traveling through the high Valley of Mexico. This was quite a bit more interesting to Edmund de Ath than to the others, who had seen it before. The Belgian was silent as they trudged over marshy plains gouged with the remains of failed flood-control projects, and splotched here and there with weirdly colored mineral springs. From cocoa and vanilla plantations rose gaudy churches and monasteries thrown up by Spaniards who had made ludicrous amounts of money, and in some cases half torn down by the thieves and Vagabonds who infested this country far in excess of Europe.

Moseh's ineffable Leadership Qualities had caused a whole retinue of *sanbenito*-and-dunce-cap-wearing crypto-Jews to fall in step behind them. They paraded through inexplicable concentrations of Negroes and Filipinos and over foamy puddles of congealed lava, past sugar-works smoking and steaming. At riverbanks they struck complicated bargains with Indians, naked except for loincloths and lines of tattooed dots on their faces, and were towed across on *balsas* made of planks lashed across bundles of air-filled calabashes, while other Indians back-carried the burros across fords. They steered clear of settlements or else rode through them as directly as possible, for now that they were out of the city, most of the townspeople were *criollos* (mixed-blood, born here) who bore a mad hostility towards Europeans. They'd have drawn much unwanted attention, and *criollo* boys would have been darting out and chucking stones at them, even if they *hadn't* been wearing *sanbenitos*.

All in all it seemed advisable to get clear of settled areas as quickly as possible, so Jack, Moseh, Jimmy, Danny, and Tomba payed very little attention to all of the Roadside Attractions that so fascinated Edmund de Ath, and bent all efforts to putting miles between them and the City. Only food was worth slowing down for, as when a miniature deer appeared at the edge of a copse or they happened upon a large tree whose branches were crowded with turkeys. Then sudden loud noises, clouds of smoke, and roadside butchery.

"Your ransom cost us a fortune," Danny remarked, "but as luck would have it, we have *several*."

"Have you been making new deals during our absence," Moseh said nervously, "or only making deliveries on the old?"

"We sold all the mercury for sixpence a ton," Jimmy answered sharply, "and spent that on whiskey and prostitutes."

Silence, then, for a mile or two. Then Moseh tried again, patiently: "As I am still part owner of the quicksilver, I am entitled to know how much has been *delivered,* how much *committed,* and how much *held back*."

"Before *we* came on the scene, the King of Spain's men were gouging the mine-owners to the tune of three hundred pieces of eight per hundred-weight of quicksilver," Danny reminded him, "and when we began selling it for *two* hundred, the Spaniards dropped the price to *one* hundred, which is nearer its natural market-price. At the time you and Dad were arrested by that Inquisition, we were takin' a breather from sellin' of it, waitin' for the price to stiffen up a bit."

Jimmy continued, "When Danny and Tomba and I came back from the Cape of Currents with a mule-train of quicksilver, and learned you'd been arrested, the price was still no higher than a hundred twenty-five, and so we contented ourselves making good on the deliveries you'd arranged, Moseh, and hidin' the proceeds in various locations 'tween here and Vera Cruz. But lately we've had nothin' to occupy ourselves, and the price has crept up to one-sixty—"

"Near two hundred in Zacatecas," Tomba put in.

"And so we've been strikin' some deals of our own, if that's all right with you."

"It is perfect," Moseh said. Three *sombreros* swiveled in his direction, looking for sarcasm, but Moseh was sincere: "Without delay, I want to liquidate my assets."

"Or since we are speaking of quicksilver, *solidify* 'em," Jack said.

"Very well, I want to take my share of the Plan, in the form of silver, or better yet gold, and strike out for the north with *them*." He looked back over his shoulder at the crowd of red Xs shuffling along in their wake. "Lately these Spaniards have conquered a new territory up beyond the pissant ditch known as the Rio Grande, which they style *New Mexico*. It can't possibly be worse than *Old*. Word has it that six hundred cavalry are garrisoned in that territory, and each one is paid five hundred pieces of eight a year, but most of that ends up in the coffers of the governor, who sells those soldiers food and other necessaries at outrageous prices. That is upwards of three hundred thousand pieces of eight a year! I am going to go up and sell them victuals at a fair price, and while I'm at it, I'm going to convert every Indian I see to Judaism."

"Er, if half of what they say of those Comanches is true," said Danny, " 'tweren't wise to go up to 'em and prate about *religion*."

"Or *any* subject," said Tomba.

"Truth be told, 'tweren't wise to go up to 'em at *all*," said Jimmy.

"That is enough!" Jack said. "Moseh has cashed out of one Plan to invest in another, and naturally the new one needs a little refinement . . . he'll have plenty of time to make improvements on the ride north."

AFTER A FEW DAYS they rode up out of the Valley and into mountains that were much less inhabited. Other than pockets of wretched Indians who'd been chased up out of the lowlands by the Spaniards, the only folk who lived up here were miners. The mines were old, deep, and famous, and surrounded by adobe houses and churches. Most of the workers were forced labor, and most were Indians. In many ways the landscape was like that of the Harz Mountains, with schlock-heaps all over the place, and large outdoor furnaces where the ore was refined, and mounds of earth in long rows where quicksilver was being used to extract silver from lower-grade ore. To Jack it was a toss-up as to whether the Harz with its icy wind and leaden skies was a bleaker landscape than this sunburnt place where nothing grew except cactus. Moseh's ruminations were bleaker yet: "They've been turning the land inside out for almost two hundred years, and here are the bones and guts strewn about . . . I'm reminded of the Expulsion in 1492. Spanish Jews fled to Portugal. They rode down roads strewn with the bodies of the ones who'd gone before them—friends and relatives who'd been waylaid by bandits and eviscerated, on a rumor that they swallowed gold and diamonds to smuggle them out of the country. These Spaniards are giving a like treatment to this country, and getting the Indians who used to own it to do the dirty work for them."

"The *coca* has worn off, I see—this might be a good time to think harder about your new Plan," said Jack.

As they worked north into Guanajuato, the mines became newer, shallower, more slapdash—typically these were owned by individual prospectors. More and more, the workers were free men. But this country had been settled long enough that some towns had been built, churches erected, and families moved in. It was in one of those towns—which a generation earlier had marked the absolute northern boundary of civilization—that they paused for a day to make a grand reckoning.

Starting from that night in the Gulf of Cadiz when they'd sacked the ex-Viceroy's treasure-brig, Moseh had kept, in his mind, a ledger-book of all that the Cabal had gained and lost. At certain times, as when they'd fallen into the hands of Queen Kottakkal, whole pages had been torn out and thrown away. Some of the Cabal had died, others had joined in late, some had taken their shares out in intangibles, such as Gabriel Goto, who only wanted to see Japan. Some of the Cabal's value was in *Minerva,* which, God willing, would continue generating revenues, other was in the quicksilver-hoard that they'd brought across the Pacific. This had been split into two batches, one for New Spain and one for Peru; the former had already been liquidated, the latter might have been sold for greater or lesser amounts of money that, now, might or might not be on the bottom of the Straits of Magellan. Whatever the current Bottom Line might be, part was owed to Queen Kottakkal and part to Electress Sophie of Hanover. But Moseh worked through all of these complications, committing it to paper so that Jack could show it to van Hoek later, and patiently explaining the difficult bits until Jack agreed.

This reckoning stretched over three days, and in the end Moseh was reduced to bringing in a sack of dried beans and making piles of them on the table, shoving them from place to place to demonstrate to Jack where the money had gone. A great many beans ended up on the floor, representing what they'd simply *lost*. But when Moseh was finished, an impressive pile of beans still remained on the table, and when Moseh told him that each bean amounted to a hundred pieces of eight, Jack had to admit that the Plan Moseh had proposed to him long ago in Algiers had been a pretty good one after all.

Jimmy and Danny and Tomba meanwhile ventured out into certain desolate places and recovered enough silver pigs to pay Moseh what was due him. Lacking banks, they had deposited their assets in holes in the ground, carefully hidden.

On the fifth of January 1702, then, Moseh and a score of others donned their *sanbenitos* and dunce-caps and formed a mule-train on the edge of this little adobe town, and set out for New Mexico. Jack rode with them until they were well out of sight of the bell-tower beside the town's church. There, every man except Jack stripped off his *sanbenito* and his cap, and they made a bonfire of them by the roadside. Jack shook every man's hand, but he embraced Moseh, and with tears washing the dust from his face, issued several ludicrous promises, e.g., that after he'd bought himself an earldom in England he'd come out to New Mexico for a social call. The parting lasted for a long time, which only made it worse when Moseh finally climbed astride his mule and hauled on one rein and got it pointed north. Jack stood there for an hour or so, making sure the *sanbenitos* were thoroughly burnt to ashes, and watching the dust-trail of the mule-train swirl up into a blue sky: ashes to ashes, dust to dust, and . . .

"Quicksilver to silver," he said, turning towards the town. "Then Jack to London."

"AS FAR AS I CAN DISCERN, all that remains here is to collect the final remnants of what was cached around Cabo Corrientes, make certain deliveries, and get the pigs down to Vera Cruz, where we'll await *Minerva*," said Edmund de Ath that evening, as they sat in front of the *cantina* availing themselves of the liquor of the *maguey*.

"It is not so easy as you make it sound," Jimmy growled.

"On the contrary, I think it is much too difficult for a man of my limited capacities," said de Ath. "Here, I'll be an impediment. In Vera Cruz, on the other hand, there is much I could be doing to smooth the way for us, when *Minerva,* God willing, arrives."

"Get thee to Vera Cruz, then," Jack suggested.

"I am interested to see the place," said de Ath. "Properly it is called *New* Vera Cruz. The old city was burnt to the ground, almost twenty years ago, by the notorious and terrible outlaw called El Desamparado . . ."

"I have already heard the story," Jack said.

WINDING UP *MINERVA*'s affairs in New Spain took several months. Jack, Jimmy, Danny, and Tomba moved north to a frontier town in Zacatecas where no one cared if Jack failed to wear his *sanbenito*—or if they did, they were too scared to say anything, because this was a town of *desperadoes,* and every man went armed all the time. When Jack had lived in Europe, he had enjoyed and even profited from being a *picaroon* in a world of Lords, Ladies, and Chamber of Commerce members. But he found living in a whole *society* of picaroons to be tiresome if not downright dangerous. So he did not linger in that border-town long, but went west over the Sierra Madre Occidental with a mule-train to recover the last of the goods they'd cached around Cabo Corrientes: a ton of quicksilver, and all of van Hoek's books—which he had left in the mountains so that they would not be seized and burnt by the Inquisition when *Minerva* called at Acapulco or Lima.

The trip back to Zacatecas was exceptionally dangerous because no fewer than three groups of *desperadoes* were waiting to waylay them in the passes. But Jimmy and Danny, as the result of their journey halfway around the world, and their exploits with the warrior-caste of Malabar, had become expert in travel through hostile mountains. And Tomba, a man who'd escaped from a sugar-plantation in Jamaica and covered a lot of ground since then, in places that were not friendly to black Vagabonds, had developed a kind of guile and subtility that Jack thought of as Oriental. There was nothing he could tell those three boys except to remind 'em, now and then, that this was not Hindoostan, and so they were only allotted one life apiece. This was cheerfully ignored, or else taken as proof that, at the age of forty-one, Jack had become a fretful old man, and toothless in more than one way.

Their trail back over the mountains was traced out by several set-piece battles in which the brigands found their ambushes ambushed, and many a *desperado*'s head was struck off by a ringing *katana*. They came back to discover that they were developing a legend, which Jack had come to believe was a good thing to *leave behind* but a bad thing to *have*.

A letter was waiting in the saloon that they used as their head-quarters; the innkeeper said it had been brought up from the south by a courier, and that it was addressed to either Moseh or Jack. Since Moseh and Edmund had gone away, the only person in this town capable of reading it was the parish priest. But the priest would turn Jack in to the Inquisition if Jack revealed his identity, for Jack hadn't been wearing his *sanbenito* or attending Mass. Jack tossed the letter for safe-keeping into the caulked trunk that contained van Hoek's books, and re-sealed it.

Now their assets consisted of a ton of quicksilver (which needed to be delivered to various mine-heads and exchanged for pigs of silver) and several tons of pigs distributed among a dozen buried caches. All of it had to be moved to Vera Cruz. Yet it would be folly to concentrate it in one gigantic wagon-train, and so the caches had to be dug up and moved one at a time, leap-frogging one another as they converged on Vera Cruz. It was a complicated business that really demanded the skills of a Moseh or a Vrej Esphahnian, and it sorely taxed Jack, who preferred things simpler. More than once he woke up in the middle of the night wondering whether they'd left a cache behind in the mountains.

The one or two broad simple concerns of Jack's early life, like the light and dark portions of a *wootz*-ingot, had been hammered out and folded over, hammered out and folded over, so many times that they had become involved and inter-tangled into a swirl of swirls, something too intricate to follow, or to be given the name of "pattern" or "design." It registered on the mind as a blunt impression that could be talked about only by smearing it into some gray word like "complicated." But he would tell Jimmy and Danny and Tomba that it was complicated, and they would not have the faintest understanding of what he meant. Jack could only pray that its complexity gave it the strength and keenness of a watered-steel blade. Much later he might be able to discern whether there was beauty in it, too.

For a month it did not seem as if the goods were making progress at all, but then Jack could no longer deny that they were spending less time in high deserts and more on roads. In moving the silver they *spent* part of it but *lost* none. This seemed implausible to Jack until he considered how wretched was their opposition. They hadn't gone most of the way around the world without acquiring a certain kind of wisdom, and if having silver made them a target, it also gave them the option to buy their way out of certain problems. Really the only persons Jack was afraid of were the Indians who controlled the river-crossings; these had a distant look in their eyes that somehow reminded Jack of Gabriel Goto when he reminisced about Japan. Their treatment by the Spaniards had left them with nothing to lose. Attempted bribery only made them angrier.

But by the end of April all of their silver was cached in eight different holes in the ground within half a day's journey of Vera Cruz, and Jack, Danny, Jimmy, and Tomba were ensconced in a house that Edmund de Ath had rented out there, waiting.

"WHERE ARE MY DAMNED BOOKS?" demanded Otto van Hoek, bending over *Minerva*'s rail to peer down into the bark.

"They tumbled into a river only a few miles short of Vera Cruz," Jack said nonchalantly, "so I'd estimate they are bobbing in the Gulf of Mexico somewhere—didn't you spy 'em on your way in?"

These were all the words they could exchange before they were drowned out by cheering and jeering from *Minerva*'s sailors, who had all come abovedecks to watch the bark approach and to see how many of the "dry" group had survived the year and a half in New Spain. They seemed generally happy and surprised, which Jack looked on as indicating that no one in the "wet" contingent had ever expected to see a live Shaftoe again. For his part Jack felt almost like a mother hen counting her chicks as he recognized one familiar face after another, and only a few new ones. *Minerva* herself had never looked better. Jack guessed from this that they'd made a good profit in Peru and that any damages suffered rounding Cape Horn had already been made good in some Caribbean port. If so, it showed excellent foresight on van Hoek's part, because Vera Cruz was both wretched and expensive, and, in sum, probably the most unfavorable place imaginable to fit out a ship for the Atlantic crossing.

"Let us load her up and be done with New Spain," Jack said when he had climbed aboard and been duly pounded on the back or embraced by every member of the complement. "Also, I would like to carry on Jeronimo's tradition, as long as we are here . . ."

"Which tradition is that?" asked Vrej Esphahnian, looking every inch the successful merchant.

"That of burning down Vera Cruz at every opportunity."

"We'll be several months sieving the Gulf for the Captain's books," said Dappa when laughter had died down. He was the only man aboard who had not aged several years, and he still had more teeth in his head than any four sailors.

"I was only jesting. We've the books, and a letter as well," Jack said.

"A letter from whom?" asked Vrej.

"I've no idea," Jack returned. "Edmund de Ath might have read it to me, I suppose, but . . ."

"You don't trust him! That is very wise," said van Hoek.

"On the contrary—in the Prison of the Inquisition I had no

choice but to trust him with my life, and he extended me the same consideration. He is odd, but harmless."

"Then why didn't you have him read the letter?"

"Because I know *you* will *never* trust him."

"Is he still in Vera Cruz?" Vrej inquired.

"As you have probably learned, the Spanish treasure-fleet is massing in Havana Bay, getting ready to bring thirty million pieces of eight to Cadiz," Jack said. "Several galleons weighed anchor in this harbor four days ago, and went thither to join that Fleet. Edmund de Ath took passage on one of those ships—I've already paid him his commission as *cargador*."

"Notwithstanding your affection for the man—" Dappa began.

"I didn't *say* anything about *affection*," Jack said.

"Very well—I'm happy he will be going home on some other ship."

"We have no time to waste," van Hoek said. "If we can embark at the same time as the Treasure-Fleet, we'll have a much easier voyage. Every pirate in the Caribbean will be hunting for Spanish galleons."

"Yes, they will, won't they?" Jack mused.

"We will be looked on as a Dutch privateer," van Hoek predicted.

"Or a heavily armed sugar-barge headed back to London or Amsterdam," Dappa put in.

"In any event, no boca-neer in his right mind will trifle with *us* when thirty million pieces of eight are afloat in the same waters."

AND SO THEY WENT and rounded up all their buried pigs and loaded them on board *Minerva,* and stowed them alongside silver from Peru and gold from Brazil. Of course van Hoek's books were loaded aboard first of all. He complained of the miserable job Jack had done re-caulking the lid, and threatened to make him pay the devil, but when the box was set down on the deck of his cabin the Dutchman looked as close to happy as Jack had seen him in years.

There was no time even to pry the lid off, though. Getting the pigs and loading them aboard only took four days, but it seemed longer to Jack than all the time he'd spent in New Spain before. He avoided going ashore, and could not set foot on dry land without entertaining a moment's phant'sy that *Minerva* would sail away and leave him stranded in that town, where anything that moved was pursued by a cloud of mosquitoes, and anything that didn't was shortly buried in wind-blown sand.

THEY DID NOT OPEN the crate and read the letter until they had cleared Bermuda, a month after departing Vera Cruz. Dappa passed it around the table first so that Jack, Vrej, and van Hoek could inspect the seal. Pressed into a daub of red wax was a coat of arms too detailed to be made out: Jack imagined he saw a fragment of fleur-de-lis in one corner and a seagull in another. But the other men were all smirking.

"Who the hell is it from?" he demanded.

"It *claims* to be from the Duchess of Arcachon-Qwghlm," said Dappa.

This bit of news hit Jack like a yard-arm across the brow, and shut him up long enough for Dappa to break the seal and smooth the page out on the table. "It is in English," he announced, and took a swallow of chocolate to whet his whistle. " 'To Jack Shaftoe, esq. The inexorable tides ebb and flow 'neath the battlements of the Castle as I pen these lines, reminding me that what is submerged and seemingly drown'd forever in fatal Seas may yet rise forth from *Neptune*'s wat'ry Dungeon if one hath only Patience to await the natural Wheeling of the Heavens. I am put in mind of a certain Man who when I last spied him seem'd to've been dragged down by the Moral Undertow which sweepeth away even strong souls who stand long in it, and to have fallen into a condition of Degradation worse than Death; and whose *Body* was scarcely more fit than his *Spirit*, as he was far gone with the French Pox and afflicted with divers Wounds and Amputations to boot—' "

"The most of notable of which was inflicted by *her*," Jack said with a gigantic wink, "but she omits that—she's too much the Lady now."

"She *writes* like one," van Hoek said, none too admiringly.

Dappa cleared his throat irritably and continued, " 'thus did this Man, whom many styl'd a *Vagabond*, vanish from Christendom's ken, swamped by Mortality's Tide; and if rumors echoed up from *Barbary*, years later, to the effect that a Man answering to his Description had been witness'd there, it signified Nothing more than when a Spar-end or Mast-head breaketh the Surface of some stagnant Cove at low Tide and reminds us that, once, a Ship was wrack'd in that Place. But all that was rumor'd concerning this Man was in an Instant overturn'd when tidings were delivered to *France* of a *bataille rangée* in the streets of *Grand Caire*, whose Reverberations seem'd to echo back and forth 'tween the rugged Pyramids and the *Barock* Monuments of Versailles, as when a Thunderbolt splits the Air 'tween two very Mountains. For the Tides of Fortune had turn'd, even as those of us, who should've known better, had turn'd our backs to advert on *inward* and *inland* Matters. Nor was this the only such occasion, for in later Years came news of a Battle won through *Alchemical* cozening in Hindoostan, and other Ebbings and Flowings I'll not tediously *enumerate*, as you are their Author.' "

"Thank God, I was afraid she was going to relate the whole story again," Jack said.

" 'In recent years, Tidings of your Adventures have, from time to time, stirr'd Admiration and Envy in the Courts of Europe. Tho' my Situation in this Castle is exceeding *remote* from such grand Places, yet it has been my Privilege to conduct a frequent Correspondence with certain rare Persons who inhabit them, and they have not been slow to inform me of all that is *claimed,* or *rumored,* concerning your *Asiatick* wand'rings. Indeed, my icy Castle hath proved a better Vantage than *Versailles* itself, for some of the Letters that come to me here originate in Hanover, and were written by a certain Lady whom you, sir, and I once looked upon there, from a respectful Distance. And lest these words seem to *demean* that same Lady by implying too great familiarity with me, who am so mean by comparison, I say to you, sir, that as a Paragon of Wisdom and Beauty she is as distant and remote to me, as she was on that Day we spied 'pon her from a *Germanick* church.' "

This paragraph was enough to make Jack's eyes cross, and van Hoek knead his temples, but after Dappa had read it a second time, Jack attempted the following translation: "All right, she's cozy with Sophie, who provided us with our cannons and owns part of this ship, and Sophie knows where we are better than the gossips of Versailles."

"We sent Sophie a letter from Rio de Janeiro," van Hoek said.

Dappa continued, " 'That incomparable Lady hath given me to believe that you may be in New Spain. I pray that this Letter hath found you in good Health there, and that you have found a *trustworthy* person to read it to you. If it is your Intention to sail for Europe with metal goods, then I wish you Godspeed, and I beg you to consider making land-fall at Qwghlm; for all your Sins have long since been forgiven.' " Dappa slowed as he read this, and there was much awkward shifting about as heads turned toward the poleaxed Jack. Seeing that he was no longer really a part of the conversation, Dappa rushed through the last bit: " 'I pray you will take this as a fair Prospect, but I know it is of no especial Value to your Partners. To them I say that, if Britain is one day to be the realm of the Lady before mentioned, that the first speck of it to owe its love and loyalty to her will be Qwghlm; and if it is to be overwhelm'd by the *Popish* legions, the last bit of soil to surrender her colors will be that on which this Castle is pil'd. London may sway to and fro 'tween Whigs and Torys, Jacobites and Hanoverians, but Qwghlm is a rock, ever loyal, and nowhere in the World will *Minerva* find a safer harbor.' What the hell is she on about there?"

Vrej said, "If the last news we had from London is true, Queen Anne will never produce an heir to the throne, which means that the *next* Queen of England will be our co-owner, the Electress Sophie of

Hanover—who has apparently become some sort of patroness to Jack's fair Eliza."

Van Hoek said, "The *harbor* beneath her castle may be safe. The *approach* is anything but—we've no way of actually *getting* there."

"Eliza—or I should say, the Duchess—addresses that matter in a final paragraph, here," Dappa said. "She instructs us to make for Derry, or as she styles it, Londonderry, on the north of Ireland, and there to find a certain pilot, name of James Hh. He'll bring us safely into the harbor beneath Qwghlm Castle."

"As Captain of this vessel, I see no commanding reason to do this when perfectly safe and well-known harbors are available at London and Amsterdam," van Hoek said, "but as a share-holder in our Enterprise I am obligated to entertain discussions."

"Sophie is a greater share-holder than any of *us*, and Eliza would appear to speak for *her*," Jack said.

"But she did not say so explicitly. Until we see a letter with the arms of Hanover on it, we can't know Sophie's mind," said Vrej.

"So you vote for London?" Dappa asked.

Vrej shrugged. "That would bring us directly to the Mint at the Tower of London. We could hardly improve on *that*. What is your vote, Dappa?"

Dappa's eyes strayed momentarily toward his cabin. "I vote for Qwghlm."

"Are you voting as a share-holder in this venture, or a chronicler of the slave-trade?" van Hoek asked. For as *Minerva* had worked her way up the long coast of Brazil, Dappa had patiently collected and written down the personal accounts of numerous African slaves, and it was no secret that he would see them in print.

"True, it's a foregone conclusion that Eliza—who according to Jack is an ex-slave like us, and a passionate hater of that Institution—would gladly be the patroness of my book, and support its publication," Dappa admitted. "But I have reasons besides that for preferring Qwghlm. To reach London or Amsterdam we'd have to sail up the Channel, practically under the guns of St.-Malo and Dunkerque and diverse other French privateer-havens. This were unwise even if France and England were *not* involved in a great war."

"We could go north round Britain, conceivably," Vrej muttered, "and approach through the North Sea, which ought to be a Dutch-English lake."

"But if we are going that route *anyway*, we may as well go to Qwghlm."

"I am coming about to your view," Vrej said, after a moment.

"I don't like it," van Hoek said.

Qwghlm

AUGUST 1702

The Seamen returned enriched with the Plunder,
not of Ships, but of Fleets, Loaden with Silver; they
went out Beggars, and came home Gentlemen; nay,
the Wealth they brought Home, not only enrich'd
themselves, but the whole Nation.

—DANIEL DEFOE,
A Plan of the English Commerce

TWO MONTHS LATER, while *Minerva* was lost in fog off of Outer
Qwghlm, a loud noise came up from her hold, and she stopped
moving.

Van Hoek drew his cutlass and went after the pilot, James Hh,
and at length tracked him down at the head. He was perched on the
bowsprit. "Welcome to Qwghlm," he announced, "you are hard
aground on the rock that we call the Dutch-hammer." Then he
jumped.

By this point van Hoek had been joined by several other men
with pistols, and all of them rushed forward in the hope of getting a
shot off at Hh. But they did not see him in that icy water (which soon
would have killed him anyway); all they saw was a faint impression in
the fog, like a woodcut pressed with diluted ink, of a longboat rowing away. That longboat fired a signal from its swivel-gun, and when
the boom had finished echoing among the Three Sghrs, the men on
Minerva could hear the distant shouting of men on other ships—a
whole squadron, arrayed all around them, riding safely at anchor,
well clear of the stony reef. All of these voices were speaking in
French except for one or two, shouting through speaking-trumpets:
"Welcome home, Jaaack!"

The men on *Minerva* remained perfectly still. It was not that they
were trying to be stealthy—there was little point in hiding now. This

was a ceremonial silence, as at a funeral. Too, there was a process of mental rearrangement taking place in the minds of the ship's officers, as they sorted through the memories of everything that had occurred in the last few months, and began to understand it all as an elaborate deception, a trap laid by the French.

As the fog began to lift, and the outlines of French frigates started to resolve and solidify all around them. Van Hoek ambled back to the poop deck, laid his right arm out carefully on the rail, and brought his cutlass down on it, a few inches above the wrist. The blade caught in his bones and he had to worry it out and chop several more times. Finally the hand—already mangled and truncated from diverse mishaps—made a splash in the water below. Van Hoek lay down on the deck and turned white. He probably would have died if he had not been aboard a ship where treating amputations was a routine affair. This at least gave the sailors something to do while the French longboats converged on them.

At some point Dappa got a distracted look on his face, excused himself from van Hoek's side, and began to walk briskly in the direction of Vrej Esphahnian.

Vrej drew one of several pistols from his waist-band and aimed it at Dappa. A whirring blade flew into his arm, like a steel humming-bird, and spoiled his aim. It was a hunting yo-yo and it had been flung by a Filipino crewman standing off to Vrej's side.

Vrej dropped the weapon and flung himself overboard. He was wearing a scarlet cape that billowed up as he fell, like a sail, and formed a bubble on the water below, an island of satin that kept him afloat until a Frenchman on a longboat flung a rope to him.

"Say the word, Dad," said Jimmy, who was manning a loaded swivel-gun, and holding a lighted torch above its touch-hole.

"It's me they want," Jack said, matter-of-factly, as if he were captured by the French Navy every day.

"It's *us* they *have*," Danny answered, pointedly, bringing another swivel-gun to bear on another longboat, "and we'll soon make 'em wish they didn't."

Jack shook his head. "This is not to be another Cairo."

QwGHLM CASTLE WAS a Dark Ages citadel that had all too obviously failed its essential purpose. Indeed, most of it was not even competent to keep out sleet and rats. Its lee corner, where it gripped the living rock of the Sghr, had, however, at least put up a struggle against gravity. It supported a row of stark crenels that finger-combed the tangled winds above the crunchy wilderness of smithereens and guano that accounted for the rest of the Castle.

To re-roof such a thing was to waste money; but to embed a whole brand-new Barock château in it, as the duc d'Arcachon had recently finished doing, was to make some sort of ringing proclamation. In the visual language of architects and decorators, the proclamation said something about whatever glorious principles were personified by all its swooping, robed, wreathed, winged demigods. Translated into English it said, "I am rich and powerful, and you are not."

Jack got the message. They put him under house-arrest in a grand bedchamber with a high Barock window through which the Duke and Duchess, presumably, could watch the comings and goings of ships in the harbor. The room's back wall, facing these windows, consisted mostly of mirrors—which as even Jack knew was an homage to the Galerie des Glaces at Versailles.

Jack lay in bed for several days, unable to bring himself to look into any mirrors, *or* to go near that window and see *Minerva* stuck on the Dutch-hammer. Sometimes he would get out of bed and hug the cannonball that was attached to his neck-collar by a four-foot length of chain and carry it into the *en suite* garderobe: a closet with a wooden bench decorated with a hole. Being ever so careful not to let the cannonball fall into that hole—for he'd not quite decided to kill himself yet—he'd sit down and void himself into a chute that spilled out onto the stone cliff-side far below.

Years ago—the *last* time a collar of iron had been locked around his neck by an Arcachon—John Churchill had warned him that angry Frenchmen were bound to come after him with pliers sooner or later. Jack could only assume that this was still true, and that in the meantime he was being kept in luxurious surroundings as part of some highly refined campaign of sarcasm.

After a week they moved him to a stone chamber. The windows were crossbow-embrasures that had recently been chocked up with pigs of glass. But they did afford him a view of the Dutch-hammer and its latest victim. *Minerva* had languished there, an object of ridicule, as gold and silver were extracted from her hold, and replaced with rocks to keep her ballasted.

"Did Vrej survive the fall, and the water?" was Jack's first question when Edmund de Ath—who had revealed himself to be, in fact, one Édouard de Gex, a Jesuit, and a hater of the Jansenists and of the Enlightenment both—came around to taunt him.

Édouard de Gex looked surprised. "Why do you ask? Surely you're not naïve enough to think you'll have an opportunity to kill him."

"Oh no, I was just wondering how it came out in the end."

"How *what* came out?"

"The story. You see, all along I've been supposing that this was *my* story, but now I see it has really been *Vrej's*."

Édouard de Gex shrugged. "He lives. He has a bit of a catarrh. When he's feeling better he'll probably come around and explain matters to you."

"*That* should be a lively conversation . . . but pray tell, why the hell are *you* here?"

"I am here to look after your immortal soul."

De Gex had traded his former garb for a Jesuit's black robes, and even his language had changed. Formerly he had spoken Sabir, but now it was English. "It is my intention to convert all of Britain to the true faith," he remarked, "and so I have made a study of your language."

"And you're going to begin with *me*? Weren't you paying attention in Mexico City?"

"The Inquisition there has grown lax. You said you were a Catholic and they took you at your word. . . . I prefer a more rigorous approach." De Gex produced a letter from his sleeve. "Does this look familiar?"

"It looks like the one Eliza sent me in New Spain . . ." Jack blinked and shook his head. "The one we opened and read on the ship . . . which was obviously a *fake* . . . but *that* one hasn't even been opened."

"Poor Jack. This is the *true* letter that was delivered to you in New Spain, and that you sealed up inside van Hoek's book-chest. But it was *not* sent by Eliza. It was sent by Elizabeth de Obregon. That fickle bitch smuggled it out of the convent where she was being held in Mexico City. Then later, when we were in Vera Cruz—"

"You took it out of the crate where I'd stored it, and substituted a fake one you'd written. Van Hoek complained that the caulking was badly done. . . . I should've suspected tampering."

"I am a better forger than a caulker, it would seem," de Gex said.

"The forgery worked," Jack allowed.

"Monsieur Esphahnian listened to your talk of Eliza for years, and knew every detail of the story by heart . . . without *his* information, I could never have composed that letter."

De Gex broke the seal on the letter of Elizabeth de Obregon. "It would weigh on my conscience, Jack, if I did not read you your mail. This is written in florid Spanish. . . . I will translate it into English. She begins with the usual complicated salutation and apology . . . then complains of persistent nightmares that have plagued her ever since she arrived in New Spain, and prevented her from getting a single good night's sleep. In these nightmares, she is on the Manila

Galleon, in the middle of the Pacific, when it falls into the hands of the Inquisition. There is no mutiny and no violence . . . one day the Captain is simply gone, as if he had fallen overboard when no one was looking, and the officers are in irons, confined to their cabins, but none of them knows it yet because they are all in a drugged sleep. A man in a black robe has seized control of the ship . . . like any other Inquisitor, he has a staff of *familiars,* who until now have been disguised as merchants' servants. They have been gathering information about their employers' blasphemies and heresies. And, too, he has bailiffs, *alguaciles,* who've been disguised as ordinary seamen but who are now armed with pistols, whips, and blunderbusses, and are not slow to use them against anyone who challenges the authority of the man in the black robe. . . . She goes on, Jack, to narrate this nightmare (*she* calls it a nightmare) in considerable detail, but much of it is well-known to you, who have such an intimate knowledge of the workings of the Inquisition. Suffice it to say that the Holy Office carried out its duties exactingly on that ship, and many of the merchants aboard were discovered to be Jews. Really, the entire Galleon was a nest of vipers, a ship of infamous degradation . . ."

"Is that what she wrote, or are you 'translating' a bit freely?"

"But even as he was decorating the yard-arms with dangling merchants, giving them the *strappado* so that they would unburden themselves of their sins, this black-robe was keeping lookouts posted for any sign of *Minerva.*"

"Does she explain the firing of the signal-cannon?"

"The hereticks mutinied. They fired the cannon in an attempt to summon help. There was general warfare—the black-robe was driven belowdecks . . ."

"Where he kindled a fire, to make an *auto da fé* of the entire ship."

"When Elizabeth de Obregon woke aboard *Minerva,* the first thing she saw was that same black-robe staring her in the face. With opium and with clever arguments he induced her to believe that the burning of the Galleon had been an accident, and that now, on *Minerva,* they were prisoners of the hereticks, who would kill the black-robe if they knew him to be a Jesuit. After that they would make her their whore. So she played the role that the black-robe devised for her . . . but after recuperating in Mexico City, and suffering diverse tortures from want of opium, and coming out from the influence of the black-robe, these nightmares had begun. She decided that they were not nightmares but true memories, and that all the black-robe's doings must have been part of a plan having something to do with *Minerva,* and something to do with the gold of Solomon, which *Minerva's* owners had stolen from the ex-Viceroy."

"And she wrote to warn us of this? That was a noble act on the lady's part," Jack mused, "but I cannot imagine why she cared whether we lived or died."

"She was of a *converso* family," de Gex said. "She was a Jewess."

"I cannot help but notice you are using the past tense."

"She lies in a pauper's grave outside Mexico City. The Inquisition there, so corrupt and pusillanimous, gave her nothing more than routine treatment. She died of some pestilence that was sweeping through the prison. But one day I will see her burned in effigy in a great *auto da fé* in St. James's Park, Jack. You'll be there, too—you'll put the torch to her pyre and pray the rosary while her effigy burns."

"If you can arrange an *auto da fé* in Westminster, I'll do that," Jack promised.

JACK HAD ASSUMED during the first days in Qwghlm that everyone aboard *Minerva* would be put to the sword, or at least sent to the galleys in Marseille. But as days had gone by it had become clear that only Jack and Vrej would be getting off at this stop—the ship and her crew, and van Hoek, Dappa, Jimmy, and Danny, were free to go, albeit without their gold. Jack liked to believe that this was because he had given himself up willingly. Later he came to suspect that it was because Electress Sophie was a part-owner of the ship. She was being shown a Professional Courtesy by whatever noble Frenchman was behind all of this—the duc d'Arcachon, or Leroy himself.

After *Minerva*'s holds and lockers had been stripped to the bare wood, they waited for a high tide and began throwing ballast-rocks overboard, trying to float her off the reef. Jack watched this operation from a battlement of the Castle, where he was allowed to carry his cannonball to and fro sometimes, under guard. After a while de Gex joined him, greeting him with: "I remind you, Jack, that suicide is a mortal sin."

Jack was baffled by this *non sequitur* until he followed de Gex's gaze over the mossy crenellations and down a hundred feet of sheer stone to icy surf flailing away at rocks. Then he laughed. "I've been expecting some Arcachon to come up here and put me to a slow death—d'you really think I'd do the deed *for* him, and spare him such a pleasant journey?"

"Perhaps you would wish to avoid being tortured."

"Oh no, Édouard, I'm inspired by your example."

"You are referring to the Inquisition in Mexico?"

"I was wondering: Did the Inquisitor know you were a fellow-Jesuit? Did he go easy on you?"

"If he had given me light treatment, you and Moseh would have detected it—and you would not have decided to trust me. No, I fooled the Inquisitor as thoroughly as I fooled you."

"That is the most bizarre thing I have heard in my entire circuit of the world."

"It is not so strange," said de Gex, "if only you knew more. For, contrary to what you suppose, I do not consider myself some kind of saint. Nay, I have secrets so dark that I myself do not know them! I phant'sied the Inquisitor might somehow wrest out of me through torture what I could not discover by prayer and meditation."

"That is more bizarre *yet*. I preferred the *first* version."

"Really, it was not so bad as the Jews are always claiming. There are any number of ways it could be made far more painful. When the Holy Office is reëstablished in London, I'll institute some improvements—we'll have a lot of hereticks to prosecute in a short time, and this desultory Mexican style simply will not do."

"I had not considered suicide when I came up here," Jack muttered, "but you are bringing me around smartly." He stuck his head out through a gap between crenels and leaned over the edge of the wall to see what the final few seconds of his life might look like. "Pity the tide is so unusually high—I'd hit water instead of rocks."

"Pity we are abjured to deliver you in one piece," de Gex said, gazing at Jack almost lovingly. "I would love to put what I learned in Mexico City to use, here and now, against your person, and get a full accounting of what you did with King Solomon's gold."

"Oh, is that all you wanted to know? We took it to Surat, excepting some trivial expenditures in Mocha and Bandar, and there Queen Kottakkal took it from us. If it's that particular gold you want, get thee to Malabar!"

Édouard de Gex shook his finger at Jack. "I know from Monsieur Esphahnian that the true story is far more complicated. He spent years in the north of Hindoostan, fighting in some infidel army—"

"Only because he failed the Intelligence Test."

"—and by the time he finally got to Malabar, the Jew had had plenty of time to insinuate himself into the confidence of that pagan Queen. A substantial part of the gold had already been diverted into the ship-building project. What became of it?"

"You said yourself it had gone to the ship-building project!"

Jack naturally turned to look towards the ship in question now. She had foundered perhaps two miles away, but seen from this tower through clear Arctic air, she seemed much closer. She was riding unusually high by this point, which was no wonder since for the last half-hour her hull had been veiled in splashes made by the ballast-stones that the crew were rolling out through the gun-ports. The waves began to nudge her back and forth as her keel lifted off the reef. Finally a cheer sounded, and several cannons were fired as signals and celebrations. Triangles and trapezoids of canvas began to cloud her spars. "Note how upright she carries herself, even when underloaded," Jack had pointed out.

"I will not be taken in by this ruse of changing the subject," de Gex said.

"Oh, but I'm not," Jack answered, but de Gex plodded onwards with his interrogation.

"Vrej claims that timber and labor are practically *free* in Hindoostan. According to his review of the accounts, too much gold was missing and whatever I may think of his *theology*, I would not dream of calling into question his *accounting*."

"Vrej has been tiresome on this particular subject for nigh on eight years now," Jack answered. "When he vaulted over the rail the other day, right out there, the first thing that came to my mind— even before I really grasped that he'd betrayed us—was joy. Joy that I'd never again have to listen to him on this subject. Now, *you* have picked up the torch."

"Vrej has related his suspicions to me. He says that whenever he raised this subject, the others would shrug it off with all sorts of vague similitudes, about 'greasing the path' or some such . . ."

"We are all old salts now, and prefer *nautickal* terms," Jack answered. "Instead of talking about some path needing to be greased, we'd more likely think of hulls that become barnacle-covered, which slows them down, and we'd speak of the desirability of keeping 'em smooth, for easy movement through the water."

"In any event—I assume this is a Delphic way of saying that bribes were paid to some Mogul or Maratha chieftain?"

"Assume what you like—that would still place the gold far away from you," Jack pointed out. He was gazing out to sea, watching *Minerva* trim her sails as she came out of the lee of the Sghr and picked up a leading wind across her larboard beam. One by one the yards traversed round, and their sails stopped shivering as the crew braced the yards and made her close-hauled. Immediately *Minerva* began to heel over and pick up speed. But de Gex now blocked Jack's view, squaring his shoulders and getting his face directly in front of his. "Your ship may be free now, Jack, but you seem to have forgotten that *you are not on her.* You are in my power now."

"I thought I was in *Leroy*'s power," Jack said, which was nothing more than an audacious guess; but the look on de Gex's face told him he'd guessed right.

"My Order is not without influence in his majesty's court," de Gex said. "In his efforts to find the gold that the Jew stole, Vrej Esphahnian could do nothing more than *bore* you. *I* can do much more."

Jack rolled his eyes. "Oh come now! If our aim had been to steal from Vrej, we'd have made a proper job of it. We were only chaffing him—we're not *thieves*."

"Where, then, is King Solomon's gold?"

"Turn around," Jack said.

De Gex finally turned around. The harbor below the Castle was crowded with French ships, most of them riding at anchor; the few that were in a position to get under way were now, however, frantically trying to raise more sail. Their decks were a-swarm with sailors coming up from below, like ants from a damaged hill. De Gex could not fathom why, until he noticed that every spyglass and pointing finger in the harbor was aimed at *Minerva*, now several miles ahead of the French ships that were trying to organize a pursuit. Van Hoek—commanding from a sick-bed lashed into place on the poop deck—had heeled her perilously far over for one so lightly ballasted, but she did not capsize, and seemed to be skimming over the water rather than plowing it up. A ship that hadn't been careened since before Vera Cruz would normally have been too encrusted with barnacles to make much headway, but *Minerva* moved as if her hull had been freshly scraped and painted. Not until she altered course slightly, and the sun glanced off her exposed hull, did de Gex understand why: the underside of the ship, below the waterline, had been sheathed, from stem to stern, in plates of hammered gold.

Only a sliver of that plating was now visible, but it shone out across the harbor like a gleam of light through a cracked door. Everyone had seen it, and a few French ships were now setting out on a forlorn pursuit, but most of the mariners were content to stand at the railings of their anchored vessels and only gaze in adoration. Jack knew what those sailors were thinking. They did not care about the value of the gold, and they certainly believed no nonsense about King Solomon's hoard. They were thinking, instead: If I were a sailor on that ship, I'd never have to scrape another barnacle.

JACK SAW IT AS ODD that de Gex had set *Minerva* free so hastily, considering that he had been pursuing this matter for above ten years, and traveled all the way around the world, survived the wrack of the Manila Galleon, given himself up to torture, &c. The next day Jack understood *why* de Gex had wanted to get *Minerva,* and most of the French fleet, clear of the harbor. Sails breached the southern horizon, a ship came into view, maneuvered adroitly round the Dutchhammer, and dropped anchor directly below the Castle. Jack recognized her from miles out. He'd last seen her in Alexandria, holed and dismasted. Since then *Météore* had been refitted and cleaned up by ship-wrights who, to judge from the looks of what they'd done, charged a lot of money.

He was taken back to his cell long before the *jacht* came close enough that anyone on its decks might have picked him out through a spyglass. This gave him another hint as to who might be aboard. His suspicions were confirmed later by faint sounds of women's and children's laughter, audible when he lay with his ear to the crack under his door. This was not a Naval Expedition but a pleasure-cruise, timed to call at Qwghlm during the magic fortnight around late August and early September when blizzards were least oft observed. The chilly cannonball that Jack had been carrying around for the last fortnight now seemed to have been implanted in his chest, and his heart ripped out to make room for it. De Gex had been oddly disinclined to torture him thus far, which had caused Jack to wonder what new, excruciating horrors might be in store for him. But he'd never phant'sied it'd be *this* bad! He could see how this would end: He would be dragged out naked and chained, and displayed before Eliza, and de Gex would relate the hilarious tale of how Jack had twice had all the money in the world, and twice lost it.

A few hours after *Météore*'s arrival, when aromas of French cooking had suffused the entire castle, large Bretons came to Jack's cell and dragged him to a part of the château that, as best as Jack could make out, was near the bedchambers. It was a windowless, hence torch-lit corridor joining an irregular series of chambers, closets, and wide spots. It had received little attention during the remodel, and still looked much as the last band of Vikings, Saracens, or Scots had left it. Here and there Jack glimpsed the backside of a wall: strips of lath, or wattle, with curls of plaster, or daub, squirting through. Casks and crates were piled in some places. They took him to a wide place in the passage where an iron grid had been leaned against the wall: a portcullis hammered out by some blacksmith a thousand years ago, torn down and thrown aside in some upheaval, and left to gather rust and cobwebs ever since. The Bretons pinned Jack against this, spreadeagled, and lashed him to it with cords. Here it became obvious that they were sea-faring men. When Jack opened his mouth to issue some remark to that effect, one of them opportunely shoved a rag-wad into his mouth, and lashed that in place, and lashed his head to the grate. They lashed his fingers down even, which struck Jack as gratuitous, unless they were afraid of his rapping out some message. When they were satisfied, they dragged the gridiron, Jack and all, down the passageway a short distance and through a curtain of mildewy sailcloth. Jack was then blinded for a few moments by sudden light. But as his eyes adjusted, he began to think he was back in the bedchamber where they had kept him for the first week. As he saw clearer, though, he came to understand he was gazing into that bedchamber from without. He was looking through the back sides of the mirrors that glazed the wall. His view of the room, from here, was total; he was positioned at the head of the canopied bed, arm's length from where a sleeper would lay his, or her, head.

"It is a style of architecture that has served me well," said a voice in French.

Jack would have jumped out of his skin, had he not been restrained, for the Bretons had taken their leave, and he hadn't suspected anyone else was in here. All he could move was his eyeballs. By swiveling these as far as they'd go, he was able to perceive movement in a dim corner of this hidden chamber.

A man came into view. He wore a periwig—powdered white, as was the new vogue—and what Jack could only assume were the most excellent fashions from France, so ridiculous were they. Something was funny about one of his hands, but, beyond that, he was splendid to look upon, and (as Jack could now detect, even with dirty rags jammed into his gob) he smelled good.

"You shan't recognize me, I'm afraid," said the only man in the room who could talk. "I scarcely recognize *you*. We last met in the Grand Ballroom of my residence in Paris: the Hôtel Arcachon. You took your leave of *most of me* hastily, and impolitely; though you did carry my hand for several miles, tangled in the bridle of that magnificent horse. Later it was found in the middle of the post-road to Compiègne with my signet-ring still on it; which is how it was traced back to me. Still you were not done re-arranging the body-parts of Lavardacs, for some years later you kindly shipped me the head of my father."

Étienne de Lavardac, duc d'Arcachon, raised now the stump of his arm so that Jack could view it. A cup had been strapped thereto, and extending from this was a black leather riding-crop. If Jack hadn't been gagged, he'd now have volunteered some observations as to how Étienne had a paltry and disappointing view of how to inflict pain, compared to the Spanish Inquisition; but Étienne anticipated him. "Oh, this is not for you. My revenge on you I have contemplated, and prepared for, these seventeen years, and it shall involve more than a riding-crop. It takes time to build a place like this, you know! I have had several of them made: there is another at St.-Malo and yet another at La Dunette. I have stood in them and watched my wife whore herself to sergeants and cryptologists. That, however, is not why I caused them to be made. Only today are these chambers being put to their true purpose. Vrej Esphahnian is in the one at La Dunette even at this moment. He is trussed up like you, staring through such a mirror, and listening as his brothers, dressed in the finest clothing, serve expensive coffee to dinner-guests.

"You see, we fooled Monsieur Esphahnian into believing that his brothers had been betrayed by you, Jack, and were perishing of typhus in debtors' prisons all around Paris. His joy at learning that this is not true will be balanced by some embarrassment that he turned you in to us for no good reason, and lost his share of the silver and gold in *Minerva*'s hold. I do wonder which of these three causes him the greatest anguish: that he betrayed his friends, that he threw away a fortune, or that he was duped. Father Édouard should reach Versailles in a few more days—he'll inform Monsieur Esphahnian that the missing gold was attached to the ship's hull the entire time—this ought to perfect his agony. It is a better torture, I believe, than anything the Spanish Inquisition could devise. But better yet is in store for you, Jack!"

He walked out.

A door opened and a woman entered the bedchamber. Jack did not know her instantly, only because he did not *wish* to. She'd changed, but not *that* much. He simply could not bear to open his eyes to her.

Nasr al-Ghuráb had told them that in the sack of Constantinople the Ottomans had discovered, in a dungeon, a device that the Byzantines had once used to put out the eyes of noble prisoners. There was none of poking or gouging. Rather, it was a great hemispherical bowl, wrought of copper, with a sort of vise in its center. The bowl would be heated first until it was glowing, and then the prisoner's head—masked, except for the eyes—would be clamped into the vise. The apparatus was so laid out that the pupils of the victims' eyes were positioned at the center of the hemisphere. When the lids were pulled up, the eyes could see nothing but a featureless heaven of red wrath that ruined even as it dazzled. The sensitive parts of the eyes were incinerated in a few moments, and the victim rendered perfectly blind without the eyes themselves ever having been touched by anything save that awful last glimpse.

In idle moments since having heard this story, Jack had sometimes wondered what thoughts went through the mind of the one who was being clamped into it. Did he resist? Could he? Were unwilling eyelids peeled back with tongs, or was the victim compelled somehow to open them himself?

It was in much the same frame of mind that he followed Eliza's entry into the bedchamber without looking at her directly. But in the end he couldn't not open his eyes, of his own free will, and gaze upon what was there, burn him and blind him though it might.

She had been at dinner with rich people, and was some time taking her gown off, washing her face, peeling off the black patches, and letting her hair down. Ladies-in-waiting came and went. A girl of perhaps nine, with eyes and face marred by smallpox, came into the room and crawled into Eliza's lap for a few minutes' rocking and snuggling; Eliza read to her from a book, then sent her off to bed with kisses all over her wrecked face. A nurse led in a boy of about seven, who had escaped the pox so far—but in a way he was worse for Jack to look upon, for his jaw had the same deformity as both of the two last ducs d'Arcachon. But Eliza smiled when he came in, and cuddled him and read to him just as she had done to the pock-marked girl. The nurse took the boy away and Eliza sat alone for some time, tending to correspondence; she read a scattering of notes and wrote two letters.

Étienne came in to the bedchamber now and twirled off his coat, and tossed his small-sword onto a window-bench. Eliza gave him a perfunctory over-the-shoulder greeting. Étienne strolled up along the side of the bed, walking towards Jack, loosening his cravat, idly swishing the riding-crop. He stopped before the mirror, pretending to study his own reflection, but in fact staring Jack directly in the eye. "I believe I shall ride bare-back to-night," he announced, loudly enough to penetrate the silvered glass.

Eliza was a bit surprised. But she mastered that quickly, and then had to hide a flush of annoyance. She finished a sentence, parked her quill in an inkwell, stood up, and peeled her gown back over her head. What greeted Jack, then, viewed through forty-odd-year-old eyes and a mottled, half-silvered mirror by candlelight, was not a bit less lovely than what he had last seen of her seventeen years ago. He could tell there had been a hard-fought dispute with the Pox and that Eliza had won it. Of course she had won it!

Her husband came up and struck her across the face with his hand, twisting her around so that she fell face-down on the bed. Then he whipped her across the arse and the backs of her thighs with the crop, occasionally looking up to smirk at Jack through the mirror. He commanded her to rise to all fours, and she obeyed. Fucking, interspersed with more whipping, ensued. Étienne did it from a position bolt upright on his knees on the bed behind Eliza, so that he could stare Jack down until the last moments when his eyes closed.

Now in the dungeons of the Inquisition, Jack had himself noted a phænomenon oft discoursed of by prisoners, namely that after a bit of torture the body went numb and it simply did not hurt that much any more. Perhaps the same thing was at work here. It had hurt just to *see* Eliza—to be so close to her. Seeing her little Lavardac boy had perhaps been the worst. This scene of "riding bare-back," however grisly it was in a certain way, simply did not trouble him as much as Étienne clearly supposed it did. If Eliza had jumped up from her writing-desk to smother her husband with kisses and then dragged him to bed and made rapturous love to him, *that* would have hurt. But instead she had shrugged, and parked her quill. Before the ink was dry on the sentence she'd been writing when Étienne had entered the room, he had exhausted himself, she had her clothes back on, and was approaching the desk with a look on her face that said, *Now where was I when what's-his-name interrupted me?*

LATER JACK WAS TAKEN AWAY and returned to his cell. The next night, the whole thing was repeated—almost as if Étienne knew in his heart that it had failed the first time. The chief difference was that when Étienne came into the bedchamber and announced his intentions, Eliza was, this time, truly astonished.

On the *third* night, she was out-and-out flabbergasted, and asked Étienne a number of probing questions clearly meant to establish whether he might be developing a brain tumor.

Jack, a theatre-goer of long standing, now saw how it was going to be. For Étienne had explained to him that his doom was to be locked up in a cell here for the rest of his life, and that once a year, when the weather cleared, Étienne was going to sail up here with Eliza and repeat this procedure a few times before turning round and sailing home. As Étienne told him this, Jack was, of course, gagged, and could not answer; but what he was *thinking* was that this was indeed an excruciating torture, but for wholly different reasons than Étienne imagined. The *premise* was excellent, granted; but the road to dramaturgickal perdition was thick strewn with excellent premises. The difficulty lay in that this show was wretchedly staged and, in a word, botched. This made it almost more painful to view than if it had been carried off brilliantly. Jack's fate, it seemed, was to languish in a chilly dungeon three hundred and sixty-odd days out of each year and, on the other few days, to be a captive audience to a bad play. He had to grant that it would be a humiliating fate *if he had been a member of the French nobility*. But as a Vagabond who'd already lived thrice as long as he ought to've, it wasn't bad at all; it was pleasing, in fact, to see how *not* under Étienne's thumb was Eliza. Jack's chief source of discomfort, then, was a feeling well known to soldiers of low rank, to doctors' patients, and to people getting their hair cut; namely, that he was utterly in the power of an incompetent.

After the third night, the set was struck, as it were. Jack was locked in his cell to begin the first year of his ordeal, and *Météore* sailed away south.

Jack settled in, and began to make friends with his gaolers. They were under strict orders not to talk to him, but they couldn't help hearing him when he talked, and he could tell that they fancied his stories.

He was there for all of a month. Then a French frigate came and took him away. They gave him clothes, soap, and a razor. Jack had a most enjoyable journey to Le Havre, for he knew that there was only one man in the world who could have countermanded the orders of Étienne de Lavardac, duc d'Arcachon.

BOOK 5

the Juncto

Hôtel Arcachon

"WE ARE VERY SORRY to hear of your little ship-wreck," said King Louis XIV of France. "But consider yourself fortunate you did not book passage on the Spanish treasure-fleet. The English Navy fell upon it in Vigo Bay and sent several millions of pieces of eight to the locker of David Jones."

The King of France did not seem especially troubled by this news; if anything, discreetly amused. His majesty was sitting in the biggest armchair that Western Civilization had to offer, in the center of the Grand Ballroom of the Hôtel Arcachon in Paris. Jack, somewhat to his surprise, had been allowed to sit down on a stool. The Kings of France and of the Vagabonds were alone together; the former had made a great show of dismissing his glorious courtiers, who had made a great show of being astonished. Now Jack could hear the murmur of their voices in the gallery outside as they smoked pipes and batted witticisms at each other.

But he could not make out any of their words. And this, he began to suspect, was all by design. This room was large enough to race horses in, but it had been emptied of furniture, except for the big armchair and the stool, which were in its center. The King could be certain that any words he spoke would be heard by Jack, and no one else.

"You know," said Jack, "I was a King for a while in Hindoostan, and my subjects would get worked up into a lather about a potato, which to them was worth as much as a treasure-chest. At first I'd want to know everything about the potato in question, and I would take a large stake in the matter, but towards the end of my reign—"

Here Jack rolled his eyes, as Frenchmen frequently did during encounters with Englishmen. Leroy seemed to take his meaning very clearly. "It is the same with every King."

"Potatoes grow back," Jack pointed out.

Louis took this as a witty and yet profound apothegm. "Indeed, *mon cousin;* and in the same way, there will always be more pieces of eight, as long as the metallic heart in Mexico City continues to beat."

Jack was a bit unsure as to why King Louis XIV was referring to him as *my cousin,* but he reckoned it must be a matter of protocol. Jack had been a king once. King of a ditch in Hindoostan, true; but no less a king.

"There is so much that is better ignored," Jack tried, hoping Leroy would agree, and apply the principle to his particular case.

"The King must not descend into these broils," said Leroy. "He is Apollo, riding above all in his bright chariot, seeing the entire world as if it were a courtyard."

"I could not have put it better myself," Jack said.

"But even bright Apollo had his adversaries: other Gods, and loathsome monsters, spawned before Time from the Earth and the Deep. The legions of Chaos."

"I never had to contend with those legions of Chaos myself, cuz, but then everything *you* do is on a much, much larger scale."

"There is another Heart that beats in London."

Jack had to ponder this ænigma for a moment. The happiest possible interpretation was that the King was speaking of Eliza, and that she was waiting for Jack on London Bridge. But given the general turn of recent events, this did not seem likely; the Jack-Eliza matter would definitely be classed as a "broil," not worth bringing up in conversation. Thinking of London Bridge reminded him of the water-pumps there at the northern end, which banged away like giants' hearts; this, then, reminded him of the Tower, and finally he got it.

"The Mint."

"Mexico beats out the divine ichor that circulates through, and animates, Catholic realms. Sometimes the treasure-fleet sinks and we feel faint; then another one reaches Cadiz and we are invigorated. *London* beats out the vile humour that circulates through the count-less grasping extremities of the Beast."

"And that would be a spawn-of-Chaos type of primordial beast you're talking about there, I am guessing, the sort of foe worthy of Apollo's attention."

"The beating of that Heart can be heard across the Channel sometimes. I prefer silence."

Twenty years ago Jack might have heard this as a baffling, eccen-tric sort of remark. Today he understood it as a more or less direct order for Jack to go up to London straightaway and personally sack the Royal Mint and level the Tower of London. Which raised more questions than it answered; but the largest of them all was: Why should Jack run errands, especially dangerous ones, for the King of France? It seemed obvious now that Leroy had saved him from the duc d'Arcachon, who had in turn preserved him from de Gex; but this King was far too intelligent to expect loyalty and service from one such as Jack on that score alone.

"If I have taken your meaning, there, Leroy, I can't say how flattered I am that you think I am the bloke for the job."

"It is a trifle, compared to your past exploits."

"I had a lot of help in my past exploits. I had a plan."

"A plan is good."

"I didn't come up with the plan. My plan man is somewhere north of the Rio Grande just now, and difficult to get in touch with . . ."

"Ah, but the plan of Father Édouard de Gex was the superior one in the end, was it not?"

"Are you saying I'm to work with *him*!?"

"You shall be afforded the resources you shall require to accomplish this thing," said Leroy, "and moreover you shall be relieved of burdens, and cut free from entanglements, that might hinder you." He took a bit of snuff from a golden box and then snapped it shut with a loud pop. This must have been a pre-arranged cue, for suddenly the doors at the far end of the room were drawn open, and three persons entered the room: Vrej Esphahnian, Étienne d'Arcachon, and Eliza.

They came on briskly, bowed or curtseyed to the King, and ignored Jack; for in the presence of the King, no other person could be acknowledged. Which was well enough for Jack. He wouldn't have known what to say or do in the presence of any *one* of these persons, had they come to him solus. To be with all three at once made him giddy, off-balance, and, in sum, even more than normally susceptible to the Imp of the Perverse. Vrej and Étienne kept Jack in their peripheral vision, which was only prudent; Eliza turned her head so that her view of him was blocked by a cheek-bone. He phant'sied she was a little red about the ears.

"Monsieur Esphahnian," said the King of France, "we have heard that you were misinformed, and that in consequence you swore a vendetta against Monsieur Shaftoe. As we have just been explaining, we do not, as a rule, involve ourselves in such broils; but in this case we make an exception, for Monsieur Shaftoe is about to do us a favor. It may take him many years. We should be most displeased if your vendetta should interfere with his work. We have heard that the misunderstanding on which the vendetta was founded has been cleared up, and from this, we presume all is forgiven between the two of you; but we would see Monsieurs Shaftoe and Esphahnian shake hands and swear in our presence that all is forgiven. You may feel free to speak to each other."

Vrej, by all appearances, had been out of pokey for a while—long enough to get some clothes made, and put on a few pounds. He had, in sum, gotten himself altogether ready for this audience. "Monsieur Shaftoe, on that evening in 1685 when you rode your horse into this ballroom and lopped this chap's hand off—" he cocked his head at Étienne "—the Lieutenant of Police came to the apartment in the Marais where my family had given you lodgings—"

"Sold, not given," said Jack, "but pray go on."

"They took my family away and threw them in prisons whence some did not emerge alive. I swore vengeance against you. Years later the flames of my passions, which had at last subsided, were whipped up again by lies sent my way by devious persons, and I looked for some way to inflict upon you the same pain I phant'sied you'd done to my family. In Manila I met in secret with Édouard de Gex, whom I believed to be my family's benefactor, and I did conspire with him against you and the other members of the Cabal. Thank God, most were either dead, or had parted from the group and found lives in places as diverse as Japan, Nuba, Queena-Kootah, and New Mexico. Of those who were still on the ship when it was driven on to the reef at Qwghlm, all have found freedom, save you. *You,* though, I have wounded grievously."

"No worse than *I* did *you* in 1685, or so it would seem."

"For what you did here in 1685 I forgive you; and for what I *believed* you had done, I hope you shall forgive me. In token of which I offer you my hand."

During this discourse Vrej had held his arms crossed somewhat awkwardly before him, as if the right was injured and wanted support from the left. Now he unfolded them and held out the right as if to shake; though he kept it curiously bent at the elbow. Postural oddities aside, Jack, who had lived with Vrej, on and off, for a dozen years, had no doubt of his sincerity. He reached out and shook Vrej's hand.

Vrej looked him in the eye. "To Moseh, Dappa, van Hoek, Gabriel, Nyazi, Yevgeny, Jeronimo, and Mr. Foot!" Vrej said.

"To the Ten," Jack agreed, and pumped Vrej's hand, hard enough to straighten the elbow. At that, something hard slid forth from Vrej's sleeve and barked Jack's knuckle. Vrej reached across with his left and slapped his forearm to keep the object from falling out altogether. As Jack could see plainly enough, it was a two-barrelled pocket-pistol.

Not knowing what Vrej had in mind, Jack let go his hand and got between him and Eliza. He'd scarcely done so when he heard a loud noise and saw Étienne d'Arcachon collapsing to the floor.

"Pardon the interruption, your majesty," said Vrej. The pistol was in his hand, a cloud of smoke drifting up from it.

Jack had got himself squarely between Vrej and Eliza by now, but she wanted to see what was happening, and kept moving about, which forced him to move as well. A door whammed open at the far end of the ballroom, and a cloud of feathers, lace, and blades—a dozen or so armed noblemen—came at them. It would be some moments before they arrived.

"I could run. Perhaps escape," Vrej went on. "But this would bring suspicion down upon my family—who are wholly innocent, your majesty, and always were."

"We understand," said Leroy, "and always have."

Vrej turned the pistol round and shot himself in the mouth.

"MONSIEUR SHAFTOE, THIS BALLROOM does not seem to agree with you. I do believe you should *not* be invited back," the King was able to remark, a bit sourly, before they were engulfed in courtiers with drawn swords.

Now Jack had always taken a dim view of Louis, but even he had to admit he was impressed by the aplomb with which this surprising turn of events was managed. There was, of course, an interruption; but only a few minutes elapsed before the conversation resumed. Jack, Eliza, and the King were in the *Petit Salon* now; the ballroom would require some cleaning-up.

First order of protocol was that the King expressed condolences to the widow d'Arcachon (for Étienne had taken the pistol-ball between the eyes). Then the King of France turned his attention once again to Jack. "Monsieur Shaftoe, it pleases us that when you saw the weapon in the hand of Monsieur Esphahnian, your only thought was to shield Madame la duchesse d'Arcachon. However, this does put us in mind of a certain entanglement that shall impede your work in London if it is not cut immediately. If the tales told of your love for this woman are true, it were useless to ask *you* to sever the tie. Madame?"

Jack, who'd been so alert to Vrej, was blindsided by Eliza. She was on him, and hugged him side-on, and kissed him once on the cheek and leaned her head against his long enough to breathe into his ear: "Sorry about the harpoon, and sorry about this; but I must do it, lest you end up in the Bastille, and I find poison in my coffee."

Jack reached out to return the embrace but caught only air, for she'd darted back as quick as any defensing-master. "I swear before

God that you, Jack Shaftoe, shall never again look on my face, nor hear my voice, until the day you die." Hastily then, before tears came, she turned to the King, who made a little gesture meaning that she was permitted to leave. She curtseyed, spun, and got out of the room as if it were on fire.

"There was to be a third part of the interview," said the King, "in which Monsieur le duc d'Arcachon would have sworn never more to molest you. But this has been obviated. Monsieur Shaftoe, you are free to depart. We must now turn our attentions back to the War; but it shall please us to learn, in a year, or several, that the money of England has been rendered worthless, and the ability of that heretic country to make war beyond its shores thus mitigated. Do take your time and make a proper job of it. No half measures. And know that as the pound sterling suffers, the widow d'Arcachon and her children shall thrive, and shall continue to enjoy all the good things that France has to offer."

BOOK 4

Bonanza

The upheavals of the last twenty years have been unbe-
lievable: the kingdoms of England, Holland and Spain
have been transformed as fast as scenery in a theatre.
When later generations come to read about our history
they will think they are reading a romance, and not
believe a word of it.

—LISELOTTE IN A LETTER TO SOPHIE,
10 JUNE 1706

En Route from Paris to London
OCTOBER 1702

THE KING WAS TOO POLITE to mention the opposite face of the bargain, which was that if Jack failed, consequences would fall on Eliza; but Jack had plenty of time to work that out on the voyage down the Seine and across the Channel. Before the end of the next day, he was on an ostensibly Danish brig pretending to smuggle French wine to England.

The last time he'd been in these waters, seventeen years ago, he'd been bound the other way, harpoon-gashed, and half out of his mind with fever. On this the return trip, his body was sound, but his mind wasn't. The full monstrousness of everything that had happened to Jack in the last weeks finally struck home, and rendered him sub-human for a long time.

The ability of sailing-ships to survive storms and tides depended on starving, drenched, terrified wretches' carrying out certain rote procedures even though their minds were absent. Jack had not sailed around the world without acquiring a few such instincts, and that probably explained how he passed the next day or so. The weather was fine; the storm was in his mind. When he came back to awareness, a day had gone by, but it seemed that he had been eating and drinking and eliminating in the meantime. He soon wished that he had remained in that semi-conscious state, because awareness brought pain.

Even so, tears did not finally come to his eyes and begin to roll down his face until the middle of the next day, when the downs of England thickened the horizon, all treeless and green, and as alien-looking as any landscape Jack had viewed during his travels. That went double for the Dover cliffs. The brig was turning now, bearing round to the north, and one morning she finally came round to a westerly heading and began to ride an incoming tide, skimming above the vast sands of the Thames, all tangled with the wracks of ships, looking like harpsichords that had yielded to the tension of their strings and imploded to black snarls. She picked her way up the estuary for the whole day, past Gravesend and Erith and various places on the Long Reach that the Shaftoe brothers, Jack and Bob and Dick, had once thought of as being extremely far away.

The river was crowded with ships far downstream of where it had been in the days of Jack's boyhood, and so Jack kept thinking that he had passed over Dick's watery death-site, only to learn they'd not be reaching it for quite some time yet. But as evening fell the captain issued blunderbusses to certain crewmen and told them to be on the lookout for mudlarks, and then Jack knew he had come full circle at last. It was strangely comforting to him. Home, as miserable as it was and had been, had some power to balm his wounds. It was all he could do not to jump overboard and wade ashore to lose himself in some Limehouse gin hole.

But that would've been irresponsible. Jack had a job that needed doing. He was a man of affairs now, a City man, and no mudlark. He told the captain to keep making way upstream until the lights of London Bridge were in view.

When they rounded the last river-bend at Wapping, light broke across the mile of water between them and the Bridge, outlining every spar and line of the countless ships riding at anchor in the Pool. Jack had remembered the Bridge as a gleaming dam of light across the Thames, but now he could scarcely make it out for the radiance of the rebuilt city piled up behind it. It was almost as if London had caught fire again, just in time for Jack's homecoming.

But the most brilliant object in Jack's vision was neither the Bridge nor the City. On the northern bank of the river, downstream of the Bridge, rose the Tower. Jack recalled this as a dull stone pile with the occasional candle gleaming through an embrasure. But on this night, anyway, the Tower was a massive stone plinth supporting a pillar of airborne light, and all the ships in the Pool below it seemed to have collected around its radiance like gnats besieging a lanthorn. Actually the eastern end of the place was as dark as ever, but at its western edge hot fires had been kindled. Piles of smoke and steam were rising up to black out the stars, and sparks careered through those clouds like meteors. The flames were concealed behind Tower walls, but they lit up their own smoke from beneath, and made of it a screen to project boiling and flaring light across the water. "Closer, closer," Jack kept demanding—it had become obvious that the captain was under orders to do Jack's bidding no matter what. So sailors were sent below to work the sweeps, and, like a many-legged insect crawling through a crowded burrow, the brig felt its way among anchored ships for hours, shrugging off curses and threats from men on other vessels who did not want to see their anchor cables fouled.

Jack could hear now the rumble of coal-carts inside the Tower, and the steady pounding beat of some giant machine inside the Mint: some massive trip-hammer coining golden guineas. When the brig had shouldered up to the front rank of ships, affording Jack an unobstructed view, he gave the signal to drop anchor, directly before the sprawling span of the Traitor's Gate. The ship swung around to point upstream and, as it did, Jack performed a slow pirouette on the foredeck so that the heat of the Mint shone always on his face.

High above, on one of the ancient towers, he could see a gentleman who had gone up there for a stroll, perhaps to get some fresh air and clear his head after too long spent down in the broiling Mint. This fellow stopped on the parapet to look out over the river, silhouetted against the burning cloud behind him, and a sea-breeze caught his long hair and blew it back like a banner. Jack could see that the man's hair was snow-white.

"That must be him, then," he said to no one, "him that was put in charge of the Mint." Raising his voice a bit he said, "Enjoy your perch up there, Mister Newton, because Jack the Coiner has come back to London-town, and he aims to knock you down; the game has begun, and may the best man win!"